h

of the
White Camelia

ICAN Press Book Publishers
San Diego, California
December 1993

Knights of the White Camelia

The evolution of the Fourth Reich

by
JAMES HESTER

Printed in the United States by
ICAN Press Book Publishers
616 Third Avenue
Chula Vista, California 91910

ICAN Press Acknowledges

ICAN Press would like to acknowlege the following individuals for their contribution to the publication and marketing of this work: Dahk Knox, Josette Rice, Steven Fellwock, Marian Denson, Paige Folkman, Mike McKenna, Ginger Adcock, Robert Hernandez, Patti Godsoe, Tina Prato, Tammi Becker, and Neil Thomas.

Disclaimer

Printed in the United States of America
Library of Congress
Cataloging-in-Publication
ISBN 1-881116-53-0

Acknowledgment

To my mother, whose kindness set the foundation of who I've been; my wife, whose faith in me nourishes who I've become, and my daughter, whose unconditional love forms the dreams of who I aspire to be.

A recruiting poster for Hitler's Student Organization

...Our main fundamental object is the maintenance of the supremacy of the White Race in this Republic.

From the Constitution of
the Knights of the White Camelia
New Orleans, 1868

...I also want to talk to you quite frankly on a very grave matter. Among ourselves it should be mentioned quite frankly, and yet we will never speak of it publicly...I mean...the extermination of the Jewish race...

Heinrich Himler
in an address to S.S. Generals
Posen, October 4, 1943

Let us no more be true to boasted race or clan, but to our highest dream, the brotherhood of man.

Thomas Curtis Clark
in *The New Loyalty*

1

The alarm clock shrieked but he was already awake. It was 5:00 A.M., the start of a new day, one more chance to carry out the Final Solution, to eliminate the disease known as Judaism.

Few people get the opportunity to make their mark in history, but he was directly involved in the evolution of the perfect race and the eradication of the source of all Germany's problems. Once the Jews, the Negroes, and other flawed creatures were extinguished, the Third Reich would be able to rise from the world ash heap. The repugnant Versailles Treaty had relegated Germany to such distinction and inhibited its true destiny as ruler of the world.

He played an active role in this noble endeavor that the führer had already initiated. His task was to round up the inferior, the weak, the dregs of the continent and bring them to their judgment day. Extermination. For a brief moment, he felt a pang of sympathy. It was necessary! he screamed at himself. It was imperative to eliminate the scourges of society in order for Germany to realize its true place in history—at any price.

Today would be a busy day. He finished dressing and affixed the swastika armband to his uniform. His boots had a high-gloss shine. He looked kingly, too royal for the position he held. Today the camp's showers would be tested for the first time. The ovens hadn't yet been perfected, but that was not his concern. His job was herding unsuspecting human filth toward the showers. Their final gasping moments would be delightful. He smiled as he pictured the stupidity and submissiveness of these Jews: old men, women, and little children as they walked their last mile on earth. He was lucky, one of the elite. He'd be able to watch this grand spectacle unfold, witnessing the panic, the screams, and the horror.

He'd heard it would be more satisfying by concentrating his hatred on a single individual. Arriving at the camp, he marched proudly to the showers, selecting the most pathetic looking Jew there. He scrutinized the Jew's every move, expression, and utterance. His subordinates were well trained, their human flotsam already in line, unaware of their destination with death. His eyes scanned the human rejects with disgust. There was his Jew, in the back, with a slight paunch. His chosen victim had a helpless and vapid look. He was apparently praying, as if God concerned himself with defective creatures like him.

Walking toward this pitiful excuse for a human being, he barked with contempt, "Juden, wie heissen sie?" Astonished by being singled out, the reply came softly without hesitation. "Madigan. Benjamin Madigan."

The guard looked at Madigan for several seconds with increasing hatred; silence filled the room. Then he abruptly walked away and smiled to himself, thinking how much better the world would be without Mr. Madigan.

After walking to his viewing place, he glanced through the window as the poison fell from the showerheads. Screams pierced his ears. Panic and pandemonium unfolded before him as death rained on the Jews. He focused on Mr. Madigan, who made no attempt to fight or wrestle himself from the death strangling him. Passively, he fell to the ground. As the life passed out of him, he mouthed the words, "Lord, forgive them, for they know not what they do."

The guard smiled as the old man succumbed.

The scene changed drastically for the guard when suddenly the screams of an elderly woman filled the room and the guard was jolted out of his nightmare.

Julia awoke to see the horrifying sight of a man placing something over the face of her husband lying beside her. The bright light from the night's full moon poured into the room. Julia Madigan could clearly see the silhouette of a menacing figure attempting to kill her mate of fifty years, Benjamin Madigan.

Although he couldn't understand what was happening, Benjamin abruptly awoke to find himself struggling against an attacker. The assailant was pressing a pillow onto the face of the elderly man, who was kicking valiantly and clawing with rapidly failing strength. Benjamin's muffled screams couldn't be heard; they were drowned out by those of his panic-stricken wife.

Within seconds, the room was flooded with light. The lady of the house, Rebecca Madigan, had flipped the switch and came running into the room, gasping and holding a baseball bat. At once, the man stopped his attack and lifted the pillow off the face of the terrified victim.

Everyone froze in astonishment as the identity of the assailant became clear. Standing cowed and dazed beside the bed was Michael Madigan, the son of Ben and Julia. Michael looked quizzically at his wife Rebecca.

"What's going on?" he gasped, out of breath from the struggle.

No one responded for several seconds. Finally, Rebecca answered, running her hands through her long brown hair.

"Well, Michael, it seems that you were trying to kill your father," she replied.

Michael, finally grasping the reality of the situation, looked at his frail, petrified parents. Ben was wheezing and coughing from the ordeal. Julia was crying and shaking with fear. Rebecca was standing in the doorway in her nightgown, still holding the baseball bat. Their three children ran into the room.

"What's happening?" yelled Joshua Madigan, seventeen and the oldest. He was clad only in his underwear.

"It's O.K. Daddy was just having a nightmare again."

Michael was overcome with embarrassment and fear of the tragedy that had almost occurred.

"Dad, I'm so sorry," Michael pleaded, almost crying. "I had the most awful dream. I..." he said haltingly.

Everyone was painfully aware of Michael's frequent sleepwalking and the nightmares that went with it. While often shaming him, dreams had never before resulted in such drastic consequences. Placing his hands over his eyes and bowing his head, he spoke in a near whisper.

"Please forgive me. It seemed so real. I was a Nazi in a concentration camp and I was trying to–to–kill you."

Recovered, Ben looked at his distraught son and struggled for the right words.

"Michael, don't worry about it, Son. You couldn't help it. God was watching out for me. Let's be thankful for that," Ben said, patting Michael's shoulder.

After several awkward seconds of silence, Rebecca spoke. "Let's go back to sleep, everyone. Tomorrow's a big day." Then gently nudging the kids out of the room, she grabbed her husband's hand.

"Good night, Michael," his mother said softly, as he and Rebecca walked toward their bedroom.

"Good night," he replied wanly, still in shock, his hands shaking.

Several hours later he shot up from his bed, sweat running down his temple, his heart pounding. Bright sunshine filled the room and the clock radio read 8:35 A.M.

"My God, Michael. Are you all right? That was one heck of a nightmare you had last night. Everything's O.K., darling. Everything's just fine."

His eyes darted around the room. With his heart still pounding, he recognized the woman beside him as his wife. They had been sleeping together in their bed.

"It was so real, Rebecca, it was so damn real. I was a concentration camp guard and I was herding people into the showers. I watched them as they died. I laughed at their screams. I was thankful to Adolf Hitler for giving me the opportunity to be a part of it all. There was one man that I watched very closely. I asked him his name, and it was—" He began to cry.

"Your father?" came her soft reply.

Hesitating, he said, "Yeah. I killed him and enjoyed it because I was a Nazi and he was a Jew."

Michael began to weep as he remembered the events of only a few hours before. "I've had these damn dreams for a while, but I almost killed my father last night. Good God, Rebecca, what's happening to me?" His wife stroked his back gently and kissed his forehead.

"It was only a dream, darling. It was only a dream."

Michael, squinting from the sunlight pouring in through the blinds, forced himself out of bed. Pushing his eyelids open, he stumbled into the spare bedroom and found his mother ironing his uniform. Rebecca entered the room just behind Michael.

"Good morning, sweetheart," Julia greeted him. "I'm sorry I didn't wake you sooner, but I wanted to make sure that you got plenty of rest after that dreadful nightmare. You have a big day today, you know. Why don't you take a shower and I'll fix you a nice breakfast. Have you finished your speech?" she asked sweetly, as if it were every night that her son had tried to kill his father.

"Julia, you're a guest!" Rebecca cried out in exasperation. "Sit down. I'll take care of everything."

"Oh, I don't mind. You know that," her mother-in-law replied. The petite, white-haired woman smiled and continued to run the iron across Michael's dress uniform.

Michael's hands were still sweating from his dream, and he'd forgotten all about his retirement today. Colonel Michael M. Madigan, U.S. Army, was turning in his uniform. It was twenty years today since he entered the service on May 31, 1969. Where had the time gone? He would take a short, well-deserved vacation with his wife, and then embark upon a new career as a professor of history at UCLA. Finally, he'd be putting to use the doctorate he'd earned.

"Is Dad up yet?" Michael asked, afraid to hear the answer. "I forgot to tell you last night that they moved it up an hour to accommodate the secretary of defense."

Among the dignitaries attending the retirement ceremony was Donald Swanson, the secretary of defense. The former general had been Michael's commanding officer for three years, and the two had worked together at the Pentagon.

"I told them, darling. Everybody's on the same sheet of music," Rebecca responded.

Still dazed and moving slowly, he was lost in thought as his mother proudly handed him his dress-green uniform. On it were the many ribbons and decorations that he had earned over two decades, including the Distinguished Service Medal, the Vietnam Service Medal, and the Purple Heart.

His mind wandered and he drifted back in time. He recalled, as if it were yesterday, his mother pinning the gold bars of a newly commissioned second lieutenant on his shoulders. She'd smiled gently, bursting with pride. The next twenty years quickly danced before him in a kaleidoscope of memories. He'd witnessed death and destruction in Vietnam, Grenada, and most recently, Panama. He'd ordered good, decent men into battle and he'd killed with his bare hands. But there had been a reason for this violence, he reminded himself, as he thought of the West Point motto: Duty. Honor. Country.

"Earth to Michael, come in. This is Houston. Do you read?" asked Rebecca jokingly.

"Sorry, Becks. I'm a little preoccupied," he responded. "I can't believe this part of my life will be over in a couple of hours. Plus, I'm still spooked by that dream. Can you believe *me*, a Nazi, spitting on my father and kicking him with my swastika-labeled boot? Then I really tried to suffocate him! What could it mean?"

"Don't let it spoil your day but promise me you'll see someone soon about the sleepwalking," she replied. "I've never seen a father and son as close as you two. You're so much alike, both survivors, never giving up, proud of your heritage and your country. This is a great day and things will be more normal," Rebecca added hopefully.

She was right, of course, as usual. She looked so beautiful today, much younger than her forty-three years, and not at all like a mother of three. Rebecca had not aged, it seemed, and her long flowing hair was as silky smooth as it had been twenty years earlier. She was still able to wear the jeans that she'd worn in college, keeping herself fit with a steady regimen of running and swimming.

He glanced into a mirror and pondered the image it reflected. Lean and just under six-feet-tall, with jet-black hair and piercing blue eyes, he looked younger than his forty-one years. God had blessed him with many gifts. He cursed himself for sometimes taking it all for granted. Most of his life had been very good, with the exception of the twenty-seven months he'd spent as a POW in Vietnam. He'd met Rebecca in 1969 as a senior at West Point. She had been a recent graduate from Princeton, a journalist for a small newspaper whose articles were mostly blistering antiwar diatribes. He couldn't understand those who protested the war, and he labeled them traitors.

Michael had grudgingly granted an interview to her, a routine ritual that the commanding officer at the Point had the power to order. Michael had convinced himself he would hate her, but despite their different perspectives, he found himself deeply attracted to her honesty, her sincerity, and the ferocity of her convictions. Just over a year later, after Michael's first tour of Vietnam, they were married. He was sure that their love was greater than any the world had ever known.

Their marriage had resulted in the births of four wonderful children: Joshua, now seventeen; Terri, fifteen; and David, nine. Remembering the loss of their eldest child, Ellen, who had not been seen since she had been kidnapped at the age of three, still caused Michael's eyes to water. He struggled to hold the tears back.

They were all great kids, with their own talents and skills. Michael and Rebecca had been tough parents, teaching them respect and values. They were a family that went on picnics and sang songs together. The only thing that kept them from being a closer family was their difference in religion. Michael was Jewish; Rebecca, Catholic. It had been difficult at times, especially with the added burden of living in Washington, a place that Rebecca had come to despise. Michael thrived on the pulse and energy of the capital. Rebecca, however, hated the hypocrisy of Washington, D.C.

No negative thoughts today, Michael told himself. Today she was very proud of him, and he of her. He was grateful for the wonderful family that he'd been blessed with and their nineteen years of marriage.

"I won't let it bother me," Michael said, snapping out of his reverie. "I've got my speech wired and I'm going to dedicate it to Dad. General Swanson let it slip the other day that I'm going to receive the Legion of Merit. Is your station going to cover it?" he asked Rebecca.

"I already told you yes. It's just that I'm not working on the story, at least not officially. But I'll be doing some investigative reporting," she said, as she kissed him and caressed his chest provocatively. Rebecca was the anchor for a local TV station and was well respected for the considerable talents and poise she brought to the screen.

"Stop that! I'll have you taken to the brig for insubordination if you're not careful," Michael protested.

"Well, on that note, I'll leave you two lovebirds alone," Julia said, blushing slightly. "I'll go check on your father and the kids," she said, exiting the room.

"I've always had this thing about men in uniform," Rebecca continued, as she playfully pressed her lips against his. "Can I make a reservation for 2100 hours?"

"Tonight it is," Michael smiled. "No excuses."

"It's about time you crawled out of bed. We're supposed to be leaving pretty soon," Ben scolded Michael, as he entered the room.

"Dad, I'm so sorry about last night. I don't know what to say," Michael stammered as he greeted his overnight guest.

"Just say that you'll see a doctor about those dreams."

"You got it," Michael said, hugging his father affectionately and without embarrassment. He'd always had difficulty showing emotion while growing up. Rebecca had helped him overcome this somewhat and he was now more able to express his feelings. He not only loved his father but respected him as a friend as well.

"You're looking great today, Ben," Rebecca said. "Are you and Julia ready?"

"She's still upstairs packing extra handkerchiefs—she plans to do a whole lot of crying," Ben replied, rolling his eyes, making Michael laugh. "She'd hoped that he would stay in a few more years and make general. But Michael never did do what his mother wanted," he added.

"Dad, you're incorrigible. You know that Mom never cared about that and neither did I. You're the only one with stars in your eyes," Michael scolded.

"Can't a father wish the best for his son? You've come so far, why stop now?" Ben asked. "But let's not argue. There's some honor in teaching young hooligans."

"For twenty years I was a soldier like you were and now I'll be a teacher like Mom was. Maybe someday I'll be a diplomat like you are now. Would you like that?" Michael asked, knowing already what the answer would be.

Michael's father was currently the ambassador to Israel, a post he'd filled two years before. Despite his stature, only about five-feet-four, he was the biggest man Michael knew. Michael glanced lovingly at his father, as the older man ran his fingers threw his thick, dark, curly hair and stroked his mustache. Ben's eyes moistened and softly he said, "Yes, I would like that very much. That would make this old man very proud."

"Well, let's round up the troops and get going. We have reservations for noon, you know," Michael reminded everyone.

"You're the one who stayed in bed all day," Ben replied.

"I know, I know. But we better get it in gear or I'll miss my own retirement ceremony," Michael warned, grinning.

"Aren't we going to wait for my folks?" Rebecca asked.

"No, I talked to Karl this morning," Ben answered, "And he said to go ahead without them." He was referring to Rebecca's father, Karl Schmidt. Rebecca had thought that they were all going together, but she didn't argue.

Three generations of Madigans squeezed into the family minivan and headed to a popular restaurant along the Potomac for lunch, with the Jefferson Memorial in the background.

After being seated, Michael said "It's hot as hell outside, Dad. What are you wearing a jacket for?" It was a typical Washington summer day with the temperature hovering around ninety degrees. The humidity made Michael's freshly ironed shirt cling to his skin, and beads of sweat had settled on his forehead.

"Well, you know how ambassadors are. We always have to be formally attired," he answered modestly.

"Ben, I can't help but notice that you seem, well, a little—bigger," Rebecca commented. Noticing his reaction, she quickly added, "Not fat. It seems like you've bulked up a little. Have you been pumping iron lately?"

The short, slightly overweight man replied slowly, "Well, just some push-ups to try and stay in shape, you know. You never know when your number's up. I'd like to delay that as long as possible." He then added, "By the way, when my day does come, I want you all to know that I love you very much." Michael and Julia were surprised by this statement, since Ben very rarely expressed his feelings in public.

"Dad, we know that," Michael replied, "but I hardly think that day is anytime soon. You're in great shape and far too stubborn to leave this world without a fight. If the Nazis couldn't stop you, no one can," Michael added, referring to Ben's experience as a young man. Ben was at Auschwitz when his parents were tortured and killed.

There was an awkward silence, and Michael at once regretted his statement. "I'm sorry, Dad. I shouldn't have said that," he replied, shaking his head.

Julia turned toward her husband, nervously fidgeting with the pearls around her neck. "Ben, I agree that this talk about dying is nonsense, but since you brought it up, I'm going to say something that will probably embarrass you, but I don't care," she said, pausing for a moment.

Ben knew what she was going to say.

"If you were to die without talking to your brother, that would be a true tragedy," Julia admonished her husband. "Rebecca, don't you agree?" she asked, putting the younger Mrs. Madigan on the spot.

"Well," Rebecca began hesitantly, "I never knew a whole lot about Ariel, except that Ben and he were at one time very close, then they had a falling-out," she said slowly.

"A falling-out is an understatement," Julia responded. "They haven't spoken in almost forty-five years and it's high time they put aside their differences and started acting like brothers."

"Dad, I don't want to interfere, but maybe Mom is right. Maybe you should try to bury the hatchet," Michael said.

Ben grew visibly angry. "Our parents were tortured and sent to the gas chambers. I was there. I know who was in charge, a despicable young Nazi officer named Herman Kepler. As you know, I've devoted much of my life to finding Herr Kepler. Ariel said that it was folly to look for him, that it would be better to get on with my life and not to allow hatred to swallow me up. He almost convinced me," Ben said, looking at the ground a moment before continuing.

"I wrote him a few years after the war. He was living in Tel Aviv. I was ready to accept his pleas and give up trying to avenge our parents' death. But instead of responding as a brother, he launched into a scathing and very personal attack on me, insulting me and our parents. I've never forgiven him," Ben said angrily. After a moment of quiet, he added reflectively. "It was like he'd been possessed by someone I didn't recognize. I don't know what happened to him, but I don't really care—I still don't," he added with finality.

No one said anything for a minute or so. Rebecca tried to change the subject.

"You know, it really is a beautiful city," she said. "Washington, I mean. But I can't tell you how glad I'll be to get away from here. I've always hated this place. Here in Washington, destroying people's lives is considered sport. I think that I'd lose my mind if I had to stay here any longer. I'll be so glad to start our new lives in California. Won't you, Michael?" she asked.

"Yeah," Michael replied slowly, the tension still thick. The rest of lunch was quiet. Both Michael and Julia wished that they had kept their mouths shut.

✠   ✠   ✠

The color guard marched smartly while the military band played. The retirement ceremony was being held at Fort McNair, the oldest active military post in the United States. Michael had attended the National War College here, the most prestigious of military schools for senior officers. The fort occupied the mile-long peninsula near the confluence of the Washington Channel, the Potomac, and Anacostia rivers.

Few Army colonels are publicly well known, but Michael was, due to his participation in numerous skirmishes, including the Libyan situation in 1986. During the past several years, he'd worked at the highest levels of government as the military aide to the national security advisor. He had had a high profile military career.

Michael and Rebecca were holding hands as they reached the parade field. They were still very much in love. It hadn't always been easy, but they had two rules that they religiously followed: they would never go to bed angry, and they would always discuss whatever was on their minds.

Today, they hoped, would be the start of a new and more peaceful life. There would be no more secret trips to various hot spots where he couldn't tell her the destination or purpose; no more calls from the White House during their vacations; no more anxiety over him coming home in a pine box.

Their children were following close behind. They were awed by the military hardware that was on hand. Ben and Julia were joined by Karl and Katarina Schmidt, Rebecca's parents. Karl was a giant of a man, standing six-feet-four and still built like a rock at sixty-seven years of age. He'd become a very wealthy businessman, owning a weapons manufacturing business. He was a nationally known expert on most weapons, serving from time to time as a consultant to the Department of Defense.

Katarina was ten years younger than her husband, and her dark eyes and hair contrasted with his blond hair and blue eyes. They had met just after the war, in Chicago. She was a student and he'd just come to the United States from Germany. It was love at first sight, and now they had been married for almost forty-four years.

It had been twenty-four years since Michael had first entered army life. Slipping back in time to when he first crossed the grounds at West Point, he remembered the horrors of "plebe summer," when the incoming freshmen were grilled unmercifully and incessantly harassed. At times it had seemed unbearable and he'd often thought that he couldn't last another day. Somehow, he held on by remembering how much more his parents had suffered. Naturally rebellious, he was almost thrown out twice for insubordination. But he had adjusted well. The values, discipline, and pride that he acquired stayed with him throughout his career.

"Are you with us, Michael?" Julia inquired, noticing that he'd drifted off into a netherworld of his own.

"I'm sorry, Mom," Michael responded, noticing his in-laws' arrival. "Hi, Karl, Katarina. How are you doing?" he asked, kissing Katarina on the cheek.

"Just great, Michael," Karl responded, in a booming voice which matched his massive physique. "Hello, Rebecca. You look stunning," Karl observed. Rebecca was wearing a bright blue dress with a red pattern that Michael had just bought her for their anniversary.

"Thank you, Daddy. Hi, Mom. I'm glad you could make it," Rebecca said to her parents.

"Mike, you seem a little preoccupied," Karl remarked.

"I couldn't help thinking back to my days at West Point. That place made me who I am today."

"You have many fond memories of West Point. It sounds as if it was all a positive experience," Rebecca answered.

"All—except for Alan Roberts."

"Who? I've never heard that name," Rebecca replied.

"He was my best friend there. We went through a lot together. We swore that we would name our children after each other," Michael answered.

"Whatever happened to him? Did you keep in contact over the years?" Julia asked.

"There was a cheating scandal our senior year, and I found out that he was involved. I was the commanding officer and as painful as it was, I reported him to the cadre. He was expelled from school one week before graduation."

"My God. Did he blame you?" asked Rebecca.

Michael hesitated before answering. "We were as close as any human beings ever were. Alan had dreamed of being an Army officer his entire life. The last time I ever saw him was a few days before graduation. He was filled with rage and threatened to get even." They were silent for several seconds. "He said that he would get me back if it was the last thing he ever did."

"Have you heard anything about him since then?" inquired Rebecca, somewhat concerned.

"Not a word. He just dropped off the face of the earth. I haven't seen him in years." No one spoke for several seconds, and then Karl and Katarina excused themselves. The silence was interrupted by the loud booming voice of General Lawrence Waters, the current commandant of West Point, as well as a former commanding officer of Michael's.

"Mike, how the hell are you? It's great to see you and your lovely family," the six-feet-six general said with characteristic enthusiasm. "The Army's going to be much the poorer without you. Any possibility of talking you out of this foolish idea? General Madigan. Has a ring to it, doesn't it?"

"Yes, sir, that does sound pretty good. But my mind's made up. I've had a great career, but I always knew this day would come. I've always wanted to teach. And I didn't spend all those years getting my Ph.D. for nothing," Michael replied slightly defensively.

"Of course you didn't. I'm just pulling your leg. But, seriously, we'll miss you. You served with great distinction," the white-haired general said, patting Michael on the back.

"General, that means a lot to me. Thanks. The two men who have had the greatest impact on me are you and my father. It makes me very happy to have both of you here with me today," Michael said.

Rebecca nudged Michael and they were both shocked to see Rebecca's brother Tommy, accompanied by his wife Adrian. Neither recognized him at first because it had been nearly twenty years since he'd been heard from. Still stunned by the sight of Tommy, Michael turned to General Waters. "Well, General, I have to get going. I'll see you later."

Tommy had always been, as Rebecca used to say, different. He was inherently bright and physically gifted, but he'd always been secretive and aloof. He'd been a Navy Seal and received the Congressional Medal of Honor. His moods were notorious and they had increased after returning home from Vietnam in 1969, partially due to losing his voice box in the war—shrapnel having torn through his larynx. He'd worked at his father's weapons manufacturing business for a while afterward and then just simply disappeared. Michael used to say that Tommy treated everyone equally, because he hated everyone, but particularly Jews and blacks. He hadn't approved of Rebecca's relationship with Michael and still didn't.

Rebecca stared at her younger brother—still muscular and lean—as if he were a ghost. After an awkward silence, she managed to speak.

"Tommy, my God, what are you doing here? I don't know what to say. It's been twenty years since anyone's heard a word from you. I didn't know if you were dead or alive," she said excitedly, not sure if she was making any sense. A cauldron of emotions clouded her thoughts. She felt betrayal, anger and a slew of other emotions, the combination of which left her confused. How could you do this to me, she thought.

Tommy looked blankly at his sister and held a cylindrical, metallic object to a hole in his neck. "I've been living in Germany, and I'm just here on business," he said, in a robotlike voice. The baton-sized object that enabled him to speak was clicking like a Geiger counter.

"Good to see you, Tom. It's been a long time," Michael said stretching out his hand. Tommy didn't reciprocate, but merely nodded as he and Adrian turned and walked away.

"I never understood him before and I still don't today. What's he got against me?" Why does he show up now after all of these years without even offering an explanation?" demanded Michael.

"I'm totally speechless. We were never close, and he was always the family outcast. But good God, it's been twenty years and he says that he's living in Germany. How could he just abandon his family like that?" cried Rebecca horrified.

Michael simply shrugged his shoulders and put his arm around her. "Who knows, darling? Who knows?"

After the music and festivities had concluded, Secretary of Defense Swanson approached the podium.

"Ladies and gentlemen; Generals Lake, Waters, and Tilden; soldiers; members of the press, it's my great honor and sad duty to salute today an officer that I've come to respect and admire..."

Michael had to hold back tears as the warm, kind words reached him. On his cue to go forward, he kissed Rebecca and walked towards the podium. He stood looking at the hundreds of faces in the audience, all friends and loved ones whose lives had influenced his own. He began his well-rehearsed speech, but was surprised by how choked with emotion he'd become.

"All that I am today and all that I have achieved is due to my father," Michael began. "His love, patience and respect gave me a soft, compassionate and gentle side. The ability to empathize, to understand the frailties and weaknesses of men helped me during my time as a commander. But, more importantly, his demands and challenges, his insistence on excellence, countered my compassionate side with a tough and demanding one. All leaders need both of these qualities if they are to succeed."

"The 'dark' side, if you will, allows for decisiveness and ambition, for discipline and toughness. When combined with the 'good' side, it results in a potent force. My dad insisted that I read history, philosophy and jurisprudence. An officer must understand the intellectual aspects of society if he is to rise above the parochial myopia that debilitates us in the profession of arms. Our duty is to follow orders, but we must never do so blindly. We will always obey our civilian superiors, but we must have the courage to point out mistakes," Michael said movingly. Turning towards Ben he felt tears welling up in his eyes.

"Thank you, Dad. Will you come up here and join me?"

A long ovation followed this touching tribute. Ben hugged his son and for the first time in many years, cried. Tears of pride and gratitude slid down his cheeks.

Michael started to release his grip, but he felt his father slump a bit. "I have to finish my speech now," he whispered.

Ben didn't respond, instead he collapsed to the ground. Michael looked down, horrified by the pool of blood that had formed on the platform around his father. Ben lay flat on his back, his eyes bulging, pleading, as he tried to say something. But he couldn't speak. His life was quickly coming to an end. He made a gesture to his son that Michael didn't understand and seemingly took his last breath. Michael, numb with horror, watched helplessly as his father's life slipped away. Ben was gone.

✠   ✠   ✠

It was a bitterly cold day in May of 1945, the mood inside was even colder than the freezing temperatures outside. There were six of them present this day, cramped in a small apartment in Munich, drinking schnapps and eating bad wurst. The thousand year reign of the Third Reich had just come to an abrupt end, after only twelve years, with the German surrender to the allies. Unconditional. Hitler was dead. He had killed himself after the disgraceful defeat.

They had come so close. There were so many ifs that could have changed the outcome of the war. If Hitler had invaded Russia in April instead of June; if they had fully developed the V2 (Germany's rocket); then they would not have been in this position. Now they were the vanquished. For the second time in less than thirty years, they were forced to bear the humiliating terms of surrender, as outlined by the victors. There were the self-righteous Americans, the pseudointellectual British, and the arrogant French, whose armed forces had collapsed pitifully in the wake of the Wehrmacht.

"We cannot accept this outcome, mein Freunden. We will not accept it!" said the tall, blond captain who was the leader of this group of young Waffen SS officers, their Sturmführer. Attired in the all black of the Schutzstaffel, he pounded the table with such ferocity that his hand began to swell. "We are the superior race. We are God's chosen people. We are chosen to rule the world. We will not permit our nation to be emasculated again, as it was during my childhood," he shouted, while waving his arms wildly.

"But mein Hauptman, what can we do?" asked one of his young colleagues. "Unconditional surrender has been agreed upon and the filthy Americans and the godless communists are already planning to carve our nation into pieces. They want to dismantle our military forces and to destroy our industry. We must be realistic. There's nothing we can do now. Germany's dead and we cannot deceive ourselves into thinking otherwise," he said, his words cutting bitterly into the hearts of these still proud and patriotic officers.

The captain was silent for a few moments; he walked slowly around the room, stretching his massive frame. All eyes were on him. When he finally spoke, the other young officers knew that this was something special.

"Germany is critically wounded, mein Leutnant, but she's not dead," said the blond captain. "The allies will pronounce their condescending homilies and will impose upon us cruel and debilitating terms. Our nation will suffer many years of subjugation, perhaps generations of guilt and submissiveness. But we will rise once again and we must begin today," he said with conviction.

"To those who read history," he continued, "thirty or forty years is but the blink-of-an-eye. How many years separated the Holy Roman Empire and Bismarck? And then more than forty years elapsed before Hitler returned us to our destiny. We in this room will do the same. We're the best that Germany has to offer. We're all in our early twenties. In thirty or forty years, we'll rule nations. We'll go out from this room today and assimilate ourselves into our conquerors' nations," he continued passionately.

"Two of us will go to America, one to the Soviet Union, one to Palestine, and two will remain in Germany—in whatever form it may ultimately take. We'll become captains of industry and finance. We'll achieve high-level status in political and military circles. We'll totally immerse ourselves in our careers and advance to the highest levels of government and business in our respective countries," he proclaimed, taking great delight in mesmerizing his fellow officers.

"But we'll never forget that our primary purpose is a goal that's right and necessary, a mission that's absolutely essential. It is our destiny," he said in a near whisper, so that his colleagues had to strain to hear. Raising his voice again, ever so slightly, he concluded his comments. "We will meet once every few years, the time and place to be determined later, to discuss our progress. We must not fail, we shall not quit, no matter how long it takes. It is our fate to return Germany to her rightful place as the preeminent world power."

"What about your brother?" one of them asked the captain, referring to his renegade twin brother, Otto.

"Don't worry about him. He was found to be dangerously lacking the character necessary to be a German officer, despite his skills. He was thrown out of the SS and I've not heard from him in six months," the captain proclaimed.

"Our concern is Germany's future. We shall be responsible for her ultimate return. Do I hear any dissent?" he inquired of the five proud men.

Not a negative word was uttered by the others, and they simultaneously stood and drew their glasses together. "Germany will once again arise," they pledged, and each swore to the others their undying loyalty to the cause— the ultimate return of Germany to its rightful place.

☩   ☩   ☩

The shots that had been fired caused panic to spread through the crowd. Michael, aware that his father had been murdered, scanned the nightmarish scene, now dominated by screams and total chaos.

What had happened? Who was responsible for this madness? Michael was having trouble comprehending the situation. It was too painful. Everything was moving in slow motion. The screams combined with the sliding of chairs and the view of people falling to the ground, cowering in fear.

"Michael! Michael, are you all right?" Rebecca shrieked hysterically. "Why?"

Michael was trying to force himself to be calm. Now was not the time to be emotional. The assassin must be found! Quickly surveying the area, he looked for any sign, any clues. But there were none. Whoever was responsible had vanished.

Within minutes, paramedics had arrived and were attending to Ben. Moments later, the ambassador was loaded into the ambulance and it sped away. Michael, starting to climb in, was advised not to come along.

"Colonel Madigan, there's a chance that we can save him. You would only get in the way. Let us do our jobs," said one of the paramedics, as another was performing CPR on his father. With tires screeching, the ambulance raced out of the parade field.

All at once, amidst the chaos and shouting, among the screams and tears, the sky was inundated with leaflets raining down. What an absurd time for some company to be hawking their products, thought Michael. Thoughtlessly, he grabbed one of the paper bombs that were drowning the stage.

Beware, it said. Beneath this message was a swastika.

Possessed with a burning rage that he'd never felt before, Michael let loose a scream that was so loud and so long that he collapsed to his knees. Rebecca grabbed his arm and propelled him toward their car.

They raced to Columbia General Hospital, hoping against all odds that Ben's life could be revived. Now they were rushing through the emergency room where Ben had been wheeled only a short time before. Michael identified himself and was met within moments by a Dr. Duc Le.

Michael, having spent over two years in a POW camp, was feeling a visceral reaction to having a Vietnamese doctor. But he immediately purged the feeling from his mind, feeling shamed by such a racist thought.

"Doctor, is there any hope?" Michael asked pleadingly.

Dr. Le shook his head sadly. "I'm truly sorry, Mr. Madigan. The wounds were too severe. There was nothing that could be done. He's gone. I'm sorry," said the doctor. Michael wasn't really understanding the words. His father couldn't be dead. Michael clenched his fists, closed his eyes, and wept.

"Michael, let's go home, dear," Rebecca said, placing her arm around his shoulder and leading her distraught husband out of the hospital.

✠ ✠ ✠

The bright rays of sunlight peeked through the blinds, waking Michael up after twelve hours of sleep. For a moment, he was unsure of his location. Slowly recognizing the surroundings of his bedroom, he called for his wife.

"Good morning, dear. I would have awakened you sooner, but you needed the rest," she said, walking into the bedroom.

"Did it really happen or was it all a nightmare?"

"I'm afraid that it happened and it *is* a nightmare. God, he was such a wonderful man. I'm so sorry Michael."

"I want you to know dear, that all the networks and newspapers have made it their lead story. We've received so many calls that I finally took the phone off the hook. I'm glad they didn't wake you."

"Are those reporters outside?" Michael asked, glancing outside at the cluster of Minicams and trucks.

"Yeah, they've descended on our house like a pack of mad dogs. Don't you just love the profession that I'm in? If I didn't tell my boss to go to hell, I'd be interviewing you right now," Rebecca replied. "Some other bizarre things happened while you were sleeping, they may be related. Maybe you better call Matt."

Matthew Bray Connors had been a good friend at West Point and they had served together in Vietnam. During one particularly bloody encounter with the Viet Cong, Matt jumped on a grenade that had been thrown at them by a five-year-old boy. This heroic act saved Michael's life and cost Matt his right leg. Matt had intended to make the military his career and had dreamed of being the first black army chief of staff. But after months of VA hospitals and searing agony, he made the painful decision to leave the army and try something else.

Matt and Michael had always been interested in world affairs. There had been scores of late night debates about politics, and the role of government, the military and economics. Matt was slightly more conservative than Michael, having come from a Republican family. Both his parents had been judges, and had been vocal opponents of affirmative action.

Matt was more interested in day-to-day policy considerations, whereas Michael tended to be more esoteric and philosophical. Matt had earned a Ph.D. in international relations and had been a professor at Georgetown for over a decade, earning a reputation that brought him into the inner circles of the Washington elite. Finally, two years ago, he was appointed deputy national security advisor.

"From your tone, I take it that this has escalated beyond Dad," Michael stated.

"I'm afraid that it has, dear," Rebecca replied softly.

Michael quickly dialed Matt's private number at the White House, a number that he'd committed to memory.

"Connors speaking," boomed a strong, powerful voice.

"Matt, this is Mike Madigan. What the hell's going on?"

"I had a feeling that you might call," Matt answered. "First of all, I'm very sorry about your dad. He was a great man and someone that I truly admired. But I'm afraid that it's grown into something of a much greater magnitude."

"What do you mean?" Michael asked nervously.

"Last night, there were three other assassinations. In New York, the Israeli defense minister was killed while coming out of the United Nations. Samuel L. Latham, the richest black man in the United States and president of a publishing empire, had his helicopter blasted out of the sky in Moscow, of all places, also taking the life of Vladimir Tokov, an up-and-coming Soviet politician," Matt explained.

"My God, Matt. Another Jew, a black and a Soviet. Do you have any idea who's behind this madness?"

"I've been here all night and we've run every hypothesis, communicated with the FBI, Interpol, the CIA, the KGB, and we don't have a clue," Matt said with some embarrassment. "I won't rest until we bring these monsters to justice. Latham was one of my best friends. I'm his daughter's godfather. And you know what your father meant to me." Matt's voice was filled with rage.

"I know, Matt," Michael said sorrowfully. "Keep me posted. As you know, I'm an outsider now. I was supposed to start teaching summer classes at UCLA next week, but I think that I'll take some time off and spend it with my family. Give Pam my best," Michael offered, referring to Matt's wife of seventeen years. "Take care, buddy."

"Hang in there, Mike. We'll find them," Matt assured him. "I guarantee it."

✠ ✠ ✠

Ben's funeral was held at the Arlington National Cemetery, behind the Lincoln Memorial. As an ambassador and former high-ranking member of the CIA, he was entitled to be buried here. The funeral was attended by many dignitaries and VIP's, including Vice President Craig Jensen. Michael had wanted to take one last look at his father, but his mother insisted upon a closed-casket ceremony.

The concept of Kevod Hamet—honor due the dead—underlies all Jewish burial customs. The dead are honored by being buried quickly. No embalming or cosmetology is done and the casket remains closed.

Both Michael and Secretary of State Christopher Watkins, Ben's boss, gave moving eulogies. Afterwards, several prayers were recited by a rabbi, including the El Malei Rachamim, a prayer that asks for the repose of the soul of the departed. The rabbi concluded with the following lines:

May the Lord bless thee and keep thee.
May the Lord let his face shine upon thee
and show thee favor.
May the Lord lift up His countenance unto
thee and give thee peace. Amen.

Slowly, the all wood coffin was lowered into the ground. Michael and Julia performed the ceremony of Keriah, the custom of tearing one's own clothing, a way of expressing feelings of grief. Michael's mind was drifting away, overwhelmed by the memories of his father and the good times they had together. As close as they were, they had both always had trouble expressing their feelings to each other. Michael had never spoken the words to his father that he had always longed to say. As the last bit of dirt was thrown onto the grave site, Michael finally spoke aloud the words he'd said in his heart a thousand times, but which Ben had never heard.

"I love you, Dad," Michael said, clutching Julia's hand, and once again, he began to cry.

2

After the funeral Michael and other members of the family went to Ben and Julia's home in Chevy Chase, Maryland, to mourn. The formal mourning period, called sitting Shivah, would go on for several days. Before entering, Michael poured water over his hands from a pitcher that had been set by the door. Upon his entrance, Julia lit a Shivah candle which would burn throughout the mourning period.

In accordance with Jewish custom the mourners were concerning themselves only with the departed soul and were not considering their own comfort or vanity. Michael saw his parents' beautiful furniture all covered with sheets and everyone sitting on wooden boxes. All the mirrors in the house were covered.

Several days of mourning had passed before Julia finally braced herself to get on with her life. Michael and Rebecca had invited her to stay with them after the assassination. But she insisted on getting out of Washington to visit her single daughter, Elizabeth, who lived in Charlottesville, near the University of Virginia, alone on a quiet lake. Elizabeth, thirty-five, was a writer who sold enough of her work to make a living but was still working on that elusive best-selling novel.

☖   ☖   ☖

Julia had spent a couple of weeks with Elizabeth and was feeling more sociable. She wanted to spend some time with Michael and had agreed to meet him at her home. She was taking Ben's death very hard.

Michael remembered that before his father had been named ambassador, he'd been with the CIA for over thirty years. In the early years, he'd been a field agent, and had been involved in some very dangerous missions. He had received several promotions and had become the number-two man in the entire agency. Michael had grown up wondering about his father's work as a spy, but whenever he inquired, Ben would sidestep his questions. Michael's imagination had always gotten the best of him and he would often lie awake in his bed pretending that they were both secret agents.

Michael was sitting on the porch step of his parents' two-story house waiting for Elizabeth when a car pulled up, snapping him out of his day-dream. He saw his mother get out and Elizabeth guide her up the walkway.

"Hi, Mom," Michael greeted her warmly. "How are you? And how are you, Liz? You look great," he said to his sister, giving them both a big hug.

"I'm fine, Michael," Elizabeth answered softly. She had always been the introverted one in the family and had spent much of her formative years in the library. She had natural beauty, Michael had always thought, but she refused to do anything to let people see it. She wore her brown hair up, had thick glasses and rarely smiled. Michael knew that she was a wonderful person, but was afraid that she would never marry.

"Oh, Michael, give me a hug," Julia said to her towering son, who proceeded to almost swallow her with his arms. She looked wistfully at the house, trying hard to suppress her tears.

Julia wiped her eyes saying, "We can't just sit here blubbering all day now, can we?" Pulling out her keys, she opened the door and walked in.

Michael was drawn to the fireplace mantle, which was covered with family photographs. He glanced at a picture of his grandparents that had been taken shortly before they were killed at Auschwitz. Ben had been a prisoner there, too, and wore, as all prisoners there did, an Auschwitz tattoo. Ben had personally witnessed his parents' deaths and it was something that had consumed him. The direction of his life had been determined by his sixteen months there and the brutal deaths of his mother and father. Deep inside, Michael knew that he too shared in their pain. His recurrent nightmares were a rude reminder of his heritage. Though he would never admit it, he shared with his father the desire to avenge the wrong.

Michael was silent, noticing that Julia was choked with emotion also. "Mom," he said, finally managing to speak, "I used to ask Dad, when I was a kid, what exactly he did in the early years with the CIA and he wouldn't tell me. Do you know?"

Julia sat down and wiped off her glasses. "Well, for almost five years, he was involved in one of the most secret projects the U.S. has ever had. He worked on the construction of a super underground place where the government would function in case of a nuclear attack or some other emergency," she explained, completely capturing Michael's attention.

"I've heard that it's practically a city itself and that it could withstand a nuclear attack," she continued.

"When I was on the National Security Council I heard talk about such a place, but never got a briefing or any solid information that it even existed," Michael said.

"Well, I don't know the details, but I assure you that such a place exists," Julia stated emphatically. "Your father never told me where it was, but he used to describe every minute detail to me. He knew every corridor, room, nook, and cranny of that place and I remember, like it was yesterday, the day that it was finished. He was so proud," she said smiling.

The three Madigans sat in the living room for over an hour telling their favorite stories about Ben. Before they knew it they were laughing and smiling together. After a while Michael moved the discussion to the present.

"Mom, I hope this isn't too painful but what was he involved in recently?" Michael asked. "Was he still really looking for that Herman Kepler, the Nazi guard?"

"Oh my, yes. He never gave up on that," Julia answered without hesitation. "But there was something else that happened recently that I never really understood," she added.

"What's that?" Michael asked.

"Well, he started getting letters from some man in prison in Chicago. He wrote back and even went to visit him in prison once," she explained.

"Who was it? What was the guy in prison for?" Michael asked, his interest suddenly piqued.

"I never knew who he was, but I do know that he was in prison for murdering someone," Julia answered.

Michael let out a low whistle. "Dad went to visit a murderer in prison?" Julia nodded. "Weird," Michael added.

They talked for another hour about Ben before Michael turned his attention to Julia. "Mom, I know that you've told us the story about how you got out of Russia many times before but I'd like to hear it again," he requested.

Julia took a deep breath and looked at Elizabeth, who merely nodded.

"Where should I begin? In 1941, when Germany invaded the Soviet Union, I was living in a small farming town. I was eighteen. All the Jews were being gathered up and buried alive in a big ditch. My girlfriend Katrina and I hid in our cellar as the Nazis came to the house and killed my parents and my eight brothers and sisters..." she said haltingly, her voice choking with emotion.

"We snuck out at night wearing only the clothes on our back and no shoes, even though it was the dead of winter. We finally got to the border and the few rubles that we had were suddenly no good. We took a job with a rich lady taking the lice out of her daughter's hair. You see, conditions were filthy and it was too cold to take baths during the winter," Julia explained.

"Katrina was caught by the Nazis," she continued, hesitating for several seconds. "They tied her hair to a horse and dragged her through town. Even today, almost fifty years later, I can still hear her screams," the frail woman remembered.

"I walked across Europe with rags on my feet and finally made it to France. I spoke only Yiddish and Russian. I stowed away on a freighter that was heading for New York. When I got there, I looked up some relatives. After the war ended, I met your father, who had just arrived from Romania. He invited me to a dance and I said no."

"Why?" asked Elizabeth, even though she had heard this part of the story before.

"I wanted to go, but was too embarrassed because I didn't have any shoes. He found out the real reason and called on me a few days later bringing me a brand new pair of shoes. We went to the dance and were married six months later," she concluded, smiling brightly at the memory.

Elizabeth wiped away a tear and even Michael was moved, despite having heard the story many times before.

"Well, I guess we'd better get going," he said. After rounding up some of Julia's personal items, they left the house, just as the sun was setting.

"Mom, I wish that you would reconsider staying with us," Michael pleaded.

But Julia had already made up her mind. She was going back to Elizabeth's for a few days, but would be back the following week.

Michael looked at Elizabeth and waved his finger gently. "Liz, I want you to take care of Mom, do you hear me?"

"Yes, big brother, I hear you," she replied.

"I know I sound like a pain in the butt," Michael acknowledged, "but she deserves the best. By the way, how's your novel coming along?"

"Pretty good, actually," Elizabeth answered. "I think I'm really onto something. We'll see."

"You'll publish that monster best-seller someday, I'm sure of it," Michael said smiling. He kissed Julia and Elizabeth gently.

"Take care," Michael said softly, waving as his sister's car pulled away.

Julia was going to spend several more weeks at Elizabeth's and then return to Washington. Elizabeth and Michael had offered to care for her permanently, but she was very proud and didn't want to be a burden to her children.

✠ ✠ ✠

Time off. Michael had almost forgotten what that was like. He prided himself on being a good father, but the truth was that he was often away and had missed many of the highlights of his children's lives. No more. Particularly Terri since she had now started high school and was dating. She was nicknamed TJ because of her middle name, Jean.

They had already bought a house in Malibu near the beach. After twenty years of constant moving, they would stay in one place, very likely for the rest of their lives, watching the kids grow and retiring peacefully. They had bought a rustic-looking five-bedroom house in a neighborhood where everyone knew each other and people seemed genuinely caring.

They had decided to stay in Washington for a short while and then head west. Rebecca had been out to the house a few weeks earlier and Josh and TJ had accompanied her, helping to get their new home ready. The movers would be coming soon to ship their belongings to California.

They were both excited about the move, but Michael was reluctant to leave Washington. He'd experienced so many incredible things and met so many fascinating people that it would be very difficult for him to move away. But not for Rebecca. She despised Washington and its phoniness and couldn't wait to get out. That was one of the reasons Michael had decided to retire from the army and not make a run for general, as he had originally planned to do.

Michael had grown up in New York, Rebecca in Chicago. The only connection either had with California was Michael's two years of graduate study at Stanford, while being stationed at Ft. Ord, near Monterey. He had fallen in love with southern California, a place where one could go snow skiing in the morning, surfing in the afternoon and camping in the desert at night.

"We're finally going to have a normal, peaceful, uneventful family life, and I love it. I love you," Michael said to his wife as they packed things into dozens of boxes.

"Don't forget, I start working next month at Channel 7 but I insisted on decent hours," Rebecca reminded him.

"And I start teaching, but I'll get a couple of sharp graduate students to help me and we'll just become a couple of horny old geezers."

They both laughed and then Michael turned serious. "How are the schools?" Rebecca had taken on the role of obtaining this kind of information.

Rebecca replied carrying a box downstairs. "I'm impressed with the quality of the schools, except that there's been an infusion of drugs recently that's really scaring the parents and teachers."

"I remember you telling me that," Michael said with concern. "How close to home is it? Do you think there's any chance of the kids getting into drugs?"

"Of course not. Josh and TJ are the straightest kids in the world and David's too young," she responded. "By the way, do you know that your daughter wants to be a rabbi?"

"You're kidding? Really?" Michael had never been an outwardly religious man and this was something that he'd never considered.

"If you were home once in a while, you would know that she's become very religious lately. However, her faith in God is being countered by her growing interest in boys. She's going to have a real hard time leaving a new boy she's fallen for. His name is Todd. She says 'It's love.'"

Michael groaned, becoming slightly flushed as he remembered what he and his friends were like at fifteen.

"Have you met this boy? What's he like? Who are his parents? Don't tell me he rides a motorcycle or I'll never sleep again," Michael said, clearly worried.

Rebecca laughed. "Don't worry. He's like Wally Cleaver and wants to be a doctor. He's an athlete and gets straight A's. He's a great kid."

So was I, Michael thought. And yet, there were many passionate weekends at the drive-in. Why couldn't kids skip their teenage years?

That night at dinner, Michael sadly realized that he'd missed countless events in his children's lives. He was almost a stranger in his own home. But time would rectify that. He would make it up to the kids from now on.

When he'd been home, he'd always been a great believer in dinner discussions about world affairs and philosophical issues. He loved debating the kids, challenging their minds and developing their values. He'd cherished the dialogue that his family engaged in when he was young, although many times he hadn't understood. But his father would insist that he contribute his thoughts, and while demanding, was never negative. Frequently, high-level members of the government would dine with them. Michael could remember discussing foreign affairs with the secretary of state and law with the attorney general.

Tonight, Michael directed the discussion towards Judaism, hoping to gain insight into Terri's religious views.

"TJ, Mom says that you're thinking of becoming a rabbi. I thought you wanted to be a lawyer," Michael said.

"It's hard to explain but I feel God calling me," she answered. "I can feel him in my heart. I know it sounds crazy, but I believe that this is my calling. Are you disappointed, Dad?" she asked, brushing her brown bangs away, her dark eyes seeking his approval.

Michael was touched by the sincerity of his daughter's words.

"Disappointed? Are you kidding? I'm so proud of you," he beamed. "I've never been outwardly religious but I do have a very strong faith in God. I'm delighted that at such a young age, you've become a person with direction. Pursue your goals and Mom and I will be there to help you however we can," he added.

As an afterthought, Michael added, "Where are you going tonight? Are you going out with Todd?"

Michael realized immediately that he'd said something totally wrong. His wife gave him a glare that could kill, and TJ rolled her eyes, and sighed loudly.

"Daddy, don't tell me that you forgot," she scolded.

"Michael, how could you? I've told you about tonight for weeks now. Tonight's the big end-of-the-school-year play. TJ has the lead role and Todd is one of the main actors, too," Rebecca lectured. Michael had completely forgotten, and he was paying the price. Rebecca's foot was tapping fiercely, and the sighs were coming rapid-fire.

"Of course I remembered, TJ. I was just pulling your leg," Michael said, feigning sincerity. He quickly realizing that nobody was buying it. "What's it about again?"

TJ had answered his same question the month before, but she responded with great excitement nonetheless.

"It's called the *Knights of the White Camelia*. It's after the Civil War ended, when a lot of white people tried to keep black people from getting their freedom," she explained. "I play a farm woman whose husband was killed in the war and I help blacks start their new lives as citizens," she added.

"What are the Knights of the White Camelia?"

"They were just like the Ku Klux Klan," TJ replied. "It was white people that felt black people shouldn't be given any rights, that they should remain slaves," she said.

"What's the name of your character?" asked Michael.

"Samantha Parker. I live on a big plantation in South Carolina," she answered excitedly. "My husband, the guy who gets killed, used to believe in slavery and so we had lots of slaves. But I always thought it was wrong and after he dies, I decide to help them," she said proudly.

"Tell your daddy what Todd's role is," Rebecca said.

"Todd's a really mean guy," she said emotionally. Her arms started to wave and her voice to rise. "He plays one of these Knights who are trying to suppress the blacks. He lynches them with his redneck buddies, calls us names like nigger lovers and burns down houses and farms, trying to scare the blacks and the whites who are trying to help," TJ said with great passion, her eyes wide in excitement.

They had finished eating when the doorbell rang. Michael answered it, fully prepared to hate Todd, whom he'd never met. He would check him out thoroughly, most certainly to the eternal dismay of his daughter.

"You must be Todd. I'm TJ's father," Michael introduced himself, shaking Todd's hand vigorously.

Todd was wearing a blue suit and had short hair that went with his muscular body. He was obviously an athlete. "Glad to meet you, Mr. Madigan. I've heard a lot about you. I'm really sorry about your father," he said sincerely.

"Thank you, Todd. Come in. TJ should be right down."

They walked over to the couch, Michael figuring to grill this deceptive-looking kid with overflowing hormones.

"I hear you drive, Todd. Is that right?"

"Yes, sir. I got my license last month."

"Since you're a junior, why would you be dating a sophomore like TJ?"

"Well, we met at synagogue and really hit it off. Even though she's younger, she seems a lot more mature than the girls in my class. She knows what she wants out of life. I guess she gets that from you," Todd replied.

Well, Michael thought, he doesn't seem so bad, as he heard TJ come down the steps. "Dad, what have you been telling Todd?" she said accusingly.

"Nothing. We've just been having man-talk. Well, I don't want to hold you kids up. I know you need to get there early and get ready. We'll be there just before curtain time," Michael said. "I hope that this doesn't embarrass you, but I'm very proud of you. Knock 'em dead."

"Thanks, Daddy. I'm proud of you, too, and I love you very much," she responded without the slightest embarrassment and kissed her father on the cheek.

Starting to leave, TJ added, "Don't forget that we're going to a party afterwards at Bill Michelson's house. I won't be home until about midnight, O.K?"

"That's fine," answered Michael. "We'll see you soon. Break a leg," he added jokingly.

"It seems just like yesterday that she was afraid of the dark," Rebecca said, watching the two teenagers get into Todd's car. She was Daddy's little girl."

"She always will be, but she's starting to grow-up. She's not a little kid anymore, Becks."

"I know, Michael," she sighed. "I know."

The proud parents headed for the high school play. Both were nervous and despite Michael's temporary amnesia, this evening's drama was something that he'd looked forward to for weeks. TJ had turned out to be a talented singer and actress. They eagerly anticipated the envy of the other parents. She was by nature very quiet but was able to come out of her shell while performing, much to her parents' delight.

The Madigans stopped by to pick up Matt and Pam Connors, who also had a member of the family in the show. Their son Albert was one of the stars of the production and they too were excited about the play.

Michael and Matt had for years played practical jokes on each other, each joke seemingly more outrageous than the previous one. Michael was determined to get even with Matt for the last trick that had been played, which had caused him great embarrassment. A couple of weeks before Michael's retirement, Matt had managed to get a hold of Michael's dress-green uniform jacket. On each shoulder were silver eagles, representing the rank of colonel. Matt turned the eagles upside down. This ridiculous posture went unnoticed until a young captain pointed it out one day, much to the colonel's chagrin. He would get even tonight.

Michael had schemed with Matt's wife, Pam, for this little joke, although it had taken a great deal of coaxing to get her to go along. The Connors had recently received a notice from the IRS saying that they owed $1,100 in back taxes. Pam intercepted this notice before Matt had seen it, and gave it to Michael. He opened it with steam and typed in two zeroes, making the amount owed $110,000. He then sealed the envelope back, making it look as if it had never been opened. Bringing it with him this evening, he eagerly anticipated Matt's reaction.

Michael and Rebecca knocked on the door of the Connors' Georgetown home. Matt opened the door greeting them with his trademark enthusiasm.

"Hey, good to see you guys. Pam will be ready in just a sec," Matt said, shaking Michael's hand and kissing Rebecca on the cheek.

"Looking pretty snappy tonight, Matthew," Rebecca teased.

"Well, this is a big occasion. I'm even wearing socks," Matt replied. Although he always wore a suit at work, off the job, Matt was notorious for wearing ratty T-shirts, faded blue-jeans with holes and rarely wearing socks.

"Matt, as we pulled up, I noticed there was a letter in the mailbox. So I brought it in," Michael commented and handed him the IRS statement.

"Oh, oh. The tax man wants us," Matt said jokingly. "Let me go see what's taking that wife of mine so long," he added and walked upstairs. "Make yourselves at home."

Michael grinned devilishly as he watched Matt disappear upstairs. He looked at Rebecca mischievously and tiptoed up the stairs with her. Standing with a view of their bedroom, he began counting. "Five, four, three, two...."

Suddenly, a shrill scream filled the house. Michael doubled over laughing. Pam was trying her best to keep a straight face as her husband sputtered and stuttered.

"What, what—" he stammered, unable to finish his sentence. His hands began sweating and his heart started pounding fiercely. He undid his tie and took off his glasses; finally, Pam couldn't take it anymore. She burst out laughing just as Michael and Rebecca entered the room.

Instinctively, he knew that he'd been had. Wiping his brow, he smiled at Michael. "You got me good, Colonel. I gotta hand it to you. But you better sleep with one eye open. Payback's a bitch, you know."

Rebecca chided both of them: "One of these days, one of you will go too far. You'll regret it then," she scolded. "Now, we have to get going or we'll be late." With that admonishment, they all hopped into Matt's white Jeep Cherokee and headed for the high school.

"Hey, guys, do you think our kids will remember us when they become big Hollywood stars?" Michael asked kiddingly, staring out the window.

Matt thought about it for a second before responding. "No, probably not," he deadpanned, taking an elbow in the ribs from his wife.

"Stop it, Matt," Pam scolded him, but then, after a well-timed pause, said, "They may not remember you and Michael but they'll always remember their mothers."

Michael laughed heartily and Rebecca was glad to see his smile return. Tonight was very important for him, she knew. He needed the warmth and laughter of being with family and friends.

The four proud parents arrived at the high school auditorium and took their seats, just as the curtain was coming up. The auditorium was packed with anxious mothers and fathers, none more so than Michael. TJ had been in several plays before, but because of Michael's work schedule, this was the first time that he would see her perform.

TJ played her role as a Southern woman who realizes, over time, the cruelty and injustice of slavery. She acted with great passion and conviction. Michael was astounded by her fiery portrayal of Samantha Parker, forgetting momentarily that it was his daughter up there on stage.

Albert Connors played the role of a slave named George whose path crosses Samantha's. She tries to help him gain his freedom, but George is captured by several of the Knights, led by Frederick Shayes, played by Todd.

The play lasted two hours but seemed to pass quickly, so enthralled was the audience. The last climactic scene was so powerful and real that the audience cringed and winced together.

George, the slave, was about to be lynched by the Knights, and was being whipped by Shayes, who laughed at George with each painful blow.

"We don't need your kind. Do you understand, nigger?" Shayes shouted, flinging the whip onto George's back. George was struggling mightily not to scream. "We won't allow our women and children to be infected with free niggers. You'll either be a slave in South Carolina or you'll die in South Carolina," Shayes shouted at the beaten man.

Shayes gestured to the others and quickly a rope was thrown up over a tree. The bloodied slave was lifted up and his neck placed into the noose and tightened.

The high school audience, and particularly Matt and Pam, were shocked to see Albert's neck in a real noose. Suddenly, there was a loud pop. It was Samantha, carrying a shotgun. She brandished the rifle at the men who were about to string up George.

"Cut that man down this very second or I'll shoot every one of you full of buckshot," Samantha demanded. When no one moved, she cocked the weapon, moving closer to the terrified Knights.

"I said take that man down. Now!," Samantha demanded. Moving slowly, Shayes and the others let George down.

She threw a blanket on George and briefly comforted him before turning back to Shayes and the others.

"Listen to me very carefully," Samantha said slowly, still pointing her shotgun. "We all just went through a terrible, bloody war. Thousands of men died, including my husband. But the war is over and the South lost. I'm sorry if you can't accept it. But this here is a man you was all whipping and this here is a man you was about to string up," she said passionately.

"He may not look like me and you, and maybe he talks a little different—but he's a human being that God made. And God don't make trash. He's got a heart and a brain, and his blood is red like yours and mine," Samantha said, softening her voice.

"Too many people from the South have died trying to keep George and other Negroes in chains. But the war's over and slavery is over. Do you hear me? Now go on home and get on with your lives. And if I ever see you harm George or any other Negro again, I won't hesitate to fill your hide full of lead," Samantha said firmly. Shayes and the others quickly disappeared into the night.

Samantha placed her arms around the battered slave. "Maybe someday, George, the hatred will stop. Maybe someday."

The curtain went down and the audience was still stunned by the gripping drama and its graphic portrayal. For several seconds there was no applause as the crowd struggled to catch its collective breath. The curtain came back up and the cast took their bows. The entire audience took to its feet to give the actors a thunderous standing ovation.

Michael and Rebecca, as well as Matt and Pam, were overcome with emotion. They had no idea that a high school play could be so powerful.

Michael couldn't get the last line out of his head, "Maybe someday the hatred will stop." One hundred and twenty-five years had passed, and still it went on unabated, day in and day out, all over the world. Would it ever stop?

After the play was over, the four adults drove to a nearby pub to get a few drinks and have a few laughs. As the waitress brought them a pitcher of beer and four glasses, Matt issued a warning. "I've already decided how to get you back, Colonel. It's gonna be good," he said, breaking out into a wide grin.

"Enough already. Would you two grow-up?" Pam chastised. "Listen, as you all know, I've gone back to school at George Washington to get a Master's in psychology," she said. "During our last class, we all had to tell everyone about some weakness we have or some big mistake we had made. I'll tell you, it wasn't easy. But I found it very enlightening. Let's give it a try," she suggested, while tugging on her gold earrings.

"That sounds interesting," Rebecca responded enthusiastically as the two men groaned simultaneously. The sounds of racked pool balls being broken filled the air, along with the smoke from the cigarettes at the next table.

"Come on, guys. Just give it a shot," Pam chided them, hitting Michael on the arm. "I'll even go first," she said flashing a big smile, her white teeth contrasting with her dark black skin and yellow dress.

Reluctantly, Michael said "We might as well give in now, Matt, because you know we're going to lose."

"So true. O.K., I'll start things off," Pam began. "I used to be what they called a black militant. I had an Afro hairdo two-feet-high and I hated all white people. I was arrested a couple of times and I even joined the Black Panthers."

"You're kidding," Rebecca said in astonishment. "I can't imagine it. You seem like the most loving, tolerant person I've ever met."

"Marrying Matt had a big impact on me. He was so secure in who he was while at the same time so loving. He helped knock the chip off my shoulder. O.K., you next, Rebecca."

"I was a troublemaker, too. I protested the Vietnam War and was arrested a few times myself. How I ended up married to a career military guy, I'll never know. I thought that Vietnam was a terrible waste and I thank God every day that Michael wasn't killed," she said in a near whisper.

"Oh, there's one other thing," Rebecca added. "Only a few people know this. I'm not very proud of it, but I used to be bulimic. I would go on binges, eating incredible amounts of food. Then I would make myself vomit. I used laxatives, diuretics and fasted a lot too. I could polish off a half-gallon of ice cream in a single sitting. Sometimes, I'd be in a grocery store, open a package of cookies and eat them all before I was done with my shopping. I was like that when Michael and I first began dating," she said, embarrassed.

"My God, Rebecca. You've always seemed like someone in total control to me," Pam commented. "Do you know why you did those things?"

"I had no self-esteem. I think it was because of my relationship with my father. It was never quiet right. He seemed distant and he always seemed to favor my brothers. I never felt good enough for him. I could never please him. I started developing self-esteem on my own, and when I met Michael everything just seemed right. Our relationship grew, I got away from my father and the bulimia stopped." She sighed and looked at Matt.

"Next victim."

"Bees," Matt said. "The little suckers scare the living hell out of me. To make matters worse, I'm allergic to some of them, and almost everything else, for that matter. I can't remember the type. But I just freak out when I see the little bastards buzzing. I mean, I saw some heavy duty combat in 'Nam, but nothing scares me like a couple bees. I can't explain it. That's just the way it is," he concluded. "All done. Short and to the point. Your turn, Cube," he said clearing his throat, a never-ending ritual caused by severe allergies.

"Before you get started," Pam interjected, "I just want to tell you that you guys have got the silliest nicknames. I mean, 'Cube,' and what do you call Matt? 'Green,' right?" she said in feigned disgust.

"Come on, woman, lighten up," Matt replied. "That's Michael M. Madigan. Three M's, M cubed. Get it? Plus, he's cool as ice."

Michael jumped to Matt's defense. "We call him Green because of his middle name, Bray. Green Bray. You know, Green Beret. Get it?" The two women shook their heads.

"Well, anyway, you all know that I'm blind as a bat. I started wearing glasses in second grade and I can't see my own hand without my contacts. Also, and this is a little embarrassing and not many people know it, but I can't swim," Michael confessed.

"You can't be serious," Matt responded. "How did you get through Special Forces schooling?"

"Believe me, it took some serious scheming to get out of the swims. But I bought off one of the cadre."

"Michael, I'm shocked," Pam said teasingly. "O.K., any other deep, dark secrets?"

To Rebecca's surprise, Michael spoke up again. He'd never talked about this topic to anyone. It had nearly devastated them.

"Matt, Pam, I don't know if you even know about this. Our first child was named Ellen. The sweetest baby you've ever seen. God, I loved her so much and was so proud of her. She was smart as a whip and so full of life..." he said pausing.

"One day, when she was three years old, back in 1973, I took her and a neighbor kid, a cute little four-year-old named Amanda, to the store to do a little shopping. I stopped in the sporting goods section and was looking at some golf clubs. Well, Ellen was getting impatient and was starting to act up. I scolded her good and told her to shut up, and swatted her butt. She had these huge tears in her eyes and I yelled at her and Amanda to sit down in a couple of chairs while the salesman showed me some golf clubs." Again, he stopped to collect himself.

"It couldn't have been more than thirty seconds."

"What happened?" Pam asked nervously.

"I looked up and they were gone. I ran frantically all over the store but they had disappeared. I began hyperventilating and screaming and I think I fainted. But I never saw either of them again. The police got involved, of course, and began a big manhunt. But I never saw Ellen again. The last thing I ever said to her was 'shut up,' and the last thing I ever did was to spank her," he said, with tears streaming down his cheeks.

After an awkward silence, Pam reached over and touched his hand. "Don't blame yourself, Michael. You couldn't have known."

Rebecca grabbed his arm as her eyes watered. Matt merely nodded.

Finally, Michael said, "Let's get out of here." They paid their check and left, and as hard as he tried, Michael couldn't stop the tears.

After arriving at home, Rebecca was so emotionally spent that she hugged Michael and went right to bed. The clock was striking midnight and TJ wasn't home yet. He was still wound up from the powerful impact of the play and from the memories of Ellen, and he was starting to worry. Josh was staying with a friend and David had fallen asleep on the floor while watching TV with the babysitter. Michael carried his little boy to bed, realizing that in the blink-of-an-eye he would be a grown man with his own life and family.

"Pleasant dreams, champ," he whispered, tucking David in bed and returning downstairs to his favorite room, the study. Their home was now covered with boxes and had been stripped bare in anticipation of the move. A large study was something that he'd always dreamed of and was his place for contemplation. Even with the boxes stacked around the room, leaving it almost void of personality, he was still very comfortable.

The study had always been his own world that the rest of the family recognized as his private space. It had, before the packing, wall-to-wall books, covering the whole gamut of Western civilization, but consisting primarily of politics, military affairs, philosophy and economics. He'd also installed a top-of-the-line stereo system, with four huge speakers that could "blow the doors off." Although from a fairly conservative family, Michael had always been somewhat rebellious and was a devoted rock-and-roll fan. He'd played guitar in several bands when he was younger and still had occasional jam sessions with Matt Connors on drums and Josh on bass guitar. They could really rock.

Looking through his record collection, consisting of about a thousand different vinyls, he lamented their demise. The compact-disk had made them obsolete. But there was history in these records, memories and remembrances of long ago days, some good, some not so good. He smiled as he pulled out his favorite record, the masterpiece by the Beatles, *Sergeant Pepper's Lonely Heart's Club Band* and wondered if his kids would ever realize the genius of the Fab Four and the impact they had had on the world.

Michael put on the record and eased into his favorite chair, which had been a gift from his father. He began reading a book about Germany. Michael had always been fascinated by Germany. He was, at the same time, repulsed by the warrior mentality and racial hatred that had originated from there twice in this century. What would happen in Germany now with the incredible changes that had occurred during the past year? It was a foregone conclusion that Germany would unify in some manner within the coming year or two. What effect would this have on the world and on Jews in particular?

Michael was absorbed in his book, barely hearing the record that was playing in the background. He stopped as one of his favorite songs started playing, slightly scratched due to the passage of many years, but it still had a powerful effect on him.

As the lyrics enveloped his memory, he began thinking of how TJ was growing up so fast. He drifted off into the past. He remembered taking her to kindergarten, teaching her to ride a bicycle, her singing songs that she had learned at school. His thoughts were interrupted by the piercing ring of the phone. Who would be calling at 12:30 A.M.?

"Hello, is this Mr. Madigan?"

"Yes, it is. Who is this?"

"I'm afraid we have some bad news. I'm Dr. Wilson at Columbia General Hospital. Your daughter Terri has overdosed on cocaine. She's in serious condition and may not survive. You better come down here," he said somberly.

Michael lost his breath. The doctor's words were too painful and shocking. He dropped the phone, and stood frozen for several seconds. It just couldn't happen.

Michael frantically awakened Rebecca. They threw a still sleeping David into the car and raced to the hospital, neither saying a word, both fearing the worst. Michael was overcome with a torrent of thoughts. Oh God, what have I done to deserve this? First Ellen and now Terri? Drugs? There must be some mistake. She wants to be a rabbi. She would never take cocaine. It was Todd, he was sure. He probably slipped something into what she was drinking to make her more susceptible to his advances. He would kill him, with his bare hands.

They arrived at the hospital at 1:05 A.M. and were greeted by Todd and his parents. Rebecca had met Todd's parents the previous month when Michael was out of town.

He ignored their greeting and immediately demanded to see Terri's treating physician. After what seemed an eternity, Dr. Wilson emerged and addressed Michael and Rebecca.

"Mr. and Mrs. Madigan, your daughter has ingested a large amount of tainted cocaine," explained the grey-haired neurosurgeon, whose long hair was combed to cover a bald spot. "It had a tremendous and immediate effect upon her nervous system and she's suffered what is called an intracerebral hemorrhage," the doctor said gravely.

"My God, what does that mean exactly?" Rebecca stammered.

Dr. Wilson hesitated for a moment before answering. "The symptoms are similar to a stroke. There's a swelling of the brain. She's in intensive care now, hooked up to an IV," the doctor explained.

"There's no easy way to tell you this, ma'am. I'm afraid that she went too long without oxygen to the brain. While she'll probably live, it looks as if she'll never be capable of independent thought. She might improve, but most likely, she'll be totally dependent upon others for the rest of her life. I wish I had better news for you but I believe you must know the truth. I'm sorry."

No matter how long he practiced medicine, it broke his heart each time he saw the anguish and pain etched in the faces of the parents.

Dr. Wilson, seeing the dazed and stunned look of the Madigans, knew there was nothing he could say or do to ease their pain. Their beautiful daughter would never go to the prom, drive a car, get married, or have a child of her own. Terri Madigan, a vibrant and dynamic girl only a few hours before with a bright future ahead of her, absent a miracle, would be a vegetable for the rest of her life.

Michael, leaning against the wall, spread his arms against the cold tile. Closing his eyes, he began pounding his head against the wall, mumbling incoherently. Rebecca began crying hysterically. Todd stared at them, not knowing what to do.

Michael stood upright and shoved his T-shirt into his blue-jeans. He then walked towards Todd and his parents. He had a dazed, almost demonic look.

"You killed my daughter," Michael said in a growling whisper. He gave the appearance of a rabid dog. "You bastard. You were supposed to be watching her. But you killed her," he repeated menacingly.

Todd recoiled at the accusations and began crying. "I'm so sorry, Colonel. I'm so sorry. It wasn't my fault."

Michael stared through him like he wasn't there, a wild, crazed look in his eyes, and then he walked away. He put his arm around his distraught wife, who was mumbling something indecipherable. The two shocked parents shuffled aimlessly along the hospital corridor. Their sorrow overwhelmed them as they walked out into the cold evening air, devoid of any feelings whatsoever.

✠   ✠   ✠

Several months passed and TJ was finally coming home. Michael and the family had already moved to Los Angeles and Rebecca had stayed behind in Washington to take care of TJ. She had lost thirty-five pounds and was incapable of talking, eating or going to the bathroom by herself. But at least now she was able to leave the hospital. She would require round-the-clock care and a lot of physical therapy.

What kind of life would they have now? Rebecca and Michael had become distant from each other, geographically and emotionally, with Rebecca immersing herself behind a wall of pity and Michael drowning himself in rage.

They had always talked things out before, had always shared their innermost thoughts and fears with each other. But they were becoming total strangers and they realized that the time had come for them to talk about the future.

Michael returned to Washington as TJ was getting out of the hospital. She didn't know who he was and was unable to talk. The thought of his once beautiful girl being like this was devastating. There were very few words spoken on the flight back to California.

Josh met them at the airport and even this normally gregarious teenager could think of nothing to say. The silence was thick as Josh pulled up outside the house that had been their lifelong dream. But now it seemed unimportant, insignificant. They walked into the house with Michael carrying TJ to her room, equipped with expensive medical equipment.

After they got her to bed and changed clothes, Michael poured himself a beer and dropped onto the sofa. They both knew that it was time to talk. Rebecca spoke first.

"Michael, I'm concerned that this tragedy is destroying our marriage," she said. "We rarely talk, we never laugh, I can't remember the last time we made love. But as important as our marriage is, we must decide about how we're going to care for TJ first. I've been thinking and I've decided to quit my job and take care of her full-time for at least a year. With your salary and military pension, I think we can make it, if we're really frugal. We'll have to sacrifice and things will be difficult, especially for David. But I don't see any other way around it. What do you think?" she asked.

Michael's eyes were wide as his wife spoke and now he hesitated. What he had been thinking of was radically different than what she had just proposed. He knew that this idea of his would cause serious problems.

"Rebecca, what's happening to our world," Michael asked rhetorically. "I don't mean just our family. Look at our society. It's being poisoned by drugs and consumed with hatred. Everyday we read about and hear on TV, stories of bombings, racial conflicts, drug wars."

After a short pause, he continued, realizing that Rebecca didn't have a clue as to what he was talking about. "Who are these monsters who killed my father and poisoned my daughter? I can't rest until this insanity has stopped. We can't just think about our children, but the sons and daughters of every American," he added.

"Michael, I haven't the foggiest notion what you're talking about," Rebecca said, clearly exasperated. "What do you think about me quitting my job?"

"Becks, what I'm trying to say is that I can't just sit back on the sidelines," Michael tried to explain, although he was failing miserably. His heart was pounding wildly and he was mumbling his words. He struggled to calm down.

"We have to look at the big picture, Becks. And so, I've decided to run for Congress and help stop this insanity," he said, with a sigh of relief, not knowing what to expect.

"You're going to do what!" Rebecca shouted. "Are you out of your mind? We have a daughter who's a mental vegetable and you want to go around kissing babies and making speeches? We've finally settled in a home and you want to move us back to Washington? Well, let me make one thing perfectly clear. If this is really happening and is not just a nightmare, then you can do it without me!" she screamed.

"If you're going to walk out on your responsibilities and leave me alone as you fly around the world massaging your ego and 'fulfilling your destiny,' I'll veto this marriage so fast that you won't know what hit you. If you decide to carry out this selfish plan, our marriage is over. Do I make myself clear?" she said, clutching her fists, until her knuckles turned white. Before he could say a word, she stormed out of the room. Michael found himself rooted in place.

He wasn't prepared for Rebecca's outburst. Divorce? It took a moment for the word to register. He didn't expect her to support his decision whole-heartedly, but he was stunned by her reaction.

He had looked forward to retirement for many years so that he could have a normal family life. But the past few months had been a nightmare. First, his father died in his arms, then his daughter was murdered, for all intents and purposes, and now his wife was threatening to leave him. What had happened to "for better or for worse?" Couldn't she see the bigger picture—or was she too caught up in her own selfish world?

He drove down to the beach to take refuge in the hypnotic effect of the waves. Michael walked along the sand for hours, the moon and the stars his only companions. For the first time in many years, he got down on his knees and prayed, sobbing uncontrollably, punching at the sky in frustration. Why was there so much misery in the world?

✠   ✠   ✠

The sound of sea gulls woke him and as he stretched his sore and cramped body the rays of the new day's light touched his face. He had fallen asleep on the beach, collapsed underneath a lifeguard tower. He got up, shaking the sand out of his pants and shoes, in time to watch the sun finish rising from below the horizon, magnificently signaling the start of a new day. He smiled as he felt the sun's warmth. He knew now what course to follow. It was all so clear on this new day. Hopefully, Rebecca wouldn't carry out her threat. But this was something that he had to do. Even if elected, there was only so much that he could do as one of 535 in the Congress. But he must try, he told himself, and waved to a lone fisherman as he walked to his car, confident that this was the right decision.

Michael would file the necessary papers declaring himself a candidate for Congress. He knew his advantages. First, he was a dynamic speaker and a highly decorated war hero. Second, he was extremely knowledgeable on most issues, particularly foreign affairs. Third, the incumbent was weak and unpopular. The disadvantages were many, however. He didn't know anything about politics, nor did he know anybody who did. Also, he didn't have the money for a campaign. And lastly, he wasn't sure that if he and Rebecca split that he could muster the strength needed to go through the rigors of campaigning. But he had never felt this strongly about anything. Despite very little sleep, he walked back to his car confidently, firmly believing in his decision.

In almost twenty years of marriage, he had never before stayed away from home because of a fight with his wife. He still couldn't get over her violent reaction. He wasn't doing this for himself, but for his father and for TJ. His primary goal in life was to provide for his family, but in the long run this would be best. And maybe, eventually, Rebecca would be by his side once again.

He drove along Pacific Coast Highway for a while, basking in the sun of the new day. But upon approaching their house he began to feel panic as he glanced at the birch trees in the yard and the toys on the front porch. He saw Rebecca's car, and like a nervous adolescent, felt his heart skip. He continued driving down the street and then pulled over to give himself a pep talk. With added resolve, he drove into the driveway, hoping for the best, but fearing the worst.

He walked inside and felt awkwardly like an intruder as he pushed the screen door open. David was playing in the living room and he put down his toys when he saw his dad.

"Daddy, daddy, will you play with me? Look what I got," he shouted in excitement.

"That's neat, David. I'd love to play with you later. But right now I need to talk with Mommy. Is she home?"

"She's in the kitchen making breakfast."

"Thanks champ. That's my boy."

Feeling as if he were walking to the gallows, he stepped into the kitchen. "Hi, Rebecca. Can we talk?"

She looked especially beautiful today. But there was an incredible sadness in her eyes and she seemed defeated.

"Sure," she responded despondently, her tone making Michael's task even more difficult.

They both sat down, and after several seconds he began. "Rebecca, we both believe in the same thing—our family comes first. But we differ on the approach. If we're confined to this house looking to TJ's every need, we'll be ignoring our own lives and our other two wonderful children. And we won't be taking any steps to prevent this from happening to others or even to us again in the future," he said standing up and walking across the room.

"Five years from now, it could be David or the Thompson kid across the street. Twenty years from now, it might be one of our grandchildren. I never thought that public service was in the cards for me, but now I feel compelled. Please, Rebecca, say that you'll support me and be by my side," he pleaded.

Her eyes were locked on the floor and she was lost in thought. Normally a woman of great emotion, when she finally spoke, her words were icy, her tone distant, her expression stonelike.

"Michael, I promised to love you and honor you and be faithful to you. All these things I've done. But it's a two-way street," she said blankly. "This is the most difficult time in our lives and you're abandoning me. You may have a legitimate long-term goal, but what about today? And tomorrow? I worry about how I'll get the strength to get out of bed tomorrow, not about the neighbor's grandchild who won't be born for twenty years. I worry about how we're going to take care of and pay for a child who will probably never be anything more than a vegetable," she said, knocking the wind out of Michael with her directness.

"And, besides," she continued, "you know how much I hate Washington—how much I looked forward to getting away from there. I just can't go back there now," she said flatly, pausing for several seconds. "Maybe you can chase your fantasies four years from now. But not now, Michael, not now. I beg of you." She hesitated for a moment before adding, "For if you do, it's over."

He walked over to her, his eyes moist with tears, and stroked her face and then kissed her lightly on the cheek. "I love you and the kids with all my heart. But this is something that I must do. Hopefully, you'll understand one day," he said without making eye contact. Michael turned and without waiting to hear her response, walked out of the house, not looking back.

3

𝕿he wind outside was howling, the temperature was far below freezing and yet the Soviet leader, a member of the all-powerful Politburo, felt a great sense of warmth. The events of the past year had been monumental, perhaps unprecedented in human history. The dismantling of the communist system and the dominolike fall of the Eastern European countries was mind-boggling. He had convincingly persuaded the Soviet president, who was overseeing the transition from communism to capitalism—from the Baltic to the Adriatic—to allow German reunification.

At first the president fought it with conviction. Eventually he quietly acquiesced to the creation of a unified and potentially hegemonic Germany that would be part of NATO. He began the year with his troops firmly rooted in East Germany, Poland, Czechoslovakia, and Hungary. He ended with agreements to withdraw all Soviet troops from foreign soil. This incredible turn of events, that seemed to catch the world by surprise, did not surprise Nicholai Ligachev. He stood gazing out the window at the fallen snow sipping cognac in his magnificent office. This was not a mere fortuitous series of events, but rather a carefully calculated plan that had been decades in the making.

Ligachev, the consummate Soviet politician, had reached the zenith of power by ruthlessly advancing through the Soviet bureaucracy for thirty-five years. He claimed not Peter the Great and Lenin as his forbears, but Charlemagne, Bismarck, and Hitler.

Despite having acquired a great taste for Russian foods and vodka, a fact to which his bulging waistline could attest, he remained German at heart. Wolfgang Weber was his real name, formerly of the SS and Nuremberg. He now wielded awesome power in the country that had divided his beloved Germany into two separate lands and had poisoned the 17 million inhabitants of East Germany with the stench of communism. The power that he had acquired, along with the wealth and privileges he had accumulated, would never diminish his hatred for the Russians. Nor would it distract him from his goal—to install Germany as the world's superpower.

Ligachev had prodded the Soviet president towards the inevitable reunification of Germany. This had been a very difficult and politically dangerous process. Historically, Germany had been the first priority of Czarist and Soviet foreign policy, and after the 1917 Revolution, Moscow's first diplomatic agreements had been with the defeated Germans. Victory in World War II had not eliminated the German problem for the Soviet Union. The very creation of the Warsaw Pact in 1956 had come as a consequence of Soviet inability to prevent West Germany's integration into NATO.

Germany represented the severest test for the Soviet president's "New Thinking," just as it had been for Lenin, Stalin, Khrushchev and Brezhnev. Ligachev had persuasively painted the picture for the Soviet leader, who came to recognize the challenge: he could not alter the Western perception of the Soviet Union as the "enemy" unless he could first do so in Germany. He could not control the arms race unless he could reduce the military confrontation in the center of Europe. And he could not transform the Soviet economy until he could win over the Germans and reduce the tension in Central Europe. Then came East Germany's sudden collapse. At first the Soviet elite had been puzzled by this event, but official policy eventually acknowledged and then endorsed German reunification.

After forty-five years, Ligachev thought to himself, Germany will once again be a great country: united and strong, dominant in Europe and free of American dependence. The deprivation imposed upon East Germany by the Soviets had come to an end.

✠   ✠   ✠

Michael had rented an apartment near the university. It was clean and inexpensive, but lonely. Its bleak walls and the deafening quiet filled him with a consuming emptiness. He had dreamed, for many years, of spending time with his family, making up for all the times he had not been there for them. He had always thought of them, whether he was on his way to trouble spots all over the world or in the corridors of the White House. He envisioned teaching TJ how to drive, throwing a football with Josh, taking David fishing, and going on camping trips with the whole family.

There had been a few family outings, Michael reminisced, as he poured himself another glass of wine. The time they had gone to Yellowstone never failed to bring a smile to his face. Rebecca had gotten poison oak all over herself and was miserable. TJ had dropped his expensive fishing pole into the lake when the live bait had scared her. David, who was only four at the time, had been scared to death when a large bear climbed onto their car. And he remembered teaching Josh the constellations when millions of stars had filled the sky. But those times had been far too few, and he had promised himself that there would be more. He had planned to attend all of the school plays, coach the kids' basketball team, and even join the PTA. But now it would never happen. His world had been ripped apart. God, what had he done to deserve this?

Michael took his guitar out of the closet and began to strum it. The music soothed his mind. God, he missed TJ. She had been such a delight growing up, but now would never know the joys of being a woman.

Michael began singing a song that he'd written for TJ some years before. He had been planning to play it for her on her high school graduation night. Now she would never hear it. He began to cry.

The emptiness inside was eating away at him and he felt that he had to call TJ. The alcohol he had been drinking helped him garner up the courage to call Rebecca.

"Hello," came her voice.

"Rebecca, this is Michael. Listen, I don't want to get into a fight, I just need to talk to TJ. It's very important."

"TJ can't talk. You know that. Michael, what do you want?"

He struggled to hold back the tears. "I want to sing to her, Rebecca. I want to sing her the song I wrote for her years ago. I know she can't talk back but will you please just put the phone to her ear. It's more for me than her. Will you just do it, please?"

"O.K.," Rebecca sighed. She went upstairs and held the portable phone to her daughter's ear.

"TJ, this is Daddy. Just sit there quietly. I want to sing you a song. O.K?"

Michael set the phone's hand piece onto the cushions of the couch and began strumming:

Dancing with my memories, I never am alone
The years have come and gone, and now you are full grown.
The time has come, my dear, to reap what you have sown.
You are a woman now with a direction all your own
But you'll always be my little girl
You'll always be my little girl
Now you have ambitions and dreams
And new worlds to find
Hope for the future will be on your mind
But I remember a snowy September
When the world first heard your cry
And the cynic in me died.
I held your little fingers and watched you grow
And now you say it's time for you to go.
I know not the roads that lie ahead
But burning in my soul and etched into my head:
You'll always be my little girl
You'll always be my little girl
You'll always be my little girl.

"Good-bye, sweetheart," he said, hanging up the phone, crying. After another glass of wine, he began to feel its numbing effects and had the distinct sensation of floating in some type of netherworld.

He looked at the empty wine bottle as if it would give him purpose, as if it could bring meaning to the hopelessness of his insignificant life. He danced with the shadows on the walls and dreamed of what once was. He cried for his beloved Rebecca and moved from consciousness into an alcohol-induced stupor. He was feeling, for a while at least, no more of that awful pain.

✠　✠　✠

The music from his clock radio jarred him back to consciousness, indicating 6:00 A.M., the start of a new day. He rubbed his eyes and stretched. His blood was beginning to circulate and his head beginning to clear. What had he done to himself, to his head? The abuses of the night before were quickly recalled by the throbbing of his brain—loud enough, he was certain, to wake up half the city. He looked at the other side of his bed in disbelief.

It was Rebecca! Had she come back to him? He couldn't remember what had happened. She must have come back, his darling wife was once again his. Together, they would solve the problems that had been thrust upon them, as they always had before. He quietly arose, the joy of his wife's return invigorated him like nothing had in quite some time. The excesses of the night before instantaneously dissipated and he tiptoed toward the bathroom for his daily shower. The gentle massaging of the hot water would rejuvenate him, and prepare him for the day.

All at once he realized that he wasn't in his apartment, but was back in their home. How did he get there? How could he not remember one of the most significant events of his life? She must have come by and brought him home. He had his family again.

He opened the door to David's room and peeked in at his pride and joy, who was sleeping peacefully. David was clutching the teddy bear that he always slept with as the watchful eyes of football players and rock stars gazed down from the walls. Boxer, the family dog, woke up and rushed to greet him, playfully licking his chops and yelping.

"Sh! Quiet boy, don't wake David. Good dog. Lay down and you can sleep for a little while more," Michael said. He quietly closed the door while patting the dog's head.

He was about to enter the bathroom, and as he glanced at the pictures on the wall, the light from the rising sun gave them a slightly eerie glow. His eyes caught a photo of his wedding day, his bride so joyful and radiant, he himself so happy and hopeful. Smiling, he thanked God for his blessings and opened the bathroom door.

Inside he found thousands of people lined up in front of him, pale and ragged with festering wounds and shorn hair. The cold shocked him and he noticed the boils on his arms that had been attacked by fleas. No one spoke and all eyes were devoid of life and hope, each shuffling, glancing at their bare feet. They were shuttled into a train by uniformed soldiers who were cursing and whipping their reluctant passengers.

A Nazi soldier struck him with his whip and ordered him to get into the train. The boxcar had no straw and was strewn with dead bodies. Fearfully, he climbed in and found himself in a quarry, shackled to a dozen or so emaciated prisoners. A guard placed a heavy stone on his back. Whenever anyone cried out or stumbled, sharp blows of the whip, to the face, back, and genitals were the result. The poor wretches who succumbed to fatigue were kicked and hit with a bludgeon.

He finally made it to the top and found himself alone and safe in his bathroom, in his quiet suburban house. He then realized that it was only a dream. Shaken, he grabbed the sink so hard that it almost came out of the wall. His heart was racing. Slowly, he stepped into the shower and eagerly anticipated the warmth it would bring.

Michael was surprised to hear music playing, softly, merry tunes from Viennese and Parisian operetta. Then he noticed that there were hundreds of people in his shower, undressing per orders of another Nazi guard. Then the shower door was slammed shut, locked and sealed. Outside, several Nazis stood ready. One by one, the guards dropped amethyst blue crystals of hydrogen cyanide—Zyklon B—into the vents. They watched their hapless prey, who were just beginning to realize what was happening, through portholes. The effect of the gas was slow, but soon everyone panicked, stampeding towards the shower door, piling up in a blood-spattered pyramid, clawing and mauling each other.

He felt the life draw out of him, but somehow he remained alive while the others, the huge mass of flesh, had finally ceased to move. The door was opened and the guards poured in, wearing gas masks and rubber boots and carrying hoses. First, they began to remove the blood and defecation and then they separated the dead. Inexplicably, he remained alive, although death could be no worse than this purgatory in which he was neither dead nor alive. His mind raced in horror, and his body was numb with pain. He seemed to be floating in a world of reality mixed with illusion.

"Oh, God!" he cried. Cringing and sobbing, he opened his eyes to a more shocking sight. He was now in the crematorium and found himself on a metal fork moving on cylinders into an oven. Flames were shooting out and he was inching closer to the furnace. Desperately trying to get off the cylinders, he kicked, writhed, and punched the invisible forces that held him. His screams were so loud that every person on earth must have heard them. The cylinders began to enter the oven door. Overwhelmed by flames, he saw, in his foggy, horror-filled mind, a shocking figure of evil. He prayed to God for death to come soon.

The figure, that of a high-ranking Nazi official, gazed into his eyes with a maniacal leer. The focused but deranged eyes belonged to Adolf Hitler himself, and as he closed the oven door the führer shouted at the prisoner, "Good-bye, Michael Madigan, you rotten Jewish swine."

Michael bolted up in his bed, sweating profusely, his heart beating wildly. My God, what a horrible nightmare! He looked up and glanced around his room to make sure he wasn't losing his mind. He was in his bed alone in his dark, empty apartment. His wife had not returned to him, nor was he in a Nazi concentration camp.

Michael calmed down and got up to fix a cup of coffee. He stared aimlessly at the yellow kitchen floor. He was forty-two years old with no family. He had always thought that he had a date with destiny. Was this his fate to fade into obscurity and grow old alone? Was this what he had worked so hard for?

He started crying and abruptly began pounding the table with all of his strength. Breathing heavily, he felt relieved, and suddenly his mind was clear for the first time in a long while. He had a job to do and there was no time for sympathy.

The professor put on his sweats and fixed the flat tire on his bicycle. It had been quite some time since he had ridden it. He had always loved a brisk bike ride. Michael wheeled his ten-speed, lavender Univega out of the apartment and felt as if new life were flowing through his body. He saw the sun coming up over the horizon. The year 1990 had started off painfully cold for California on this January day. He could see his breath as he carried the bike down the creaking stairs. He took solace in the stillness of the morning and the quiet soothed his mind. He glanced toward the upcoming sun and smiled.

Michael pedaled down Pacific Coast Highway. His hair was being blown back by the strong wind. He had no gloves and his fingers felt numb on this cold day. He would ride to the Santa Monica pier and watch the ocean. He passed the fourteen-block long Palisades Park and finally reached the Pier, at the foot of Colorado Avenue, which had become, over the years, a well-recognized landmark. He parked his bicycle and locked it to a lamppost with a thick, unbreakable kryptonite lock. It was still early, yet Michael saw dozens of joggers, fishermen and others who were walking and taking in the fresh air.

He popped into a coffee shop for a quick shot of caffeine and a croissant, then walked along the pier, trying to ward off the effects of his nightmare. He smiled at a pretty young girl that walked by him and then leaned over the side of the pier and gazed at the sea below. The beauty of nature never failed to awe him and this morning was no exception. He couldn't help but smile as he gazed at the sea gulls and listened to the crash of the waves. He watched intently a lone surfer who was braving the cold.

The young girl that had walked by him a few moments before had also stopped and leaned over the railing. Michael hadn't really noticed too much about her. She was bundled up in a loosely fitting, grey sweat suit with a fanny pack and was wearing sunglasses and a baseball cap. She was about ten yards from Michael, who was now feeding part of his croissant to the hundred or so sea gulls that had flocked to the pier in search of food.

Michael reveled in the sunlight that warmed his cold face and was making shadows on the wooden pier. He closed his eyes and turned to face the ocean. Then he leaned far over the railing, looking at the water below. He didn't notice the girl as she sauntered towards him. Starting to walk by, she dropped something and bent over to pick it up. Glancing quickly about to make sure that no one was watching, she grabbed Michael's ankles and threw his legs up in a mad thrust.

Totally unaware of what was happening, Michael was unable to stop his body's momentum from flying over the edge of the pier and plummeting into the ocean below.

His scream terminated quickly as he plunged into the cold water and began thrashing his arms wildly. What was happening? He couldn't swim! The waves crashed unrelentingly onto his near-limp body. He started to yell, but instead swallowed a mouthful of salt water. He tried to remain calm, but he was going down and there wasn't much time. Frantically glancing upward, he realized that no one had seen him fall. Even if someone on the beach had seen him, it would be too late for them to do anything.

After several frantic and panicky seconds, he started to sink into the blackness of the freezing water. He asked God for forgiveness, realizing that his life was about to end.

As Michael sunk below the surface, the surfer that he had been watching earlier paddled ferociously towards the drowning man. Wearing a full-body surf suit, he dove powerfully off of his board at the point where he had seen Michael disappear. For several seconds, he could see no sign of anyone. Finally, grasping blindly around in the surging water, he grabbed an arm and pulled up kicking with all of his strength.

The two of them surfaced. The surfer pushed his long blond hair out of his eyes and shoved Michael onto the brightly colored surfboard. Michael gasped and hacked for air as the surfer began paddling towards shore. He opened his eyes, uncertain of what was happening, but knowing one thing. He was alive.

The surfer kicked his muscular legs as fast as he could, rapidly reaching the shoreline. No one on the pier or the beach knew what had happened as the two of them walked onto the sand. Michael took a few wobbly steps out of the cold water and collapsed, shaking with fear and cold.

"Are you O.K., man?" asked the surfer.

Michael didn't respond at first but finally managed a nod.

"Hey, I'm not one to butt in," said the rescuer in a slow drawl, "but just what were you doing jumping off the pier with all of your clothes on?"

"I assure you," Michael answered slowly, his teeth chattering, "it wasn't planned."

"Well, you better get some warm clothes on right away. Do you live around here?"

"About twelve miles away. I rode my bike."

"Listen, tell me to get outta here but I don't think that you're up for it. My name's Alex and I'll be glad to give you a ride home. What do you say?"

Michael managed a smile. "O.K., Alex. I'll take you up on that. Let's get going," he said, struggling to his feet. Alex held the board under his arm and they headed towards his car.

They reached his apartment with Michael still coughing and shocked by what had happened.

"Alex, someone pushed me over the railing. You didn't see it?" Michael asked.

"Sorry, man. I saw you hit the water but I didn't see the fall. I was just sitting on my board peacefully waiting for the next wave when I heard you screaming. I couldn't believe it," Alex explained. "Hey, I don't want to be critical but can't you swim?"

Michael looked embarrassed and grinned sheepishly. "No, Alex, I can't. Maybe now would be a good time to think about taking some lessons. But seriously, you saved my life. I owe you a lot."

"Hey, don't sweat it. It was no big deal," Alex said modestly. "I gotta split, man. You O.K.?"

"Yeah, I'm fine. Let me give you my phone number. If there's ever anything I can do for you, give me a call," Michael said, scratching his number out on a scrap of paper. "Take care," he said as Alex pulled away.

Still out of breath and stunned, he hopped into the shower and turned the hot water on full blast. He allowed his mind to go blank, placing his hands on the shower wall and letting the pounding hot water soothe him. He couldn't let this stop him. He hadn't gotten a good enough look to identify his assailant. He would just have to carry on with his plans as before.

The first thing he would do, before his 1:00 P.M. class, would be to call his father-in-law, who was in town at his west coast home in Marina del Rey, just a little bit south of his place in Santa Monica. While not a political heavyweight himself, he was an extremely successful businessman with many connections. Maybe he could give him some ideas.

Michael made the phone call to Karl Schmidt and received an invitation to join his father-in-law for breakfast.

After cleaning up and gathering all of his things for his afternoon class, Michael hopped into a pair of faded jeans, jumped into his 1967 Mustang convertible, and raced towards Marina del Rey. Karl lived just a little bit inland, a mile or so from the world's largest small craft harbor where over six thousand boats are berthed.

Michael's mind was racing with a million things and before he knew it, he had arrived at Karl and Katarina's three-story house. Michael bounced up the stairs two at a time and seconds later was met at the door by his massive father-in-law.

"Come on in, Michael, come on in. How are you doing?" Karl asked, vigorously shaking Michael's hand.

"I'm hanging in there, sort of," Michael said wanly, kicking the sand off of his shoes before walking in.

"Follow me. We're going to have breakfast on the patio," Karl said, and they walked through a garishly decorated room and outside onto a large patio. "Katarina isn't feeling well so she's still in bed. Have a seat," he said, pulling out a chair for his guest. "I'll be right back."

Michael took a deep breath and exhaled powerfully, basking in the sunlight. He closed his eyes searching his mind for some peace in the quiet. Meanwhile, Karl was in his den, slowly opening a locked top drawer. He pulled out a small pistol and placed it into the pocket of the blue windbreaker he was wearing and returned to join his guest.

Michael wasn't sure where to start. "I guess you know about the situation with Rebbeca and I," Michael said sadly, pouring himself a cup of coffee.

"Yes, I do, unfortunately," Karl said. "I never thought I'd see the day. I thought that you were the perfect couple," he lied. He had never approved of their marriage and was determined that it would end today. He felt the pistol in his jacket and glanced around nervously.

Just then, Michael let out a loud groan and ran his fingers through his hair.

"Karl, I gotta get something off my chest. Rebecca knows about this, but obviously I can't talk to her," he said anxiously.

"Sure." He would at least hear Michael out before killing him, Karl decided.

"Well, I keep having these bizarre dreams about Nazis and Hitler," he began, catching Karl's attention.

"Really? Go on."

"I just had one last night and each one seems to be more real than the one before. They're just wiping me out."

Karl paused briefly before responding. "As you may know, I believe strongly in dreams and reincarnation. Maybe, these dreams mean that you've lived another life and you're just now remembering it."

Michael furrowed his brow and shook his head. "No offense, Karl, but I can't swallow that. I just can't believe that I used to be a Nazi."

Karl, forgetting about the weapon under his jacket, became very animated. "Michael, do you ever wonder why some people are born brilliant while others are dumb as rocks? Or why some people are beautiful and others ugly as sin? Reincarnation is the only explanation. Life is nothing more than living one life after another. It's the only thing that makes sense."

Michael stroked his chin and stood up. "Who were you in your last life?" he asked skeptically.

"You don't believe so you'll laugh," Karl replied.

"I promise. I'm really interested."

"O.K. In my last life, I was Otto von Bismarck," Karl said seriously, referring to the chancellor of Germany during the late nineteenth century.

Michael nodded and spoke slowly. "You know, everybody who believes in reincarnation is always a past king or something. Why is that? Why never a slave? Or a blacksmith?"

Karl laughed. "I've been both, believe me. You just asked for the most recent."

Michael was silent for a few seconds. "You really believe that, don't you?"

"I certainly do," Karl said emphatically.

"Maybe you're right. Who knows? Maybe I used to be a Nazi guard and maybe I killed my grandparents," Michael said, not really believing it. "Do you really think it's possible?"

"All I'll say is that it's not something you can rule out," Karl responded. He, too, didn't know for sure about Michael, but now he couldn't take the chance and kill him like he had planned. He didn't need any bad karma coming back at him later. Michael could possibly be one of the elite—the chosen. Time would tell. He excused himself in order to put the gun back in its drawer.

Karl reentered the room and poured them both a glass of orange juice. "I really thought you two would be together forever."

"So did I," Michael responded, resembling a whimpering puppy. "I could understand it if I cheated on her, or went out drinking with the boys every night. But my crime is that I care about this country and want to do something for TJ and my dad. How can she leave me for that?"

"I know it seems unfair as hell to you. And I agree with you one hundred percent, Mike," his father-in-law assured him. "I think that she's totally off base. It's her duty as a wife to support you. But who cares what I think? I'm not married to you, am I?" he laughed heartily.

Michael grinned. "Thank God for that. I've heard you snore and can be a real bastard sometimes. At least, that's what Katarina has told me."

"If that's what she told you, then it must be true. God never made a finer woman than my Katarina. I'm really sorry Mike, but I don't think you called me to sing the blues over Rebecca, did you?" Karl surmised.

"No, I didn't," Michael admitted. "I called because I filed papers to run for Congress. But I don't have a clue about how to get elected. I feel that I'm qualified, but I don't know the political game. I don't know the players, don't have connections, and don't have any financing. Other than that, my campaign's in great shape," he joked.

"Well, Mike, as you know, I'm not a politician. Don't like them and never will," Karl said candidly. "But, not to toot my own horn, I've done pretty well for a hardheaded immigrant and I've made a lot of connections. I might be able to help you get started. Do you know Peter Volhard?"

"The congressman from Los Angeles? I've heard of him. He's possibly the next speaker of the house, isn't he?"

"That's him. He's one tough son of a bitch, but honest as they come. And he's a good friend of mine who owes me a few favors. Why don't I set up a luncheon with him for you? He's been in the House for twenty-five years. He has a lot of respect for military types like you. What do you say?" Karl inquired, slapping Michael on the back.

"Sounds great. I owe you."

"Don't mention it. I'll expect you to do me a few favors when you get to Washington, O.K?"

"No promises, but I'll do whatever I can."

"Great. By the way Mike, I think that I can do something about filling those coffers with some campaign contributions. I know a few fat cats who respect my judgment. Get a bank account and a treasurer and let me know where to send those checks," Karl instructed. His mind was racing in a new direction. Maybe this could work to their advantage.

"Thanks, Karl. I'll make you proud of me. And Rebecca, too. God bless you," Michael said, bidding Karl good-bye. He was heading off for his first class as a new professor. Michael left sprinting down the steps. Karl Schmidt spread out his massive arms and cupped his hands behind his head. "Just maybe you will," he said out loud, laughing as he walked back into his house.

Michael drove onto the UCLA campus in Westwood thinking about when he first saw it as an awed teenager almost twenty-five years ago. He had been a star basketball player in high school, and despite his size, he'd been offered a scholarship to play at the most successful basketball program in the country. Instead, he surprised everyone, including himself, when he turned the offer down and went to West Point.

Michael had always loved teaching and enjoyed challenging young minds, debating every word that came out of their mouths by playing devil's advocate. In this forum he had the opportunity to mold students, to shape their thinking processes and help them make the most of their abilities. It didn't really matter, he felt, if they remembered what they learned. Actually, he knew they would forget most of it. What was important was that they learn how to think, reason, and analyze. He looked forward to teaching them how to compartmentalize, and filter out irrelevant matters. If he could accomplish this with dozens, and even hundreds of students, then he would be very proud.

Today felt different, because he knew, for the first time, that he was really going to be elected to the Congress. It was one thing to teach politics and government as an outsider, but he would soon be on the inside—a member of the government. He started daydreaming about serving in the House of Representatives and thinking about the grand history of that august body while walking from the faculty parking lot, carrying a gym bag and his guitar.

This reverie took him back 200 years and was the reason why he walked absentmindedly into a student, knocking her and her books to the ground.

"I'm really sorry," Michael pleaded, helping the young girl to her feet. "Are you O.K?" She didn't respond and Michael was afraid that he'd hurt her. He looked directly at her and spoke louder.

"Are you all right?"

She brushed off her faded blue jeans and replaced her baseball cap that said "Bruins."

"I'm O.K.," she said in a muffled voice.

"I'm glad of that," Michael said, relieved. "When you didn't respond, I thought that I had hurt you."

She threw her backpack over her shoulder and replied. "I didn't respond," she said in the same garbled tone, "Because I'm deaf. The second time, I read your lips." Michael wasn't sure how to react, but kept staring at the young student. There was something vaguely familiar about this young deaf girl. After a few moments of awkward silence, he finally said, "I'm Michael Madigan. I'm a new professor here." He racked his brain trying to remember the sign language he had learned before, and amateurishly signed, "What's your name?"

She broke into a wide smile. "Judy. It was nice meeting you. I'm late for class. Good luck with your new job. Good-bye," Judy said, walking away from the dazed professor. Michael smiled as he approached the Graduate Studies building and quickly made his way to his new office, where he opened the gym bag and pulled out some bizarre looking clothes, which he quickly donned.

Michael walked confidently into the classroom on this brisk, bright January day. His class consisted of eighteen graduate students, all working towards a Masters Degree in International Relations. He much preferred graduate students because they wanted to be there, unlike most undergraduates.

Quickly scanning the class he saw a very diverse group, roughly equal in gender and consisting of almost every ethnic group. He noted with fiendish delight the horrified looks his students gave this outlandishly dressed "person," none of whom realized that he was their professor. Michael's appearance was unrecognizable, which was the effect that he wanted.

He glared defiantly at the students while smoking a cigarette and carrying a guitar. He'd slicked his hair back, sporting a Rudolf Hess white T-shirt and high black boots, and he carried a heavy metal truncheon—a batonlike weapon. On one arm he wore a black armband that read "Deutsche Alternative" (German Alternative) and on the other he displayed a deceptively real-looking tattoo that said "White Power."

"We're sick and tired," he spat out angrily in German, "of being blamed for the German past." He then repeated the same phrase in English as he picked up his guitar and began strumming the strings.

"I'd like to play you a little song," he said, and began strumming his guitar.

> *When you see a foreigner on the street*
> *and he is looking at you or your wife.*
> *Go over and cut his skin*
> *and end his filthy life.*

As Michael finished singing, his students sat mesmerized, by this bizarre individual. They feared this neo-Nazi skinhead that was singing songs of hatred. Recalling the class roster that he had earlier memorized, he called a Mr. Turner.

Somewhat nervously, Alex Turner acknowledged his presence. Michael's mouth nearly dropped when he realized that this was the surfer that had saved him earlier. But because of Michael's outrageous attire, Alex hadn't recognized him yet.

"Mr. Turner, what do you think will be the ultimate outcome of Germany's reunification?" The muscular student with the blond ponytail was still in shock. He relaxed somewhat as Michael rubbed the tattoo off with alcohol and removed the armband. He answered hesitantly at first but gained momentum as his response gathered cohesion.

"I believe that it will take at least a decade before reunification is possible," Alex began. "East Germany is essentially a third world country in comparison to the West and they are, despite their common heritage, two different peoples. Easterners will be thrown into shock as they find themselves suddenly without the safety net of the omnipotent government, and forced to deal with unknowns such as inflation and unemployment."

"They'll resent the West more than ever," Alex continued. "Due to the large number of immigrants that will be competing with them for jobs, they will be more likely to display xenophobia and react violently. The only way to truly unify will be for the Westerners to give billions in aide to the East. The latter will resent being patronized and the former will resent the sacrifices they'll have to make for this foreign people," the surfer concluded.

"That's quite an incisive analysis, Mr. Turner. Thank you," Michael said with admiration. "O.K., I think I caught some of you off guard, but I am, believe it or not, your new professor and this is how I plan to conduct my classes. I wanted to shock you today and I think I did." The class breathed a sigh of relief.

"I rely heavily on what's called the Socratic method," Michael continued. "It's popular in law school, but is definitely applicable here. If I do my job properly, you'll never know my beliefs. My position will be the exact opposite of yours. You'll be the focus of this class, not me. If you intend to sit passively and just take notes, then this is the wrong class for you. Do I make myself clear?"

"Yes, sir," shouted the class in almost total unity.

"Good, then I think you'll learn a lot and have some fun as well. Before we debate one of the seminal events of the twentieth century, the reunification of Germany, let's get to know each other a little better."

Michael sat down on a stool and gave a short summary of his background. Despite no one recognizing him at first, most of the students had heard about him.

"Let's go around the room and each of you tell us a little bit about yourself," Michael proposed. "We'll start with Mr. Johnson. Is he here?"

"Here," answered a tall, articulate black student. With all eyes trained on him, Darrell Johnson started. "I'm from San Diego and did my undergraduate work here at UCLA, getting my degree in economics. I'm here because the world's getting so small and interdependent. No real understanding of economics can be complete without an appreciation for how the countries of the world interrelate politically, economically, and ideologically."

"Well said, Darrell. Glad to have you," Michael replied, walking towards the window and calling the next student.

"Judy Solomon." Getting no response, he turned back towards the class and repeated himself. This time he received an answer and was embarrassed to see why she hadn't responded initially. Judy was the deaf girl that he had run into earlier. She spoke in a rather garbled manner, but confidently and with no trace of nervousness. She was, Michael thought, the youngest and prettiest student in the class. She had piercing brown eyes and long, flowing hair that shined in the sunlight.

"I'm Judy and I'm from New York. I got my degree in political science from NYU," the petite young woman began. "I'm Jewish. I was adopted at an early age by a strange man who used to beat me. The beatings caused my deafness when I was twelve, and I ran away when I was seventeen and changed my name. He used to call me a dirty Jew. Because of the abuse and my heritage, I've become obsessed with studying the Holocaust of World War II. I'm interested in knowing how other countries interact and what makes people, entire countries, hate each other to the point of engaging in genocide."

Looking up, rather pale, was the next student, Alex Turner, the carefree surfer who had been the first one to speak. "That was pretty heavy, Judy, I'm sorry to hear that," replied Alex. "I'm almost afraid to say that my parents are German, they came here after the war. My father was merely a beer maker, who by the way, makes the best damn beer in the world. And yours truly can get kegs for almost any social occasion for a nominal fee. Why am I here? Despite many attempts to flunk out from the University of Florida, the damn place gave me a degree. And I'm not here to save the world, or the whales or anything like that. I just don't want to get a job yet and I always wanted to live in California. The women are fine and the waves are bitchin'. What more can a guy ask for?" Alex said to mixed laughter.

This went on for the remainder of the class and Michael was impressed by their overall degree of diversity, intellect, and enthusiasm. This was a distinctly dedicated and gifted group of students.

Suddenly, he had an idea. While he would seek the powers that be for his campaign, such as Karl and Peter Volhard, the grass roots could not be ignored, nor could youthful excitement. As the end of the period approached, he stood speaking slowly.

"I told you that you would never know what I'm really thinking or what positions I actually hold. That's true, at least in this class. But I have very strongly held opinions and they'll soon become widely known outside this classroom. That's because I've just become a candidate for the congressional seat in this district. I also teach a class in Contemporary American Politics and have noticed that many of you are in that class as well. I'll offer you a chance to earn credit by working on my campaign, instead of attending classes. For additional information, see me during my office hours," he said, feeling energized as he noticed that a few students seemed interested.

"For our next class, read the first three chapters of the textbook and be prepared to contrast it with the recent developments in Germany. See you next time," Michael said to his young troops. He felt excited about the future for the first time since Rebecca had left.

✠   ✠   ✠

One by one they arrived at the German economic minister's house, located on the outskirts of Bonn, West Germany, along the Rhine River in the state of Westphalia. All were present for their thirtieth meeting since that fateful day in 1945. Their second meeting was in 1950, five full years after they made their sacred pledge. The time was necessary for them to adjust to their new lives. After that, they met every other year, but recently they were meeting much more often.

All were now in their late sixties. Very soon the time would come to implement their grand scheme. A plan that had been hatched almost half a century ago amidst the destruction of a conquered nation.

"Guten Abend. Welcome once again," said the evening's host, a small man with thick glasses. He spoke slowly, and in a distinctively husky voice.

"We've labored diligently for so many years. Soon, we will again rendezvous with history to retrieve the fate that providence has meant for Germany. Our plan is close to fruition. The godless communist empire is collapsing before our very eyes and will soon find itself on the ash heap of history. The 'shining city on the hill' in America is dissipating in the face of racial conflict. The melting pot mentality is evaporating. But we must act quickly."

The West German economic minister paused for a moment while surveying his colleagues. They had exceeded their wildest dreams. Before him sat one of the richest men in America, a Congressman who would perhaps soon be speaker of the house, the secretary general of NATO, the world's foremost expert on guerilla warfare and terrorism, and a Soviet general who was also a member of the Politburo. Despite the many years in their adopted countries, they remained dedicated and obsessed by their mission to return Germany to her greatness.

"Gentlemen, we've discussed our plans over the decades in general terms, always postponing for later the specific details of our mission," proclaimed the economic minister. "But we can no longer operate on general platitudes and high-sounding homilies. This is our plan. It's been fermenting for over four decades and now is the time for us to pour it into the chalice of history."

"First, we have already achieved our major goal: reunification. We are finally a united nation after so many years."

"Secondly, we must cause chaos in both the Soviet Union and the United States. We will concentrate on doing this along racial lines, dividing these would-be superpowers into numerous ethnic blocs, each hating and distrusting the other. But we must also work to foster good relations between the two nations, so that they dismantle their military forces and remove troops from Europe."

"Third, we must destroy the dollar as the world's predominant currency and replace it with the deutsche mark."

"Fourth, we must eliminate that bastion of human filth known as Israel."

"Fifth, we must obtain nuclear weapons of our own. Since it would take too long to develop them, we must acquire them clandestinely, or by force."

"All this will take large amounts of money, much more than even we can imagine. As you know, we are deeply involved in one of the world's wonders, the first truly international bank, The International Commerce Bank, or ICB. One of our esteemed colleagues is head of what is called the black network. We will discuss this in more detail later, but suffice it to say that the primary goal of this unit is to obtain money. Lots of it," he emphasized.

"The quickest and most profitable industry that exists today is the drug market. I'm not proud of our involvement in this despicable trade, but there's such an incredible demand, and that is not of our making. We can achieve two goals at once: one, we will add to our growing resources of hard currency and secondly, we will destroy the fabric of American society, and then with its increasing openness, we will lay waste the minds of the Soviet youth."

The six men toasted each other and talked long into the night about their respective missions. Their plan was finally coming together. It wouldn't be much longer before Germany would be reborn, rising to reclaim what, by divine right, belonged to her alone.

There had been many gatherings over the years since their initial meeting over four decades before. But this was their first since Germany had been unified. As promised that day over forty years ago, they had dedicated their lives to rebuilding Germany into the power mandated for her destiny. They had separated and assumed new lives and had reached the pinnacles of power in business, politics and the military in their adopted homelands. But always burning in their minds and hearts was their mission to restore Germany to the greatness that she deserved.

They were very secretive, and with one exception even their families had been kept in the dark about their backgrounds as Waffen SS soldiers and their sacred mission to establish a Fourth Reich. They did not use their real names but instead used code names that each had chosen after a favorite German historical figure.

Their leader was known as Bismarck, after the Iron Chancellor that unified Germany in the 1870's, making it a great power after centuries of division and struggle. Bismarck raised his wine glass and spoke eloquently and with passion.

"My comrades, we have almost accomplished our mission that we pledged ourselves to almost a lifetime ago," he said, proudly. "We have achieved beyond what we in our wildest dreams could have imagined on that day back in 1945 as our great nation was being destroyed. Our country is once again unified. Wir sind wieder wer (We are again somebody)."

"Historic opportunities are often wasted, but an unusual combination of forces, including the efforts of the six of us here tonight, has altered the political map of the northern hemisphere." Bismarck spoke in his usual grandiose manner. "We must thank God that our nation is once again whole. But we are not finished. In fact, we've only just begun. We must move on to the next phase and demand our rightful place in history," he added.

The next to speak was Charlemagne, his code name taken from the leader of the First Reich, known as the Holy Roman Empire. He had adopted the Soviet Union as his homeland, and his love for Russian foods had added about a hundred pounds to his once-trim frame. He had risen to a place in the Politburo and had been instrumental in persuading the Soviet president to acknowledge the inevitability of German reunification.

"Prost! How magnificent it is to be here to implement Germany's destiny," he said enthusiastically. "We can be proud of our efforts, which are perhaps unprecedented in world history. But as our leader has said, our work has just begun. We must lash out against the cruel half century of subservience that we've been forced to endure. We are warriors, let us not forget— German warriors. All of this talk of a new world order makes me ill. Mankind knows only violence and power. History unfolds in layers and cycles, our time has come once again to retrieve our position as conquerors," he said to applause.

"Guten Abend," spoke the white-haired American politician, the most intellectual of the group, who was known as Rommel. His code name was taken from the great and elusive general of the Third Reich.

"Who would have thought that we'd be here tonight, just as we said we would be?" Rommel said, rising to his feet, punctuating his words with sharp hand gestures.

"To think that I am an American politician is just incredible since I despise Americans and their self-righteousness," he said emphatically, pausing for effect. "Their hypocrisy never fails to amaze me with all their platitudinous ramblings of democracy, constitutional rights and the like," Rommel continued. "History has shown that the only nations that remain as powers are those who take, not those who let themselves be taken. America is collapsing, drowning in a self-induced melting pot of diversity, ethnicity, and cultural distinctiveness. They have forgotten that the whole is greater than the sum of its parts. Each special interest and ethnic group insists on its own selfish interests and this can only lead to ultimate defeat for the country as a whole," he said with certainty.

The group members applauded his passion. Following Rommel's plea was the physically most imposing member of the group, Wilhelm, his name taken from the well-known Kaiser of World War I.

"I empathize with Rommel, who has had to endure working with the egocentric Americans who consider it their God-given destiny to engage in self-aggrandizement. But I have had to submit to an even less appealing environment. I work in the most hypocritical, contradictory, and arrogant organization that the world has perhaps ever seen. As you all know, my comrades, I've risen to the top of the North Atlantic Treaty Organization. The only bright spot in this despicable organization is that its basic premise is an underlying hatred for the Soviet Union," he said with disgust.

"But sixteen back-stabbing, petty, namby-pamby countries working for world peace? Please excuse me while I vomit. Germany has been a pitiful subservient excuse for a country. No more, my friends. Germany has returned and will once again rule the world!" he said, absolutely convinced that it was in the hands of the gods.

"Thank you for those inspiring words, Herr Wilhelm," spoke the next man, a short balding man with glasses. He called himself Frederick, named after the great German general of over 200 years before.

"I'm not a military man, I'm ashamed to say. I'm merely an economist. But my convictions cannot be questioned, and my dedication equals all of yours. A man must realize his strengths and understand his weaknesses. As the world gets more 'civilized,' and I use that term loosely, military power is not as important as it once was. Look at America. Its main enemy is not the country with the most bombs or missiles, but rather Japan, a nation of cars, electronics and economic know-how. Economics is the key to our return," he said convincingly.

"The American dollar is the dominant currency and as a result, the United States is the strongest country. We must make the deutsche mark the standard currency. I have a plan to achieve this and we'll take our rightful place in history once and for all. I've worked with the Bundesbank in West Germany for 20 years and have recently become the economic minister for the new unified nation. Remember, money rules," Frederick said.

"I concur with Frederick," spoke the next man, the only one with a beard. "I am Krupp, as you all know, and you remember Krupp's legacy," he said in reference to the great weapons industrialist. "I've been forced to bear perhaps the heaviest burden of all in this esteemed group. I've lived in Israel all of these years, surrounded by Jews. But I've learned much in this tiny nation, the most militaristic in the world," he said, pausing slightly.

"Conventional military might has lost its significance over recent decades. What has taken its place is guerilla warfare, low intensity conflict, and terrorism. Now that the cold war is over, the world does not fret about ICBM's being launched between the world's superpowers. But now, small regional wars are breaking out everywhere. Rather than being a result of ideological poppycock, they are based upon, more often than not, ethnic and racial grounds."

"Let's face it. Some people are superior to others. The different races of the world were not meant to live in harmony. How can thousands of years of warfare be explained otherwise? My job has had the lowest profile of all of the six, but I might add, perhaps has been the most productive. I've been developing and training terrorist groups, soldiers of fortune, arms merchants, all over the world."

"Frederick has modestly neglected to mention his significant contributions towards our success in establishing the ICB, the first truly global institution. On the surface, it seems to be an Arab bank, but in reality it is run by us and based in Europe. Frederick has been heavily involved in the economic growth of this phenomenal organization. And I've been involved in the black network, an immense and almost omnipotent terrorist faction, dealing in the drug trade, money laundering and assisting foreign leaders plunder their nation's treasuries," Krupp said rather sinisterly.

"I'm not ashamed to speak of my involvement in these activities. Drugs and terrorism at first blush seem perhaps immoral. But they are a means to an end," Krupp said defiantly.

"We must engage in all-out war, and I use that term in a different context than it usually is used. It must be a combination of conventional military forces, nuclear weapons, and terrorism, combined with economic warfare. I, too, have a plan. Now is the time for us to coordinate our plans, to mold together our dreams and strategies in order to achieve our true destiny. I drink to Germany!" Krupp said, raising his glass.

After a couple of minutes of hearty celebration, cheers and festivity, Bismarck stood and asked for silence.

"Gentlemen, we have each spoken tonight, saying, for all intents and purposes, the same thing in different ways. We agree on the goals. Now we must implement Phase II," he said, walking across the room.

"We've already achieved unification and have seen the collapse of the Soviet Union. Now, we must carry out the rest of our plan," he said passionately.

"Comrades! Let us sing to Germany!"

> *Deutschland, Deutschland über alles*
> *Über alles in der Welt*
> *Wenn es stets zu Schütz ünd Trutze*
> *Bruderlich zusammenhalt*
> *Von der Maas bis an die Memel*
> *Von der Etsch bis an den Belt*
> *Deutschland, Deutschland über alles*
> *Über alles in der Welt!*

(Germany, Germany, above all things/Above all things in the world/If in defense and in offense/We like brothers hold together/From the rivers Meuse and Nieman/From the Adige to the Belt/Germany, Germany, above all things/Above all things in the world.)

4

Michael awoke abruptly to loud knocking on his door. It was 7:00 A.M. He was usually an early riser, but it was Saturday. Who could it be?

He opened the door, still rubbing his eyes, and was quite surprised to see his oldest son, Josh, standing there.

"Josh, how are you doing, Son? Come on in. It's great to see you. This is really a surprise."

"Hi, Dad. I thought I'd come by and check out your new babe lair."

"My what?"

"You know, where the women flock to," he said jokingly.

"I'm not looking for women," he said flatly, pausing briefly. "Pretty impressive for a rat hole, isn't it? It only took me a lifetime of hard work to achieve it."

"Hey, chill out, Dad, it's not that bad and it's only temporary. You and Mom will be back together soon. I'm sure of that," he said confidently, trying to make up for his thoughtless comment.

Michael noticed, for the first time, that despite an earring that he despised, his son was one good-looking young man. It surprised him to see that he was a man and not the little boy he had remembered.

He and Josh had never been real close and he wasn't sure why. They had a lot in common; both were athletic, fiercely independent and ambitious, and they always spoke their minds. Now he remembered why they were never close. They fought constantly. Josh was never one to blindly obey. He had always challenged Michael and Rebecca, as well as teachers, coaches, and any other authority figure. This was anathema to a military man and Michael never really understood what made Josh so anti-establishment. Perhaps it was because he was never there for him. Maybe he had missed one too many birthdays or football games.

"So, Josh, to what do I owe this honor?"

Josh, like his father, had great difficulty expressing his emotions. Mostly, when he spoke his mind it was without displaying emotion.

He had grown quite a bit, Michael realized. He was at least six-feet-two and had filled out. Michael could see muscles rippling through his shirt.

Josh pushed his blond hair out of his eyes and speaking slowly, said, "Dad, I know we've never been real close, but it's not too late you know. I know you're going through a real tough time and I want to be there for you. I just started at UCLA and I figure we could help each other out."

"What do you mean, Josh?"

"Would you like a roommate?"

"Are you serious?" Michael asked, suddenly feeling like he was back in school himself. "That would be fantastic, or as my students would say, awesome. But what about your mother? She needs your help with TJ."

"To be truthful, Dad, I haven't been, like, real helpful in that regard. I'd do anything for TJ, but Mom is home full-time and she's hired a part-time nurse as well. I've been living on campus in the dormitory and help out as much as possible, but TJ wouldn't be any worse off if I moved in with you," he explained.

Michael drifted back in time to when he was a boy. Ben had always been there for him and had been the world's greatest father, a hero in Michael's eyes. But for reasons he couldn't explain, he hadn't done the same thing for his kids. Josh was now a man and Michael barely knew him. He didn't know what kind of music he liked, what football team he cheered for, whether he had a girlfriend, or what he wanted to do for a living.

"Joshua, I'm sorry for all the times I wasn't there for you. Maybe it's not too late." He hugged his son and thanked God for this great gift.

"Well, Dad, if you've got the morning free, I've made some plans for us. Are you feeling adventurous today?"

"What do you have in mind?"

"I can't tell you just yet but it's a new thing I've just taken up and I thought you might enjoy it, too."

"Let's go, champ. You lead on. I had some tentative plans, but those can be changed. Let me eat, take a shower, and make a few phone calls. I'll be ready in a flash," Michael said enthusiastically.

After a quick breakfast, they hopped into Josh's car heading west on the freeway. Josh was driving a 1957 Chevy. Michael thought that this was one of the few cars that could truly be considered a classic.

"Nice wheels, Son. In my day, a car like this was the ultimate in cool. I'm surprised that someone your age would be seen in an antique," Michael commented.

"One thing that I've learned from you, Dad, is that new things aren't necessarily good and old things aren't automatically bad. Class, style, beauty, all transcend generations. Without getting too heavy, this car is bitchin' and the chicks love it."

"I guess that's what counts," Michael said with a laugh. "I'm impressed. I have to agree with your philosophy, Son."

"People get so wrapped up in their lives, but when you look at the big picture, a single individual doesn't mean shit," Josh said a bit cynically. "Sorry for the language, Dad, but we're insignificant in terms of our relative importance. Most of my friends think the world started around 1980 and know absolutely nothing about events that happened before. I try to have a broad perspective and look back to the way things were before I was around. Can you believe that I actually like big band music? And I dig the music from the sixties. Then there were so many songs with social significance," said Josh excitedly.

"I love watching the old movies on the late show, without the sex and violence of today," he continued. "I love football and I get off on watching the film clips of the old NFL, before Astroturf and instant replay and all the specialization. There were guys that played both ways and kicked ass, like Paul Hornung, Jim Brown, Alex Karras and Johnny Unitas. Those guys were bad. That's why I'm majoring in history. We can learn a lot from what's already happened."

"Josh, I can't tell you how pleased I am to hear you say that," Michael said with great pride. "I always told you that history moves in ebbs and tides, in cycles, and that those who learn history, who master its lessons will succeed in this world. Those who don't will be doomed to repeat the mistakes of the past. I never realized that you were such an intellectual. My memories of you are riding your bicycle down that steep hill on Roosevelt Street when you were three, or that damn fool thing you did last year, that bungee-jumping out of a hot-air balloon. If I'm not mistaken, you've broken about every bone in your body at one time or another. I didn't realize that you were the studious type too."

"I guess that's why we were never close, Dad, because there are many things about me that you don't know."

The truth of Josh's statement saddened Michael.

"I never meant for it to be like that, Josh."

"I know. You just got caught up with other things and before you knew it, your little boy was gone. But I'm beyond all that now and I'm not trying to lay a guilt trip on you. I know we love each other. Let's leave it at that and move on," Josh said flatly.

Michael had been so absorbed in their conversation that he had not realized where they were heading. Looking up he saw that they were approaching a small airport on the outskirts of the city.

"Are we going on a trip?" Michael asked.

"In a matter of speaking, yes, we're going on a trip. We're going skydiving, Mr. Green Beret. That's if you can handle it, old man," Josh teased.

"Skydiving? Good God!" Michael exclaimed. "I haven't done that in years. When did *you* start jumping out of perfectly good airplanes?"

"A couple of months ago. I did it on a dare to impress a girl, whose name I can't even remember now, and found that I love it. I joined a skydiving club and we jump every Saturday morning. What do you think, Colonel? Nothing like a little free fall from ten thousand feet to get the heart pumping."

"Free fall? You must be joking. I haven't done anything but static line jumps from low altitudes in...since I can't remember when. Ten thousand feet! Are you serious?"

"Serious as a heart attack, Pop. If you can't deal with it, I'll understand. I guess you have to slow down when you get to be your age," Josh said, poking fun at his old man.

"Don't try and con me with that psychology crap. I can't honestly say that this is the way I prefer to spend my weekends, but since we're here, I'll show you how it's supposed to be done. I was jumping at night with people on the ground shooting when you were watching cartoons."

They both grinned and raised their hands up and slapped palms. Josh brought the car to a stop outside a small hangar on the landing strip.

Michael and Josh walked towards a group of eight or nine people in various stages of donning their parachutes. Surprisingly to Michael, four women were part of the group. How times have changed, he thought. But why not?

Joshua began the introductions. "Everyone, this is my dad, Colonel Michael Madigan. He's a little bit on the old side, but he's going to join us today."

A spirited yell went up from the group.

"Despite what Josh says, I'm not quite ready for the retirement home just yet," Michael said good-naturedly. "By the way, my name's not Colonel. It's Mike."

"Well, it's an honor to meet you, Mike. I'm Tim Garrison and I'm the pilot today," said the confident ex-Air Force pilot, who still carried the swagger of a fighter jock. "I'd love to join you guys today, but I'm the designated driver, so to speak. Let me introduce you to everyone."

The tall, husky pilot with the contagious smile made Michael feel at home as he shook hands with every member of the group. This should be fun, he thought.

"O.K., everyone, let's get going," Tim yelled. "I assume you've all done your pre-jump drills so let's not waste anymore time. The winds are going to start picking up. How many of you are going to air surf today?" he asked. Two of them rose their hands, one was Josh.

"What's air surfing?" Michael whispered, not wanting to appear ignorant.

"That's where you hold on to a small board, called a boogie board, and while you're free falling, you lay on it like a surfboard. You can traverse laterally at tremendous speed," Josh explained. "You can spin and tumble and it's just a real rush, Dad. When it comes time to pull the cord, you put the board between your legs and hit the ground with it still there. Want to give it a try?"

"Not in this lifetime. I'll be lucky if I survive the jump, much less try any fancy stuff," Michael declined.

"O.K., Dad, but watch me. It's really awesome."

Everyone boarded the plane after going over each other's equipment one last time and receiving a safety briefing from Tim. Michael looked around at the others' faces and noted the calm that they all seemed to possess. He would never admit it, but he was scared. He had made over 300 jumps, many in combat, several dozen free falls and had received his Halo badge in the army for high-altitude jumps. But he wasn't sure why he kept jumping because it scared the hell out of him every single time.

Most of his jumps in the army had been by static line, one end of the rip cord had been attached to the inside of the plane and the other end to the parachute. This way, the chute would pop out automatically after several seconds, even if you panicked and blacked out. But in free fall, you had to have the presence of mind to pull the cord yourself. He had never frozen, but had known two people who had. They had hit the "automatic stop," otherwise known as the ground. With skydiving there were no second chances.

He thought back to his days at Ft. Benning, Georgia, when he had been in airborne school. They had been three torturous weeks, pushing up the "red clay of Georgia." Military parachutes, he remembered, were quite different from the ultralight, brightly colored chutes seen on TV. With the ultralight chutes, skydivers can land on a dime standing up. Military chutes are rather heavy, and to turn them requires real arm strength to pull down on the riders. For this reason, the "black hats" would make their students do pushup after push-up, hundreds a day, to develop upper body strength. Before going in the mess hall to eat, students had to traverse a set of horizontal bars. Anyone who couldn't cross it wouldn't eat.

As the plane gained altitude, he continued his airborne reverie. The noise inside was incessant, but not deafening. Michael saw the apparent lack of fear on his new friends' faces, but he didn't believe it for a second.

"Want to sing some songs I learned in airborne school?"

One of the girls, a striking blonde named Kelly, broke out into an enthusiastic smile and said, "Sure thing, Mike. We're a fun-loving group."

"O.K., everyone, now I'll sing a few words, and then you repeat the same words. Got it?"

"Got it," shouted Kelly.

Josh looked at his Dad and good-naturedly rolled his eyes.

"I want to be an airborne ranger." *I want to be an airborne ranger.*

"I want to live a life of danger." *I want to live a life of danger.*

"Stand up, hook up, shuffle to the door." *Stand up, hook up, shuffle to the door.*

"Jump right out and count to four." *Jump right out and count to four.*

"I want to go to a combat zone." *I want to go to a combat zone.*

"I don't ever want to go back home." *I don't ever want to go back home.*

"If my chute don't open wide, I got another one by my side." *If my chute don't open wide, I got another one by my side.*

"If that one don't open wide, I'll be part of the countryside." *If that one don't open wide, I'll be part of the countryside.*

"Tell my wife I did my best." *Tell my wife I did my best.*

"Bury me in the leaning rest." *Bury me in the leaning rest.*

"All right! You guys are O.K. for a bunch of civilians," Michael said, grinning widely. The singing seemed to loosen everyone up. Suddenly, Michael noticed the green light—it was time.

As they were getting ready to jump, Michael looked over at Josh, feeling very proud. This was once the little boy he had rocked to sleep. He was a man now, brave and strong, and Michael felt truly blessed.

One by one they exited the plane. The cold onslaught of air shocked Michael, stunning him for a few seconds. This is where the static line would pull out the chute, he thought. Free falling in a basic spread position, he quickly reached a terminal velocity of 174 feet per second, approximately 120 miles per hour. It was both exhilarating and absolutely terrifying. He had forgotten how incredibly quiet it was at this altitude and how tremendously focused he could become. He knew that he was descending fast, but felt no falling sensation. He could no longer feel the pull of gravity because it was being equalized by the wind resistance against his body.

Michael looked around him at the other jumpers. They all wore bright colors, he suspected, so that they could spot one another. He picked out Josh, who was wearing a neon green jacket. Josh was now air surfing and was streaking horizontally across the sky, spinning like an out-of-control top. Josh's legs were extended and slightly spread, while his arms were swept back. His hands were flat, his fingers together, acting as ailerons, giving control on the latitudinal axis. Then he started tumbling, end over end. Michael was mesmerized. Maybe he would try it sometime.

He remembered Tim's instructions. It was now time to pull the cord. He saw two, three, four other chutes pop open within his sight. "Now," he said to himself, as he pulled the cord.

Nothing happened, and for a moment he didn't understand. It didn't seem real. He pulled again and the chute still wouldn't deploy. His heart started racing faster than the speed he was tumbling. Keep cool, Madigan, he thought to himself. This had happened to him once before. Stay calm. Pull the reserve. All jumpers carried two chutes for this very reason. A failed chute was very rare, but you could always count on the reserve.

He pulled the reserve, but again, nothing happened. It seemed surreal, now, as he plummeted closer and closer to the earth.

"Damn it," he shouted, and yanked with all his strength. He pulled and pulled and screamed to no avail. He had no way of stopping his rapid descent. He began to pray, once again asking God for forgiveness.

All the others were now drifting slowly to the ground, except for Josh, who had jumped last and was still falling. Josh noticed that one of the jumpers had not deployed his chute. What the hell was going on? It's now or never, he thought. Josh knew that something was radically wrong, and that someone was going to die if drastic action wasn't taken.

Josh estimated the location and direction of the plummeting jumper and literally aimed himself in that direction on his boogie board and took off. There wasn't much time, he knew. But he had to make it. Don't let it be Dad. God, don't let it be Dad.

Josh knew that direction and rate of descent could be altered and increased if he changed his position. He reached up with both hands and adjusted his goggles. He then bent his legs back at the knees to reduce the drag at the rear while extending his elbows to increase drag up front. Drawing his body into a tighter position he became a human shuttlecock, resulting in increased acceleration to about 200 miles per hour.

Josh spread his body in the basic spread-eagle position slowing his rate of descent as he approached the troubled jumper, who appeared to be passed out, his head and limbs limp like a rag doll. The ground was only about a thousand feet below. He reached the seemingly lifeless jumper, tackling him much like a linebacker would a running back. The impact almost knocked him out, and for a second, he couldn't breathe. Slowly, he regained his presence of mind and amazingly was still holding on to this out-of-control jumper. He couldn't tell who it was or even if he was still alive. All he knew was that if he didn't pull his cord immediately, they would both be dead.

His arms were wrapped around this deadweight of a person and he couldn't quite reach the cord. He stretched farther and finally reached it, sending the parachute popping out. Seconds later they hit the ground at a speed that was much too fast for a safe landing. Josh bore the brunt of the weight, and the two bodies tumbled like weeds. As the others came running over, Josh realized that the person he had saved was his father, who lay in a crumpled heap, his face covered with blood. But he was alive and Josh cried tears of joy.

"I love you, Dad."

✠   ✠   ✠

Michael woke up in a hospital bed and looked up to see Josh gazing down at him, holding his hand. He couldn't remember what had happened. He looked around confused.

"Dad, do you know where you are? Do you remember what happened?"

Slowly, hesitatingly, Michael responded. "Well, it looks as if I'm in a hospital bed. The last thing that I remember was singing airborne songs in the plane. And then we jumped. My God, it was so cold and so quiet." He was silent for a few seconds.

"Josh, my chute didn't open, did it? My God, that's what happened. What about the reserve? I can't remember."

"Dad, neither chute opened. I don't know how to say this, but we checked out your chutes and found evidence of deliberate sabotage. Someone was trying to kill you."

"Then how did I survive? I don't seem to have any broken bones. I'm just a little sore and I've got a giant headache."

"I'll tell you all about it later. The doctor said you can leave. Let's go home, Dad."

Michael slept fourteen hours and was still sore when he awoke. But he was going to be all right. Someone had tried to kill him. Why?

Josh walked into the room with a cup of coffee. Michael had forgotten that Josh had moved in the night before. "What are you doing here?"

"I live here, remember? You take it easy, understand? I'll take care of you."

"I appreciate that, Josh, but I'm all right. I have things to do. A candidate for Congress can't just lay around all day, you know. Hey, I wonder if I got any free publicity from this little incident. Maybe something good will come from this after all."

"You're right about that, Dad. We made the papers and the TV news."

"What do you mean, we? What did you do?"

"Why don't you read the paper and find out?" Josh asked, smiling and shaking his head.

As they were eating breakfast, Michael asked a question. "Josh, I can't top your little adventure that you talked me into, but there's a meeting that I'm attending tonight and I'd like you to come along. It's at the synagogue and will be sort of a town meeting between local Jews and blacks. There's always been an affinity between us, but lately this friendship is dissipating into violence. The meeting was called to try to turn this situation around."

"We need to break down the barriers through education. We need to know more about their backgrounds, lifestyles, and experiences. They, in turn, need to learn more about Jews—what makes us tick. And besides, this is a good opportunity for me. I'll be the main speaker and I hope to pick up a few votes. What do you say?"

"You're becoming quite the political animal, aren't you?" Josh noted. "I've never been wild about going to synagogue, but I'd like to go to this. Count me in," he said to Michael's great pleasure.

The temple was one of the largest in southern California and there were about 400 people on hand, Michael estimated. The format for the program was somewhat unstructured. They planned to just talk, basically, ask questions, and have some cookies and punch. Michael had prepared a speech outlining a brief history of the Jews. Several black leaders would speak after him, and the floor would be open to questions at all times.

As the crowd took their seats, the rabbi, Lisa Boehm, welcomed everyone. This was the first synagogue Michael had been to with a woman rabbi.

"Ladies and gentlemen, we're here tonight because of something that's become a very real problem," Rabbi Boehm began slowly, looking elegant in a simple but sophisticated purple dress.

"Adults and children are being hurt and even killed because of hostility between us. History's made it difficult enough for both of our peoples without this senseless behavior. Let's not point fingers, nor cast stones tonight. Let's acknowledge that there's a problem that must be stopped before any more blood is spilled," she said, to the nodding approval of many.

"I'm pleased to introduce to you tonight a man who most of you already know and who will soon be working in Washington as our representative in Congress. We're doubly blessed to have him here tonight because, I'm sad to say, there was an attempt on his life yesterday. It's only because of his son's heroism and the grace of God that he's alive. Ladies and gentlemen, Michael Madigan."

Michael stood up and walked towards the podium. Josh gave him the thumbs up signal and he smiled to himself. Public speaking had once terrified him but he was becoming quite a skilled orator.

"Thank-you, thank-you very much," Michael said to the applauding crowd. "We're less likely to fight among ourselves if we know more about each other. It's hard to hate someone that you know well. It's easy to hate strangers, foreigners, people with strange and different customs that we don't understand. It's probably true that much of our society, including our guests here tonight, don't know much about Jewish history. Hopefully, I can tell you something about our history and I'll try not to bore you."

"There are over four billion people on this planet, of whom only a small fraction are Jews. Statistically, they should hardly be noticed, but they are."

"The Golden Era of Ancient Greece lasted only 500 years while the Jews' creative period extends through their entire 4,000 year history. Their contributions have been absorbed by both the East and West."

"And yet, up until 1948, for almost 3,000 years, the Jews didn't even have a country of their own. Great nations of the pagan era, which appeared at the same time as the Jews, have totally disappeared. The Babylonians, Persians, Hittites, and Philistines, all have vanished, after having once been great powers."

Michael had always prided himself on his knowledge of Jewish history and was thoroughly enjoying himself. For a moment he recalled how TJ had wanted to become a rabbi. His eyes watered, this would never happen.

"The most recent and evil example of the anti-Semitism that Jews have had to deal with is the Holocaust of World War II, the so-called Final Solution, where Hitler and his madmen tried to wipe Jews off the world's map, taking over six million lives in the process. We can never forget."

"Ladies and gentlemen, the Jews have had a long, arduous history," he continued. "We've been called God's chosen people, but there have been times that many of us have felt as if we were God's forgotten people. Why have we been subjected to so much misery, pain and hatred from other people? I cannot answer that. But I have confidence that God will reward us for our strength, perseverance, and faith. We will not give up and we will not be defeated."

"We can identify with African-Americans because they too have felt the sting of hatred and oppression. But we ask you, as we have attempted to do over our history, not to give into the temptation of blind, retaliatory hate. I ask you not to resort to violence which leads to only more violence. Do not get caught up in a vicious circle of violence."

"We ask you to try to understand us better and we pledge ourselves to learn more about your culture, experiences, history and contemporary perspective."

Michael concluded his prepared remarks and then fielded questions. After several inquiries, he concluded.

"Thank you very much and if there are no more questions, I will be followed by Dr. William Collins, the esteemed professor of sociology from USC, who will share with us a history of African-Americans. Dr. Collins?"

"Thank you, Colonel Madigan, for those most informative and thought-provoking words." Dr. Collins, a heavyset man with a full beard, began his speech.

All at once, from one of the back rows, a middle-aged man rose his hand. "Dr. Collins, excuse me. May I say a few words before you begin? I would like to add to Colonel Madigan's inspirational comments."

Michael looked at Dr. Collins who nodded in return. The man looked very familiar, but Michael couldn't quite place him.

"We would welcome your observations," Collins said.

The man stepped up to the podium and began speaking in a loud, booming voice while the audience listened with anticipation.

"My name is Alan Roberts," the speaker said.

Michael's face went white. Alan Roberts! My God, is this the same man who was expelled from West Point a generation before? It was, Michael realized, as he took a long look. Roberts spoke to the crowd with passion and authority.

"As George Lincoln Rockwell pointed out, since the beginning of time man has fought a never-ending battle with the forces of nature. Death in childbirth, in earthquakes, diseases, droughts, famines, and death at the claws and fangs of ferocious animals have plagued humanity for thousands of years. Only the strongest have survived."

"Weaklings did not last long. Those called 'Aryan white men' eventually rose to complete domination and civilized much of the savage world." The audience was shocked by the stranger's comments. His implications were becoming more obvious. Michael was aghast by his discovery and Dr. Collins was starting to feel great anger. A number of people began to jeer. But Roberts went on.

"The natural enemies of humanity have forced the naturally inferior groups to accept the domination and leadership of the superior white group. People's revolutions were always temporary, and power sooner or later fell back in the hands of the Aryan race. As a result, the world has benefitted by the exceptional whites of England, France, Spain, Portugal, Germany, Italy, and the like, but most of all by the Nordics."

Dr. Collins rose to his feet. "You are no longer welcome. Please leave or I'll call the police!" he shouted.

Roberts kept speaking and the crowd was becoming ugly. "Over the centuries, Man fell in love with his own intellect. With this went a degradation of physical force. There was one group which had been schooled in this intellectualism for thousands of years—the Jews. Naturally weak and nonaggressive, this group even developed a religion which glorified intellectual paranoia."

As the audience yelled louder, Roberts spoke stronger and became more animated as he continued.

"Meanwhile, Negro rights stride forward. The UN gives cannibals and spear-chuckers from Africa equal treatment and they're called 'statesmen' by our liberal toadies. We forget that struggle is the father of all things. When the Negro and Jew stand against the Nordic man, the one who is racially pure, the Nordic, will be the survivor," Roberts concluded.

The crowd reached fever pitch, and in unison exploded into an emotional frenzy, charging the podium and throwing objects of all types at Roberts. Amidst the chaos a deafening explosion rocked the temple and the majestic glass windows shattered, spewing rock, glass and other debris in every direction. Columns began to collapse and flames were shooting from the building.

The rage that had been escalating against Roberts had now been replaced by the instinct to survive. The entire building was on fire and the hundreds of people who had shown up for fellowship and prayer stormed the doorways in a wave of panic. Bodies were trampled and shrieking screams pierced the night.

Once outside, the crowd was met by a burning symbol of racial hatred. Against the black sky rose a burning cross, some thirty feet in height. The flames from this hastily-built cross paled in comparison to those coming from the burning temple. But the flames of the cross were hot with hatred and they burned to the soul of everyone present.

✠   ✠   ✠

Rebecca had brought dinner up to TJ, and no matter how many times she had looked at her daughter she still couldn't believe what she saw. This once beautiful, charming girl, who had been so full of life and ambition had become practically a vegetable. She never spoke, never smiled and never showed emotion. Rebecca cried as she put down the tray in front of her listless daughter.

"Darling, it's dinner time. I made up your favorite dish, lasagna. Remember how much you always liked it before? Come on, dear, sit up and I'll feed you," Rebecca offered. Slowly, mechanically, TJ took the food.

Rebecca finished the feeding, which had become a ritual that never failed to leave her completely drained. She felt wiped out. She was incredibly tired. She walked downstairs and sat on the couch absently staring at the TV. Curse you, Michael, she thought to herself. You should be here helping me. Why did you desert me?

Rebecca, once a strong, proud woman, broke down and cried until the pain subsided and she fell asleep on the couch.

She remained in a contorted position for over two hours, until just before 11:00 P.M. She awoke with a kink in her neck from sleeping in a strange position and she noticed that the TV was still on. She was about to turn it off when a reporter noted that there had been a major fire and cross burning at the Temple Israel. She rubbed her red-rimmed eyes and listened intently.

"Good evening everyone and welcome to the eleven o'clock edition of Eyewitness News," said the anchorwoman, Alicia Hill.

"Tonight, we start off with a tragic story involving a brutal crime of hate. Earlier this evening, Jewish and black leaders met with one another trying to put aside their differences. The purpose was to learn more about each other in an evening of brotherhood and worship. This attempt to soothe their differences ended in disaster as the temple was firebombed. A cross was burned in front of the fiery wreckage of what was once the city's largest synagogue."

"Let's go live to the scene where reporter Ken Reed is standing by. Ken, could you tell us what happened?" asked the anchorwoman.

"Thank you, Alicia," replied the reporter, who was standing in front of the wild inferno. "As you can see in the background, the fires are still burning and the temple, a once beautiful and majestic building, is fast becoming a pile of ashes. Scores have been injured and there is one confirmed death. It's been difficult to tell exactly what happened, because of the confusion," Reed reported.

"Congressional candidate Michael Madigan was one of the guest speakers for tonight's prayer meeting. He is standing by to tell us exactly what happened."

"Colonel Madigan, could you tell us what led to the conflagration that we see?" asked the reporter, shoving a microphone into Michael's face.

Rebecca bolted up off the sofa in disbelief. Despite their difficulties, she still loved him and was concerned.

"This evening's program was structured to bring the Jewish and black communities together in a relaxed atmosphere, to pray and learn more about each other," Michael explained. "There's been considerable hostility and acts of violence toward and between our peoples in recent months and we wanted to try to put an end to it. Everything was going smoothly until a man in the congregation asked if he could be recognized to make a few comments."

"We welcomed his observations and led him to the microphone where he proceeded to give the most racist, hateful diatribe against Jews and blacks that I have ever heard," Michael continued. "As the crowd began jeering and booing, he became more passionate. He finished just as several people rushed towards him. And then, there was a loud explosion, all the windows shattered and there was smoke and fire everywhere. People panicked and began running towards the doors in a frenzied state, stampeding towards safety. Some couldn't get out, but those who did probably wished that they had not," he said.

"In addition to seeing this beautiful building crumble to the ground, once outside, we were met by a giant burning cross. Ku Klux Klan members were watching from the top of the hill before they got into a car and sped away," finished Michael.

"Colonel Madigan, does anyone know who the speaker was that got the crowd so agitated—do you believe that he was connected to the firebombing?" the reporter asked.

"I know he was connected," Michael said emphatically. "In fact, I know who he is. His name is Alan Roberts and he and I were close friends over twenty years ago, when we were attending West Point. He was involved in a cheating scandal and was expelled from school shortly before graduation. I never saw him again until this evening. After the explosion, I saw him run out a back entrance and get into the car with the KKK members," Michael said.

"Colonel, I've been told that there was an attempt on your life yesterday. Could you tell us about that?"

"My son Josh and I went skydiving and my chute failed. Josh managed to defy the laws of physics, catching me and pulling his chute just before we hit the ground. It was a miracle that we survived," he explained.

Rebecca's heart almost stopped when she heard that Josh had almost died. It was bad enough that his foolhardy father had risked his own life, but he had risked her baby boy's life as well.

"Damn you, Michael. You won't be happy until our whole family is dead!" she screamed at the TV.

"Colonel Madigan, do you think that there is any connection with the skydiving incident and tonight's firebomb? And if so, what does it all mean? Is it simply a matter of people who don't like your politics or is it something more?" inquired Ken Reed.

"Good question," replied Michael, pausing before fully answering. "I believe these events are connected with the death of my father, Benjamin Madigan, and others who were killed recently. These were deliberate assassinations of accomplished and respected men who were black, Jewish or communist."

"It appears that there's a growing intolerance of racial and religious minorities. There seems to be an organized effort to stir up tension between various ethnic and religious groups," Michael continued. "I hope I'm wrong, but I think that there's some organization responsible for these violent acts. Unfortunately, I don't think that we've seen the last of them."

"Thank you, Colonel Madigan. This is Ken Reed reporting live from the Temple Israel. Back to you, Alicia."

Rebecca felt overwhelmed by the continued onslaught of events against her family. They were being destroyed and it was happening on TV. When would it end? Rebecca cried herself to sleep, as she had done many times before over the last few months.

5

Michael could faintly hear the door chime as he gradually woke. It was 4:30 A.M. Who could it possibly be at this ungodly hour?

He stumbled to the door and opened it.

"Sorry to wake you, Mike, but I tried to call you last night and couldn't reach you. I guess you had your hands full." It was Karl Schmidt, who at this hour of the morning seemed even bigger than normal.

"Yeah, I guess you could say that. But is that why you're here?" asked Michael, still groggy and rubbing his eyes with his hands.

"No, it isn't," Karl admitted. "I'm heading off to Washington to meet with my friend Peter Volhard and I thought that you might want to tag along. I'm being offered a 'mission' by the government, involving the dismantling of the Soviet nuclear forces. Peter is recommending to the administration that I head up the U.S. delegation. I figured that this would be a good opportunity for you to meet Peter, who will probably be the next speaker of the house," suggested Karl.

"Really, what about Lyman?" Michael said, becoming interested. "I thought Lyman was entrenched in that position at least to the end of the century."

"Don't spread this around, but apparently he got drunk the other night and got behind the wheel of his car. The son of a bitch ended up killing a teenage girl and now I'm told that he's a basket case. I hear that he'll probably step down."

"That's awful," Michael replied. "I guess I should join you. When does your flight leave?"

"In an hour and a half. You better get your butt in gear."

"I can't be ready that soon. I have meetings today," Michael protested.

"Screw your meetings. This is much more important. You'll find out that who you know counts much more than what you know. And you can't miss meeting with the future speaker of the house, can you?" Karl remarked.

"I guess you're right. Let me make a few phone calls and I'll be ready in half an hour."

Eight hours later, they arrived at Peter Volhard's office and were shown right in.

"Karl, how are you?" Volhard said warmly, shaking his hand vigorously. "It's always good to see you. This must be your esteemed son-in-law, the very resourceful Colonel Madigan. I've heard much about you," Volhard said, displaying his well-known charm.

"Thank you, Congressman. Your reputation precedes you as well," Michael said with respect.

After a meeting of about three hours, they adjourned to a quiet, discreet watering hole where they could talk in a more relaxed mode. They were seated in the back where they could be assured privacy.

"So, Michael—may I called you Michael?" asked the white-haired Volhard.

"Of course, Congressman. Please do."

"Tell me, why do you want to leave the quiet of academic life for the dirty world of politics?"

"Congressman, my life has not been quiet," Michael said with a touch of anger. "And it has not been peaceful. My father was assassinated, my daughter's mind was poisoned by drugs, several attempts have been made on my life, and there have been repeated attacks on racial minorities in my district. Just recently I've witnessed the firebombing of my temple by the Ku Klux Klan. I have no ulterior motives. I only want to represent my district in Congress. I feel that I have the ability and the desire. I would welcome whatever assistance you could provide," Michael said firmly.

"I told you he was a hard charger didn't I, Peter?" said Karl, smiling. "This young man will go far."

"I've been impressed with your military career and am even more so after having met you," said Volhard, although Michael wasn't sure that he was being sincere. It could be just a politician shine, he thought to himself. "You have that intangible something the voters will love. And besides, you'd be doing your constituents a great service if you got that fool Arthur Rusing out of there," he said, referring to the incumbent.

"The key is money and organization. Karl has already lined up a number of wealthy friends who have agreed to contribute handsomely to your campaign. I can point you towards some professional people in southern California. You have knowledge and experience in foreign affairs, but people don't give a damn about that now," he said, explaining the realities of this election. "They're concerned with their pocketbooks, their jobs, their families. The economy is dead right now and the rest of the world is outperforming us. The public wants solutions. You need to develop some expertise in economic affairs and come up with some ideas, something novel, something exciting, something to lead this country into the twenty-first century," Volhard expounded.

Michael was begining to feel panic. He couldn't even balance a checkbook. He remained calm and looked confident.

"I'm working hard in the economic arena, Congressman, and your words ring true. Could you elaborate on your suggestion for something novel?" Michael asked deftly, putting the ball back into Volhard's court.

"The key is globalization. The world's growing smaller, Michael, and we're becoming more interdependent. There's talk of a North American Free Trade treaty, the Pacific Rim countries are trading heavily with the U.S., and Europe is taking strong steps to become more united. I think that we shall see a United States of Europe before the end of the century," predicted the congressman.

"Do you really think so?" asked Michael, in disbelief. "After centuries of warfare, do you think that they'll really be able to put aside their historical differences?" Michael queried.

"Yes, I really do. It's in their own best interest to do so. If they can work together, all will be enriched and will benefit. But I will add one caution. You're correct in your assessment that centuries of mistrust exist. I don't foresee the countries of Europe all working together unless one nation takes the lead."

Michael became intrigued. "Who would that be?"

"Well, both France and England are in a state of decline and most of the other nations are not yet strong enough. Germany is the only logical choice. Germany needs to assume a more prominent place in world affairs and become more assertive. Germany is the only country that can pull this off. Much as the U.S. assumed leadership of the free world after World War II, Germany must do the same in Europe," Volhard said.

"That's very interesting, Congressman," Michael responded. "But don't you think that the rest of the world will be wary of a nation that has brought the planet to the brink of destruction twice in this century?"

Volhard bristled, but replied calmly. "Colonel, World War II and Adolf Hitler are ancient history. I'm talking about the next century, the future. Germany cannot be shackled, forever forced into submissiveness. How long must she carry her guilt for the misdeeds of a few overly ambitious people?" he asked.

"Misdeeds? My grandparents died in the gas chambers and my father was in a concentration camp," said Michael loudly, trying to control his temper.

"Colonel, I'm not trying to rewrite history. What happened was a tragedy and I don't believe it will ever happen again. I was merely trying to think of the future, how best to make possible the well-meaning plans that have so far been proposed. That will be your main challenge as a politician, Colonel. How to change mind-sets and work towards the future," said Volhard softly.

Before Michael could respond, Volhard changed the subject. "One other thing, you need to debate that spineless Rusing. Once the voters see you face-to-face against him, you'll be in like Flynn."

This brought a smile to Michael and the three men raised their glasses together, toasting Michael's new political career.

"Call me tomorrow, will ya Mike?" Karl shouted as Michael got up to leave the bar. He was due at the Connors' house.

"I'll call first thing. Good night, Congressman. I appreciate the advice," Michael said.

"Don't mention it," Volhard said, barely able to stand up. "I look forward to working with you here in Washington. Let's get together in about two weeks when I'll be in California. We'll plan some more strategy."

Karl and Volhard started to leave as well when they were approached by a new waiter who had just come on duty. He gave his name as Frank. He looked to be in his mid-twenties. "Would you gentlemen like another round?" Frank asked.

Volhard, deeply intoxicated, looked at Frank as if he had seen a ghost. His stare penetrated the waiter's eyes. After several seconds of awkward silence, Frank felt very uncomfortable.

"O.K., I guess the answer's no," the waiter said, moving briskly away.

"What in God's name is wrong?" asked Karl. "You look like you just caught a glance of the Grim Reaper."

"That young man. He is the spitting image of..." Volhard started but didn't finish.

"Who?" Karl demanded.

"A dead man. The man I killed when I first came to the states," answered Volhard, suddenly feeling a chill.

"Oh, God, I haven't thought of that in years," he said, visibly shaken.

"I'm not sure that you ever told me the details," Karl stated, curiously.

"You remember, I'm sure, when we arrived in New York. It was June of 1945," Volhard recounted. "I came to Los Angeles and you went to Chicago. You took a train and I hitchhiked all the way to California. It was a rainy night and I was soaking wet. No one would pick me up until finally a young man stopped. He looked very similar to me. He was second generation German. Both of his parents had just been killed in a car accident," Volhard said, combing his memory.

"He had just been to their funeral in Dallas and had decided to start all over again in California. His name was Peter Volhard. He was a charming young man. I remember that we had gotten a flat tire. We went out into the rain to change it and I'll never forget how he smiled when we finished. When he walked back towards the trunk I crushed his skull with the tire iron."

"I took his wallet and identification and pushed his car off the embankment. I hitched a new ride about twenty minutes later assuming my new identity. It's been so long, I've almost forgotten my real name. Well, anyway, our waiter is a dead ringer for the late Peter Volhard, God rest his soul." Volhard raised his glass. "Here's to Peter," he toasted.

"*I'll* never forget who you are, Dietrich Luther," replied Karl. "And neither will your comrades. Your story is similar to mine. I, too, killed a young man and assumed his identity. Karl Schmidt, 1946, south side of Chicago. Another man was framed for the murder, fortunately for me. But that was years ago. Let's go home. We both have busy days tomorrow."

✠   ✠   ✠

Michael was feeling the numbing effects of the schnapps, or perhaps it was just too much excitement. It was all beginning to come together. Politics was primarily who you knew, and he was getting to know people in real power.

He hailed a taxi for the drive to Matt Connors' house, in an old section of Georgetown, the pedestrian heart of the city. Georgetown was a combination college town, diplomatic community and wealthy suburb, complete with politicians and socialites. Michael drifted back to when he and Matt used to debate politics and international affairs until the early hours of the morning. It was one thing to argue in the abstract, to say that you'd do this or formulate that policy if you were in office. And it was something else, he realized, to really have the power. If elected, he would be making decisions affecting thousands of real people with real problems. The thought sobered and excited him.

The taxi came to a stop alongside an old brownstone which housed Matt, Pam and the three Connors children. He paid the driver and briskly strode the stairs.

After knocking, the door was opened by a beaming Pam, whose wide smile seemed to light the night.

"Michael, how are you? It's so good to see you," she said warmly. They gave each other a long hug and he kissed her gently on the cheek.

"You haven't changed a bit," Michael greeted her graciously. "You're still as beautiful as the day you married Matt."

"I'll gratefully accept that compliment even though there isn't a word of truth to it. These bones couldn't come close to fitting in my old wedding dress," she said laughing, although it wasn't true. Pam Connors could still get into her high school cheerleading outfit and she kept herself in top shape, befitting a former college athlete.

"Nonsense. I bet you can't even buy a drink without being asked for an ID," Michael continued. "Now where's that old warhorse of yours?"

"Warhorse? Who you calling a warhorse, young man?" Matt said, coming down the stairs. "Haven't you learned to respect your elders yet, you young whippersnapper," Matt yelled good-naturedly while limping to the front door. He concealed it so well that Michael often forgot that Matt had only one leg, his right was artificial. But he couldn't forget how Matt had lost his leg. His bravery, or perhaps foolhardiness, had saved Michael's life. He could still visualize Matt jumping on the hand grenade that had been thrown by a wide-eyed boy who had been walking along the Mekong Delta.

"Come in, come in. I gotta warn you now that if you get elected, you won't be welcome in this house. I have a policy against socializing with rapscallions," Matt bellowed, slapping Michael on the back and doubling over with laughter.

"Everyone knows that the world is run by the renegades in the White House basement," Michael retaliated. "All they do in Congress is campaign, go on junkets and bounce checks," he joked.

Matt laughed heartily. "Well, this renegade is starving. Could I twist your arm into eating some of Pam's cooking?" he said.

"I suppose, if it will make you happy," Michael joshed. He was ravenous and knew that Pam was in a league by herself when it came to cooking.

They were joined for dinner by three very intelligent and articulate teenage kids: Albert, sixteen, a talented young actor who had, along with TJ, mesmerized Michael the night of the year-end play; Danielle, fifteen and an honors student, with stunning eyes and a gorgeous smile just like her mother's; and John, thirteen, an up-and-coming star athlete.

The dinner discussion focused on the destruction of nuclear weapons, a subject that they had addressed earlier. The Connors family also believed in the dinner table forum for discussing serious topics. The children were encouraged to participate and offer their views.

Matt was often surprised by how incisive children could be. He noticed that their views were not encumbered by the artificialities of politics and pretense.

Michael thought the topic a little too heavy for dinner and switched gears. "How's your job going?" he said to Pam.

She paused for a moment to finish swallowing. "Just great, Michael. We're making real strides forward and can do things now that we couldn't imagine a year ago."

"Holograms, right? You make those things like they use on Star Trek, the 3-D images. How do they work again?"

Pam truly loved her job and never tired of talking about it. "Well, conventional holograms are made by splitting a laser beam into two parts. One beam illuminates an object that reflects light onto film. As the direct beam from the laser also strikes the film, the two beams interfere with each other. When laser light is spread through the film, the spread is re-created to provide depth cues. It's reconstructing the rays just as though the object were still there. Got it?"

"Oh, yeah, I got it," Michael replied, even though most of it went over his head.

"Well, let me show you," Pam said excitedly. "Follow me."

Michael followed her into the guest bedroom that he would be using, and saw all sorts of computer equipment and assorted paraphernalia. He let out a low whistle.

"I don't know what this stuff does but it sure looks impressive," he remarked.

Pam became more animated as she started describing everything. "See this plastic tubing? We put some film in here and take an object, like this book, and place it right here. An overhead laser shines its beam through a diverging lens and onto the film and then onto the object. Light falling from the object interferes with light falling directly on the film from the lens. See?"

"And this stuff makes a hologram?"

"Yes, sir," she said, smiling widely.

"Can you show me one?" Michael asked.

"I'm afraid not right now. I was working on it before you came and it's not quite ready. Maybe later."

After the hologram tour Michael and Matt adjourned to Matt's study for some fine cognac.

"Green, what do you know about Peter Volhard?"

"He's from the old school," Matt retorted. "He's been in Congress since God was a corporal. He's articulate, sharp as a tack, and well respected. He's a real gentleman, too. He's incredibly persuasive. I've heard stories where he got rival factions to compromise on a vote where only moments before they were ready to rip each other's throats out. He's smooth, Mike. If you're looking for something bad for me to say about him, I can't think of anything. He's a truly class guy and the U.S. will be the better if he's the next speaker of the house."

"Wow, that's quite a ringing endorsement. He's promised to help me in my campaign," Michael said.

"Then you're practically in. What Peter Volhard wants, he almost always gets."

"That's great to hear, Matt. Now, let me ask you a little bit more about this dismantling program. Are the U.S. and the Russians really going to destroy all of these weapons?" Michael asked skeptically.

"It certainly looks that way, Mike," said Matt, shrugging his shoulders. "At least that was the plan before the 'commies' collapsed into a million pieces. It's hard to say now what the hell's going to happen. But I'll tell you that the U.S. is prepared to act unilaterally if need be. The president is adamant about this. We'll start getting rid of these things real soon," he said with certainty.

"It's just mind-boggling, Matt, what's happened in the last few years. I mean, our whole foreign policy for over forty years was based on this tremendous fear of the Soviet Union and now, in the blink-of-an-eye, they no longer exist."

"It's a mindblower, all right. We're running out of enemies."

"I don't believe that for a second," Michael countered. "I bet right now, as we speak, some group of generals is meeting somewhere plotting to take over the world. It's in our blood, old buddy. Humans are violent creatures, we're predators. No matter how civilized we become or how many international peace conferences we call, there will always be war. I wish it wasn't true but I'm afraid that it is," he said cynically.

"You may be right. I hope that you're not but..." Matt paused for a moment to sip the last of his cognac. "What else was it that you wanted to ask me about?"

"I almost forgot. I don't know if you heard about my skydiving incident and the firebombing at the temple?"

"I heard about it. It's been the scuttlebutt for the last two days. People in Washington still know who Colonel Madigan is. Did they catch anyone?" Matt inquired.

"Not yet. But I think there's some connection between these events and the earlier assassinations."

"You mean on your father and the others?"

"Yeah. I can't quite put my finger on it, but I can't help but think that it's all a part of some master plot," Michael speculated. "But why now? And why blacks, Jews and communists? How are they all connected?"

Matt thought carefully before replying. "You could be right, Mike. Let me look into it a little closer. What group would be against all three?" he mused.

"Hey, Cube, remember Alan Roberts? I saw him the other day," Matt said, changing the subject suddenly.

Michael started gagging. "You saw Alan Roberts?" he said, his face flush.

"Yeah, I saw him all right. It's been twenty years, but I recognized him. He said he was going to get you."

Michael became silent. Matt wasn't aware that Roberts was involved in the temple firebombing. "Green—" he started, but didn't finish, as Matt once again changed gears suddenly.

Matt's face broke out into a huge smile. "Follow me, Mike," Matt said excitedly, rushing out of the study. He ran up the stairs quickly and ordered Albert to come with him. The three then exited the house and walked out to a large garage, dominated by musical equipment.

"Mike, did you know that Albert's a very talented drummer?" Matt said, picking up a bass guitar. Albert took a seat behind a huge set of drums.

Michael smiled, realizing what was going on. Matt handed him a guitar and Michael quickly tuned it. Matt checked out the amplifier and the rest of the equipment that surrounded them.

Michael couldn't stop grinning as they prepared for their impromptu jam session. Matt gave the signal and began laying out a riff that caused a shiver of excitement to go up his spine. Albert followed his father's lead and pounded out a very inspiring beat on his drums. Michael quickly strummed the lead guitar as the three harmonized, belting out the Beatles' *Get Back*. Both Michael and Matt were fans of the Beatles. Michael's personality was eclipsed by the rock-and-roll rebel within as he shouted the lead vocals into the microphone. Pam and the kids quickly ran into the garage as the infectious rhythm engulfed the whole house. Pam watched Danielle and John dance and smile as the trio played several of their favorite songs for about forty-five minutes. Finally, Pam put a stop to things, over the protests of Michael and Matt.

"We have neighbors, you know?" she said firmly but good-naturedly. "How would it look for a White House official to be arrested for disturbing the peace?" she said.

"Every party has a pooper—" started Matt.

Michael reluctantly put down his guitar. Laughing, he said, "Come on, Matt. Maybe Georgetown is too stuffy for Hendrix and the Stones."

"You know, instead of peace talks at the UN, we should have jam sessions," Matt proposed. "I can see it now. The Security Council would be sort of Lawrence Welkish, but I bet the General Assembly could get down, don't you think?"

"You bet," Michael replied. "I think that you should propose it to the president."

Matt groaned at the thought. "Andrew Tolbert's idea of letting loose is to have the Marine Corps band play John Phillips Sousa," Matt laughed.

"Oh, I'd be willing to bet that even he couldn't keep his feet from moving on a couple of the songs we belted out tonight," said Michael, as everybody walked into the house laughing and smiling. "I'm going to hit the sack, guys. I'm bushed."

Pam started fixing up the guest room. A few minutes later it was ready. Michael closed the bedroom door while waving good night to Matt and Pam, who were standing in the hallway.

Matt started laughing and rubbing his hands. "Oh, this is going to be so sweet. Revenge is delicious," he said excitedly.

"It's the Y chromosome, isn't it?" Pam said, with feigned disgust. "One day you two will go too far with your practical jokes and will regret it," she said, wagging her finger. But Matt was too excited.

Michael wasn't exactly drunk, but he wasn't completely sober. That's O.K., he thought. It was a productive evening with Karl and Peter and it was more fun than he had experienced for a while with the Connors'. He relived the jam session in his mind. Thinking back to the meeting with his father-in-law and Volhard, he was satisfied. There had been a few laughs, he had learned some valuable things and made some vital contacts. Colonel, you done good, he thought to himself. "You deserve a good night's sleep," he said out loud, hitting the pillow and immediately falling asleep.

The rain pounded his bare back like hard pellets. The wind was howling with such velocity that he could barely see. His hands were swollen and he could barely grasp the oars anymore, but he knew that if he didn't, the taskmaster's whip would crack against his bloodied skin. He could accept his fate on this prisoner of war boat, but the Nazi bastards meted out the same punishment to his children.

My God, he thought, what kind of animals could whip a child—a girl for that matter? He looked behind and saw TJ screaming and writhing in pain, mouthing words that he couldn't understand because of the howling wind and rain. Next to her, a Nazi soldier was cracking his whip on David. He's only ten years old, for God's sake. Leave him alone, you sons of bitches! Behind David, Michael saw Josh, who was suffering the wrath of some screaming idiot with a rifle. Josh wouldn't take any crap from anybody! Tell him to go to hell, Son. The Nazi hit Josh soundly in the head with his rifle butt, sending blood squirting as the skin on his face broke open.

Michael was beside himself with anger and hatred, when suddenly there was a loud explosion. A bomb had hit the starboard side and the ocean began pouring into the shelled boat. It was sinking! Panic set in aboard the sinking boat. Michael realized that he might die, but he took some solace in seeing the terror and fear in the eyes of his German captors.

Out of nowhere he thought he saw something. Off the port bow. It looked like a periscope. It was a submarine and it was surfacing. A tall German officer raised his head up out of the vessel and forcefully began issuing orders. They were being rescued. The guards and prisoners began climbing onto the submarine.

One by one they hoisted themselves into the partially submerged craft. Everyone was on now, except Michael and the kids. He had gone first so that he could help the half-beaten children on board. As he reached out, the German captain shouted, "Choose one. There is only room for one more."

Michael screamed. "Choose! You can't be serious. These are my three children. I can't choose."

"Choose one, you Jewish swine, or all four of you can drown. Choose now!" As he spoke, the prison boat was sinking. Josh, TJ and David screamed. Michael grabbed Josh and pulled him aboard as TJ and David's eyes locked onto his. The hatch to the submarine started to close as the prison boat finished capsizing. TJ and David were swallowed up by the sea.

"God forgive me," Michael said, weeping uncontrollably.

Michael bolted upright, his whole body tense, his heart pounding. It had been a dream. But what was that? He could barely make out a figure, standing in the corner of the room. At first, it was amorphous, translucent. But it began transforming right before him, taking shape, adding colors. It was a West Point cadet, about twenty some years old, in a dress uniform. The cadet stood at attention, a rifle at shoulder arms. Michael looked closer at the image. It was Alan Roberts, tall and lean, his jaw jutting out, his uniform glistening in sunlight, from twenty years before. What was going on?

It couldn't be, but there he was. "Alan, is that you?" Michael asked, shifting in his bed.

There was no response. The cadet remained at attention. Michael stared.

Then all at once there was a voice. "I'll get you Madigan, if it's the last thing I ever do."

Michael's entire body became taut and his eyes darted madly across the room. This was the bastard who had firebombed his temple. His eyes became fixed on a set of golf clubs that were standing in the corner of the room. He jumped quickly off the bed, grabbed a club and began swinging it at his former best friend.

Michael let out a scream, slashing the club wildly at Roberts, but the image of the cadet remained motionless. Michael swung madly again right through Roberts' neck, cursing as the golf club knocked over a lamp, but the West Pointer remained standing.

"You son of a bitch," Michael yelled at the motionless figure.

Matt suddenly appeared and flipped on the lights. He saw a wild-eyed Michael brandishing a golf club at a holographic image. Michael was holding the golf club like a baseball bat and was startled to see Matt and Pam standing there. Slowly he looked around him at the destruction that he had caused.

"Michael, calm down man. Oh, God, I'm sorry, Cube. It was just a joke, man," Matt explained. "It was just a joke, Mike. This isn't really Alan Roberts. It's just a hologram."

"I knew that one day you guys would go too far," Pam scolded. "Are you all right, Michael? I'm sorry that I let him talk me into this nonsense," she said, giving Michael a hug.

"I had a humdinger of a nightmare, another Nazi one. I awoke in a panic only to see our old friend Mr. Roberts."

"Mike, I never thought that you would react that way. I know that you and Alan had a bad parting, but you were homicidal just now. Why?"

"I guess you weren't aware that the man who led the firebombing at my temple was our friend, Alan Roberts, who now likes to ride around in white sheets," Michael explained.

"Oh, man, I had no idea. Roberts did that?"

Michael merely nodded and Pam chewed out her husband something fierce. "Why don't you get your sorry butt back to bed before I nail it to the smokehouse wall?" she said. Matt sulked out of the room like a whipped puppy.

"Michael, I'm so sorry. Will you forgive me?"

"Hey, don't sweat it, Pam. I guess I had it coming. Matt gave me fair warning. Payback's a bitch."

"Well, try to go back to sleep. See you in the morning, O.K?"

"O.K. Pam. Good night."

A couple of hours later, Matt woke his houseguest. Michael sat quickly upright, his heart racing.

"What time is it?"

"It's five thirty in the morning. I think I forgot to tell you that we're going skiing today, just Pam and I. We're taking two days off and heading up into the Poconos. Want to come with us?" Matt inquired.

"I'd love to, Matt, but I have to get back. I have some meetings to attend this afternoon," Michael explained.

"Well, I tried. You know what they say, all work and no play..." Matt said smiling.

"Maybe next time. I'm just going to take a quick shower and take off. Where exactly are you going?"

"We're gonna try a new place this time. It's called Camelback and its right off Interstate 80 in Pennsylvania. They've got an 801-foot vertical drop there. I can't wait. I haven't skied in two years and I'm psyched. Listen, Mike, we're going to be leaving in about an hour. Why don't we drop you off at the airport on our way?" Matt offered.

"Sounds great."

"And, Mike, in all seriousness, I'm really sorry about last night. I had no idea it would go down like it did," Matt said seriously. He smiled. "But I had you going, didn't I? The voice sounded like him, didn't it?"

"You had me going, Green. I'll give you that. But you better watch over your shoulder from here on out. I'm going to hang your gonads out to dry one day," Michael warned, smiling.

Matt and Pam pulled into Dulles airport around 6:45 A.M. and bid Michael good-bye.

"Give them hell, Mike. We hope that you'll be living in Washington again soon," Matt said, shaking Michael's hand.

"Me, too. It depends on the voters. You never know why people vote the way they do. Thanks for everything. Give my best to the kids," Michael said. He kissed Pam on the cheek and then headed into the terminal.

A couple of hours later, the Connors' arrived at the ski resort. They parked the car, got dressed and headed right for the slopes. Matt and Pam were both experienced skiers and there was plenty of fresh powder. Camelback had a reputation as a tough mountain with very few intermediate or beginner slopes. This slope was for young, aggressive skiers for the most part and Matt began to feel his age after a few heart-pounding runs.

After getting to the bottom of one particularly difficult run, Matt waited for Pam to catch up. It was just as well that she usually ran a couple of minutes behind him on each run. It gave him the chance to catch his breath.

"Hey, babe, over here," Matt shouted, raising one of his poles skyward. Pam skied up with a look of exhilaration.

"That last run was fantastic. Did you do the moguls on the side?"

"No, you know those damn things eat me up. I just went straight down the middle. I was really hauling down that long stretch," Matt exclaimed. "Hey, what time is it?"

"It's a quarter after twelve, I'm starving. Let's break for lunch," Pam suggested.

"Why don't you go ahead and grab a table, babe?" Matt replied. "I'm gonna do one more run." He gave her a quick kiss and headed for the chair lifts.

Apparently, a lot of people were stopping for lunch as the long lines they had seen all morning were now much shorter.

The people in front of him paired off as they got onto the two-man chairs that whisked the skiers up the mountain. Matt looked around for someone to join him. A short woman in a ski mask that covered her whole face approached him from behind.

"Single?" she said.

"Yes," Matt replied, and the two of them got onto the chair together. He wasn't quite ready and almost got knocked down by the chair.

"Whoa, I almost bit the dust there," Matt said laughing, but his new companion didn't respond.

"Beautiful day, isn't it?" he asked, trying to make small talk. She just nodded her head.

Quite the social butterfly here, Matt thought to himself. Maybe he should just keep his mouth shut and enjoy the view. He closed his eyes, relishing the absolute quiet of the mountains and feeling the splash of the sun on his face. Nothing could be better than this.

"Mr. Connors. I have some important information for you," said the woman skier, snapping Matt out of his daydream.

"How did you know my name? Who are you?"

"My name's not important. But there's a connection with all of the things that have been happening," she said mysteriously.

"What do you mean? What are you talking about?" Matt said heatedly.

"Look to Germany. That's the connection," she said softly.

"Germany? Are you talking about Ambassador Madigan and the other assassinations?"

"Yes. It's the Germans," she repeated.

They were almost to the end of the lift and Matt was puzzled. "Are you CIA or something? What's your name?"

"Listen, I know a lot. I'm going to be contacting you from time to time and will give you more information as I get it. You can call me Sgt. Pepper," she said jumping off the chair.

"Sgt. Pepper? You mean like the Beatles?" he asked, but she was already about twenty feet away. He was so astonished by the mysterious skier that his legs crossed causing him to fall face first into the thick, powdery snow.

He pulled his face from the snow and desperately looked for his chair-mate in the bright blue ski suit, but she was long gone. What was she talking about? What did she mean by "look to Germany?"

espite the many demands made upon the attorney general, Tony Peterson managed to work some type of workout into his busy schedule every day. This morning he had just played racquetball with a young, aggressive attorney in his office named Paul Hampton. The attorney general had just turned fifty but was still "hot" on the court.

"Great game, sir. I'd heard that you were still pretty good," the blond-haired Hampton said, out of breath.

"What do you mean *still*? You mean I did O.K. for an old guy?"

Hampton laughed. "All I know is that you whipped me."

Peterson slapped him on the back and walked away smiling. Hampton would never know that he was so sore he could barely walk.

Peterson showered, changed and quickly headed back to work. He would be giving a press conference later about the administration's new drug enforcement policies.

While he was reviewing the briefing books his staff had prepared, his private phone rang. Only three people had this number: his wife, the FBI director, and the president.

"Peterson here."

"Good morning, Mr. Attorney General. How are you this morning?"

"Who is this?"

"Let's just say friends. Friends do things for each other, do they not?"

"What are you talking about? How did you get this number?"

"You don't seem to be very friendly. Well, that's O.K. Let's get down to business. We want you to exclude certain portions of your new drug enforcement policy and not address them at your press conference," said the mysterious caller.

"Are you crazy? Do you know who you're talking to? I'll have you behind bars for the rest of your life," Peterson barked.

"I don't think so, sir. I'm sorry you're so uncooperative. We'll have to resort to other means. Mr. Attorney General, someone would like to speak to you," said the sinister voice.

There was a moment of silence and Peterson's anger grew. The nerve of these bastards.

"Daddy, help me please. They're hurting me." It was the pain-filled voice of his daughter, Melanie. He began shaking, feeling an emotion he had never known before, a combination of intense fear and hatred.

"Melanie, are you all right? Where are you?"

Before she could respond, she was cut off. "Sorry, Mr. A.G. Wish we could chat longer but we have business to take care of. Melanie is really built for a thirteen-year-old. I bet she could keep all of us satisfied for a long time. Am I right?"

"If you lay one hand on her, I'll personally rip your heart out. Do you hear me?"

"I hear you. We're not just some piss-ant irritant. We're for real, Mr. AG. We'll be calling the shots and you'll do what we say, or everyone you love will die a very painful death. You do what I've instructed or Melanie will pay the price. End of discussion." The line went dead.

✠   ✠   ✠

During the cross-country flight back to California, Michael feverishly worked on his campaign. Karl had made good on his promises and money was coming in quicker than he had ever imagined. The radio and TV ads were working well, and he had been campaigning tirelessly. Fourteen hours a day was the norm. He had been greeting workers as they arrived at their construction sites, shaking hands with shoppers at the mall and speaking on college campuses. And he tried to stage at least one event per day that would make the evening news.

Most important, however, was the small group of students working on his campaign. They had originally signed up for the class credits but soon it became much more to them. Gradually, they came to believe that they could make a difference and that their efforts could actually change people's lives. The most important thing for Michael was that they believed in him. In him, they saw a man who cared and would not compromise his principles.

Michael landed at LAX and was met by Alex. Both of them were very excited. Tonight was the biggest test in the campaign so far. Michael was debating Arthur Rusing and the event would be televised. Michael was well prepared and thoroughly familiar with the issues. He knew every vote that Rusing had ever made. He was confident. His "staff" of college students had made him so.

During preparation for the debate, Alex played the part of Rusing and the other students acted as reporters who would be asking the questions.

Darrell Johnson concentrated on economic issues while Alex handled foreign policy and social issues. Judy Solomon had been working directly with Michael: summarizing, collating, and digesting the tons of available information into a workable series of notebooks. She quizzed him endlessly, trying to trip him up by playing devil's advocate. He was ready.

"Colonel Madigan, remember to stress jobs over and over," Darrell reminded him.

"Don't forget to emphasize military budget cuts in the post cold war era," chipped in Alex, the new resident Soviet expert.

"Be prepared to get some off-the-wall hypothetical, like what you would do if your daughter was raped and killed, would you favor the death penalty?" Alex added, then instantly regretted saying it, remembering TJ. An awkward silence followed. Michael's thoughts began to drift, but he quickly snapped out of it, realizing that everyone was looking at him.

"Sorry, Colonel, that was pretty stupid of me. I just meant for you to be prepared for some strange question."

"I know, Alex. I appreciate the warning. I'm very grateful for all of your work, energy, and enthusiasm. You've made sure that I'm prepared and you've given me confidence. No matter what, I'll always be able to say that you are my friends," Michael said with emotion.

He saw Josh enter the room where the debate was being held, holding hands with a striking blonde woman.

"Hi, Dad. Knock him dead," Josh advised. "Do you remember Kelly? From the jump?"

Michael suddenly remembered. He knew he had seen her somewhere before. Now he envisioned her with a helmet on, singing songs, ready to jump from the plane.

"Hello again, Colonel. Last time we saw each other, things didn't go too well. If the questions get too tough, remember your reserve," Kelly suggested.

Michael laughed and said, "I'll keep that in mind. I never thought of it that way. Hopefully, I won't crash and burn like last time."

Michael pulled Josh aside. "Josh, I just wanted to tell you how much it's meant to me to have you living with me and helping me with this thing. You're the only one in the family that seems to understand."

"I believe in you, Dad. I agree that this is the best way to make things better. I know that you'll make it and I'll be right there beside you."

"That means more to me than you'll ever know. Off the subject, are you and Kelly an item now?" Michael said, teasingly.

"Well, Dad, I have you to thank for that. Seems that she was so impressed with me saving you that day that she can't live without me."

"Hey, that's what fathers are for, to risk their lives for the sake of their son's love life," Michael said with a straight face. "But if things start to go sour between the two of you, don't expect an encore. I think I've done enough."

"Agreed. Seriously, Dad, I think that I'm falling for her in a major way. She's not like the other girls."

"You're lucky, from what I've seen. Well, I have to get going. I love you, Son."

"I love you too, Dad. Give 'em hell."

Michael had Judy apply some makeup to his face. The heat from the TV cameras could be overwhelming and he had to make sure that he didn't sweat profusely. He had to project strength and calm.

Michael saw Rusing arrive and thought he detected some nervousness. Rusing had been serving in the House for eighteen years and had never been seriously challenged, a fact that Michael couldn't understand. He thought Rusing was intellectually inept and morally corrupt.

Last second preparations were being taken by the television crew and the candidates. Each candidate stood behind a podium and a five-person panel sat behind a table strewn with notebooks.

"Good evening, ladies and gentlemen, and welcome to this live debate between our two candidates for Congress. On my left is the incumbent who has been elected to this seat for nine consecutive terms, Arthur L. Rusing; and on my right the challenger, a first time political candidate, retired military officer and professor of history, Michael M. Madigan. I'm Henry Marsh with K-AMP television and I'll be the moderator for tonight's debate," said the journalist.

"Joining me are four respected members of the news media. On my left is the Pulitzer Prize winning writer for the Los Angeles Times, Burke Sellers. Next to him is Marian O'Neal of Channel 12. On my right is political reporter, Harris Atkins. And next to him, Sandra Lewis, economic reporter for the Wall Street Journal."

"Tonight's format will be as follows: the candidates will each make an opening statement, which will be followed by a series of questions from the panel on a variety of topics. Congressman Rusing, will you begin, please?"

"Thank you, Henry," Rusing began. "I'm pleased to be here tonight. As you know, I've been representing this district for almost two decades. I have the experience and knowledge that's necessary in these trying times. My opponent is, to be perfectly candid, inexperienced, and we simply can't allow for on-the-job training. Your elected Congressman must be thoroughly familiar with the issues and with the major players," he added, condescendingly.

"With all due respect to Colonel Madigan, he has been hopscotching around the globe for the last twenty years and has been a resident of this district for only the minimum time required by law for a candidate. There is no way for such a newcomer to witness firsthand the problems that the people here face, or to learn how the system works."

"I offer continuity and steady progress towards a fully employed economy, with good jobs for all, and a foreign policy that projects both strength and compassion. This is a unique time in our nation's history and it's imperative that the most qualified people be at the helm. Thank you."

"Colonel Madigan, you may now give your opening statement," said Marsh.

"Thank you," Michael began. "I agree that during these times of great change and challenge we need strong leaders. Mr. Rusing has been a weak leader and an ineffective congressman. His major reason for asking you to vote for him is that he is an incumbent. Well, ladies and gentlemen, that's not enough. It's time to move away from the stale politics of the past and move towards the future, aggressively and with conviction."

"First, with respect to the economy, I've prepared a twelve-point program that will create jobs and lower interest rates, and provide incentives for saving and investing. We must be able to compete in the global market by improving our children's education, and by quality training for our workers. If not, Germany and Japan will pass us by like we were standing still."

"Second, the cold war is now over. The time has come to put aside the tired dogma of the last forty-five years. We no longer face the possibility of World War III with the Soviets. That doesn't mean the world is safe or that we have no more worries; the world may even be more dangerous now. The balance of power between the United States and the Soviets has kept the peace. Now the emphasis will shift to regional wars and ethnic struggles."

"The United States is once again the sole superpower, just as it was after World War II. We must use our power and influence intelligently if the world is to be free of constant war. Military might and economic power are interrelated. We must keep our economy strong if we are to have a viable foreign policy."

"Thirdly, there are several issues that confront us as a community. Racism has once again raised its ugly head and intolerance is becoming epidemic. I'm sure most of us feel the same disgust and outrage over these cowardly incidents and are prepared to vigorously combat prejudice."

"Similarly, our neighborhoods are drowning from the plague of drugs pouring into our society. We must stop this poison from infiltrating any farther. Drugs are getting into our grade schools, and because of the tremendous profit potential, the violence accompanying them is unprecedented. Drive-by shootings, automatic weapons, explosives, and other resources that often outmatch those of the police cannot be allowed to continue unabated. We must declare war on drugs and take back our cities. We must punish the dealers, educate our young people, and stop the drugs from getting into our country. I pledge to you my body and soul in this effort," he promised.

Michael lowered his head and almost whispered. "I'm a father of three beautiful children. My daughter Terri, a once vibrant girl, is now almost completely brain dead and is kept alive only by modern technology. Sadly, I missed much of her growing up and was determined to be there for her as she grew into adulthood," he said softly. "Cocaine robbed me of that privilege."

"She'll never graduate from high school now, never go to college, never marry and have children, and will always be faced with the indignity of having to be helped by someone to go to the bathroom or to eat. Drugs destroyed my daughter. Ladies and gentlemen, I vow to you that I will do everything in my power to make sure that you are not robbed of your sons and daughters."

"Thank you, Colonel Madigan and Congressman Rusing. Now, we will begin the questioning portion of the program. Mr. Sellers, if you could begin, please."

"Thank you, Henry. This first question will be directed to Congressman Rusing. Congressman, the economy seems to be the main topic with the voters today. How do you propose to jump-start it?"

"Burke, your question presupposes that the economy is dead," Rusing replied. "I beg to differ. More people than ever are working. Inflation is low. Interest rates are close to an all-time low and Wall Street is booming. True, there are too many people out of work, but overall the economy is solid. We need to encourage, however, further investment. We need to lower taxes, especially the capital gains tax, allowing people to invest those monies into the market, making the economy stronger. And we need to concentrate on America first. We cannot kowtow to the Japanese and the Europeans like trained dogs. We must stop buying their products and stop selling our country off to wealthy samurais."

"Colonel Madigan, the same question to you, sir," Sellers added.

"I can't believe that Mr. Rusing is trying to sell the people the same old story," Michael said, staring directly into the camera. "The economy is not fine. It's sick and needs some drastic action. He talks of capital gains taxes as the whole answer, but when has that really worked? It may be a great theory, but look at the state of our economy! Mr. Rusing is insulting our intelligence when he says that if we prop up the rich and the privileged, maybe some scraps will fall from their table. It's a tired old theory that never worked before and never will."

"Mr. Rusing further tries to tell us that we must resort to protectionism because of the evil ways of the rest of the world. Protectionism is based on misplaced patriotism and is out of touch with reality. Like it or not, the world is connected. What happens in Tokyo and London affects us here in California and vice versa."

"Try telling the unemployed construction workers that our economy is fine, or the owners of hotels whose rooms are empty. Or to the airlines who are jumping over each other in their efforts to file bankruptcy. Or to the real estate agents who have to get second jobs at McDonalds at night to feed their families. And try to tell forty-five percent of black teenagers who can't find a job that everything is fine. I'm sorry to say, Mr. Rusing, that if you ever talked to your constituents or ever attended the votes on crucial issues that you were elected to do, you would know that everything is not fine," Michael said, facing his opponent.

"How dare you attack me personally," shouted a visibly stunned Rusing. "My record is beyond reproach."

"Then why did you miss thirty-five percent of the votes on the floor of the House last year, the poorest record in Congress? And why don't you ever visit your district, Mr. Rusing? I'll tell you why. You've lost touch with your constituency, with the issues. You now seek reelection in order to maintain your privileges. Tell us, Mr. Rusing, why you bounced ninety-four checks at the Capitol Bank last year? Or why you used taxpayers' money to take seven foreign trips last year to such strategically important places as Fiji and the Bahamas. And tell us why you spent $50,000 of the taxpayers' money to mail fund-raising requests to people outside your district. Tell us why," Michael demanded.

Henry Marsh looked at the other panelists in horror.

"Gentlemen, please. You must refrain from talking to each other. The format that we've agreed on calls for you to answer the questions of the panel. I urge you to do so."

"Mr. Marsh, Mr. Madigan has made some accusations that I would like to respond to right now," growled Rusing, his face flushed with anger.

"I'm not out of touch with the voters. I've been a Congressman since you were a green second lieutenant and I've served these people with distinction. How dare you try to take the moral high ground, you hypocrite," Rusing shouted, to the astonishment of the panel.

Rusing's voice lowered. "I didn't walk out on my wife and my children. I never had an affair with my secretary like you did when you were on the National Security Council. I never killed anyone with my bare hands like you've been known to brag about. So don't try to be high-and-mighty with me, boy." Rusing's face was beet red and he was almost hyperventilating.

Michael and the members of the panel were stunned. The situation seemed nearly out of control. Michael struggled to avoid the temptation to lash back at his opponent, and managed to keep his composure. He was not going to sink to Rusing's level.

"Congressman, evidently I've touched a nerve here. I stand by my comments about the economy and your lack of leadership. And I'm a little embarrassed to be a part of this debate," Michael began, but stopped short as Rusing began clutching his chest. The Congressman grunted out loud several times and collapsed to the ground, knocking over his podium. Members of the audience and panel gasped in horror, and a few people started shouting for help, but no one seemed to know what to do. Michael stood motionless for a moment, gazing down at Rusing with contempt. He deserved to die. Let the bastard choke, thought Michael.

"Is there a doctor anywhere?" someone shouted. "Does anyone know CPR?" yelled another.

No one came forward and Rusing's life seemed to be draining away. Michael took his eyes off the dying man and his gaze met Josh, whose eyes were desperately pleading for his father to intervene. Michael, who knew CPR, shook his head violently as if to do away with the demons that made him want to let this man die. His moment of hesitation ended and Michael rushed to the side of his fallen opponent.

"Give him some room," Michael ordered and several people quickly moved back. He undid his tie, loosened his shirt and began to administer CPR. Tilting Rusing's head back and clearing the airway, he blew in two quick breaths. Then he pressed hard on Rusing's sternum and applied fifteen compressions for every two breaths. Within a minute, Rusing had regained consciousness. An ambulance arrived and paramedics swiftly loaded Rusing onto a stretcher and raced him off to the hospital.

Michael was so disturbed by what had happened that he was momentarily breathless. His students rushed to his side.

"No wonder he had a heart attack. You nailed the bastard, Colonel. He didn't know what hit him," Alex said. "The dramatic ending aside, you outscored him on points and issues. It wasn't even close. Plus, you have a more commanding presence than that spineless jellyfish," chipped in Darrell.

"It's amazing that after eighteen years, he doesn't have a better command of the issues. You had a much tighter grasp of the issues, especially in foreign policy," added Judy.

"I think that you should sue that son of a bitch for slander, if you ask me. Especially that crap about you having an affair. People are tired of that kind of dirty politics, especially when it isn't true," Alex said.

"My first impulse was to wring his neck, break him into little pieces and let him die," Michael said in a hushed tone. "I knew what to do to save him but for a moment I was prepared to do nothing." His face was pale and he felt shaky. "I was willing to let a man die because I wanted to win an election," he whispered, and began walking aimlessly. The press started hovering around him for comments, but Alex quickly ran interference. Michael needed to go home and rest. He left the building without saying another word.

✠   ✠   ✠

The day had been set months before. Today was a summit meeting for all of Colombia's cocaine lords, along with a powerful American politician. They were meeting at the family ranch of Jorge Ramirez at Hacienda Veracruz on the Caribbean coast near Barranquilla. Ramirez was the kingpin of all of the Colombian drug lords.

Not all were looking forward to the meeting. Their wealth and power had made them almost the equivalent of a sovereign nation as far as influence, but to meet with an American politician? Insanity. Who could say if he would bring the FBI, DEA or some wannabe Rambo? He cannot be trusted, counseled Pedro Escoban, head of one of the drug families.

Several others felt the same way, but Ramirez was adamant about this meeting. He had received certain assurances that the American politician could be trusted.

The invited guests began arriving by private plane at the ranch's 6,000 foot paved landing strip which was large enough to accommodate commercial aircraft. Hacienda Veracruz could encompass several small towns within its borders. It was completely self-sustaining and had its own private lake. Armed guards prowled everywhere. The leader of the Cali cartel, the most powerful drug smuggling operation ever, took no chances.

All of the meeting's participants were now assembled with the exception of two. The American Congressman and an unnamed colleague would soon be arriving. Ramirez shouted orders out to his staff, threatening horrible things if his demands were not met.

The quiet sky was interrupted with the sound of an airplane coming in from the horizon. They were here.

For so many years they had struggled, thought Ramirez. Although they wielded incredible power, now a breakthrough was possible that they had never envisioned. Even he could not comprehend the enormity of the offer.

As the plane's engines came to a halt, two distinguished-looking men stepped out. Ramirez could see that these were men who were used to having their orders obeyed. They had an innate sense of superiority in their manner and in their walk. They were escorted into the magnificent, sprawling country-style mansion. There were eight others present. Ramirez spoke first.

"I would like to make a toast to all of us here today. Gentlemen, please raise your glasses for what will surely be a historic day. To health and wealth!"

As everyone finished toasting, the two guests stood up. The American politician was known by his comrades as Rommel and his colleague was known as Krupp. Rommel spoke.

"I suspect that there are several guns pointed at me at this moment because of my capacity as an elected representative of the United States government. But I am sixty-eight years old and in poor health. I couldn't harm a flea and would be most appreciative if your weapons were aimed elsewhere."

Ramirez glanced at several of his guards who had taken obscured positions behind various structures. Without saying a word, his look had the desired effect. All of the guards quickly left.

"Thank-you. My name, by the way, is Peter Volhard. I am a member of the United States Congress and my associate, who shall remain nameless is, shall we say, a soldier of fortune. He was one of the founders of the Baader-Meinhof organization and he has trained soldiers all over the world in low-intensity conflict and guerilla warfare. And indeed, gentlemen, we are in a war. The so-called 'civilized' nations have declared it so. You must be prepared to resort to force comparable or greater to that which is being used against you. That's where my esteemed colleague comes in.

"While it's true that I'm a politician in the United States, I have my own motives for my actions here today which need not concern you. Suffice it to say that I'm determined to accomplish my objectives, and leave it at that. That is why I need your help," he said. The audience was puzzled.

"The theme today is expansion of your organization and most important-ly, of your ability to transport your products. I've been informed that you have accumulated so much cocaine that you've not been able to efficiently move it into the United States. That's where I can help," Volhard offered.

Krupp stood up to speak. "Let me add to Herr Volhard's comments. I would like for you to consider another market, perhaps as lucrative as the

United States. What we used to call the Soviet Union. For many years, they have been isolated from the world. But much has changed. Now is the time to strike. We propose to provide you with the means to infiltrate your goods into Russia, the Ukraine and all of the other republics."

Krupp had everyone's attention. "We also propose to assist you in getting your products into the United States, and I can assure you that at certain times and places there will be no security: no police, no DEA and no FBI to hinder your transportation into America. We can also provide you with planes and men. You will easily quadruple your sales during the first year and that doesn't even include the Soviet Union."

He looked around the room to gauge the impact of his statements. No one moved, no one spoke.

"I know that you are very skeptical of my words and that some of you are thinking of ways to slice out my tongue or remove my testicles. But I am speaking the truth," Krupp said forcefully. "As it happens, we are German but you need not concern yourself with our motivations. Just let us show you our goodwill to you with a gesture of sincerity," Krupp offered, turning to Volhard.

"Today, in Washington, D.C., the attorney general of the United States, Anthony Peterson, is speaking on Capitol Hill before a committee on Drug Abuse and Enforcement," said the Congressman. "He has been instructed by our organization to delete certain provisions of the administration's new drug policy. As an incentive for him to act accordingly, we kidnapped his thirteen-year-old daughter. He was told that she will be raped and killed if he doesn't comply so we believe that he will."

"But it doesn't really matter if he does. As a symbol of our good faith, Mr. Peterson and his daughter will be killed tonight. I hope that this will show our noble intentions," Volhard said, coolly. He knew he held the Colombians in his grasp.

ony Peterson was beside himself, pacing furiously about his office. He'd been chain-smoking all morning and was now pounding his desk and cursing subordinates.

"Who the hell are these bastards?" he screamed. "I want them found, do you hear me? They've got my baby. If they harm one hair on her head, they're dead men. Do you hear me? I don't care what those friggin' sons of bitches on the Congressional oversight committee say, I'll commit 100 per- cent of the U.S. law enforcement agencies to find them!" he shrieked.

"Leonard, what time is it? I'm a basket case. What time is my press conference?" he shouted, practically in tears.

"It's 10:35 A.M., boss. T-minus twenty-five minutes," responded Deputy Attorney General Leonard Silva.

"I can't risk Melanie's life, Leonard," said the attorney general. I just can't do it. Maybe I'm not strong enough for this job. I know I shouldn't give into these spineless bastards but I have no choice. I'm going to comply with their demands and probably hate myself the rest of my life. But I'll still have my baby and we can pursue our original policy later when things have calmed down," he said to his chief deputy.

"Have you talked to the president, Chief?" Silva asked.

"No, I haven't," replied Peterson. "You want to know why? Because I'm afraid. I'm fifty years old, one of the most powerful men in America and I'm afraid to fight a group of stinking cowards and I'm afraid to tell my boss."

Peterson walked into the press briefing room as he had dozens of times before, but never before had he felt such a sinking feeling in his gut. God, get me through this, please, and protect my princess, he prayed. He looked around and saw basically the same contingent of reporters that normally covered these briefings.

He hated reporters because he had, on many occasions, been misquoted. Sometimes he envied totalitarian regimes because they didn't have to put up with these wolves.

Silva approached him just as he was about to speak. "Boss, we found this sitting on the podium." He handed Peterson a small, gift-wrapped box.

"What is it?"

"I think you had better take a look at this."

"Has it been cleared by security?"

"Yeah. They ran it through the metal detector and x-ray. It's definitely not a bomb, but considering the circumstances...you had better just open it."

Peterson had a sick feeling in his stomach. Something was wrong. He knew Silva well enough to figure that out. "O.K., let's see what it is." Peterson opened it up.

The inside of the box was packed with cotton. A folded piece of paper lay on top. Peterson opened it up.

"What the hell is this!" The note seemed to have been written in blood. It read: *Melanie wanted to wave good-bye to you one last time.* He went ice cold. He reached in and pulled out some cotton to reveal a small, thin finger.

Before a crew of television and print reporters, the attorney general began yelling, shouting obscenities and crying simultaneously.

"You bastards. I'll kill you. I told you if you harmed one single hair on her head, I'd personally shoot your balls off. Oh God! Not my Melanie, my angel baby." He began crying uncontrollably and collapsed to his knees.

The press pool was stunned. No one knew what had caused the attorney general's incredible outburst and everyone was too shocked to do anything. Everyone's eyes were glued to the attorney general who was bent over on the ground, crying and shrieking.

In the midst of the chaos there was a pop. Peterson grabbed his throat. Blood was oozing out from between his fingers. Within seconds, the United States' top law enforcement official was dead.

Pandemonium broke out and everyone was shouting. Silva didn't know what to think. He quickly ordered an aide to help the attorney general and ran to the only exit in the room, expecting the assassin to make a run for it. But no one did. He glanced across the room and saw a pistol on the ground.

He realized that every eye, every camera had been focused on the attorney general and that probably no one had seen the assassin, who by then had dropped the murder weapon.

That's exactly what had happened, making this one of the most incredibly bold criminal acts in American history—not a single witness.

✠　✠　✠

Jorge Ramirez watched in disbelief at the scene on his television—brought into his living room in Colombia via the Global News Network. For once, the feared drug lord was stunned. My God, he thought. He would soon be one of the most powerful men in the world. Volhard had made good on his promise and he couldn't help but feel great respect for him. A televised assassination with no witnesses! Perfect. They were dealing with men who meant what they said, men who had no fear. Absolutely perfect.

✠　✠　✠

That Monday morning, Michael met with his advisors, who were grilling him on the speech he was giving at a luncheon later that day. His speech consisted of his economic proposals to the Santa Monica Chamber of Commerce. Due to the recent tragedy, much of their talk concerned Peterson.

"Colonel, what do you make of what happened? How could anybody be killed on national TV and the murderer get away?" asked Darrell.

"Yeah, there must have been some type of conspiracy, some organized set-up, don't you think?" inquired Judy Solomon.

"Everyone is always quick to assume a conspiracy. Why is that so? Is it because we've lost all trust in our government?" Michael wanted to know. "Let me ask you this. Most of you were either very young or not even born when Kennedy was assassinated. How many of you think that there was a conspiracy to kill him or a cover-up? Let me see a show of hands."

To his astonishment, everyone raised a hand.

"Really? Even though there's no hard evidence?"

"Colonel, c'mon. There were just too many weird things, too many inconsistencies. Someone, or something, must have masterminded it. My guess is the CIA. Or maybe the mob," speculated Alex.

"But you're just guessing. You're forming an opinion where there's nothing to substantiate it. What about the Warren Commission?"

"With all due respect, Dad, the Warren commission was nothing but a bunch of corrupt, greedy old men who were just trying to cover their rears. They're all a bunch of crooks."

"Do you really think so?" said Michael, surprised by his response. "If all of our leaders are dishonest and corrupt, then what does that say about us? If that's the case, and we do nothing to change it, then we get what we deserve," said Michael, clearly exasperated.

"That's why we need you, Dad," exclaimed Josh. "We're tired of being lied to and ignored. Maybe you can make a difference. Now go give all those fat, stuffy, old farts a kick in their collective ass that they won't forget for a while."

Michael and his motley gang of students drove to the Loews Santa Monica, the most luxurious beachfront hotel of Los Angeles, where the luncheon was being held. As he walked in the ultramodern lobby with its five-story atrium and window overlooking the ocean, he smiled at the organ concert being presented.

He went over in his mind, for what seemed the hundredth time, the various economic terms and phrases, hoping like hell that he didn't mess up. As he was always told in the army, "Keep it simple, stupid." Wise advice, he thought to himself, as he and his staff stepped up the escalator and entered the hotel banquet room.

The candidate walked briskly into the dining room with an air of confidence. He waved to the crowd that had assembled, one of whom approached him and spoke.

"Colonel, I have some papers for you," said the nondescript man.

What the hell is this? I don't have time for any nonsense, he thought. But he opened the folded papers anyway and took a quick glance. It was a Summons and Petition for dissolution of marriage.

Divorce papers! My God, this can't be! His thoughts became frozen and the gentle buzz of the crowd was suddenly silenced. He felt as if he were in a surreal kaleidoscope with images flashing but not taking form.

The audience had taken their seats. After some brief remarks, Michael was introduced by the president of the chamber. He didn't move, however. The light that had been sparkling in his eyes was gone. The glow on his face had dissipated. He had been wounded in battle before but this was much worse.

Finally, after several awkward moments, Michael approached the podium and began to speak. He was lacking his usual forceful style.

"Good afternoon, ladies and gentlemen. I'm Michael Madigan and I'm a candidate for the U.S. Congress. I've worked diligently the last several months to prepare a comprehensive economic blueprint which I believe will help us remain competitive in a vastly changing global economy. I had intended today to talk about this package which will jump-start our economy and help us remain an economic superpower," Michael said. His staff became nervous at Michael's apparent intention to depart from his prepared remarks.

"But," he said, pausing awkwardly, "during the past hour, I've been consumed by frustration at the cynicism, the hopelessness, the distrust, and the 'throw the bums out' mentality that seems to have reached epidemic proportions. As I was preparing for my speech, several of my aides, all much younger than I, made me realize that no one trusts the government or the system anymore. Political leaders are presumed to be crooked and everyone is in it merely for themselves. I find this very disturbing."

"Uh, oh," Judy whispered. "He finds it disturbing."

Michael walked away from the podium and spoke without a microphone. In a booming voice that had once commanded soldiers in combat, every eye became fixed on him.

"I have some thoughts that I would like to share with you."

Josh groaned. His father was about to "speak his mind" as he often had in the army. This had usually resulted in some type of reprimand from his superiors. His dad was no diplomat. "I hope he doesn't blow it," Josh said to Kelly.

"If any of you think that I'm corrupt, dishonest, greedy or anything of the sort, I pray for your children's sake that you don't vote for me," Michael said. "If you think of my opponent in those terms, I hope you won't waste your vote. If you believe that one man can't make a difference, that the system is too entrenched, too stacked against average folks, too far gone, then please do me a favor. Keep your apathetic, indifferent, fat ass home on election day. America doesn't need you and I have no interest in representing you in Washington. If you think that all politicians are corrupt and you don't do anything about it, then you're no better than the bums you curse. You'll get exactly the representation you deserve."

Michael wondered if he had gone too far. He felt a tremendous tension in the air. Perhaps he should have stayed with his prepared speech. He glanced around the room and focused on one older gentlemen who seemed angered by Michael's words. Reacting instinctively, he raced across the room and began speaking to the obviously peeved listener.

"Sir, what's your name?"

"It's Cyrus McCormick and I resent your remarks. I had planned on voting for you but not now. How dare you insult us like that!"

"If you were insulted, please accept my apologies," Michael said, trying to mollify the angry voter. "There was no disrespect intended. I was only trying to make a point. There's such a web of cynicism that many of us throw up our hands and say 'what the hell.' I can understand that. But we can't give into that temptation. Each of us is a shareholder in this company and we have a duty to make the board of directors accountable. And if we don't, then we don't deserve a share of the profits. Many of our leaders are perk-happy, pork-dispensing, self-centered cretins. But who elected them? We did. And we'll always reap what we sow," Michael said, to scattered applause.

"I'm determined to give my all to represent you in Washington and to make you proud again. I'll try not to let you down, although I'll certainly make mistakes. I expect the same of you. Please make me proud." Michael was pleasantly surprised to receive a standing ovation.

✠ ✠ ✠

Rebecca cried softly as she looked at her once-beautiful daughter who was sitting in her bed in a catatonic trance. TJ had lost forty pounds and her skin was sagging over her protruding bones. Her face was drawn and pale, her hands clammy, her eyes void of life.

My God, Rebecca thought, will I ever have my daughter back? Will my little girl ever return to me? Is this what the balance of my life will be like? No husband, no job, only caring for a living skeleton.

What was that the doctor had told her? Something about how the overdose had damaged certain biochemical reactions which allow for the normal turnover of key neurotransmitters. She didn't understand it when he said it and she didn't give a damn about it now. All she knew was that her baby had been taken from her.

She sat on TJ's bed feeling as depressed, lonely and miserable as she was sure any one person could. She had just been to a lawyer's office and had instructed him to file divorce papers and serve Michael with them. It was one of the most agonizing and draining experiences of her life. She had never dreamed this would happen. She had truly believed that her marriage would last forever. Divorce was for other people, not her and Michael. They had loved each other too deeply to consider divorce. She thought they had reached the point where their love could handle anything.

She collapsed alongside TJ, sobbing loudly, her thoughts confused. Eventually she calmed down and for some reason thought of her wedding day. Michael had looked so dashing and he had told her many times that she was his fairy princess. Although almost two decades had passed, she envisioned it as if it were yesterday. She recalled every detail of who was there, what the guests were wearing, what music was playing, what words were spoken. She remembered the words that she spoke that day, in her own personal vows to Michael. And she remembered the vows he spoke in response, in front of all their friends and family.

"We leave behind today our past and separate lives and begin our new life together, where we'll be not only a team and a partnership but we'll merge to become a single entity, pooling our talents and strengths, balancing our fears and weaknesses. We'll share the chores, pleasures, and frustrations of daily life as well as our hopes, dreams, ambitions, and prayers."

"Love is often difficult for me to express, particularly in front of an audience, because it is personal and private. But I want to say to you, in front of all the people who mean so much to us, that I love you, Rebecca, and I thank God for having allowed you to come into my life."

"I waited a long time for you and endured many difficult periods. But the wait has been well worth it because I have been blessed a thousand times over. You are my reward. You've believed in me and encouraged me, made me laugh and renewed my spirit. In return, I pledge to love you, be faithful, be a good father and to try to keep alive these feelings of romance that we know today for all the days of our lives."

"So let no one cast asunder what God hath joined together. We'll be grateful for the sunshine and survive the stormy weather. Will you merge your heart with mine and fuse with me your life? Will you call yourself my wife?"

She fell asleep beside her daughter, who would probably never understand why her mother's heart was filled with pain and why the tears wouldn't stop.

✠   ✠   ✠

The winter winds were just beginning. This was the last week of the political campaign. Rusing had recovered and was being portrayed a hero. The following week would be a battle for Michael. He had crisscrossed the district, had spoken at every school, every union hall, every Rotary and Kiwanis club imaginable. He had addressed bankers, lawyers, business men and women, laborers, students, retirees and every other conceivable group. He was proud of the fact that he didn't tailor his comments to suit the group he was addressing. He refused to be a political chameleon, changing his colors every time he spoke. He had certain views which he fervently adhered to. Many didn't like his message. So be it.

Michael's gang of dedicated students had been an invaluable help to him. They formed the backbone of his staff. Alex had proven to be an incredibly talented fund-raiser. Judy had a talent for public relations and her responsibilities included logistics. She was also in charge of his schedule. And Darrell was the main force behind the presentation of substantive policies.

Michael had finally developed a rhythm. He had hit his stride. He was gaining confidence and hammering Rusing unmercifully on a wide variety of issues. He was no longer a political novice, although he still had much to learn. He spent countless hours meeting with the "heavyweights" of his campaign, including Peter Volhard, but relied equally on the grass roots upon which his campaign was based.

He knew now that he was going to win. He and Josh had grown very close during the last few months. Josh had a wisdom that was very unusual for someone his age. He reassured Michael that it was all right to follow his instincts. Michael had always been one to act with his gut and Josh helped encourage this. They complemented each other.

If only Rebecca was still with him. Her filing for divorce had devastated him and came close to knocking him out of the race. She had been his soul mate. They had been partners. How could she do this to him? He was filled with anger and his sadness had nearly drained his reason for living. Despite the flood of destructive emotions, he stilled loved her and he prayed everyday for a reconciliation. He was certain that she still loved him, despite the spiteful things that her high-priced attorney had been saying.

Attorneys, what a curse to society they are, he thought. What do they accomplish? Nothing constructive, he was sure. They always seemed to be attacking and destroying everything. Rebecca had hired a bloodthirsty warrior who would not be happy until he had destroyed whatever part of their marriage remained. The goal was total victory for Rebecca. This included custody of the children with limited visitation for Michael and the bulk of their assets, including his military pension, their house and an ungodly amount for child support. They could probably have come to an agreement among themselves on everything. Now thousands would be spent. It was the adversary system at its worst. Both parties would eventually end up crippled emotionally and drained financially. The only winners were the damn attorneys.

⌖ ⌖ ⌖

The Sunday morning before the election, Michael was speaking at a church. He was expressing his concern at the recently increasing number of racial incidents that had occurred in the district and around the country.

At the same time, in another part of the country, there was another gathering. Their topic was also race relations. But this one was of a much different tenor.

Alan Roberts was delivering a message of hatred and bigotry. He had spoken of white supremacy on many occasions but never to such an audience as had gathered this evening. The audience consisted of only six men. They were men who considered themselves to be racially superior and hoped to soon control the world. They had all assembled, for the first time, in the United States. They had come to solidify their plans to escalate racial violence. Roberts was visibly nervous about speaking to these "supermen."

"Gentlemen, I'm honored to speak to you tonight. Collectively you hold great power. Perhaps, more power than any group in history. I'm humbled to be in your presence. We have yearned for a world that is devoid of inferior beings, particularly Jews and niggers. Our homelands have a rich history of ethnic cleansing attempts. Unfortunately, they weren't entirely successful. But we will continue the quest for a white, Christian world." He could see that the six men were receptive to his speech and began to gain confidence.

"Tonight, I'll give you a brief history of race relations in America. There is a secret society that never became well-known but whose basic tenets we hold dear..." he paused briefly.

"You wish to create tension between the races here in America and I have ideas on how best to do that. But first I ask you to look to the past. This will help accomplish your goals."

"Most people have heard of the Ku Klux Klan but there was another organization that was founded in New Orleans in 1867 called the Knights of the White Camelia. Its principle aim was to maintain white supremacy in the South during Reconstruction. The Knights employed any tactics necessary to protect their families and maintain a pure white Christian race and that included any methods necessary to control the nigger."

"Things have changed since 1867, but these goals are just as worthy today and can be expanded to include Jews. Members of the Knights were required to take an oath vowing to employ all necessary steps to wipe out those of inferior stock. They were charged with the following:

> *Our primary objective is to maintain the supremacy of the white race. We belong to a race which nature has endowed with superiority over all others. God has given us a dominion from which no human laws can deviate. This dominion has always remained in the hands of the white man, while all others have occupied a subordinate and secondary position.*
>
> *Among those who have left traces of their greatness, we find only those descended from white stock. We see, on the contrary, that most of the countries inhabited by the other races have stagnated in a semi-barbarous condition. The more remote a race of men is from the white, the more fatally that stamp of inferiority is affixed, irrevocably dooming them to eternal degradation.*
>
> *The government of our republic was established by white men, for white men alone. They never contemplated that it should fall into the hands of an inferior race. We believe that any attempt to wrest from the white race the management of its affairs is an invasion of the rights guaranteed by the Constitution and a violation of the laws established by God himself; that such encroachments are subversive and that no individual of the white race can submit to them without humiliation and shame.*
>
> *It becomes our solemn duty, as white men, to strenuously resist those attempts against our natural and constitutional rights, and to do everything in our power to maintain the superiority of the white race.*

"This charge was written over a century ago but its words ring true today," he said, urgently. "As a leader in the KKK, I uphold this oath. Our world has been overrun with refugees of inferior stock. They take our jobs, rape our women, and receive preferential treatment in employment. We white Christian men seem to be afraid to stand up and fight for what we have earned, for our rights. Gentlemen, you are about to begin a mission of historic proportion. The KKK will assist you in whatever way we can." Roberts finished his speech and sat down.

Krupp, the German who had devoted his career to encouraging terrorism and specializing in guerilla warfare, stood to speak.

"Mr. Roberts, thank you for your very insightful and inspirational words today. It's true that before any plan can be implemented, it must be well-thought-out and calculated to the minutest detail. And that's why it's important to study history and learn from its lessons. However, the time has arrived for us to act, not talk; to strike, not debate; to attack, not analyze. It's true also that we have an agenda which cannot be fully addressed today. But that does not mean that we're precluded from action. Our goals are many and global, but our primary objective is essentially the same as that of the Knights of the White Camelia—racial superiority at any cost. Our hope is to accomplish this worldwide but we'll start with the United States. The incredible diversity of the U.S. will play in our favor."

"We must now begin to lay the groundwork for our future actions," Krupp commanded. "We must continue to create in this nation a climate which identifies the need for the protection of white Americans. We must whip into a frenzy the tension that is already in place. Charles Manson had the right idea, although his was certainly a weak and disturbed mind. He had intended to create a race war that would result in, how did he put it, "Helter Skelter." Well, now is the time for Helter Skelter, my fellow Knights. We must infiltrate into the ethnic cracks of society and exploit whatever tensions that can be found. People will have to die. Neighborhoods will have to be destroyed. This mission will not be an easy one."

"We are growing increasingly disgusted with governments trying to legislate morality and trying to force us to atone for the so-called sins of our forefathers. We adhere to the ideas of Nietzsche, who believed that contemporary morality is an inversion of true morality. Life's true task is to fulfill man's instincts and not to inhibit them."

"Nietzsche's principle that might makes right is the verdict of nature. In contrast, civilized religions, such as Judaism and Christianity, have always opposed this ethic. They preach humility and compassion."

"Religious leaders have used religion to inhibit natural instincts. We cannot allow the master race to become the slaves," he said forcefully.

There was complete silence in the room. "The six of us have dedicated our lives to this sacred mission and we are destined to succeed. Join us, Roberts, in our quest to rid the world of these pathetic second-class dregs who have been the recipients of governmental largesse for too long. We must claim our rightful heritage."

"Do I hear any dissent?"

"No!" shouted the others. The group assembled here today was just the right combination needed to carry out their goals.

"Before we adjourn," the lantern-jawed Roberts interjected, "I have an idea that I'd like to share with you. As you know, I am one of the leaders of the Ku Klux Klan. It is our desire to ship all blacks back to Africa, but even I have to admit that's not realistic. I've got another idea..."

"Don't keep us in suspense," said Krupp.

"I've already contacted a few, white, God-fearing police officers that I know in Los Angeles who, like us, are tired of what's happening to our country. They will do anything for our cause," Roberts said, smiling at his plan.

"Spit it out, Herr Roberts," said Bismarck.

"Well, with your approval, this is what will happen. These police officers will arrest some nigger and beat the living crap out him," Roberts explained.

"That sounds good to me," said Wilhelm, "but what will this accomplish for us?"

"You see, I will be present when this beating takes place. And with my video camera, I will bring it into the living rooms of millions all around the world. I think this will be all we need to stir up the already disillusioned masses of inferior stock. There will be clear evidence of police brutality which they've always alleged and believe me, this videotape will further our plans."

Rommel nodded his head and glanced at his colleagues. He then turned back to Roberts. "Interesting idea, Alan. Go to it," he ordered.

Roberts smiled. "You'll see. This will be big. I promise."

✠   ✠   ✠

Michael had fallen asleep in his clothes around 4:00 A.M. as the television reporters kept saying that it was too close to call. He was staying at a hotel and three television sets were still blaring.

"Congressman, wake up. Time to get up, you're due in Washington," Josh softly said to his slowly waking father.

"What did you call me?"

"Congressman. Has a ring to it, doesn't it? I don't know why they were calling it a dead heat. You won fifty-four to forty-five percent. You better get out of bed and go bounce some checks or something. You're now a member of the least respected institution in America. On the trust scale you're just between attorneys and used-car salesmen," Josh teased.

"I really won? You wouldn't be kidding an old man, would you?"

"You really won, Dad. And all kidding aside, I'm very proud of you." Josh gave his father a hug.

Michael got himself out of bed and splashed some cold water on his face. "Josh, I'm going to take a shower real quick and then we've got a full day ahead of us. Get Alex, Darrell and Judy together and schedule a press conference for 9:00 A.M. Get me the *Chronicle* and the *Times* and get your grandfather on the phone. And..."

While Michael had been issuing directives, Josh had made a telephone call and was talking softly. "Dad, there's someone here who wants to speak to you."

"Who is it?" Michael demanded. "Well, are you going to tell me or do I have to rip your ears off? Give me that phone," he barked, in mock anger.

"Hello, who is this?" he asked.

"Congratulations, Michael. I knew all along that you were going to win."

It was Rebecca. His heart began pounding and his palms began sweating. Why was he reacting like this?

"This is a surprise. How are you?"

"I'm doing pretty well, actually. It was real tough at first, but I've more or less adjusted to a new lifestyle. I thought that I was going to go stir-crazy for a while there but I've gotten used to it. When will you be moving to Washington?" she asked.

"I don't know. I haven't even thought of things like that, I was so intent on winning first. You know me, one day at a time."

"Yeah, that's true. Now that I think about it, it was me who always did the planning, wasn't it?"

"Yes, it was. I guess I was always too busy to, uh, think things out," he said, defensively.

"Anyway, despite what's happened, I'm very proud of you, and the country is lucky to get you. I mean that."

Tears started trickling down his face. "Michael, there's someone who wants to speak to you. Just a moment, will you?"

It was probably Karl, he thought. He was anticipating Karl's voice, but was stunned to hear a weak female voice at the other end.

"Hi, Daddy," came a feeble voice that he at first did not recognize. "Congratulations, I'm proud of you." The words came slowly. It was TJ! More tears wet his cheeks.

"TJ, is that you, darling?" Michael stammered. "I--I love you, sweetheart. How are you feeling?" There was so much that he wanted to say but the words wouldn't come.

"I feel a little better, Daddy. When are you coming home?"

Michael began babbling like a tongue-tied schoolboy. "I don't know, darling. Hopefully soon."

"That's good. We miss you. I'm tired, Daddy, I got to go now. Love you, bye," she said softly.

"I love you, too." Michael could not remember ever feeling so stunned and affected.

Rebecca resumed the conversation. "Surprised?"

Michael was having trouble responding. "God, you know I love her. I didn't abandon her, I swear. Please tell her that I love her, that she's my little girl."

"Michael, I know you do and she knows it also. She's been making great progress and just started talking again a few days ago. She seems fairly coherent for short periods of time. She's improving," Rebecca exclaimed.

"Michael, I know that we've disagreed on how best to help TJ, but please do everything you can in Washington to help her. And get rid of these god-awful drugs, will you?"

"I'll die trying, Becks. Thanks for calling. It means a lot. Maybe someday I'll be able to tell you how much."

✠   ✠   ✠

Karl flew into Moscow directly from Washington. He had been to the Soviet Union once before, about seven years earlier when the cold war was at its zenith. Although he fervently despised the Soviets, he begrudgingly respected them and their tremendous military machine. Now this once powerful country had collapsed almost overnight and their vaunted armed forces had been stripped. They still possessed weapons by the thousands—both nuclear and conventional—but no longer had the will, political or otherwise, to use them. They were a defeated people who would soon be fighting internally, he was sure. They had agreed to destroy many of the weapons that had made them such a powerful nation.

The president had asked Karl, at the recommendation of Peter Volhard, to lead an American contingent to Moscow for the purpose of overseeing the destruction of Soviet nuclear weapons. It had been suggested to the president by Volhard that it might be more palatable by the proud Russians to send a civilian as opposed to an American military officer or government representative.

Karl was accompanied by several other Americans, including a navy admiral, Jonathan Hawkins, and a career diplomat from the State Department, Charles Worthington. But it had been made clear to Karl that he was in charge. He would communicate his recommendations directly to the president and the chairman of the joint chiefs of staff.

Karl flew into the Russian city on Aeroflot, the former airline of the Soviet government, once the largest airline in the world. He noted that the plane was very large and cold-looking, much like its makers. The flight was troubled by several delays and he arrived forty-five minutes late, a fact that didn't surprise him.

He had had a chance to speak with the other members of the team back in Washington. Overall, they were bright and industrious. They felt that this was a historic opportunity and were all caught up in some type of idealistic nonsense.

Hawkins was a commanding presence and a forceful leader who had seen action in several military campaigns. But Karl surmised that he suffered from military myopia and paranoia. Hawkins had been the type who saw the Soviet Union as the "evil empire," and saw communism as the reason for every malady in the world. Hawkins didn't trust the Soviets and believed that despite the momentous changes of the recent past, they were still the enemy. Karl could take advantage of this.

The remaining member of his team could prove to be more difficult. Worthington was a career diplomat who had specialized in Russian history and affairs. He spoke the language fluently and knew many of the key players. He was forceful yet not obnoxious and an expert negotiator. Karl had gotten the feeling that this Bostonian resented an "outsider" being placed in charge. But Karl would take care of that.

Karl was greeted at the airport by Colonel Vladimir Dostevesky, Deputy minister of defense in the new Russian Republic. The Russian colonel had a noticeable limp, the result of a grenade exploding in his tank during the German invasion of the Soviet Union in 1941. He had been only sixteen at the time and had lied to get into the army. He was full of resentment for his infirmity and the fact that he had been passed over for promotion to general. In fact he was resentful toward life. Most of all, he still hated Germans, after all these years.

"Good afternoon, Mr. Schmidt," came Dostevesky's greeting in heavily accented English. "I trust your flight was comfortable. Please let me escort you to your quarters where you can tidy up and rest. I am sure that you must be very tired."

"Thank you, Colonel. I most certainly am. We could all use come sleep," Karl replied.

"We will do our best to make you feel at home. Follow me, please," said the Russian officer.

8

ichael felt absolutely exhausted as he drove down the freeway. His was one of the few cars on the road at 2:30 A.M. He'd believed that one man could make a difference. But was it really so? And at what cost? He'd already lost his father and his wife. Even though he had won the election he was beginning to wonder if it was worth the price. He envisioned the events of the upcoming weeks. He had to go to Washington to receive a new congressman's briefing. Immediately upon his return he had to be in court concerning his divorce. Divorce. Just thinking of it hurt his head.

Will I ever get home, he thought to himself, impatient with the long drive. Finally, he reached his exit and headed west. He had fallen asleep at the wheel for a few seconds before realizing it and jerked up with a start. He was so tired, he didn't think that he could make it one more mile.

"I'll just pull over for a moment," he said out loud. He pulled over to the side of the road, stopped the car and lay his head back on the seat.

His mind began drifting and he could feel the cold air against his skin. His breath seemed to freeze in midair. The cold metal of his rifle pierced his bare hands. The prisoners were walking wearily along the path. Their sunken eyes were wide with fear—like scared animals.

The silence was broken by the sharp shouting of the oberleutnant. "Move, you pigs. Faster, faster...or I'll whip you until you pray to die."

There were approximately 200 prisoners, barefoot despite the intense cold, consisting of men, women and children. They were marching in the woods with tall green trees on either side; sharp rocks on the path, causing cuts and bruises to their feet.

Where are we going, he thought? This looks familiar, said a voice in his head, but he couldn't remember. He looked at his colleagues, all seven of them, in neatly pressed uniforms and polished boots, a picture of health and vitality. He gazed, with some sorrow, at the prisoners, whose emaciated bodies were in stark contrast to his own body. They were plodding along the trail. Was he feeling guilty or smug? He couldn't be certain.

Finally, they came to a halt. The sergeant shouted at the prisoners to take their clothes off. What in hell? Did he hear right? It was just above freezing. They would die without their clothing, what little they had.

"Now!" the sergeant yelled as the soldiers pointed their weapons at the skeleton-like prisoners who obeyed to save their lives.

"March forward, over there, you swine!" yelled the sergeant, pointing towards a ditch that paralleled a small creek.

Like scared sheep, numb with cold and fear, they moved towards the ditch. As the last prisoner reached its edge, the oberleutnant ordered, "Fire!"

All of the guards, except him, sprayed bullets at the prisoners. Since they were at fairly close range, death was immediate. The bullets ripped open their heads like ripe melons, splattering blood and brain tissue everywhere. The rain of bullets continued for several minutes, until the screams stopped. The prisoners lay dead, having tumbled into the ditch in a heap, some with the assistance of a Nazi's boot. He watched in horror as dead children, with no faces, were rolled into the mass.

The ober-leutnant said to him, "Soldier, your job is to fill in the grave. Here's a shovel. Get started."

In shock, he mechanically reached for the shovel and now remembered why this looked familiar. He had done it before when the ovens at the camp were not working efficiently and mass firing squads were necessary to expedite the Jews' deaths. His job was to fill in the graves.

He started shoveling the dirt over the naked bodies. Looking up, he found himself alone in this field of death. The other guards must have gone back to the camp already. He was the only person alive here. An eerie feeling passed over him as he saw strange faces whose eyes seemed to stare at him.

He must dig faster, he must bury these corpses. He couldn't stand it anymore. A shock of recognition startled him as he poured dirt over one young face.

My God! he thought, that person looked familiar. He must be dreaming or losing his mind. No, he knew that face, now obscured by the dirt. He must see it.

He climbed into the hole, seven or eight bodies deep. He slipped and fell onto the body of what appeared to be an old woman, whose ear had been severed. He started brushing away the dirt with his hands and suddenly came upon the youthful face he was searching for. It was the face of a young boy unmarked by bullets, but the youth's arms had been shot completely off his body.

He brushed aside the dirt and the splattered blood from the boy's face. It was his son, David.

Michael bolted up in his seat so fast that he hit his head on the steering wheel, letting out a scream loud enough to be heard by the police officer who had pulled behind his car.

The officer could clearly hear the man's shouting now. "You murderers! You killed my son and you make me bury his body. I'll kill all of you, I swear, if it's the last thing I do. You're all dead, you bastards!"

The officer radioed in his location and then spoke to Michael through the loudspeaker. "Come out of the car with your hands up." Using his car door as a shield, the officer crouched behind it with his gun drawn. Officer Tim Woodings couldn't afford to take chances. This guy, he thought, sounded really whacked out. He repeated his request over the loudspeaker.

Michael recognized his surroundings and could see the flashing multicolored lights of the squad car in his rearview mirror. By the second command from officer Woodings, he exited the car and stood with his hands high, fearing to move.

"What's happening here!" Woodings shouted, gun still drawn. "Anybody else in the car? Who were you screaming at?"

"There's no one else, I'm sorry officer, but it's really just a big misunderstanding. You see I was having this dream and..."

"Down on the ground, now. Put your hands on top of your head and cross your feet...cross them now...do it!" demanded Woodings, still suspicious.

Woodings moved from behind his door with gun drawn and walked carefully towards Michael's car. Flashing his light in the car revealed no other occupants. He patted him down for weapons and then let him stand up.

"Have you been drinking tonight, sir?" inquired the officer.

"Drinking? I should have been. I deserve to get rip-roaring drunk with everything that's happened. However, I haven't had a drop of alcohol tonight."

"Any drugs?" the officer continued.

"No drugs—it's all really quite simple, sir. I was just having a nightmare and..."

"You're the new congressman, aren't you? Hey, I voted for you. I liked your style. Are you messed up in here? You were screaming like nobody's business, saying you were going to 'kill them,' calling someone 'murderers.' What was that all about?"

"Well, as you guessed, I'm Michael Madigan and I just had the worst day of my life. I was heading home, I just live a few blocks from here, but I was too tired and had to pull over for a minute. I fell asleep and had the mother of all nightmares. I dreamed that my young son was killed and that I was digging his grave. You can't imagine how real it seemed. I'm really embarrassed but I can assure that you that I'm not drunk," he explained.

"I like you, so I'll take your word for it. You don't smell drunk and your eyes just look tired, not drugged. I'll give you an escort home if you want. Do you always have dreams like that?"

"I've had a few gruesome dreams lately, that's for sure."

"Well, you better go right to bed. And say... why don't you see somebody about those dreams."

"You're absolutely right about going to bed. I've been up for about thirty hours now and I could use some shuteye. I think that I can make it without an escort. I live over on Flushing Drive, just a few blocks from here."

"Well, I'll follow you just to be sure. By the way, give them hell in Washington, will ya?"

"I will, officer, thanks."

✠   ✠   ✠

Krupp was at the controls of the Lear jet. He had taken up flying soon after the war and had flown to almost every continent on earth. This time he was heading for Colombia, to the Hacienda of Jorge Ramirez. They had met once before. They had made a proposition to Ramirez and had demonstrated their sincerity by executing the attorney general of the United States, along with his teenage daughter.

Krupp saw the remote landing strip and gently landed the plane. He was met by Ramirez and seven of his associates, five of whom were brandishing automatic weapons.

"Señor, it's a pleasure to see you again. Come in and we'll drink to the future. Yes?"

"Yes, let's do that."

"Please, please, put your weapons down," Ramirez said to his body-guards. "This man is our friend and guest." Despite the assassination of

Peterson, many of Ramirez' men still didn't trust this German. But they complied with orders and put their weapons down.

They walked passed an immense swimming pool and into the main house, which seemed to be a monument to lavishness. Gold ornaments and paintings of masters, whom Krupp recognized, hung on the wall.

"Ah, I see you are a connoisseur, my friend. This painting here is a Rembrandt," Ramirez said proudly. "A priceless original. Breathtaking, isn't it? It used to hang in the Louvre; don't ask me how I got it. That aspect is not quite so beautiful."

"Señor, please look at this painting. I would like to show you something very interesting. This is a seventeenth century Dutch painting called the *Sale of Tulip Bulbs*. It was for many years in a famous museum, until I acquired it. As you can see, it shows two men at a table, engaging in a business transaction," Ramirez said excitedly, pointing to the large painting. "But look closer. We put this painting under an infrared camera and look what we discovered," he said, outlining a form with his finger.

"It looks like a face," Krupp said.

"It is, my friend. It's someone looking over the business transaction. For what purpose? Who knows? But this mysterious face has been there for over two centuries peering out but no one could see it. I get excited every time I see it. Please forgive me," Ramirez said smiling.

"There's no need," replied Krupp. "Maybe somebody will be looking out over our business dealings," he suggested.

"Perhaps so. Care for some cognac, Señor?"

"No, thank you. I must fly back tonight."

"You are welcome to stay here if you like. My home is yours."

"That's very gracious of you, but I must decline. I have much business to attend to."

"I'm sure you do, amigo. And with that said, why don't we get down to our business here?" Ramirez remarked. "I was, to be quite candid, stunned to see the attorney general gunned down, just as you said. I know that was no small task. And the way it was done! Magnificent! Am I correct when I say that no one has been arrested?"

"Yes, you are. In a crowded press room with a live TV audience and there were no witnesses. You're dealing with experts. We will accomplish much more before we are through. But we need your help," Krupp stated.

"Name it. What is it that you want?"

"Could we be alone?"

"Certainly." Ramirez nodded his head and the room was emptied.

"Señor Ramirez, we want to purchase as many drugs as you can produce. If you have 100 people working around the clock, it will not be enough. Money is no object."

Ramirez said nothing for a moment. "What may I ask, do you plan to do with such quantities?"

"Simply put, our agenda is personal and I will not go into detail. Trust me Señor, when I say that I can insure no police, no DEA, and no FBI in the states. Can you satisfy our demands?"

Ramirez hesitated before speaking and then his words surprised Krupp. "I have never been, how you say, a man of morals. And I have no great love for America or especially the Soviet Union. I sell drugs to make money, but I do not have the desire to destroy a culture. Is that your personal agenda—to destroy the American culture. If so...I am not a monster."

"I didn't realize that you were such a humanitarian, Señor Ramirez. I am too busy to debate you. If you do not wish to sell us what we want, then I will find another buyer." Krupp stood up quickly and headed for the door.

"Not so fast, my friend. Of course, I will sell you what you want. I am a businessman, first and foremost. I am one of the most powerful men in Colombia. But I feel small next to you, my friend. There is a look in your eyes that I have never seen. I don't know what it is that you and your colleagues have in mind, but I suspect that it is something very, very big. Am I right?"

"Let me just say that we have been working for over forty years and that the world will not be the same when we are finished. So, do we have a deal?" asked Krupp.

"Yes, we do," said Ramirez smiling.

"An associate will be in touch with more details. I must leave now. Auf Wiedersehen," Krupp said, in his usual no-nonsense manner and departed as rapidly as he had arrived.

✠   ✠   ✠

Michael woke up early despite having only slept a few hours. His thoughts were filled with David. The past year had found him consumed at first with TJ's tragedy and later with Josh. But he had hardly spent any time with David. He would remedy that right away.

He showered quickly and threw on some casual clothes. He was taking a day off from politicking to spend with his youngest son. Michael realized that they barely knew each other. A horrible thought struck him. What if David didn't want to spend time with his old man?

For the first time since he received the divorce papers, he called Rebecca. His heart was beating fast and his hands were sweating. He felt like a teenager calling the captain of the cheerleaders for a date. After the phone rang twice, he was ready to hang up. But then his wife answered.

"Hello."

He had trouble getting his mouth working and finally he managed, "Hi, Becks. How are you?"

"Michael. I'm, uh, fine...I guess. How are you?"

"Still in shock from being served with divorce papers. I can't believe that it's over. Do you really want this?"

"No. Are you kidding? I've cried myself to sleep almost every night these past few months. I want it to be like it was in the early days, before you became consumed with saving the world." She hesitated. "I'm sorry. I don't suppose that you called to hear me lecture you."

"I have to agree with you there. The last thing I want to do is fight. How is TJ?"

"She's much better than she was six months ago, but after some tremendous improvement, she's stabilized, or more accurately, stagnated. I don't know if my daughter will ever come back."

"Our daughter, both of ours. Don't forget she's mine too," he snapped. Realizing that he had raised his voice, he said softly, "I'm sorry. I didn't call to fight. I'm so tired of fighting."

"I know you've had some tough times lately," Rebecca said softly. "With the riots in Los Angeles and people trying to kill you, I just don't know what to make of the world anymore. Has God forgotten us?"

"No, God has not forgotten us, Becks. But there's a lot of evil in the world and we just have to teach our kids about the good things and how to deal with the bad."

"The reason I'm calling, Rebecca, is that I want to visit with David for a while. I really miss him. Would that be all right?"

"I don't know, Michael. It seems that being around you is an occupational hazard and I'm not sure if it's the best environment for a ten-year-old."

"For God's sake, I'm not the plague. I'm not going to put him in danger. Don't you know me better than that? Things have been rough between us lately but you know that I love my kids and would do anything to protect them. Damn it, you know that."

"I know that. It's just that my attorney advised against it until everything's sorted out."

"Your attorney told you to keep my kids away from me? Well, screw the bloodsucker! What the hell does he know about our family, about me?"

"Michael, let's not fight. You can see David for a while. It would probably be good for him. But don't you have to do a zillion things to get ready for your new job? Don't you have to go to Washington?"

"There's a lot to do, but I can do it later. I need some rest. I deserve it."

"I know you do, Michael. I don't know how divorce ever came into the picture. It's something that I never envisioned. But I want you to know that I'm proud of you."

"Thanks Becks," he said sincerely. "I want to take him to Washington. Before you scream, I'm taking a week off and doing nothing official. I might see the sights and stay with Matt and Pam. I swear. I have to look for a place to live, too. But I promise that David will be with me every minute and that he'll have a great time. What do you say?"

"You know that I can't say no when you use that voice. When do you want to pick him up?"

"The day after tomorrow and I'll return him in exactly one week. Thanks, Becks. This is very important right now. I had another nightmare and David was in it."

"One of those Nazi dreams? Good God, Michael, are you still having those? When are you going to see a doctor?"

"Maybe I will one of these days. But anyway, take care and I'll be by on Friday. Good-bye."

✠   ✠   ✠

Friday morning came quickly, and Michael was very excited. It had been some time since he and David had done anything together. Three years before, they had gone fishing and David had caught his first fish. Michael had been so proud. David had clapped each time someone caught a fish. He was so cute, with dark brown eyes just like his mother that sparkled with excitement. He was so full of life and despite his young age, very gregarious. TJ had always been more introverted and Josh had been somewhere in between. But David liked to be the center of attention.

Michael drove up to the house that he had thought he and his family would live in the rest of their lives. He had dreamed of retiring one day and working in the garden, and bouncing a grandchild on his knee. He sat in the car for a few minutes and tears filled his eyes as he realized that would never happen.

Wiping the moisture from his eyes, he walked up to the door and softly knocked. It seemed strange that this had been his home and yet now he had to knock. Rebecca answered with David right behind.

"Hi, Daddy. I've missed you."

"How's my champ? How's my boy?"

"I'm kicking butts and taking names."

Both Michael and Rebecca looked at each other in amazement. "Where in the world did he hear that? Is that what you're teaching him?"

"Of course not. I have no idea where he picked that up. David, where did you learn that?"

"Petey's dad always says it."

"Petey Bensen is the neighbor boy whose father is a police officer," said Rebecca sheepishly.

"Well, on that note, what do you say we hit the road, champ? Say bye to Mommy."

"Bye Mommy. Oh, Daddy, can I ask you something?"

"Shoot."

"Why don't you love Mommy anymore?"

Rebecca rolled her eyes in embarrassment and Michael felt hurt. Slowly, he answered. "David, listen very carefully. You used to be too young to understand but now you're a big boy. Is Petey a friend of yours?"

"He's my bestest friend in the whole world."

"Well, have you ever been mad at him? Have you ever had a fight?"

"Yeah. He had a birthday party and didn't invite me. I was really mad at him but I found out that he sent me an invitation and it got lost."

"But you still like him, don't you?"

"Yes."

"Well, Mommy and I are fighting a little bit right now, just like you and Petey did. It's a little more serious but I hope that we'll be able to work things out. But David, when I married your Mother many years ago, I promised God that I would always love her. And you can't let God down, can you? We might not be able to work our problems out, but I'll never stop loving Mommy or you kids. Does that answer your question?"

"Yes, Daddy. That makes me happy. Bye Mommy. See you later, alligator."

Rebecca was trying to hide the tears that Michael's words brought and with a sigh replied, "After a while, crocodile."

The two Madigan men walked down the driveway. The flight went quickly and they were in Washington in no time. The kids had lived there for many years, but he never had the time to take them to any of the sights. They arrived at Dulles Airport about 6:00 P.M. and rented a car.

They were expected at the Connors' by 8:00 P.M., where they would stay for the next week. David knew the Connors' kids even though they were older than him. But he liked John, the youngest, and remembered the time they had got caught dropping water balloons off of a hotel balcony.

"David, before we go to Mr. Connors' house, I want to make a stop, O.K?"

"Where, Daddy? The White House? Is the President going to give you another medal, like he did that one time?"

"Not tonight. We're going to the Lincoln Memorial."

As they pulled into a parking lot beside the Memorial, David stared at the large statue of Lincoln facing them. They walked up the steps of the Memorial just as the sun was going down. The Reflecting Pool was beginning to light up with the lights of the city.

"David, Abraham Lincoln was probably our greatest president."

"I know about him, Dad. I learned that in school," David said proudly.

"I know it's dark, but over there is some writing on the wall. It says 'In this temple as in the hearts of the people for whom he saved the Union the memory of Abraham Lincoln is enshrined forever.' That means that people are going to remember the great things he did for our country many years from now. In my new job, I'll have to be strong like President Lincoln."

"You're not afraid of anyone are you?" David said.

"Well, I'm not afraid," replied Michael, "But I know it'll be tough. I hope I'm big enough for the job."

"Let's get going. Mr. and Mrs. Connors are expecting us," Michael said. He put his arm around the boy and the two of them walked back to the car.

Michael and David reached the Connors' house on time and were greeted on the doorstep by a giant Irish setter who barked a greeting heard by the entire neighborhood.

"Caesar, down boy. Down boy! It's just a politician," called out Matt, opening the door and walking out onto the porch.

"He could make quite a sergeant-at-arms on the House floor. And wouldn't bounce any checks, either," replied Michael.

"That's a big dog you got there Mr. Connors," exclaimed David, hugging the dog.

"Well, come on in before my neighbors see me cavorting with a Congressman and send my property value down," Matt teased.

"Hi, Michael, it's great to see you. I'll guess we'll be neighbors again pretty soon," said Pam, kissing his cheek.

"It's always a pleasure to see you, Pam, and maybe we'll really be neighbors. That's one of the reasons why I'm here this week, to look for a place to live. I'm sure you remember David. He's my chief of staff this week."

"I can't believe how much he's grown," Pam said in amazement. "The last time I saw him he barely came up to my knees. Why, he's practically a man now. I bet you're hungry, aren't you?"

"Yes, ma'am. I'm hungry enough to wrassle a bear and kiss a pretty girl."

This drew a look of mock horror from his father. "Where in the world did you pick that up?"

"From Petey's father. He's got lots of neat sayings like that. Want to hear some more?"

"I think that will be enough for right now, young man. Could we put our things away?" Michael said, turning to Matt.

"Sure thing. Albert will help you carry those to your rooms. When you get cleaned up, maybe we could talk a little bit in the den before dinner. O.K.?"

"I'll clean up later. David, you go with Albert and Mrs. Connors and I'll join you pretty soon."

They walked into a huge library surrounded by books and historical documents. Matt made a hobby of collecting them.

"Look at this, Mike. This is the original document that Napoleon signed when he surrendered at Waterloo to Wellington. Just picked that up last week. Napoleon was one of my favorites but even the greats lose sometimes, don't they?" Matt shrugged.

"That's for sure. There have been some weird things going on lately, Matt. What can you tell me about Peterson? Any more clues?"

"Nothing. It's the damnedest thing I've ever seen. The murderer must have been in the room and yet the whole press corps consisted of regulars. They've all been interrogated by the FBI like you wouldn't believe and still nothing."

"Any idea on the motive?"

"Well, we think that it has something to do with drugs, but we're not sure. A young attorney in the A.G.'s office, a Paul Hampton, was present when Peterson received some type of threat on the telephone. Apparently some organization called Peterson on his private line and told him that he should delete a key provision of the administration's new drug policy or they would kill his thirteen-year-old daughter, Melanie."

"Is she O.K?"

"I'm sorry to say that her body was just discovered a short time ago, with evidence of sexual abuse."

"Christ. What kind of world do we live in, Matt, where they go after our children?" Michael asked in disgust.

"That's not all. The young attorney I just told you about, Hampton?"

"Yeah?"

"He was found dead yesterday, strangled in his apartment."

Michael just shook his head.

"Mike," Matt continued, "I've been approached by someone, a woman actually. I don't know who she is but she's trying to tell me something."

"What do you mean?"

"Well, it's sort of like 'Deep Throat.' I've met her once, but didn't see her face and she gives me clues and uses code names and a bunch of weird shit. It seems she's into the Beatles and calls herself Sgt. Pepper."

"What kind of clues? What's she trying to tell you?"

"She won't come right out and say it, which makes it pretty frustrating. I can't quite put my finger on it yet, Mike, but she seems to be saying that there's some type of organization out there trying to wipe out key members of these groups."

"We don't have enough problems of our own, do we, without some crazy rednecks running around creating havoc?" Michael asked, shaking his head.

"I wish it were only that. I think we're possibly facing something much more serious than a bunch of rednecks," Matt said, pausing. "But I don't want to speculate any more until I get some more information. I'm hoping to hear from Sgt. Pepper again soon."

Michael laughed to himself before speaking. "Well, as you know, the big thing in California has been the riots in L.A." he said. "Some guy videotaped a police brutality case and it hit the news. The rest is history."

Unknown to Michael, it was Alan Roberts who had caught it all on videotape. Alan Roberts was right. It was big.

"Green, what do you think of it? And before you answer, tell me what you think as a high ranking member of a conservative government and also as a black man."

"Let me answer the second question first. As you know, I grew up in south L.A., went to school in Compton and was in Watts on August 11, 1965, when the riots started back then. I actually knew Marquette Frye, the guy who was pulled over by a white police officer for speeding and reckless driving at 116th Street and Avalon Blvd," Matt said, becoming more animated.

"This motorcycle cop radioed for a patrol car to carry Frye to jail," he said, telling a story that he had told hundreds of times before. "A crowd gathered. A scuffle broke out and Frye's brother and mother were arrested too. The crowd grew angry. Rocks and bottles were thrown and the riot was on. Six days later, thirty-four people were dead. Now almost thirty years later the same thing happens. I can't believe it," said Matt. Then, he paused for air.

"The same damn problems: no jobs, poor schools, police brutality, poor housing and public transportation. But the worst thing of all is the feeling of hopelessness. There's a whole segment of society that feels that they don't have a chance. I know that some of us can make it, like I did, but I can't blame most people for feeling so hopeless. We've got a whole underclass of people filled with despair and rage. I don't share it but I can understand it."

"What about the police brutality thing?" interjected Michael.

"Well," answered Matt, "Police brutality has always been a complaint of the black community but it's always been their word against ours. And guess who was believed. This time the whole world saw it and it still didn't make any difference. To answer your first question, as a black man I feel frustration and anger by the verdict. And I'm greatly sorrowed by its aftermath. Now I'm not saying that the verdict justifies looting, burning and murder. The police response was pathetic, and it took too long for the National Guard to be deployed. A lot of the troublemakers were just taking advantage of the verdict and the chaos. But the problem isn't just 'rotten people' as one political candidate put it. And rounding up thousands and putting them behind bars is no real answer. We need to get to the roots of the problem, and that's going to take some time."

Michael, who had been listening intently, asked, "Do you see any connection between these other events we've been talking about and the riots?"

Matt nodded his head and said, "I have a theory, and I think there's a connection. I need more information from this informant. But if I'm right, we're going to be facing much worse than what happened in L.A."

As they talked about the bizarre events of the recent past and about the responsibilities of his new job, Michael made a sudden decision to take David to Israel. He had come to Washington to find a place to live and to get to know David better. But he could always find a place to live later. He might never again have the chance to share his Jewish heritage with David. He made reservations on the 10:00 A.M. flight to Jerusalem. After thinking about it, he decided there was no real reason to tell Rebecca because she would probably object. No reason to worry her unnecessarily, he decided.

Michael was excited to have this opportunity to teach David about the history of the Jewish people. He remembered his first time in Jerusalem, how his father had been so excited and had talked nonstop about Jewish history. Was David too young to understand the wanderings in Canaan, the enslavement in Egypt, the captivity in Babylon, the conflict with the Greeks, the oppression under the Romans and most recently, the concentration camp victims in World War II? Could a ten-year-old absorb or appreciate how the Jews have struggled over four continents, through six civilizations and forty centuries?

Morning came quickly. "C'mon, Congressman. Get your butt out of bed. You're only supposed to sleep when the House is in session."

"Is it six already? I just went to bed."

"I can remember when you'd get by on two hours of sleep. You must be getting old," Matt teased.

"Don't give me that crap. I can still run rings around you," Michael shot back.

"Well, then get moving. You have a plane to catch, remember?"

9

ichael and David took off on a DC-10 from Dulles Airport and began the long flight to Israel, changing planes in Rome. David was full of questions.

"What's Israel like, Daddy? I saw on TV pictures of soldiers on the street with big guns. Is it always like that?"

"Well, David, I'm afraid it is to some degree. You see, Israel has to fight to exist. It's a small country surrounded by enemies. Over the last forty years there have been five wars. They don't have lasting peace and so there are many soldiers."

"Why does everyone hate Israel?"

"You keep asking me questions that I can't answer. My Dad used to say that maybe it's because there are no hairs on a sea gull's chest."

"What does that mean?"

"It doesn't really mean anything. That's the point. It goes back to the same thing I was telling you before. People are different and when they don't understand the differences, they hate and fight. Israel's neighbors don't agree on a lot of things so there's a lot of fighting," he added.

"Do the children fight too?"

"Not quite. The sad thing is that children are taught by their parents to hate their enemies so the problem continues. When they grow-up, they teach their children and so on. It never seems to end. David, even though other people may hate you because you're a Jew, it's important that *you* not hate other people just because they're different. All people are God's children. You must never forget that," Michael emphasized.

"Grandpa Ben lived in Israel for a long time, didn't he?"

"Yes, he did. He fought in the Israeli Army before returning to the United States. He was in the Israeli War of Independence, the war that saw the birth of Israel."

"Wow, was that like the American War of Independence?"

"Yes, it was. You see, for a long time, Jews lived in a country called Palestine. Then, many years ago, they were chased out and didn't return for over thirteen hundred years. In 1947, Palestine was divided into a Jewish part and an Arab part. On May 14, 1948, the same day I was born, Israel was born, too. That morning they proclaimed their independence and the next day they manned the front lines to defend it," Michael told the excited boy.

"Your grandpa used to tell me that they had only 19,000 men to fight the Arabs who were attacking on five fronts. Most had never held anything in their arms except wives, children and the Torah. The Jews were outgunned by the Arabs who had all kinds of modern weapons. In just a couple of days, Jerusalem fell to the Arabs."

"But they didn't give up, did they?" David asked.

"No, they didn't, David," answered Michael, excited by his interest. "They were outnumbered but they had a great will to win. They were determined not to yield even one inch of soil and they kept on advancing."

"The Arabs thought that the war would be over in a week but after a month of fierce fighting, they gratefully accepted the truce terms," Michael continued. "Israel was then an independent nation. But its future has been scarred with more wars and constant threats."

"Daddy, are Jews really God's chosen people?" asked David.

"Well," Michael responded, "For 4,000 years we've survived every crisis imaginable. God must be keeping his eyes on us."

"But Daddy, if God really was watching out for Jews, why has it been so hard?"

"That's a very good question, Son. The world's a dangerous place and a lot of terrible things happen. Some people say if there was a God, he wouldn't let there be wars and despair. But life is not supposed to be easy, David. Life's a struggle and those who work hard and treat others with love and respect and keep their faith in God are the ones who prosper in the long run. And I don't just mean with material goods," he emphasized.

David nodded his head as if he understood. Quickly, he started laughing. "Mr. Connors told me some neat words for things on an airplane. Want to hear them?"

Michael shook his head. "I guess so," he said laughing.

"OK. The small sandwiches they serve are hockey pucks. Overstuffed bags are called mobile homes. The lazy flight attendant who hides out in the galley is a galley, queen and bags of peanuts are called pilot pellets because the pilots eat so many. Funny, huh, Dad?"

"Right, champ. I think I'll have a few hockey pucks. What do you say?" Michael asked, grinning at his son.

"OK, Dad. Some pilot pellets, too."

After dinner, the flight attendants began retrieving the trays. It had been some time since Michael had watched a movie and he was looking forward to it.

Right then, Michael saw a familiar face and almost doubled over in surprise. The man coming out of the rest room was his uncle Ariel, whom he hadn't seen in years.

"Ariel, over here," Michael shouted.

Ariel saw Michael and looked as if he was going to faint. "Michael, what are you doing here?" Ariel was thinking quickly, trying to imagine how Michael could have ended up on the same plane.

"That's some greeting, Uncle. Glad to see you, too."

"I'm sorry," Ariel stammered. "I'm just surprised to see you. You're going to Israel?" he asked, amazed.

"Yes. Sorry I didn't call you in advance but it was a spur of the moment thing."

"I see. I thought I saw you back in the terminal getting onto another flight," Ariel said.

"That was probably me. We were getting onto another flight to Jerusalem, but I decided at the last minute to go to Tel Aviv first. So we changed planes at the last minute."

"I'd better go sit down for the movie," Ariel said, standing up. "You're welcome to stay with us while you're in Israel. Of course, you know that you're always welcome." Ariel made his way back to his seat.

A tall, dark-skinned man walked past their seat toward the back of the first-class section. Michael had seen him earlier and had noted a prominent scar on his face. While Michael watched, the man with the scar quickly pulled out a gun and began shouting orders to the astonished passengers. Michael heard similar orders being screamed in the coach section by a another man. One of the men appeared to be an Arab and the other an European. And then, another Arab man emerged with a gun.

Several frightened passengers grabbed for their children, while others began sobbing, mouthing prayers or clutching their seats, fearing the worst.

There seemed to be a total of three hijackers. The European stormed into the cockpit with his gun drawn.

"Captain, please be advised that this plane is now under our control. Refusal to cooperate on your part will mean instant death to many innocent people. We are willing to die for our cause. If any of you decide to be a hero, you'll be a dead hero. Let me speak to the passengers."

Reluctantly, the captain handed him the microphone. "Good afternoon, ladies and gentlemen. I'm sorry to say that today's movie will not be shown. Instead, you'll have the unique opportunity to participate in a hijacking. We are very determined to carry out our mission. For those whose friends and loved ones are planning to meet them at the Tel Aviv airport, they will unfortunately have a long wait. This plane is not going to Israel and we are prepared to kill anyone who tries to interfere. If you cooperate with us you will be rewarded. If you do not you will die. Any questions?" he added sarcastically.

The European was replaced by one of the Arabs, who repeated the threats in Arabic.

"Daddy, what's happening?" David said, fear in his voice.

"This is called a hijacking, David," Michael whispered.

"These men are taking over the plane and are going to force the captain to fly the plane to somewhere besides Israel."

"Where are we going?" David asked nervously.

"I don't know, David."

"Maybe we can jump them, Daddy."

"That's brave of you, Son. But just do what they say and sit here quietly. Can you do that for me?"

"Boy, this is something that the guys at school aren't going to believe," David exclaimed.

"Sh, David, no jokes right now," Michael ordered.

Michael noticed that the two Arabs had started going down the aisle, seat by seat, demanding each passenger's passport. What the hell was going on?

"Passport!" barked the tall one, who was called Amin. The middle-aged couple in the first row of coach nervously handed over their passports. Israeli passports were handed to him and were not returned. The next passenger was a blond young man around twenty-five. His name was Charlie Hooper and he was from Florida. He received his passport back.

This procedure was repeated for the entire coach section. It quickly became obvious that the gunmen were keeping the passports of all those who were Jewish or had Jewish sounding names. There were half a dozen black passengers who did not receive their passports back either.

Michael watched as the terrorist, named Abdul, reached Ariel's seat. He was wondering what Ariel's response would be. Ariel was known for his hot temper. Michael hoped that he wouldn't get himself into trouble. Michael was too far away to hear their conversation.

"Your name?" asked the terrorist.

Ariel shot the terrorist a glance of pure hatred. "Ariel Madigan," the man answered slowly through clenched teeth. After a moment of puzzled thought, Abdul suddenly seemed to recognize the name.

Abdul swallowed hard and began to sweat nervously. "You are Ariel Madigan?" he asked hesitantly.

Ariel nodded.

The hijacker stood in place for a moment, seeming at a loss as to what to do. Finally, he regained his composure and moved on.

He was obviously agitated by the time he reached Michael. Abdul demanded to see Michael's passport and he obediently produced it. Abdul's eyes widened, "Madigan? What is going on here?"

"Are you related to Ariel?"

Michael knew a "yes" would place him in more danger. But he was proud to be Jewish and would not be made to feel ashamed.

"Yes, I am," he answered, praying that he would not regret his pride.

"And a little Jewish boy, too. How old are you?"

"Ten," David blurted out.

"Are you afraid, little boy?"

"No, because my Daddy is a congressman and he'll have the whole US Air Force after you if you don't let us go," David said defiantly.

Michael grimaced. He had hoped to keep that information hidden. The gun-toting bastards might value high-level government hostages.

"A Congressman? Stand up and come with me," shouted Abdul, who seemed nervous.

Michael's main concern was David's safety. He grabbed his son by the shoulders and looked directly into his eyes. "Son, you be a big boy now. I'll be right back, OK?"

"OK, Daddy. I'll be all right."

Michael stood up, not knowing what to expect. As they neared Ariel, Abdul gave him the same order.

Michael and Ariel walked the few steps towards the cockpit with guns pressed into their backs. As they approached the front of the plane, they were ordered to stay outside the cockpit door for a few minutes. Michael looked at his uncle, who was seething with anger. Abdul slammed the door, leaving Amin out with the passengers. Once inside he glanced frantically at his leader, Fritz Streicher.

"Streicher," gasped the hijacker anxiously. "We have problems."

Streicher ran his fingers through his long blond hair. He did not like problems or surprises.

"Ariel Madigan is on board. Actually, we have two Madigans. Congressman Michael Madigan and Ariel Madigan are on board," he said, loud enough for the crew to hear. "We're screwed, now..." he continued, blurting out sensitive information. Streicher interrupted his tirade.

"Quiet, you fool! Why don't you tell the whole plane while you're at it." And then lowering his voice, "We're toast if anything happens to Ariel. Where are they?"

"Right outside the door," came the anxious reply.

"Is that a fact?" said Streicher, struggling to maintain his composure. "Who planned this thing? I can't believe it. Someone has a sick sense of humor. We followed Michael, but Ariel wasn't supposed to be on the same plane. I bet the mix-up happened when Michael switched planes at the last minute." And then under his breath he said, "The pilots have heard too much, they've got to go. I hope Ariel can fly this thing."

"Captain, how close are we to Rome?" Streicher asked, his voice cracking.

The captain was an ex-Air Force fighter pilot by the name of Martin Andrews. In his mid-forties, he still had the build of a college athlete.

Reluctantly, he answered. "We're about 200 miles from Rome. Do you mind telling us just what the hell you're doing? Are you forcing us to fly to Beirut or some other horse shit place? If you are, just say so and quit jacking us around."

"Oh, Captain, that was not very nice. My mother is from Beirut," said Abdul. "I am afraid that you will have to pay for that remark."

Captain Andrews grimaced and realized that no matter how much he despised these cowardly shits, he had to keep his big mouth shut for the safety of the passengers.

Streicher hesitated for a few minutes. Finally, he grabbed the microphone. "Is this on the proper frequency to reach Rome? I have a few things that I want to say," the German stated.

As the drama was unfurling in the cockpit, one of the passengers in the middle of the plane had something else on his mind. Right across from him was an in-flight telephone. He had to get it, but Amin was keeping a close eye on everybody.

The passenger's name was Greg Purcell and he was a reporter for GNN. He slumped over and began groaning and gasping for breath. This man appeared to be having a heart attack.

The five flight attendants had all been ushered to the back of the plane. Susan Treverton, a student at Georgetown who worked as a flight attendant part-time, saw Purcell and began to rush to his aid. She was quickly stopped by Amin and his gun.

"Please, that man is very ill," responded the flight attendant. "You must let me help him. If you don't and something happens to him, there will be a panic and you may not be able to control everyone," she warned.

Amin saw that there was some logic in this and gestured for her to proceed. She was a premed major. She reached Purcell, he was grabbing his chest, seemingly not able to get his breath.

"Sir, tell me what the problem is. Where does it hurt?" she asked.

Purcell pulled her to him and whispered, "I'm not really hurt. I need for you to get me the telephone and help me to the bathroom."

Susan was stunned. The tall redhead was about to tell him off for risking the passengers' safety with his foolishness, but Amin was standing nearby, weapon drawn. If she didn't do as he wished, the gunman would learn that it was all a ruse. If she did as he requested, this fool might be endangering the lives of everyone aboard.

Think quickly, quickly. What do I do? she asked herself. Suddenly, the plane hit some intense turbulence and everyone not wearing a safety belt lurched forward. Amin almost dropped his gun. Susan and the other flight attendants fell to the ground momentarily. Now was the chance!

Amin was distracted by the screams of the already tense passengers. Susan grabbed the telephone and quickly handed it off to Purcell like a relay runner hands off a baton. He stuck it down his shirt before Amin could turn around. So far, so good, Purcell thought.

I hope the son of a bitch chokes, thought Susan. What a fool! Who was he going to call, the police?

Amin came back to where Purcell was and yelled at Susan. "Can't you keep him quiet? All of his moaning is driving me crazy."

"He's got severe cramps and needs to get to the rest room immediately."

"Then go already. Just get him to shut up," he said impatiently.

Susan and Purcell's seatmate, a young student, helped Purcell stand and helped him to the rest room.

Susan opened the door and assisted Purcell into the small space. She asked him pleasantly, "Will you be all right, sir?" while glaring at him with contempt.

"Yes, I think so. Thank-you very much. I'll ring the bell if I need your assistance," mumbled the reporter.

The door closed behind him and he quickly dialed a series of numbers that his telephone charge card required and reached GNN European headquarters in London.

"GNN. Can you hold, please?" asked the receptionist.

"No, I can't hold!" demanded the reporter. "This is Greg Purcell and this is literally a matter of life and death. I need to speak to Everett Mitchell or George Hackett immediately."

"Yes sir, I'll connect you right away."

After what seemed an eternity, senior editor Everett Mitchell came on the line.

"Greg, this is Mitchell. What the hell's going on?"

"I'm on American flight 342, Washington to Rome. We've been hijacked by three gunmen, two Arabs and a German. I don't know what organization they're with, but they checked everyone's passport and kept those belonging to Jews and blacks."

"Jesus Christ," yelled Mitchell. "Where the hell are you calling from?"

"I'm calling from one of those in-flight phones from the bathroom of the plane."

"You mean to tell me the hijacking is in progress right now? My God." Turning from the phone he yelled to a subordinate. "Get me a mike hooked up to this call, this second."

"Everett, let's monitor this for a second and we might want to break in," Hackett directed. Mitchell nodded.

"Greg, this is one hell of a journalistic coup but you better not endanger the lives of innocent people. Be extremely careful."

"I'm going to return to my seat and I'll have the telephone stuffed in my shirt. I'm wearing a jacket so no one will know. Make sure that there's no unnecessary noise coming from your end," Purcell whispered nervously.

"OK, buddy. We're ready. Go to it," encouraged Mitchell.

"Real quickly, let me tell you that we should be very close to reaching Rome," Purcell explained. "I've been watching the route closely. I don't believe there's been a change in the flight path. I thought for sure that we would be heading for Tunisia or something but it doesn't appear that we are. By the way, Michael Madigan, former army bigwig and present congressman -elect from California is on board and he's been brought up to the cockpit along with some Israeli passenger. OK, that's it for now. Keep your ears open," Purcell said, signing off temporarily.

Purcell opened the door and Amin was standing there, looking intense and angry. Purcell came out just as the impatient terrorist was about to storm in. Susan rushed to his aid and asked if she could be of assistance.

"Thank you, ma'am," Purcell said graciously. "But I feel much better. It's amazing how some serious vomiting can do the trick. Guess it was something I ate." He walked slowly back to his seat and sat himself down.

Back in the cockpit, tempers were getting short. First Officer Lloyd Albert demanded an explanation.

"Listen, I don't know what your plan is but we're getting awfully close to Rome. Is there a point to this hijacking? I'm Jewish, by the way, and if you want to kill me, go ahead, but quit jerking me around," Albert shouted angrily.

"Well, well, well. A feisty Jew," Streicher said sarcastically. "I thought that you were all passive as sheep. But never mind with that, you will now learn of our mission. Connect me with the passengers on your intercom. Do it now, I say," he ordered, trying to think quickly. The presence of Ariel Madigan had changed everything. Their plan had to be aborted or changed. He was trying to think of a solution but he could see only one way out of the enormous blunder that had been made. They would abort and leave Ariel to work his way out if he could.

Andrews turned on the intercom and handed it to Streicher. "Good afternoon, ladies and gentlemen. Let me introduce myself. My name is Fritz Streicher. For those of you who can not pinpoint my homeland from either my name or my accent, let me help you. It is Germany. My Arab friends and I, as well as our colleagues back home and around the world, have grown quite weary with the disgusting manner in which the United States keeps arming Israel with weapons. Israel is a puny country of parasites, existing this long only because of the might of its hypocrite neighbor, the United States."

"We will no longer tolerate this interference," he announced authoritatively. "If it continues, many innocent people will die. This is only the first of many statements we will make in protest."

"All you Jews on board, no matter what happens in the future, I am sorry to say that, at least for today, you are not God's chosen people. But take heart. For those who believe in life after death, you may soon meet your creator." He put down the microphone and the astonished crew watched him in stunned silence.

Streicher gestured to Abdul, who pulled out a large bag, opened it and poured the contents onto the floor. "Get the Madigans," the German ordered.

Abdul did as he was told and pulled Michael and Ariel into the cockpit. They all could see that the bag contained parachutes. Streicher and Amin picked up the parachutes and proceeded to put them on one at a time. When they were both done, Abdul went out into the plane and traded places with Amin, who then put on a parachute himself.

What kind of hijacking was this? They were going to jump out of the plane and not do anything? It couldn't be that simple, Albert thought. All of a sudden, he had a sick feeling in his stomach.

Finally, all three had donned their chutes and were ready. For what?

Ariel spoke slowly but with intense anger, "What are you doing?"

Streicher wouldn't make eye contact with Ariel and refused to answer his question. The German nervously continued speaking to the passengers and through Purcell's hook-up, to the entire world. GNN had broken into its newscasts and was broadcasting clearly everything that was happening.

Since all three of the gunmen now seemed occupied, Purcell took a chance and started talking into the phone, which was still in his shirt, but held up near his mouth.

Purcell felt strongly that they might not be alive much longer and so he risked describing to the global audience what was happening. He explained how all of the terrorists had donned parachutes. His voice could be heard on the broadcast, slowly and distinctly to those listening. A worldwide audience was chilled by the eerie reality of this live broadcast.

"Just what are these people doing, you might be asking yourself?" Streicher said mockingly to the others in the cockpit. "Are they really going to jump out at 30,000 feet? That is exactly what we're going to do."

"You see," the German continued, "we had other plans but circumstances have forced us to adapt. In case you're wondering, we're bundled up quite warmly because it will be below freezing at this altitude. Also, we're wearing rib protectors because sometimes ribs get crushed when the chutes open. Speaking of which, we'll each fire a parachute deployment gun which will extract a small drogue chute as well as the main chute. This will be necessary because of the high speed. Also, we each have oxygen tanks. Impressed?" he asked, still refusing to make eye contact with Ariel, who glared at him hatefully.

Streicher ordered the three members of the crew to walk out of the cockpit and stand in the aisle in front of the side door at the front of the plane. He and his fellow hijackers followed the pilots. Michael and Ariel were ordered to stay inside the cockpit with the door shut.

"Ladies and gentlemen, I'm afraid we must now bid you adieu. We are no longer welcome, I'm afraid," Streicher said, stretching the microphone cord as far as it would go. "Please say your good-byes to your brave crew. Martin Andrews, your pilot. Lloyd Albert, your first officer. And Ted Griffin, your flight engineer." After a second thought, he added, "And also, you might want to grab onto something. We might hit some turbulence. We hope you've enjoyed your flight."

With those words, Streicher pulled out a .45-caliber pistol and fired three bullets into the side door, causing it to fly open. The freezing air sucked out everything that was not fastened down, including the three crew men and a flight attendant that was standing near the door. Right behind them were the hijackers, who also were sucked out, but they were prepared for it.

"Auf Wiedersehen," yelled Streicher, as he was sucked out of the plane.

Michael and Ariel heard the screams of the passengers and quickly realized what must have happened. With no one at the helm, the plane started diving.

The passengers panicked as objects were sucked out of the plane. Two other people were violently pulled out of doorway. Purcell had to shout to be heard over the screams and was now speaking directly into the phone.

"Oh, my God. The pilots are gone! They've been sucked out the door," Purcell shouted. "There's no one flying the plane and we're starting to dive.

The gunshots ripped a hole in the side door, and flew open. There's a suction in here that is pulling people out of the plane. The hijackers are gone. They've parachuted out. There is no one flying the plane," he shouted into the phone. The GNN audience could barely hear his voice above the screaming passengers.

Purcell was trying to keep calm but even in all of his experience, he had never been this frightened. Three more people, two men and a flight attendant, were sucked out of the plane. "Good Christ Almighty, three more people just got sucked out of the plane and the plane is going into a nose dive!" said Purcell into the phone.

All across the world, millions were glued to their TV's listening live to what would probably soon be the end of 107 innocent people. This went beyond journalism, Hackett thought to himself. He was about to give the order to end the coverage on live broadcast. But Purcell's next words gave some hope and the linkup was kept.

"The plane has leveled out," said Purcell, calming down somewhat. "I can only suspect that either Congressman Madigan or the Israeli gentleman I mentioned earlier is now flying the plane. At least we're not diving anymore."

Michael had his pilot's license and had flown on a regular basis for a time. But those were small planes and that had been years ago. There was no comparison as he sat behind the controls and pulled the plane out of its nose dive. He struggled to remain calm. Hearing the screams coming from the passengers he knew he had to try something or they would all be dead.

He had at least stopped the dive and they were momentarily safe. But there was no way that he could land this monster with its thousand different instruments and dials.

He grabbed the intercom and was about to speak when Ariel grabbed his arm.

"Michael, I'm a pilot. I've flown commercial jets, although it's been a few years. I think that I could land this plane. I'll need help from the control tower and I'll need your help."

With adrenaline flowing through him, Michael looked his uncle in the eye. "Do I have a choice? We're dead anyway."

"That's the spirit, Mike," said Ariel. "We just might stand a chance."

"I guess we don't have a whole lot of options, do we?" Michael said, thinking of David.

There were so many gauges and dials that he couldn't even figure out how to call on the radio. He picked up what he judged to be the radio and started speaking, while pushing the button.

"Anybody, any channel. Mayday. Mayday. This is flight 342 approaching Rome," he said urgently. "Mayday. Mayday. Anybody out there? All pilots are dead. I repeat. All pilots are dead. We have some flight experience but need assistance. This is an emergency. Please respond."

Ariel and Michael waited for a response, fearing that they hadn't gotten through to anyone. Michael hung his head.

"Flight 342, this is Rome. Do you hear me?" came a welcome voice.

"You bet I do. Can you tell us how to land this thing?" Michael asked looking up.

"Is this Colonel Madigan?"

Michael was shocked to hear his name, but at this point he didn't really care about how they knew.

"Yes, it is. Can you help us?"

"I think so but we need you to stay calm and pay attention very carefully. My name is David Eshkol and I'm going to help you and your friend down. By the way, do not go out into the plane. The side door has been shot off and everything is being sucked out."

"What is going on!" Michael exclaimed. That's what he had assumed, but how did the air traffic controller know that?

"OK, Colonel, do exactly as I tell you and I think you'll be eating kosher tonight. Are you ready?"

"Ready as we'll ever be," Michael responded. At least the guy had a sense of humor, he thought.

"All right," Eshkol said, monitoring a long range radar screen that covered a circle 200 miles in diameter, centered upon Rome. Flight 342's transponder responded to the radar signal by sending back an electronic transmission. This signal was fed into a computer, allowing the ground control to calculate the altitude and ground speed. Eshkol checked the blips on his screen and issued clearance for the aircraft to begin its descent.

"American 342 cleared present position to land on runway thirteen. Maintain 7,000 feet, and gently head north-northwest," Eshkol directed, as communication was switched from his headset to a direct speaker system so that all controllers in the room could hear.

Ariel glanced about nervously as he tried to descend to 7,000 feet from their present altitude of nearly 30,000 feet. Ariel put the plane into a gentle right turn, toward Rome. They were now 118 miles from the airport.

Ariel throttled back the engines, producing an immediate response, as if someone had applied the brakes. The plane suddenly began to descend. Passengers all throughout the plane began screaming.

"We'll help you determine your gross weight, your maneuvering speed and the flap settings. Remember, that your weight may have changed by as much as 200,000 pounds since you took off. Now, you need to start making adjustments for crosswinds and initial flap extension. When you land, you want your flaps at thirty," instructed the controller.

Ariel nodded his head. The flaps were set. He knew that flaps were usually lowered to their maximum angle of thirty degrees for landing. This would enable a jetliner to fly at a considerably lower speed, producing a safe, controlled descent and landing. The airport came into view.

"Don't forget to reduce your air speed."

"Roger," Michael responded.

"OK, your approach speed should be 141 knots, touchdown at 121 knots. Your present weight is approximately 98,000 kilograms. OK, set your bugs," Eshkol instructed.

"Our what?" Michael asked.

"Little white tabs on your primary air speed indicators. They're movable and should be set. They give you a visual reference for the proper approach and landing speeds." Michael saw what Eshkol was talking about and set the tabs. By now, they had descended to 18,000 feet. "Listen, you don't want to come in short of the runway. Come in high over the airport to make sure that you have sufficient altitude, then circle for a landing. If you come in too high, put it into a side-slip, kill altitude quickly and correct for the high approach."

Eshkol had lost Michael but Ariel recognized the terminology. He had done side-slips before in small planes but didn't know that he could do it with a jetliner. He would have to twist the control yoke in one direction, setting the ailerons to produce a turn and simultaneously jam his foot into one pedal, pushing the rudder into the opposite direction. Ariel prayed that this would not be necessary.

Eshkol transmitted the weather to the substitute pilots. "We have scattered clouds at 5,000 feet. Visibility is sixteen miles. There's a five knot wind blowing from 320 degrees." The controller continued. "OK, go ahead and gear down."

Michael looked about in a daze for a moment and finally figured it out. He pulled the hydraulic undercarriage selector to the down position. Within seconds they heard the sounds of the gear dropping into position and the controlled vibration caused by the increased drag.

"At about twenty to sixty feet above the runway, ease back on the control column and round out the glide with the main wheels just a bit above the runway. Then reduce power to idle. Got it?"

"I think," responded Michael.

"After you touch down," Eshkol said, "maintain directional control by using the rudder. And apply full and steady braking force to the pedals. Retract the flaps so that there's more weight on the tires," he added.

Meanwhile, Purcell continued his commentary. This would make him an instant star in his field. Millions were listening around the world. Rebecca, former GNN reporter, sat glued to the broadcast. Her husband was attempting to land an airplane in Israel.

Israel? He said he was going to Washington. My God, what about David? He's going to kill this whole family.

"Damn you, Michael Madigan. I hate you!" she screamed. She passed out, expecting a crash. She missed the commentary on the landing.

The plane was now only a few feet above the ground, but it was going too fast and wasn't level. The wheels made contact with the ground and the plane suddenly bounced. They had not slowed down enough and had come in at an angle. The screams of the passengers started again.

Again, they touched the wheels to the ground and this time the plane was level. The plane was on the ground and a cheer went up from the passengers who had not gone into shock. The plane was still traveling too fast. It was careening forward at 170 knots. Two tires blew in the right main landing gear. Ariel was using the brakes as directed but it still seemed out of control. He saw dozens of emergency vehicles on the runway and several fire trucks. He prayed that they would not be necessary.

"Reverse thrust," shouted the controller.

The plane passed the control tower and there wasn't much runway left. At the end of the runway was an airplane that wasn't moving. It must be empty, Ariel surmised, as it sat there, unable to do anything else. His speed had been greatly reduced but he couldn't get it to stop. They were going to crash.

A new obstacle appeared. A low metal guardrail was in the middle of the runway. Ariel leaned heavily on the right brake and the plane veered slightly, skidding. The left side of the nose glanced off the metal rail, taking off the round wooden posts at their bases.

"Prepare for a crash, brace yourselves," Ariel told the panicked passengers.

The two planes collided with a thundering crash, as the smaller stationary plane shattered into pieces like a broken ice formation. Flight 342 took a huge jolt that threw everyone forward and then back. Seconds later, the plane came to a grinding stop.

Michael could hear the whoops of joy and relief. But he sat in silence for a moment to regain his stomach, collect his thoughts and thank God.

David pushed his way through the crowd and into the cockpit. His eyes met his father's and they embraced.

"I'm so sorry, Son, for taking you on this flight. Are you all right?" Michael said, crying.

"I'm fine, Daddy. Are you OK? Did you really fly the plane?" the boy asked proudly.

"C'mon, Son. Let's get out of here." Michael looked at his uncle with a sense of awe. It was unbelievable what this seventy-year-old man had accomplished. "God was with us, Ariel."

Ariel looked close to collapse but responded weakly.

"Yes, he was nephew. Yes, he was."

10

ikolai Ligachev and his two sons, Gunther and Konrad, had just completed a twenty kilometer volksmarch. Ligachev, also known as Charlemagne, had married a German woman and after only a few years, they divorced. She had returned to Germany with the children where they had grown up under Communist rule in East Berlin. Ligachev was now seventy years old and his sons were well-educated and highly respected men. They both idolized their father, even though he had missed their childhood. They had spent the majority of the walk discussing Germany's recent reunification.

They finished their walk and gladly sat down at the tables surrounding the oompah band. The table was filled with plenty of bratwurst and cold Löwenbräu beer.

Gunther, tall and thin, was a publisher for a large newspaper. Konrad, shorter and quite a bit heavier, was a college professor. They were both married and had children. They led peaceful lives and tried to avoid getting involved in politics. Gunther had the opportunity to leave the country for the first time the year before and he was shocked to see the freedom and wealth in other parts of Europe.

Neither son knew of their father's true identity or his past. They had on several occasions broached the subject of his early years during the war, but he wouldn't talk. And they never pressed it.

After they had downed their last wurst and beer, Ligachev suggested that they walk another two kilometers down to the lake. He had decided to talk to his sons about his beliefs. They reached the lake just before sunset. He figured that there would be about forty-five more minutes of light left.

"What's on your mind, Dad?" asked Konrad. "Is it about Mother?"

"Don't worry, your mother is fine. This is very difficult to explain...please sit down."

Both sons sat on the ground and listened intently, knowing that it was something very important since their father was never at a loss for words.

"Sons, I've never talked to you or anyone about the war. Not even your mother. But the time has come for me to tell you. What I'm about to say may shock you and even disgust you. You may no longer wish to claim me as your father. You can walk away from here and I will understand." His sons looked at him with puzzled expressions.

"By telling you this, I'm violating an oath that I swore to uphold over forty-five years ago. Then, I would have preferred to die rather than break the promise, but now I feel differently," he said, looking each one in the eye.

Gunther and Konrad turned to look at each other and then back at their father. To them it was inconceivable that he could say anything that terrible. They waited for him to continue.

"Sons, as I'm sure you know, I was a lieutenant in the war. What you don't know is that I was in the German Army, and not the Russian..."

"The German army?" Konrad asked. "But you are Russian."

"I didn't go to the Soviet Union until after the war. My real name is Wolfgang Weber, and I was born in Nuremberg."

"Why did you lie to us? You told us you were Russian!" Gunther asked angrily.

"It's a long story. I had to kill Russians during the war. I was following orders," he said defensively.

After the initial shock, Gunther spoke up. "Dad, no one can blame you for Hitler and the Nazis. You were a young man and you had orders. You had no choice."

"Ah, there lies the rub," Ligachev said, shaking his head. "You see, I respect those men. Hitler, Hess, and Göring were great men that were trying to restore Germany to power. Before you judge me, please hear me out."

"You are both familiar with Germany's history and are proud of her heritage. Germany was a world power until her loss in World War I. The allies crippled her by imposing impossible war reparations, including a 'guilt clause' in the Treaty of Versailles. Germany was humiliated."

"Father, that does not justify—" Konrad started, but was abruptly cut off.

"Hear me out Son," Ligachev continued, "and maybe you will understand my thinking. "Twenty years later, as a young man, I joined the army and quickly became a lieutenant. For six long years, I fought for Germany, only to see her humiliated again. I was powerless to prevent Germany's surrender to the allies and that was painful. That pain was doubled by the Nuremberg Trials of 1945 and 1946."

"The trial began on November 20, 1945, at the Palace of Justice. Germany was charged with four counts, including crimes against humanity and war crimes. The self-righteous allies sat in judgment wearing black gowns and dress uniforms littered with ribbons." Ligachev's eyes were staring distantly.

"Twenty-one Germans were placed on trial. I witnessed these absurd proceedings. These once powerful men were pale, waxen figures. I remember their names: Fritzsche, von Neurath, Speer, Seyss-Inquart, Jodl, Sauckel, Raeder, Doenitz, Schact, Funk, Streicher, Frick, Frank, Rosenberg, Kaltenbrunner, Keitel, von Ribbentrop, Hess and Göring and a couple others. I can still see their faces as if it were yesterday. I admired these men and I had to watch them humiliated by this sanctimonious mockery of a trial. The proceedings lasted 284 days and I died nearly every day." He stopped speaking and looked at his sons, trying to gauge their reaction. Gunther was upset and Konrad seemed more stunned.

"Dad, we can get you some help or something. Maybe..." Konrad's voice trailed off. He was out of words.

"I'm not finished yet, Son. On October 1, 1946, sentences were proclaimed. Three were acquitted but they requested that they remain in custody due to fear of reprisals. Seven received prison sentences and the other eleven were sentenced to be hanged. That day set the course for my future. It set in motion a quest so sacred that the last forty-six years have been in preparation." Ligachev was disappointed in their lack of understanding.

"I attended the executions on October 11. Just before Göring was to be hung, he bit on a potassium cyanide capsule and died instantly. Part of me died that day. Five other patriots and myself sketched out a plan to undo the injustice."

"On a cold spring day, we met and vowed that Germany would rise again. We dedicated the rest of our lives to this mission. We went off to different countries and now have reached positions of power. We're now in the last stages of our mission, we are still obsessed with finishing our objective. We've succeeded beyond our wildest dreams and are very close to conquering the world."

"Close to *what!*" Konrad asked, astonished. "You are insane!"

Gunther spoke bluntly. "You're telling me that you're involved in some clandestine effort to conquer the world? It's preposterous."

"It's not preposterous. We fielded the most powerful army the world had ever seen with the Wehrmacht. We would have won the war had we finished the V2 program. It's technology, Sons, that wins the battles. The United States is the dominant military power because of its superior technology."

"Yes, but what does that have to do with Germany? Germany is decades behind the U.S. in weaponry and we don't even have nuclear weapons," argued Konrad.

"Germany will have nuclear weapons within one year," Ligachev said simply.

"Nonsense. I follow this closely," snapped Gunther. "We're a decade away technologically and politically, the other nations of the world would never allow it."

"There are other ways. We have infiltrated the highest levels of the American and Russian governments where we'll have access to nuclear weapons. I am a general and member of the Politburo. We will steal them."

Gunther jumped to his feet. "Madness! This is absolute insanity. The man I've respected all of these years tells me that he admires Adolf Hitler and that he's sacrificed his life to conquer the world. As if that wasn't enough, he's going to steal nuclear weapons. This can't really be happening. You were right, you're no longer my father. I hope you rot in hell!" Gunther shouted, and stormed away.

Ligachev knew that he would probably never hear from Gunther again. He also knew that he would not go to the authorities. Who would believe him?

He looked at Konrad, who appeared stunned and scared. He did not seem as angry as his brother. Perhaps they could talk some more and just maybe, he would see things differently.

☦   ☦   ☦

As Michael got off the plane in Rome, he had no idea of the magnitude of the press' reaction to this hijacking. He was incredulous over the hundreds of reporters that crammed the airport terminal and how they seemed to already know exactly what had happened.

It became apparent to Michael that he would not be able to leave for his connecting flight to Tel Aviv until he answered some of their questions. Just before he was to field the first inquiry, Greg Purcell introduced himself and gave a quick explanation as to why there was so much interest.

Michael's mouth dropped open.

"You're a hero, Colonel, whether you like it or not. And so am I. The old guy, too. Millions have listened to my commentary. We're superstars now, Mike. What do you think?" Ariel grabbed Michael's arm and squeezed it tight. "Listen, I want none of the spotlight. I want nothing to do with TV cameras, do you understand? I don't care if you have to lie," he requested, and disappeared into the crowd.

Michael looked at his uncle as if he wasn't even there and thought of the three dead pilots and how their families must be feeling. He was momentarily sickened. He looked down at David, who seemed petrified by the mob of press. And then he thought of Rebecca, who would now hate him even more now for almost losing David. Oh, God, I just want to go to sleep, he thought. But the flashbulbs clicked like firecrackers, microphones were everywhere and the reporters' questions sounded like a roar.

Michael began to speak and a hush went through the crowd. "Ladies and gentlemen, I'm overwhelmed by the response to this hijacking. Please remember that a tragedy has occurred. Three brave pilots died tonight as well as several others. I think that they should be first and foremost on our minds. Families are grieving tonight over the senseless loss of their loved ones. Please think of those men and women in your prayers as well as their families."

"I'll be glad to speak with you tomorrow after my son and I get some rest. Good night," he said abruptly, and attempted to escape the mass of reporters that surrounded them.

He looked around the airport for Ariel, who had seemingly evaporated into the frantic crowd. He finally spotted him. Ariel gestured for Michael to join him. Moments later, they boarded the flight to Tel Aviv. The press bombarded them upon landing, but Michael and Ariel weren't speaking. Ariel found his driver parked outside and flagged him down. All three climbed into Ariel's chauffeured car which quickly sped away.

"We can get our luggage later," Ariel said, as he stared out the window.

David was quivering with excitement and fear. He had no idea that the experience they had just gone through had been broadcast around the world, nor could he understand the reaction of the crowd. It was a day that he would never forget. Despite the ordeal, he was glad his father had taken him on this trip. That night a bond was formed between father and son.

"Michael, I've been so nervous these last two hours," Ariel's young assistant exclaimed. "My name is Menachem. I was listening to GNN the entire time. It was horrible. We heard the shooting, the screams of passengers and Mr. Purcell's account of your heroics. Your wife must be so proud of you right now."

Proud was not the word Michael was thinking of when he envisioned Rebecca's response. No, that was definitely not the word.

They arrived at Ariel's home and were warmly greeted by his wife, Lenore. "God's countenance was shining on you tonight, Michael. Thank God you are safe!" She invited them in and turned to the boy. "This must be David. I've heard so much about you. You've grown so much since I last saw your photograph. Why, you're practically a man."

"David, this is your Aunt Lenore. Give her a hug," Michael instructed.

David shyly and reluctantly obeyed, hugging her politely.

"You all must be famished. Let me warm your dinner. It will be ready in just a moment," said Lenore.

Michael and David didn't realize how hungry they were until the food was put in front of them. They devoured the meal, much to Lenore's pleasure.

After dinner, they retired to the living room and talked for about an hour about the hijacking. David was rapidly fading and despite the excitement, was close to falling asleep.

"Ariel, can I ask a favor? May I make a telephone call?"

"Michael, my house is your house. Please don't insult me by asking such a question."

Michael was dreading this phone call. He was afraid that it would result in shouting, so he decided to call from their bedroom. He dialed Rebecca's number with a trepidation that far exceeded anything the terrorists had done to him that night.

The phone rang three times. Michael prayed that she was not home.

"Hello?" came a weak voice.

"Hi, Becks. I—"

"How could you take him out of the country without telling me! You bastard! You won't be satisfied until you kill off our whole family, will you? Is he all right?"

"Yes, he's fine. He really is. I'm so sorry..." Michael stammered. "I never imagined anything like this could happen. We got to talking about Dad and Israel and I realized that I might never get a chance to take my kids there. It was completely spontaneous and I'm sorry."

"Let me talk to him this very minute!" she shrieked..

"David, come here," Michael called. "Mommy wants to talk to you."

"Hi, Mommy. Did you watch us on TV?" David asked excitedly.

"Oh, baby, are you O.K? Are you hurt at all?"

"I'm fine, Mommy. Daddy's taking good care of me. Tomorrow, we're going to the place where granddad used to live. We're staying with Uncle Ariel and Aunt Lenore. They're nice, but he has a funny-looking beard and she's fat," he said, and Michael rolled his eyes.

"I'm glad you're all right, sweetie. You've had a very big day. You go to bed, O.K? Remember that Mommy loves you. Night, night. Let me talk to Daddy again," she said.

"I told you he was fine," Michael said defensively. "Please don't make me out to be some monster, will ya? I just wanted to spend some time with him."

"Well, then take him to Disneyland like most fathers, for God's sake. You listen to me very clearly, Michael. You bring him home tomorrow, do you understand me? I won't debate you on this. Maybe when he's older, you can go back. But you bring him back tomorrow or I'll march into court and demand that all visitation be terminated. Do you hear me? Good night," she said abruptly, hanging up the phone.

Even though they were divorcing, he still couldn't get over the intensity of her outbursts lately. She had never been like that before. She never once inquired how he was. He had almost died. The whole world thought that he was a hero and she was treating him like a criminal. She didn't give a damn about him anymore. For the first time, he realized that he had truly lost her. He sat on Ariel's bed and cried.

After composing himself, he found David and headed to the guest bedroom. They both collapsed instantly into a sound sleep. Ariel stayed up alone for a while, still shaking.

Ariel washed his hands for the third time since they had been home. He had been obsessed with cleansing himself for decades, a reaction, he believed, to living amongst Jews.

He walked slowly, towards the back of the house to a locked door. No one, not even Lenore, had ever been in his secret room. He opened it and turned on the light and sat in a single chair in the middle of the room.

Everywhere, on the walls, the floor, and even the ceiling, were German and Nazi memorabilia. On one wall was a recruiting poster for Hitler's National Student organization. It pictured a handsome Nordic youth, his blond hair blowing in the wind and blue eyes flashing, carrying a Nazi flag. The youth wore a short-sleeve brown shirt and a black tie with a Nazi symbol. Ariel, also known as Krupp, smiled back at the youth.

Turning his eyes towards another wall, he felt awed as he glanced at a large photograph of the first Nuremberg party rally in 1933, just after Hitler had come to power. Three Nazi flags reached into the sky and Hitler was surrounded by hundreds of thousands of faithful followers.

On another wall was a painting depicting Hitler as a knight, straddling a black horse and wearing white armor. In sharp contrast to this image was a photograph of a line of Jews in prison garb, eight across along a narrow road, stretching to the horizon. He wasn't sure where this was. Perhaps Belsen, or Ravensbruck. Maybe Buchenwald. He only knew that the majority of the hapless people depicted died violently.

Throughout the room were different uniforms, insignia, hats and other regalia of the Waffen SS, including swastika armbands. He smiled as he reverently picked up an SS service dagger with its sheath and chain, worn by commissioned officers. He glanced at a copy of Das Schwarze Korps (the black corps), the official newspaper of the SS. His mind went back in time.

He felt as if he were really back at Auschwitz. He was thumbing through his party membership book. Next, he looked at a wreath band, a green banner attached to a wreath, which was sent by local SS leaders to the funerals of fallen SS men. So many good men had died in the service of the SS. He sat alone in his secret room, transfixed in spirit and transported in time, to another and better place where Germany ruled.

It would be like that again soon, he told himself. He and the Six would return Germany to its former greatness, as long as they could keep from being associated with bungled terrorist attempts. That was unbelievably stupid of them.

✠   ✠   ✠

The next morning, after a quick shower, Michael spoke to his uncle, who had only slept a few hours.

"Ariel, I'm afraid I have to go back to the U.S. right away," Michael said to his uncle's astonishment.

"Right away? You can't be serious," Ariel said perplexed. "If for no other reason, the jet lag will kill you. You can't ask David to sit on an airplane for twelve hours after last night. And you can't bring him all the way to Israel with promises of seeing his family's homeland and then send him back to California," Ariel scolded.

"Ariel, I was too embarrassed to tell you last night, but Rebecca and I are divorcing. I brought David here without telling her and she's threatened to take me to court and keep me from ever seeing him again if I don't bring him right back ASAP."

"Divorce? That can't be. You were the perfect couple. I've always heard how much you loved each other."

"Well, the crazy thing is, we still do love each other. Or at least, I still do. Running for Congress is what ended it. I thought that was the best way to respond to the madness that took my dad and destroyed TJ's brain. She thought that I should stay home and concentrate on our family. She told me I was an egomaniac. I think that she's selfish and narrow-minded. And so she filed for divorce. This has been one hell of a year."

"I always thought that I'd get her back and that we'd work it out," he lamented. "Until last night, that is. That was the first time that I realized our marriage is really over. So now I'm a congressman and a big hero and I'm more miserable than I've ever been. I'm a man of faith, as you know, Ariel. But I can't understand this. Why has God let me lose my family? What's his reason for this?"

"Michael, you can't possibly understand why God does what he does. But have faith, and it will work out. You shall see. You must always have faith," he implored, patting his nephew on the back. "God has his reasons and he will not let down those who have faith," Ariel insisted.

"Ariel, can I ask you a personal question?"

"Of course, Michael. What is it?"

"It has to do with my father. Mom said that you two had a falling out years ago and that you never spoke again. She told me what the fight was about but I would like to hear it from you."

"Your father was a stubborn man, Michael. But then, so am I. As I'm sure you know, our parents were killed at Auschwitz. Your father was there and saw them in their dying days and he was never able to get it out of his head. The rest of his life was consumed by an obsession. He became totally controlled by his desire to one day track down a particular Nazi guard. Don't get me wrong. I was devastated by their deaths, too. But life goes on, Michael. You cannot live in the past and you cannot let hatred consume you."

"Mother said that he tried to iron out your differences. But that you wrote him a scathing letter telling him to stay out of your life."

"What? I don't believe it," Ariel said in amazement. "Oh, I suppose that I should not be shocked. That makes sense. Yes, it makes sense."

"Are you saying that you didn't write him a letter like that?"

"No, I didn't. I swear on my mother's grave. As a matter-of-fact, Ben's the one who wrote the letter to me."

Michael was stunned. "He wrote it to you?"

"Yes, I hate to say. It was many, many years ago but I remember it as if it were yesterday. It was so full of venom and hatred that I'll never forget the pain that it caused. He called me a race traitor and said my parent's lives meant nothing to me," Ariel said slowly, his eyes beginning to tear up. "I never stopped loving him but we never communicated after that. I always regretted it. When he died, a part of me died, too," he said painfully.

Michael spoke after a few minutes of awkward silence.

"Well, I think that we have to go now. I'm sorry to come and go so fast but Rebecca insisted. Thanks for everything," he said, giving his aunt and uncle a hug.

"Give Aunt Lenore and Uncle Ariel a hug, David," Michael instructed.

"Take care, Michael. We'll say a prayer for Rebecca," Ariel said. "And for Ben, too," he added with a smile.

Ariel drove them to the airport and because of Michael's instant celebrity status, his uncle lent him a fake beard so that he could travel without publicity. This all seemed so incredible to him. David was pouting about leaving so soon and Michael couldn't blame him. It was all so crazy.

Despite their long hours of sleep, they were both still tired and slept much of the flight. This flight was even longer than the previous one. Tel Aviv to Washington and then on to Los Angeles. David was very restless when he wasn't sleeping and thought the flight would never end.

They finally landed in Washington, D.C., and before changing planes, Michael tried to call Josh but he wasn't home. As they got closer to Los Angeles, Michael asked the flight attendant if he could use the in-flight telephone. He needed to call Josh again to see if he could pick them up.

After five rings he was just about to hang up when a woman answered. Michael stammered and said, "I'm sorry, I must have the wrong number."

"Colonel Madigan, don't hang up. This is Kelly, Josh's girlfriend. He's staying at his mom's and he asked me to stay here in case you called."

"Hi, Kelly," Michael said. "I almost didn't recognize your voice. I'll be arriving at LAX in about an hour and a half. Do you think that you can call Josh and ask him to pick me and David up?"

"No problem, sir. By the way, how's it feel to be on the front page of every newspaper in the world?" she asked.

He thought of his wife's screaming and looked down at the ridiculous fake beard that was about to fall off. "It's very lonely, Kelly, but you probably wouldn't understand. Tell Josh that it's flight 444, coming in from Washington. O.K? I'll talk to you later. Bye," he said and hung up.

As they began their final descent, Michael asked David how his beard looked. "Is it slipping? Do I actually look as stupid as I feel?"

"No, Dad, it looks cool. It's slipping a little bit so just don't make any sudden moves, O.K.," David advised. "Are there going to be reporters there when we land?"

"I don't think so. Nobody knows that we're coming on this flight, except for Josh. He's going to pick us up."

Michael looked at his youngest son. "Champ, are you upset with me for having dragged you clear around the world and practically getting you killed? Please tell me the truth," Michael said in all sincerity.

"Heck, no, Daddy. This has been the coolest thing that's ever happened to me. It's funny, I was scared for a while on that plane, but I knew you would make things right," David answered, beaming at his father.

"Thanks, Son. That means a lot. I love you."

"I love you, too. You're the best Daddy in the world."

Michael was close to tears and he probably would have sobbed all over his beard but for the sudden jolt of the landing. They were home. The best thing about first-class was the fact that you could get off the plane quickly. Tonight, they exited the plane first and headed for their baggage, which was ready within minutes.

Michael began looking for Josh. His eyes scanned everywhere, but there was no trace of him. Oh, God, don't be late tonight, please, he moaned to himself. As he was about to let out a curse, he noticed a familiar face. There was Kelly, Josh's girlfriend. And she looked a lot different then he remembered her. She was wearing a short leather skirt with boots and a tight blouse that she filled up rather convincingly. She was a gorgeous young woman. Josh was very lucky.

He shouted to her several times and then remembered that he was still wearing that ridiculous beard. He walked right up to her and she still didn't recognize him.

"Kelly, it's me. Me and David."

"Colonel Madigan? Is that you? What in the world?"

"Don't ask. I feel foolish enough but I don't want to give a press conference. Where's Josh?"

"I couldn't reach him so I figured I'd pick you up. I couldn't let a hero take a cab home, could I?" she said, shrugging her shoulders.

"You can stop it with that hero crap and let's just get out of here."

"You got it, Colonel. I'm parked right over here. Let's go," Kelly said, and led them towards her car.

David fell right asleep in the car. Kelly noticed that Michael's eyes were glassy from fatigue. "I'm sure you're very tired so I won't bother you about what happened if you don't want to talk about it. But I would love to hear about it sometime," she said excitedly.

"I hope that you don't take offense if we talk about it later. But I just can't keep my eyes open," Michael said yawning. He peeled off the beard and then fell asleep.

Kelly made the one-hour drive to Rebecca's house with Michael still sound asleep. She woke David up gently and helped him into the house. It was 2:00 A.M. and although Josh was long asleep, Rebecca was awake and pacing the living-room floor.

She practically threw herself at David and squeezed him so hard that she suddenly let go, thinking that she might have hurt him. He was so sleepy, though, that he didn't notice.

"Thank you so much, Kelly. I can't tell you how worried I was. Maybe when you're a mother one day, you'll understand. Where's Michael?" she asked, more out of curiosity than concern.

"He's sound asleep in the car, Mrs. Madigan. I know that it's none of my business but he loves his children very much. I hope you know that."

"Yes, I know Kelly," answered Rebecca in a hushed tone. "Please take him home and I'll have Josh call you tomorrow."

Kelly drove her white Volkswagen Rabbit convertible to Michael's house, about forty-five minutes away. She was starting to nod off so she turned the radio on and sang along with the songs to pass the time. They arrived sooner than she thought.

"Colonel Madigan, wake up, sir. You're home," Kelly said, shaking him gently.

For a moment, he was completely disoriented. Who was this woman? Slowly, he realized it was Kelly and that he was home.

"Where's David?" he asked, frantically .

"I already dropped him off at Mrs. Madigan's house. You were both out like a light so I didn't bother to wake you. You've had quite an ordeal the last couple of days so I figured that you wouldn't mind."

"Well, thank you. That was very considerate of you," he said in a sleepy voice. "Where's Josh?"

"He was asleep at your wife's house so I guess I'll see him tomorrow. That reminds me. I left some of my things up in your apartment. Do you mind if I come up to get them?"

"No problem, Kelly. I want you to know how grateful I am for all you've done tonight. Let me know if there's anything that I can do to pay you back."

"Don't worry about it. It was the least I could do."

Michael fumbled for his keys and opened the door. He threw his suitcase into the middle of the living-room floor and collapsed into his favorite chair. "Kelly, don't mind me. Go ahead and get your things."

"Here they are," she said. "I guess I better get going."

"Thanks again for everything. I'll see you later," he said, almost falling asleep in the chair.

"Colonel, there's just one more thing. You know how you said to let you know if there was anything that you could do for me? Well, there is one thing."

"You name it, kid. It's yours."

Softly, Kelly purred, "I want you, Mike. And I want you right now."

Michael was shocked as she unbuttoned her blouse and dropped her skirt. She had a stunning body.

He knew it was wrong, but he hadn't made love to a woman in over eight months and he felt his blood rushing. He stood up and kissed her, and in their embrace they dropped to the floor.

11

elix Klaus, secretary general of NATO, also known as Wilhelm, sat in his office in Brussels reminiscing about the past. He had fond memories of his father, Boris, who was killed during the first week of the war in 1939, during the invasion of Poland. At least he had seen Poland fall, in a matter of days, to the powerful Wehrmacht. Boris would have been proud to have seen his son commissioned as an officer two years later. It was such a shame that this strong and courageous man was one of the war's first casualties.

Klaus sat in his plush office and stared into the magnificent fireplace. A sudden knock on the door removed him from his reverie.

"Come in," said Klaus, swiveling around to face the door.

The commanding officer for one of NATO's regional commands walked in. He was in charge of the central region known as AFCENT, a position which was always controlled by a German officer. General Dolf Punder was a dedicated officer who had been in his position for two years. He had been summoned by Klaus to talk about Germany and the alliance.

Klaus had made building up the German army a priority. The stated objective was to allow Germany not to be so dependent upon American assistance. The real mission was something quite different.

All of the regular forces of what was once called West Germany were assigned to NATO in peacetime. This consisted of three corps and twelve divisions, with sixteen armored and fifteen armored-infantry, two mountain and three airborne brigades. These forces had recently been supplemented by the forces of the German Democratic Republic, or East Germany.

Klaus had made sure that Germany paid attention to the issues of mobilization and making reinforcements readily available. In the mid 1970's, a Standby Reserve had been created which the Defense Minister could call up in emergency without prior recourse to Parliament. Plans had been made for a number of cadre formations to be quickly expanded to war strength.

The training and equipment for reserves had been reasonably good. The majority of the Bundeswehr's tanks were the Leopard II's with Chobham armor for better protection against antitank warfare, and advanced, smooth bore, 120-mm guns. Artillery had been modernized and included U.S. self-propelled guns and the FH-70 medium gun jointly developed with Britain and Italy. Helicopters provided antitank support and battlefield mobility. New multiple rocket launchers enabled mines to be sown in the face of advancing enemy tanks. All in all, the Bundeswehr was powerful.

One of the primary goals of the Six had always been to reduce or eliminate the American presence in Germany. The U.S. Army in Europe numbered about 200,000, the vast majority being in the U.S. Seventh Army. This army consisted of two corps, V Corps based in Frankfurt and the VII Corps headquartered in Stuttgart. American troops were leaving now after forty-five years. The problem was that there would still be many Americans in Germany. They were not leaving fast enough for the Six. Their plan would be carried out with the Americans or without them.

General Punder was one of the few German commanders who had seen action in World War II. Punder had never met Klaus and nervously entered the magnificent office.

"Guten morgen, Herr Klaus. It's a great honor to meet you. I am at your disposal," said the general respectfully.

"General, please sit down. Would you like a cigar?" asked Klaus. "There's nothing like a good smoke."

"I'll pass, Herr Klaus, but thank you for offering."

"Very well. Let's get down to business. I will be direct, General. To whom is your loyalty, NATO or Germany?"

"I don't understand, Herr Secretary General," responded the puzzled officer. "I've been a German officer for over forty years but I'm currently assigned to NATO."

"What do you think of the growing strength of the German forces?" asked Klaus.

"It's a result of the new assertiveness of Germany. She is no longer a second-rate power."

"No, she isn't. Let me ask you a question, General, that you may not wish to answer," said Klaus, pausing briefly. "Would you have any hesitation in using this newfound strength that we have discussed?"

"Do you mean if Germany was attacked?" he asked incredulously. "Of course not. I've spent my entire adult life as a military man and have prepared for that possibility. I would give my life to protect my country. But that possibility is slight. The Warsaw Pact scarcely exists and we've taken steps to rectify historic differences, primarily with Britain and France," Punder said assuredly.

"You've misunderstood my question, Herr General," Klaus said, staring into the fireplace. "I have no doubt that you would act heroically in the face of an enemy invasion. Would you consent, however, to preemptive moves on Germany's part to reclaim its rightful place as the dominant country in the world?" he asked matter-of-factly.

"What in God's name are you talking about? Are you asking me if I would agree with German belligerence! Absolutely not! There is no place for German aggression. Twice in one century is enough. And the moral aspect of it aside, it would not be realistic. Who would we attack? A devastated Soviet Union? England? As you know, any attack against a NATO member requires a military response by all the signatories," Punder said emphatically.

"Then I take it by your response that you do not support a predominant Germany. Is that correct?" Klaus asked, this time looking straight at the general.

"I'm not really sure what it is you're asking," Punder replied, feeling very uncomfortable. "I am 100 percent in support of Germany playing a strong role in international affairs. But I would have no part in an unprovoked strike against another nation. We've worked too hard to develop Germany these last forty years to have it destroyed by some maniac's delusion of grandeur. Mr. Klaus, I hope these questions are hypothetical, and designed to test me. I pray that there's no other reason for such inquiries," Punder said forcefully.

"You are correct. These questions are mere abstractions but they have some foundation in current events," Klaus lied. "As you know, there's a growing belief that Germany should assume a more aggressive posture. But peace must be our primary goal and I thank you for your candid response. I'm quite pleased with your reaction. We are a multinational organization," he said smiling.

"Thank you, General, and give my best to Eva," Klaus said, shaking Punder's hand and then abruptly walked back behind his desk.

General Punder slowly walked out of the secretary general's office. He was puzzled by this meeting. If Klaus was testing him, then he was very angry. His loyalty and integrity were not things to be "tested" by politicians. But if Klaus was planning some secret German war strategy then that was dangerous. He decided to check into it.

Lost in thought, Punder crossed the spacious parking lot of NATO headquarters and was greeted by his personal driver, an American named Staff Sergeant Ray Brown, newly arrived from Ft. Benning, Georgia. He was fluent in German.

"Good afternoon, General. Are you ready to go home?" he asked cheerfully.

Punder did not readily answer, still deeply distressed by the meeting with Klaus. He mumbled something indistinguishable and climbed into the vehicle. Brown knew better than to ask any more questions and quickly closed the door behind the General and got behind the steering wheel of the HUMVEE. Within seconds they were on the highway and Punder replayed the meeting over in his mind. Brown occasionally glanced in the rearview mirror and twice started to speak but each time thought otherwise.

Brown was just getting used to working for such heavy brass. This NATO Headquarters was some gig, he thought. He had never even seen a general before coming here and they were now practically a dime a dozen. This German general was really cool, too. He wasn't some tight-ass that never smiled, treating others like dirt. Punder was known for joking around and sharing a few beers with the rank and file. Brown liked this assignment.

Punder continued to gaze absently out the window of his vehicle. He wondered what would happen if he spoke to Larry Waters, the SACEUR (Supreme Allied Commander, Europe). He decided that Waters would never believe it and he would be laughed out of his position.

A bomb detonated, sending a massive explosion through the vehicle. A thousand little pieces flew into the air and fire burned what remained. The burned-out remains of the HUMVEE would be found later that afternoon, along with the charred corpse of one of the most powerful men in Europe.

✠ ✠ ✠

Michael woke and thought that he was still dreaming. He looked to the other side of his bed and saw a naked, beautiful woman. He shook his head and realized that it hadn't been a dream. He'd had sex with his son's girlfriend. What could possibly be lower than that? But there was no denying the fact that he had enjoyed every single second.

My God, what a woman. She'd made him feel like a twenty-year-old. He glanced at his watch. It was now 10:00 A.M. He panicked. What if Josh came home?

"Kelly, Kelly, wake up. Come on. You have to leave right away," he said, shaking her.

She stretched and yawned, without embarrassment. She kicked the blanket off and playfully exposed her nude body.

"Hey, Mikey, was last night great or what?" she said, breaking into a smile. "Are you up for an encore? Can you think of any better way to start the day?" she purred, and reached for Michael.

"Kelly, last night was fantastic and I won't forget it," Michael said. "You are a sexy woman. But I can't allow it to happen again. If Josh ever found out, he would never speak to me again. What I've done is unforgivable," he said, consumed with guilt.

"Calm down there, Mike. We're all adults here. Josh and I aren't married and you're going through a divorce. Josh is a big boy. If you don't want to start a relationship, that's fine. I'm not looking for one. But last night was wonderful and nothing can change that. I'm very attracted to you and I know you like me. If you ask me, you needed to get laid something bad. I hope that we can still be friends. O.K?" Kelly said, putting out her hand.

Michael relaxed and grinned. "O.K.," he said, taking her hand.

"By the way, if you don't mind me telling you, you're a great lover," Kelly added. "Better than Josh. You took it nice and slow. I loved it. You were awesome," she added.

Michael could feel his confidence coming back. She was right. He did need that. He wasn't sure how he felt about being compared sexually to his son, but it didn't really matter. This was a onetime thing never to happen again. But he would definitely remember it.

"By the way, Michael, you were talking in your sleep last night. You must have been dreaming. I guess it was some dream because you were yelling and cursing," Kelly commented, starting to dress.

"I was? What was I saying?" he asked curiously.

"I'm not sure exactly but you were calling someone a Nazi bastard. Do you remember it?"

"Not totally, just fragments," Michael responded, struggling to remember. "But it's an ongoing nightmare that I've had for over a year now. The details and the people are different, but it's always about Nazi Germany. Several members of my family were killed in concentration camps but I wasn't there, of course. I was born after the war ended. What's weird is that the details are so clear and seem so real."

"Well, Mikey," Kelly said, tucking her blouse into her tight skirt. "I gotta go now. Take care and don't get too uptight about last night. I'll always cherish it." She kissed him lightly on the cheek and left.

Michael sat in bed in silence for a long time, lost in thought, bombarded by feelings of guilt, relief, and exhilaration. He replayed every second of the night before in his mind. "Time for a shower," he yelled out loud and jumped off the sofa. He smiled as he showered and quickly dressed. His flight for Washington would be leaving and he looked forward to getting there. As a congressman he had a lot of work to do. But before he started working, he would take one more day off.

✠ ✠ ✠

Michael was spending the day with his mother. Today was her birthday. Julia had been living in Maryland in their old house since Ben had died. She had stayed with Michael's sister, Elizabeth, for the first couple of months but had recently moved back into their old place.

She had become almost a total recluse. Between losing his father, TJ's accident, Rebecca's filing for divorce and his appointment to Congress, he had nearly forgotten his mother. He wanted to make it up to her today.

Julia lived alone on the outskirts of town. She had been a teacher almost all of her life and had taught many years at a local college. She and Ben had bought a house at the foot of the mountains in 1967 and lived there all the years that Ben was with the CIA, until he was named U.S. ambassador to Israel. They had moved to Israel after the appointment, but kept the house. Michael was saddened that Ben had never seen the Maryland house again. The first thing that Michael noticed when he arrived, was that Julia hadn't changed a thing since Ben's death.

They hugged each other as usual, and Michael thanked God for his mother. She had taught him right from wrong and it was her strong faith in God that gave her the ability to hold more love in her heart than anyone he knew. He looked at her small frame and knew that she would always be a giant to him.

He remembered when she was younger. She had always told him to not be discouraged by the evil in the world but to find the good that lies in all people. She was an eternal optimist. It was these thoughts of her that had kept him going through the tough times.

"Mom, you look great. How are you? Happy Birthday. Here, I got a little present for you," Michael said, handing her an obviously quickly wrapped present. "We'll open it later. Tell me how things are going."

"Pretty good. You know that I stayed with Elizabeth for a while," Julia recounted. "But I finally decided to come back here. This is my home. I've become active in a few groups they have for old geezers and I've been busy bragging to anyone who will listen to me about my son, the congressman. I'm so proud of you, Michael. I just wish your father was alive to share in your success."

"Me too, Mom. What do you say we go out for breakfast and make up for lost time? It's the least I can do for you today. Wherever you want to go, just name it."

"I have a real craving for pancakes. How about if we go to that place on First and Elm?" she asked excitedly. "Do you remember it? We used to go there on Sunday mornings, the whole family."

"I sure do, Mom. That sounds great."

Michael escorted his mother to his car. He was glad to see her smile. She deserved to be happy, he thought.

"Mom, how's Elizabeth doing?" asked Michael. "Is she finished with the great American novel yet?"

"Almost, I think. She tells me that it won't be much longer," Julia answered proudly. "Won't that be great to have a famous novelist in the family?"

Michael laughed. "Yeah, that would be something. How's her social life, do you know? Does she have a boyfriend?"

"I think that she goes out with a few different men, but no one special. She was never really the dating type. She's always been more interested in her books," Julia replied.

"I think that she lacks confidence in herself, or something. She's always been a little on the, you know, mousy side. I wish she would take an assertiveness class," Michael expressed.

"I think she's happy just the way she is. And besides, she's a little more capable than you give her credit for, Michael. She gets by just fine."

Julia quickly took over the role of tour guide and pointed out all the things that had changed since Michael was last in the area.

"Mom, let's sing some songs. What do you say?"

"My Lord, Michael. It's been years since I sang anything but I'll give it a shot. What do want to sing?"

"Follow my lead, Mom," he said, starting to sing.

O Susanna, O don't you cry for me,
I come from Alabama with a banjo on my knee.

Julia smiled widely, "Michael, I haven't sung that in over thirty years."

"Do you remember singing that song to me when I was a kid? You used to take my leg and play it like a banjo while singing. I used to laugh like crazy," he said fondly.

"I remember. I would just touch your leg and you would laugh hysterically. Elizabeth and Jacob would get into the action too," Julia said, laughing at the memory.

The mood turned somber for both of them. The mention of Jacob brought tears to them both. Jacob had been the eldest son and everyone had been convinced that he would be very successful in life. But he was killed in Vietnam in 1965.

"Do you ever think of Jacob, Mom?"

"Just every day, Son. Just every single day."

"Me, too. Why do you suppose we've had so much despair in our lives, Mom? Do you ever wonder about that?"

"And why do you suppose we've had so much joy as well? Your father was an ambassador and you're a congressman. I was married to a man I loved for over forty years and I have two wonderful children and three lovely grandchildren. Life's not meant to be easy. Some people don't have enough to eat or have never felt loved. I'll not hear of any sorrow today, especially on my birthday," she scolded.

"You're absolutely right, Mom."

They came in sight of the restaurant and he found a parking place.

"Come on, Mom. I'll buy you the biggest blueberry pancake you've ever seen."

After Michael helped his mother from the car, they walked arm in arm across the large, crowded parking lot. She looked younger than her sixty-eight years and was smiling ear to ear. Michael was thinking about the times when they had come to this unpretentious breakfast nook. He didn't see the car that was coming in their direction. A dark late-model sedan was barrelling down towards them, increasing its speed.

Julia stopped in her tracks, frozen in fear. Michael, snapping out of the past, realized that this was a deliberate attempt to kill them. With only seconds to spare, he pushed his mother and dove out of the car's path. The "weapon" just missed Michael by inches and thundered by at high speed. The driver managed to avoid hitting the cars in the parking lot and flew over the curb onto the street and was quickly out of sight.

Julia had been pushed directly into the pavement by Michael and her entire face was bloodied. She was unconscious but breathing. Michael was unscathed and his only thoughts were for his mother. He knelt over her crumpled body as a crowd began to gather. It broke his heart to see her in this condition.

✠   ✠   ✠

Rebecca hadn't slept well in several weeks, worrying constantly about the upcoming court date in their divorce proceeding. The judge would address such issues as child support, property distribution and visitation. She glanced at the clock and noticed that it was 4:30 A.M. and that she had been awake for almost an hour. Finally, she decided to get up and do something besides cursing Michael.

She put a robe on and walked first into TJ's room and then into David's. TJ was getting much better and her doctor had offered encouragement. And despite the fact that she was furious with Michael for taking their son to Israel, the hijacking and its aftermath had made David a hero in the eyes of his friends and classmates. He was now completely enamored with his father and had even talked about living with Michael for a while. Rebecca understood his excitement but it hurt her to think that he would rather be with his father.

She put on some coffee and lit a fire in the fireplace. She pulled out her Bible for the first time in many years. It had been given to her by her mother, Katarina. It was dusty and she wiped it off. She sat down in her favorite chair and began reading.

Lately she had been so confused and uncertain about what to do next that there were days when she didn't think she could handle it. She was occasionally reduced to uncontrollable sobbing and had constant battles with sleep problems. Her life was not supposed to be this way. The good times were supposed to be ahead of her.

She selected the book of Proverbs in the Old Testament and remembered her mother reading passages to her years before. Was she really once a little girl, she thought to herself. It seemed so long ago.

She read the pages out loud as if her vocalizing the words would give them increased effect. She read them slowly and with meaning, and found comfort in their message.

She came to one passage that her mother had made her commit to memory when she was just a schoolgirl.

"Put all thy faith in God. Lean not towards thine own understandings. Acknowledge him in all ways and he will determine thy path."

It was as if she had read those words for the first time. What did it mean? She didn't understand why her life seemed such a mess and that's what was so frustrating. She wanted a clear, simple answer and wanted to know why certain things were happening. She couldn't understand it.

Rebecca continued to read for almost two hours before she heard David stir. Where had the time gone? She helped him get ready for school and then went into TJ's room to assist her. David was smiling widely and TJ seemed to be in a good mood. Maybe things weren't so bad.

As she was cooking breakfast the phone rang. She let the answering machine catch it, allowing her to screen the calls. It was her mother. Rebecca had not spoken with her in over a month.

"Good morning, Mamma. I was just thinking of you this morning," she said, picking up the phone and turning off the machine. "I couldn't sleep and got up early to read. Guess what I read? The Bible that you gave to me on my sixteenth birthday. I read Proverbs from beginning to end. I know I've been a pretty crappy Catholic but believe it or not, I got a lot out of it this morning. So, anyway, how are you?" asked Rebecca.

"I'm doing just fine, darling," replied Katarina. "Your father is still in Moscow, involved in all sorts of hush-hush stuff with the government. Whenever I ask him about it, he clams up and mumbles National Security, or some such nonsense. But how's my favorite daughter?"

"I'm your only daughter, Mom," she reminded her, "and I'm doing pretty good, all things considered. TJ's getting better and David is so jazzed about what happened last week that I wouldn't be surprised if he starts signing autographs. You did hear about that, didn't you?" Rebecca asked unnecessarily.

"Of course. Michael's certainly becoming quite well-known. He's in the paper practically every day."

"Well, much of it is for one disaster or another. I swear, he'll manage to get this whole family killed somehow," Rebecca said with disgust.

"Did you hear about what happened to him yesterday?"

"God, I'm almost afraid to ask."

"He took dear old Julia out to breakfast and there was an attempt on their lives," she explained excitedly. "Some maniac tried to run them over and Julia broke her nose."

"Good Lord, is it ever going to stop? Can you see why I had to get out, Mom? Can you understand now?"

"I hate to not take your side, dear, but I don't see," Katarina said firmly. "You promised to love him and be by his side, in good times and bad. You vowed to support each other and your children and look at your family now. Everybody's distraught and confused and empty. Your father met with Michael recently and said he was emotionally despondent over not having his family. He worked so hard for you and the kids all those years and now imagine, he's a United States Congressman."

"But Mom—" Rebecca tried to interject.

"What an incredible accomplishment and he has no one to share it with," Katarina continued. "He has to move to Washington and live alone and you'll be in California alone. What kind of life is that? Darling, I want to ask you a question and I would like an honest answer. Do you still love him?"

"Of course I do," she whispered softly. "I love him with all my heart. But Mamma, TJ needs constant care and David has friends out here now. And damn it, I don't want to live in Washington," she said emphatically.

"Sweetheart, can you really say that it's better to have your family torn apart in California than it would be to have everyone together in Washington?"

Rebecca began crying. She felt like a child again, when her mother would somehow make the pain go away. "No, no, I don't know. Mamma, I'm so confused, I don't know what to think," she said, now weeping.

"One more question, dear," Katarina said, waiting a moment for her daughter to calm down. "Do you really believe that he abandoned the family when he decided to run for Congress?"

"Oh, Mamma, I know he didn't even though I accused him of that. I know that he feels that he can make a difference in Washington..." She was unable to go on for several seconds, feeling too emotional. After she calmed down, Katarina added, "Darling, I have to go now, but please remember to put all your faith in God and he will determine your path."

"Thank you, Mamma. Give my best to Daddy. I love you."

✠ ✠ ✠

The emergency-room doctor told Michael that his mother could be released. Her injuries, while painful, were not serious. Michael let out a sigh of relief and thanked the physician profusely. Somehow, another member of his family had escaped death, a situation that was becoming almost routine. But he couldn't just quit. He would not let himself be defeated by these cowardly bastards.

A nurse wheeled Julia out into the lobby in a wheelchair. She seemed rather pale and her nose was bandaged, but was in good spirits.

"Michael, I want to say something to you," Julia said. "I've seen the look of despair in your eyes and I can understand it, with everything that's happened to you recently. But you can't give up, Son. Your father wouldn't want you to. He'd expect you to fight these people. I hope that you can see him in your mind and heart like I can. He's constantly in my thoughts. His death mustn't be in vain. For it to make sense, you have to do something about it. That's your destiny."

Julia hesitated before continuing. "Please forgive me for telling you how to live your life," she said.

"You're absolutely right this time, Mom," Michael acknowledged. "I can't let his death be for nothing. It's not about revenge. It's justification. I've got to make some good come of his death. I'm sorry about yesterday, Mom, but I won't let you or him down. I promise."

12

The "Gang of Three," Michael's young advisers, had all been offered jobs with Congressman Madigan. Judy, Alex and Darrell had all accepted and would be working in Washington. This evening they had planned a party for the congressman-elect. Judy was in charge of the evening's festivities, which would serve as a prelude to Michael being sworn in the following day. They were excited and willing to meet challenges head on. They felt that they were making a difference.

Since none of them, including Michael, had found permanent housing yet, the party was being held at Loews L'enfant Plaza, a large luxury hotel with 372 rooms in the southwestern part of town. No one knew until just a few days before that this ornate and elegant hotel was owned by Dietrich Turner, Alex's father. Alex "the surfer" was rich.

"Alex, I can't believe that you're a member of the bourgeois," needled Darrell. "We all thought that you were a 100 percent, unsaturated, proletariat party man. If you can't trust a beer maker's son, who can you trust?"

"Well, he must have sold a lot of beer to buy this place," exclaimed Judy, signing excitedly. "This place is unbelievable."

"Hey, Alex, all kidding aside, how did your old man end up with a place like this?" inquired Darrell.

"Well, I'm not really certain of the details, but I swear to you that he was a beer maker for years and years. One day he started messing around in real estate and before you could say 'toga party at the frat house' he was stinking rich. Go figure," Alex said, shrugging his shoulders.

Judy feigned a look of disgust and admonished them with an ultimatum. "Look here, you clowns. The colonel will be here in a few minutes, along with Matt. And the speaker of the house will be right behind, so let's get your collective butts in gear," she ordered.

"Judy, you're so beautiful when you talk dirty," added Alex, who had become an expert at signing. "But no sex discrimination. If we men have to rev up our tushes, so do the women. Am I right?"

"You got that right," said Darrell.

"You guys are impossible," sighed Judy, trying to look disgusted. "But seriously, we have to hurry up. He'll be here any minute."

Michael arrived right on time. Matt had told him to meet him at the hotel under the pretext of having dinner there. Matt and Pam greeted him as soon as he walked in the door.

"Matt, I thought I was going to meet you in the restaurant. Hi, Pam, how are you? You look lovely as always," he said, kissing her on the cheek.

"Well, old buddy, I just wanted to introduce you to someone. He's giving a lecture tonight in one of the conference rooms and I'd like for you to meet him. He's a genius on economic matters and I thought this would be a good opportunity for you two to meet. O.K?" Matt asked.

"Sounds great. Lead on, Green. Age before beauty," Michael teased.

"Yeah, right. You're no spring chicken yourself, you know," Matt retorted, grinning. "Well, follow me."

They walked across the lobby and made a turn down one of the long hallways. Michael followed Matt and Pam into a conference room that had been labeled "In Use" and was puzzled to find the room in complete darkness.

"Hey, Matt, I don't want to question a White House official but I think we're in the wrong place."

"You may be right, Congressman, but I don't think so. Where's the light switch?" Matt asked, as he fumbled for it.

The lights flickered on and music blasted out. Michael found himself the totally stunned recipient of a surprise party.

"Oh, man, this is too much. This is really great," Michael said breaking into a broad smile.

Josh was the first one to shake his hand. "Dad, I'm a little bummed about losing my roommate. Now I have to pay all the bills myself. Congratulations. Dad, I love you," said Josh. Michael was moved by his son's display of affection.

Kelly came up and stood next to Josh. She was dressed in a low cut blouse and short skirt. Michael felt a surge of passion.

"Congratulations, Colonel," gushed Kelly, rather excitedly. Turning to Josh, she continued, "Josh, you have to promise that your dad dances at least one song with me tonight. I've never danced with a congressman."

Josh looked at Michael and said, "Hey, Dad, what gives here? First you dump me with all the bills and now you're stealing my girl?"

Michael knew he was joking but the words left him feeling guilty. "What can I say, Son. I've got to please my constituents, you know."

Josh laughed and before he could say anything else, Peter Volhard walked in. Michael practically sprung to attention, out of twenty years of habit.

"Good evening, Mr. Speaker. It's a great honor to see you here tonight. A few minutes earlier and you would have been completely in the dark."

"Isn't that always the case with Congress?" asked Volhard. As the small crowd roared with laughter, a waiter served drinks.

Volhard raised his champagne glass and said, "Ladies and gentlemen. Let's make a toast to my new colleague. May you always remember that you're here to serve the people of your district. I know that you'll do so with great honor and distinction."

"Hear, hear," came the unanimous reply.

The hotel had gone to tremendous lengths to prepare for this party, a fact which Michael quickly picked up on. "Hey, throwing me a party is one thing but an extravagant wingding like this is something else. Who's paying for all this?" Michael asked Judy.

"Relax, Colonel. This whole event is being paid for by one of your staff."

"What are you talking about? None of you can afford the cab fare to get here," Michael said.

"Apparently you're not aware that our very own Alex Turner is stinking rich. His father owns this monument to opulence," Judy added.

Michael quickly looked around the room for Alex.

"Alex? Are you serious? Our little surfer and party animal is a member of high society? Surely you jest."

Alex heard and said in his defense, "Sorry, Colonel, but I swear that I didn't earn any of this money. I mean, you can't blame me for my parents, can you? It was out of my control," he said defensively.

"But I thought he was a beer maker, Alex. Beer makers don't normally become billionaires."

"Well, he diversified. I think that's the word for it. What do I know? He'll be here later on this evening if you want to meet him. By the way, he gave fairly generously to your campaign," Alex said.

"In that case, make sure you let me know when he arrives. I want to thank that man profusely," Michael teased.

"Well, there's no time like the present. Here he is," Alex said, gesturing towards a white-haired man that had just entered the room.

"Dad, over here," Alex shouted across the room.

"Ah, Alex, there you are."

"Dad, I want to introduce you to Colonel—that is, Congressman Madigan."

"Congressman, it's a great pleasure. I am Dietrich Turner," he said in a thick German accent.

"Nice to meet you, Mr. Turner. I want to thank you for hosting this party. You have a beautiful place here."

"Thank-you," replied Turner. "You know, I am from Germany and I knew your father-in-law and his wife Elena. She was my first grade teacher, as a matter of fact and I used to have a terrible crush on her. But she left to come to the United States and I never saw her again. I was crushed for years," he said with a smile.

"But...my father-in-law's wife is Katarina, not Elena," Michael pointed out.

"It is? I always thought it was Elena. Well, perhaps I've been wrong all of these years. It wouldn't be the first time," Turner said. "I must be going. It was nice meeting you, Congressman. Alex, I would like to speak to you later, O.K?"

"Sure, Dad," Alex said, as his father exited the room. He then turned to Michael. "Colonel, I'll talk to you later. I'm in charge of the refreshments and I think that I just spotted a waiter with a few bottles of champagne. Gotta run."

Michael walked away shaking his head. He never would have believed that Alex came from money. Michael was somewhat puzzled by Mr. Turner's comments about Karl's wife. He had seemed quite certain that her name was Elena. Michael spotted Judy and flagged down the waiter with the champagne.

"Judy, I just want to tell you how much I appreciated your efforts during the campaign. Your contribution was enormous and I'm very grateful."

"You're very welcome, Congressman," Judy said. "I guess I'll have to get used to that one, won't I? You know, I signed up with you at first because it was something different and a way to get out of the classroom. But the more that I got to know you, the more I began to believe in you. I feel as if I've known you all my life. There's something about you that's so familiar. I think that you won't be stopping with Congress. Is that true, Senator? Mr. President?" she goaded him.

"Good God, Judy. A year ago I didn't know a filibuster from a veto and I couldn't even tell you who my congressman was. I still don't know how I'm going to put half of my campaign promises into action, and you're talking about me running for president."

"Well, we've never had a Jewish president, you know. Maybe you'll be the first."

"I wouldn't bet the farm on it. Let's come back to reality. Cheers!" Michael said, raising his glass.

Judy drank the sparkling contents of her glass very slowly. "I'm not much of a drinker, Colonel. A couple of glasses of this stuff and I'll be comatose. But I'll make a toast to my boss. To your political career, Colonel. May it be long and fruitful."

"Thanks, Judy. That means a lot." He noticed her rub her eyes. "Are you okay?"

She hesitated before answering, "I'm all right, really. I'm just tired and the champagne just hit me. I told you, I don't do alcohol very well. If you don't mind, I'm turning in. Alex got me a room here tonight. Can you believe it? Room 1522," she said while pulling the key from her purse. "I'm going to call it a night. Is that O.K? I feel exhausted," she apologized. "The guys can handle everything, although I'm sure that someone will mess something up without a woman around," Judy said grinning.

"I'm sure you're right about that, Judy, but we'll muddle through somehow," Michael laughed. "You go on up to sleep. We need you refreshed for tomorrow. Good night. Thanks again for all your help. I couldn't have done it without you," he said sincerely and kissed her on the cheek.

Judy bid the others good night and exited the banquet room. Michael was about to seek out Volhard when he saw Kelly coming his way. Kelly had caught a glimpse of Judy as she left. Kelly froze, and with a puzzled expression asked Michael who she was.

"She's one of my student advisers. Her name is Judy Solomon. I'm surprised that you never saw her before," Michael replied. "Why do you ask?"

"Uh, I think I know her. Where's she going?"

"Well, she's staying here at the hotel tonight. Room 1522, I think she said. She told me that she was going to sleep real soon so if you want to talk to her, you better hurry."

"First things first, Colonel. You promised me a dance. Or did you forget?" Kelly said, in a sexy voice.

"I didn't forget. But the band hasn't started..." As he was speaking, the band came out and started warming up.

"They're just getting ready to let it crank and the first song will be a special request that I just made." The music began and the lights were turned down. While most bands start with something fast and furious, they commenced the evening's festivities with a love ballad.

They joined hands and Michael laughed. "How did you know about this song? It's absolutely my favorite."

"There's a lot that I know about you. But I bet that you don't know much about me. Did you know now that I'm incredibly wet and that I want you inside me?" she purred.

Michael was looking into her very inviting eyes. He was fighting to maintain his self-control. "Kelly, I don't know what to say. You're a gorgeous woman, but this can't go on. I can't do that to Josh. However much I want to be with you, my love for my son will be greater. And in all candor, I don't think that a relationship with someone half my age is a real wise career choice. I'll be in the public eye constantly and I just can't afford to take the chance."

"You're getting divorced, aren't you? And correct me if I'm wrong, but voters don't normally go for bachelors. I don't really think that an attractive young girlfriend is going to ruin your career. In fact, I think that it would help. And I think that what I feel brushing up against my leg right now is an indication that you're thinking about something other than your career. Am I right?" she teased.

Michael actually blushed, feeling like a complete fool before this girl. "Kelly, I don't know what to say..."

As the song ended, she replied provocatively, "Just say that you'll dance another song with me. But I have to go to the little girl's room. Will you wait for me?"

Michael shook his head, not knowing what to say. Kelly winked and left the room, while Michael looked frantically around to make sure that Josh had not been watching.

Kelly walked past the rest rooms and got onto the elevator, taking it to the top floor. She walked briskly to room 1522 and stood outside the door for a moment, formulating her plan. Kelly had not seen her sister in years and she needed to decide quickly how Judy's life would end. Kelly looked in her purse and made sure the safety on her .38-caliber pistol was off. She reached for the door handle and was surprised when it turned. The traitorous Jew had not even locked the door. It would be her last mistake, she thought, opening the door.

Judy was standing out on her balcony despite the freezing temperature and the light snow that was falling. She looked down at the rooftop pool two floors below and thought that she saw the reflection of the Washington Monument in the water's shadows. She closed her eyes and replayed in her mind the excitement of the last few days. She couldn't remember the last time she felt so happy.

Kelly walked gingerly into the room and saw Judy on the balcony. She smiled as she realized that Judy's deafness, which had always rankled her, would now allow her to put an end to her miserable sister's life.

Kelly was now only a few feet away and the daydreaming Judy had no warning of her presence. Kelly gazed over Judy's shoulder to see if anyone was out on the pool deck below. When she saw no one, she lunged forward grabbing Judy's ankles. Thrusting upwards with all of her strength, Kelly threw the unsuspecting Judy over the balcony railing.

A muffled scream filled the air as Judy plunged to the cement below. Seconds later, Kelly brushed herself off and stared at the still body below her. Then she turned and walked calmly and slowly out to the elevator and headed back towards the party. A certain congressman owed her a dance.

✠   ✠   ✠

Konrad Ligachev put his children to sleep and kissed his wife Heidi good night. He told her that he was going to work in his study to prepare for his classes the following day.

The thirty-five-year-old son of Charlemagne was still reeling from the shock of his father's confession. His father was not a Russian as he had always thought, but a Nazi! Incredible! and even more mind-boggling was their plan to conquer the world. He couldn't think clearly. He retired to the study and put Wagner on the stereo. Wagner always helped him to clear his mind.

He was as astonished as his brother Gunther, but his reaction was not immediate hatred or condemnation. Instead, he was fascinated. His mind was racing in a thousand different directions. He wouldn't get much sleep tonight. The Fourth Reich? Was his father serious? Could it really happen?

He paced furiously and quickly downed two glasses of brandy. He felt the need to talk to someone before he exploded. But Gunther was out of the question. There was no mistaking the fury in his older brother's eyes. He knew that their relationship would never be the same. He would like to talk to his father, but not now.

His father had spoken briefly of his colleagues, some of whom went to other countries. He didn't know who these other men were but he began to speculate. He had met Karl Schmidt on several occasions and knew him to be a successful American businessman originally from Germany. Was he one of the Six? He couldn't be, thought Konrad. He was always so articulate, not the brutal image of a Nazi.

He tried to deduce who the others were. He had met Felix Klaus a couple of times. On each occasion, he couldn't understand why his father, a Soviet general, would be meeting with the secretary general of NATO. Why would he meet with an American businessman, for that matter. Could Klaus and Schmidt be involved?

Konrad wondered if he and Gunther were the only offspring who knew. His father had said that he was breaking a forty-five-year-old vow of silence. Could all of the other members of the Six resist telling their sons?

Suddenly, he thought of Steven Schmidt, who he had met the year before in Paris. The younger Schmidt's wife was with the World Bank and had been part of the American contingent exploring the possibility of extending membership in the World Bank and International Monetary Fund (IMF) to the Soviet Union and its former satellites. Konrad had talked at great length with him that weekend and a friendship had been born. Konrad had been quite pleased to have received a Christmas card from Steven and Ellsbeth the previous holiday season.

Maybe he should give Steven a call. He ransacked his desk drawer frantically looking for the number and finally found it. What would he say? Even if Steven knew about everything, would he admit it? He took a deep breath and decided that there was only one way to find out. He dialed the number and waited with a combination of dread and excitement. Due to the time difference, he was sure that someone would be in.

A female voice came on the line and said in English, "First Federal. How may I direct your call?"

With some hesitation he said, "I would like to speak to Steven Schmidt, please."

"Just a moment, sir. I'll connect you."

Konrad's heart began to pound faster with each passing second and another voice came on the line. "Mr. Schmidt's office. How can I help you?"

"Yes, could I speak with Mr. Schmidt, please. My name is Konrad Ligachev."

"Let me see if he's available, sir."

After a short interval, Steven picked up. "Konrad, Steve Schmidt here. How are you? This is quite a surprise. Are you in town or are you calling from Germany?"

"I'm calling from Berlin, Steven. I was just thinking about some things and you came to mind. Do you have a few minutes?"

"Sure. I was just working on some incredibly boring reports and I could use a break. What's up?"

"Well, I'm not really sure how to put it," Konrad stammered. "Let me just say that either you'll know what I'm talking about or you won't. If you don't, please don't ask any questions because I won't answer them."

"That's about as mysterious an introduction as I've ever heard. You've certainly got my attention. Shoot," replied Steven.

"What do you know about our fathers' role in the war?"

Steven was silent for a few seconds before answering cautiously. "Why do you ask?"

"My father told me a little about his experiences during the war and although he didn't mention any names, I think that he was somehow connected with your father. And I think that there is some connection still today."

Steven was astonished and uncertain how to respond. The protracted silence made Konrad think that he was onto something. He decided to gamble.

"I also think that Felix Klaus is involved and that the three of them, and a few others, have some far-reaching plan for Germany."

"My God, Konrad. Did he tell you about the Six?"

"Then you know, too? Do the other sons know?"

"I don't think so," Steven replied. "They all vowed that nothing could ever force them to divulge their secret. My brother Tommy and I found out years ago by accident. We weren't supposed to know. If your father told you, then as far as I know, he's the only one to voluntarily do so. Don't you have a brother?"

"Gunther. My father told both of us and Gunther flew off the handle, saying that he was no longer his son."

"Will he go to the authorities?"

"Probably not. Gunther might never talk to my father again, but I don't think that he'll take any steps against him. Besides, who would believe it?" Konrad pointed out.

"That's for sure. Let me be blunt here, Konrad. What do you think of this? Are you supportive?" Steven asked, greatly worried about this possible leak.

"I'm not really sure what it is I would be supportive of. My father only told me a little bit. I just had to talk to someone about it. Thank God I was able to reach you. So, Steven, just what the hell is this Six up to?"

"In a nutshell, it's about restoring Germany to a superpower. The Fourth Reich, if you will.

"How is this suppose to happen? What about the United States?"

"Konrad, the telephone isn't the best place to discuss this. I'll be in Germany a week from Tuesday. We'll meet then and go over everything. O.K? In the meantime, don't mention this to anyone, including your wife. Well, I better go. I'll give you a call when I arrive. Good-bye."

"Thanks, Steven. I'll talk to you next week. Bye." Steven hung up the phone and looked at Tommy, who had just flown in from Germany and was in the room during the entire conversation. "What do you think, little brother? Can he be trusted? It would be nice to have another son that's in, wouldn't it?"

"Yeah, it would," Tommy said, in his metallic voice. "But this ain't some Sunday trip to the park. Not everyone is cut out for this kind of thing. Let's wait until your meeting with him before we decide."

✠   ✠   ✠

Michael hardly slept, tossing and turning all night with the image of Judy falling off the hotel balcony. He was scheduled to be sworn in this morning as a member of the House of Representatives and he looked like death itself. He had alternated between crying and drinking to help ease the pain. A bottle of Jack Daniels whiskey lay alongside his bed three-quarters empty. And since he hadn't even started drinking until 2:00 A.M., after returning from the hospital, he was still feeling its effects.

Michael lay in his bed wondering if anything was worth this much pain. Everyone he had cared for had either died or been hurt in some way. His family had been dismantled, he had slept with his son's girlfriend, his daughter was nearly a vegetable and he was losing his faith in God.

He pulled the covers over his head and doubled up his naked body like a baby and wept. Maybe he should just forget the political life. Maybe Rebecca was right. What good would he possibly accomplish? With all of the lobbies, the political action groups, the bureaucrats—the list goes on and on. How could he ever change things? All that he had managed during the past year was to lose everything he held dear. He pulled himself out of bed and went into the bathroom. He looked in the mirror at himself and hated his reflection.

"You're nothing but a fake. You're a lonely, bitter failure and you can go straight to hell!" Michael yelled into the mirror.

He grabbed the bottle of whiskey from off the floor. Just as he was about to put it to his lips the phone rang, startling him for a second. After four rings, he picked up.

"Colonel Madigan?"

"Yeah, who is this?"

"This is Amanda Nolan with the Washington Post calling about the Judy Solomon incident. Will you confirm a rumor that says she and other members of your staff were taking drugs all night long celebrating your election to Congress?"

Michael was enraged. "Listen to me, you stupid bitch. A woman I care for is close to death. She wasn't using drugs. Judy Solomon is one of the straightest and most decent people I have ever had the privilege to know. So take your microphone and note pad and shove them about three feet north!"

He hung up the phone and collapsed on to the floor. Reporters. They were worse than lawyers. They all could go straight to hell.

He sucked out the rest of the whiskey and threw the empty bottle as hard as he could into the mirror in the bedroom, sending glass flying. He slumped to the floor and fell asleep.

Michael was awakened by a knocking at his door. It sounded to him like a jackhammer. His head was pounding from the alcohol.

"All right. I'll be there in a second," Michael shouted.

"But you better not be a reporter or I will put sharp pieces of broken glass into your eyes. And I'm not joking." He wrapped a towel around himself and slowly opened the door. He wasn't prepared for who was on the other side. Michael stood in the doorway for several seconds. A scratched whisper was all he was able to utter. "Rebecca."

Rebecca looked at him in a way she hadn't for quite some time. She looked back at him with affection.

"Good Lord, Michael, you look positively awful. May I come in? I realize that I'm probably the last person in the world that you expected to see this morning but I want to talk to you if it's all right."

"Of course, sure. Come on in," he stammered, suddenly feeling nervous. "Sorry the place is a mess. You know that I've always been a slob," Michael quickly tried to clean up the broken glass.

Rebecca noticed the shattered mirror and the remains of the whiskey bottle and was able to put two and two together. "I see that you still have your famous temper," she said half jokingly, and then felt bad when Michael didn't smile.

"I want to tell you, Michael, how terribly sorry I am about Judy Solomon. There was nothing that you could have done to prevent it. You mustn't get down on yourself. And you can't let it stop you from carrying out your goals. Or your seat in Congress." She added the last sentence with a warm smile and touched his shoulder.

Michael wasn't quite sure what was happening and his brain wasn't operating as efficiently as usual.

"Rebecca, I don't mean to be rude, but just what are you doing here? I have a million things to do and I'll be glad to talk to you later, but right now I really am running late," he said impatiently.

"Michael, I've thought long and hard about us over the last six months and especially during the last week or so..."

"Are you going to ask for more child support or less visitation or something?" he asked angrily. "If you are, now's not the time. Just write out what you want. I'm not going to hire a bloodsucking lawyer and you can have practically everything. But I just can't get into it right now."

Rebecca sighed and asked him to sit down. "Michael, you're not making this any easier. This is difficult enough. Please sit down and listen."

Michael sat down. "O.K., you have my attention. What is it?"

She wrung her hands and began pacing the floor, as she often did when she was nervous. "Michael, I don't know about you, but just because I filed for divorce doesn't mean that I ever stopped loving you. Signing that petition for dissolution was the most painful moment of my life."

"Well, it wasn't the highlight of mine either."

"I'm sorry if I hurt you. We had the same goal—to help our family. I reacted to all of this turmoil differently than you did. Another daughter was taken from me and I didn't want to go back to that life we had before when you were at the Pentagon. And I didn't fully understand your desire to be elected to Congress. I guess I thought it was some ego thing and I didn't really appreciate that you were doing it out of love for TJ and your father."

For a moment, Michael felt a glint of hope, despite his headache. "And?"

Rebecca looked as if she were on the edge of tears. "And," she said slowly, "What I'm trying to say is that if it's not too late, I want to try again."

Michael felt elated. "Are you serious? Do you mean, uh, that you want to forget about the divorce and live with me again? Here in Washington?"

"Yes, that's what I mean. I'm so sorry that I hurt you. I never stopped loving you. I want us to be a family again."

"I'm sorry too, honey," Michael said. "Oh, Becks, of course it's not too late. I never stopped loving you, either. I prayed that this would happen but I had just about given up hope." He embraced her and whispered, "Thank-you God for giving me back my family."

After several minutes of embracing, Michael looked deep into Rebecca's eyes. "Sometimes it takes something awful to make us realize how lucky we are. I promise not to let you down. Maybe I'm naive but I really think I can make a difference. With you in my corner, I know I can do it," he said excitedly, pausing before continuing.

"I have to admit, though, had you not shown up this morning, I don't think that I would have made it for the swearing-in ceremony. I was just about ready to give up."

"Michael, I'm proud of you. You've become a real leader."

"To be honest," said Michael. "I'd prefer to live a life of leisure, teaching a few classes and hanging out on the beach. But I can't just sit by and watch my country go down the tubes. I have to try and make a difference."

"I know, Michael, and I love you for it." Then she asked, "will you excuse me for a minute, please?" and walked out of the room.

Michael heard her whisper something he couldn't make out, but soon in walked Josh, David and TJ, all smiling. He had not seen TJ in quite some time and when she said, "I love you, Daddy," Michael nearly broke down. He had his family back and TJ was walking and talking almost as if she had fully recovered.

Michael stared at them amazed. Rebecca broke the silence.

"Well, we can't just stand here crying all day. Somebody has to get sworn into the House of Representatives. Let's let Daddy get ready and we can all go over to Capitol Hill together. Is that O.K., Michael?"

"That's just perfect. Absolutely perfect."

13

$\mathscr{S}$teven arrived in Berlin and after attending to some routine matters concerning his itinerary and accommodations, he decided to make one more phone call before continuing his conversation with Konrad Ligachev. He would call his father. Every night since he had received the shocking news that an outsider knew of the Six, he had gone over in his mind a million times whether or not he should talk to Karl. He had finally decided that he had no choice.

Steven placed a call to Moscow. Direct dialing was nonexistent and Steven discovered that he would not be able to get through right away. He would have to wait for the operator to call him back.

He began unpacking and ordered some room service. He had left a message that he was going to take a hot bath and that if he didn't come to the door right away, to just leave his dinner. He undressed and sank into the hot tub, contemplating whether he was doing the right thing. He realized that he could be serving a death sentence on Konrad and Gunther and possibly even Charlemagne. He knew that there was no other choice.

After a long hot bath and a delicious supper, he opened a bottle of wine just as the phone rang. It was the operator informing him that his call had finally been placed. "Go ahead, sir."

"Steven, is that you, Son? What the hell are you doing in Germany?"

"Hi, Dad. I'm here on business, for a conference. How are things in the country without a name?"

"Everything's moving along just as planned. We're actually reaching a point where we'll really be destroying some weapons soon. And our other plans are right on schedule. We can talk about that later. Is there a reason for this call or did you just want to hear my voice?"

"There's definitely a reason and it's got me quite spooked, to be frank," Steven confessed. "I don't want to go into a whole lot of detail on the phone, but apparently Charlemagne told his two sons about everything and one of them called me and started asking questions."

"What did you tell him?"

"Not much since he seemed to know quite a bit. He caught me off guard and I acknowledged the existence of the Six. I hope that I didn't screw things up, Dad."

"No, of course not," Karl replied. "If anyone has, it was Charlemagne. I took a lot of heat when you and Tommy found out and that was an accident. I was very fortunate that the two of you felt that our cause was just. Not everyone will, particularly of your generation. What's your gut feeling on his reaction?"

"Ambivalence. He's not sure what to make of it and asked to meet with me to discuss it further. I told him that when I got to Germany, we'd get together and talk. Should I still meet with him?"

"Yes, of course, but since this is so important, I'll be there, too, and I'll have Charlemagne there as well. You mentioned another son. What about him?"

"Apparently, he wants nothing to do with any of this and has severed himself from the family."

"Will he go to the authorities?"

"Konrad said that he wouldn't, but you can't be certain."

"No, you can't. When you and Tommy found out about us, had you taken any steps to interfere with our mission I would have killed you," Karl said bluntly. "Nothing will set us back. You know what must be done with the defiant son. What's his name?"

"Gunther."

"Yes, Gunther. I'm afraid that the sun will not shine much longer on him. We shall see what the fate of Konrad and our esteemed Charlemagne shall be. He better not have set us back or he will rue the day he was born. Set up a meeting for tomorrow. We will meet you outside the Zoological Gardens at 4:00 P.M. Have you discussed this with Tommy?"

"Yes, he knows all about it."

"Very well. Auf Wiedersehen, mein Sohn."

Karl was beside himself with anger. "How could he do this without consulting us?" he shouted. "Who does he think he is? He's placed our mission in jeopardy after so many years." Bismarck pounded the glass-top kitchen table with all of his considerable strength, shattering it into pieces.

Still consumed with rage, he picked up his phone and called Charlemagne. He would kill him with his bare hands if need be. They had come too far for any problems to surface now. They were too close.

Karl finally got through to Charlemagne, who was stunned by Karl's anger. None of the Six had talked to each other like that since the war, when Bismarck commanded them in battle. Perhaps he had committed a blunder that would cost him and his two sons their lives. Regret bombarded his mind all night and as a result, he barely slept until the time for their arranged meeting.

Steven arrived first and walked around the edge of the park, which was bound by the Spree River. Karl arrived next, and father and son talked for several minutes before Charlemagne arrived. No greetings were exchanged and the Soviet leader was feeling extremely uncomfortable. Finally Konrad appeared and it was time to get down to business. Both Konrad and Ligachev were nervous. Only Karl seemed composed.

The four men paid the admission into the Animal Garden and walked in the direction of the world's largest bird house. Karl began speaking, knowing better than to refer to their code names.

"Konrad, good afternoon. Please excuse me if I dispense with pleasantries and get right down to business. What exactly do you know and do you intend to share your new found knowledge with others?"

Konrad's suspicions were now confirmed. If he didn't join with them, he was a dead man. And he realized by Karl's intensity that he would never see his brother again. He was also painfully aware that his father's life depended on his answer.

He had thought about nothing else ever since the confession by his father. And the words he was about to speak were not based solely upon fear for his physical safety but partially by belief.

"I still don't know much about your group but I understand that you wish to return Germany to its proper place as ruler of the world," Konrad proclaimed. "I'm an academician and not a military man. I don't fully understand just how you will accomplish this. But after days of soul searching and sleepless nights, I will support your endeavor," he said, trying to sound convincing.

"I too, have been embarrassed at the passivity of Germany," Konrad continued as Karl stared at him intensely. "But I thought that there was nothing that could be done. When I first heard the plan from my father, I thought him mad, not because I didn't embrace the concept but because I didn't think it feasible. Our military has been suppressed by the allies and we have no nuclear weapons. If we could acquire nuclear weapons, then the plan is feasible. And even then, it would be most difficult."

Karl watched him closely, looking more to how he said it than to what he said.

"Wolfgang," Karl said, calling him by his real name, "You are certainly aware that you've placed our entire mission in jeopardy by revealing our existence to your sons. Their lives and yours will be determined by what you say. Answer my question carefully. Can Konrad be trusted and are you willing to stake your life on it?"

Charlemagne spoke firmly. "Konrad is a man of his word. If he says that he is one of us, then he is."

"Very well," spoke Karl, and he turned to Konrad. "You'll have to be tested, of course. You'll be asked to carry out a very difficult task and will be required to undergo some intense training. You'll work with Krupp. Are you willing to give up everything?"

Konrad found the words to say with some conviction "Yes. What about Gunther?"

"Will he join us?" asked Karl.

"I'm afraid not," Konrad answered. "He thinks that we're lunatics. He'll never join but I would stake my life that he won't go to the authorities."

"Can you be positive?" inquired Karl.

"As sure as I can be."

"That was not my question," Karl bellowed. "Can you guarantee that he will never speak to anyone about this?"

"No. Of course not."

"Then your task is quite clear. Konrad, you shall kill your brother before the week is out. Only then will you be accepted into our group. And I would advise you, for your own health, to be successful."

Konrad was too shocked to speak. Charlemagne was stunned. He was going to lose a son. Oh God, what have I done?

✠   ✠   ✠

Michael was afraid to have his entire family present in the same room at the same time. Disaster seemed to follow him. Security was heavy and it would be almost impossible for someone to try something in the U.S. Capitol, he told himself. Nonetheless, he could not relax.

He was still distraught over Judy's accident but Rebecca's return helped him to go on. His family was finally back together again. He had prayed for this and God had rewarded his prayers on this very special day.

The swearing-in ceremony went very smoothly and Michael could see the pride in Rebecca's eyes. TJ had made an amazing recovery and for a moment he had cursed himself at not being around for her these last months. Despite his new responsibilities, he vowed that they would always come first. In fact, he would have to take a few days off to go back to California and finalize the move for the whole family to Washington.

Michael's mother was present also. She had recovered from the incident with the car.

"Mom, you're looking great," he said. "Rebecca and I are back together for good," Michael said happily.

"I'm so happy for you," his mother answered warmly. "I knew that you would patch things up. I've always felt in my bones that your marriage was something special and that it would last until your dying days. And Michael, I'm proud of you. Your father was never one to get emotional but I know that if he were here, he would be crying tears of joy to see his son in the United States Congress."

"Thanks, Mom. Rebecca and I have to go back to L.A. to take care of some things. The kids are going to stay with Matt and Pam Connors for a few days until we get back. You remember Matt, don't you, from the army?"

"Yes, dear, I do."

Micheal began making his rounds and noticed that Josh and Kelly had just arrived. His heart started racing as his eyes rested on Kelly. Surely the whole world could see the effect this girl was having on him. Calm down. Stay cool. For God's sake, don't let Rebecca catch on to anything.

"Hi, Dad. I'm sorry we're late," Josh apologized.

"I probably would have been more surprised had you been on time."

"I know, I know. I'm trying to work on that."

"I don't know you that well but Josh has told me so much about you that I feel almost like a daughter," gushed Kelly. "Congratulations, I know that you'll do a great job. And I see that congratulations are also due in your personal life," she remarked, looking at Rebecca.

"I'm glad you could make it, Kelly," Rebecca said warmly.

Michael was thinking of the night he had just had with Kelly, and he needed to excuse himself to get some fresh air. The rest of the event went smoothly.

✠ ✠ ✠

Michael was reluctant to leave town when he was supposed to be starting his new job. But his family was more important. And besides, he needed some time alone with Rebecca. They had much to talk about and some romance was definitely in order. But he would have to tie this trip to business in some way.

Michael had been following closely a civil rights bill that would soon be voted on. In the aftermath of the L.A. riots, he thought that it would be a good idea to get some input from the people who were involved in the violence. While his district was outside the South Central area that was mostly affected by the riots, they still needed to be addressed by both local and federal officials. They had to come to grips with an entire segment of society that had no hope.

Michael instructed Darrell to arrange for him to meet with actual residents from South Central L.A. as well as gang members. These were the people whose minds he had to get into, whose emotions and feelings he had to try to understand. He could empathize with them intellectually, but he couldn't totally understand. He was white and a member of the establishment.

Darrell thought that Michael was totally out of his mind but he was able to actually arrange a meeting for Michael with the leader of one of the biggest gangs in L.A., the Bloods. They would meet at the intersection of Vernon and Vermont, one of the first areas hit by the rioters. Looting and fires left the Vermont Square Shopping Center a tangle of charred wood and metal.

Darrell felt that this meeting was madness but if Michael was determined to go through with it, he had to learn some of the lingo of the street. Darrell had grown up in the ghetto and had almost been killed in a drive-by shooting when he was thirteen. He had recovered slowly and discovered books during three months of hospitalization. Education saved him from the streets.

"O.K., Colonel, listen up," Darrell said, as they drove towards South Central. "A *blob* is a Crip's name for a Blood, and a *crab* is a Blood's name for a Crip. *Gaffle* up means to arrest, and to *pop-a-cap* means to shoot at someone."

"Pop a cap?"

"Yeah, as in 'I popped a cap at that blob,'" Darrell said, with a straight face.

"What about drug slang?" Michael asked.

"Well, if you're *amped*, you're high on methamphetamine. *Grinding* means to deal drugs. *Slamming* is injecting a drug, and *tweaked* means being stoned."

Michael shook his head as they drove through the urban devastation. Every block now had abandoned homes. Iron grillwork covered the doors and windows of many of those still inhabited. Religious symbols were scattered about a few of the yards and the paint on many houses had peeled down to bare wood.

In front of many of the houses, people were selling their furniture—some having been evicted, others needing money to buy crack. Stripped and demolished cars dotted the streets and littered the vacant lots while groups of hopeless men stood aimlessly in front of carry-outs and restaurants. Michael felt hopeless and let out a sigh.

Darrell spotted the group they were to meet and pulled the car over. Michael could feel the piercing glances of about a dozen skeptical gang members sizing him up as he got out of the car and approached them. Darrell started the introductions.

"Congressman Madigan, this is Johnny Green, leader of the Bloods." Directing his attention to the other gang members, Darrell continued.

"As I told you guys, this is Michael Madigan and he's just been elected to Congress from Los Angeles. He wants to talk to you about the riots and what can be done to make sure it doesn't happen again."

Before Michael could speak, he was challenged. "What part of Los Angeles do you represent, Mr. Congressman?" The title was practically spat out by Johnny, who was not impressed with Michael.

Michael felt a twinge of anxiety. He knew what their response would be to his answer. "I represent Malibu, Agoura Hills..." He didn't get the chance to finish.

"Malibu?" sneered the gang leader. "What was your platform, Mr. Concerned Politician? A black chauffeur for every Rolls Royce? You ain't shit. You'll leave here and fly back to Washington thinking about how to keep people like us out of the same school that your daughter goes to. So don't try to jerk us, jack. 'Cause we ain't buying what it is you're selling."

Michael had known this wasn't going to be easy. "I'm not trying to sell you anything," he said, attempting to appear forceful. "I'm not trying to make you my friend or win your vote. As you've already pointed out, I don't represent your district."

"Then what the hell you doing here, man? You make the wrong turn to Disneyland?" shouted Johnny, a tall and lanky twenty-year-old. He was wearing a black jacket and his hair was in corn rows.

"I just want to talk," Michael said simply. "The riots happened on your turf and I'm afraid that it will happen again in other areas. I want to prevent that from happening and I need to understand what's going on inside you."

"You want to know what's going on inside me?" asked Johnny. "You ain't never gonna know because you're rich and white. You're never gonna be fucked over by the cops just for walking down the streets. You ain't never gonna see a friend of yours gunned down in front of your eyes. You come here wanting to know what it is we about. Well, maybe we don't want you to know. So why don't you get your white, rich ass off our turf. We got important things to do."

Michael hesitated for a moment. Then he decided to gamble.

"You guys think that you're pretty tough, don't you?" Michael taunted.

"We hold our own. What's it to you?"

"I hate to inform you of this but the plain, honest-to-God-truth is that you ain't shit," said Michael. Darrell looked at him with horror.

"Say what?" asked Johnny, stunned. "Could you repeat that? I'm afraid that I'm a little hard of hearing. I thought you said something that you couldn't possibly have said. So what was it you were saying?"

"I said that you're all just a bunch of wimps. Anybody could run you out of here if they wanted to. Especially you, Johnny. You couldn't even whip an old man like me."

Johnny was shocked and looked at the others in disbelief. He suddenly began glancing nervously about.

"All right man, where are they? I know that you couldn't be as stupid as you seem to be. You want to start something and then the police will come out of nowhere like fucking John Wayne and throw my black ass in jail. I'm not stupid."

"There's no police. I guarantee that," said Michael. "I'm just tired of punks like you who talk big but can't back it up. Listen up, Johnny. I'm challenging you, one on one, me and you. No one else. And I want a simple answer. Are you man enough?" said Michael, relying on his former Green Beret experience.

Johnny wasn't sure what to make of this. All of the other gang members were psyched up by Michael's bold talk. They wanted him killed. Johnny felt that he could certainly take this trash-talking fool of a white man but he couldn't get rid of the feeling that it was a set-up.

Some of the others began fueling the fire. "Man, you ain't going to let this motherfucker get away with this shit, are you? You could whip his ass with your eyes closed."

Michael decided to gamble some more. "I'll tell you girls what. First, I'll whip Johnny and then I'll take your next toughest dude. If one of you gets tired, the other can come after me. How's that sound?"

Johnny fell for the bait. "All right, old man. You got yourself a fight." The gang spread out and surrounded the area. One man took a guard position up on a rooftop and others cordoned off the "arena."

Johnny took off his shirt and started jabbing the air. He gestured at a tall kid named Duane Eddy to do the same.

Michael took off his tie and said, "Why don't we make it interesting? Let's make a little wager."

"Loser pays $500," shouted Green.

"You boys disappoint me. Let's make a real wager, something with some guts," Michael said arrogantly.

"I'm listening."

"If you win," said Michael, "I'll give you a brandnew machine pistol. My father-in-law owns a weapons manufacturing company and he can get plenty of them."

Eddy shook his head and said, "You think we're chumps or something, man? Do you expect us to believe that a congressman is going to give us a gun?"

"I give you my word. If I lose, Darrell will make sure you get it. Won't you, Darrell?" Glancing over at Darrell, he saw the young aide absolutely stunned.

"I said, 'Won't you, Darrell?'"

"Uh, whatever you say, Congressman."

He was still skeptical but more or less satisfied. One of the other members shouted out, "What if the white dude wins?"

This inquiry brought loud, raucous laughter. "Ain't gonna happen," said Johnny, grinning.

"Not in this lifetime," added Eddy, shaking his head.

Michael answered the question. "If I win, you have to talk to me. And I don't mean just for a few minutes. I want you to come back to Washington with me and talk to Congress. There's a vote next week on a civil rights bill and urban aid. I want you to tell them your concerns. I want you to stop fighting and tell America how we can stop the bloodshed in the cities."

"Shit, man, you be dreaming. What kind of nonsense you talking?" asked Johnny.

"Just as I thought. The stakes are too high and you haven't the guts. I'm risking my career by offering you a gun but you aren't man enough to go after it. I was right. You really ain't shit."

"Listen fool," Johnny said angrily. "I'm tired of your big mouth and your lecturing. We accept your terms and the bet. Now get ready to have your ass whipped and you better have your boy get that weapon or you're going to see some real violence."

"O.K., Johnny," Michael said calmly. "Let's make a few ground rules. No weapons can be supplied to either of us by anyone else. We can use any weapons we might find on the street, such as a tire iron or stick. And you and your guys can only fight one at a time. Agreed?"

"Yeah, yeah, now come to Johnny and wish that you were never born."

Michael and Johnny started circling around each other as the other gang members began taunting Michael.

Johnny made the first attempt at contact by swinging at Michael, who deftly sidestepped the punch and countered with a blow to the stomach, a punch which lifted Johnny an inch off the ground. The others reacted in shock, realizing that this was not going to be a cakewalk.

As Johnny doubled over in pain, Michael followed up his punch with a swift kick to the head, drawing blood and knocking Johnny to the ground. The Blood's leader was dazed and Eddy saw his chance.

"I'm in, man. I'm in," shouted Eddy.

Eddy's eyes were filled with hatred. Who the hell did this white man think he was? He rushed Michael by putting his head down and tackling him. They both hit the ground with a thump, and Michael was momentarily dazed. Eddy flipped him over so that Michael's face was looking up at his and was about to strike it with his fist as he straddled the congressman's legs. But the former Green Beret kicked his right leg into Eddy's groin and leaped up as his opponent grabbed the hurt area of his body, grimacing in pain. Michael pivoted his left foot and spun clear around and with tremendous momentum, landed a roundhouse kick to Eddy's face and broke his nose.

Johnny had found a tire iron and came rushing at Michael like a man possessed. As the weapon was racing towards his head, Michael picked up a trash can lid and deflected the swing and then shoved the lid into Johnny's face. Johnny screamed in pain and fell to his knees. Michael followed this with a barrage of karate punches to the face and then another kick to the head, taking out three of Johnny's teeth.

Eddy stumbled towards Michael with a switchblade he had pulled out of his pocket.

"That's not allowed, man. That's cheating," Michael admonished him.

"Cheating my ass. You said no weapons given to us by anyone else. I didn't get this from anyone else. Now get ready to get cut up," warned Eddy.

Michael couldn't argue with his logic. He was right. No mention was made of weapons already in the combatant's possession. He was starting to tire.

Eddy swung at him, ripping Michael's clothing and just missing his body. Michael looked at his cut shirt in disbelief and the crowd let out an approving roar. Michael thought back to the fight that he had to earn his black belt six years before. Instinctively, he jumped into the air and let loose with a quick kick of his right leg to Eddy's hand, knocking the knife to the ground. As Eddy stood in shock, Michael kicked again to the chest area, causing Eddy to double over. Michael stood over his opponent and came down on his neck with a crushing blow, sending Eddy to the ground.

Michael stood back and saw the two gang leaders, both on the ground. He looked at the others. Their contempt was gone, replaced by grudging respect. Michael had taken a great risk but felt that the only way he could get through was on their terms. But he would have to move quickly.

"Good fight, guys," Michael said. "You're both really tough. But I think that I had an unfair advantage. I spent twenty years in the army. I'm also a karate black belt. And you almost won anyway."

Michael extended a hand to Johnny, who was struggling to his feet. At first he wouldn't take it, but Michael waited and finally he did. Michael dusted off his back and started to help Eddy, whose face was a bloody mess.

"I know a few things about gangs and I know that you are men of honor," Michael said. "Johnny, I know that you'll carry out your part of the bet and come to Washington with me. We leave tomorrow morning at 7:30 A.M. Darrell will come by to pick you up. Please don't be late. I'll see you then."

Michael and Darrell walked away. Darrell was certain that they should be running. He whispered under his breath, "Congressman, we better beat feet. Let's get the hell out of here."

"No, we can't act afraid. That would be a sign of weakness. We'll walk slowly out of here with our heads up."

"I just hope that this isn't a sign of things to come, Congressman," said Darrell, shaking his head. "I hope that you don't get into messes like this too often. You promised to give a gun to a gang leader? How in the world could you have done that?"

"Simple, Darrell. I didn't expect to lose," Michael replied. "You've got to act as if it's impossible to fail and if you really believe it, then you won't."

"But what if you did?" Darrell insisted. "Let's assume for a moment that one of them got a lucky punch or something. Would you have really given them a gun?"

"Of course," Michael said, without hesitation. "I made a bet and I don't believe in welching. I took a calculated risk."

✠　　✠　　✠

Konrad arrived home still in a state of shock. He was greeted at the door by his wife, Heidi. She was a petite woman with bright red hair and penetrating green eyes. She quickly sensed that something was wrong.

"What is it, darling? Can I get you something?"

Konrad didn't want to worry her and so shrugged it off to fatigue. "Nothing's wrong, dear. I'm just very tired. Those idiots at the university are having me jump through hurdles again over some foolish nonsense," he lied.

"Again? I thought that they finally had stopped chasing ghosts and were just letting you teach," replied Heidi, clearly irritated. "You come sit down and I'll have your dinner ready in just a minute. Oh, by the way, Gunther called. He sounded quite upset."

News of his brother piqued Konrad's interest but he tried not to sound too excited. "What did he want?"

"I'm not sure but he sounded very agitated, which is unusual," she commented. "He said something about going to the airport, although he wouldn't tell me where he's heading. He has a flight somewhere at 11:30 P.M. tonight and wanted to speak to you before he left."

Konrad looked at his watch and saw that it was ten past seven. He began sweating nervously. He believed in the Six but was not sure if he could accept their methods. To kill his brother was insanity. He wouldn't do it, even if it meant his life. He started to pick up the phone when a loud knock on the door interrupted him.

Heidi shouted from the kitchen, "Konrad, will you get that, please? I've got my hands full."

Konrad walked to the front door and opened it. Two men stood at the door, one small with a beard and the other, tall and powerfully built.

Konrad sensed trouble. "How can I help you, gentlemen?"

The small man spoke first. "Herr Ligachev, we are friends of yours and associates of your father. We would like to speak to you."

Konrad felt a sinking feeling in his stomach. "Come in, gentlemen. Let me get your coats."

The tall man, who was quite a bit younger, said, "That's quite all right, Mr. Ligachev. We will only be a few minutes. Can we talk alone?"

Just then, Heidi walked in. "Guten Abend. Are these friends of yours from the University, Konrad?"

"Yes, they are. This is, uh..."

The younger man quickly filled in. "Good evening, ma'am. Sorry to barge in at supper time but we need to speak to your husband for a few minutes. My name is Gerrhard Meyer," he said, without introducing the older man, who was known as Krupp.

"I'm pleased to meet you. I suppose that you can talk in the study. Konrad, I'll have dinner ready in about ten minutes. Would you gentlemen like to stay for dinner?"

"Thank you very much, Frau Ligachev," responded Meyer, "but we must really be going in just a few moments."

"Perhaps another time. I'll be in the kitchen, Konrad."

"You're a lucky man, Herr Ligachev," observed Meyer. "A loving wife is a precious prize, wouldn't you agree?" asked the younger of the two mysterious men.

Konrad didn't respond to the question. The two strangers followed him into the study, which was surrounded by thousands of books. Krupp commented on Konrad's study.

"Very impressive, Professor. It's a sad commentary on our times that many younger people waste their minds in front of the television. I hope that you're passing on to your children the desire to improve their minds through reading. Quite admirable," Krupp remarked.

"Let's cut the crap," ordered Konrad, nervously. "Who are you and what do you want?"

Krupp sat down and continued. "I think you know the answer to both of those questions. The short answer is that we are Germany and we want to secure Germany's future. And now, whether you like it or not, you are a part of that future. Sit down and listen."

The old man's tone changed drastically with his last sentence and Konrad did as instructed.

"As you already have unfortunately come to know, we are a group of former SS officers who after the war, banded together to create a plan to resurrect Germany," Krupp explained. "It's taken us over forty-five years but we're close to success." The former Nazi continued. "My domain has been unconventional warfare and what is often referred to as "terrorism." Perhaps such words shock a professor. But I'm not some rabid dog who kills innocent people for no reason. Everything we do has a purpose. We simply don't have the time to wait for history to happen in the normal course. We must expedite it and we're faced with people who do not often wish to cooperate," said Krupp with distorted logic.

Meyer spoke next. "I'm not one of the original members but rather a part of a small collection of younger members. We're a warrior people. We take what we want. I'm not trying to justify it, it's destiny."

"Konrad, we're close to achieving our goals and could use assistance from young people like yourself," Krupp said, in a friendly tone that camouflaged the hatred that he really felt. "But we also know that not everyone will agree with our methods. And so I ask you: Are you with us?"

"Yes, I'm with you," replied Konrad. He had no other choice.

"Excellent," responded Krupp. "You're a scholar and there's a great need for that in our organization. But first you must learn some other skills. We have a mission that must be carried out and you will assist us. We will leave tonight. Tell your wife that an emergency has come up and bid her good night."

"But first, we'll stop at the airport," interjected Meyer.

Konrad's mind began racing. He briefly thought of escaping, perhaps by climbing out the back window and disappearing into the blackness. Maybe never to see his family again. However, his new colleagues would not allow this to happen.

"Professor, please go pack some clothes," said Krupp. "Hurry, Herr Ligachev. Your new life awaits you."

Konrad nervously went into his room and began packing a bag. He replayed in his mind what he just heard. "Your new life awaits you." Good Lord, what kind of nightmarish life was he facing? He was a scholar, not a terrorist. He wasn't sure if he could kill. Maybe it would be him who died.

Konrad, carrying a bag, walked into the kitchen, where his wife was cleaning up. He leaned over and kissed her neck gently.

"Heidi, I must leave right now on business. Please don't ask me what it is because I can't tell you. It has to do with my father and that's all I can say. I'll tell you about it later. Tell the children I love them and will call as soon as possible."

"Konrad, you're scaring me," Heidi exclaimed. "You're a University professor and are acting like some type of secret agent. What's going on? Does it have to do with those two men? Who are they? And what does your father have to do with it?"

Konrad placed his finger on her lips before she could ask another question. "Hush, my darling. I don't understand it all myself and will try to explain it to you later. I must leave now. I love you, Heidi," Konrad kissed her lightly on the lips and stroked her cheek.

With what sounded like a final good-bye, Konrad walked out of the house and into the unknown.

"Very good, Professor. Now get in the truck and listen very closely," ordered Krupp.

Konrad obeyed and climbed into the cab of a large truck. Konrad sat between Krupp and Meyer, who drove. They looked at each other for several minutes. Krupp broke the silence.

"Herr Ligachev, you have every reason to be nervous. You're about to embark on a journey that some of us have been on for over forty-five years. This world is foreign to you. I too, am an educated man and there have been times when I shuddered at the world's brutality. Can mankind solve its problems through intellect and logic alone? The answer, my friend, is no."

"We're not all the same, no matter what the idealistic, naive fools may tell you," Krupp continued. "Germany's destiny is to rule the world, by whatever means necessary. Do you understand?"

Konrad hesitated before answering, finally mustering the strength to reply defiantly. "I understand but there's one thing that I can't do," he said. "I won't kill my brother. I'll die first."

Meyer spoke from the driver's seat. "We know that. We could not ask you to do such a thing. A brother must not kill a brother."

Konrad heaved a sigh of relief. He felt a great weight released. "That's wonderful. I feel 100 percent better," he said, smiling.

"You will not have to kill your brother, Professor, because he is already dead."

Konrad was shocked at this news which Meyer delivered as if describing the weather. He sat in silence for the rest of the journey, gazing out the window into the blackness, wondering what the future held.

Hours passed as the truck drove into the night. Konrad fell asleep and Krupp went over some paperwork, utilizing a small overhead light. Finally, Meyer pulled over and came to a halt. Konrad awoke with the jolt of the abrupt stop. He was momentarily dazed. He glanced outside and saw a flurry of activity, as several men scurried about. Konrad felt a twinge of intense anxiety.

Krupp exited the vehicle and began issuing orders to several men, all of whom had been in the back of the truck. Each responded quickly to his directives. Konrad realized that this was some type of military operation.

"What's going on?" Konrad asked Meyer.

"You'll find out soon enough. Now just do what you're told."

"Can you at least tell me where we are?" inquired Konrad.

"Herr Ligachev, you will be told when it is necessary and not before. So if you value your health, be quiet."

Konrad felt as if a blunt instrument had been shoved into his stomach. *I'm not a soldier.*

Krupp called out with an air of authority. It was clear he was in command and it was obvious that he had done this kind of thing before.

"Gentlemen. We're just outside the American chemical depot on the outskirts of Frankfurt. You all know your assignments, with one exception. Herr Ligachev will act as a lookout. Here, you will need this."

Krupp tossed Ligachev a .45-caliber pistol. He looked at it scared and confused.

"We're breaking into an American military base?" Konrad asked incredulously.

"That's exactly what we're doing."

"Why? You won't get away with it."

"Of course we will. We've practiced this particular mission a lot," answered Meyer. "The only new variable is your presence. If you do anything to jeopardize this mission, I will kill you. Is that clear? You'll be a lookout and nothing else. Yell if anyone is coming. Do you understand?"

Konrad understood. He should be home sleeping with his wife. He cursed his father for getting him involved in this.

He glanced about him and saw six other men, all dressed in black, each carrying an assortment of weapons. Meyer disappeared for a moment and returned dressed as the others.

Krupp had only a few more words to say. "Gentlemen, our mission is the primary objective. Everything else is secondary. You all know what to do if you get caught," he said. Everybody made sure that they had their cyanide tablet, to be taken in case of capture. Like the Nazis before them, they would not live to see failure.

"Good luck, Gentlemen. Let's do it," ordered Krupp.

After applying black and green camouflage stick to their face, all members of the team hopped into the back of the truck again, except for Konrad and Krupp. The elder leader of this mission handed Konrad the keys to the truck.

"You will drive tonight, Herr Ligachev. Let's go."

Krupp climbed in the passenger seat and Konrad crawled into the driver's seat.

"Just act calmly and do what I say," ordered Krupp.

Konrad put the truck in gear and began driving out of the secluded wooded area and in a few minutes reached the road. He drove in silence for about ten minutes, as every few moments Krupp would direct him one way or the other with hand signals.

The American installation came into sight as they drove around a sharp curve. There were several armed guards posted and Konrad began to panic.

Krupp saw the sweat pouring from the professor's forehead and hoped that they had not made a major mistake bringing him along.

"Herr Ligachev, please relax. There's nothing to worry about," Krupp said plainly.

Konrad tried to slow down his heartbeat but he was sure that everyone could hear it. He stopped the truck alongside the guard post and was greeted by an American corporal carrying an M-16.

"Good evening. May I see some identification?" asked the young soldier, whose name was West.

Krupp responded to the question. "Good evening, Corporal West. I am a representative of Felix Klaus, the secretary general of NATO. We are here on a surprise inspection of your facility on his direct orders. Here are our papers," he said with an air of authority. Krupp handed the papers to the guard, all the time smiling pleasantly. The documents were indeed from NATO and were signed by Felix Klaus.

West had strict orders not to allow anyone on base without checking with the staff duty-officer. "Your papers appear to be in order, sir. Let me just run this by the officer on duty. It should just take a minute."

"Corporal West," Krupp responded firmly, "I'm under direct orders from the secretary general of NATO. If you have any questions, I suggest you place a call to Brussels. But do not inform your superiors of our presence. A surprise inspection is just that. There is to be no advance knowledge by the people being inspected or the whole purpose is defeated. We've made arrangements for a room, where we'll clean up. We will have a quick breakfast and then pay a visit to your commanding officer. Am I making myself clear?" Krupp said impatiently.

West hesitated and said, "Just a moment, sir." He walked over to the guard building and huddled with the other guards, Corporal Sullivan and Private First Class Boldt.

"Hey, guys, what do you make of this?" asked the twenty-three-year-old from Arizona. "This is supposedly some bigwig from NATO here to do a surprise inspection. He says that he's under direct orders from the secretary general of NATO and that we're not to tell the SDO."

"Bullshit, man," responded Sullivan. "Even if they're telling the truth, we got our orders. If they're worried about tipping everybody off about an inspection, it's too late to make any difference. It's 4:30 A.M. now and there's no way anybody could get ready that quick. Either they're ready or they're not," pointed out Sullivan.

"And besides," added Boldt, "Captain Howard would have our ass. He gave us direct orders to let him know about anyone coming on to the base."

"I guess you're right. I just hope this foreign brass doesn't hit the roof," said West.

West walked backed to the truck. "I'm sorry, sir. I have my orders and inspection or not, I'm going to have to contact my staff duty-officer and let him know that you're here," he said, struggling to appear confident.

"Very well, Corporal," Krupp said politely. "I certainly understand orders. I myself am a military man of many years. But could you and your men do us a favor? There are some things in the back which are quite heavy. Could you help us move them to the front of the truck, please? I would be most grateful," Krupp said.

"Sure thing, sir," answered the corporal. "Sullivan, Boldt, come over here. Help these guys for a second. They need to move something."

The three young guards were eager to help. Standing post all night was boring and this was at least something to do. They walked to the back of the truck.

"Please open the back of the truck and you'll find a large box. That is what needs to be moved."

Konrad was beginning to realize what was happening and he felt sick to his stomach. He had seen the back and knew that there was no box.

West opened the back of the truck and immediately caught two bullets in his head and was dead before he hit the ground. Sullivan and Boldt also received point-blank executions. The six men in back quickly jumped out and picked up the corpses and loaded them into the truck.

Meyer cursed this unwanted event but they had all known it was possible. This would not thwart their mission but they would now have to move more quickly to insure that they were gone before anyone discovered the missing sentries.

Konrad was gasping for air. He felt as if he were choking. He had only been involved in this nightmare for a few hours and already four men had lost their lives. He didn't know if he had the stomach for it.

Krupp's abrupt order brought him back to reality. "Let's go."

Konrad started the truck again and headed onto the base, wondering what other horrible things would happen. Good Lord, for what reason?

Konrad was still in shock; three Americans had just been executed. Krupp ordered him to drive. He was temporarily unable to respond.

"This is not preparation for a final exam, Professor Ligachev," said Krupp, in a sinister tone. "This is the real world and unless you start moving a little quicker, you'll never move again."

Brandishing a .45-caliber handgun, Krupp ordered, "Drive, Professor. And do not stop until I tell you."

The truck passed several housing areas and then the PX and Commissary, all dark due to the early hour. Their destination was the far end of the base, where in nondescript Quonset huts and earthen igloos, lie a considerable percentage of the U.S. chemical weapon inventory. Their objective was primarily artillery shells and bombs but also BZ. Their plan was bold. They were to drive right up to the huts and igloos and kill anyone who might try to stop them.

As they had been briefed, there were several guards posted, three to be exact. The man in charge on this particular evening was Sergeant Ray Manning, a five-year-man from Southern Mississippi. Manning was "short," meaning that his tour was almost up and that he would soon be returning to "the world"—the U.S. He was joined this night by Eric Dettlinger and Andre Edwards, both corporals, both from Philadelphia. This assignment was punishment from their top sergeant.

The six men in the back of the truck donned their protective gear. They each put on a battle-dress overgarment, consisting of a two piece suit in a camouflage pattern. The garment's material was an outer layer of nylon-cotton and an inner layer of charcoal impregnated polyurethane foam.

Their gear included chemical protective gloves and footwear along with protective masks and hoods. Filter elements in the cheeks of the face pieces could remove any agents from the air entering the masks. Microphones in their masks allowed for communication with the others.

Konrad watched horrified at their alienlike uniforms. Oh, God, what am I doing here?

It was now close to 5:00 A.M. and would be light soon. It would not be long before West and the others were found missing. They had to move quickly. Krupp's team was able to proceed instinctively. They knew exactly where they were going and what they were looking for.

Konrad was sweating profusely. He couldn't believe what was happening. They could not possibly just drive onto a U.S. military base, kill several soldiers, steal chemicals and drive away. What would he tell Heidi?

Sergeant Manning and Corporal Edwards saw the truck driven by Konrad pull up. They were not expecting any visitors. All three guards drew their M-16's.

"Stay calm, Herr Ligachev," ordered Krupp. "Perhaps you should remember that your failure to do so may result in your death. I will do all of the talking."

Manning walked up to the driver's side window as the other two men stood, weapons drawn.

"Good morning, Sergeant," Krupp said with considerable charm. "We are members of a NATO inspection team and are here on behalf of the secretary general, Felix Klaus. Here are our papers."

Krupp handed the papers to the suspicious sergeant, who looked at them askance. They appeared to be real but something didn't seem right, Manning thought.

"Did you check in at the main gate? Didn't Corporal West direct you to the SDO, Lt. Maxwell?"

"He did indeed. However, normal procedures have to be modified somewhat in this case. This is a surprise inspection ordered by the secretary general himself. The USAEUR commander has been fully apprised, but no one else in the chain of command is to be notified, including the commander of this post. We are to go directly to the site and conduct our inspection. Our orders are quite clear Sergeant," Krupp said.

"I'm sure they are, sir, but so are mine. I'm not to allow anyone to come in here unless the SDO directs me to. I'm sorry, sir, but you can't conduct your inspection unless Lt. Maxwell gives me the go ahead," Manning said nervously.

"I commend you for your steadfastness, sergeant. Orders are to be followed at all times. Could you contact your Lt. Maxwell? We will play by your rules," Krupp said disarmingly.

"Very well, sir," answered the guard. The young sergeant walked over to the guard booth to call the lieutenant.

Konrad knew what was coming next and thought that he was going to vomit. Out of the back of the truck, three men who had not yet put their protective clothing on slipped quietly out. One of them snuck up behind Edwards and placed a six-inch steel blade into the young man's back and just as quickly pulled it out. The soldier died instantly.

The other two aimed their AK-47s and placed three rounds each into Manning and Dettlinger before the phone call could be placed. Both crumpled to the ground in pools of blood.

The three assassins quickly dragged the dead bodies into one of the earthen igloos where they would not be found for a while. The remaining members of the team, in full protective gear, jumped down from the back of the truck and slipped quietly into the huts and igloos.

Inside lay a combination of different weapons, ranging from blister agents related to modern pesticides. Some were in artillery shells, mostly 155-mm howitzer rounds and 4.2-inch mortar rounds. There were also drums of bulk chemical agent, but at one ton each, were beyond the team's ability to move.

They would just concentrate on the artillery shells. Most of the chemicals were in binary form, which made their protective suits unnecessary. But they couldn't take any chances.

Konrad was sickened by the brutal murders he had witnessed. He was astounded by their indifference.

Konrad sat still as the six men in their chemical suits loaded the weapons into the truck. He couldn't imagine for what purpose they would be used. Even the Nazis had refused to use such monstrous devices. He prayed that he would be killed before long so that he would not have to endure any more missions like this one.

14

The crew was making its final check before pulling out of the harbor. The captain of the *Ocean's Daughter* was glad to be leaving this Colombian port. Armando Concepcion's crew had spent several drunken nights in the company of certain ladies of the evening. This had resulted in an almost complete breakdown of discipline. To add to his problems, he had to procure penicillin to ward off venereal diseases.

He cursed Colombia as the ship pulled out of the harbor on the northern coast of the country. Their shipment was a rather sweet one, he had told the crew, smiling at the pun. Their delivery was 1,200 blocks of fine chocolate. This load was much preferable to their last one, where they had transported 1,000 drums of powdered lye to Miami. The crew was uninformed of the true contents of the shipment and their destination.

All of the crew drank excessively and chased women. But despite their flaws, they weren't criminals and would not appreciate the real cargo. They had loaded chocolate onto the boat, but 5,000 kilos of cocaine were wrapped in the bars of chocolate. And on their last shipment, 10,000 kilos of cocaine had been hidden at the bottom of the drums of lye. Concepcion was only in it for the money and he was paid well.

The captain had been promised dozens and maybe even hundreds of similar shipments if he was successful. He knew the risk but he also knew that only about three percent of the shipping containers that enter United States ports annually actually get checked by Customs. And with such creative containers—chocolate bars and lye—he would never get caught.

He had already decided what he was going to do after the last shipment. He was going to spend the rest of his life on an island in the South Pacific, rich beyond his wildest dreams. He deserved it, damn it.

Concepcion was without peer as a sailor. He and his crew set out for a very long and difficult journey. He didn't really understand his orders but he wasn't being paid to understand. He set sail out of Barranquilla and headed northeast into the Caribbean Sea.

They sailed east, more or less along the Tropic of Cancer, until they reached longitude thirty degrees west, at which time the ship headed north, past the Azores and then through the Strait of Gibraltar and into the Mediterranean Sea. No one except Concepcion knew where they were headed and the crew was defiant as the days passed with no answers.

The *Ocean's Daughter* passed the northern tip of Tunisia, Crete and then reached the Suez Canal, and by this time the tension was unbearable.

Concepcion was in his quarters preparing to retire for the evening. He swigged directly out of an old bottle of Scotch and started mentally counting the money that he would make from this trip, when his door burst open and three burly, drunken crew members stormed in. One was carrying a knife.

Two of them threw the unsuspecting captain up against the wall. The bottle of liquor crashed to the floor and the knife was pressed against his throat.

"Tell us where we are going, old man, or we'll kill you," threatened one of the men, whose hot breath reeked of alcohol. "Why are we going through the canal and when will we reach our destination?"

Being drunk himself, Concepcion was more reckless than usual. "My comrades, is this any way to treat me? I'm the one who is making you rich."

"Answer us," said another in a deep growl. "Quit playing games!" The knife drew blood as it pressed harder against the captain's throat.

"Put the knife down and I will tell you. Otherwise, you'll have to kill me," he said calmly.

Reluctantly they put the knife down and let him go. The three men stared at him suspiciously.

"We're headed for Karachi. Are you satisfied?"

This knowledge seemed to mean nothing to these crewmen, who looked at each other blankly. "Where's that?" one of the men asked.

"Pakistan—we're going to Pakistan. We'll sail through the Red Sea and then pass under Yemen and into the Arabian Sea. We'll head north, to off the coast of Oman. Then we'll reach Karachi."

"Why are we delivering expensive chocolates to Pakistan?" asked the knife-wielding man suspiciously.

"Listen," he said, and then speaking slowly and forcefully he continued, "We are in the transportation business. We get paid for shipping things. We don't ask why or how. Do you understand?" Then in a shout, he finished, "Now get your sorry asses back to bed and I'll try to forget this ever happened!"

The three men looked at each other and bowed their heads. Mumbling to themselves, they walked meekly out of the captain's room.

Several days later, the ship arrived at Karachi. It was after midnight when they pulled silently into the dock. They were met by a team of men dressed in black. Under normal circumstances, they would have been greeted by customs officials, but not tonight. The crew was confused by the men in black and the lack of officials. They whispered amongst themselves.

The crew was directed to load the boxes of chocolate onto a truck and this was done within minutes. Much to the dismay and resentment of the crew, Concepcion ordered them to sleep on the ship.

"I will not waste my time explaining orders. I am the captain. You'll do as I say or you'll be without a job. Stay on this ship or don't bother returning."

The crew backed down and did as instructed. Concepcion met with one of the men that had greeted them and they climbed into a truck with several others. As the truck sped out of the harbor, one of the men spoke.

"Good evening, Señor Concepcion. My name isn't important," said a short man with a German accent, known by others as Frederick. "I would like to commend you on your ability to make such a long journey."

"Where is this shipment going?" Concepcion asked bluntly. "I know that you wouldn't go to all the trouble to ship this stuff all the way from Colombia to Pakistan."

Frederick surveyed the captain's face and decided to tell him. There was no harm in it now. "This shipment is going to Miami."

"Miami. Are you insane?" Concepcion asked incredulously. "We just travelled thousands of miles across the Atlantic Ocean and you're going to send it to the U.S? Who's running this show?"

"Fortunately, I don't have to answer to you," Frederick said, looking at the captain with contempt.

"Listen, I meant no disrespect. I just don't understand," the captain said realizing his mistake.

"You did notice that there were no customs officials at the Karachi harbor?" Frederick asked condescendingly.

"Yeah," the captain said, wondering where this conversation was heading.

"That privilege cost about $100,000 in bribes to arrange. We're now headed for the airport, where this shipment will be loaded onto an unmarked plane. It will head to Czechoslovakia in place of a regularly scheduled Pakistani commercial airline and land in Prague, where it will then head for Miami," Frederick explained proudly.

"What about the jet's radar transponder? They're going to know that this plane is not a commercial airliner," Concepcion pointed out.

"I'm most impressed, Señor," Frederick said, patronizingly. "Most sailors wouldn't know about the airliner codes that identify planes."

"I used to be a pilot," Concepcion said, feeling that he needed to explain himself.

Frederick continued unabated. "The jet's radar transponder has been altered to beep out the code of a commercial airliner. The plane won't even arouse suspicion. And you, Señor Concepcion, will be a very rich man."

Concepcion said nothing as the truck arrived at the airport. The boxes were loaded onto the plane and he stood by the truck smoking a cigarette. As the last box was packed into the cargo bay, Frederick approached Concepcion and handed him an envelope.

The captain counted the money and smiled. It was more than he had been promised.

"Gracias, my German friend. I do not understand your methods, but I understand money," Concepcion said and turned to walk away.

Frederick gestured to one of his subordinates who struck the back of Concepcion's head with a club. Concepcion dropped the envelope of money and slumped to the ground. The money was picked up and Concepcion was loaded into a wooden crate. No loose ends, no evidence, Frederick thought, pleased.

The crate was quickly hoisted up onto the empty truck. It would be returned to the harbor and dumped into the water. Probably in a few weeks, the body of Armando Concepcion would be found and not a single person in all of Pakistan would care.

✠   ✠   ✠

Darrell Johnson still couldn't believe that he was picking up a gang leader to take to Washington. Michael Madigan was not an average congressman.

He was praying that Johnny wouldn't be there. But unfortunately for Darrell, honor was something that the gang member took seriously. It didn't make sense, he thought, that they could engage in horrible acts of violence against others and view honor as important.

Darrell spotted Johnny Green right where he said he'd be, exactly on time. Darrell pulled up and opened the door. "Get in."

Johnny was alone. He had that look that said, "Don't mess with me."

"Where's Madigan?" Johnny demanded.

"He's already at the airport," Darrell said.

The gang leader shifted awkwardly in the car several times. Finally, he asked, "Just what the hell is it I'm supposed to do, man? What do you dudes want with me?"

"You know, Johnny, I'm not really sure," Darrell answered truthfully. "I don't really understand what the Colonel's got in mind. He has a feeling that to make things better, you have to talk. He thinks that on the one hand, you have this white power structure that's been running things for ever and on the other hand, you have an underclass, mostly minority, that has lost hope and is full of rage. He believes that they have to be reconciled. Do you understand what I'm saying?"

"I'm not stupid, man," Johnny said angrily. "I didn't go to school as long as you maybe, but I got a head on my shoulders. You think I'm a loser, don't you?"

Now it was Darrell's turn to look confused. "I didn't say that."

"You don't have to say it. It's written all over you face. You know what's sad, man?" Johnny said contemptuously. "The people who can help the most, who can talk to gang members, are the people who used to live here but made it out and moved away. They're the ones who should come back and help the rest of us."

Johnny continued. "I bet you ain't been in a neighborhood like this in a long time, have you? You want to pretend that we don't exist. Well, we're here, man. This is our home, with the crime, the drugs and the hookers. This is our school, man, where the kids learn. They don't get to go on pony rides at birthday parties. They don't join fraternities or play tennis. They worry about staying alive. So don't judge me, man. Don't judge me."

"I would never think to judge you," Darrell said defensively. "If you work hard, you can get past all of that. I put myself through college and..." He didn't get a chance to finish.

"Well, congratulations Mr. College Boy, but you're the exception. When you live in this kind of shit and things happen every day, you don't think about taking the SAT's or what you're going to major in," Johnny said passionately.

Johnny saw that Darrell looked surprised. "You seem shocked that I know what an SAT is. Well, I scored 1250 on it and got accepted to three colleges. I had some dreams, too. But my mother went to jail and there were three mouths to feed. So don't give me all that jive about making something of myself. I am who I am and I don't really give a damn if that pleases you or not," he said.

They sat in stony silence for the next fifteen minutes. Darrell glanced at this brooding, angry man and didn't know what else to say. He had grown up in the same environment, but he had made it out. Why couldn't others escape as well?

✠   ✠   ✠

Frederick, the economist, arrived at the Brussels airport from Karachi to see Wilhelm, the NATO leader, before continuing his flight to the Cayman Islands. As a high-ranking member of the government, it was difficult for him to get away without notice, so he would make a stopover in Brussels and meet with Felix Klaus, if only for appearances' sake.

He took a taxi to the country home of Wilhelm who lived in a large house on the outskirts of Brussels. He was greeted at the door by a servant who informed him that the secretary general was out on the grounds riding one of his horses. Wilhelm was an expert horseman and kept a stable full of horses, including several Arabians, his favorites. Frederick was shown to the stables and was impressed with the size of the grounds, which seemingly went on as far as the eye could see. After several minutes, Wilhelm rode up to greet his old friend.

"Whoa, there," he said to the animal. "Calm down, girl," he said, as he dismounted. He stroked its neck with one hand and reached out to shake Frederick's hand with the other.

"Guten Tag," Wilhelm said to Frederick, "Wie geht's?"

"Sehr gut," Frederick responded.

"This is an Arabian, one of the finest horses in the world," Wilhelm said proudly. "It's a beautiful animal," said Frederick, admiring the well-muscled animal.

"It certainly is," Wilhelm said, handing the reins to a stable hand. And then he shouted orders to a couple of servants and within seconds, refreshments were brought. The men sat down at a large table with an umbrella and laughed as they quenched their thirst.

"It never ceases to amaze me how skillfully we've carried out this charade," Frederick said. "Look at this place. It's befitting a king and they let you live here, while you plan the demise of NATO. The same is true of Charlemagne and Rommel. It's truly astounding."

"It's ironic indeed," agreed Wilhelm. "I don't mean to rush you, but let's get down to business. I have a meeting in a short time with some more of those naive so-called statesmen," he said with a grin.

"Very well, Felix. As you know, Krupp and I are involved in another organization which you may be familiar with but only in general terms," said Frederick.

"Are you talking about ICB?" Wilhelm asked, taking a large gulp of wine.

"Yes," Frederick said. "It's coming apart quickly, I'm afraid," Frederick warned. "I'm on my way to the Cayman Islands to see what I can retrieve."

"What do you mean *retrieve*?" Wilhelm asked.

"Well, U.S. investigators have acquired evidence that a large Washington bank is controlled by ICB. As a result, the Federal Reserve immediately ordered that the transfer of money and assets between the two banks be terminated," Frederick said, feeling a familiar knot in his stomach.

"How did this happen?"

"Some overly ambitious district attorney supposedly had his suspicions about the Washington bank and applied pressure on the Feds, who in turn have started twisting arms over at Justice. That's one of the reasons Anthony Peterson was terminated. Besides the drug thing, he was about to start a criminal and civil investigation."

"I was aware of that," Wilhelm said matter-of-factly. "What else?"

"Well, the Feds are starting to breathe down our necks a little too closely. We've bribed a lot of people," the economist emphasized, "but that hasn't stopped the self-righteous holier-than-thous who think they must promote truth, justice and the American way," he said mockingly.

"What bank is it that you're talking about?" asked Klaus. "It's not First Federal, is it?"

"Yes, it is," answered Frederick. "As you know, Steven Schmidt recently became its executive vice-president. ICB essentially bought control of the bank, along with others in the U.S.," he explained.

"Forgive me my ignorance, but I don't understand how that happened."

Wilhelm signalled a servant for another glass of wine before continuing.

"Felix, let me start at the beginning," Frederick said, sipping his wine. "You never really understood why I married a Pakistani woman, did you?"

Klaus shook his head.

"I understood a long time ago that there was a place for an international bank that moved money for wealthy people, from dictators to arms dealers. There was a need for a global institution that laundered money for dictators, carried with total impunity," said Frederick excitedly.

"But in the industrialized countries there is too much government regulation. A bank such as this could never be based in the U.S. or Europe. The only place the ICB could prosper would be in the so-called third world," he explained.

Wilhelm interjected. "I know that it was created supposedly to be a Muslim bank."

"It had to be done in the Arab world because they share our hatred of Jews," Frederick elaborated. "Now while it's true that I came to love my wife in time, I married her only for the connections it brought me in the Pakistani banking industry," he said.

"You see," he said, "the bank was supposed to be a Muslim institution, although we incorporated in Luxembourg and made the headquarters in Germany. Even though it soon developed hundreds of branches around the world, and although the majority of the shares were owned by Arab investors from the gulf countries, it has always been, in its heart, a Pakistani bank," he added.

"O.K., how does First Federal play into it?" he inquired.

"I'll get to that," Frederick said. "Things happened that were not initially planned. When the Soviets invaded Afghanistan in 1979, Pakistan acquired added strategic importance. The U.S. wanted to supply the mujahedin rebels in Afghanistan with Stinger missiles and it needed the cooperation of Pakistan. The black network just grew from there," he said.

"The black network?" Wilhelm asked.

"Yes. To the Pakistanis, I presented ICB as Pakistan's nuclear bomb project," Frederick said. "In the Muslim world I would encourage them with promises of global domination by the accumulation of oil dollars. And the thing that always kept them going was the promise that we would deliver the bomb," he added.

"How can a bank buy weapons?"

"What it has done is act at times simultaneously as a bank and a broker, which has given it a tremendous advantage," Frederick explained.

"How so?"

"Let me give you an example. ICB brokered the sale of F-15 jets to Iran from the U.S. ICB learned from its sources in Iran that it wanted to buy spare parts. The bank then surveyed the supplier market to obtain the price of the materials. Because U.S. restrictions on the sale of such equipment to Iran made this deal illegal, ICB then provided a falsified end-user certificate that the jet parts would be sold to Israel. The bank then opened a letter of credit in favor of the seller and arranged to ship the parts," he explained, pausing for a second.

"Because it's such a large bank," Frederick continued, "ICB can afford to pay off the seller immediately, then turn and collect a vastly larger sum from Iran," he explained.

Wilhelm shook his head in amazement.

"But now we're starting to pay the price for some of this freewheeling," Frederick warned. "Investigators in several countries have determined that over ten billion dollars in deposits are missing," he said.

"Ten billion?" Klaus asked in astonishment. "How?"

"Well, the bank operated virtually without regulation the world over," Frederick explained. "We organized it in such a convoluted manner that no one would be able to figure it out. We had dozens of shell companies, offshore banks, subsidiaries and the like in seventy different countries. We used the Cayman Islands extensively and had this weird type of accounting, where we did everything in longhand in a rare Pakistani dialect," the German official stated, much to his comrade's astonishment.

"You see," he continued, "using these Cayman Island accounts the bank would lend massive amounts to curry favor with governments or to buy secret control of companies."

"Did they buy control of First Federal?" the NATO leader asked.

"Yes, and two other American banks as well," answered the economist.

"About ten or twelve years ago, a group of Arab investors bought First Federal. The bank lent the investors the money they used to buy the stock in First Federal, with the shares pledged as collateral. Of course, these loans were never repaid. I'm sure that you can guess what happens then," he asked.

"The bank gets the collateral."

"Exactly. But the collateral was the shares in First Federal," said Frederick smiling. "And so a group of unregulated foreign investors takes over an American bank without U.S. regulators knowing about it," he added. "And these same investors happened to own controlling shares in ICB."

"Sounds pretty good to me. What went wrong?"

"Well, it was only a matter of time," admitted Frederick. "The bank gathered deposits, looted most of them but kept enough new deposits flowing in so that there was always sufficient cash on hand to pay anyone who asked for his money. In the 1980's, the bank became a magnet for drug money, capital flight money, tax evading money, and money from corrupt government officials. It got a reputation as a bank that could move money anywhere and hide it without a trace," the economist noted.

"What about this black network? And what is Krupp's role?" asked the NATO leader.

"Well, its original purpose was to pay bribes, intimidate authorities and quash investigations," Frederick acknowledged.

Wilhelm was clearly impressed. "Maybe you're right. Maybe money is what makes the world go round. I've always thought that it was the barrel of a gun," he said.

"It's both. To be a true superpower requires both. Germany must be strong militarily and economically," said Frederick. "If so, then she'll be invincible."

"But what of these problems that you referred to? Is ICB still operating?" Wilhelm asked.

"No, it's not. But it's served our purpose. The ten billion I mentioned is safe in the Cayman Islands. I'm on my way there now and I will be meeting with Steven Schmidt. ICB has come to an abrupt end but it has accomplished its goal. We now have the means to finance our plan. But we have only enough for a short time. We must carry out our mission soon," he warned.

Wilhelm raised his wine glass. "Let's drink to the Fourth Reich. May it last forever," he said, as the two men toasted the inevitable resurrection of Germany's greatness.

✠   ✠   ✠

Michael talked briefly with Johnny Green on the flight to Washington and was quite impressed, although saddened at the same time. The young man clearly was bright and had natural leadership skills but had chosen to channel his talents into negative and destructive forays.

Johnny still wasn't sure what to make of Michael and this trip. And he was still seething at the beating he had taken from this older man. But he wanted to know just how it was that he had been whipped so convincingly.

"Can I ask you something?" Johnny asked, careful not to appear too eager or enthusiastic.

"What is it Johnny?"

Johnny hesitated for a second. "I gotta tell you. You messed me up good, man. And I want to know how you did it," he said.

Michael knew how hard it was for Johnny to say this and he took it as high praise. "Well, Johnny, as I said, I was a Green Beret for many years and we learned some pretty lethal stuff. And I studied karate for a long time."

"You in Vietnam?" Johnny asked.

"Yes."

"Ever kill anyone with your hands?"

Michael became sad and waited a while before responding. "Yeah, I did. I'm not proud of it but it was either me or him."

Johnny tried to steer the conversation away from Vietnam. "Could you teach me some of those things?"

Michael perked up. "What do you want to know?"

"Well, you knocked me on my ass that last time before I even knew what hit me. I felt a punch to the back of my neck and then the next thing I knew, I was kissing asphalt."

Michael laughed but saw that Johnny didn't take it as funny. "Well, you always want to go after as many targets as possible. At least two. I hit you at the base of your neck and then quickly followed up with a swift kick to the back of your knee."

"Hitting someone on the base of the neck is something that you always see on TV," Michael explained, "and the person always goes right down. But this isn't always so. This is the so-called karate chop but its effectiveness is overrated. But if done correctly, can bring you down quick."

Michael straightened his hand and simulated a quick blow to the back of the neck. Michael demonstrated on Johnny. "The target area is right here," he said.

"Once your opponent has been struck, you gotta move quickly for another target. The back of the knee is my favorite. Even a small person can kick the back of the knee with enough force to be effective. The greatest advantage of kicking into the knee is putting your opponent on the ground."

"You sure put my ass on the ground, that's for sure," Johnny said, trying to conceal a smile.

"I'll give you another lesson if you want later," Michael said.

"You better be careful about teaching me too much or I'll whip you next time," Johnny said, this time laughing.

"Well, I won't let you in on all of my secrets," Michael said as he sank back into his seat. His mind was spinning in a million directions. The past months had been an emotional roller coaster: the divorce proceedings, Rebecca's return, his dalliance with Kelly and the tremendous guilt concerning Judy's close call. It never seemed to end. Maybe he should just write a book and leave the backstabbing pain of the real world to others. But he felt compelled to do something, even if he didn't succeed.

Rebecca was going to meet him at the airport, along with the kids. Josh had decided to transfer to Georgetown and while he would not be living with them, they would be able to see each other frequently. He was surprised at how close he and Josh had become. His son was a bright, hard working articulate young man. Perhaps a little too much of a dare devil but Michael couldn't see much wrong with that.

Michael's eyes began to moisten as he thought of TJ. He was ecstatic that she had improved so much. His intense love for her was sometimes overshadowed by hatred toward those who had tried to destroy her mind. His number one priority while in office would be to try to eliminate drugs from society. It was a promise he wouldn't break.

David had seemingly grown up right before his very eyes with their escapade to Israel. The incident had given him increased confidence and he had talked about his father nonstop since the hijacking.

Then there was Rebecca. She had come back to him. He would no doubt be extremely busy with his new career, but his family would always have priority.

15

Each of the seven young guests arrived at Peter Volhard's house as instructed. They were eager to be briefed on their upcoming missions. Volhard, also known as Rommel, lived in a large colonial-style house in Virginia. His guests gathered in his den, which was covered with the heads of dozens of animals.

The highly trained and very select group ranged in age between twenty and thirty-seven. They all spoke fluent English in addition to German, and some spoke other languages as well. They had received university degrees and most important, each of them had military training. They were all single and had no ties to anything other than Germany.

Rommel gestured, speaking in a manner that commanded respect and they all rose to their feet. He signaled with a short wave of his hand for them to sit down.

"Guten Abend. Welcome to my home." He sat down in an easy chair just below the head of the first lion he had ever killed.

"All have some knowledge of our mission but tonight, you'll be told everything. The one thing that we demand from you is loyalty. If after what you hear tonight you cannot provide your 100 percent loyalty to the Reich, than you will be asked to leave. No questions asked. But," he said, rising from his chair, "if you remain with us and are not dedicated, you will be killed," he said bluntly. "In a most painful manner, I must add."

Rommel tried to gauge their reactions. He saw nothing to indicate anything but loyalty. He knew they were fully prepared to die for the cause.

Rommel paused, shuffling the ice cubes in his vodka before continuing. "My friends, in 1945 my colleagues and I were all young officers in the Wehrmacht and had just suffered a humiliating defeat at the hands of the Allies," he said with anger.

"What choice did we have but to accept defeat?" Rommel asked. "The United States had become the superpower and was the first to develop the nuclear bomb. But our leader would not allow us to accept defeat. He persuaded us to formulate a plan to restore Germany."

"Many of us were skeptical but he convinced us," Rommel explained excitedly. "He knew that Germany was only defeated for the time, but that she would return. He demanded we look to history. History moves in ebbs, tides and cycles. Germany had gone through many other peaks and valleys in its long history and it would return he insisted."

"'We are the superior race,' he told us that day. Our people must reign. We had been dealt a setback but had forty or fifty years to work with."

"The man known to us as Bismarck convinced us to devote our lives to this mission and we have. We sit in the halls of the highest levels of government in the three most powerful nations in world history. Not in my wildest dreams did I believe that it would actually work out just as we planned so many years ago. But it has, my friends, and we are almost there. And each of you will contribute."

Rommel again paused, glancing around the room. Before he disclosed anymore, he would ask a few questions. He looked at the young man to his right.

"You are Lothar Freitag, are you not?"

"Yes, sir, I am," replied the recruit nervously.

"Are you prepared to die for this cause?"

"Yes, I am."

"Very well, Herr Freitag."

He went onto the next person, a very tall blond named Ludwig Schuler. "Mr. Schuler, have you ever killed anyone?"

Schuler's eyes grew large and he hesitated somewhat before answering. "No, sir. But I will if necessary."

"We'll see quite soon. That brings us to the woman in our group, the talented Kelly Adkins. Why have you chosen this life? Would you rather not marry and have children?"

She was the smallest but there wasn't one shred of doubt in her body. "Herr Volhard, I've decided for the time being against a family. Even though I was born in America, I've spent many years in Germany. I want to be a participant. This is Germany's destiny. And I want to be a part of it." She paused briefly but locked her eyes on Rommel's, not flinching.

"Perhaps I'll have children later. After all, I'm still young. I have plenty of time."

Rommel was impressed with her steely coolness. She was small and thin but a warrior. Next was the oldest member of the group, Dietrich Lietz.

"Herr Lietz, what are your feelings towards Jews?"

Lietz pondered the question and replied slowly. "We cannot be so naive as to think that Jews are the cause of all our problems. The so-called Final Solution would not have solved anything, I'm afraid. They are inferior, but we cannot become preoccupied with Jews. During World War II, this intense anti-Semitism caused us to lose Albert Einstein. The outcome of the war would have been radically different had Mr. Einstein remained in Germany. There would be no need for meeting here tonight. Germany would already be ruling the world."

"A very incisive analysis, Herr Lietz." He glanced at his watch and then to another member of his team. "Herr Bruckmann, war today is much different than in my day. Nuclear weapons have radically altered the battlefield, making Armageddon possible. We'll be dealing with nuclear weapons and they may be unleashed before our mission is accomplished. Are you prepared that millions may die?"

"Herr Volhard, we must focus on the ends and not on the means. I would prefer to accomplish our mission with as little bloodshed as possible. But our cause is just. If there is bloodshed, so be it."

Rommel felt good about this group. They seemed to complement each other well. But time would tell. He would not hesitate to kill them for interfering.

The latest mission was called Operation Volk and only five other people were aware of it in its entirety. None of the other members of the Six had shared all of it with their team members but he felt compelled to do so.

"My esteemed colleagues. Our mission has many aspects to it, many stages, many layers. This is Operation Volk. Throughout the cold war period, we've witnessed the emergence of a bipolar world, with the U.S. and the Soviet Union emerging as the predominant powers, our primary targets. Their power and strength must be eliminated."

"This has been easier to accomplish in the Soviet Union than we had ever anticipated. The sudden collapse of the Communist Bloc was a shocking event, and now it's developing into ethnic conflict and potential civil war. We can use this to our advantage."

"In America recently, we've seen tremendous rage manifested vividly in the recent riots. America is divided. We will exploit that division."

"It's our intention to take by force our rightful position," Rommel proclaimed. "And to do this we must acquire nuclear weapons and economic power. And we've set out to replace the dollar with the Deutsche mark as the world's primary currency."

"Herr Lietz has eloquently pointed out that Jews are not the only cause of Germany's problems, but we will be much the richer without them. Therefore, we'll finish their genocide."

"Large amounts of money are necessary to accomplish these goals. As Herr Bruckmann has so clearly stated, we must focus on the ends and not the means. The sale of drugs in the U.S. and former Soviet Union will fund our mission and at the same time, poison our enemies."

Volhard could tell his audience was impressed with the plan. The seven new members waited for him to continue.

"I will tell you how we will accomplish this. First, here in the United States, I am the second person in line, behind the vice president, should anything happen to the president. Our plan will soon cause a scandal for the vice president, who will then be forced to step down. It is our hope to influence the president to nominate as his new VP a man that we will be able to control."

Rommel saw the eyes of each of his new underlings light up in amazement and he continued.

"The United States president is a powerful man, but even he can't launch a nuclear weapon by himself. He needs the simultaneous input of the secretary of defense. The current secretary will soon find himself the victim of a tragic accident and, again with the influence I have with the president, it is our plan that one of us will soon be named the next secretary of defense."

"Prior to that, we hope to accomplish a vital mission in the former Soviet Union. One of our group is currently leading a United States delegation to oversee the dismantling of Soviet ICBM's in accordance with the recent arms reduction treaties. He will acquire at least one ICBM with multiple warheads. It will be kept in Russia until needed. Additionally, we've successfully acquired chemical weapons and bombs. Another goal is the large scale introduction of narcotics into the former USSR and the U.S."

"We will also continue to exploit racial differences in the United States and eventually in the former USSR."

Rommel was taking great pleasure in witnessing the awed eyes of this young team. He was their führer and they would sacrifice their lives for him. He raised his glass and all of the others followed his lead.

"To the Reich," they shouted.

✠   ✠   ✠

Michael arrived at his office by 6:30 A.M. He still couldn't believe that he was a United States Congressman and his entire family was with him.

Michael had been told by many people that freshmen legislators were rarely able to acquire power very quickly. They had told him it would take time and he needed to be involved on the "right" committees. Again it was more who you knew than what you knew. Michael decided to team up with Peter Volhard.

Michael wanted to sit on committees and subcommittees involving drugs, civil rights and intelligence. He was smart enough to realize that economic matters were not his forte. He needed to stick to what he knew.

He was going over his schedule for the day when the phone rang, and since he was the only one there he answered it.

"Michael Madigan."

"Michael, I thought I'd take a chance on calling. I know that you're an early riser. This is Nate Wallace. How the hell are you? And by the way, congratulations, Congressman. It's going to be great to have you in Washington."

"Nate, how are you doing, buddy?" Michael replied enthusiastically. "You know, I'm nervous as hell, to be honest, and it's really comforting to hear from old friends. Thanks for calling. What's up at the DEA?"

Nate Wallace had served in the army with Michael and they had been young officers in Vietnam in the same Special Forces battalion for a while. Nate now worked at the Drug Enforcement Administration.

"Mike, I'm sure you've heard about that recent Supreme Court decision that said that U.S. agents can seize fugitives overseas without a host country's permission," Nate said.

"You bet, and to tell you the truth, I don't think that I agree with it," Michael acknowledged. "Who do we think we are? We just ride in on our white horse and kidnap whoever we like? I know that the liberals are up in arms and frankly, I don't blame them," Michael noted.

"You always were a closet ACLU'er," laughed the arch-conservative Wallace, "but we think that it's great over here. These bastards have always been beyond our reach and now we can do something about it. Recently in Colombia, leading figures of the Medellin cartel got an offer that guaranteed them no extradition to the United States and reduced sentences for confessed crimes. So they turned themselves in. They'll serve a couple of years at some country-club prison and be out in no time. That stinks."

"I'll have to agree with you there," Michael admitted. "But I'm sure that you didn't call this early to debate Supreme Court decisions. Is there a point to all of this?"

"That's what I like about you, Mike. You get to the bottom line. Well, you're right. I didn't call you this early to debate the current makeup of the court." He hesitated and Michael started to get irritated.

"Nate, would you say what's on your mind? No offense. but I've got a ton of things to do."

"Sorry, Mike. I think I have something that might interest you," Nate offered.

"What is it?"

"Well, I don't want to go into the details over the phone, but it has to do with TJ."

"My TJ? Nate, don't screw around with me. What are you talking about?" he demanded.

"I was really affected when TJ overdosed," admitted Nate. "I always loved her and thought of her as the niece I never had. When I heard about what happened, I was devastated."

"Nate, cut to the chase."

"After it happened, I managed to get myself involved. I dug and dug and made it a mission to find out who was responsible. And Mike, I know who was responsible and where he hangs his hat."

"Nate, what are you getting at? First, of all, I don't see how you could pin a particular overdose on any one person and second, even if you could, I don't think that it will be the administration's top priority," noted Michael.

"Maybe not. But I figure that maybe it would be a top priority for someone. Perhaps you. And me. And maybe a couple of our friends."

"What are you suggesting? That we sneak into Colombia, or wherever, on some covert type mission, and grab these guys? You can't be serious," Michael remarked.

"Serious as a heart attack, Mike. Back in our Special Forces days, we used to do this stuff and be back for breakfast."

"Nate, I don't know if anyone has informed you but I'm a sitting U.S. congressman. We don't parachute into foreign countries and kidnap people. There's no Kidnapping Drug Lords Committee," Michael said sarcastically.

"Listen, Mike, I don't blame you if you think I'm nuts but I've put a lot of time and thought into this. Will you do me a favor at least?" Nate asked.

"What is it?"

"Will you join me for lunch and hear me out? Will you do that much for an old buddy?" Nate asked innocently.

Michael reluctantly agreed. "I guess so. What do I have to lose except for my life and career?"

"That's the spirit," said Nate. "How about that place we used to go to all the time when we were in the Pentagon? What was that called?"

"Alfredo's."

"That's it. Best lasagna in town. How's one o'clock sound?"

"I'll probably regret it but I'll be there."

"Mike, I think that once you see what I have, you'll agree with my plan. Remember, it's for TJ. O.K., pal?"

"O.K.," Michael whispered hanging up the phone.

✠   ✠   ✠

In another restaurant on the other side of town, another congressman was meeting with a new colleague to discuss the drug war. Peter Volhard was having lunch with a chief lieutenant of the notorious Jorge Ramirez, whose ranch Volhard had visited earlier in the year. Volhard had wanted to meet with Ramirez himself, but knew that it would be too dangerous for someone of his notoriety to come to the United States and possibly be seen with a U.S. congressman. This was Alejandro Lopez' first trip to the United States but the Colombian would not have time to sight see. He would be in the country for only about twenty-four hours.

Volhard had arranged for a luncheon at a very discreet place named Roberto's. It was on the outskirts of town and usually was not very crowded. At 12:30 P.M., when Volhard arrived, there were only two other people in the restaurant.

He sat and ordered a glass of water. He rarely drank liquor and never during the day. Seven minutes after his arrival, Lopez appeared.

The drug lord looked amused by the seediness of the place, but said nothing.

Volhard didn't stand up but did extend his hand. "Señor Lopez, how are you? How was your flight?"

"Fine, Mr. Speaker, just fine. And how are you doing?" asked the short, swarthy man.

"Splendid," responded Volhard. He signaled the waitress and they placed their orders.

The Colombian started things off. "I must tell you how impressed I was with your attorney general's last press conference. I have never seen anything like it," he said in an awed tone. "I had my doubts before, but after that I was convinced. Have the authorities any clues?"

"None whatsoever. They're too stupid," Volhard said contemptuously. "No one will ever know. Of course, in one way, it didn't accomplish a damn thing. The president just appointed the deputy to be the new attorney general.

He's almost an exact clone of Peterson. But it was very theatrical," the speaker added.

"It's still the hot topic in my country," Lopez added.

"Let's get down to business, shall we?" Volhard said in a no-nonsense tone. "Tell me how you're going to sell me your product. We have a ravenous appetite. We want everything that you can produce. Can you give us what we want?"

"Part of that is up to you," Ramirez' aide replied. "Can you stop the federales, the FBI, the DEA and all of those other wannabe Rambos from running around like crazy all over Latin America? And your Supreme Court's recent decision has a lot of people nervous, including Señor Ramirez. How do we know you wouldn't send your thugs down there to seize him?" asked Lopez.

"You don't, except to take my word for it. That will never happen," Volhard responded. "I have too much on my mind to worry about some Latin American drug dealer. No offense intended. And besides, what I am doing is highly illegal. I will not go out of my way to advertise my actions, if you understand what I mean."

"Understood. Let's begin," Lopez said, spreading his arms out on the table and running his hands through his slicked-back hair. "We're expanding our operations so that we can accommodate you."

"How so?"

"We're creating other routes, other drugs, other means," he exclaimed. "We're not just operating in Colombia, but in all of Latin America. As you know, while Colombia is the world's largest refiner and shipper of cocaine, it's not the largest producer of the coca base. That distinction lies with Peru. We've been working feverishly to improve our Peruvian connections."

"After about ten years of the Colombian authorities doing nothing, they've recently started cracking down hard," Lopez continued. "These new hard-ball tactics have angered all of my associates. And they're not backing off, at least not yet. But we can play hard ball, too." The Colombian hesitated. "Forgive me for being so candid. I still have this fear that you're carrying a wire and any moment, FBI agents will jump out of the walls."

"Alejandro, may I call you that?" responded Volhard with considerable charm. "I have only told you very briefly who I am. I am not an American and I have a mission that dwarfs anything you can even comprehend. Please continue," Volhard said, very businesslike.

"We've solidified our contacts in Peru, specifically in Uchiza, in the Upper Huallaga Valley. We're trying to manufacture more. It takes 500 kilograms of coca leaves to make one kilogram of finished cocaine powder. And it's becoming more and more difficult. Many of the cocaleros are leaving and getting out of the business. I tell you in all candor, Mr. Volhard, it is not so easy as it once was. You must listen so that you can help."

"You have my undivided attention," Volhard replied.

"First of all, coca was a legal crop in Peru until just a few years ago," Lopez explained. "It's been a staple there for centuries and the Andean Indians still chew coca leaves. And now it's illegal. Great efforts are being taken by the authorities to stop it."

"I've been told by many reliable people of stories of American helicopters landing, with soldiers coming out with spray guns, releasing clouds of yellowish or reddish mist that kills within days all of the coca fields," he said in an accusatory tone.

"Preposterous. If that's going on, it's not with American involvement," rebuked Volhard.

"I merely tell you what I've been told," Lopez said defensively. "The spray is supposed to be a soil fungus that attacks the roots of coca bushes. The helicopters supposedly come from Santa Lucia, an anti-drug base in the southern part of the country near the Bolivian border staffed with Peruvian police and American DEA agents."

"Also, last month, the Peruvian Air Force took control of the Uchiza airstrip in an effort to stop cocaine traffic. Further, in the past six months, two radar installations in northeastern Peru were used to spot drug planes for Peruvian Air Force interceptors to chase," he said in an exasperated tone.

"It doesn't sound like you're capable of meeting our needs. Perhaps I overestimated your abilities," said Volhard.

"Mr. Volhard, I did not say that. But we can no longer do this in our sleep. We could use your considerable influence. But be that as it may, we can still deliver. Listen to me, my American friend," he said, as he lowered his voice.

"First, we're spreading into less developed places in the Middle Huallaga Valley," Lopez continued. "We control the airstrip at Campanilla. Also, further south, out of the range of the helicopters from Santa Lucia, our business is rapidly expanding. We're planting in other valleys: the Ene, the Aguaytia, the Ucayali, the Tambo, the Apurimac and the Madre de Dios," he said to Volhard, although the names meant nothing to the American.

"Also, we're spearheading the move into heroin," continued the Colombian. "Cocaine demand is no longer expanding in the U.S. and all of these anti-narcotics efforts have had a dramatic effect on the price of cocaine. Also, the cocaine seized last year was four times what was confiscated in 1988. That's why the move to heroin."

"Don't forget the USSR," said Volhard. "We want cocaine shipped to Europe and beyond."

"I know. We're working on that with great diligence," Lopez said with some irritation. "We're developing routes from Argentina and Brazil, sometimes through Africa. Some cocaine base is transported via motorized canoes down the Amazon river tributaries into Brazil, where it's shipped to Europe and into the former USSR. We're having great success with that," he said with pride.

"We're also trying other routes to the U.S.," Lopez continued. "As you probably know, cocaine base is made mostly in Peru. For the most part, it's been transported by light plane from the Peruvian Andes directly to Colombia, or indirectly by routes that cut across Ecuador or Brazil. In Colombia, it's then refined into powder and flown out by private plane and arrives at a staging area in southern Mexico or the northern tier of Central America, primarily Guatemala and sometimes Belize. From there, it's transported to large U.S. cities by various methods," he said. The drug dealer paused for a moment.

Volhard kept stirring his drink. After some awkward silence, he spoke. "Please continue."

"We've created other routes where the powder is sealed in water-tight containers and air-dropped into the waters off Puerto Rico, the Dominican Republic or the Virgin Islands," he said excitedly. "They're then picked up by boats and shipped into the U.S."

"Until recently, we were sending cocaine powder from Colombia into Mexico by private plane and then into the U.S.," Lopez continued. "However, interdiction efforts have pushed us into southern Mexico and Guatemala."

"So, you see, we're trying to meet your demands. But Mr. Speaker, there are things you can do to help us," proclaimed the drug dealer.

"Such as?"

"Your DEA and Justice Department have pushed plans to deploy modern Blackhawk helicopters against cocaine traffickers in Guatemala, the Dominican Republic and Jamaica. I've also heard that the plan has led to a turf struggle with the Treasury Department's Customs Service. We would hope that you could lend your talents to encouraging this bureaucratic fighting," the Colombian requested.

"Consider it done, my friend."

"I believe that we'll both profit from this relationship," said Lopez.

"Give my best to Señor Ramirez. He is a most impressive man," observed Volhard, as he stood and shook Lopez' hand.

"That I will, Mr. Speaker. Buenos tardes."

☩   ☩   ☩

Donald Swanson was a workaholic and the secretary of defense was still in his office at 9:00 P.M. as usual. His wife, Sandra, had long ago grown accustomed to his absence. Mrs. Swanson almost dreaded her husband's retirement, which would probably be at the end of the president's second term, if he was reelected. Maybe it would come sooner.

The former general was meeting this evening with Matt Connors, the deputy national security counselor. The meeting was at Connors' request.

"Mr. Secretary, thank you for meeting with me," Matt began, as he entered the massive Pentagon office.

"Good to see you, Matt," said the secretary, who had changed into casual clothes to be more comfortable. He was wearing jeans, a flannel shirt and cowboy boots. "What's on your mind?"

"This is all speculative but I've been looking into it for some time now," Matt began nervously. "I have a source who's fed me a lot of information but I don't have much hard evidence. It's a little crazy but I'm convinced I'm onto something."

"Well, spit it out, Matt. I promised Sandra I'd be home before she went to bed for a change."

"Yes, sir," Matt replied with deference, even though he was basically a peer of Swanson. "As you know, there have been a series of assassinations, murders, bombings and the like, all directed against three different groups: blacks, Jews and Russians. Someone's trying to exploit racial tensions here in the U.S. and ethnic differences in the former Soviet Union. And neo-Nazi rallies have been popping up all over Germany."

"What's your point, Matt?"

"I think that all of these things are connected."

"How so?"

"This is the crazy part, General," Matt said, beginning to pace the room, which was covered with photos of fighter planes. "It's my hunch, based on what my source has told me, that this is a highly sophisticated effort by a group of former Nazis who all served in the same SS battalion during World War II."

"Good Lord, Connors, the war's been over for more than forty-five years. Are you saying that a group of senior-citizen Nazis are plotting to take over the world?"

"I know it sounds bizarre but just hear me out," Matt requested. "My sources have reported seeing six men together in different places in Germany, the U.S. and the old USSR during the past five years. Each one has reached a place of great power in various countries."

"What do you mean? I thought that you said they were German," the secretary of defense responded.

"I did General, but only two of them stayed in Germany after the war. The four that left Germany have all amassed great power in their new countries and now each time there's an incident, one or more of them is somehow in the background."

"Matt, I've heard some wild ones before but something's really crawled up your ass this time," Swanson said. "O.K., I'll play along. Who are these people? Let's start with the Americans."

"Please realize that at this point it's mere conjecture on my part," Matt said defensively, dreading Swanson's response. "I'm still lacking hard evidence. So, here goes." He took a deep breath. "I don't know who the second American is but I think that one of them is Peter Volhard," he said cringing slightly, waiting for the famous Swanson temper to erupt.

"The goddamn speaker of the house is a Nazi?" Swanson shouted. "My God, Connors, what kind of drugs have you been smoking? Listen, I know you've got a solid head on your shoulders and you must have something to base this cockamamie theory on. I've always respected you Matt, but I'm a busy man. You get me some hard evidence and we'll meet again. I've really got to be going or the wife will make me sleep on the couch again. You know your way out," Swanson said, making it clear that the meeting was over.

Matt walked away feeling like a schoolboy who just got turned down for a date. My God, what a fool he must think I am, he said to himself. I shouldn't have said anything until I had some more evidence. He trusted Sgt. Pepper but he needed more details, something more concrete. He left the Pentagon's dark corridors and headed home.

Secretary Swanson worked about half an hour more on some paperwork and then decided to call it a night. He summoned his driver, Lou Caskey, to meet him in the garage.

"Good evening, Mr. Secretary," called the good-natured Caskey.

"How you doing tonight there, Lou? How's that gorgeous wife of yours?"

"She's just fine, sir. She just got promoted at her job."

"That's great, Lou. What do you say we head to my abode and let me see what my better half is up to?"

"You got it, sir."

The dark sedan pulled out of the parking garage and headed down the Jefferson Davis highway towards Alexandria, Virginia. The secretary was a man of many moods. Sometimes he was the funniest, most charming man and occasionally he was very abrupt and cold. Not surprising, Caskey thought, when your job is to think about war.

Tonight, however, he wanted to talk. "Lou, don't tell anyone this but I had a meeting tonight with someone who tried to convince me that the Nazis are conspiring to take over the world again. Does that take the cake, or what?" Swanson said sarcastically.

"That's a new one, sir."

They were now out on a dark stretch of highway and Caskey steered around a sharp curve without slowing down.

"Whoa, Lou, what you trying to do to me? How about hitting the brakes around those curves?" Swanson yelled.

Caskey was mashing the brakes furiously but with no success. "The brakes are gone, sir. We're out of control!"

Those were the last words that Swanson would ever hear as the secretary of defense and his young driver plunged through a guardrail and plummeted a hundred or so feet to the rocks below. The sedan exploded upon impact, in a fiery eruption, spewing fire and shrapnel from the remains of the car dozens of feet into the air.

16

The Soviet president was on vacation with his family, and had, for once, been able to totally relax at his dacha on the Black Sea. It was now nearly over and he would have to head back to Moscow to sign a treaty that would strengthen the republics at the expense of the central government. He had decided this was necessary if the country was going to enter the modern world.

It was almost time to leave and he would finish his vacation with a typically Russian form of masochism. Leaving his ornate office he walked across the grounds to the banya, or bathhouse. The one here at Foros was much grander than those visited by average Russians but its purpose was the same, to make you sweat. It was a cross between a Finnish sauna and Turkish bath.

He often missed just being an average person. Much of the joy of going to a bathhouse was the ritual, the camaraderie. Soaping, steaming, rinsing, weighing in, joking with others. He had often thought that the bathhouse was the only place in society that was truly classless. The men sat on wooden steps naked, except for a bundle of leafy birch twigs called a venik for a covering.

This afternoon he would be joined by his security chief, Yuri Khudenko, a scowling, unfriendly man who was known for his crassness. For reasons of his own, the Soviet president liked and trusted this offensive man.

"Yuri, how are you?" the Soviet president said eagerly, as he took off his pants and placed them on a hook outside the glass window that was starting to steam.

"Excellent, Mr. President," replied the security chief, who was already starting to sweat.

"Let's go torture ourselves!" shouted the president, walking briskly into the steam room.

They both stepped up to the top row, the hottest position. "Ah, this is where we see who the men are. It is so hot that the air burns your nostrils," the president said, sticking his chest out and breathing in.

"What we need is some beer and vobla," suggested Yuri, referring to a dried, salted fish. "What do you say, Mr. President?"

"Not today, Yuri. I have work to do tonight. I can't tell you how much I dread tomorrow," sighed the president.

"More water?" asked Yuri.

"Da," answered the president.

Yuri carried his heavy frame down to the floor and poured a pitcher of water onto the bricks. Steam enveloped them, sending heat upward. The president winced in pain and said, "Ah, just right."

At that moment, the door to the steam room swung open and a fully clothed man looked inside.

"Who the hell is that?" demanded the president, unable to see through the thickness of steam. "Close that door."

"It is me, Mr. President, Valerie Petrovich," came the reply. The former professor was the president's current communications director. "There are some people here to see you," he continued.

"What people?" he said in exasperation. "I'm not expecting guests." He bounded down the steps and stepped out of the steam room. He grabbed a towel and reached for one of many telephones that were in every room throughout the compound. The line was dead. He tried another and then another. All the lines were dead.

He knew something was terribly wrong and quickly dressed and left the banya. The president, still sweating, rounded up his wife and two children and told them of his suspicions and then went straight to his office, preparing himself to face whatever was about to happen.

Several men were already in his office.

"Who are you? What do you want?" he demanded.

"We've been sent by the Committee," the spokesperson answered.

The Soviet leader *knew* that there was no such committee. "What do you want?" he repeated.

"For you to support our cause," came the reply. "And for you to sign over all of your powers to Nikolai Ligachev."

"To hell with you and to hell with Nikolai Sergeyevich!"

"Oh, but you will support us. We will give you one last chance to sign these papers. If you refuse, military troops will be deployed and people will die," said the spokesperson.

The Soviet president stood mute. Inside he was trembling and praying, but his exterior showed a stubborn resolve.

"You fool! So be it," he said contemptuously.

"As we speak, the airport has been closed. You will not be able to return to Moscow. We have destroyed all of your communications gear and your security officer has been arrested. And the Soviet people are now under a strict curfew. Also, several war ships are blocking any possible escape route you might be considering by way of the Black Sea," he said with an air of superiority.

The Soviet leader looked disgusted. "You people make me sick. You amateurs are doomed to fail," he said defiantly, as he was escorted out of the room. He and his family were locked in their living quarters. He was made to be the prisoner while the real criminals were planning to destroy the country.

The next morning, the rest of the world was made aware of the events in the Crimea. Soviet radio gave a brief and incomplete account of what was happening: *Nikolai Ligachev has taken over the duties of the president of the Soviet Union in accordance with Article 127, Clause 7 of the Soviet Constitution.* This was all Soviet radio said to millions of stunned listeners. No mention was made of the Soviet president's whereabouts.

Soldiers loyal to the new Committee had been deployed into Moscow and various capitals throughout the republics. They confiscated the Soviet president's briefcase used to activate nuclear missiles.

The next day the Committee gave its first press conference. Nikolai Ligachev was the leader of the coup and was responsible for presenting their goals at this conference. He was trying to look authoritative and display a commanding presence but his heart was not in it. He was still troubled by the events with Konrad and Gunther. His colleagues in the coup, as well as the members of the Six, were disturbed by his disheartened performance.

"My fellow countrymen. Our committee has been established to head off national disaster. Our leader is simply too tired after these last few years to lead us into the future. It is our task to restore our country to greatness," he said, rather unconvincingly. He glanced nervously at his five comrades, all of whom looked disheveled, tired and in one case, very hung over.

Ligachev gave no valid reason why power should be turned over to the Committee, nor did he explain the whereabouts of the president. Nor did he explain what it was that they hoped to accomplish. Ligachev's speech left a befuddled nation even more puzzled. No one seemed able to give an adequate explanation for what was going on.

Back in the United States, Bismarck and Rommel met. Rommel had spent the last two days in high-level meetings with members of the administration and the Congress.

Rommel was furious. "What kind of coup is this!" he shouted. "What the hell is wrong with Charlemagne? He looks as if he's been drinking for days. The whole coup is a complete failure because they can't get their act together. The idiots!" yelled Rommel.

Bismarck was seething with anger. "Are they sleepwalking? I can't believe this! They take over the Telegraph Office but let cables get sent. They stopped the Soviet Press from broadcasting but let goddamn GNN continue to broadcast to the whole world. And these ignorant, sons of bitches come up with a name that makes Russians keel over with laughter. They named themselves the State Committee for the State of Emergency. In Russian that translates to, if you can believe it, the State Committee on Accidents."

"You've not heard the worst of it," Rommel said quietly, dreading Bismarck's response. "Word is that military command is back in the hands of the government. Several of Charlemagne's colleagues have quit and one has committed suicide. There are reports of riots across the country. It's total chaos. Charlemagne doesn't stand a chance. If he doesn't get out of there quickly, he'll die."

"It's a disaster," Bismarck said, placing his large hand over his face. Then he uncovered his face and sighed, "It will be over within twenty-four hours, if not sooner. But perhaps some good will come out of it."

"I don't see how," Rommel countered.

"Charlemagne and his group of stooges have failed miserably, but the Soviet Union will never be the same. You saw the people knock down the symbols of the Communist Party? Lenin—no less. He's no longer a god. The communist party is in shambles and Soviet ideology is waning. Despite Charlemagne's buffoonery, Russia is playing into our hands beautifully. There will be such confusion in the months to come we will be able to carry out our plans unabated, possibly more so than if the coup had been successful."

Rommel was not sharing Bismarck's optimism. "What now?" he said dryly.

"We can focus our efforts more here in the U.S. This will speed our plans up immeasurably," Bismarck said excitedly. He clapped his hands together and then slapped Rommel on the back.

✠　✠　✠

Charlemagne sat in his office in the Presidium of the Supreme Soviet within the Kremlin. The coup was over. Three of his colleagues had been arrested, two others had committed suicide. He knew that he would probably either be arrested or killed before sunrise, if not within the hour.

Ligachev called his driver who was, despite his twenty years in the Soviet Army, still a low ranking soldier. Anatoly Yakolev promptly entered the room.

"Anatoly," he said with warmth, "what is your opinion of what is happening?"

"I don't really know, sir. It's all a little bit over my head," said the driver, trying to take a safe position.

"I believe that you are too modest, Anatoly," Charlemagne said. He reached into his drawer and pulled out a gun with a silencer. He aimed it at his driver and pulled the trigger, firing two shots into his face. He hit the floor with a thud.

Charlemagne undressed and quickly donned the soldier's uniform. If anyone saw him up close, this masquerade would never work, he was much too old for an enlisted man, and the few specks of blood would be questioned. But perhaps in the darkness he could escape. He swiftly grabbed his long overcoat and left the room.

He exited the building by a door known only to several of the highest government officials. He gazed at the tallest of the five Kremlin towers with its stars in three-layer ruby glass and then walked briskly through the Kremlin. He would try to get to Leningrad, now called St. Petersburg, where he would then try to get to the West, perhaps Helsinki.

Ligachev walked into Red Square, passed the Spasskaya Tower and Lenin's tomb and turned onto Ilyinka Street, heading for the Metro station. The first streetcar of the day pulled up seconds later and he took it to the Leningradsky Station, one of several railway stations in the city. Pulling his coat up as high as it would go, he purchased a ticket to Leningrad and hopped on the train. The new day was just beginning.

As the train pulled out of the station, he reflected on the past few weeks. He had sentenced his sons to death and now had failed his duties to the Six. Would he still be welcomed by the others? He couldn't think clearly. What had happened to his life?

He stared out the window, afraid of being recognized from the disastrous press conference he'd given a few days before. Charlemagne tried to cover his face by pulling his hat forward and placing a hand up. The compartment was crowded with people who were all talking excitedly about the failed coup. Finally, he buried his face with his hat and pretended to sleep.

When the train arrived in Leningrad, Charlemagne was one of the last to get off. He wasn't sure where he would go or what he would do. He played over in his mind a thousand times the disastrous plot and its humiliating collapse that the whole world had seen. But there were really only five men whose opinions he valued. He cringed at the thought of them cursing him or calling him a fool.

Amidst all the thoughts of the coup, there was the numbing pain of what would happen to Gunther and Konrad. He was lost in his thoughts, moving along the darkened streets of Leningrad, surrounded by fog. Suddenly, out of an alley in front of a butcher store, three youths jumped in front of him, surrounding him.

They started shouting at him in an unfamiliar Russian dialect and making menacing moves. Then the tallest one, a long-haired man of about nineteen, pulled out a knife, terrifying Ligachev.

"I don't speak Russian," he lied in German, trying to keep his identity secret.

"Ah, Deutscherer! A German. Heil Hitler!" mocked the young man with the knife.

"Please don't hurt me," he begged.

"We don't want to harm you, old man, unless you don't cooperate," spoke the oldest-looking one, in German. "Just give us all of your money."

He had always made it a habit to never carry money on the street, but tonight he was carrying a large bundle of cash. He wasn't exactly sure how much it was, but it had been his escape money.

He was too old and tired to fight them. He knew he had no choice as he slowly reached for his wallet. He reluctantly handed it to them.

"Oh, look at all the pretty money, comrades. We are rich!" he shouted and raised the money in the air for his partners to see.

"Well, well, the old German lives the good life, doesn't he? This is what we call redistribution of wealth. Communism at its best, don't you think?" carped the one with the knife.

Ligachev began to relax. They seemed to be happy with the money. Why would they want to harass an old man who just made them rich?

"Remember how I said that if you cooperated, we would not harm you?" asked the one with the knife.

"Yes," Ligachev whispered.

"Well, I was lying." Taking the six-inch blade, he stuck it into Ligachev's chest and pulled it out. Charlemagne gasped and began choking on blood. He grabbed his chest and fell to his knees.

The thieves ran off laughing and bragging about their success. They left Nikolai Ligachev to die in a darkened Leningrad alley.

He was bleeding profusely and tried to call out but couldn't. With all of his remaining strength, and leaving a trail of blood, he crawled out of the alley and onto the main street, hoping to be seen by a passerby. The pain was excruciating and by the time he reached the cold cement, he collapsed.

A couple of men passing by just minutes later discovered the body of the unconscious old man.

"Look, there's a man," the first yelled.

"Is he dead?" the other demanded.

"I don't know, you fool. You call an ambulance and I'll stay here with him." The younger man took off running while the other man stayed with Charlemagne. Charlemagne had suffered a tremendous amount of blood loss and the Good Samaritan prayed that if this old man was to die, that God would take him peacefully.

✠ ✠ ✠

Michael couldn't concentrate on anything after the conversation with his old buddy from the DEA. Was he actually going to propose a covert mission into some godforsaken South American ranch to kidnap a drug lord? Michael was certain that he must have misunderstood Nate.

He was burning with rage. If he could face the person responsible for TJ's overdose he would kill him with his bare hands. It wouldn't be the first time. While in Vietnam, he had been forced to kill in hand-to-hand combat along the Mekong Delta.

That incident had given Michael nightmares for years, but with counseling he had worked through it. Thinking about it now, he vividly recalled the wet paddies, the deep ditches, the steep-sided and booby-trapped dikes, and the searing heat. The eighty inches of annual rainfall had made the delta a living hell. He remembered the young Vietnamese whose head he had crushed with a rock.

Get a grip, Madigan, he told himself. He stood up to stretch, as if this would exorcise those painful memories. But he was a soldier then. As much as he regretted taking a life in such a manner, he didn't feel guilt or remorse, just sadness. It was the only thing to do under those circumstances. But it was different now. He was a member of Congress.

Michael remembered Johnny Green. What was he going to do with him? As was often the case, he had shot from the hip and hadn't fully considered the details. What was he going to do with this gang leader?

He would deal with Green later. He rushed to get all of the pressing items through before lunch, make a few phone calls, and meet with his staff to set his itinerary. Michael finally finished his last phone call shortly after noon.

There was just enough time to run over to Alfredo's to meet Nate. Even with his reservations, he found himself filled with anticipation.

They arrived simultaneously and Nate grabbed him in a bear hug. "Michael, old buddy, how the hell are you? It's been, what, three years?"

"Something like that. It's great to see you, Nate."

"I always knew that you wouldn't be satisfied with the boring life of a professor," Nate said, slapping Michael on the back. Nate was wearing a stylish suit with a cowboy hat. His thick, dark curly hair showed in wisps from beneath the hat. A familiar gold-toothed grin flashed at Michael.

Michael felt as if he had just been transported back to when they used to be a team. The feeling was reassuring. "Well, believe it or not," Michael started to explain, as the waitress escorted them to a corner table. "I was really looking forward to the academic life. The day that I retired from the service, I had no political aspirations. Things just started getting crazy...I felt obligated. I guess you heard about Rebecca."

"No, but my wife Christine told me that she had heard something."

"We just got back together about a week ago. When I announced that I was going to run for Congress, she went ballistic and filed for divorce." Michael still had trouble saying that word.

"You can't be serious? I thought that you two were, to be perfectly candid here, disgustingly devoted to each other. I can't picture it, Mike. But you're back together now?"

"Yeah, and I have to tell you Nate that if she hadn't come back, I might have given up my seat before I served a day," Michael confessed. "She came back at the absolute lowest point in my life. One of my chief aides was almost murdered and it was only one of a whole series of tragedies that's happened this past year. The morning I was to be sworn in, I had a hangover after drinking myself into a near coma. And who shows up at the door?"

"Rebecca."

"You guessed it. God must have known I couldn't take anymore," Michael said honestly.

"Well, I'm glad to hear that everything worked out. You've been through the ringer lately, what with your dad, TJ, Judy Solomon, the defective parachute, the temple explosion, the hijacking, and anything else you can think of. Did I miss anything? You're a regular advertisement for the six o'clock news."

"It's really been a crazy year," Michael acknowledged, but then quickly became focused. "Let's talk turkey. What exactly were you trying to tell me this morning?"

"This is from the heart, Mike," started Nate. "I took what happened to TJ very hard. I considered her a member of the family. I began snooping and ingratiated myself with the local cops and the FBI. I soon found myself a full member of the investigation."

"What did you find out?"

"We found that TJ was at a party and didn't even know that she was taking cocaine. Apparently, it was slipped to her by someone else," Nate explained.

"Don't tell me it was her boyfriend Todd or I'll break every bone in his body," Michael said, his blood pressure beginning to rise.

"Calm down, Mike. It wasn't him," Nate assured. "There was an older kid there that night trying to turn people on. He sold some stuff, gave some away and slipped some to others. His name is Kenny Livingston and he's currently doing six months for violation of parole."

"Why would anybody do that? Is it just sadism, or what?" Michael asked, struggling to hold his rage.

"No, Mike, at least not completely," Nate said, trying to keep Michael from losing control. "Pushers think that if everybody would just try the stuff, that they'll like it and be a future buyer. He gives them a freebie or slips one in a drink and hopes to find himself a convert."

"That's positively sick!" Michael exclaimed. "Where did this Livingston get it from?"

"Exactly what I wanted to know. He was just a small link in the chain. He steered us toward a pretty big dealer in New York by the name of Jesse Conrad," Nate replied. "Conrad has some connections in Colombia. We traced him to Jorge Ramirez, one of the kingpins in Colombia. He's been almost impossible to find but lately he's become very visible. Either he's getting lazy or planning some huge operation because we know every step he's been taking lately. I could tell you the next time he takes a crap."

"Spare me, please. What's the bottom line?"

"I propose we bring him back to the U.S. for trial," Nate said bluntly. "The Supreme Court says it's cool, he's involved in something huge, we know where he is and he's been getting a little sloppy lately. And besides, he's the cause of what happened to TJ." He let this last statement sink in for a few seconds.

"Now, Michael, I don't think you'll say I'm out of bounds about proposing this," Nate speculated, "but the thing that might be the sticking point is your involvement in the operation. Now before you give me your 'I'm a sitting U.S. Congressman' speech, let me just say that the only reason I'm proposing this is because you're the best, Mike. I've already assembled a team of four, and myself, but we need one more. And I think that you could help us carry this crazy thing out," Nate said with reverence.

"Nate, I'd be lying if I said that I wasn't interested. You know that I always got off on covert missions. But let's get real here for a minute,"

Michael said, assessing the scope of Nate's proposal. "If we failed, it could have broad-sweeping ramifications. All family and personal concerns aside, if word got out about a secret mission headed by a renegade congressman, it would be a great embarrassment for the U.S. government and could affect our foreign policy for years to come."

"I don't agree with you there," Nate said, shaking his head. "Covert missions are a fact of life, although you're always going to have your bleeding hearts crying about due process or some horse shit like that. The world's still a dangerous place and the military and intelligence agencies serve a necessary function. If the word got out about this mission, the country wouldn't automatically have a fit. O.K?"

"I'll buy that," Michael agreed.

"I know that we'll be successful because I've planned it to the most minuscule detail. But even if we didn't succeed, it wouldn't necessarily be a failure. You've been on a dozen aborted missions so you know what I'm saying."

"So, would your presence mean the world as we know it coming to an end?" Nate concluded.

"Nate, don't get melodramatic on me. I know that the world doesn't revolve around me, but I don't think it would do a lot to advance my career," Michael said skeptically.

"First of all, Mike, I think the man on the street would be entirely supportive," Nate predicted. "In fact, I think that you'd be seen as a hero. The public has this mental image of Congress as a bunch of do-nothings who go on junkets and write bad checks. Just think of what would happen if word got out that there are really guys in Congress who do something more than sit on their ass waiting for their pension."

"I don't know, Nate, although I have to admit it sounds very intriguing. But Good Lord, I might have the shortest career in history," Michael said with uncertainty.

"You never seemed like the type who played it safe, thinking of only his advancement," Nate said. "And besides, if you're not going to do it now, you never will later. You'll become fat and lazy. Pretty soon the most exciting thing you'll do is give a speech to the local Rotary club. Now's the time, Mike. Promise me you'll at least think about it. If you want to come over to my office, I can fill you in on the details."

"I'll think about it," Michael said hesitantly.

"That's my boy. Hey, did you hear about Swanson?"

"No, what happened?"

"Well, apparently on his way home from work last night, he flew off the side of the road and bought the farm big time," Nate said indifferently.

"Oh, my God, that's awful," exclaimed Michael. "Does anyone know what caused it?"

"Well, the rumor mill has it that it was sabotage through and through. Brake line cut clean, I hear."

Michael shook his head. Was it ever going to stop?

he meeting with the president was scheduled for 10:00 A.M. The participants were the chairman of the joint chiefs of staff, General Ronald T. Lund; the secretary of state, Christopher Watkins; Matt Connors, filling in for his absent boss, Davis P. Elliot; and several congressional leaders, including Peter Volhard. Also present was the president's chief of staff, the hated Phillip Gordon.

President Andrew Tolbert walked into the Oval Office, after everyone had been assembled and the meeting immediately commenced. He was the only one not in a suit, wearing a yellow sweater and blue jeans that complemented his blond hair and blue eyes.

"Well, boys, you all know what we're here for," the president began, his voice hoarse. "I want to know what happened to Don Swanson and who's responsible, or if it was just some horrible accident. Because of what's happening in the USSR, we have to move quickly. Phil, I want you to prepare a list of candidates and begin the selection process," he directed his chief of staff.

"Yes, sir," Gordon answered, chewing on his pencil.

"Matt, you were the last person that he met with. Did he give you any indications about anything unusual going on? Did he mention any threats? And, if you don't mind me asking, just why were you meeting with him at such a late hour?" the president asked.

Matt felt all eyes on him. He had nothing to be nervous about but still there was something unsettling about the way the question was phrased.

"Mr. President, I requested the meeting about a certain theory I've developed," Matt explained. "I'd prefer for the time being not to discuss what we had talked about. There are a lot of holes in it and I'd hate to raise eyebrows over something that's potentially half-baked. As a matter-of-fact, Swanson thought it was crazy and basically threw me out of his office," said Matt.

"Well, Matt, I hope I didn't imply that I considered you a possible suspect," said the president diplomatically. "And if you don't want to talk about your discussion with Swanson, I'll accept that for the time being. But if things start getting crazier, you'll have to spill the beans. Fair enough?"

"Yes, sir."

"What I was trying to get at," the president continued, "was did anything seem wrong?"

"He never conveyed that to me," Matt said. "Our meeting was real short. I started to tell him this theory of mine and before I could get too far, he threw me out on my ass. He said he'd promised his wife that he'd be home at a decent hour."

"O.K., anybody else have any theories on whether this was a murder or just a freak accident?" asked the president.

No one answered for a few moments. General Lund broke the silence. The silver-haired military man pushed back in his chair.

"Sir, I don't have any evidence to back it up but my gut tells me that this was no accident. Someone's responsible and I'm convinced that we'll find out if we keep digging."

Volhard interjected. "No offense, General Lund, but I think that it's counterproductive to speculate on something that's not supported by evidence. It accomplishes nothing to start out with a premise that may not be true. We can only make decisions based on the information we have. As of right now, it appears that this was a horrible accident. If we find to the contrary, fine. But for right now, the temptation to find an enemy lurking or a conspirator conspiring without any supporting evidence is the height of paranoia," Volhard said forcefully.

Lund appeared offended. "I wasn't saying that we should go off on a wild-goose-chase. It's just that we have to consider all possibilities and not rule anything out."

The president tried to calm the waters. "I agree with both of you. We can't allow ourselves to get wrapped around the axle looking for a bad guy where there is none. But we also can't rule it out. I want to know the cause of Don Swanson's death," he ordered.

The president went on. "Obviously, we're not going to solve this here today. Let's move on. Any recommendations for a replacement? I want to move quickly on this."

General Lund spoke up. "Time is of the essence. For that reason, I propose that we bump up Ashworth."

This suggestion caused several heads in the room to simultaneously shake, including the president's.

"Sorry, General, I don't agree," said the president. "Ted Ashworth is one brilliant guy but the man's a policy nerd. He doesn't have a leadership bone in his body. Gentlemen, all cabinet positions, particularly defense, must go to men with some guts. Leadership is what counts. Technical expertise must be secondary."

Secretary of State Watkins interjected. "I agree that we should, for time considerations, promote from within. But I concur with the president that Ashworth is not the man. I suggest that we nominate Elliot and move Matt here into the national security adviser position."

Matt looked stunned and despite his ambitions, had never actually considered the possibility of being the president's chief adviser on national security issues.

The president nodded. "Davis is sometimes a pompous ass but I could accept that. And Matt could fill Elliot's shoes here very capably."

Matt suddenly began feeling very warm. Before anyone could respond, Tolbert's secretary walked in.

"Excuse me, gentlemen. I'm sorry but there's a very urgent call for Mr. Connors. The caller said it's an emergency," said the secretary nervously. Matt excused himself and left the room. Who could be calling?

The meeting continued as the speaker of the house commented again. His eloquence and persuasiveness commanded their complete attention.

"With all due respect, Mr. President, I think nominating Davis Elliot would be a huge mistake. I hate to attack a man who's not here to defend himself, but he's more than a pompous ass. He's downright insufferable and I think that he would soon be out of control."

"Peter, you definitely have a point there. Davis can be a prick sometimes, can't he? You got anybody in mind?" the president asked.

"As a matter-of-fact, I do," replied the speaker. "Now, I know the sentiment here is to promote from within for time reasons. But it would be much better to have the right person. With the collapse of the Soviets, there's no critical reason to blindly rush in with a less than qualified candidate."

Watkins was clearly anxious. "Well, come on Mr. Speaker. Enlighten us, for God's sake."

"Karl Schmidt," came the immediate answer. "Mr. President, he's been in the weapons business for forty years. He knows the principles in almost every country in the world, allied as well as enemy. He's currently doing a tremendous job in Moscow overseeing the destruction of their ICBM's. He's tough as nails, is a great negotiator, thoroughly knowledgeable, and can definitely make things happen. I think that he would be an excellent choice."

No one had even considered Schmidt but it made sense. All eyes looked to the president.

"I have to admit that he wasn't on my top-ten list, Peter," said the president "but now that you mention it, I've always been very impressed with Mr. Schmidt as someone who could get things done. He always struck me as a man who wasn't afraid to get his hands dirty. What do the rest of you think?" Tolbert asked his advisers.

Phil Gordon, the quintessential imperial chief of staff that all of Washington was afraid of, spoke up.

"Mr. President, I've met with Mr. Schmidt on several occasions and he's definitely a can-do personality. He could be just what we're looking for."

Several others shook their heads in agreement.

The president looked at Gordon. "Phil, get on this right away. I want every bit of information available on Schmidt and get him back here from Moscow for a meeting. Peter, why don't you give him a call and see if he's interested."

"Glad to do it," smiled the speaker of the house. "I think that he'd be an excellent choice."

Matt Connors retreated to his office after leaving the meeting to find that the mysterious Sgt. Pepper was on the line. This was the first time that she had ever called him at his office.

"Matt Connors here. What's up?"

"Listen, I have some information on one of our former SS boys. The Russian one," said the mysterious informant.

"What about him? If you're going to tell me that he was involved in the Soviet coup, I already know it," Matt said with obvious irritation.

"Well, I don't believe you know that he apparently was attacked in Leningrad by some street thugs. No reason to think that it was anything other than a robbery. They got a good chunk of change from what I hear."

"Mugged in Leningrad? What the hell was he doing there?" said a puzzled Connors. "What's his condition?"

"He's in a hospital. I have the location and name. He's in pretty bad shape and might not survive the night. If you want to talk to him, you'd better do it quickly."

Connors began mulling in his mind about how he was going to explain a sudden trip to Leningrad. But there wasn't time. Elliot was currently in Jerusalem and wasn't due back until the day after tomorrow. And he couldn't go to the president. He would just have to go and accept the consequences. If his theory was half-baked, he'd have some fast-talking to do. If it was on target, his bosses would damn well be interested in what he would have to say.

"Where is he?"

"I can't do it over the phone. Get a pen," the informant directed. "Meet me in the Library of Congress. Find the nonfiction shelves and the following book: 943.086 SNU. Got that?"

"Yeah, I got it. I'll be there in half an hour," Matt replied, and he heard a click on the other end.

It was now 11:00 A.M. He picked up the phone and directed his chief assistant to make the necessary arrangements. After he met with Sgt. Pepper, he was going to Leningrad.

Matt quickly got a few things together that he would need on his hastily scheduled trip and headed for the Library of Congress, which was located on First Street between East Capitol and Independence Avenue.

He arrived within minutes and gazed intently at the wildly decorated lampposts and the powerful Neptune fountain with nude women astride horse fish. He took the steps above the fountain two at a time and felt the stare of the stone faces above him that seemed to be watching his every move.

He had been here dozens of times but was still awed with each visit. He bolted in through the revolving doors on the ground floor and quickly grabbed the elevator at the rear of the lobby. He rode it to the vistor's gallery, which was far above the highlight of the structure, the massive eight-sided expanse of the Main Reading Room.

Matt gazed down at the hundreds of readers below him, looking far away, as they paced or sat at one of the five concentric rings of dark old desks. Looking up at the 160-foot-high domed ceiling with its murals that chronicled the progress of civilization, he took a deep breath.

The heart and soul of the library was its miles and miles of stacks, usually only penetrable with a guide. But he had been here numerous times before, doing research on a variety of topics. Matt felt that he could find the book that his mysterious informant had specified. But even with his knowledge of the library, it wouldn't be easy. Almost 100 million pieces were stored here and to find a single book would be a monumental task. But he could not call attention to himself.

After almost giving up in frustration, he found the row of books and walked slowly, looking intently for the Dewey Decimal number that he had been given. He saw that the surrounding numbers all covered subjects about Germany and he finally zeroed in on the call number he was searching for.

He pulled a dusty book off the shelf entitled "History of the Waffen SS." On the cover was the image of an SS officer staring with cold and penetrating eyes. He opened it up and began to read. He became totally absorbed as he scanned the pages. SS stood for Schutzstaffel, or Protective Squad. They were initially supposed to act as Hitler's personal bodyguards, but their function expanded greatly over the years into more sinister areas.

Matt felt a shiver up his spine as he gazed at pictures of some of this elite corps, decked out in black caps, black ties, black-bordered armbands and black breeches. He read that only "selected personnel" could apply. Applicants had to meet Himmler's genetic prerequisites.

Lost in fascination and revulsion, Matt was startled by a voice that came from the other side of the stack.

"Mr. Connors?" asked the soft female voice.

"Yes. Sgt. Pepper?" Matt responded, as he tried in vain to catch a glimpse of her through the crack where the book used to be. But he couldn't see her face.

"Yes. I think that you should check out this book, Mr. Connors. You might learn a lot about who you're dealing with."

"What do you have on our favorite coup leader?" he inquired, feeling foolish talking through a stack of books.

"The name of the hospital is in the book you have in your hands. You must speak to this man. If he survives, I believe that he will talk. He's grown very despondent recently and may not wish to continue fighting. He may tell you what you want to know," she predicted.

Matt shook his head. "All you've told me is some nonsense about the Germans. What about them?"

"It's the Fourth Reich. Former Nazis are still alive and their plan is to take up where Hitler left off. They must be stopped."

Matt was puzzled. "Why all of this 'Deep Throat' crap? Why can't we just talk like normal people. If what you're saying is true, then the president has to be informed."

"No, not yet," she said emphatically. "This must remain a black operation for a while more. We need more information. You're the connection, Mr. Connors."

"What do you mean I'm the connection? To what?" he said, raising his voice. "Listen, I'm going to walk over to the other side of these books and you're going to tell me what this is all about." He then proceeded to do just that, but she was gone. What was going on? He was the connection? To the Germans? What did that mean?

He looked at his watch. It was time to get to the airport for his hastily planned trip to Russia. He walked briskly along the stacks, lost in thought. Suddenly he became aware of footsteps. He stopped and listened.

Someone was on the other side of the tall rows of books. Was it Sgt. Pepper, a library employee or a reader? He didn't know and now, didn't care. He shrugged his shoulders and continued walking.

All at once, he saw a man in front of him who had just rounded the corner of books. The unknown man assumed a stance, reached into his jacket and pulled out a gun. He then aimed it at Matt and pulled the trigger.

After a split second of paralyzing astonishment, Matt managed to dive around another corner of books, just missing being hit. His heart was pounding so hard he thought it would explode.

The initial shock over, he was now thinking clearly. He raced as fast as he could through the endless web of books. Looking over his shoulder, he saw the assailant again, who let another bullet fly, this one catching his jacket and actually nicking his arm. But it had just grazed him.

Matt sprinted as fast as a man with only one real leg could and finally reached the visitor's gallery. He felt solace in being surrounded by other people and let out a sigh of relief. But still he ran, glancing over his shoulder for his would-be murderer.

Racing around the octagon-shaped room, he encountered a heavyset library worker who was coming out of one of many cubicles pushing a cart of books. Matt didn't see her in time and he flattened the unsuspecting woman. The violent collision sent books flying in all directions.

Matt was sprawled on the floor, dazed and shaken, and after several seconds, pulled himself up. He started to help the equally stunned employee, but froze as he saw his assailant about ten feet away. The man again pulled a gun from his jacket and aimed it at Matt.

"Good-bye, Mr. Connors," said the sinister voice. Matt closed his eyes and prepared for his death. He heard the loud sound of a gunshot, quite distinct from the quiet pop the other two rounds had made. He heard screams but seemed puzzled that he didn't feel anything. He opened his eyes.

The unknown assailant had blood dripping from his mouth. He had dropped his gun to the ground and was slumping against the railing. Horrified employees and visitors watched the bizarre events unfold. Matt spotted out of the corner of his eye a woman on the other side of the room with a gun. It must be Sgt. Pepper! She had shot his attacker. But she quickly disappeared out a side door.

The momentum of the two bullets had pushed the man onto the railing, where he dangled for a moment before finally falling over it completely. Matt watched in astonishment as the man plummeted towards the terrified readers below, who were scurrying from their desks like panicked rats.

The shot man somersaulted in midair and landed on the outer ring of desks. The violent crash broke his neck. Matt looked at the havoc below.

He didn't have time to get involved in this now. He quickly put his arm in front of his face to prevent anyone from identifying him and headed out a side door. Matt walked as fast as he could and would not learn until much later that the name of his assailant was Alan Roberts.

Matt decided that the details of this attack would have to wait. His prime objective now was to head to Russia and talk to Nikolai Ligachev before the failed coup leader died.

✠   ✠   ✠

Rebecca groaned as she realized how much more work was involved in fixing up their new home in Virginia. She had been working for two days and had barely made a dent.

She still couldn't believe that she was back in the fishbowl life she had sworn to leave behind. But she felt great pride in Michael's accomplishments and actually had convinced herself that maybe, just maybe, he was right.

Washington was really a beautiful city, she admitted to herself, and their new home was everything she had dreamed of in a house. Two-stories, with a huge backyard, four bedrooms, a large patio that would be great for entertaining and, much to Michael's liking, a basketball hoop in the driveway. She could remember the early days of their marriage when he would play basketball on summer evenings until dark with Matt Connors and some other friends. Michael had always been a frustrated jock.

Rebecca was preparing for a dinner party that night with some new friends. This would be the first party since she and Michael had got back together. She was excited and nervous, eagerly anticipating the evening while simultaneously dreading it. Maybe they needed more time to renew their relationship. But Michael had seemed pleased when she suggested it.

Their guests for the evening would be Sterling and Linda Shannon. Rebecca had just met the Shannons and instantly hit it off with Linda, a very outgoing and vivacious reporter with the Washington bureau of GNN. How they met was part of a surprise that she wanted to spring on Michael at dinner. Sterling Shannon was a senior partner with a large D.C. law firm: Bracken, Seagrave, Shannon and Randel. He was very connected politically and was one of the finest trial lawyers in the country.

Josh had promised to come over and help his mother, but he was late, as usual. He finally pulled up in his 1957 Chevy accompanied by Kelly. He bounded up the walkway, Kelly in tow, rapped twice on the screen door, and then walked in before anyone could respond.

"Mom, I'm here. Anyone home?"

"Over here," came the response from an out-of-breath Rebecca. She was panting, trying to move a couch into a certain position in the living room.

"Hi, Mrs. M.," gushed Kelly. "The house looks beautiful."

"That's very nice of you to say, even though there's not an ounce of truth to it," Rebecca responded, clearly pleased. "I can't believe that I'm giving a dinner party tonight. This place looks like it's been condemned by the Department of Health."

"No way. It's not that bad," replied Josh. "The Kellster and I'll help and it'll look bitchin' in nothing flat."

"Josh, please watch your language," admonished his mother. "The Kellster?"

"Yeah, you know, the Kellmeister—my squeeze."

"For heaven's sakes, the way you kids talk today it's amazing that anyone knows what you're talking about," Rebecca said, shaking her head and smiling.

"Right, like your generation never used any slang. Groovy man, far out. Can you say groovy in a sentence and keep a straight face?" Josh teased.

"How am I supposed to get ready tonight if I'm spending all my time jabbering with you? Let's get going," Rebecca instructed.

"Where's TJ and David?" asked Josh, who was starting to move boxes out of the dining room.

"They're both with Grandma Katarina."

"How's TJ doing?" asked Kelly.

"She's improving greatly. I thought the move would be very disruptive but it didn't seem to faze her a bit."

"That's fantastic," answered Kelly.

Josh ended up hauling boxes while the two women arranged things and moved things around. Rebecca and Kelly talked all the while and began to develop a real rapport.

"Mrs. Madigan, I heard that Colonel Madigan has dreams about Nazi Germany. Do you know why?" asked Kelly.

"How do you know that?" asked Rebecca.

Think quick, Kelly, she told herself. "Well, Josh told me. You know, they lived together for many months and got pretty close," she blurted out quickly.

"Of course," Rebecca replied, nodding her head. "Michael's been having these dreams for about two years now. I don't know what triggered them and neither does he. His father died after he started having those nightmares. They really scare him and he wakes up sometimes literally shaking and sweating buckets."

"What does he dream about specifically?"

"One time he was a Nazi working at a concentration camp where he killed his father. Another time, he was told that he had to choose which one of his three children would live while the other two died. Horrible things like that," Rebecca said.

"Good Lord. Those must be terrible! I hope they stop soon. The Colonel's an awfully good man."

"Thanks Kelly, that's sweet of you." Rebecca said fondly.

"Mrs. Madigan, may I use your rest room?"

"Of course, Kelly. There's one down the hall and one upstairs. Take your pick."

Kelly walked slowly up the stairs and glanced downward when she reached the top. Everyone was busy but she had to move quickly.

She stepped quietly into the master bedroom and tiptoed up to a bureau by the side of the bed. She reached into her purse and pulled out a small bugging device and placed it on the back side of the bureau. She then placed another device underneath the bed. She double-checked both to make sure they were secure and out of sight, and then walked silently out of the room. In all, it had taken less than thirty seconds.

✠   ✠   ✠

Michael returned from his lunch with Nate Wallace very preoccupied. But he remembered that he had brought an LA gang leader with him to Washington. He buzzed Darrell and directed him to send Johnny into his office right away.

Despite fundamental differences, Darrell was very impressed with Johnny. He was clearly no one's fool and had a good head on his shoulders. Too bad, Darrell thought, that his energies had been channeled in such a negative way. Maybe they could do something about that.

Johnny walked into Michael's office and Michael could see that he had changed since their fight on the LA streets. The "attitude" was gone and so was the street jargon and dialect.

"I have to tell you, Mr. Madigan, that I don't quite know what to make of all this. Johnson here's been showing me around all morning and gave me a brief history of how the government works. On the street, no one has a clue. You dig?"

"I know what you mean, Johnny. But this is where the rubber meets the road. The decisions that are made in this building affect 250 million people. Pretty heavy, huh?"

"I guess so. But I still don't believe that all these marble statues and high-sounding documents apply to the 'hood,'" the gang leader remarked. "We still got nothing to hope for, no future to dream of, and the police still mess with us. So, why don't we do whatever it is we're going to do and let me get my black ass back to L.A."

"Sit down, Johnny. I want you to listen closely," Michael directed. "There's a civil rights bill in Congress right now that the administration is pushing. I don't think it goes far enough. The Judiciary Committee is discussing it and I want you to say a few words. I want it straight from the gut. Don't sugarcoat it. I want you to tell the committee what it's really like to be poor and black in America and why young men like you join gangs," Michael requested.

"You want me to give a speech to all you congressmen? What you been smoking?" mocked Johnny.

"I'm dead serious, Johnny. This country is the best in the world but we got some problems," Michael pointed out. "One of them is racism. We've got a quarter of a billion people here, 100 different ethnic groups. We've got to get along. We can't keep on fighting or pretty soon there will be nothing to fight for. People are bigoted not because of something in their blood but because of ignorance, and fear. Did you ever notice that kids of different races get along? It's not until later that they develop prejudices," Michael said passionately.

"You're right," Johnny admitted.

"Let me ask you a question. Do you ever want to have a son?" Michael asked.

"Yeah," said Johnny.

"Do you want him to be in a gang?"

"Hell, no. We don't plan to be in gangs, it just happens. There's nothing else. For many guys, they have no other family. The gang's their family."

"Then let me challenge you. Tell these out-of-touch congressmen to get off their fat asses and do something. Tell them that if they don't, what happened in L.A. will happen in every major city in America. Will you do it, Johnny?"

"Yeah, I'll do it, Mr. Madigan," Johnny said reflectively, amazed by his own words. "But do you think they'll listen to me? Or will everyone laugh?"

"They'll listen to you, Johnny. And no one is going to laugh," Michael pledged, hoping he was right.

Matt arrived in Leningrad alone and immediately checked into a hotel. He was flying as a private citizen and not as a high-ranking government official. He was amazed at the chaos he saw as a result of the attempted coup. Nobody knew if they were coming or going.

He arrived at the hospital and told the admissions clerk, in passable Russian, that he was an old friend of the patient in room 343 and that he must see him immediately.

"I'm afraid that is not possible, sir. He has only been out of surgery for a few hours and I'm afraid that he is very weak. He may not make it," the woman said.

"All the more reason that I talk to him," Matt said excitedly. He decided to gamble.

"I'm a high-ranking member of the U.S. government," Matt said. "It's imperative that I speak to him immediately. It could be the difference between peace and World War III. I can't put it any more bluntly than that. I beg of you," he pleaded.

The nurse was clearly uncertain. After several moments of hesitation, she decided to take a chance on this distinguished-looking black United States official. If he was telling the truth, nothing could be more important.

"I'll let you see him but only for a few minutes. It could mean my job. And I have two children to feed."

"Bless you, nurse."

"Follow me. Quickly," she ordered.

They took the stairs to the third floor and headed to room 343, where Ligachev was lying, with tubes protruding from different parts of his body. He certainly didn't look like someone who could conquer the world.

"I'll give him a stimulant to awaken him," said the nurse. "He'll be coherent for only a few minutes."

She gave him a shot in the right arm and within seconds, he opened his eyes.

"Where am I?" asked the disoriented old man.

"You were attacked by some hooligans and robbed of your money," the nurse replied. "You were badly hurt and are now in a hospital."

"Am I going to live?"

"I believe so. But there's a man here with the U.S. government who says he absolutely must talk to you. Let me know if you are too weak."

The old and frail patient looked at Matt puzzled. "What do you want to know?"

"Are you Nikolai Ligachev and is that your real name?"

He hesitated and gasped in pain before answering. "I've sworn never to reveal this but I will tell you. I am Ligachev but my real name is Wolfgang Weber."

"Were you a member of the SS during the war?"

"Yes, but for the last forty years I've been a Soviet officer," he answered, coughing loudly.

"Are you involved in an organization now that is made up of former members of the SS?"

Ligachev didn't answer for several minutes. Matt repeated the question. Finally, he nodded affirmatively.

"What's the purpose of this group? And how many members are there? And was the coup tied to this group?"

Ligachev began to fade. Matt shook him hard. "You must tell me!" he shouted.

The nurse was clearly angered by this interrogation, her face turned red and her jowls tensed. "You must stop. Can't you see he's dying?"

Matt paid her no mind. "Answer my question. What is the purpose of this group?"

Ligachev struggled to get the words out. "Our purpose is to restore Germany to a major world power."

"How is that to be accomplished? How, damn it?" Matt was getting frustrated.

"By force," whispered Ligachev.

"Who are the members of this group, besides yourself?"

There wasn't much strength left in the old man. "We are known as the Six and are named for great German historical figures. I am Charlemagne..." His voice started to trail.

"Who are the others? The Americans first."

"Rommel and Bismarck," he whispered.

"What are their real names?" he demanded.

Wolfgang Weber passed out again. Matt prayed that he had not pushed the old man too much. Dear God, let him live, he said to himself. For the sake of the world, let him live.

Matt groaned at how close he had come. This dying man had confirmed his worst fears. Sgt. Pepper was right. There was an organized group of former SS officers in existence. What were they plotting? How could any small group take over the world? He put his face to his hands in frustration and looked at the elderly German man lying beside him.

Matt noticed a note pad on the table beside the bed. It was a letter, in a shaky handwriting, written in German. Matt called upon his college German courses as he attempted to read the letter:

Dear Konrad,

I've had a most unfortunate accident and am not sure if I'll survive. I'm not a young man anymore and do not have much strength. I will make this short.

I've been lying in this hospital bed and have thought much about the plans of the Six that have been so much a part of who I have been for over forty years. This was more important to me, I am sorry to say, than my family. I now regret that I wasn't a better father and a better husband to your mother.

Unfortunately, it's too late to do anything. My actions have resulted in the death of your only brother, my oldest son, and I've condemned you to a life that's contemptible. I have very likely placed your life in jeopardy as well. What a foolish old man I am. And because of that ridiculous coup, now the whole world knows.

Years ago, our plan sounded so right, so noble. But what's the point now? Is it really worth the death of millions? Is that what we really want? I always thought the answer to that question was yes. But I have now changed my mind.

Konrad, you must stop them. I'm very tired now and will try to continue this letter after I get some rest. I'll give you details and pray that you can stop the madness.

Always your father,

Wolfgang Weber

Matt's mind was racing to take in the words of the letter. This was written to his son, who knew about the Six and apparently had mixed feelings. He must get to him immediately. He would have to find Konrad. The letter talked about the deaths of millions. What kind of madness? They must have nuclear weapons. Good God, Matt thought. He must find Konrad.

✠ ✠ ✠

Karl was reading an English newspaper about the coup when the phone rang. He wasn't expecting a call and immediately became cautious.

"Schmidt here."

"Karl, Peter Volhard. How are you, my friend?"

"I'm fine although I cannot say the same for the Soviet Union and our esteemed Herr Ligachev. How goes it in the U.S. Congress, Mr. Speaker?" asked Karl, who had returned to Moscow.

"Things are progressing excellently. I think that you were right about this coup not affecting us much. I have some big news for you. This could be a major step in executing our plan. I think I have convinced the president to name you the next secretary of defense."

Karl was stunned. It had been the ideal plan but he was shocked that it might actually happen. "Are you serious, Peter?"

"Very serious. The president wants to meet with you tomorrow. Do you think that you could spare a few hours?"

"Tomorrow? We have a very busy day scheduled but I'll rearrange things. But if he actually appoints me, I must insist on some time to finish up here. We're very close."

"Karl, I'm afraid that I disagree with you," Volhard said firmly. "If you get the position, we'll probably have to abort your mission. Too risky. Combined with the chaos from the coup fiasco, I think that we should put the USSR on the back burner, or turn it over to one of the subordinates. But we can discuss that later."

"Very well. But there's something I must tell you. Charlemagne is apparently dead."

Peter Volhard didn't respond at first. Then, "Please don't tell me suicide like those other cowardly morons or I'll be ill."

"Nothing like that. He apparently killed an enlisted man and snuck out of Moscow wearing the dead man's uniform. He made it all the way to Leningrad and, believe it or not, was robbed by a gang of street thugs. Evidently, they didn't know who he was and it was a simple robbery. They took his money and stabbed him for good measure. From my sources, he hung on for a short time but just didn't have the strength. Last I heard he was breathing his last in a hospital bed. What a pity."

Volhard thought for a moment before responding. "If you get that post, perhaps we won't have to worry about the Soviet Union. And I have another idea. It involves the vice president. I'll tell you when we speak. I think that we should all meet to discuss Charlemagne's death."

"Of course. Let's meet tomorrow morning. Let's meet in Germany," Bismarck directed. "I don't think that you could get away without causing some suspicion but Frederick, Wilhelm and Krupp should be there. Make the arrangements and contact them."

"Yes, Mr. Defense Secretary. That sounds good, doesn't it?"

"Yes, it does, Peter. Yes, it does."

✠   ✠   ✠

Michael had been working feverishly on the civil rights bill that was being debated on the Hill. He thought the U.S. government needed to take drastic action, not just a token Band-Aid approach. He fervently opposed the administration's weak bill but wasn't sure if he had the influence to persuade any of his colleagues to vote against it.

Through his connections with Volhard, Michael managed to get himself on the highly prestigious Judiciary Committee. He had thought hard about the pros and cons of having Johnny Green appear before the Committee. It was dangerous and Johnny was so unpredictable. What if he said something totally inflammatory? It would destroy everything.

It was now 6:30 P.M. and Michael still had a ton of work to do, but he had promised that he would be home by seven for their dinner guests. He looked forward to the dinner party mostly because Rebecca was excited. She had talked about nothing else for the past two days and he was ecstatic that she was going to make the best of their life here in Washington.

He got into his car and resorted to the best reliever of stress that he knew: rock-and-roll music. His selection for the ride home was the Rolling Stones' *Goat's Head Soup*. He had the cassette tape at the beginning of his favorite song, *It's Only Rock and Roll*. Before he knew it, he was home and it was 6:59 P.M. He had made it with a minute to spare.

Despite having worked a twelve hour day, he was buzzing with energy. As Matt used to say, he had more energy than a three headed hound dog in hot stink. He was never sure just what that meant, but it seemed fitting.

Michael wasn't into large Georgetown parties but he relished socializing with small groups of people in positions of power. He loved to debate and challenge his guests, but always within boundaries. No matter how much he disagreed with someone, he would never say anything mean or vindictive. That was his unwritten rule. At work, he could rip someone a new one, but not at the dinner table.

He smiled, walking in through the garage, feeling more in love than when he and Rebecca had married twenty years before. She still looked just as beautiful now.

He raced up the stairs and was amazed by how nice the house looked. A lot of work had been put into their new home and it looked great. As Michael was about to sneak into the bedroom to surprise Rebecca, David came rushing out of his room chasing the dog, and the three of them crashed into each other. Michael collapsed to the ground, hitting it with a thud.

Rebecca heard the crash and came running into the hall, only to find Boxer licking David's face and Michael laughing hysterically, sprawled out on the floor.

"For goodness sakes," Rebecca proclaimed with mock indignation. "What am I going to do with you guys? David, get up from there and take Boxer downstairs. And Michael, get into that shower and get ready. The guests will be here in twenty-five minutes."

"Yes, ma'am. David, the boss has spoken. So let's get a move on. Do what Mommy says."

"Daddy?" asked David with big, innocent eyes. "I'm glad you're back and we're a family again."

"I am too, champ. And I'm never going to leave again." He gave David a hug and looked at Rebecca, who had never looked as angelic as she did now.

David ran downstairs and Michael kissed Rebecca. "I guess you never know how much you love something until it's taken away from you. But I guess I better get into the shower or else I'll receive an awful beating from you. Am I right?"

"Most indubitably," she confirmed. "Now get moving. You remember how our guests always seem to show up early."

"O.K., O.K. I'm going," Michael pleaded with feigned exasperation. "By the way, how did you meet the Shannons?"

"It's a long story. I'll tell you at dinner. Sterling is a pretty important lawyer in town, you know," she said.

"Great. We'll be eating dinner with a bloodsucker."

"Don't call him that. He's a very dedicated and talented lawyer, extremely well connected and very knowledgeable about civil rights. Maybe he can talk to you about the administration's bill," Rebecca suggested.

"That watered-down thing can't in all seriousness be called a bill," Michael shouted from the shower. "I think that I'm going to have Johnny speak to the committee tomorrow. What do you think?"

"I really don't know, Michael. A gang-banger? It seems pretty risky to me. What's the benefit?"

"It's the shock value that I'm looking for," Michael explained. "None of us really has a clue what it's like on the streets, with the homelessness, the drugs, the crime. I'm hoping Johnny can at least get people to look at it from the inside out."

He started to tell her about the proposal made to him by Nate Wallace but decided against it. He didn't like keeping secrets from his wife but there was no need to worry her.

As Michael was putting on his shirt, he asked, "Who's going to take care of TJ and David?"

"Josh and Kelly are going to watch them over here."

Michael felt frozen when he heard Kelly's name.

"Michael, Kelly and I talked for hours today. She and Josh helped me straighten things up. She's really a delightful girl. She asked me about your dreams."

Michael stopped in his tracks. The only reason Kelly knew about that was because of the nightmare he had when they were sleeping together. Oh my God, she didn't tell Rebecca, did she? He started to panic.

"She told me that you and Josh had become very close and that you told him the details about your dreams. It seems so unlike you, opening yourself up, being vulnerable. I'm very proud of you, Michael," Rebecca said, giving him a kiss.

"You are?" he asked, letting loose a loud sigh of relief.

"Yes, I am," she said breezily. "You never would have been able to express yourself like that to one of the kids before. I think that it shows a real sense of strength to not be so wrapped up in that macho crap like you always were. You've changed, dear."

That was way too close for comfort, Michael thought, just as the doorbell rang and he ran out of the room to answer it.

"You must be Sterling and Linda," Michael said to the handsome couple on his doorstep. "I'm Mike. Come on in."

The Shannons seemed to radiate the aura of a true Washington power couple. For some reason, he couldn't picture either one without the other.

"Follow me into the living room. What's everyone drinking?"

Michael played the role of bartender. Rebecca entered the room and was clearly relishing her role as hostess.

"Linda, I just have to show you the house," she said, bursting with pride, and turning towards her husband. "Michael, will you boys be all right alone for a few minutes while I take Linda on a tour of the house?"

"We'll survive."

Michael gave Sterling his drink and the two men adjourned to the den. Dropping into a well-worn chair that had taken him years to break-in, he started the conversation.

"So, Sterling, your reputation precedes you. I hear that you're about the finest private attorney in town."

"Well, I wouldn't say that exactly. But I give it my best shot," Sterling said modestly. He was about fifty years old and very thin. He had a long, aquiline nose that had earned him the nickname Hawk, which he despised.

As the ladies returned, Michael noted that Linda's designer dress probably cost several thousand dollars and that she seemed to be wearing half of the Crown Jewels. Michael then looked at Rebecca, with enthusiasm. He knew her so well, despite their separation.

"Michael, I was going to tell you during dinner, but I just can't hold it in anymore. I've been offered a job at GNN, at the Washington bureau. That's how I met Linda. Michael, I really want this. I haven't worked for a year and I really miss it. Please say you'll support me," Rebecca pleaded.

Michael hugged her and said, "Of course, I'll support you. I think that it's great. I'm proud of you, Becks."

"I also have some other news but it's not definite yet. I think that my father is going to be the next secretary of defense," Rebecca said proudly.

"You're kidding," Michael said, totally stunned by the news. He had no idea Karl was being considered. "Well, I think that a little celebration is in order."

He excused himself and came back with a bottle of very expensive, aged champagne. Michael filled everyone's glass and made a toast.

"To Rebecca, the greatest and most beautiful journalist that Washington has ever seen, as well as the most wonderful wife that any man could have," he said. They all raised their glasses.

"Hear, hear," came the reply, to the sound of clinking crystal.

18

Matt boarded the Aeroflot plane that was heading towards Berlin. He knew that Ligachev's sons were from there. He must find Konrad. The letter mentioned the death of his oldest son. What had happened to Gunther?

Matt played the scenario over in his head. A group of Germans trying to conquer the world? Secretary Swanson was right, it was preposterous. Even though Sgt. Pepper's cryptic clues had been confirmed by Ligachev's dying words, he still had no hard evidence. He couldn't go to the president with this. Nor could he go to his boss, yet. For the time being, this would be his secret project.

He was disturbed by the mention of the deaths of millions. Matt, more than almost anyone in the government, was aware of troop movements, war preparations, and the like, by every country in the world. Germany, while recently more assertive, wasn't even close to developing nuclear weapons. He had just recently met with the chancellor of Germany and was certain that this wasn't the policy of the government.

That meant it was outside the government. Some secret group was plotting to overthrow the German government. And then what? The world? It was too crazy. If it were true, how could it possibly happen? Theory aside, Matt told himself, the logistics would probably be too overwhelming.

"Would you like anything to drink, sir?" a stewardess asked Matt.

He snapped out of his reverie to see that her name was Michelle.

"Yes, Michelle, could you get me a vodka and tonic? I could certainly use one."

"Of course, sir. I'll be right back," the flight attendant promised as Matt stared out the window.

Perhaps he was jumping to conclusions but his instincts told him that he was on to something. And he was maybe the only outsider in the world that knew. But knew what?

"Here's your drink, sir," Michelle said with a smile.

"Thank you very much. Excuse me, but you don't look Russian. Are you an American?"

"I sure am. Lincoln, Nebraska," she replied. "I've always had an interest in the Soviet Union. I studied Russian history at the University of Nebraska and I decided to spend a summer in Moscow, just sightseeing, you know. My Russian is actually pretty good. And then this job became available. I really like it a lot. My steady flight is from Moscow to Bonn and sometimes Berlin. Do you work with the government?" Michelle asked.

Matt took this as a compliment. It must be that look of authority, he told himself. "Yes, I do. Why?"

"I don't know. It was just a guess," she admitted. She bent over and began whispering. "I'm not supposed to talk about other passengers but there's a man aboard today who I think works for the government too. I've seen him on this flight several times during the past month. He's that big man up in the front," she said, gesturing with her head towards the front of the plane. "I've always wondered if he's a spy," she said with a smile.

Matt was now curious and got up and walked a few steps towards the front but quickly returned. It was Karl Schmidt! He knew that Karl was working in Moscow but why would he be making frequent trips to Germany? His mind started wandering. No, no, it couldn't be. Impossible.

"Are you all right, Mr.—?"

"Connors. Matt Connors. I'm sorry, Michelle," Matt said, somewhat embarrassed, trying his best to appear nonchalant. "I thought he might be someone I know."

Matt froze. He needed time to think this out. He told himself that Karl couldn't possibly be involved. If he was, how am I going to explain my presence in Moscow.

Michelle asked him, "would you like for me to tell him you're on board?"

"No, not right now," Matt said slowly, finally coming out of his little daydream. "Listen, Michelle, could you do me a favor? Could you walk by that man and tell me if he's reading anything, or talking to anyone?"

"I was right. He's a spy, isn't he?" asked the excited redhead from Nebraska.

"Let's not jump to any conclusions. I just would like to know what he's doing. O.K?" Matt said calmly, hoping not to get her too worked up.

"O.K. I'll be back in a flash."

Matt got a twinge in his back and felt nauseous. Was Karl Schmidt one of the Six? Was he Rommel or Bismarck? It was too incredible for words. He had known Karl for years and had always thought of him as a man of great integrity. Could he be a Nazi?

His heart was racing as Michelle came back to report.

"Sorry, Mr. Connors. He's sleeping. Nothing very sinister about that, is there?" she said with a sweet smile.

"No, I guess not. Sorry it's nothing more exciting," Matt said, trying to downplay their conversation.

Michelle laughed. "Well, I guess, I'll have to wait a long time to get another chance to be a spy. But I'll keep my eyes open, O.K? Have a good flight, sir," said the young American.

The plane landed right on time. Matt realized that he was very visible. He and Karl knew each other well and he was the only black man on the flight. But he would follow Michael's father-in-law and see what turned up. Hopefully, nothing would. He began thinking of reasons why this crazy scenario couldn't be true. They had shared many meals and had even played golf together. It must be just a coincidence. After all, Karl was from Germany. It wasn't so crazy to think he might visit his home country occasionally. But he would follow him anyway.

Matt grabbed his on board luggage from the overhead compartment and headed off the plane, careful to pull his coat up so as to partially block his face. He wished he had a hat. What if Karl saw him? He would have to think of a plausible explanation for being in both Russia and Germany.

Matt walked slowly across the tarmac and into the terminal, careful to remain inconspicuous. Behind a stone pillar he saw Karl enter the building, and then walk over to a telephone and place a call. Matt gazed from behind the pillar and positioned himself so that he could see Karl but not be seen himself. After a few minutes, Karl came out of the telephone booth and headed outside onto the street. He had no luggage, other than the briefcase he was carrying. Matt had luggage but would have to come back for it.

Karl hailed a taxi and disappeared into the night. Matt did the same thing and told the driver to follow the cab in front. The cabby gave Matt a cold stare and said, "It's your money."

Matt felt silly pretending to be some type of spy. He was an analyst, not a field agent. But how hard could it be? Just follow him and see where he goes. Easy.

They drove for twenty minutes, heading east out of town and into a suburban neighborhood. Finally, Karl's taxi came to a stop and Matt's cabby pulled over, about a quarter mile behind. Karl got out in front of a large private home and walked briskly up the walkway to the door. He rang the bell and moments later, a man answered and escorted Karl inside.

What should he do now? "Pull forward just a little," Matt directed the driver, who did as he was told. He saw that it was surrounded by a six-foot-tall wrought-iron fence. He saw shadows from one of the rooms and could make out several people. He had to get closer.

"Stay here. I'll be back in a few minutes," Matt said to the driver, who shrugged his shoulders indifferently.

Matt quietly walked up to the fence and tried in vain to make out the figures in the window. He would have to climb the fence. His mind suddenly had a frightening thought. What if there was an alarm or, worse yet, what if it was electrified? He started looking for something metal. He saw a trash can sitting on the curb in front of the home next door. He opened it and pulled out a wire clothes-hanger. His cab driver watched from his perch and was now convinced that his fare was crazy.

Matt stepped up to the fence and threw the coat hanger against it. No sparks flew, so at least it wasn't electrified. He walked up and grabbed the fence and shook it hard for several seconds and then ran back to the cab. "Let's wait here for a few minutes," Matt whispered.

Matt and the cab driver sat in silence for about five minutes. Nothing. Apparently, there was no alarm.

Matt had instructions for the cabby. "I'll be gone for about ten minutes. If anyone looks out of the window, I don't want them to see a car parked here. I want you to drive up and down the street. But don't leave," he ordered.

"As long as the meter's on, I'll do whatever you want."

Matt pulled his coat up to his face and walked up to the fence. He then put his foot on one of the bars and hoisted himself up and over. Very impressive, he told himself, for a desk jockey with a bum leg. He quietly ran across the lawn and positioned himself outside the window where he had seen the figures. He glanced around the yard and plotted his escape route in case anything happened. He was sure that he could be up and over the fence in seconds if detected. He crawled up to the window and peered in.

He could see Karl, who was walking across the room with a glass in his hand. He was speaking to three other men, none of whom he recognized, although one looked familiar. But he couldn't hear what was being said.

One of the other men began speaking. It was Frederick.

"Perhaps we are fortunate. I think that Charlemagne was greatly disturbed after the failure of the coup, devastated by what happened to Gunther, and worried about Konrad." He shook his head. "Charlemagne made a monumental mistake. I don't know if he would have been able to live with it. Maybe this is the best thing."

Bismarck nodded his head. "Was this really as it seems? Was he really attacked by ordinary street thugs? Krupp, I want your word of honor that no one from the Six was involved in his death."

"I swear, Herr Bismarck. It was, pure and simple, an unrelated death. But I agree that perhaps this is for the best," answered Krupp honestly, although he wouldn't have hesitated for a second to slit the fool's throat.

Frederick continued the discussion. "But what of our plans? Charlemagne was invaluable. How do we replace him?"

Bismarck responded with great vigor. "Perhaps we don't need to. I've not yet had the opportunity to tell you the news. I'm on my way to meet with President Tolbert about possibly being named the secretary of defense."

Both Frederick and Krupp immediately stood up. "That's fantastic news," said the economic minister, shaking Bismarck's hand.

Krupp was excited by this news. "That was our hope but to see it actually happen is incredible. We have a bout with destiny, gentlemen. Congratulations."

"Well, it's not definite yet," Bismarck cautioned. "Rommel said that he sold the president, but you never know. And then there's the Senate. So, it's not a done deal."

"Well, it is as far as I'm concerned," said Frederick.

Bismarck went on. "If I do get this position, we might be able to forget our plan in the former Soviet Union. We may not need to stir up ethnic trouble there. I propose that we dispatch Charlemagne's team to Germany to get the German people and military behind us." No one spoke. "Then it's agreed. Gentlemen, I would like to make a toast to Germany."

"Prost," they shouted joyfully, as their glasses clanked together.

Matt, straining to hear, lost his balance and fell to the ground. Matt couldn't be sure that they hadn't heard him. He froze and waited.

Inside, Frederick said, "Did anyone hear anything?"

Bismarck shook his head. "No," added Krupp.

"That's funny. I thought I did. Maybe I was just imagining it."

The evening's host walked to the kitchen and opened the back door. "Come here, boys," he ordered.

Two very large Doberman pinschers began panting and growing excited. They were muscular and powerful. Frederick patted them and unlatched the patio door.

"Go see what you can find," he said to the dogs and they raced across the large backyard and then around the house, growling louder and louder, baring all forty-two of their razor-sharp teeth.

Matt heard the pounding and panting. His instincts told him he had only seconds to act, and he raced for the gate as fast as he had run since the grenade explosion in Vietnam. But the two dogs caught up to him and threw him to the ground, gnawing his good leg and chewing on his blood-soaked skin.

He let out a loud scream and the men inside came running out. The two dogs and Matt were rolling in a tangle of blood, teeth and legs. Matt was losing blood and lacked the strength to throw the dogs off. His head was doubled back and he saw out of the corner of his eye a branch of a tree that had fallen to the ground. He strained to reach it and just barely managed to wrap his fingers around the bottom part of the branch.

He squirmed and struck one of the dogs on the head with the branch with all the strength he could muster. The dog whined and swayed dizzily before collapsing. The other animal stopped just long enough to give Matt a second to wind up and smack it in the face. He would only have a few seconds, and the four men were rapidly approaching.

He threw himself onto the fence, and with every fiber of strength crawled over it and fell to the ground. He looked around but didn't see the cab.

"Damn it, where are you? Where are you?" he screamed.

He started limping out into the street, picking up speed as he saw the taxi heading toward him. The men had opened the gate onto the street and were after him, with the dogs sprinting ahead. Puncture wounds in his leg and several lacerations were bleeding profusely.

He was gaining distance on the elderly men, but the dogs were gaining fast.

The cab driver, seeing his predicament, threw open the door. Matt tried to throw himself into the moving car, but part of his legs were dragging along the street. He reached for a last burst of energy and with great effort, pulled himself up into the car and closed the door. The dogs had just reached the cab and were barking viciously at it as it sped away. Matt was about to pass out from shock and loss of blood but he managed to look out the back window at the men. It was more than he could handle—he collapsed, much to the chagrin of the driver, who just wanted to go home.

The driver cursed, but he couldn't let him die, which, judging by the amount of blood on the floor of his cab, would soon happen. He drove to the nearest hospital, carried Matt into the emergency room and disappeared into the night.

✠   ✠   ✠

Karl Schmidt landed at Dulles airport outside Washington and headed right to the White House for his meeting with the president. Andrew Tolbert had a reputation for being extremely knowledgeable but somewhat weak. He would always know all possible sides of an issue but often lacked the where-withal to make an unpopular decision. He was cautious. Quite often a decision would be based upon which adviser had spoken to the president last.

This morning's meeting would be attended only by Schmidt, the president and the White House chief of staff, Phillip Gordon. The prospective secretary of defense arrived right on time.

"Good morning, Karl. How's Katarina?" Tolbert said warmly.

"Good morning, Mr. President. She still loves me, for reasons which escape me."

"Tell me how things are going in Moscow," the president instructed. "Give it to me straight."

"Mr. President, we're making tremendous strides," Karl replied. "We've come to an agreement regarding the mechanics of how the weapons are to be destroyed. We've established a timetable and are ready to proceed with the unprecedented step of destroying weapons."

"Marvelous. That's exactly what Davis told me," said the obviously pleased commander in chief. "Tell me, Karl, what do you make of these new Russian leaders? And the leaders of the other republics, for that matter? How is it different than the past with the Soviets?"

"The people haven't really changed, sir, but the system sure has," Karl responded with a sigh. "It's like night and day. Everything still moves in slow motion, but just wait until they get the hang of it. Then you're going to see some ball-busting action."

Tolbert laughed heartily, slapping Karl on the back as he moved from the center of the room to his desk.

"Karl, let's get down to the matter at hand. I'm sure you know why I asked you here," said the president. "Peter Volhard has avidly recommended you to be the next secretary of defense. Let me be blunt, Karl. Why would appointing you not be a big mistake?"

"Well," replied Schmidt, "I've never held elective office but I've run a large corporation for years, I've negotiated with government officials, I've traveled all over the world. I'm a leader. I can be eloquent and I can kick some ass when it's necessary. I can do this job, Mr. President."

"I'm sure you can, Karl. How do you see the role of the military in the post cold war era? Do we really need a large peacetime army and navy?" asked the president.

"Of course we do," Karl responded. "That nonsense about this being the end of history is a total crock. War is not obsolete. A strong military is as necessary now as ever before. Yes, we must scale back, prioritize and focus on a lighter, more responsive force. The Soviets are no longer the threat, but there are new threats we must look out for," he cautioned.

"Such as who? Anyone in particular?" asked Tolbert.

"Japan," was the prompt reply. "It's a new world we live in. Economic might is almost as important as military strength. The country that will lead is the one that recognizes this and develops both," he said, mouthing Frederick's often-proclaimed advice.

"Are you a hawk or a dove?" quizzed the president.

"I'm neither and I'm both," answered Karl. "I reject the simplistic use of such outdated labels. I believe in the overpowering use of force if it's in the best interest of the nation. War is something to be avoided, but once the decision is made, we need to be able to react quickly and with lethal force."

"Let me ask you a blunt question, Karl," said the president. "You've said that our most likely enemy is Japan. I've had other advisers who say it's Germany. You're originally from Germany. What's your opinion on the new assertiveness of the Germans and do you think you could be objective in analyzing any potential German threat?" asked the president.

"Let me make one thing clear, sir," Karl said forcefully. "I was born in Germany, yes. But I've lived here for over forty-five years. I am an American. I don't think we need to be overly worried about Germany. Germany is moving towards a unified European defense.They're light years from acquiring the Bomb. To be a military power in today's world, that's essential," Karl said flatly.

"I'm glad you brought that up," Tolbert said."I'm sure you know about the 'football.'"

"Yes, sir. Wherever you go, you're accompanied by an aide who carries a box with the codes to launch nuclear weapons."

"Exactly. And I'm sure that you know that I can't launch them by myself, nor can any president," said Tolbert, a fact Karl assuredly knew. "The creators of our current system took into account the possibility of an irrational president who might throw the world into nuclear holocaust for no good reason. The secretary of defense is an integral piece in the launching sequence," the president said.

"Let me ask you a hypothetical question. Suppose we get a call right now and I'm told that Russia has launched numerous ICBMs and that they'll hit various targets in the U.S. within fifteen minutes. Should we launch a retaliatory strike immediately or wait until they hit?" The president's pleasant tone became extremely somber and he looked straight into Karl's eyes to gauge his response.

"There's too much at risk here to launch on notice," said Karl. "You might not have complete information. Many of the weapons might not arrive where they were targeted. Some might malfunction. No attack, no matter how massive, could wipe out our ability to retaliate. That's why there's so much redundancy. Our sea-based weapons are almost invulnerable. Our land-based weapons are based at too many locations. I believe in hardened silos, and in mobile storage, so as to keep the enemy guessing. An immediate retaliation on the part of the president would be a foolish mistake of unprecedented consequence," Karl said emphatically.

"I see," said the president, clearly impressed. "Continue."

"Command and control in such a situation is critical," Karl proceeded. "The National Command Authority would, in the event of a nuclear attack, either become airborne or go underground to be immune from attack. It would be imperative that command and control be functioning at all times. The body cannot act without the head."

"No matter how awful the results of a nuclear strike might be," he continued, "It would be ten times worse if command and control was eliminated. Let's say that Washington, New York and Boston are wiped out. We still have military forces worldwide and hundreds of millions of people still alive. They would need for the key leaders to be alive to defend or fight."

"Very well, Mr. Schmidt," replied the president. "I'm very impressed. As they say in the business world, we'll be in touch." He shook Karl's hand vigorously and gave him the famous presidential grin.

"Thank you, sir. I hope we can work together. I would like to be a part of your team."

With that, Karl left the Oval Office. Phil Gordon remained uncharacteristically silent.

19

elix Klaus, also known as Wilhelm, sat in his magnificent NATO office. He had just been thinking of Charlemagne's death and felt a combination of sadness and anger. What a fool to have almost jeopardized their mission. But at least now they would not have to have Charlemagne killed.

His more pressing problem was to fill the position of AFCENT commander who, traditionally, was always a German general. He had had hopes that General Dolf Punder would have been able to place Germany first, but he too had been caught up in the idealistic fantasy of peace.

He was suddenly drawn out of his reverie by the buzzing of the intercom. "Herr Klaus, General Steigrich is here to see you."

"Send him right in," Klaus directed.

In walked a specimen of Nordic perfection. Mannfried Steigrich, six-feet-four, 225 pounds, with broad shoulders and small waist, blond hair and piercing blue eyes. He possessed an air of arrogance, without a trace of nervousness about meeting the NATO commander. He was a man used to being obeyed.

"Guten Morgen, Herr Klaus. It's a great pleasure to meet you," barked out the German general.

"Likewise," responded Klaus, clearly impressed. "Would you like a smoke?"

"No, thank you. Never touch the stuff."

"Well, I've been smoking cigars for fifty years and I'm still ticking," said the NATO commander, lighting up. "Please sit down. Tell me why you're interested in the AFCENT position."

"To be perfectly honest, sir, I'm not interested. I was told that you summoned me so, here I am," said Steigrich, looking somewhat puzzled.

"Why would you not be interested in the AFCENT post? It's considered to be a very prestigious position and is usually offered only to the most worthy candidates."

Steigrich looked somewhat uneasy. "Can I speak freely?"

"Of course."

"I am German, first and foremost. I'm not a diplomat, I'm a general. All this hand-holding between the allies disgusts me. We Germans have to recognize what we are. We're warriors, nothing more and nothing less," he said bluntly, starting to worry that his outspokenness would land him in trouble, as it had many times before.

Klaus looked him over slowly, carefully studying his face. "Well spoken, Herr Steigrich. Your beliefs put you in the minority."

"Yes, I know, which is why I've accepted the fact that I've ascended as far as I can," Steigrich said with no regret. "The higher positions all involve the allies and I'm afraid that I just can't stomach that. I'm only forty-five and it distresses me that my career has leveled out."

"Let me ask you a question, General," stated Klaus. "Do you believe that certain races are superior to others?"

Steigrich looked uncomfortable.

"Please speak your mind. There's no right answer."

"Every time I speak my mind it usually gets me in hot water. My views are different than most," Steigrich conceded. "But I do believe that Germany and the Aryan race are superior."

"Please elaborate," said the NATO chief, still not displaying his approval but encouraged by what he was hearing from Steigrich.

"Certain nations and specific races have dominated throughout history, in cycles," replied the General. "In the fifteenth and sixteenth centuries, it was Spain and Portugal. Then the French during the seventeenth and eighteenth centuries and then Great Britain. The last century has been dominated by the United States and Germany, although Germany should have prevailed."

"Why do you believe Germany lost the last war?" asked Klaus, who detected a note of anger in Steigrich's voice.

"Military ineptness on Hitler's part, and plain bad luck. Hitler's biggest mistake was putting off the invasion of Russia from April to June of 1941. Had he not been so determined to punish the Yugoslavians, had the invasion commenced in the spring, it would have been finished before the winter set in. You don't invade Russia in the winter! Hitler should have learned from Napoleon."

"What was the bad luck?"

"We were this far from developing the V2," said Steigrich, holding his fingers an inch apart. "A lucky break here, a month or two there, we would have completed the project. Had we not been so depleted from the disaster on the eastern front, we could have held on for several more months. Remember, the Americans didn't develop their bomb until August 1945 and we surrendered in May 1945. Those months could have made the difference."

Klaus studied the young general for several minutes. Steigrich began getting nervous.

Finally Klaus spoke. "Herr Steigrich, I want to tell you something that may or may not sit well with you. I barely know you. But I've checked into your background and that's why I asked you here."

Again Klaus paused, then continued. "Would you be willing to be part of an army that restores Germany to its proper place, to take by force that which Germany deserves?"

Steigrich hesitated but Klaus continued.

"General, I will not tell you the specifics until later. But I want your answer to my general question. There is a plan for Germany to assume its place as the preeminent world power. Would you be willing to lead her army?"

The General was stunned. "NATO has a plan—I don't understand."

"Not NATO," chided Klaus. "Outside the alliance. Germany alone. There's a plan in existence for Germany to conquer the world within the coming year."

Steigrich hastily stood up. "Within the coming year? With all due respect, sir, that's ridiculous. Nothing of the sort is in existence."

"Herr Steigrich, I don't blame you for your skepticism but rest assured that I am speaking the truth. Let's assume that what I say is correct. Would you be willing to lead the army?" repeated the NATO leader.

"Yes, I would, without hesitation. It's just that I cannot believe it," said the visibly shaken Steigrich.

"Then you don't oppose it in theory?" posed Klaus.

"Not at all. I believe Germany is destined to reign. I just didn't think that it would be in my lifetime," confessed the general.

"Well, dreams do come true, General," said Wilhelm. He handed Steigrich a piece of paper with an address written on it. "Meet me at this location at seven o'clock tonight," he directed.

"I'll be there, sir. Until tonight." The general walked out of Klaus' office in a state of excitement, not sure of what he was getting himself into but ready to take a chance that might get him into trouble yet again.

Klaus wondered briefly whether he had made a mistake by revealing too much to Steigrich. But you must go with your instincts, he told himself. Everything about Steigrich felt right. And besides, Germany's reemergence was destined by the gods and nothing could stop it from occurring.

✠　✠　✠

Matt awoke in tremendous pain. He had no idea where he was. He took a few minutes to shake the cobwebs out of his brain and to take in his surroundings. He was in a hospital, in a barren room, and his one good leg was heavily bandaged. Slowly, it started to come back to him. He remembered being chased by the men and the dogs.

He instantly panicked. Had Karl recognized him? Good Lord, he said to himself, I might be a dead man. He felt overwhelming anxiety and became nauseous. He tried to get out of bed but the pain made it impossible. He rang the nurse and tried to block out the pain.

After what seemed forever, nurse Rita Altierst walked into his room. Young and very pretty, with long blonde hair tied in a ponytail, she spoke in fluent English.

"Good morning, Mr. Connors. How are you this morning? You've been asleep for over twelve hours. You lost a lot of blood and came very close to having your leg amputated. But Dr. Friedreich was able to salvage it, fortunately. What can I do for you?" she asked sweetly.

Amputation? The word stunned him and he gasped in disbelief. Rita saw his response and reassured him.

"Mr. Connors, you're past the danger point," the nurse said. "Everything is O.K. now. The doctors saved your leg and you're going to be just fine. We saw from your wallet and papers that you're an important man in Washington and we notified your superiors. Mr. Elliot would like for you to call him as soon as you feel up to it."

This revelation was worse than amputation. Elliot knew! He would go through the roof to know that his chief aide was running around the world chasing Nazis and getting attacked by dogs. Matt's head throbbed unrelentingly.

"Nurse, would you help me to the rest room, please?"

"Of course, Mr. Connors. Let me have your arm," said the beautiful nurse, wrapping her arms around Matt's waist. But he was in no condition to enjoy her youth or beauty. After emerging from the rest room, he realized that he was very hungry.

Rita helped him back into bed. "Would you like some breakfast, sir?"

"Yes, I would. By the way, where am I?"

"You are in St. Gregory's Hospital. You were dropped off in the emergency room by a cab driver about eight o'clock last night. You were rushed into surgery for two hours and you've been asleep for the past thirteen hours. It's now eleven in the morning."

Rita brought him breakfast and he devoured it.

"My, my, weren't we hungry?" said the good-natured nurse.

"Where did you learn such good English?" asked Matt.

"I went to college at the University of Virginia. I started off premed with hopes of being a doctor. But there were problems for my family back home so I had to return before completing my studies. Since I love helping sick people, I became a nurse."

"Are you from Berlin originally?" inquired Matt.

"Born and raised. Things have sure changed during the last couple of years, I suppose for the better. Time will tell. I'm not really very political," she confessed.

Matt pursued a long shot. "Do you by any chance know the Ligachev family? The father is Nikolai and the sons are Gunther and Konrad."

Rita beamed. "I sure do. I went to the same school as Konrad's daughter, Alexandra. She's a good friend."

Pay dirt! Matt couldn't believe his luck. "Could you tell me how to reach Konrad? I need to speak with him urgently."

"I can call his house right now if you wish. Would you like me to?" asked the nurse.

Matt hesitated for a moment. His head was still pounding and his mind was unclear. "Not right now. Perhaps this afternoon after I shower and clean up. But my German is not very good. Would you place the call for me?"

"I'd be glad to. I get off work at three o'clock so let me know before then, O.K?"

"Sure, Rita. And thanks for all the help and warmth. I appreciate it."

"Just doing my job. Let me know if I can get anything for you."

He stared nervously at the phone for several minutes before picking it up and calling Elliot. The national security adviser was in a meeting but had left instructions to interrupt him if Matt called. This made him even more nervous.

After several seconds, Elliot's gruff voice came on the line. "Matt, what the hell's going on? What are you doing in a German hospital?" He was shouting.

Matt held the receiver several inches from his ear. After Elliot's eruption subsided, he finally spoke. "Davis, it's a long story. I'll explain it all when I get back. Please give me some latitude. I think I'm on to something really big."

Elliot paused. He had never known Matt to do anything improper and for the most part, trusted his judgment.

"All right, Matt. I'll give you some leeway, this time. But I want it all when you return. None of this crap about wanting to further develop your theory. Do you understand?"

"Thank you," came Matt's reply. "I think I'll be O.K. to leave the hospital tomorrow and I've tracked down the person I need to speak to. I'll be back in two or three days."

"O.K., Matt. I'll cover for you until then. I'll say that you're sick. But for God's sakes, don't get attacked by any more dogs."

"Believe me, that's a priority. By the way, any progress on the defense job being filled?"

Elliot replied, "It's not definite yet but I think that the president's going with Karl Schmidt—runs a weapon's manufacturing business, heading up the team in the former Soviet Union destroying weapons. Bit of an odd choice, I must say. Do you know him?"

Matt didn't hear a word after "Karl Schmidt." He still didn't have the evidence he wanted but if his theory was correct, the United States was in big trouble.

"Matt, you still there?" demanded Elliot.

"Yeah, I'm here. Who pushed for Schmidt?"

"I wasn't there, but I've been told that it was suggested that I take the post and you move into the NSA position," Elliot told his deputy.

Matt felt a twinge of exhilaration recalling that he had been considered. "Obviously, that got shot down."

"I wouldn't say shot down, Matt. The president still hasn't made up his mind. But Volhard pushed for Schmidt. The president met with him today, and from what I've heard, he was very impressed. He should be making a decision in the next day or two," Elliot added.

Matt's head now felt like it was going to explode. He desperately needed more rest.

"Davis, I have to go now. I'll talk to you soon. Good-bye." He hung up the phone and fell fast asleep.

✠   ✠   ✠

Michael walked into the room where the House Judiciary Committee was meeting. Being a student of history, he couldn't help but be overcome with awe and amazement. This was the room where the Committee had met in 1974 to approve the articles of impeachment against Nixon.

Michael was excited and ready as he took his seat. Although nervous about how Johnny Green would testify, he felt battle-ready. He felt more alive than he had in years. This is what he was born to do, he knew it, could feel it. His entire life had been a training ground for this new career.

Slowly, the conference room began filling up with the members of the Committee and their staff, some spectators and a few reporters. Chairman Brian McMullen's gavel brought silence to the room.

McMullen, a veteran legislator from Illinois, and a steady force in the House, was often able to get opposing sides to reach a consensus. He was also worried this year about the state of race relations. He knew that every major city was on the brink of a riot or similar disturbance. Almost anything could ignite the flammable situation.

The Committee heard testimony from two esteemed professors, a Hollywood actress, and a black minister. All were intelligent advocates who brought different perspectives to the issue before the Committee.

McMullen looked down toward the end of one of the two long tables where his colleagues sat and nodded to Michael.

"Members of the Committee, we will now hear from one more person. Would the Representative from California introduce him, please?"

"Thank you, Mr. Chairman," Michael said confidently. "I would like to introduce to you someone that I've met recently who, somewhere along the way took a wrong turn. He's twenty years old. Ladies and gentlemen, I believe that before we vote on this bill, we must put ourselves in the shoes of the people in the street. We must feel what they feel and see what they see. I would like to introduce you to Johnny Green, a member of a gang called the Bloods from Los Angeles," Michael said while glancing about the room, trying to gauge his colleagues' reactions.

Michael looked up at Darrell and signaled for Johnny to be seated at the witness table. Darrell had been in charge of making him presentable and Johnny was wearing a jacket and tie for the first time in his life. Johnny walked up to the table and took his seat. He glanced at the sea of mostly white, male faces of the Committee and almost lost his lunch. He frantically sought out Michael, who winked at him and gave him the thumbs-up sign.

McMullen had reluctantly agreed to what he thought was grandstanding by Michael. He wanted to get it over.

"Sir, could you tell us your name and where you're from?" the Chairman asked the gang leader.

He paused. "My name is Johnny Green. I'm twenty years old and from Los Angeles. I'm the leader of a gang. Mr. Madigan asked me to speak today to you all and I'm not really sure why," Johnny said, forgetting what he was supposed to say.

"Mr. Green, I believe that Congressman Madigan wanted you to tell us about gangs and why young men like you join them," McMullen said condescendingly.

"Yeah, that's it. He asked me to talk about what it's like to live in the ghetto and to be in a gang. Well, it's not a whole lot of fun. I didn't grow up hoping to be in a gang. I wanted to be a doctor. Believe it or not, I'm actually sort of smart. I just haven't had the chance," Johnny said, looking down at the table.

Congressman Gerald Cook from Ohio cleared his throat and gazed intently at the gang leader. "Mr. Green, what's stopping you from working or going to school? You appear to be healthy."

"Yeah, I'm healthy," Johnny said, shaking his head. "I've heard some of you say today that anyone can achieve whatever they dream for in America. They just have to work hard. But they have to believe there's a chance. The people I know don't work towards a dream. Not because they're lazy or don't care. It's because they know it won't come true," said the gang leader, who was amazed that every eye was focused intently on him.

"Now there will always be exceptions," the leader of the Bloods continued. "One kid out of a thousand will make it and you'll say, 'See, it can be done.' Yeah, it can be done for those with real talents but the average kid needs a chance, too. Most of us aren't geniuses but just regular people. We can't be forgotten. We count, too."

Johnny looked at Michael. "I don't really understand this bill you're voting on except that it seems to say that everything's O.K., let's just keep things the way they are. Well, things are not O.K. They stink. I don't know how to fix it but I hope that you all do. There's a lot of hatred and rage on the streets. And a lot of crime and drugs."

"I've killed two men in my life," Johnny said, and immediately noticed the horror on many of the faces in the crowd. "I'm not proud of it and I think about those men every single day. Maybe this shocks you and maybe you won't listen to what I'm saying. But I hope that you do. If you just keep looking at the floor like most of you are now, then our cities will continue to burn," Johnny warned.

"I don't have the answers. I just hope you listen before what happened in Los Angeles happens again. You know, Congressman Madigan wanted me to speak to you and I thought that he was crazy. I told him to get lost."

Michael felt a sinking feeling in his stomach.

"He probably doesn't want me to mention this," Johnny continued, "but he challenged me to a fight and said if he won, then I'd have to speak to you. Well, I'm pretty tough but I have to tell you that Mr. Madigan kicked my ass," explained the gang leader bluntly. "He communicated with me in the only way I knew. Violence. I hope that you do something about it. Thank you."

Johnny stood up as he finished, not knowing what to expect. McMullen adjusted his glasses and looked on either side of him. A buzz of voices was spreading across the room.

Michael gazed around the room and wondered if his colleagues were impressed or laughing at him under their breath. He was quite sure it was the latter. But he wouldn't be deterred from what he thought was right. There was a point to having Johnny speak. Did they hear?

Johnny began to walk away from the table. He noticed that the Committee members were all averting their eyes from him. Their attitudes filled him with rage and he turned around and sat back down. His move stunned the Committee and a hush went through the crowd.

"Did you have something to add, Mr. Green?"

Johnny sat and took a deep breath. "Yeah, I do, Mr. McMullen. You all is looking at me like I'm some bum, something that got on your shoe. You all have been polite but you ain't listened. Maybe you'll listen to this," he said. Michael winced.

"We're listening, Mr. Green," McMullen replied.

"Maybe I'm not high and mighty like all of you with your fancy degrees and all of that. But people like me didn't start those riots in LA. It was people like you," Johnny lashed out to the shocked Committee.

"And how is that, sir?" interjected Gerald Cook.

Johnny glanced around nervously at Darrell and then at Michael. He took a deep breath and exhaled. "That video was rigged by one of your boys," he said.

McMullen signaled to one of his staff. "What do you mean?"

"I mean that one of your brothers set up that whole beating on purpose. It was all a set-up by one of your homeboys to start a riot between blacks and whites," Johnny spat out.

McMullen's jaw dropped about a foot as he realized what Green was saying. "Do you mean to tell me that the beating of that black man by the police in L.A. was intentionally set up by a member of Congress?" he asked incredulously.

"That's exactly what I'm saying. It was all a puppet show and one of your buddies was pulling all the strings," Johnny said slowly. A roar of voices talking over each other suddenly enveloped the room as the stunned Committee seemed to simultaneously erupt.

"Mr. Green, I hope that you realize the seriousness of your accusation," McMullen admonished. "And—"

Johnny interrupted him. "I ain't saying another word without an attorney. You looked down at me and tried to judge me. But you all are a bunch of hypocrites."

Michael's whole body tensed. What have I done?

✠ ✠ ✠

Matt woke after another twelve hours of sleep. He was finally starting to feel like a human being again. He played the events of the last forty-eight hours over in his mind.

Rita walked in and her smile lit up the entire room. "Good morning, Mr. Connors. Did you have a restful night?"

"Yes, I did, Rita. I feel much better, thank you. Listen, I don't want to press you but I think that I'm ready for that call. Could you try to reach Mrs. Ligachev?"

"Sure thing. Now?" asked the nurse.

"Yes, if you don't mind."

She dialed the numbers and Matt's thoughts were racing wildly.

"Hallo," came the response from Heidi Ligachev, who answered the phone.

"Guten Tag, Frau Ligachev. This is Rita."

"Rita, how are you, dear? What can I do for you?"

"Mrs. Ligachev, there's a gentleman in my hospital who needs to talk to your husband urgently. Is he available?"

"No, he's been away for several days and I don't know for sure when he'll be back."

"Mrs. Ligachev, would you be willing to meet with this man? He works for the U.S. government and has some questions that you may be able to answer. Would that be O.K?"

"I suppose so but I'm not sure how helpful I'll be," Heidi said.

"Can he come over this afternoon?" the nurse inquired.

"Yes, that will be all right. Perhaps around four o'clock?"

"Four o'clock," said Rita, looking at Matt, who nodded.

"Four o'clock it is. See you then."

Matt ate breakfast, showered, had lunch and took a nap. He woke around 2:30 P.M. and felt much better. A doctor looked at him and gave the green light for him to be released. Rita gave Matt his final marching orders and told him to get into a wheelchair, which at first he refused.

"Mr. Connors, don't make me use force. This is hospital policy. You don't have a choice," she said forcefully but good-naturedly.

Matt caved in and sat down in the wheelchair and smiled.

The nurse continued. "Do you mind if I go with you? I know the way. I can introduce you to Mrs. Ligachev. She's really a nice lady. What do you say?"

"How can I say no to that face?" asked Matt. "And besides, I probably don't have a choice, do I?"

"No, you don't," she laughed.

"Well, in that case, let's get going."

Rita wheeled him out of the building and from there they walked a few blocks to the strassenbahn, or street car. They headed down Unter den Linden, the central thoroughfare of old Berlin. Translated, it means "Under the linden trees." They passed Humboldt University where Karl Marx and Friedreich Engels were once students.

"See that building there?" Rita pointed out. "That's the Museum fur Deutsche Geschichte, or German History," she said enthusiastically, like a tour guide.

They crossed over the Gertraudenstrasse river and were just about there. "This is our stop," Rita said, as the streetcar came to a halt.

They walked about a quarter of a mile, and stopped in front of a large two-story house. Matt became visibly nervous. Did this woman know anything? Would she be able to lead him to Konrad? He had to talk to Konrad!

Matt was still feeling somewhat groggy and his body was stiff and sore, causing his movements to be slow.

"Rita, I can't tell you what I need to talk to Mrs. Ligachev about and I appreciate your not asking. It's not the kind of thing that I can discuss with you at this time. I hope you understand," said Matt.

"Of course I do, Mr. Connors. Believe me, I'm not the pushy type. If you want to tell me later, that's fine. If you don't, that's fine too."

"And another thing. Will you call me Matt? You make me feel old by calling me Mr. Connors."

"Sure thing, Matt," Rita said as she knocked on the massive door.

A very sad-looking middle-aged lady opened the door and identified herself as Frau Ligachev. "Come on in, please. How are you, Rita?"

"I'm fine, ma'am. This is the gentleman I was telling you about, Mr. Connors. He works for the U.S. government and would like to talk to you," Rita said.

Matt looked at her and shook her hand. He said in his best German, "It is nice to make your acquaintance, ma'am. Thank you for seeing me on such short notice."

"Please, don't mention it. You said it involved Konrad and so I am very much—how do you say—interested. He left last week and I'm very worried," she replied, giving the appearance of a distraught wife.

Matt frowned. He had been hoping to hear something more hopeful. "Exactly what happened the last time you saw him?"

"Let me think a minute." Heidi paused for a moment before continuing. "I was in the kitchen, getting dinner ready. Shortly after Konrad got home two men came by and they left rather suddenly with him. I haven't seen him since and I've been a nervous wreck," she said, wringing her hands even though her voice wasn't emotional.

"Do you know who the men were? Had you seen them before?" asked Matt.

"I had never seen them before. One was older, around the same age as Konrad's father. The other man was younger and his name was—I can't remember."

"Please think hard. It could help find Konrad."

"I'm trying, Mr. Connors. I'm trying—I'm sorry, I just can't remember."

"Please continue. What else happened?"

"Well, Konrad talked to the men in the study for a few minutes and then he went to pack a bag. I can remember almost his exact words," said the woman.

"What did he say?" asked Matt.

"He said, 'Heidi, I must now leave on business. Please don't ask me because I cannot tell you. Tell the kids I love them and I'll call as soon as I can.'"

"Did he say where he was going?" asked Matt.

"No. I'm sorry, Mr. Connors. He kissed me and left with the two men. My Konrad is a professor, not a secret agent." Heidi began crying.

"Ma'am, please try not to worry. I'm sure that he'll call as soon as he can," Matt reassured her.

"Thank you, Mr. Connors. You said that you had some information for me."

"I'm afraid to tell you now," Matt replied. "I'm not sure if it'll accomplish anything to make you worry more."

"I'm a big girl, as you say in America. Please tell me what you know," she pleaded.

Matt paused and let out a sigh. He began talking slowly but his speech became faster and faster as he went on. "Mrs. Ligachev, I have a lot of theories, some shreds of evidence but for the most part, I'm flying by the seat of my pants. I work for the president and his national security adviser. Not to blow my own horn but I hold a pretty important position. My absence is not easily explained. I took off first for Russia and then here without telling anyone, searching for I'm not sure what. Maybe I shouldn't be telling you but if I don't tell someone, I think that I'm going to bust." He decided to take a chance.

"Mr. Connors, I don't know if I can help you. But I don't think that telling me will hurt anything. You look like you need to get something off your chest. Go ahead, it's O.K."

"Where should I begin?" Matt asked as he began pacing. "I must tell you some bad news. Konrad's father is dead."

"What?" shrieked Heidi. "You must be mistaken."

Matt handed her his handkerchief. "He died yesterday in a hospital in Leningrad, the victim of a mugging. I was the last person he spoke with."

"You? What did he say?" demanded the German woman.

"You see, I've developed this rather bizarre theory about a group of former Nazis whose goal is to conquer the world. I was in his hospital room to ask him questions."

"Nonsense," shouted Mrs. Ligachev.

"That seems to be everyone's response. Please let me finish," requested the deputy national security adviser.

"Of course, I'm sorry. Please forgive me."

"I don't have the time or the hard evidence to go into all the details. But I challenged Mr. Ligachev with this accusation and he confirmed it." Matt pulled out the letter that he had found in the hospital room addressed to Konrad.

"Is this his handwriting?" he asked.

She looked at it closely. "Yes, I believe it is. He had a very distinct writing style. Let me finish reading it." Matt stayed quiet as she read the letter.

"Also, I'm afraid that Gunther is dead too." Matt tried to soften the blow but she started crying.

Heidi tried to speak but couldn't say anything.

"I don't think you need to be involved, Rita," he said nervously to the nurse.

Heidi came to Rita's defense. "Rita is family. She and Alexandra are like sisters and I'm her godmother. Whatever you have to say to me can be said in front of Rita. So, Mr. Connors, please continue," she said.

Nobody in the U.S. administration would take him seriously and yet here he was talking about a plan to take over the world with two German women. But what else could he do? He took a deep breath and showed her the letter.

Fear resonating in her voice, Rita said "The deaths of millions? Only nuclear weapons can cause such tragedy. Germany has none," she stated emphatically.

Both pairs of eyes turned to Matt, who shrugged his shoulders. "He told me that his real name was Wolfgang Weber and that there exists a group of ex-SS officers whose goal is to restore Germany to power."

"You can't be serious," Heidi said in disbelief. "Are you saying that my father-in-law is a Nazi? If what you say is true, how could such a thing possibly happen?"

"I don't know the specifics," answered Matt, "but he said by force. He also said that there were five other members and that they were known by the names of great German historical figures. His name was Charlemagne."

"Charlemagne," said Heidi aloud. "He often spoke of him with great admiration."

Matt continued. "He said that there were two members of the group who were living in America and that their names were Bismarck and Rommel. He said to ask Konrad. And then he was gone."

Rita couldn't believe what she was hearing. "Excuse me, but this sounds just a little too far-fetched. Mr. Connors, please."

"Hey, I agree with you. It's insanity, it's too crazy to believe. But he confirmed it and he wrote this note. Now whether you believe it or not, I have to find Konrad. I'm sorry ladies, but I have to get a hotel room for the night and some rest." He stood up abruptly.

"No hotel for you, Mr. Connors. You will stay with us," she said with authority.

"I'm afraid that I'm going to have to decline. I've many phone calls to place and I need total quiet to recover from my injuries," he said with finality. "I'll call you soon and I'd appreciate any information about Konrad's whereabouts. And so, ladies, I have to leave now. Please don't breathe a word of this to anyone." He looked into their eyes. "Promise?" he asked.

"Promise," the two German women answered in unison.

Matt asked, "Would one of you call me a taxi?"

"I'll call," Rita said with a smile and ran to the phone. Within five or six minutes, they heard the horn of the taxi. Matt bid them good-bye.

"Please let me know if you have any news. I'll be at the Hotel Frankfurter." He shook their hands and thanked Rita again for all of her efforts. "Keep in touch, Florence," he said, walking out of the door.

"Florence?" she asked quizzically.

"Florence Nightingale," he said with a smile and disappeared into the taxi.

The two German woman talked about the night's events for about an hour before Rita left. Then Heidi Ligachev walked into the kitchen and dialed the telephone. She waited four rings before anyone answered. "Hallo," came the voice on the other end.

"This is Heidi Ligachev. Matthew Connors of the U.S. government was just here. He knows all about the Six. He's staying at the Hotel Frankfurter." She looked out the window and smiled as she hung up the phone.

20

The president arrived at the Oval Office 7:00 A.M. and immediately summoned Phil Gordon.

"Phil, I've decided to name Schmidt for defense. Ordinarily, I think that the Senate would have his lunch but I believe they'll confirm. What do you think?" Andrew Tolbert asked.

"Mr. President, he has a lot of negatives," answered the chief of staff.

"Are you saying we should take the path of least resistance? Phil, I'm disappointed. But my mind is made up. Get Schmidt on the horn and issue a press release. Then set up a meeting with the Senate leaders," the president said, breaking into his famous smile.

"Yes, sir, Mr. President." Gordon knew it was pointless to try to change his mind. "I'll let you know when we get a hold of Schmidt."

"Thanks, Phil," Tolbert replied. "What the hell was that about a Congressman duking it out with a gang member?" he asked, changing the subject. "Sometimes I wonder why I'm not retired playing golf like most people my age. I mean, what's next?"

"We live in a strange world, sir." Gordon said with a shrug of his shoulders and quickly got out of harm's way. Tolbert had a terrible temper and would frequently scream, curse and even throw things.

A few minutes later, Gordon rang the president. "I got Schmidt on the line, sir."

"Thanks, Phil. Maybe he can control that damn fool son-in-law of his." The president picked up the phone and got right to the point.

"The job's yours, Karl, if you think you can stand the heat. Before you answer, tell me straight, Karl. Any skeletons in your closet? Ever bed down a boy or smoke dope or anything that might cause problems on the Hill?" Tolbert asked.

Tolbert could sense anger in Karl's voice.

"Nothing like that, Mr. President. Only that I never served in the military, and my brother died in jail after serving a life sentence for murder. I tried to enlist but they wouldn't take me—flat feet."

"I don't think that you have to be military to do this job right," the president said. "We're entering a different era and I think, if I put a general in the post, he'd just tell me that he needs more weapons and more men. And I know that you can't pick your relatives."

"I want you to lead the charge, Karl," the president continued. "We're issuing a press release soon so be prepared to be barraged by the media boys. Give them hell."

"You won't regret your decision, Mr. President. I'll make my country proud," Karl said ironically.

"That's what I like to hear," said the president.

☩   ☩   ☩

Michael barely escaped the crush of the media as they probed and prodded with their questions regarding Johnny Green's startling revelations. Johnny was totally unprepared for such an onslaught and even Michael was overwhelmed by their tenacity. When he pulled into his driveway around 8:00 P.M., he discovered, much to his chagrin, that the media was camping out in his frontyard.

As he walked up the driveway, a hundred microphones were stuck into his face and he was blinded by the flashbulbs.

"No comment, folks. Maybe tomorrow. It's been a long day," Michael said politely but firmly. With that, he opened the door and slammed it behind him.

Rebecca was standing right there and their eyes locked.

"Michael, what am I going to do with you?" Rebecca said, in mock exasperation. "You made my first day on the job a living hell." She grabbed him and pulled him to her. "But I'll forgive you if you give me a kiss."

Michael didn't argue, and he complied with her wish, pressing his lips against hers in a long, passionate kiss.

"Well, that's the way a congressman should be treated every night when he returns home. Where is everyone?" Michael whispered.

"David and TJ are asleep and Josh's at Kelly's house. Are you thinking what I think you're thinking?"

He didn't answer but instead grabbed her even more passionately. "Oh, Michael—" Hearing a knock at the door she abruptly stopped speaking.

"Don't those damn reporters speak English?" he shouted in anger. He looked out the peephole but saw no one at the door. "That's odd. I know I heard a knock."

Just then, another knock was heard coming from the back door. Michael ran through the house and peeked out the kitchen window. It was Nate Wallace and another man.

Michael opened the door. "What in God's name are you doing? I thought that you were one of those media slugs."

"I can't believe those jackals. They'll be going through your garbage soon," Nate said contemptuously. He took his coat off and started to introduce his companion.

Rebecca walked into the room. "Hi, Becky, remember me? Nate Wallace. Mike and I served together in 'Nam. Anyway, as I started to say, this is Charlie Stevens."

Charlie shook Michael's hand vigorously "Good to meet you, Mike. And you too, Becky."

"You didn't waste any time causing controversy," Nate interjected. That's what I like about you, bud. Why do something quietly when you can make a lot of people sweat?"

Michael knew he was joking but it offended him. "I'm not a publicity hound," he said defensively.

"I know, Mike. Don't get all bent out of shape about it. I'm just messing with you," said Nate.

Rebecca chimed in. "At least you kept me busy on my first day back," she said with a smile. She then added, "Would you guys like something to eat or drink?"

"A beer might do the trick," Nate responded.

"Same for me," replied Stevens.

Michael went to the refrigerator and pulled out three beers. "Becks, would you mind if we talked some business for a little bit?"

Rebecca took the hint. "Not at all, darling. I'll be upstairs." She turned to their guests and said, "It was nice meeting you. Good night."

As she walked out of the room, Michael whispered, "Your timing stinks, guys."

"Sorry, Mike, but this is important," Nate said seriously.

"I suppose it's about that crazy idea of yours to go down and kidnap Ramirez," Michael speculated.

"Yes, it is. We've planned everything down to a gnat's ass. The team leaves on Friday. We want you to come. If everything goes to plan, we should be back home by Sunday. Nobody will even miss you," Nate said convincingly.

Stevens spoke up. "Michael, I'm the pilot for this mission. I'm CIA. This is a joint operation with DEA and it's been approved by the brass. No one knows about you and no one needs to. The team's a crackerjack outfit and very nonpolitical. I'd doubt the others would even know who you are," the CIA man said candidly.

Michael shook his head. "But why me? If your team is as good as you say, you certainly don't need me."

"We need you, Mike," Nate said, "because you're the best special ops guy I've ever seen. I mean, they're still talking about you in SF about the things you did in 'Nam."

"That was twenty years ago, for God's sake."

"Maybe so, but you've been involved in more recent operations, like Grenada and Panama and a couple of others," Nate added.

"I see that you've got some sources, Nate. No one should know about those," Michael said.

"I have some connections," conceded the DEA man. "Listen, Mike, Ramirez has been impossible to corner and we know where he's going to be this weekend. He's taking a vacation and his security will be minimal. Now's the time, Mikey boy. Join us. If not for you, or your constituents, do it for that sweetheart daughter of yours. This bastard deserves to fry. Let's get him."

✠   ✠   ✠

Steigrich followed the servant through the ornate house, the walls of which were covered with photographs. Klaus was an avid and skilled photographer and had actually sold many of his prints earlier in his career.

Steigrich stopped to look closely at one of the photos and was very moved at the black-and-white shot of a German soldier, who appeared to be in great pain.

As he was studying the photo, Felix Klaus, otherwise known as Wilhelm, approached. "General Steigrich, guten Abend."

"Guten Abend," Steigrich replied, somewhat surprised. After collecting his composure, he asked Wilhelm about the photograph on the wall.

"Ah, that is one of my favorites. I took it myself during the Battle of the Bulge. That soldier had just been hit. But he wouldn't stop. He refused medical assistance. He insisted on leading the charge, despite having a bloody pulp for a leg," Klaus reminisced.

"What happened to him?

"Actually, he died a few seconds after I took the picture. Artillery shell hit him. Took his face clean off," Klaus said sadly. "I keep that photo for inspiration."

Before Steigrich could respond, Klaus gestured to Krupp, who had just entered the room. "I would like you to meet an associate of mine," Wilhelm said.

Steigrich looked at Krupp and felt that there was something familiar about him but he couldn't be certain.

"General Steigrich, I've read much about you," Krupp said. "Your credentials are impeccable and your loyalty to Germany is beyond reproach."

Steigrich looked at Krupp with skepticism. Krupp was an unknown quantity. He began to feel ill at ease.

Wilhelm detected the tension. "Let's get down to business, shall we?" he said. "General Steigrich, would you be willing to lead Germany's army against the other powers in what would be, essentially, a preemptive attack?" Klaus' directness unsettled him and he began to wonder if he was being set up. Maybe Krupp would arrest him if he answered Klaus' question in the affirmative.

"Herr General, you're probably wondering if what Herr Klaus has told you is for real or if this is some type of trap. I assure you that I'm not with the police and you will not be arrested," added Krupp.

Steigrich looked a little embarrassed. "Excuse my hesitation but this is a little hard to believe."

"I know it is," replied Krupp. "But it's the truth. Let me tell you who I am. I prefer to think of myself as a soldier but some might call me a terrorist. I am, in all modesty, perhaps the world's leading authority on guerilla tactics and small arms. I'm an expert in what is now being called low intensity conflict. But our mission requires a conventional military man. And that man is you, General. But let me make one thing crystal clear," he said slowly, pausing for effect.

Krupp walked over to a large desk by the fireplace, opened up the top drawer and pulled out a pistol. He pointed it at Steigrich's head and cocked the hammer.

"General Steigrich, we're running out of time to carry out our plan so we must act quickly. Are you totally loyal to Germany and are you willing to die for her?"

"Of course," came the nervous reply. "I believe 100 percent in German supremacy and in her destiny to rule the world."

"Very good, General," Krupp continued, taking another step towards Steigrich and placing the weapon against his head. "But if you ever sway, even display the slightest doubt, I will be glad to pull the trigger that blows your brains out. Do we understand each other?" asked Krupp.

"Yes. I understand," answered Steigrich, his heart pounding.

"Good," interjected Klaus. "Please forgive us, Herr General, for such a crude demonstration, but we must be certain of your loyalty. There is too much at stake." Krupp put the pistol down and Steigrich let out a sigh of relief.

"One other thing, Herr General," added Krupp. "How is your daughter Erika doing these days?"

Steigrich's eyes widened at the mention of Erika's name. "She is doing fine. She and her husband just had a baby, my first grandchild. Why do you ask?"

"I would hate to see anything happen to such a beautiful family, that's all," replied Krupp.

Steigrich understood. "You can trust me. I swear."

"Very well," answered Wilhelm. "Let me tell you who we are. Sit down, Herr Steigrich. Make yourself comfortable."

Steigrich sat down and listened intently for the next hour as Wilhelm told him about the Six and their mission.

"Incredible. Absolutely incredible," said the astonished Steigrich. "It's beyond belief. Germany will actually be able to recapture its greatness after all. I never thought that I would live to see it."

"And you might not," interjected Krupp. "I'm sure that you realize the dangers involved. Despite our success, make no mistake that the odds are against us."

"I realize that," responded the general. "But I also think that this is Germany's fate. Her destiny. It's meant to be and I will be proud to be a part of it. What exactly will be my role?" asked Steigrich.

"Very simple. To assemble an army that is loyal to our objective. At first, it should be very small, perhaps one brigade. At our first meeting, I asked if you were interested in the AFCENT position. But that was just a ruse. Your real task will be to assemble a small, loyal, elite force that will grow in time to be the largest in the world. Do you accept this challenge?" asked Wilhelm.

"Yes, sir, I do. You've come to the right man."

"I don't wish to belabor the point," said Krupp, "but perhaps you heard about General Punder's death?"

Steigrich look puzzled. "I heard that he was killed by a car bomb—" He stopped and suddenly realized the truth.

"It was not an accident, General. So I hope that you will not follow in his footsteps. Give my best to your daughter," said Krupp, making his point very clear.

Wilhelm added. "My colleague is a little more direct than I, but please heed his warnings. Do not contact me at my office. All of your dealings and communications will be with him. He will contact you tomorrow and we will meet sometime next week. Good night, General."

"Good night, Mr. Secretary General," said Steigrich as he walked out into the darkness. He was to assemble an army to lead Germany. He looked to the stars above him. God, don't fail me, he said to himself.

☩   ☩   ☩

Matt was still recovering from his wounds. He walked very slowly to his room at the Hotel Frankfurter. He had tried the elevator but it was out of order. Why did he pick such a dump? he asked himself.

He turned the key and flipped the light switch on. He was very tired and needed a good night's sleep. He pulled out a beer that he had just bought and cursed as he realized that he didn't have a bottle opener. He looked all around the room for something to help him open the bottle. The radiator. He walked over to the old-fashioned radiator and put the bottle between the grooves in the top of the antiquated heater and popped off the bottle cap. Some of the foam rushed to the top and he quickly put it to his lips. He kicked off his shoes and sat on the bed.

What a day. He still couldn't believe that he was running around the world on a half-cocked lead. What was he dealing with? Hitler's ghost?

He had to talk to Konrad. What if Heidi didn't hear from him? He couldn't stay in Germany more than a couple of days. He must talk to him.

Matt sat in his bed, swigging the warm beer, his thoughts racing in a million directions. His body was begging for rest. He fought to stay awake and develop a plan of attack, but he finally passed out into a deep sleep, fully clothed.

A key turned silently in the lock. A slight noise jolted Matt causing him to drop his beer bottle to the floor. He found himself facing two masked men with guns. He started to yell out but before he could say anything, one of them pulled out a club and smashed it into Matt's temple, quickly rendering him unconscious.

The men carried him down the back steps and into an awaiting car and drove away into the night.

Matt awoke several hours later, his arms tied behind his back, sitting on the floor of a dimly lit and damp room. Where was he? The only person that knew where he was Davis Elliot. No, there was one other person. Heidi Ligachev. It couldn't be, but there was no other explanation. The sweet little German woman he had opened up to was a Nazi.

Matt tried to loosen the rope around his arms but couldn't do it. His circulation was being cut off. Squirming and twisting only made it worse so he finally stopped. He had to urinate desperately and when he couldn't hold it in any longer, he relieved himself, soaking his pants with urine.

Matt had seen death close up before but he began to worry that he might be joining the dead soon. Was this to be his fate, to die in a German prison?

✠   ✠   ✠

Pam Connors had just put her youngest son, John, who was sick, to sleep. She now had the house to herself. Silence was something that was normally in short supply in the busy Connors household and she was going to cherish every moment.

She had stopped worrying about Matt and his secret missions years ago. She was a realist and knew that her worrying would accomplish nothing. She had no control over it and would not allow her imagination to run away with her.

She put a record on the stereo and laughed, remembering how her daughter had chided her for holding onto them. Danielle had a date tonight and that was cause for worry much more than anything Matt might be doing. She had developed into a beautiful and shapely young lady.

Pam poured herself a glass of wine and put her feet up on the coffee table. Her eldest son, Albert, was spending the night at a friend's and the house was all hers. The combination of a whirlwind day and the wine had its effect and Pam was soon sound asleep, still clutching the glass of wine. The record reached the end of the last song and began skipping repeatedly, while Pam peacefully slept in ignorance of the irritating sound.

Outside, two men sat in a dark sedan with long range surveillance equipment and knew that everyone in the house was asleep. They moved quickly towards the house, dressed all in black and wearing ski masks. They each carried rope, and a pistol with a silencer. The men expertly picked the back door lock and silently made their way into the house. One moved into the living room, while the other proceeded upstairs towards the Connors' youngest son.

Pam detected a noise and abruptly awoke, shocked to see towering over her a masked man with a club in his hand. She instinctively screamed and lunged off the couch but the intruder caught the side of her head with a sharp blow of the stick and she collapsed to the ground.

Upstairs, the other intruder had reached the bedroom of the sleeping young boy, but despite years of hardness couldn't bring himself to harm him. He pulled a hypodermic out of a bag around his waist and plunged it into John's arm. He would be out cold for many hours. He put the boy on his back and proceeded downstairs.

The man who had hit Pam noticed how appealing she was, but he quickly put such thoughts aside and hoisted her onto his shoulders. Within seconds, both men were out of the house with their victims and they drove away into the darkness.

✠   ✠   ✠

Michael was driving frantically through the dense traffic. He had just been summoned by the president for a private meeting. Why would he, a freshman legislator, be singled out? Maybe it was about his father-in-law, the next secretary of defense. No matter. This was an important moment in his career and he wanted to make a favorable impression.

A guard escorted him to a room near the Oval Office, and he was surprised to find himself alone. He opened a door that led to a hallway and called out. But there was only an eerie silence. He realized he was just outside the Oval Office and still he encountered no one. He heard voices, coming from the Oval Office.

For a moment, Michael stood outside the door, uncertain. He just couldn't barge into the President's office. He decided to make some noise. Surely, someone would hear and come out to greet him. He began coughing and shuffling his feet but no one noticed.

He couldn't just stand there all day. He was just about to knock when he clearly heard one of the voices inside. The words were in German.

Michael tiptoed to the door and positioned himself so that he could glance in the room. He saw the president, Chief of Staff Phil Gordon and Secretary of State Watkins. Gordon was shouting excitedly and pacing around the room flailing his arms while Tolbert sat quietly at his desk. Watkins sat with a briefing book on his lap.

After several moments, Gordon stopped his harangue and Tolbert and Watkins began speaking. They too were speaking in German. What was going on? Michael then saw the president reach up and place his hands upon his forehead and saw him grab what appeared to be his skin. He slowly peeled back a mask. Michael thought that his heart was going to jump out of his body. Tolbert shook his head and pushed his hand through his hair. Michael could now clearly see the president's true appearance and thought that he had just seen the devil. He managed to stifle a scream and quickly ducked out of sight.

After several minutes, he stole another glance into the Oval Office, hoping that what he had seen was just his imagination. But it wasn't. Sitting at the desk of the president of the United States was Adolf Hitler himself, shouting at Phil Gordon and the secretary of state, who were responding to him in German. Michael took one more glance and saw a swastika on the wall. He felt like vomiting.

He began running blindly through the White House. He made it to the streets and ran about two blocks before stopping. He threw himself on a bus-stop bench in near exhaustion. He revisited, in his mind, the events that he'd just witnessed.

Michael spotted a telephone booth and madly dashed towards it. He yanked the receiver off and began dialing, in a near catatonic daze.

"White House," said a voice.

"I need to speak to the vice president immediately. This is Congressman Michael Madigan and it's an extreme emergency."

"Just a moment, sir," came the reply.

Soon another voice came on the line. "Craig Jensen here," said the vice president.

"Mr. Vice President, we've never met but I'm Michael Madigan, a new congressman from California."

"Yes, I know quite a bit about you, Mr. Madigan. I heard about your gang-member friend."

"Listen, there isn't time to talk about that now. I'm calling about something that's perhaps unparalleled in American history. You must believe me."

"What is it Madigan? You sound almost hysterical," said Jensen. "Have you been drinking?"

"Of course not," shouted Michael. "O.K., I'll try to calm down." He took a couple of deep breaths and spoke slowly. "Listen, what I'm about to tell is almost incomprehensible but I swear I'm telling you the truth."

"Well, spit it out, Madigan. What has you so riled up?"

"I was just in the White House. The president had called me there for a meeting," Michael explained. "None of the staff was around and I walked right in the West Wing and proceeded to the Oval Office. I heard several voices coming from there and realized that they were German."

"German?" asked the vice president surprised. "Are you certain?"

"Positive. I was stationed in Frankfurt for several years and used to be almost fluent in German," said Michael.

"Who was in there? Did you see?" inquired Jensen.

"Yes, it was the president, Phil Gordon and Secretary of State Watkins," answered Michael.

"Which one was speaking German?" asked Jensen.

"They all were, absolutely fluently."

"That's impossible. The president doesn't speak German," said Jensen, irritation showing in his voice. He was starting to lose his patience.

"But that's just it, you see. That wasn't Andrew Tolbert in there," Michael said quietly.

"What are you talking about?"

"I saw what appeared to be President Tolbert sitting at his desk. He then reached up to his forehead and pulled off a mask. You'll think I'm crazy but it was Adolf Hitler."

"What? Are you insane?" replied Jensen.

"I probably wouldn't believe it, either. But I swear on my father's grave that Adolf Hitler is either impersonating the president or is the president. Either way, he must be stopped. Andrew Tolbert must be killed immediately. Do you hear me? He must be assassinated for the good of the country and the vice president must quickly take over. There's no other solution. That man in the Oval Office, whoever he is, must die, or this country will never survive. Do you understand what I'm saying?" Michael shouted.

Jensen didn't say anything for several seconds and then spoke very slowly. "Madigan, I suggest you get some help and that you get it right away."

"If you're not going to do anything, then I'll kill him myself. For the good of the people of the United States, I'll kill that impostor in the White House," Michael said with a tone of finality and hung up the phone.

Michael suddenly woke and shot upright, sweat dripping from his forehead. He saw the light of the moon shining in his bedroom and realized that he had been dreaming again. What a nightmare! This had been perhaps the worst one of all. Every detail had been so vivid, so clear, that he found himself shaking like a leaf.

He quickly glanced around the room and reached out for Rebecca. She wasn't there, and for a second he panicked. He got out of the bed and walked into the hallway. He heard Rebecca's voice coming from downstairs and saw a light on. He headed down the stairs.

Michael walked into the kitchen just as Rebecca was hanging up the phone. She noticed that he looked pale and that he was drenched with sweat.

She knew right away what it was. "Another dream, Michael?" she asked softly.

"Yeah, and this one was the worst I've ever had," he said, hugging her tightly.

"Who was that on the phone?"

"That was Danielle Connors," Rebecca answered. "She just got home from a date and found the house empty. Matt and Albert were away for the night and she was surprised to find John and Pam gone. Pam's car was still in the driveway and she can't imagine where they could have gone. Pam had told her only a few hours ago that she was going to stay home because John was sick. She sounded quite worried."

"What time is it?" asked Michael.

"Just after midnight."

"I better talk to her," he said as he dialed the phone.

"Do you think anything's wrong?" she asked nervously.

"I don't know. I hope not but...Hello, Danielle? This is Mike Madigan. Rebecca just told me everything. Do you have any idea where your mom might be?"

"No, Colonel Madigan and I'm really scared." She was crying now. "My dad and brother are out of town and I don't know what to do. John was really sick and I can't imagine where my mom would go without her car. Also, I just found some dirty footprints in the kitchen." She began crying inconsolably and Michael couldn't understand her.

"Danielle, I'm going to call the police and come right over there," Michael said reassuringly. "Do you hear? Lock all the doors and don't let anyone in unless it's me or the police. Or your mom, of course. O.K., sweetheart?"

"O.K., Colonel. Thank you."

"I'll be right there and everything will be all right." Michael hung up the phone. "Rebecca, call the cops and have them meet me at the Connors' house."

"O.K., but you be careful, Michael," she said, and kissed him. He threw on some clothes and headed towards the Connors' house, praying that everything was all right.

✠   ✠   ✠

Matt woke after many hours of sleep feeling very disoriented. The pain was excruciating and that was the only thing of which he was sure. Slowly, it came back to him. He had been absconded from his hotel room and the German woman must have turned him in. They now knew that he knew. Certainly, they wouldn't let him live. He must escape.

He quickly realized that that would not be easy. The room was pitch black and his hands and feet were tightly bound, almost to the point of cutting off his circulation.

After what seemed like several hours, the door suddenly swung open and a light was switched on, causing Matt to cringe from the sudden brightness.

It was an elderly but still powerfully built man, known among his colleagues as Krupp. He was accompanied by a tall, muscular man carrying a rifle. After a short pause, he spoke. "Mr. Connors, do you know who I am?"

Matt had seen the German terrorist before but he wasn't sure where. He shook his head, wincing from the pain.

"Your memory is not so good. We met, although not formally, the other night, as you found yourself compelled to break onto the property of a colleague of mine. That kind of antisocial behavior is not favored by certain Dobermans, I'm sure you would agree," said Krupp.

Matt now remembered Krupp. Matt tried not to show fear. "I don't know what you're talking about," he spat.

"Mr. Connors, I'm afraid that you do. At least, that's what Heidi Ligachev tells us. She says that there are many things that you know about us," Krupp proclaimed.

It had been Konrad's wife after all. How could she do it? It didn't make sense.

"Are you going to kill me?" Matt asked.

"Yes, we are," said Krupp coldly.

"But not just yet. We have some things that we could use your help with. You're a very capable man, Mr. Connors," Krupp said in an ingratiating tone.

"What in God's name makes you think that I would help you bastards? Excuse me but I'll pass," Matt lashed out angrily. "My only regret is that if you do kill me, I won't be able to see you and your 'colleagues' go down."

Krupp smirked at Matt's response. "Mr. Connors, your attitude is very negative, I'm afraid. It definitely could use some adjustment." He walked over to the other side of the room and picked up a phone and began dialing. After several seconds, he spoke into the phone. "Put her on."

Krupp turned towards Matt and handed him the phone. "There's someone who wants to speak to you."

Matt felt a sinking feeling in his stomach.

"Matt, they have me and John," screamed Pam. "What do they want?" she shouted hysterically.

Krupp took the phone from Matt and said, "Sorry, Mr. Connors. She'll have to call you back later."

Filled with rage, he flung himself against Krupp, but with his hands and feet tied, his attempted tackle was not very effective. He made contact with the old German but quickly fell to the ground.

"You sons of bitches. I'll kill you all," he screamed.

"You'll do nothing of the sort," Krupp retorted. "In fact, you'll do whatever we say and will help us. If you refuse, your family will be fed to those Dobermans you made so angry. Do you understand what I'm saying?"

"Yes," Matt said, weakly. "I understand."

21

Michael arrived at the Connors' house just as the police did and quickly introduced himself to the officer in charge.

"Sergeant Mendez," Michael said, noticing the officer's name tag, "I'm the one who called. The girl inside is Danielle Connors and her father works at the White House. Her mother and brother are missing and she called me. Her father and I are good friends," Michael explained.

"O.K., Congressman. Let's go see what the girl has to say," said Mendez, as he and his partner walked up to the door and knocked.

There was no answer. "Ms. Connors, this is the police. Please open the door. We're here to help you."

Michael yelled so that Danielle could hear. "Danielle, it's Mike Madigan. Open the door, sweetheart. It's O.K."

A few seconds later, she opened the door, visibly upset. "Come in," she said, so softly that she could barely be heard.

Sergeant Mendez spoke first. "Other than your mom being gone, have you noticed anything unusual?"

Danielle quietly handed him a note that she had found in the kitchen. He read it and handed the note to Michael. "Congressman, read this and see if it makes any sense to you." The note read: *Your husband is interfering with our business. He and his family will pay the price.* It was signed "The City of Orchids." Michael knew instantly and was sickened.

He comforted Danielle and helped her to the couch. "It's going to be all right, sweetheart. I'm going to do everything I can to get your mamma back. Now, you sit here for a minute and let me talk to the sergeant."

Michael grabbed Mendez' arm and escorted him out of Danielle's earshot. The policeman asked impatiently, "What's this City of Orchids bullshit? Do you know?"

"Yeah, I know. Matt Connors has been trying to convince the president to take a very active role in the war on drugs. Most of the cocaine entering this country comes from Colombia; specifically, from the Medellin region. Medellin is in the Colombian Andes and is called the "City of Orchids."

Mendez looked confused. "What are you saying exactly? That some drug lords have kidnapped Mrs. Connors because of what her husband has been doing?"

Michael nodded.

"Where did you say the Mister was again?" asked the cop.

"I'd bet either Colombia or at the bottom of the ocean," Michael said, feeling nauseous. "If both of them aren't dead yet, they soon will be. These people don't mess around. They're vicious and brutal. I think that I'm going to be sick," he said and rushed to the nearest bathroom.

Mendez was in over his head. He was a patrolman and was used to domestic violence and liquor store robberies. International drug lords and White House officials were definitely not his domain. Michael returned with all the color drained from his face.

Mendez yelled to his partner, "Hey, Jackson, get the Feds over here. I can't stand them but we're out of our league."

"Congressman, the FBI will be here shortly. Will you stay here until they come?" the sergeant asked.

"Sure thing," Michael said. He walked over to the sofa where Danielle was and put his arm around her.

✠　✠　✠

The alarm clock went off at 5:30 A.M. and Michael groaned as he turned it off. He had not gotten to sleep until after 3:00 A.M. The combination of that nightmare, the kidnapping of Pam Connors and just two hours sleep made him feel like the living dead. His body ached but he had decided that he would go on Nate Wallace's crazy mission. Things were out of control.

He splashed water on his face and brushed his teeth, trying not to wake Rebecca. To think that Medellin drug lords were kidnapping Americans was just too much for him. Maybe this mission was insane but he just couldn't sit around reading reports. Somebody had to do something.

He knew that the conviction of a single drug dealer wouldn't solve the whole problem but it would go a long way towards that goal. Ramirez was the biggest trafficker in the world. Perhaps his capture would not only curtail the flow of drugs but have a psychological impact on other dealers and distributors. Kidnaping the chief kingpin from his own home would send a strong message.

He agonized over whether he should wake Rebecca and say good-bye. He might not ever see her again. He stood by the bed and gazed lovingly at her. She was his berscheta, the Hebrew word for soul mate. He kissed her forehead and quietly left the house, praying that he would return safely.

Michael made the short drive to Maryland, where Nate lived. He knocked and within seconds, Nate opened the door, fully dressed in jungle fatigues.

Nate smiled. "Mike, I take it that you're not just here to wish us good luck."

"I'll probably regret this but I'm in, Nate. We've got to get this bastard. They kidnapped Pam Connors and I think they have Matt too."

"Connors? Are you serious? Man, that's heavy shit," Nate said. "Come on in and tell me what happened. Can I get you some coffee?"

"Yeah, I need a pitcher, I think. I only got about two hours of sleep," Michael said, letting out a loud yawn. Nate yelled out to the CIA pilot Michael had met, " Hey, Charlie. Get Mike some coffee, would you?"

"Right away," replied the agent.

"So, tell me what happened with Connors, Mike. This is incredible," said Nate.

Michael filled him in and added his analysis that if Pam had been kidnapped, Matt must have been as well.

"Now, we don't know that, Mike. Let's not jump to conclusions. You know how it is over in the White House basement. Matt used to be a special ops guy like us. He gets off on running around the world on secret missions. It's what he lives for."

"Ordinarily, I'd buy that, Nate," responded Michael. "But it's just too much coincidence. They kidnapped Pam for a reason—to send a message to Matt. Either they've got him holed up somewhere or he's at the bottom of a hole."

"He's my best friend," he paused and then continued, "we've got to get that bastard, Nate. Let's pin him to the wall!"

"I hear you, pal," Nate said. "It looks like you rushed out of the house in a flash this morning. I don't think that you're wearing the right apparel for a covert operation. Those clothes will definitely clash with a jungle environment," Nate said, hoping that some humor would steady Michael's nerves. "Let's see, you look like a forty regular. Could we interest you in something in a khaki, perhaps?"

Michael smiled. "I'd prefer a drab green, actually."

"O.K. Let's see, a thirty-six waist?"

"Thirty-six?" Michael said, offended. "Does this flat stomach look like a thirty-six? Try thirty-two, pal."

Nate laughed. "Coming right up. Do you want to call your office? We're going to be leaving in about an hour."

"Yeah, that's a good idea." He looked at his watch. It was 6:30 A.M. There was probably no one at the office yet and so he dialed Alex Turner's home number.

"Hello," answered Alex sleepily.

"Alex, I'm glad I reached you," Michael said.

"Is that you, Colonel? What's up?"

"I have to leave town for a couple of days and I can't tell you where I'm going. Cover for me. It's pretty important stuff. I hope to be back by Monday. O.K?"

"You got it, Colonel," Alex said sleepily.

"One other thing. Sometime today, call my wife for me. Tell her that I'll be gone for a few days and that it has to do with Matt. She'll understand."

"Colonel, are you sure everything's all right?"

"No, I'm not sure about that at all, Alex," Michael said, and hung up the phone.

✠   ✠   ✠

Rebecca arrived home exhausted. She wasn't used to the drain of the rat race or Friday evening traffic. She greeted Christina, the housekeeper, found that TJ had gone to bed early and that David was outside playing. She begged Christina for a little bit of quiet time and collapsed onto the couch.

There was so much for her to learn, so many of her skills had eroded and she had lost much of the "killer instinct" that she used to have. But she desperately needed the mental stimulation. As important as she had viewed her task of taking care of TJ, she had often thought that she would lose her mind.

But now her thoughts were filled with Pam Connors. And what of Matt? Had he been kidnapped as well?

They had known Matt and Pam for years and had shared many different experiences that had made them the best of friends. Dear Lord, please let them be alive, she prayed.

"Mrs. Madigan?" Christina whispered. "I'm sorry to disturb you, but your father's on the phone."

"Thank you, Christina," she answered as Christina handed her the portable phone.

"Hi, Daddy. How are you?"

"I'm great but you sound down. Is everything O.K.?"

"Did you hear about Matt Connors and his wife?"

"No, I've been pretty busy today, testifying on the Hill. What about them?" he asked.

"Well, actually, I'm not sure if anything's happened to him, but Pam was kidnapped."

"What? By whom?"

"We don't know. There was a note signed by the "City of Orchids." It said that Matt had stuck his nose in their business and that his family was going to pay the price. Do you know what that means?" Rebecca asked.

"I'm not sure, honey," he said. "Did Michael tell you what he thought it meant?"

"He went over to their house about midnight, got back about three-thirty this morning and left before six. So I never talked to him. And this afternoon, I got a call from one of his staff who said that he had to leave town for a couple of days. If it wasn't for this thing with Pam and my new crazy job, I'd be very upset," she said quietly.

She paused for a moment. "But now that I think about it, I'm pretty ticked off. He didn't even call me, one of his junior gestapo agents did."

"What did you call him?" Karl asked.

"Sorry, Daddy, but that's what his young staffers call each other," Rebecca explained.

"You don't know where he is?" he asked.

"Not a clue. But he's a big boy, I suppose. I'm sure he'll call tomorrow," Rebecca sighed with resignation.

"Listen, Becky, what do you think about dinner with your whole family tonight? Both Steven and Tommy are in town. And Mom, of course. Also, Elsbeth and Adrian. I'm buying. I knocked those senators on their butts today. They didn't know what hit them. I think that you're talking to the next secretary of defense," Karl said proudly.

"Congratulations, Daddy," Rebecca replied. "I have great confidence in you. But are you serious about all of us getting together tonight?" she asked in disbelief.

"Why do you sound so surprised?"

"Well, I honestly can't remember the last time that happened," Rebecca explained. "Tommy, especially. The only time I've seen him in twenty years was at Michael's retirement and he was in one of his antisocial moods."

"Then you don't want to come?"

"I didn't say that. Of course, I'll go. I always wanted us to be a family. You know that. It just seems that you were always at work, Steven was always studying and Tommy was always busy hating the world," Rebecca said sadly.

"I didn't want it to be like that. I wish that things had been different. But maybe it's not too late. Can we pick you up at eight o'clock?"

"Sounds great, Daddy. I'll be ready. Where are we going?"

"I don't know. That's up to your mother and she's already changed her mind twice," he said with a hearty laugh.

"Surprise me, Daddy. I'll see you at eight," Rebecca said hanging up the phone, suddenly feeling very energized. She had always dearly loved each member of her family and had often regretted that they rarely spent time together. Maybe it wasn't too late.

✠　✠　✠

A rough hand and a gruff voice woke Pam and John. "Get up," the man growled at them. Their fear made them instantly alert.

"Hey," yelled Pam. "We're going. Don't push me. And keep your mitts off the boy," she snapped.

"Just do as I say if you ever want to go home," barked the man with no name.

Pam looked at John and nodded. "Do what he says," she assured him. "Don't be afraid, sweetheart."

"I'm not," answered John, bravely managing a smile.

"That's my boy."

They walked down a long corridor and into another room, which was dark and damp. The unidentified man pushed her again into the room.

"Hey, what's going on?" Pam shouted.

"You're going for a ride. Now, stay still or I'll have to hurt you," he threatened, applying blindfolds to them. "Do you understand?" he added.

They didn't answer but understood clearly. Their captor finished tightening the blindfold and pushed them back into the corridor.

"We're going for a little ride," said an unidentified voice. "And so you don't get cute, we'll be taking a little detour. Now get in the car," he shouted at them.

Pam and John did as he said and within seconds the van took off. Pam grabbed her son's hand.

"Are you O.K., sweetheart?" she asked.

"I'm fine, Mom. Do you think that he's taking us home?"

"I don't know, baby. I hope so," Pam answered, trying to sound brave. They spent the rest of the trip in silence.

After about an hour of driving, the vehicle came to a halt. They were still blindfolded as their captor spoke to them.

"Listen to me very closely, Mrs. Connors," said the voice. "I will not repeat this. Right now you still have a husband and your boy still has a father. But if you call the police or stir up any trouble, you will quickly become the widow Connors and little John here will come from a single parent family. Do I make myself clear?"

Pam was trying to hold it in, to sound brave in front of John but she couldn't do it.

"What do you want? Why do you want to harm my husband? And what was the purpose of putting us through hell tonight if you're just going to let us go?"

"Your husband has made some enemies. Tonight was to make him realize the severity of his actions. His deeds will end up hurting either him or his family. Do we understand each other?" the kidnapper asked, grabbing her wrist tightly.

"Yes, yes," she said.

"Do not do anything foolish like recording your calls or posting a cop in the house. You would regret that, I assure you. Your husband's cooperation will determine when you hear from us again. Now get out of here." He pushed them both out and they fell to the ground, their blindfolds still tightly bound around their eyes. The vehicle squealed away.

John was crying. Pam did her best to comfort him. Pam wrestled her blindfold off and immediately took John's off and hugged him.

"It's O.K., darling. Everything will be all right," Pam assured her son, looking around to see where they were. It was dark but they seemed to be in a park.

John noticed the silhouette of a swing set and a merry-go-round. He knew where they were. "We're in the park down the street from our house."

"Are you sure?" asked Pam, afraid to get her hopes up.

"I'm positive. See that basketball court over there? That's where me and my friends play ball all of the time. I'll show you how to get home, Mom," he said bravely.

He grabbed his mother's hand and began confidently walking toward home. Pam laughed at this role reversal. "O.K., John, take us home. Take us home, baby."

✠   ✠   ✠

Thousands of miles away, Matt was being interrogated by a couple of brutes who enjoyed inflicting pain.

"Talk," ordered the biggest one, "or you will pray for death." He held a whip in his hand.

Matt was almost incoherent from the pain. "I've told you everything I know. I swear."

"We don't believe you. Did we tell you that your wife is an appealing woman? She could keep several white men satisfied all night, don't you think? Am I right, Mr. Connors?"

"Go to hell!" Matt spat.

"I guess that's a yes," the big man said to his colleague. Following his lead, the smaller man said, "I've always wondered if brown sugar is as sweet as they say."

"So I've heard. I bet I could make her squeal," laughed the big man, displaying two missing teeth.

"There's a young girl in the family, too, isn't there? Leave her for me. I've always liked the young ones."

Matt glared at them full of hatred and rage. The torture session was interrupted when Krupp walked into the room. The two men snapped to attention.

"What have you found out, gentlemen?" Krupp asked.

"He's a stubborn one. Won't say a word," responded the tall one, as he held up the whip.

Krupp looked impatiently at the two men. "Every man has a weakness. Do you know what yours is, Mr. Connors?"

Matt glared at him. "Shove it up your ass."

Krupp laughed. "Mr. Connors, I would like to introduce you to some colleagues of yours from Africa. Maybe they can convince you of your foolishness." Turning, he shouted at the others. "You two come with me," and they all walked out the door. "Kommen sie hier," Krupp commanded and immediately a man in a strange protective suit came in carrying a bizarre-looking box, which he put on the ground. A loud buzzing was coming from the box.

Matt stared at the box in disbelief. How did they know? he wondered.

The man carrying the box was wearing a boiler suit, made from a close weave, white cotton material with a zip fastening in the front. The wrist and ankle bands were elastic. He wore gloves made of soft leather with fabric gauntlets and a black transparent veil over his face.

Matt began hyperventilating as the man in the strange suit poked at the box with a pole, knocking aside its top. Matt screamed as the bees flew out of the box by the thousands and hovered in a thick cloud in the middle of the room. African bees travel and attack in a mass.

Matt started bouncing frantically off the walls as the bees swarmed around him. He was beyond reason as he shrieked at the top of his lungs, running panic-stricken around the small room, his arms flailing madly. He could stand it no more as he dove to the ground and assumed a fetal position, shaking violently and sweating.

Krupp watched through a small window and smiled. He caught the attention of the man in the suit and signaled that it was over. Matt was in shock and the men had to lift him from the floor. A few bees escaped into the hallway as they left the room.

They dumped Matt on the ground, pathetic and beaten. Krupp stood over him.

"Please forgive the crude interrogation," he said. "I just wanted to get my point across. You've interfered in something that is, as you say in America, way out of your league. Think about it," Krupp said forcefully.

Not wanting to revisit the bees, Matt said, "I just have bits and pieces. All I know is that there's a group of former SS members who are determined to return Germany to power." He paused, trying to catch his breath. "I don't know any details, I don't have names. Nothing. I'm no threat to you. I had hoped to find out more from Konrad Ligachev, but I never found him," Matt added, his voice cracking.

"Ah, yes, the young professor. He met a most unfortunate fate. An accident, I'm afraid. Very unexpected."

Matt shook his head. "It doesn't surprise me. After all you're just a bunch of murdering Nazis," he said, and spit at Krupp.

"Mr. Connors, I'm going to attribute that very undiplomatic outburst to the pain you're feeling. If I thought that you meant it, I would have to return you to your buzzing little friends. Do you want that?"

Matt shook his head.

"I didn't think so."

"Do you really think that you're going to take over the world? You can't be serious," Matt whispered.

"We're very serious, Mr. Connors," Krupp replied rapidly. "That's one thing you will discover quickly. We'll be the leading power on earth within one year. The other nations of the world will bow to Germany and the Fourth Reich will begin a long and glorious reign."

Matt looked into Krupp's eyes and realized that this old man truly believed what he was saying.

"And, Mr. Connors, if you want to leave here alive, and if you expect your wife and son to survive, you will help us," the German ordered. "If you don't, you'll cause the very painful deaths of every member of your family. Please think about that tonight as you nurse your wounds."

Krupp abruptly turned and walked away, as his henchman grabbed Matt and threw him into a dark, cold room. Matt shivered on the floor and cried like a baby.

✠   ✠   ✠

The doorbell rang and Rebecca looked at her watch. Right on time. She yelled to her housekeeper. "Christina, will you get that? It's my father. I'll be right down."

Christina opened the front door, expecting the huge man she had seen in the newspapers the last few days and was quite surprised to see a younger man.

"Can I help you?" Christina asked.

"I'm Becky's brother," the sullen young man said.

Christina appeared frightened by the metallic, alien voice of Tommy Schmidt.

"My name is Tommy. *¿Dondé esta Rebecca?*" he said condescendingly, and walked right in, pushing her aside.

Christina instantly disliked him. "I'll get Mrs. Madigan," she said and quickly left, wanting to be out of his presence.

"Yeah, you do that."

Christina raced upstairs and knocked on Rebecca's door.

"I'll be right out," came the reply. Seconds later, she opened the door. "Was that my father?" she asked.

"No, ma'am. It is your brother."

"Steven? Really? Is his wife with him?"

"It's not Steven. His name is Tommy."

"Tommy? Are you serious? Tommy's here?" she asked in disbelief. She walked to the edge of the stairs and peered downward. It was him all right.

"Well, isn't this a surprise," Rebecca said out loud.

"Mrs. Madigan, please take no offense but I don't like your brother. If it's all right with you, I'll go make sure that David's ready for bed," she said.

She understood. "That's fine, Christina. Tommy is not one to win friends. Tell David I'll be there in a moment to kiss him good night."

Rebecca walked downstairs. "Hi, Tommy. This is quite a surprise."

"Yeah, I've always been full of them, haven't I, Sis?"

"That you have," she answered. She always held a soft spot for Tommy but she couldn't bring herself to kiss him.

"You ready?" Tommy asked.

"I guess so. Are we meeting everybody at the restaurant?" she asked.

"Yep. The whole loving family together again. Makes your heart warm, doesn't it?" he asked caustically.

She didn't respond. His robotic voice caused her to shiver. "Let me say good-bye to David." She went upstairs and was back within two minutes. "Let's go."

Rebecca was surprised to find herself actually nervous and even a little afraid. She knew that Tommy was just a little different, not really a bad person, but still his hatred for the world bothered her.

They drove in silence for several minutes. Rebecca was searching for small talk but for some reason she couldn't think. Finally, she blurted out, "How is Adrian?"

"She's still breathing," he said absently.

I don't know why Adrian stays with him, she thought. Minutes more went by before she spoke again. "What do you think about Daddy becoming the secretary of defense?"

"He ain't got it yet," he said, and then he lifted his voice. "Those damn Senators can't see the glasses at the end of their nose and they're determined to keep a German out. Those ignorant bastards won't confirm him."

Rebecca's anger was rising. "What's wrong with you, Tommy? Why are you always so angry? Why do you hate the world? How could you disappear for twenty years and show up like nothing happened," she asked with intensity.

"Why do I hate the world? Because it sucks," he spat out angrily. "Maybe it's because you and Steven were always treated better than me. Maybe its because I had the goddamn Viet Cong stick grenades in my pants and bayonets in my eyes. And maybe I don't feel like being a part of the Fourth fucking Reich."

Rebecca was shocked by his violent reaction and lost her breath for a moment. "Tommy, you've always shut me out of your life," she said with resentment. "I would love to talk to you about our childhood and about your war experiences. I really would. We've always seemed like strangers. I never wanted it that way. Daddy said tonight that maybe it's not too late to reunite our family. And, what did you mean about the Fourth Reich?"

"Nothing, Sis. Nothing at all," Tommy said, clamming up. The rest of the drive was in silence. Rebecca wondered just who she was sitting next to and whether she had ever known him.

"now what really gets my goat, Mike?" asked Nate Wallace, as he finished packing his bag.

"What's that?" Michael asked.

"Well, all of the politicians talk a lot about fighting the 'war on drugs' but they don't put their money where their mouth is. It's all just smoke and mirrors."

"I thought that the administration was real serious about it. Aren't they spending a ton of money on anti-drug programs?" asked Michael.

"You'd think so with all the hoopla, but not really," Nate replied with a groan. "Let me give you the straight scoop, Mike. You boys on the Hill passed this thing called the Anti-Drug Abuse Act a few years ago and the President made a big deal about it. But ninety days later, he sends his budget for the following year to Congress a billion dollars lighter than the year before. And it's been the same every year since," Nate said, with a sigh of frustration.

"Why do you suppose that is?"

"Who knows?" Nate shrugged. "But with the spread of crack cocaine, the Pentagon's been sticking their big nose in it, and the DEA opposes that big time. Of all the money that's being spent, they want to squander it on this fancy high-tech crap and interdiction. All a waste of time if you ask me," Nate said in frustration.

"I would think that you would support interdiction."

"Let me tell you why I don't, Mike," Nate said. "First of all, they've been installing all of these new radar systems on the border to detect what they call 'low and slow' aircraft penetrating United States airspace from Mexico. Existing radar installations picked up nothing that flew in lower than 10,000 feet. Cold war thinking said that no enemy plane could drop an atomic bomb from lower than that."

"The cold war's over," added Michael.

"You said it, pal," Nate concurred. "So, now, you see, out of nowhere, there's this 'soft underbelly' of U.S. air defenses. Now, there's money in the budgets for radar balloons and military surveillance aircraft to be deployed along the southwest border. The drug-war hawks envisioned this impenetrable radar net," he explained.

"What's so bad about that? It makes sense to me. Stop it before it gets in," Michael said.

"The feeling at DEA is that interdiction is futile. You could have the whole country surrounded, but people who want drugs are going to get them. You got to stop the demand."

"Then what's the use of going on this, uh, this whatever it is that we're going on?"

"Well, in any war, if you chop the head off, the body dies," stated Nate. "Ramirez controls a massive empire. Without his direction, there will be chaos. Plus, it sends a message, you know. I mean, if we can swoop down in the middle of the night and throw this guy's ass in an American jail for a couple of decades, it's going to have an impact."

"Well, it's 'Miller time.' You all ready?" Nate asked.

"Not really," answered Michael, "but let's get it over with."

"That's the attitude," Nate laughed. "Try to keep the excitement down, Mike. Don't get too riled up."

"Let's do it," Charlie said, and the three men climbed into Nate's car and drove to the edge of town, where they would meet three more members of the team and then fly to Peru for a midnight meeting with Señor Ramirez.

"Where exactly in Peru are we going?" Michael asked.

"Tingo Maria," Nate answered. "It's in a section called Huanaco, northeast of Lima. It's in the mountains and is full of guns and big money. You see, Peru is a refining state. A few years back, the Colombian government cracked down on the cocaine trade and the refiners fled into Peru and set up shop. They've been there ever since," he explained.

"South America was never my area of specialty," Michael began, "I've been hearing a little bit about this Shining Path. Who are they?"

"Ah, Sendero Luminoso. A fine bunch of terrorists. They're a strange outfit," Nate said.

"What do you mean?" Michael asked.

"Unlike most of your hardworking terrorist groups, they don't have a coherent political thrust. They just flat out love being terrorists and wreaking havoc. They terrorize for the sake of terrorizing. They specialize in bombing government installations, railroads, power lines, you name it. They fight the army or whoever's in the neighborhood," Nate explained.

"Tell me more about Ramirez' refining capability."

"Well, what you see is not what you get."

"What's that supposed to mean?" Michael asked.

"What you see on the surface are grass huts but if you look closer, you'll find centrifuges, diesel generators, water pumps, hydraulic presses, drying facilities and underground warehouses for storage," Nate counted off. "The infrastructure is solid, far reaching and very sophisticated." Nate shook his head in disgust.

He continued. "These bastards can refine 500 pounds of cocaine a week in some of these labs. The traffickers use barges to bring in bulldozers to make landing strips, and at one laboratory complex there was a paved all-weather airfield 2,500 feet long and 125 feet wide. They utilize elaborate communications systems, have fleets of trucks, and boats. Another complex had seven dormitories, each capable of housing 120 people, complete with a video entertainment system. It hurts my head just thinking about it, and Ramirez controls it all."

"How do you know where he is exactly?" Michael queried.

"If I tell you, I'd have to kill you," Nate laughed.

"C'mon, Nate. I want to know," Michael insisted.

"We've got a plant. Actually, you might know him. Larry Steele, ex-Green Beret," Nate said proudly.

"I know him," Michael said excitedly. "He was in SF for a while but then he became a commercial pilot. Right?"

"Exactly," Nate said. "He flew 747's for Eastern Airlines but got bored. Then he contracted to fly explosives for some nut case who said he belonged to an anti-Castro group. Unfortunately for Steele, the dude was a government informant and this was a Customs' sting. The case against him was thrown out for lack of evidence but he lost his job with the airline. He became an airline broker, bouncing around Central America, buying and selling planes."

"How did he get involved with you guys?" Michael asked.

"Well, he stumbled into the smuggling business and became a specialist in moving shit for Latin trafficking organizations. He was a genius at developing complex schemes to avoid radar," Nate said with admiration.

Michael listened intently as the DEA man described Steele's techniques for evading capture.

"He would take off at night from Texas," Nate said in a hushed tone. "As he reached the Gulf coast, he'd slow down and drop to 500 feet so that anybody watching FAA radar would think that he was a helicopter cruising out to the Gulf oil rigs. Eventually, he'd climb and head south, entering Colombian airspace during a predesignated 'window' of time that had been bought from Colombian officials."

Michael whistled.

"He'd then land at some rinky-dink strip in northern Colombia, load up and head back, flying low and slow. He'd sink to 200 feet at a prearranged drop-zone," the DEA man explained. "He would then toss out the coke, packed in duffel bags, and some dudes below would gather it up."

"Unbelievable," Michael said.

"Yeah, and he got stinking rich, too. The man started charging ungodly rates per kilogram and sometimes made over a million per trip. Million!" Nate emphasized.

"Unbelievable!" the CIA pilot chimed in. "I can see I made the wrong career decision," he said, with a half -laugh.

"Our boys down in the Gulf got suspicious and started keeping their eyes open but couldn't get him. He was real slick," Nate said, picking up where he left off. "But a few years ago, we linked him to some crack and he was convicted and sentenced to ten years."

"What happened to him?" Michael wondered.

"He was sweating real bad, I'll tell you," Nate said, smiling at the memory. "Until then, he was the cockiest, most arrogant son of a bitch you'd ever seen. He thought that his shit didn't stink and he thought that he could squirm his way out of anything. But he couldn't get out of this and so he decided to make a deal."

"What kind of a deal?" the congressman asked.

"He proposed becoming a double and was so eager to head off a long prison sentence that he agreed to provide his own airplane and pay his own expenses."

Nate shouted at the driver, "Get off at the next exit!" He then continued with Michael, "Where was I?"

"Steele's becoming a double" Michael provided.

"Oh, yeah. Anyway, he flies to Medellin to plan some big-ass shipment. He told us that some of the big boys, Ramirez included, were moving their operations to Nicaragua."

"Nicaragua? Really?" Michael asked, surprised.

"Yeah, believe it or not," the drug agent said. "Steele was supposed to pick up a couple thousand kilos at some big ranch south of Medellin, refuel at a military base outside of Managua and fly into the States. He was sweating bullets about flying into Nicaragua but was assured that the proper arrangements had been made. Then the nosey-asses at Langley had to put their two-cents-worth in." Nate looked at Charlie, who responded in mock horror.

"Hey, don't pick on us," the CIA agent protested.

"Well, when you boys heard he was going to fly into contra-land, you decided that he had to have a camera aboard," Nate said, rolling his eyes. "Steele couldn't believe it. Nicaraguans with guns were not the most camera-happy people he could think of," he added, as Michael laughed.

"The CIA boys come up with this ridiculous plan to hide a couple of automatic cameras in the plane, one in the nose and the other in the bulkhead, pointing backward towards the cargo door," Nate said, laughing. "But after the cameras were installed, he realized this was no piece of cake. The remote-controlled shutter had a fuckin' five-foot antenna. As Steele clicked it, the motorized cameras squealed like a pig in heat," Nate chuckled, and shook his head.

"What did they do with the antenna?" Michael asked.

"Good question. The CIA boys suggested that he cut a hole in his pocket and run the antenna down his leg. Can you believe this shit?"

"So, what happened?" Michael demanded.

"Well, he headed for Nicaragua and landed at the airport. The camera in the nose failed, but the other one worked and snapped some up-close and personal shots of a couple of the big boys loading bags of coke. A U.S. intelligence satellite trained on the area took some high-resolution photographs," Nate said excitedly. "But we screwed with the guy."

"What do you mean?" asked Charlie.

"Well, the poor sap is told that they'll drop his sentence if he just does this one mission. But then one more. And one more. I've lost track now but supposedly, they're going to let the guy go after one more mission. Anyway, he's in tight with the Ramirez crowd and he was kind enough to fill us in," the DEA man said with a smile.

The six men arrived at the airport and headed off for Peru. Michael looked out the window. He was having very serious doubts about this whole thing again. Good Lord, what have I got myself into this time, he asked himself.

☩   ☩   ☩

Rebecca and Tommy arrived at the restaurant and for the first time in years, Tommy smiled at her.

"Listen, Sis, maybe it's not too late. Maybe I can still be your brother," he said, with a warmth that Rebecca had never known before.

"Oh, Tommy, I'd love for that to happen. I really would. Me and you and Steven and Daddy, a big happy family. That's all I ever wanted," Rebecca said excitedly, and hugged him.

"I'm not so sure about all that "Leave it to Beaver" shit," Tommy said cynically. "Let's take it one step at a time. There's a lot you don't know. Maybe you should."

Rebecca didn't understand, but she didn't care.

"Tommy, anytime you want to talk, call me. I'll be there for you," she said, with moisture in her eyes.

They exited the car and walked into the restaurant, a chic Washington place that Katarina enjoyed. Everyone was already there, including Josh and Kelly. Rebecca stopped short and shot Josh a stare. "What are you doing here?"

"Glad to see you, too, Mom. Boy, a guy can't even have dinner with his family," he answered in mock exasperation.

"Sorry, Josh. Of course, I'm glad to see you," she said, giving him a hug. "And you, too, Kelly. How's school?"

"Just great, Mrs. Madigan. I'm applying to law school in the fall. Do you think your husband would write me a letter of recommendation?" Kelly asked.

"I'm sure he would," she answered.

Karl gave Rebecca a kiss on the cheek and a hug. "Hi, Becky. I invited Josh. I thought the whole family should be together, although we're going to miss that congressman husband of yours," he added.

Steven overheard his father's last comment. "I'm sure he's making the world safe for democracy," he interjected with a touch of sarcasm, which Rebecca noted.

"I'm not sure, but I think you just insulted my husband," she said, good-naturedly and gave Steven a hug.

"Not at all, little sister. I'm just teasing. Elsbeth, come here and say hello to Rebecca," he called to his wife, who made her way across the room.

"Give your sister-in-law a kiss," Elsbeth gushed. "It's been too long. We say it every time but we really do have to see each other more often," she said emphatically.

Everybody engaged in small talk and walked around the bar as they waited for their table. Rebecca was amazed to find herself really enjoying the evening. The worries of her job and Michael's whereabouts evaporated.

A waitress appeared and announced that their table was ready. The group sat down and Rebecca sat next to Adrian, Tommy's wife. She had never been overly friendly to the family but she hadn't displayed her husband's hostility either. Maybe Rebecca could talk to her tonight.

As everybody began ordering their entrees, Karl stood up to make an announcement.

"Can I have your attention, please?" he asked,and received immediate silence. "I've just been informed that the Senate confirmed me. I'm the new secretary of defense."

The table broke out in applause. Katarina shot her husband a death glare as she was hearing this news for the first time. "When did you find that out?" she demanded.

"Sorry, darling, about not telling you," he said apologetically. "But I just found out ten minutes ago. I left messages to contact me here if there was any news. The vote was fifty-two to forty-eight, one of the closest in history." He gazed lovingly at his wife and said, "doesn't this deserve a kiss?"

Rebecca asked, "Does this mean we'll be dining at the White House on a regular basis?"

"We? What is this we stuff?" he laughed in response.

"Up-and-coming congressmen have to hob-nob with the powers that be, you know," she added.

"Well, I'm glad to see that you're making the transition to political wife," her mother added. "I didn't think at first that you'd be able to."

Rebecca was hurt by this veiled reference to their separation, which everyone had thought was her fault.

"I've made the mental adjustment, Mom. Politics is a game and you have to play. I accept that. Michael's very ambitious and I'm determined to support him."

"Well, well," Karl added. "I'm happy for you, baby."

"Thank you, Daddy."

Steven chimed in. "Ambitious? What are we talking about here? Are we looking at the future First Lady?"

"I don't think so. I just mean that Michael hopes to move on. I'm not sure to what."

Karl joined in on the conversation. "I think that Michael has a tremendous future. He's only been in office a short time and he's already made a name for himself. He's got a reputation as a can-doer. The public has this picture of Congress as these fat, greedy do-nothings marking time, and passing the buck. Michael caught a lot of attention with that hijacking. He's a hero in a lot of people's book."

"Are people really saying that, Daddy?" Rebecca asked.

"You bet they are," Karl said without hesitation. "And that incident with the gang leader turned some heads. I thought it would hurt him but people are eating it up. A member of Congress duking it out with the leader of the Bloods. Incredible! The vast majority of the public thought it was great," Karl said, shaking his head.

"That's my Michael," Rebecca said somewhat facetiously. "He likes to stir things up."

"That he does," Karl continued. "There's talk going around that the president's gonna dump that fool Jensen and pick up someone new, someone young, aggressive, with a reputation as a pit bull. The president is catching some real political heat recently and all Jensen does is babble bullshit. He needs someone who can do his dirty work." Karl paused, and looked around before continuing.

"Don't hold me to this, but there are some rumors that Michael's a possible replacement for Jensen."

Rebecca just about swallowed whole the carrot stick she was eating. "Daddy, you can't be serious. I mean, he's capable, but he's a political babe in the woods."

"Change, baby, change."

"What's that suppose to mean?"

"People want change," Karl replied. "They're tired of the same old status quo. I'm not saying that it's going to happen. I'm just saying that people want some fresh blood in there to shake things up. A thousand things could happen and maybe I'll look like a fool for even bringing it up. But it's a possibility. Your husband could one day be a heartbeat away," he said with a wink.

Rebecca looked shocked. She considered her father's statement and found it unbelievable.

The atmosphere became more joyous and Rebecca was beaming at the warmth that was emanating from the room. But she couldn't stop thinking about Tommy. She had tried all night to get Adrian into a conversation. Then when Tommy excused himself to use the rest room, Rebecca pounced on Adrian.

"Adrian, it's good to see you and Tommy. I was never so surprised as when he picked me up tonight," Rebecca said.

"It was his idea, you know," Adrian replied.

"Really?" Rebecca was surprised. "It just doesn't follow the pattern. We were never close and then we didn't hear from him for nearly twenty years. But tonight, we actually shared a few nice brother-sister things. I still can't believe it," Rebecca said smiling.

"Well, he seems a little different lately, not quite himself, you know," Adrian admitted.

"What do you mean?"

"I can't really put it into words. He seems distant."

"I don't mean to criticize your husband, Adrian, but he's never been a social butterfly. In fact, he's always been angry at the world," Rebecca said.

"I know. When I say distant, I mean it in a different way. Maybe I'm just imagining it. He's done a lot of traveling lately and he's gone for weeks at a time."

"Where's he been going?" Rebecca asked.

"He doesn't always tell me but I know he's been back and forth between the U.S. and Europe several times and to South America a couple of times."

"Really? Trips with Daddy's business?"

"I don't know," Adrian said, shrugging her shoulders.

Rebecca decided to gamble. "Let me throw a phrase at you. The Fourth Reich. Has he ever talked about that?"

"What do you mean? Is that some Nazi thing?"

"I don't know, Adrian. I thought that you could tell me."

"Sorry. But I do know that Tommy was involved with the Ku Klux Klan and something called the Knights of the White Camelia."

The mention of the Ku Klux Klan made Rebecca's heart freeze. Her head began throbbing. The Ku Klux Klan? Good Lord! Tommy returned to the table.

"What are you gabbing about?" Tommy said with a smile.

Adrian was as surprised as Rebecca was to see this lightened attitude. "Nothing. Just girl talk."

"Every time two women talk," Tommy said, turning his head towards Steven, "it's nothing but trouble for the men." He smiled again. Rebecca shuddered as she stared at her brother—a stranger.

Kelly interrupted a conversation with Elsbeth and headed for the ladies' room. Karl excused himself and followed her. He cornered her in the hallway.

"Hello, Ms. Adkins. How are you tonight?" Karl asked.

"I'm fine, sir, or should I say, Mr. Secretary of Defense. Congratulations. That's very exciting news."

"I've heard a lot about you from Peter Volhard. I was wondering if you'd be interested in a certain project. I've already talked to Peter about it," Karl said.

"What is it?" asked the young neo-Nazi.

"Well, it depends on how a number of things turn out in the coming weeks. But it could be historically significant. Would you be interested?"

"If it will help Germany, I'm interested."

"Great. You'll hear from me soon. What is your relationship with Josh?" Karl asked seriously.

"Mr. Schmidt, you should know there's no relationship. I let him bed me once in a while but I'm loyal only to the Reich," she said coolly.

"Of course," Karl said. "It was a pleasure talking with you," he said, and walked back to his table.

Over the course of the next thirty minutes, everyone finished their meal and started leaving. This time, Karl and Katarina drove Rebecca home.

She returned to the pensive and worried mood of before and there was a long stretch of silence as she was gathering her thoughts. Pam Connors, Michael, Tommy, the Fourth Reich and the Ku Klux Klan. Sitting beside her was the new secretary of defense, who had mentioned earlier that her husband could wind up being the next vice president. It was all too much for her and she felt exhausted.

Karl knew better than to probe any further. He realized how tired his daughter was and he let her alone to her thoughts. Before Rebecca knew it, she was home.

"You're home," Karl said softly, nudging her gently. She sat up as if shot by lightning.

"Relax, Becky. You look like you could use a good night's sleep," added her mother.

"Oh, Mom, I sure could. I'm exhausted."

"Then you march up those steps and go right to sleep," Karl commanded, in his father-knows-best tone. "Do you want me to tuck you in and tell you a story?" he teased.

She laughed, "Daddy, can we really be a family again? Is it really not too late?"

"I hope we can, sweetheart. I hope we can." He reached over and kissed her. "Pleasant dreams, baby doll. May all of your wishes come true."

"Your's too, daddy. Love you both," she said, and got out of the car, practically bursting with happiness.

✠   ✠   ✠

The covert team headed by Michael and Nate approached its destination. The night was pitch black. It was 4:00 A.M. when the plane landed on a small airstrip in the jungle, where they were to make the switch.

Michael discovered that there was one other member of the mission, a CIA helicopter pilot named Ron Castillo. He flew a Blackhawk helicopter and had been involved in numerous missions in the war against drugs. In the mid-eighties, he had participated in an airborne assault on the Bolivian cocaine industry, a joint exercise with the Bolivian authorities. Highly-trained squads descended into the El Beni rain forest and dismantled countless laboratories that produced tons of cocaine each year.

The plane landed and Castillo was already there waiting. The six men covered the plane with branches and other cover, hiding the small aircraft. They began making their final preparations.

They changed their clothes, each donning an all black flame-resistant suit. Next, they put on bulletproof assault vests. Each wore a Balaclava mask and special night goggles that were able to amplify ambient light up to 60,000 times.

They applied black tape to all the exposed shiny parts on their weapons. Each of them carried a weapon, an HK MP5 submachine gun, and their pockets were filled with extra ammunition and grenades. Radio communication devices were attached to their chests and each wore assault gloves.

As Michael adjusted his LBE (load bearing equipment), which he had strapped a red-filtered flashlight to, as well as a canteen, he reminded himself that he was a sitting U.S. Congressman. What had he gotten himself into?

Nate looked around to see if everyone was ready. Each member of the team had finished his final checks. Nate smiled and said, "Show time!"

The team boarded the helicopter and Castillo took off from the jungle airstrip. They proceeded towards Ramirez' ranch on what Nate had labeled Operation Retrieval. All men aboard had been involved in similar missions. There was still some nervousness as they flew over the Peruvian jungle in complete silence.

Within twenty minutes they approached the outskirts of the ranch. They would land the chopper a short distance away and walk the last few hundred yards. Castillo would stay with the helicopter, prepared for a hasty takeoff.

The six black-clad men moved toward the ranch without a sound. One of the team produced wire cutters and they were through the large fence that surrounded the estate within seconds. They spread out and descended towards the main house. So far, there was no resistance.

Within moments, they were just outside the house and still no guards or dogs, contrary to what was expected. This might actually work. From Steele's description, they knew exactly where Ramirez slept. Although the sky above was blackened by the moonless night, they all moved easily across the terrain. The night goggles made their vision as accurate as if it were day.

They walked up the steps to the back door. Nate grabbed the doorknob and turned it. The door was open.

This is too easy, Michael thought. Was Ramirez getting lazy? Four of them proceeded silently into the house with their weapons drawn, while two stayed outside. Nate was leading. Still wearing their night-vision goggles, they could see that they were in a massive room with a staircase. For a few moments they stood still, getting their bearings and orienting themselves. There were still no guards. Ramirez's room was upstairs. By prior arrangement, three of them would proceed towards his room.

✠   ✠   ✠

On the south side of Chicago, detective John Gandara received a call about some human remains that had just been discovered. He gulped his coffee, grabbed his partner, Sam Adams, and dashed out to their car.

Apparently, a road crew had been digging alongside the highway and discovered the bones.

Gandara thought out loud as his partner drove. "You know, from the report I got, these bones look to be pretty old. We might want to get Daniels involved in this with that high-tech DNA stuff."

"You mean the PCR?" asked Adams.

"Yeah, I think that's it. You've been reading up on it more than I. How's it work again?" Gandara inquired.

"Well, I don't know all of the details but it does involve DNA. PCR stands for, and give me a second to recall this, uh, polymerase chain reaction. Yeah, that's it."

"How do you know all of this stuff, Adams?"

"Unlike you, John old boy, I can read," said the younger partner, laughing. "Anyway, the way I understand it, this polymerase is the enzyme that triggers the replication of DNA inside dividing cells."

"What does that have to do with the price of tea in China?"

"With this PCR, they can take a single strip of DNA, stick it in an aluminum box with a bunch of test tubes and come up with a billion copies of this stuff."

"What does that have to do with these bones?"

"I'm trying to tell you, if you'd give me a chance. What this PCR does is to allow researchers to study the faintest, most fragmentary traces of DNA found in specks of dried blood, strands of hair, chips of bone, you know, stuff like that. Now, check this out, John," the young cop said excitedly. "They used this stuff recently to identify a murder victim from skeletal remains over ten years old."

Gandara looked skeptical. "How can they do that?"

"The way I understand it," Adams continued, "is that they extract bone cells from the femur and they can then identify the person. They used it recently to identify the remains of soldiers who died in combat. Also, they'll be able to solve some historical mysteries."

"Like what?" inquired Gandara.

"Remember back in 1979, some guy drowned in Argentina and they thought that it might be that Nazi dude, Josef Mengele, but they couldn't be sure?"

"Yeah, I remember reading about that," Gandara pretended.

"Well, with this stuff, they'll be able to tell for sure. Also, Abraham Lincoln, no less, supposedly suffered from some disease, but nobody's really sure. I forget what it was called but this PCR stuff will help them find out."

Gandara wasn't impressed. "Who gives a rat's ass?"

Adams was waving his arms. "John, this stuff has unlimited potential. The DNA in a single sperm cell can link a suspect to a rape victim and this

PCR stuff amplifies it. Also, a cell found in saliva can supposedly be traced back to a person who, say, licked a stamp on a letter bomb."

"I don't swallow that one. You mean, they can catch a perp by his spit?" Gandara asked, in amazement.

"That's what I've heard," Adams answered. "The head shed in the Department is working with some professors at the University on this. Supposedly, they have some scientists over there who can do this shit."

"So, you think they can tell us who this poor son of a bitch buried on the side of the highway is?"

"Yeah. Pretty awesome, isn't it?" asked the younger cop.

"Let's see what we can find," Gandara said, pulling up to the sight. "What will they think of next."

✠   ✠   ✠

Karl was finishing breakfast when the doorbell rang.

"That must be your driver," Katarina said.

"Can you believe that I'm actually the secretary of defense?" he said in amazement. "I still can't believe it."

"I'm very proud of you, dear. I just know that you're going to do a great job. Have a good day," she said, giving him a hug and a kiss as he left for the Pentagon.

"Good morning, sir. I'm your driver, Sergeant Mullin," said a sharply dressed Marine.

"Good morning there, Sergeant. It's a fine day to be a soldier, isn't it?" asked Karl.

"I wouldn't know, sir. I'm a Marine. Soldiers are in the Army," Mullin said without thinking, but then began worrying that he had sounded too cocky.

Karl realized that unknowingly he had insulted this young sergeant. "No offense, sergeant. I take it you think that the Marines are tougher than the other branches."

"It isn't my opinion, sir. It's just a fact," Mullin said. "The sun rises in the east, the Pope's Catholic and a Marine will kick an Army dude's ass without breaking a sweat."

"I see," Karl said, getting into the car. "Then I'm glad that you were assigned to be my driver. What do you say that we get to work and start earning our paychecks?"

"You got it, sir," Sergeant Mullin replied enthusiastically. "Next stop, the Pentagon."

As they made the half hour drive to the "office," Karl picked up the car phone and dialed.

A sleepy female voice answered. "Hello," mumbled Kelly.

"Kelly, this is Karl Schmidt. How are you?"

She sat up quickly. "Mr. Schmidt, this is a surprise. What time is it?"

"It's six o'clock. Sorry to wake you but I wanted to follow up on that conversation we had the other night."

"That's O.K., sir. I'm listening."

"I want you to come to a party this Friday night. I want you to wear your sexiest dress," said the elder Schmidt. "Is Josh there with you?"

"Yes."

"Tell him hello for his grandfather. But I want you to come alone to this party. Craig Jensen will be there and I want you to be very friendly to him."

"You mean the vice president?" she asked.

"That I do. His wife won't be there and I think that he'll take a very deep interest in you."

"What do you want me to do, Mr. Schmidt?"

"It's very simple, Kelly. I want you to use those stunning good looks God blessed you with and seduce the bejeezus out of the vice president of the United States. Do you think that you can do it?" he asked.

"Of course I can do it," she said annoyed. "I'd rather be gang-banged by all the niggers at San Quentin, but I'll do it if it's important," said Kelly, the daughter of Alan Roberts.

"It's very important," Karl added. "I've told Josh very selective things about his grandfather. I've got him all excited about his father possibly becoming president one day. Just tell him that this will help Michael's career. Now, can you do that?"

"Yes," she said simply.

"That's my girl. I'll be in touch with you before Friday. Tell Josh hello. Good-bye."

Josh was still half asleep but saw Kelly's reaction to the conversation. "What was that all about?" he asked.

"It's the strangest thing, Josh," she said innocently. "Your grandfather wants me to seduce Craig Jensen. And he said that you wouldn't mind."

Josh sat up. "Baby, I'll mind all right. To think of that bastard in bed with you will drive me crazy. But I'll go along with it because it's all part of a plan. My father could be the next vice president," Josh said, and then kissed her cheek.

"Do you mind if I try to get a little more shut-eye?" Josh asked, pulling a pillow over his head.

Kelly answered slowly. "Sure. I can't sleep now so I guess I'll get up." Josh didn't hear her finish her sentence—he had already fallen asleep.

✠ ✠ ✠

Nate led the team into Ramirez' room and flipped the light switch. Ramirez immediately bolted upright in his bed, as did a young girl about half his age. He started to reach for a pistol but changed his mind when Nate stuck a rifle in his nose.

"I'm afraid not, Señor," Nate said sarcastically. "This is your morning wake-up call. Congratulations. You've won an all expense paid trip to Washington, D.C."

"Let me guess," Ramirez said. "CIA? DEA?"

"Bonus points for that correct answer," sneered Nate. "Michael, would you be so kind as to grab some of Mr. Ramirez' clothing out of the dresser? Make sure he dresses warmly. We don't want him to catch the sniffles." Michael tossed Ramirez some clothing. Suddenly, he heard shouting coming from downstairs. He rushed into the hallway and found that the rest of the team had several of Ramirez' aides standing with their hands up.

"Good job," Michael yelled, and returned to the bedroom. He glanced at the terrified young girl, who had wrapped a sheet around her naked body. "Señorita, why don't you go take a hot bath, or something?" he said to the girl, who scurried into the bathroom.

"So, Señor Ramirez, you wouldn't mind coming with us, would you? You walk out that door and if any of your goons make a move, you're a dead man," Nate warned. "So I suggest that you order them to back off. Do you understand me?"

Ramirez didn't answer but nodded his head. He looked up at the ceiling where the camera was. He was smiling as he thought about how embarrassed these fools would be when the rest of the world witnessed this kidnapping. The six Americans marched out of the house and Michael had his weapon buried in the Colombian's back. Walking outside, a dozen or so more guards appeared but quickly realized that they could do nothing without getting their boss killed.

They walked slowly through the woods to where the chopper was. Nate had run ahead to inform Castillo and the rotor blades were swirling, ready to take off. Michael shoved Ramirez into the chopper and as the last man boarded, it took off. They reached the airplane and to their relief, no one had discovered it. Within seconds, the brush was cleared and the seven men boarded the plane.

Castillo took off and Michael didn't relax until the plane reached cruising altitude. He sighed loudly and looked at Nate, who was laughing.

"We did it, buddy," Nate exclaimed. Everyone let out a cheer, except Michael, who looked deep into the Colombian's eyes and wondered if he still had a career.

elix Klaus, also known as Wilhelm, gazed absentmindedly out the window of his massive and ornate office in NATO Headquarters. He decided to call the new U.S. secretary of defense, Karl Schmidt.

He buzzed his secretary. "Elena, please get me Karl Schmidt at the Pentagon."

"Yes sir," came the immediate reply.

After about thirty seconds, Elena buzzed her boss. "Mr. Schmidt is holding for you, sir."

"Thank you, Elena." He picked up the flashing line. "Karl, how are you? Are you alone?"

"I'm fine and yes, I can speak freely."

"Good. I just spoke with Rommel and he suggested some distractions and that we try something in Iraq. What are your thoughts on that?" asked Wilhelm.

"Iraq? That's very interesting. I had been thinking along the same lines in Yugoslavia. Ethnic battles are raging there between the Serbs, the Croatians and God knows who else. But maybe Iraq is simpler."

"Yugoslavia is too complicated," Wilhelm cautioned. "Too many nationalities, too many ethnic groups. We need one recognizable villain. The whole world knows of the modern Hitler, as your president has said. With the U.S. election coming up, he could use an international crisis to regain some popularity that he's lost in recent months."

"That's certainly true. And Iraq has not been complying with UN resolutions. Military action would be justified."

"It would certainly make our job easier if we could get all of those American troops out of Europe," stated Klaus.

"Last year during the war, more than 70,000 army soldiers and 40,000 tanks and artillery pieces were moved from Germany to Saudi Arabia," Schmidt explained. "Out of the six armored or mechanized divisions that had been deployed with NATO, only two remained in Europe as the war progressed. Half the Marine Corps was in the gulf and about one-fourth of the Air Force's tactical aircraft."

"That's exactly what we want to do now," Wilhelm added. "Spread out the U.S. arsenal and distract it at the same time. With the collapse of the Soviet Union, the end of the cold war and the recession in the U.S., there's much pressure to cut back the American military. Am I right?" asked Wilhelm.

"You certainly are," replied Karl Schmidt. "I'll be leading that charge vigorously. The army will be reduced from twenty-eight divisions to twenty. I hope to close more than 225 military bases around the world and reduce the current military of 2.1 million by about one-fourth."

"Also, I plan to cut back on weapons," the new head of the U.S. military continued. "The M1A1 tank. Gone. The AH-64 Apache and AH-1S Cobra helicopters. History. The Navy will scale back its Trident submarines and reduce its carriers from thirteen to twelve. There are other things, too."

"Great. What do you think of me meeting with the Iraqis?" asked the NATO leader. "Perhaps we can persuade them to proceed with their deviant behavior. Then you could convince the president that a strong U.S. response is needed. Acceptable?" asked Klaus.

"Agreed. But you're too visible. Perhaps Krupp."

"Krupp," the secretary general whispered. "He would be a good choice. I'll talk with him immediately." After decades of dreaming, all of their goals were finally coming together.

"I'm meeting with the president later this morning," replied Schmidt. "He's so worried about the election he probably wouldn't even notice a little war," he said with a laugh. "Auf Wiedersehen."

✠   ✠   ✠

General Steigrich had assembled four of his top officers. None had any idea of the true nature of their gathering. They had speculated that Steigrich had been offered the AFCENT position and was looking for a staff. They were all eager for a move up the ladder.

Steigrich began, as he poured himself a drink. He had known these men for over twenty years and they were fiercely loyal and patriotic. Germans to the core.

"Gentlemen, thank-you for coming here this evening," he began, somewhat nervously. "There's been speculation among yourselves as to the purpose of this meeting. I believe the consensus is that I've been offered the AFCENT job and am looking to build a staff. Am I correct?"

The four officers looked at each other before anybody replied. Colonel Reindel, an infantry officer, spoke. "That would be logical, Herr General. You've met with Felix Klaus and there's a vacancy, with the death of General Punder," he postulated.

Steigrich smiled. "Yes, poor General Punder. Well, gentlemen, Punder was not a true German. He believed in alliances and world peace and all of that rot. I have asked you here because of your dedication to Germany."

The officers were somewhat confused. Colonel Graf, an armor expert, responded. "I think I can speak for all of us, Herr General. We are all patriotic Germans."

"Of course you are. But how much so?" He paused briefly. "How many of you would be supportive of efforts to restore Germany to its proper place as the world superpower?"

Graf stood up and spoke in a loud booming voice. "We would all support such a plan, Herr General, but it is not realistic. What are you saying?" he asked.

"Here it is, gentlemen," Steigrich said. "There exists a plan for Germany to take by force what she was stripped of twice in this century. World domination."

"Preposterous," bellowed Reindel. "With all due respect, General Steigrich, that's not possible."

"Ah, Colonel, but it is," the general responded. "I too, was a disbeliever at first. But an extraordinary group of men have been formulating this plan for over forty years and have dedicated their lives to it. Let me tell you about these men," he said sitting back in his chair and placing his hands behind his head.

Steigrich talked for the next half hour about the Six and the four officers were clearly astonished.

"If it is as you say, General, I, for one, am with you. I have dreamed such a thing all of my life," stated Reindel.

The others echoed his feelings and all four of the assembled officers expressed their loyalty to the cause.

Steigrich continued. "Let me be blunt, gentlemen. General Punder did not share your enthusiasm and you have seen his fate. If you have the slightest doubt, you must leave now or you, too, will meet an early and painful death," he said, pausing to let the words sink in. No one moved.

"Then I take it that you are all in agreement," Steigrich said. "Germany shall return," he said, as the five men joined hands and let out a rousing cheer.

✠ ✠ ✠

Michael stared out the window as their plane began its approach to the Washington airport. He had a gnawing feeling that something would still go wrong and that people would find out that he was involved. If that happened, would it launch his career to a higher level or end it abruptly? How would the public take it? How would his colleagues feel? The uncertainty made him rather nauseous. The plane's landing gear touched down.

"We're home," shouted Nate Wallace, looking at Ramirez. "Let's see you bribe your way out of this, Mr. Big Shot. Jorge, you're going to the big house for many years, and with that soft skin you'll make someone a nice cell mate. Don't drop the soap in the shower," he said, laughing raucously.

Michael turned to Nate. "Are you personally taking him to DEA, or what?"

"You got it, buddy," Nate replied. "We're going to put this man away." He looked at Dan Booker, the other member of the DEA and said, "Book him, Danno," laughing even louder. "I always wanted to say that."

The six members of the covert team disembarked from the plane, with Ramirez in handcuffs. It was 7:30 A.M. The plan was to make a big media splash about Ramirez' capture, but first, Michael had to be out of the picture.

Michael and the others walked across the tarmac. He turned and said to Nate, "I don't know if I should thank you or crucify you, but I have to admit, it was a kick. I hope I still have a job." He put out his hand and shook Nate's.

Nate grew serious. "We did it, Mike. It's too bad you can't take some of the credit because I think you'd be a big hero over this." He gave Michael a salute. "Good job, buddy, and good luck."

"I'll need it," Michael said, with a wry smile. The CIA pilot offered to drive Michael home. They left the airport and reached Michael's house as the sun was shining brightly.

"Take care, Charlie, and thanks for the ride," he said to the pilot, who nodded and drove away. Michael walked gingerly into the house.

Rebecca heard the front door open and her heart started pounding. She picked up a baseball bat and walked into the hallway and saw Michael ascending the stairs.

"Michael," she said in exasperation. "What did you think you were doing?" She didn't know whether to feel anger or relief but she hugged him.

"Do you know about it?" he asked in astonishment.

"Just me and the rest of the world. Michael, what were you thinking? You've got a family, you know. And for God's sake, you're a United States Congressman. You can't be running around the globe playing Rambo."

"How did you know?" Michael demanded, panic beginning to set in. "I had to do it, for TJ. We caught the bastard who poisoned her. But how could you possibly know?"

"GNN's been playing live footage of it for the past hour. Apparently, Ramirez filmed the whole thing and it was turned over to the media," Rebecca explained.

"Dear Lord," Michael said.

"The phone's been ringing off the hook," she added.

Michael was speechless for a moment and then kissed her on the cheek. "We'll talk about it more later. I've just got to catch some shut-eye," he said blankly as he walked upstairs in a zombie-like trance.

Michael quickly undressed and was asleep within seconds. Rebecca watched him sleep and wondered what this would do to his career.

Michael woke up about 11:30 A.M. and turned on the TV. The news was dominated by Ramirez' capture. Rebecca heard him shuffling about and came into the room. Michael didn't know what to think or say. "I'm sorry if I worried you. It won't happen again. I just had to do it for TJ. Please understand that."

"I'm trying, Michael, I'm really trying. Things always work out your way but you take such risks. One of these days you'll gamble and lose and your family will suffer," Rebecca said, beginning to cry.

Michael stood up and grabbed Rebecca's shoulders. "Look at me. There's nothing more important to me than my family but sometimes I do take risks. I feel that God won't let me lose. Do you understand? I knew that we would be successful. I knew it," he said emphatically.

"I wish I could share your faith, Michael. I've really tried. But the important thing is that you're alive and that I love you," Rebecca said, and they kissed passionately.

"I guess I should call the office," he said, dialing the phone. A pleasant voice answered "Congressman Madigan's office."

"This is Michael Madigan. Let me speak to Alex Turner."

"Just a moment, sir."

Seconds later, a very excited Alex picked up the phone.

"Colonel Madigan, are you all right? Where are you? You wouldn't believe what's going on. Half of the people want you removed from office and the other half want you to run for president. This place is nuts."

"I'm sitting on my bed with my wife right now. I got back early this morning and zonked right out," Michael explained. "I'll be in the office in an hour and a half. I'll see you soon," he said and hung up the phone.

"Alex said I'm not like most congressmen. Do you think that's true?" he asked his wife.

A wide smile crossed her face. "They broke the mold when they made you. Sometimes you infuriate me and I'll probably lose my mind, but I'll never be bored. Now let's get you ready, Mr. Rambo. You've got a big day ahead of you and so do I. I'll probably have to work a lot of overtime this week, thanks to you," she said, trying unsuccessfully to suppress a smile.

☩   ☩   ☩

For the first time in days, the door opened and a light switch was flipped on. The light blinded Matt and he grimaced as Krupp walked towards him.

"Good morning, Mr. Connors," he said condescendingly. "I hope you've had a chance to think about your future and your family," Krupp said with a devilish laugh.

"What is it that you want, you Nazi bastard?"

"Mr. Connors, I thought by now that your attitude would be less confrontational," Krupp said, shaking his head. "I have to commend you, though. Most men wouldn't have survived what you have so far. I respect you very much."

"Spare me your phony praise," Matt spat out.

"It seems that we're going to have to let you think a little deeper about your predicament, Mr. Connors. Perhaps three more days will make you a little less hostile," Krupp threatened, watching closely for Matt's reaction. "Or maybe you'd like to visit with your friends, the bees, again?"

Matt hesitated. Think quickly, he told himself. If he sat in this cell and rotted away, he would accomplish nothing. If he cooperated, perhaps he could escape.

"O.K., you win. What do you want?"

"That's more like it, Mr. Connors," said Krupp. "You'll see that it's much better to cooperate."

"I want some assurances that my family is all right. If you've harmed any one of them, you can forget it. You'll have to kill me," Matt said.

"Very impressive, Mr. Connors. Always loyal to your family. Perhaps you and I are not really so much different. I too, am loyal but my 'family' is Germany. I'm as dedicated to her as you are to your Pam and Danielle."

"I want to speak to them. Right away or you'll get nothing from me," he demanded.

"That can be arranged. They're safe, you have my word."

"Your word? Why doesn't that make me feel really warm and fuzzy?" Matt asked. "Come with me, Herr Connors. You'll see that your precious family is fine. Then we have much work to do. Follow me," Krupp said as he exited the room.

Matt was surprised by how little strength he had as he stumbled down the corridor. Matt reached the end of the dark corridor and was shoved by a brutish guard into an empty room. He was slammed into the wall and he grimaced in pain, but refused to shout. He would not give his captors the satisfaction.

"What do you want of me? For God's sake, tell me. Do you want ransom?" demanded Matt.

"Ransom? My good fellow, we're not so crude to go to all this trouble for something as unimportant as money," the German said, as if he had been deeply insulted. "We're politically motivated. Mr. Connors, we have at our disposal literally billions of dollars. We don't need or want your money," said Krupp contemptuously.

"Then what do you intend to do with me? Why don't you just kill me and get it over with?"

"You're an asset to us, Mr. Connors," Krupp said. "To dispose of you would not be prudent. And since you have a wonderful family that you care for deeply—well, must I say it? You would do almost anything to save them from pain. Wouldn't you?" asked the German.

"You bastards! I'll kill every one of you."

"A very irrational position, Mr. Connors," Krupp replied menacingly. "First, you will not escape. You will be kept very secure. And, must I say it again? Pam and the kids would not appreciate your attitude. Please don't make me lose my patience. I don't wish to have my associates continue their interrogation. If they're not supervised, they often become rather overzealous."

Krupp looked long at Matt. "So, tell me Mr. Connors, do we have your cooperation or not?"

Matt groaned and was close to tears, but managed to say, "yes, yes. I'll do whatever you want but don't hurt my family. I beg of you! Please!"and he slumped to his knees.

"Ah, that's more like it, Mr. Connors. Or may I call you Matt?" the Krupp asked. "Now Matt, you will go clean yourself up. Then you will record a message. That's all that will be asked of you. It's all very simple, really. But rest assured that we're rather determined. If you help us, you'll be released," Krupp said innocently.

Matt stared at him intently, his eyes burning with hatred. Thirty minutes later, he had showered, shaved and been treated by a nurse, then given some expensive casual clothing. Next, a German woman named Elsa helped apply makeup to his facial wounds.

Elsa led him into what appeared to be a studio with a pleasant background set and a mountain of photographic equipment. He was led to a desk and chair and instructed to sit down. He was left alone for several minutes before Krupp and three muscular henchmen returned.

"Hello again, Matthew," Krupp greeted him. "You look much more presentable now, don't you? Elsa did a fine job. Let's proceed, shall we? Look into the cameras and read the document I have in my hand. That's it! If you do this one thing, you'll be returned to your family. It's very simple, Matthew."

Matt locked eyes with Krupp and softly asked, "Who's my audience? And what if I deviate from the script?"

Krupp smiled. "Very good questions, Mr. Connors. Your audience is primarily the United States general population although your words may be carried internationally. After all, you are a very high-ranking U.S. official."

After several seconds of silence, Krupp continued. "As to your second question, this broadcast shall not be, how do you say, live. We reserve the right to edit. And we might have to bring the bees back. And lastly, Herr Connors, remember your wife and children. Don't underestimate us."

Matt paused for a moment. "Let's get on with it. What do you want me to read?"

Krupp said with a slight smile, "You're making the right decision. Your family will thank you for it very soon." He handed Matt a two-page document, printed in English. Matt read it quickly and paused before speaking.

"You can't be serious. This is pure bullshit."

"Ah, Matthew, I ask you to remember your lovely Pamela and Danielle," Krupp said shaking his head.

"Listen to me," Matt said in protest. "Even if I read this, nobody will believe it. I'm not like this. Davis Elliot won't believe this. Neither will Andrew Tolbert or anybody else in the government. This is racist crap and I'm not a racist. Anybody who knows me knows that."

"Matthew, we don't care what Andrew Tolbert thinks," Krupp said. "Your audience is the American public, particularly the black population. Your words will ring true with many people. Please, I'm too old to debate with you. Read this or we'll act accordingly," warned Krupp.

"May I say hello to my family?" he asked.

"Yes. Just hello and proceed with the script. Do you understand?"

"Yes. I'm ready," said Matt.

The attendant made some adjustments to the camera equipment and gave Matt the signal.

"Good Evening. My name is Matthew Connors and I'm currently the deputy national security adviser in the Tolbert administration. I hereby renounce my position for the following reasons and have fled the United States. This is a message to the African-American community."

"First of all, I wish to address my family. Pamela and Danielle, I love you with all of my heart. To my youngest son, John, who we call Touchdown because of his football skills, be strong. And my oldest, Albert William, you're the man in the family. Take care of everyone."

Matt glanced out of the corner of his eye to see if this message drew any response from the Germans. When it did not, he proceeded to read.

"My fellow African-Americans. I am a high-ranking member of the current administration. I worked very hard to achieve this position but the price has been much too high."

"I've prostituted myself, doing whatever the white establishment directed me to, hoping that one day I'd be rewarded with a few crumbs that they might throw my way."

"But I won't be a puppet anymore nor an Uncle Tom, sacrificing my principles for approval by the white man. We've been asked for many years to proceed nonviolently, to act within the system, to follow the white man's laws and become acclimated to the mainstream."

"But I say no more. I refuse to remain a slave to this corrupt and bigoted system. The black man must rise up and strike out in the only language that will be understood. The system is unfair and blacks cannot and will not be given a fair shake."

"You must act in the only way that they will understand. Violently. Only when the blood of the white man pours and his women are humiliated and his children abused by our anger will the system change."

"The time is now. You must strike terror into the heart of this racist nation. We must not fail."

Matt quivered in disgust as he finished reading the scripted words. His only hope was that Pam would remember their talk of many years ago and contact the appropriate people. "Very good, Matthew," said a smiling Krupp. "You know, much of what you said is true. White America has never given your people a fair chance, has it?"

Matt gazed into his eyes and said, "Go to hell!"

Krupp merely laughed. "Only the losers go to hell, Mr. Connors. Please remember that."

✠ ✠ ✠

Michael arrived at his office on Capitol Hill and despite all attempts at escaping notice, he was caught by a web of reporters.

"Please, let me go to my office. I'll be giving a press conference soon and will answer your questions in due course. That's all for now," he said as he entered the building.

He arrived at his office and Alex began issuing orders nonstop. "Alex, contact the speaker's office and set up a meeting for me ASAP. And I want you to contact Sterling Shannon and see if I've broken any law."

"Yes, sir," responded Turner.

"Darrell, I want you to deal with the press. Everything needs to go through you."

Darrell nodded.

"Also, I want you to contact our ambassador in Peru. See what kind of mess we've made," he instructed. "I happen to think we accomplished quite a bit."

Michael looked at Darrell. "Any word on Matt Connors?" he asked, half afraid to hear the answer.

"Not yet, Colonel," Darrell replied. "His wife and son were released and are safe, but we've heard nothing on Mr. Connors. I'll let you know the minute I know anything."

Michael retreated to his office and closed the door. For a few moments, he closed his eyes and relished the quiet. He knew that it would not last long.

Seconds later, Alex knocked and walked in. "Colonel, I've arranged for you to meet with the speaker."

Michael felt like a schoolboy being sent to the principal's office. He took a deep breath and headed for the speaker's office. Michael discovered to his chagrin that Volhard was accompanied by the other leaders of Congress, including the senate majority leader.

Volhard sat behind an enormous desk and silently gestured to Michael to have a seat. The other three men all stood. No one spoke for several seconds. After what seemed like half a lifetime, Volhard spoke.

"Mr. Madigan, I know that you're rather new to political life. Please explain to us what you've been doing," he asked, with a note of anger in his voice.

Michael wasn't sure how to respond and struggled to keep his cool.

"What is your response, Mr. Madigan? Please enlighten us," Volhard demanded.

"I'm a maverick, perhaps even a renegade. But I'm also a patriot and I love my country," said Michael forcefully. "I'll stand by my actions and will testify at Mr. Ramirez' trial. I'd hope that you not condemn me but if you must, I can live with that."

The four congressional leaders were stunned by Michael's words and said nothing as he stormed out of the office and headed down the corridor. Despite his bluster and outrage he was scared to death. What have I done? he asked himself.

✠　✠　✠

Rudolf Himmler, former member of the elite Soviet Special Forces team, was staring out the window of his Moscow hotel. He had been working with Karl Schmidt in Russia. With Schmidt's appointment to secretary of defense, Charles Worthington had been officially named by Tolbert to head the delegation to destroy weapons. Himmler had now been placed in charge of completing Bismarck's mission in the USSR. Himmler's assignment was to steal nuclear weapons from the Russians in this time of confusion.

There was a knock at Himmler's door and he opened it and smiled to see the only female member of the team, Ludmilla Kolkov.

"Good morning," Rudolf said cheerfully.

"I hope that I'm not bothering you. May I come in?"

"Of course," he said, gesturing her in. "Would you like a cup of coffee? I just made some," he said with a smile.

"Thank you but no. I want to talk about our mission. We lost some momentum when Herr Schmidt left but we can still succeed without him."

Rudolf quickly concurred. "I agree. We must pursue two courses of action and they both involve money. Lots of it. Now that communism is dead, capitalism and greed are very much alive. Bribes will work. And if they don't, there's always sex," he said mischievously, leering lustily at the stunning redheaded Ludmilla with the bewitching green eyes.

"Yes, I know your preoccupation with things below the belt, Herr Himmler," Ludmilla said with a grin, "but I would prefer to keep my clothes on."

"But it may be necessary. You don't rule it out, do you?"

"Of course not. I will do whatever is necessary," she declared emphatically.

"We'll see," Himmler retorted. "O.K., tell me what we have so far."

Ludmilla began walking around the tiny room, gesturing with her hands and becoming quite animated. "I've been looking for former Soviet scientists who are suddenly out of work. For decades, they've had the ultimate in job security. Now they face the prospect of not being able to feed their families. With the splintering of the USSR, there's suddenly fifteen different republics, all with nuclear weapons on their soil. They're confused, disorganized and uncertain. We can bribe one or more to help us to build weapons, or steal them ourselves."

Himmler continued where she left off. "I've been working with the U.S. delegation, whose job it is to oversee the destruction of nukes. Now that Herr Schmidt is gone, our best bet is to grease some palms to help us steal them."

Ludmilla inquired, "Do you think one of Herr Schmidt's assistants could be persuaded to help us?"

"I've spent a lot of time with both of them. Worthington is hopeless. He does everything by the book. He doesn't seem the slightest bit interested in making a quick profit."

"What about Hawkins?" Ludmilla responded.

"Yes, Admiral Jonathan T. Hawkins, U.S. Navy," Himmler said, imitating the admiral's characteristic gravelly voice. "I think he's vulnerable. He's proud of his career but has always resented the fact that he was never able to become financially well-off. He fancies being a CEO, sitting on a few boards and pulling down a six figure income. Plus, I've just found out what could be the coup de grace."

"What's that?" she asked.

"I've just been informed that his wife has cancer."

"That is terrible news. We'll lose him," she said in exasperation.

"Perhaps. But he doesn't know yet, and I've been trying to figure how we can use this to our advantage. She's not in danger of immediate death but has less than a year to live, the physicians predict. So—" he said slowly, waving his left hand, "if we move quickly, he may be willing to make some money. But I think that it would take a lot. He's basically straightlaced but has some cracks in the armor. He has a penchant for the finer things in life. He's always driven cars he couldn't quite afford, dressed in clothes from the finest stores and lived in villas that were always just a little beyond his means. His wife, Roberta, is a moderately successful author, who generally puts out a book a year and takes in more money than he makes. He's now facing the loss of her income."

Ludmilla perked up. "Roberta Hawkins is his wife?" she asked. "I've read all of her books. She writes romance novels." She saw the look that he shot her at this admission.

"You read that stuff?" Himmler asked in mock horror. "A revolutionary like you reads romance novels? I never would have guessed."

"Yeah, I know, it doesn't fit my profile," she said.

"I always knew there was a girl in there somewhere. All women want to be swept off their feet by some prince and go off and live happily ever after, raising a brood of little ones. Isn't that so?" he asked with a tone of hopefulness.

"I wouldn't mind having a husband and kids someday. But I have other things to accomplish first. So get off my back and finish telling me about Hawkins."

"Well, as I said, he doesn't know yet. I'm going to make him an offer he can't refuse, as they say in the movies. But there's a risk."

Ludmilla knew the answer but asked the question anyway. "What's the risk?"

"Despite his problem, he might refuse a bribe and report it. It could jeopardize the mission," he said, stating the obvious.

"Then he would have to be eliminated," Ludmilla said simply. "End of story."

"Now that's the cold-blooded murderer we've all come to love," he said laughing.

She laughed, too. "O.K., we have to move quickly. But let me tell you about my end of the game."

"You have my undivided attention."

"As I said, there are many former Soviet scientists out there in desperate financial straits. I think that both weapons and knowledge can be bought. I have two meetings set up today, one with a Russian army commander and another with a scientist."

"Who's the commander?"

"Colonel Alexander Polov. And the scientist's name is Boris Semneyov."

"Never heard of either one," said Himmler.

"Well, believe me, they're both movers and shakers. Or at least, Semneyov used to be. But he's been relegated to oblivion after twenty years as a nuclear weapons expert. And he's a real prima donna."

"So, you think both men can be bought?" Himmler asked.

"I can't be sure, but I think that they're prime candidates. Polov dreamed of making general but that won't happen now with the collapse of the country and Semneyov is suddenly without a job. And he has eleven kids," she added.

"Eleven?" he said in amazement.

"I know. I can't imagine it myself. But as I started to say, the break up of the Soviet Union has really created a dilemma with nuclear weapons."

"How so?"

"Well, the Soviet nuclear arsenal contains some 27,000 nuclear warheads scattered across the republics. Four of them, Russia, Ukraine, Kazakhstan and Belorussia have inherited all of the long range strategic weapons and about ninety percent of the tactical weapons. Some of them have talked of dismantling these arms. Ukraine and Belorussia insist that they eventually want no nukes whatsoever on their soil."

"Do you think that will happen?"

"I don't know. The Ukraine and some other republics fear that they'll be unable to resist Russian dominance if they turn over responsibility of their nuclear arsenal to Russia. The danger would become greater still if a military or right wing coup overthrew the Russian government, which is possible, especially if there's a hard winter or food or fuel shortages which could touch off street riots."

Himmler thought about that last statement before commenting. "I talked a lot with Herr Schmidt before he left about the collapse of the USSR. The real fear of the U.S. government is a breakdown of the former Soviet command structure that would put easily mobile tactical weapons into dangerous hands. These nukes, such as artillery shells, warheads on short range missiles, nuclear mines, and all the rest are much easier to seize than ICBMs stored in underground silos."

"But we actually need both," Ludmilla said. "And already the southern republics of Georgia and Azerbaijan have 'nationalized' all military property on their soil. It's essentially a turf battle. Before, ideology held all of the republics together. But now they're disorganized and confused, prime candidates for either theft or bribes."

"Agreed. Also, we have another possibility. Some weapons have already been disabled but not destroyed. I think that it would be easier to go after those because they won't be as heavily guarded," Himmler added.

"How are they disarmed?"

"It's pretty simple, really. And it's very effective, immediately making these monster weapons totally harmless. Just remove their tritium bottles and krytron triggers."

The two Germans looked at each other and knew what they had to do. "Ludmilla, what are we waiting for? Let's get to it. After all, we have to get busy so that you can find your Prince Charming."

✠   ✠   ✠

Kelly was watching TV in her apartment. The lead story on almost every channel was the daring kidnapping of Ramirez led by Congressman Michael Madigan. Many commentators were taking shots at Michael, calling him a dangerous renegade who could not be trusted with the important decisions of America's future.

She was fascinated by the response of the average American. The vast majority of the American public supported his actions. To them someone was finally actually doing something rather than just talking about it. He was quickly becoming a folk hero.

Josh walked in and saw his father being interviewed on one of the networks. "Can you believe it, babe? Dad's a friggin' hero. He could run for king and win hands down."

"There's a lot of people knocking him and calling for his removal. They say he's dangerous and unstable," Kelly said.

"Well, of course. All of those pompous, self-inflated commentators will say that. What else can they say? But times have changed. There's a lot of frustration out there.

"People are tired of the Washington set that seems to be out of touch. Dad's really hit a chord. It's unbelievable the response he's getting, especially coming after the hijacking and the Johnny Green thing."

The phone rang. It was Karl Schmidt. "Good morning, Kelly. How are you?"

"It's your grandfather," she whispered. "I'm fine."

"Tonight's the night, Kelly. Are you ready?"

"I suppose so. Jensen's not exactly my idea of a dream date, you know."

"Listen, Kelly, the primary sexual organ is the brain. While you have a knockout body, if this is going to work, you have to have the right attitude. It won't work if your heart isn't in it," Karl admonished her.

"I know, sir. I'll get my head on straight," she whispered.

"Well you better. A lot is riding on this. Now you better go put on your sexiest dress, drown yourself in perfume, and go to the party and give Mr. Jensen a presidential hard-on. Can you do that? If you can't, tell me now and we'll get someone else," he said harshly.

"I can do it, Mr. Schmidt. I promise you."

✠   ✠   ✠

Matt's coerced speech was now being shown across America, having found its way into the living rooms of millions of homes across the country by the GNN feed. The speech was causing such a furor that it was almost overshadowing the onslaught of publicity for Michael. Most of the Washington elite watched in stunned silence, not even knowing that Matt had been gone. Andrew Tolbert watched in amazement.

"The ungrateful son of a bitch. I don't know what's going through his mind, but he just ruined a promising career," shouted the president.

Davis Elliot was in the room with several other of the president's top aides and while everyone was ripping Matt apart, Elliot remained uncharacteristically quiet. It didn't go unnoticed.

"Davis," said Tolbert, "you're the one that I would suspect would be ready to flog him publicly and yet I don't hear a peep. What gives?"

The national security adviser hesitated briefly before responding. He adjusted his thick glasses and loosened his tie.

"Mr. President, I know Matt Connors better than anyone. I can't believe that he said those words voluntarily."

"If you mean that he's been kidnapped, that was the first thing that went through my mind. But where are the kidnappers? They usually publicize their cause and if they had kidnapped him, I would think that they just might say something. Wouldn't you think so?" asked the president.

"Yes, sir. But there's something that you're not aware of." He shifted uneasily in his seat.

"You've got my undivided attention," said Tolbert.

"Connors has been gone for a few days. I spoke to him forty-eight hours ago. He was in Russia and was on his way to Germany. He asked me to give him some leeway, that he was onto something big but that he couldn't tell me," Elliot responded meekly, knowing that he was about to be lambasted.

"Russia? What the hell was he doing there?" demanded the president. "I don't like my top aides scurrying around the world on secret missions. Damn!" Tolbert shrieked. Pausing for a moment, he shook his head in disgust. "Did he tell you anything?"

Elliot could see that the president was furious. He should have told him earlier.

"That he left on a hunch but had obtained some hard evidence of something really big. He wouldn't tell me what. But he had been roughed up and was calling me from a German hospital," Elliot explained.

"Roughed up? What the hell is going on here?"

"I don't blame you for being upset, sir," said Elliot. "But I don't believe Matt spoke those words without being severely coerced. In Vietnam he was tortured as a POW because he wouldn't tell them a damn thing. He wouldn't talk unless they were putting some pretty heavy screws to him. Also, even if I believed for one minute that Matt meant those things, he couldn't just leave his family. Matt was the ultimate family man. Nothing was more important to him," he added.

The president stroked his forehead. "That's true. Why don't we get his wife on the horn here and talk to her?" Tolbert said and buzzed his secretary.

"Janet, will you get me Matt Connors' wife on the phone? Try her at home first, O.K.?"

"Yes, sir."

"I wonder if she's seen it?" Elliot asked, referring to the tape that they had just seen.

"Probably. And if she hasn't, she will shortly. They're playing the hell out of it. Which brings us to our next problem. What's the response to this going to be? Is black America going to go along with that nonsense?" pondered the president.

"I can't believe that people will riot just because of one disillusioned government official, but who knows? Race relations are not what they should be. With those riots in LA., anything could happen," warned Elliot.

After several minutes, the president's secretary buzzed her boss.

"Pam Connors is on the line, sir."

"Thank you, Janet," he said and picked up the phone. "Hello, Mrs. Connors. This is Andrew Tolbert."

"Hello, Mr. President," she said in a tearful voice. "Are you calling about that speech of Matt's?" she asked.

"Yes I am, Pam. I have to admit that it caught me by surprise and we've been wondering if that speech represented his true feelings or if he had been coerced," Tolbert asked.

"Of course it was coerced," shouted Pam. "He's not a racist and is not capable of saying those things."

"How can you be sure?" asked the president.

Pam was stunned that there could be any doubt. "Certainly you know the man enough to know, don't you? Or at least Davis Elliot knows, for God's sake," she shrieked, fighting to hold back the tears.

"I'm sorry to upset you, ma'am. I just have to be sure," said the president.

"Well, if it's evidence you want, I got plenty of it," Pam said forcefully. "First, my son and I were kidnapped the other day and our captors called Matt for us, who was being held somewhere in Europe. I talked to his kidnappers."

"You talked to him? And you were kidnapped yourself?" Tolbert asked in disbelief.

"Yes, we were taken by some group that left a note saying that Matt had stuck his nose in stuff that was not his concern and that his family was going to pay the price. They signed it 'City of the Orchids,'" Pam explained.

"What does that mean?" asked Tolbert.

"It supposedly has something to do with Colombian drug lords. I don't know for sure." She paused for a moment and then added, "Then there's the code that Matt sent."

"What code? What do you mean?" asked Tolbert.

"When Matt first got into the upper echelons of government, he always said that he might be kidnapped. And that he might be forced to say something against his will, so he devised a way to let us know. And he let me know in his speech. We had rehearsed it a million times, and again just last month, as a matter-of-fact," Pam explained.

Tolbert was now fascinated. "What was the code? I heard him say hello to you and the kids. Was it in there?"

"Yes. As you know, my name is Pam. Our oldest is Albert, followed by Danielle and the youngest is John. So, the plan had always been if referred to us in that order, everything was O.K. But if he said our names in a different order, then there was something wrong," Pam explained.

"So, by saying your names out of order, that means trouble?" asked Tolbert.

"Yes," she said weeping. "I'm sure he's being tortured."

"Pam, every asset the U.S. government has will be utilized in searching for him. He's a strong man and not easily defeated. I've heard that he went through some tough times in Vietnam and came out without a scratch. We'll find him. I promise you."

Pam regained her composure. "I know you will, Mr. President. Let's see if there's anything that I can tell you that will help." She hesitated for a few moments, trying to think of something. "Both the thugs who kidnapped me and the bastards who took Matt had German accents. Does that help?" she asked.

"German accents?" Tolbert repeated. "I don't know if it means anything or not. I'll run it by my staff. Listen, Pam, if there's anything that Mary Alice or I can do to make things easier, let us know," he said, referring to his wife.

"That's very kind of you, sir. Just bring Matt home. That's all that I want," she pleaded.

"We'll do our best, Pam, and God bless."

☩   ☩   ☩

Kelly arrived at the party wearing a black dress that hugged her skin tightly. It was exactly what Karl Schmidt had wanted to see.

Karl was already there and walked across the room to greet her. "Hello, Kelly. How are you doing?" he asked, giving her a kiss on the cheek.

"I'm fine, Mr. Schmidt," she said, her breasts practically pouring out of her low cut dress.

Karl whispered into her ear. "Remember that you're a new member of my staff, in case anyone asks." She nodded. "Well, let's introduce you to a few people," he said. He noticed Chris Watkins walking across the room with his wife Wendy and motioned to them.

"Chris, Wendy, how are you tonight?" Karl gushed as if he had known the secretary of state all of his life.

Watkins looked a little awkward at this sudden familiarity. "Uh, hello. I take it you know my wife."

"Of course. I'd like you to meet a new member of my staff, Kelly Adkins. She's fresh out of Georgetown but is brilliant. She's got a real future." Karl beamed like a proud father.

"Well, it was nice seeing you, uh, Karl, and it was a pleasure meeting you, Ms. Adkins," said the secretary of state, and he and his wife walked away.

The new defense secretary cursed to himself. "I hate these damn parties. Let's get to the reason we're here so I can get the hell out of here," he said as they headed across the room with Kelly in tow towards Jensen.

Craig Jensen was holding a drink and talking to the assistant secretary of labor. The vice president saw the new defense secretary and his charming guest approaching. He decided to initiate a conversation.

"How's the first week on the job been, Mr. Secretary?" said Jensen, managing to cover up his indifference and sound like he actually cared.

"Very interesting, that's for sure," Karl responded. "I'd like you to meet a new member of my staff, Kelly Adkins." He noticed that Jensen was sizing her up with obvious approval.

"Hello, Ms. Adkins. I'm Craig Jensen," he said and kissed her hand. "If you're as smart as you are beautiful, then ours is a very lucky government."

"Thank you, Mr. Vice President," she said with a flashing smile.

"Where are you from originally?" Jensen asked, engaging in small talk. Kelly had rehearsed this part.

"From western Pennsylvania. Beaver Falls. I hear you're from the same area. You're a big hero in those parts and it's a real honor to meet you," she said.

"You're from Beaver Falls? No kidding? I haven't been there in a while but it's always held a special place in my heart. It will always be my home and some of my family still lives there. Did you go to Beaver Falls high school?" Jensen asked.

They exchanged a few more lines of small talk until Karl interjected, "Mr. Vice President, I need to speak to Mr. Watkins. If you would excuse me for a minute," he said and walked to the other side of the massive room.

Kelly looked at her shoes in a very bashful manner. "It was nice meeting you, sir," she said and held out her hand, as if to let the vice president know she understood if he needed to attend to other important business.

"Ms. Adkins, or can I call you Kelly?" he asked.

"Kelly's fine, sir."

"O.K., Kelly," said Jensen. "I don't like these kind of parties, but I have to at least show my face. You know it's been a long time since I've met somebody from Beaver Falls."

"Is your wife from Beaver Falls, too, sir?" she asked.

"My wife? Uh, no. She's from Iowa. I met her in college," he stammered.

"Where is she tonight?" Kelly asked.

Jensen grew visibly nervous and began running his hand through his thick brown hair. "She's visiting her folks this weekend." He looked around and noticed a few people glancing at him with the blonde bombshell in the painted-on dress. He had already had a few drinks and suddenly felt very hot.

"Kelly, I'd really like to talk to you about Beaver Falls but unfortunately if I spend too much time with a beautiful woman, tongues will soon be wagging. But it would be so nice if we could finish up this conversation."

Kelly smiled. "I'd like that. But there's not many places we could go where you wouldn't be recognized. Unless—" she didn't finish.

"Unless what?" asked Jensen excitedly.

"I was just thinking, if you wouldn't mind, maybe going to my apartment. It's just a few blocks from here. I live there alone and we could talk without having to worry about what everybody else is thinking," she said softly.

"That sounds great," Jensen said, trying hard not to sound too desperate. "You can't imagine what it's like living in this fishbowl. Everything you do and everywhere you go, some reporter wants to tear you down. They call it investigative reporting but they don't care whose life they destroy," he said bitterly.

"It sounds like you could unwind a bit. It must be very hard to live the kind of life you do," Kelly said sympathetically. "Why don't you meet me in about twenty minutes or so," she asked with a smile, writing her address on a piece of paper.

"That's just fine, Kelly," he said, turning and heading for the secretary of health and human services. He would talk to this boring moron for a few minutes and then excuse himself and join the stunning Kelly Adkins in an "unwinding" session, he thought, smiling to himself. A few minutes later, while talking to Glendon Mead about the housing crisis in America, he suddenly found himself suffering a terrible "headache" and feeling somewhat flush.

Jensen put his hand to his forehead. "Whoa," he mumbled. "Sorry, Glendon, but I just got hit with a monster headache. It feels like a jackhammer splitting my skull."

Mead put his hand on Jensen's back. "Anything I can get for you? Do you need some help to the couch?" Mead asked.

"No, thanks. These last couple of weeks have been crazy. I just need some sleep." He called for his driver and made apologies to everyone before leaving. And then he headed out, his hand to his head, to the apartment of Kelly Adkins for what he hoped would be a very therapeutic evening.

Kelly would not be Jensen's first indiscretion and his driver understood fully when he was told to wait, no matter how late. The vice president got out and walked up the stairs, pulling his coat up above his eyes. He would be hard pressed to explain his presence here at night.

Jensen quickly discovered the back stairs and ascended the four flights to Kelly's level. It seemed safe and he walked briskly to apartment 419. He put his head down as he knocked on the door and was relieved when she opened it within seconds. He rushed into the apartment.

"You look like you just evaded a squad of KGB agents," Kelly said laughing.

"I don't mean to be overly paranoid but it would be a bitch explaining what I'm doing here. I can't take any chances, you know."

24

"I understand," said Kelly. "I can't even imagine a life where every-thing you do is on the evening news."

Jensen sat down and she offered him a drink. "A beer would be great."

She headed for the kitchen to get the vice president a beer. "I'm still listening," she shouted from the other room.

"Well, it's to be expected for the president because he is, after all, the man. But I get the same scrutiny and none of the power," said a clearly-bitter Jensen.

Kelly returned to the room and handed him his beer, which he chugged from the bottle.

"I guess it depends on the president, right? Some are secure enough to share the power, aren't they?" she asked.

Jensen put his feet up on the coffee table. "I suppose, but in general, the vice president doesn't have the power. I'm not even close to being the second most powerful person in the government. I'm not even in the inner circle.

I get sent to funerals and basically stick my finger up my ass waiting for the old man to croak."

"Is it really that bad?" Kelly asked softly.

"Hell, I don't mean to complain. There are some good perks. But I much preferred the Senate. Then, I was somebody. Now, I'm nothing. Even my wife will tell you that," he said clearly disgruntled. He finished his beer. "Could I bother you for another one?" he asked.

"No problem," she responded, going quickly back to the kitchen. Upon her return she handed another beer to him, and once again he ignored the glass.

"I'm sure your wife must be proud of you. I know that I would be," she said, sipping a drink of her own while sitting down next to him.

"My wife was excited at first, but that didn't last long. Back in Ohio, as a Senator, when I entered a room or gave a speech, people listened. I was the man, particularly since the other senator was weak and unpopular. But Tolbert gives me nothing to do, except go to funerals. I've met more dead foreign leaders than live ones," he said sarcastically.

Kelly laughed and brushed her arm against his. "Too bad your wife couldn't be here this weekend," she said seductively.

"She went to visit her folks in Iowa. No particular reason other than to get away from this place. And me," he said, looking at the floor.

"I'm sure that's not true. It's just the situation. She probably loves you very much," Kelly said softly.

"Don't bet on it, Kelly. By the way, I don't get a chance to wear my hair down too often. Call me Craig."

"O.K., Craig," Kelly answered hesitantly. "I feel a little funny about calling you by your first name."

"Hey, I'm just a man. This town has all these marble statues and sometimes people get lost in all of the pretension. I'm just a bureaucrat, no more, no less." He hesitated for a few seconds before continuing.

"I don't mean to get philosophical on you so please excuse my ramblings," he apologized.

"I find it very refreshing. There's no need to apologize," she said, gently caressing his arm.

"Where was I?" he asked out loud. "Oh yeah, you were saying that my wife must love me. I'm afraid not. Her love for me died some time ago. We were just about to get a divorce when Tolbert asked me to be on the ticket. She wanted to stick it out then and see what happened. She'll hang on for a while to see if Tolbert kicks the bucket. But we're just going through the motions. We haven't slept in the same bed for over a year now," he said.

"My God!" Kelly exclaimed. "With the pressures of your job? How do you handle the loneliness?"

"Mostly, I just do without. But there are times when I just have to have someone to hold, to touch," he said with a tinge of desperation.

"What do you do?" she asked.

"I look elsewhere. And believe me, it's not easy. I really miss just talking to someone intelligent." She looked warmly at him, still caressing his arm.

"What do you do?" Jensen asked.

"I start law school at Georgetown next year."

"That's what this country needs. Another lawyer," he said with a laugh. "I'm just joking, Kelly. I'm a lawyer, too, you know. There are some good ones out there."

"Did you really want to be a lawyer or was it just a steppingstone to politics?" Kelly asked.

"You caught me," Jensen said. "I never intended to practice law. I did it for about a year and hated every minute. Then I ran for a House seat when the incumbent unexpectedly died. He was in perfect health and just keeled over during a speech one day. I got elected by a hair and the rest is, as they say, history," he said laughing.

"Do you love your wife?" Kelly asked bluntly, getting up to get him another beer.

As she was getting him a beer, he thought about the question. "Do I love her? Hell no. But what can I do? If I get a divorce, my career is over. Americans wouldn't stand for a single president."

"Do you really think so?" she asked handing him the beer.

"Absolutely. If a candidate never marries, he must be gay. And if he divorces, it's a sign of bad judgment. I don't think that we'll ever see a single president," he said, and then gulped the beer, almost emptying it in one swallow.

"That doesn't seem right," she said, shaking her head. She stood up and walked over to the stereo. She put on a soft record and said, "Would you like to dance?"

"I'd love to," answered Jensen. "I can't remember the last time I danced. I suppose it was at the inaugural ball," he said, placing his arms around her as the music started.

He nodded approvingly at Kelly's selection. "Very nice, Kelly. This was big when I was in college. I thought that all of you young people liked rap and heavy metal."

"I guess some do but not me. I like ballads, romantic songs. I know all of the songs from the forties and fifties by heart. My parents used to play them all of the time," she said, as they began to sway to the music.

Neither spoke until the song was over. Jensen fell prey to the hypnotic effect of the music, the alcohol and Kelly's perfume. Kelly looked into the mirror on the living-room wall. As they danced, she signaled to the cameraman to get into position.

The song ended, and Jensen looked into Kelly's eyes, bringing her closer to him and then kissing her gently on the lips. When she did not resist, he pulled her tighter and kissed her more firmly. Kelly pulled away, to his immediate chagrin, but then brought back his smile when she grabbed his hand and said, "Let's go to my room."

He followed her like a puppy, feeling overwhelmed by the urges that he had kept repressed for too long. God, she's beautiful, he thought to himself. When they reached Kelly's bed, she stopped and looked at him with a piercing glance and quickly slipped off her dress.

He practically ripped off the rest of her clothing. Standing before him completely naked, the light from the moon bouncing off her silhouette, he was awed by her perfect shape.

"Your turn, Craig," she purred, helping him to remove his shirt and pants. They fell into the bed and began a long and intense night of passion. Their first attempt at lovemaking was over rather quickly. He apologized for its brevity but she praised and comforted him, allowing his confidence to return.

After a second time, Jensen almost collapsed, totally spent. "My God, Kelly. I haven't felt like this in years. You're incredible," he gasped. "If you slept with the president, he'd have a heart attack and I'd be moving into the White House. What do you say?" he said with a laugh.

"I don't think the First Lady would approve," she said smiling. "And besides, he doesn't do a whole lot for me. They say power is an aphrodisiac but I can't imagine in my wildest dreams going to bed with Andrew Tolbert. But I would have made love to you even if you were just another attorney. I find you very attractive," she lied.

"Really? That makes me feel very good. Yes, that might just get me through the rest of this damned term." He looked at his watch and saw that it was about 3:00 A.M.

"As much as I hate to, Kelly, I've got to be going. I have to wake up in my bed and I can't come home when everybody is up. My only hope is to sneak in. Tonight was fantastic. I have to see you again. May I?" he asked.

"Yeah, I'd like that, Craig," she replied sweetly.

He finished dressing and kissed her as he left. "I'll call you, O.K.?"

"I'll be waiting," she said as he walked out into the hallway. "Or maybe you'll hear from me first," she said when he was out of earshot, laughing as the cameraman walked in.

"Hope I didn't embarrass you too much," she said naughtily.

"Hey, no big deal," answered the cameraman, Mark Metcalf. "I've done a bunch of these. I hardly even pay attention. Really. But this is my first vice president. It threw me at first. What's the plan, do you know?" he asked.

"I think we might have a new vice president soon," she said, whistling to herself. "Well, a girl has to get some sleep. If you don't mind, Mark, I'll turn in."

"Sure thing. You have a good night," the cameraman replied, wondering if she had believed that nonsense about his not noticing. He had noticed, all right, and watched intently every single second. Before he turned in the photos, he would make copies for himself.

"Kelly Adkins, you're one fine woman," he said to himself, wondering if it was too late to stop by his girlfriend's house. He was as worked up as he could remember being in quite some time.

✠   ✠   ✠

Boris Gunther turned off the television as soon as the American movie was over. The German truck driver lived alone, escaping by watching the Hollywood movies that he rented. Boris looked into the mirror while brushing his teeth. He hadn't shaved recently but there was still that resemblance that three more people had mentioned in the last two days. He was the spitting image of Felix Klaus, secretary general of NATO. He had been told this almost daily over the last two years and he was getting sick of it.

"Klaus can kiss my ass. He doesn't live in a dump like I do, screwing prostitutes," he grumbled. He was a burly part-time truck driver. He picked up a shot of schnapps and polished it off with a quick tilt of the head. That being the last of many, he collapsed into bed and lamented on his miserable life. "Felix Klaus can go to hell!" he shouted and fell asleep within seconds.

A short time later, two men entered his dingy apartment, expertly picking the lock. They moved quietly through the rubble of his dwelling and quickly reached the bedroom. One of them picked up a pillow and shoved it onto the drunken man's face, and stood watching him kick while hearing his muffled screams. Due to his inebriation, there wasn't much fight in him. Within minutes, he was dead. For added insurance, one of the attackers struck Gunther's jaw with the butt of his 9-mm gun, breaking his two front teeth.

The killers carried his lifeless body out of the bed and to their automobile. They drove without saying a word until they reached the office of Dr. Frederick Van Heuven, general dentistry. They unloaded the body out of the trunk into Van Heuven's office and placed the corpse onto a gurney.

Van Heuven walked in and nodded to the two men without saying a word. One of them broke the silence.

"This is him, doc. You know what to do."

"I know what is expected of me," he said, looking at his watch. "You'll return to remove the body?"

The other gunman spoke gruffly. "Don't worry about us. Just pull his teeth out and don't ask questions. O.K?"

"Yeah, I got it," he responded, sounding annoyed by these thugs who thought they were big men. He started the job as they left the room and wondered aloud how he got mixed up with this gang of mobsters whose names he didn't know and whose objectives he could not fathom. But they paid him well and that was all he needed to know.

The dentist called out to his nurse, who came running into the room, followed by another dentist who would assist in the surgery.

Dr. Van Heuven gave the orders. "Nurse, prop open the patient's mouth. Dr. Fritz, hand me the plastic bin with the extracted teeth."

Looking puzzled, Fritz picked up the bin and opened the lid. Inside were posterior teeth arranged in sequence on wax blocks. He admired the numerous gold inlays and onlays that covered the teeth, which had earlier been removed from Felix Klaus.

"What's going on?" Fritz asked, alarmed by the bizarre scene.

"Dr. Fritz, I'm going to systematically inlay these gold restorations into our dead friends dentation and you are going to assist me," Van Heuven explained.

"Are you insane?" Fritz protested. "That's impossible! The bite wing x-ray will show some variation."

"I will not debate you, doctor. Your only concern is to do what I tell you," Van Heuven said firmly. "Now, please begin by removing the existing gold work."

Van Heuven slowly motioned to the nurse to x-ray Boris' mouth and thought carefully about the one obstacle they faced. Boris was missing an upper-right bicuspid while Felix Klaus was not. Van Heuven would have to create a custom-sized socket into Boris' auxiliary bone structure and implant Klaus' bicuspid.

He instructed the nurse to do several consecutive x-rays to create the fit. On final insertion, he carefully coated the root surface with calcium hydroxide to mimic the attaching ligament at the tooth-bone interface.

Fritz then took over, removing old amalgam filling and existing decay in Boris' less well kept mouth. Tooth by tooth, the inlays were meticulously placed.

The work continued through the night. The killers would return at 8:00 A.M. to retrieve the body. The final details would include the placement of a few anterior resin fillings to duplicate those of Klaus. In addition, a crown on his front incisor would be made to match the broken portion of Boris' right incisor which had been cracked by the gun butt. Leaving the loose crown in the mouth cavity would help complete the ruse. Van Heuven had been told that Boris' body would be consumed in a fire where the only way to identify the dead man would be by the teeth. It was possible that people would actually think that the soon-to-be-found charred corpse belonged to the secretary general of NATO, Felix Klaus.

Van Heuven lit a cigarette as the sun started to come up through the window. Although the money he would receive for the macabre task was more than he made in a year, he would have no more to do with these assassins. He motioned to the nurse to take away the body of the late Boris Gunther and stormed out into the dawn of the new day, a disgusted but richer man.

✠   ✠   ✠

Michael wasn't able to get any work done because the capitol was set aflame by what had happened in Peru. He left for home early and called Rebecca at work. Things were frantic at GNN, mostly because of Michael.

He was put on hold for several minutes and was about to hang up when she came on the line. "Michael, is that you?"

"Yeah, it's me, the national hero or national embarrassment. Take your pick," he said dejectedly. "Probably the latter."

"I think you're wrong. The polls are showing that the average American can't get enough of you right now."

"They're not the only ones," Michael said. "Every TV show, every magazine, all the dailies and networks, they all want a piece of me. Nightline called. Good Morning America called three times. Half the country wants to crucify me and the other half wants to crown me king. I don't know what to think. My mind is going twenty different directions all at once. Will you take me away from this madness?" he pleaded.

"You can't be serious? Because of you, I'll probably have to work overtime," she answered.

"Come on, Becks. Your turf is the White House. This has nothing to do with the president," Michael replied.

"Well, let me tell you something, Mr. Rookie Politician, yes it does. The president has already held a press conference, the primary topic of which was you and your buddies. And there are rampant rumors that he's considering dumping Jensen and taking on you. You know, the election is approaching and Jensen's a liability," Rebecca explained.

Michael was stunned. He had never for a second ever conceived that such a thing was possible. Vice president? Good Lord.

"You know, my dad said the same thing the other night. Oh, did I tell you about Saturday night?"

"No, you didn't. What did he say?" Michael asked.

"Well, let me tell you something else first. Our whole family had dinner together. The whole family, Michael."

He didn't understand. "I know that you've never been a close-knit family, but what's the big deal?"

"Tommy was there, too," she explained.

"Tommy?" he stammered. "Your brother Tommy? I thought he wanted nothing to do with any of you."

"So did everyone else. After he came back from Vietnam, he just disappeared. I thought that he had died until I saw him at your army retirement," Rebecca explained. "I almost fainted when he stopped by the house to pick me up."

"What did he say? How did he explain it? What happened to what's her name? Uh, Adrian?" Michael inquired.

"He didn't really go into it, just that the war had a tremendous effect on him and that he had to get away. He picked Daddy's hometown and began his life over basically. He wouldn't go into specifics, Michael, but he looked good. He really did. He opened up to me and was warm and gentle. Can you believe it?" she asked in amazement.

"That doesn't sound like the antisocial, mad-at-the-world Tommy that I remember," Michael said.

"Well, part of him still was, but there was another side of him that wasn't like what I remembered." Rebecca paused before mentioning the thing that had been disturbing her.

"He referred to something that didn't make sense and wouldn't explain what he meant. And it's bothering me quite a bit, Michael, so much so that it's the only reason I wasn't sick from worry this weekend over you," she said.

"What is it, Becks? What did he say?"

"Well, I asked him why he had always been so angry at the world and he said it was because Daddy always preferred me and Steven, because of the war and because he didn't want to lead the Fourth Reich," Rebecca answered.

"The Fourth Reich? What does that mean?"

"I haven't a clue. He wouldn't say anything else. But I've had the weirdest thoughts the last few days. The Fourth Reich...it gives me shivers to think of Hitler and swastikas and that nonsense. What do you think?"

"You got me. I always thought that Tommy was a few fries short of a Happy Meal. Who knows what's in that head of his? Anyone who drops out of sight for twenty years isn't all there." They remained silent for a minute, both thinking about what Tommy could have meant by that statement.

Michael continued. "I almost forgot what I called for. I have to get away from here. I'm just not into doing the Today show right now and the phone is ringing off the hook. Will you take me somewhere that doesn't have a phone and make love to me until my eyebrows fall off?" he pleaded.

"Oh, that sounds like an offer I can't refuse," she said softly. "Listen, let me finish up here quickly and I'll meet you at home in an hour."

"Sorry, no can do. The buzzards are setting up shop in our frontyard, I've been told. Meet me at L'enfant Plaza in an hour. We will have complete privacy. What do you say?" Michael said.

"What about the kids?" she asked, and then answered her own question. "I know, Christina will take care of everything. O.K., Michael, you're on. I'll meet you in the hotel lobby in an hour."

"Not to brag, sweetheart, but if I sit in the lobby of a crowded hotel, it'll cause a stir. At least this week. Just go to room 1425, I've already arranged it. And bring your toothbrush. And Rebecca, one more thing."

"Yes?"

"I love you, darling. I hope this crazy thing doesn't ruin my career but if it does, we'll go back to California like we had planned originally and I'll teach. But no matter what, I'll love you with all of my heart."

"I love you too, Michael. See you soon," Rebecca said, and hung up the phone.

Craig Jensen was going over his itinerary for the next week with his staff. The election was coming up quickly and the convention was to be held the following week. There was talk of dumping him, but the president assured him that he would remain on the ticket. Although at times he despised his job, he wouldn't give it up without a fight.

Bill Wright, the chief of staff, walked into Jensen's office and closed the door. The normally combative Wright stared at his shoes. Jensen sensed something was wrong.

"What is it, Bill?" the vice president asked.

"We have a problem. There's a guy out there who's been demanding to see you. Diana buzzed me and I was prepared to tell him to hit the road or I'd call security."

"Well, what then?" Jensen asked impatiently.

"He said that maybe before he left, I'd like to take a look at something first. And then he showed me some photographs," Wright said.

"Photographs of what?" he demanded.

"You need to talk to him," Wright replied. "Right away."

Jensen was alarmed by his usually unflappable chief aide's concern. Wright was even sweating.

"O.K., Bill, I'll meet with him if you think I should" said Jensen, in a tone just above a whisper.

"I'll show him in" replied Wright somberly, and seconds later he walked back in with the unexpected visitor.

Their surprise guest started things off. "Good afternoon, Mr. Vice President. It's an honor to meet you."

"Cut to the chase. Who are you and what do you want?"

"I'd rather not use a name but I do have something for you to review," the man said mysteriously, and handed the vice president an envelope full of 8X10 color glossies of him and a certain young woman in various positions of passion.

Jensen grew white as a sheet as he realized that they were pictures of him and Kelly writhing in her bed. He was enraged and frightened at the same time as he realized that he had been set up. By whom and for what purpose?

"You son of a bitch. I'll have you arrested for trying to blackmail the vice president of the United States."

"Whoa, Mr. Vice President, calm down. I'm just a lowly messenger. I'm not even sure who I'm working for. I was hired through a third party who doesn't even know. I was just told to give these to you with a message," he answered.

"What message?" Jensen asked.

"That the originals are somewhere else, very safe and that they'll be released to the press unless you resign."

Wright glared at the messenger. "Anything else?"

He shrugged his shoulders. "That's it. I'll be on my way. I'll show myself out," he said, and walked quickly out of the office, his heart pounding, afraid that he would be arrested. He held his breath until he reached the street and hailed a cab.

Jensen and his aide were silent for a minute as the two men thought about these photographs. Wright broke the silence.

"You know," said the chief of staff, "With all of the speeches you've made recently on family values, this could sink you and the president. I hate to give in to blackmail but I just don't see what choice you have. I really don't."

Jensen's rage was now gone and he was practically in tears. "I'm not a hypocrite. I believe in the family. But my wife has all but deserted me. I need a woman's touch once in a while. Is that so much to ask, Bill? Is it?"

Wright responded as he started to leave the room. "No it isn't, boss. Maybe you should go home early, get a good night's sleep and we'll talk about it tomorrow. O.K?"

Jensen nodded as Wright closed the door. He broke out in uncontrollable wailing as he slowly realized that the only thing in his life that he valued, his career, was over.

✠ ✠ ✠

Felix Klaus, also known as Wilhelm, was early for his appointment with the German chancellor. He had met with the leader of West Germany on many occasions in past years, but this was the first time since the unification.

The chancellor's secretary let Klaus know that the German leader was now ready. "He'll see you now, sir."

"Thank you, Fraulein" said the old man to the charming young woman, and he walked into the chancellor's office and was met by a tall and grinning man with a large and very noticeable birthmark on his cheek.

"Good morning, Herr Klaus. It's a great honor to meet with you today. I apologize for making you come to me. Next time, I will come to Brussels," said Ernst Luther, as he vigorously shook Wilhelm's hand.

"Nonsense," said Wilhelm. "I'm German and you are the leader of Germany. I gladly come to you."

"Please sit down. Can I get you anything?"

"No, thank you. I'm just fine, Herr Luther. By the way, do you plan on attending the Olympics? They start this Saturday, you know," Wilhelm reminded the chancellor.

"Yes, I do hope to attend at least one event. Isn't your grandson participating?" asked the Chancellor.

Klaus beamed proudly. "He certainly is. He's in the 100- and 200-meter races. I'm certain that he'll be declared the world's fastest person, the first time ever that a German will hold that distinction and the first time in quite a while that that honor will go to a white man."

Luther continued. "That's wonderful. I suppose it's in his blood. Were you not an Olympic athlete yourself?"

Klaus was impressed that Luther was aware. He responded modestly.

"I was only seventeen. I was a long jumper at the 1936 games. I didn't win a medal but I think that I could have in 1940, but the games were cancelled because of the war. I remember it like yesterday. My teammate Lutz should have won but in the middle of the competition, while leading over the American Negro Jesse Owens, he actually gave Owens advice on how to improve his jumps. Owens took his advice and just barely beat Lutz. I never spoke to Lutz again and to this day I cannot understand it," Klaus said, shaking his head.

"I hope that your grandson wins but if he doesn't, you can still be proud of him. He is incredible," Luther said.

"That's true. He is evidence that Germany is the greatest nation on earth," Klaus said, and then paused. "Which brings me to the purpose for my meeting. How is the unification going?"

Luther lit a cigar and inhaled before responding. "It's much more difficult than I imagined. Eventually, everything will work out but these first couple of years are so taxing. None of us really understood how far behind our Easterners were. They're decades behind. Remember, they went directly from totalitarianism to communism and now they're expected to make the immediate jump to capitalism. They've been like Rip Van Winkle, asleep for forty years."

"Is it really that bad?" Klaus asked.

"Oh, yes. And to make the transition will require massive sacrifices and money from the West. And the West Germans resent it," Luther explained.

"But they're all Germans," Klaus stated emphatically.

"After forty years of communism, we're not the same anymore, I'm sorry to say. Right now, we're two different people. It will be very difficult," the chancellor stated.

"But it is Germany's destiny," Klaus said flatly.

"I believe this also, Herr Klaus." He reached into his drawer and pulled out a bottle of whiskey and poured two glasses. "Let's drink to Germany."

"To Germany," the two men said, and gulped down the drinks. Klaus smiled and then spoke.

"Which brings me to my second point, Herr Luther. If Germany is to be a powerful nation, she must act like it. Last year, during the Persian Gulf War, Germany did almost nothing and was criticized heavily by other nations. And rightly so, in my opinion. We should have taken more of a leading role," Wilhelm said.

"Our Basic Law prohibits us from military action for other than purely defensive measures. The world is still wary of an aggressive Germany," Luther said, defensively.

"The Basic Law does not expressly say that. Everyone interprets it that way because they're so paranoid after the war. But with the collapse of the Soviet Union, and now that we're unified, Germany must take a stronger position. There are two crises breaking out and I urge you to react with strength. Iraq apparently didn't learn from Desert Storm. And Yugoslavia is truly a crisis," Klaus stated strongly.

"What do you suggest?"

Klaus leaned over. "First, take immediate steps to build up the army. Secondly, if hostilities break out with Iraq, Germany must lead the way, along with the United States. And third, we must take immediate steps to defuse the situation in Yugoslavia. I can sympathize with the Serbs; when there's a mixture of many different ethnic groups, it spells disaster," he said, pausing for a moment.

"Lastly, I recommend that you take immediate steps to reduce immigration. There are simply too many foreigners in Germany and it's diluting her strength. The world's breaking up before our eyes, Herr Luther, while we're the only ones uniting. Look at how things have changed," Klaus said, walking over to the large globe on Luther's desk.

"We've seen the disintegration of the Soviet Union into fifteen different republics and either they'll break up into smaller splinters based on ethnicity or there will be civil war," Klaus predicted. "Look at Yugoslavia, now gone, replaced by Serbia, Croatia and Bosnia-Herzogovina. You have seen within the publicity of the Olympics that Catalonia is threatening to leave Spain."

"Czechoslovakia may split into two nations and there is talk that Brittany will break away from France," Klaus continued. "There will be nations this year at the Olympics that you have probably never heard of, more than 170. Four years from now, I predict that there will be more than 200. We must stop the flow of immigrants into our nation. They are sapping our strength." Klaus finished, out of breath.

Luther listened intently. "There's much truth in what you say, Herr Klaus. I'll take your words to heed. I promise you that." He then changed the subject. "What of NATO's future?"

"I will be out of a job fairly soon. NATO is obsolete. Its primary purpose was to deter the Soviet threat, which no longer exists. America is focusing on domestic problems and no longer sees the need to spend billions on the defense of Europe. The American presence will be gone within five years, except for possibly a nominal force," Klaus stated.

"Do you really think so? What will take its place?"

"A European defense force led by Germany," Klaus said firmly. "The death of NATO is but another reason why Germany must take a strong stance. History shows that weakness invites aggression. There will be a huge vacuum created by the loss of the Americans. We must fill it quickly and in numbers. Germany has learned its lesson and will never again take a posture of belligerence. I trust that there is no chance of that happening," Wilhelm said.

"I can assure you of that," Luther stated emphatically. "We have no design on starting another war. We've had forty years of democracy and it works. We're a prosperous and powerful country," said the chancellor.

"I agree, Herr Chancellor. But things have changed. There will be an imbalance of power once the U.S. leaves. We simply need to take more of a leading role in international affairs. For our children," Klaus pleaded.

"Your advice is, as always, very sound," Luther said, standing up and putting out his hand. "I'm going to try to make it to the Olympics this year. We will see."

"Say hello to your family for me, Chancellor. I know how much they mean to you," Klaus said, and exited the room.

"That's true. They're much more important than my career. I'd resign in a second if they needed me."

"I hope that day never comes. Germany needs you. God bless you," Klaus said, as he left the Chancellor's office wondering if his words would influence Luther's actions. It would be helpful if Germany built up its army, but their mission would be carried out one way or the other.

✠   ✠   ✠

Ludmilla Kolkov was early for her meeting with the former illustrious scientist, Boris Semneyov. She hoped to conduct the meeting in strict business terms, but just in case, wore a short, sexy dress and just the right amount of makeup.

Ludmilla Kolkov! God, she despised that name and hated pretending to be a Russian. Hopefully, this charade would not be necessary much longer.

Only a few minutes late, Semneyov appeared, looking exactly as she had imagined, like a disheveled scientist.

"Good afternoon, Comrade Semneyov," she greeted him, in fluent Russian. "It's an honor to meet you."

He grunted a few words that were nearly unintelligible and they sat down. He was not interested in small talk.

"Let's get right to business," she said, and he nodded his head. "I work for an organization that wants to acquire nuclear weapons. It wants both the knowledge to build weapons of its own as well as receiving access to nuclear sites so that it can obtain such weapons," she said bluntly.

"Steal them, you mean," he clarified.

"Yes, that's basically what my group wants," she answered.

"Do you represent a government?" the scientist asked.

"We choose not to get into specifics. We're merely a prospective buyer looking for a seller. Who we are is irrelevant. We can make you a very rich man," Ludmilla added.

This offer caught his attention, since he had not worked in some time and was struggling to feed his family. "I have two questions," stated Semneyov. "I will probably do what you wish if the price is high enough. But I will not harm Russia. Will these weapons be used against her?"

"Absolutely not. We hope not to use them at all but if we did, it would be against the United States most likely."

He thought about this for a moment before asking his second question. "How much will you pay?"

"We're prepared to pay you ten million rubles for helping us to obtain warheads and one million rubles a year to work for us developing new weapons."

These figures were almost unfathomable for the Russian scientist and were much higher than he had even dreamed of. Ludmilla realized he was impressed.

"Do you know Colonel Alexander Polov?" she asked.

"Yes, I do. I know that he's very bitter about his career and the collapse of the nation. And I know that he has serious financial difficulties," Boris responded.

"I'm meeting with him later today to ask him the same questions that I'm asking you. Do you think that he would be agreeable to such a proposal?" she asked.

"I know that he's very despondent. We were good friends at one time but have drifted apart. He's very bitter and I think that he would not resist such a generous overture," the scientist added.

"Then you agree? You will help us?" she asked.

"I want the ten million up front," he demanded.

"That's no problem," she added, nonchalantly.

He felt overwhelmed. He would be rich. "What else?"

"Since you know Polov, I would like you to come to our meeting. Will you do that?" she inquired.

"I don't mean to repeat myself, but I will come if I am paid first," he said flatly, somewhat uncertain of himself.

"You follow me and you will be paid within the hour. Do we have a deal?" Ludmilla asked.

"We have a deal," he said enthusiastically, as they shook hands.

"One more thing, Comrade. We have the utmost confidence in you. But and I'm sure that this is unnecessary, if you fail us or we find that you cannot be trusted, you and your family will meet a most unhappy fate. My organization is rather adamant about loyalty. Please us and you will live a long and wealthy life. Displease us and..." She left the sentence unfinished.

"I understand, Comrade. I'm too old to be a hero and all I care about is my family. I will make no trouble for you," said the Russian.

25

ichael woke up in his hotel room and glanced at Rebecca, who was still sleeping. They had not had such a passionate evening in many years. Their relationship had been a little awkward since they had gotten back together and they knew that it would take a while before they could resume a normal marriage. He had forgotten everything last night. He gazed lovingly at Rebecca and thanked God for her.

She began stirring and broke out into a wide smile when she saw his face.

"Well, good morning," she purred, reaching towards him and pressed her lips against his. "Care for more?"

"That would be suicide," he said grinning, as he embraced her and began kissing her neck. He moved his hands along her back and started to lightly stroke her thighs.

She arched her back and whispered, "Oh, darling, don't stop." Michael threw off the sheet that was covering both of them.

The sudden ringing of the phone startled them. He glanced at his watch. It was 9:30 A.M. and he was late for work. But the only person who knew they were here was Christina. He looked at Rebecca with a fearful glance and picked up the phone.

"Hello."

"Congressman Michael Madigan, please."

"This is he. Who is this?" Michael demanded, shrugging his shoulders in response to Rebecca's asking look.

"Sir, this is the White House operator. Will you hold for the president?" said the operator.

"Uh, sure," Michael replied, startled.

"Who is it?" Rebecca whispered.

"It's the White House," Michael said, cupping his hand over the phone. "The president..." He didn't get to finish as a voice came on the line.

"Michael, this is Andrew Tolbert. I'm sorry to bother you. It took a little bit to track you down, but these White House operators can find anyone," said the president.

Michael was still trying to figure out why the president was calling him.

"You're not bothering me, Mr. President. What can I do for you?"

"Despite the irregularity of it all, I was very impressed by your little mission. The American people were too. They're ready to proclaim you as the new emperor," joked Tolbert.

"I don't know about that, sir. I hope that I didn't embarrass the government. I just felt that there's too much talk in Congress and not enough action."

"I'll vouch for that," said Tolbert. "Politicians want to protect their own jobs and no one wants to rock the boat. You didn't give a damn about your career, just doing what was right. I have a lot of respect for that."

Michael was ecstatic to hear that from the president. But he knew Tolbert didn't track him down in a hotel just to compliment him.

"Thank you, Mr. President. But I'm sure you didn't call just for that," Michael responded.

"Ah, the famous Madigan directness. I'll be glad to get to the bottom line. Michael, there's about to be a major player leaving my administration and I want to know if you'd be interested in filling the position," Tolbert said bluntly.

"Sir, I've only been in the Congress for two years. I don't know if I could abandon my constituents." As an afterthought, he said, "I guess it depends upon the position."

"I was told you would respond like this," laughed Tolbert. "Why don't we talk about it in person? Are you available for lunch today at the White House?" asked the president.

"Today? Of course, sir. What time?" he inquired.

"How about twelve-thirty? Is that O.K?" asked Tolbert.

"That's fine, sir. I'll see you then."

Rebecca was beside herself in anticipation. "Well, what did he say?" said Rebecca.

Michael replied coyly, "Oh, nothing in particular. Why do you ask?"

Rebecca hit him with a pillow and shrieked, "What did he want?" laughing so hard that she almost fell off the bed.

"He offered me a job," Michael said.

Rebecca squealed with excitement. "VP? Right? Daddy was right!" she shouted, pounding the bed.

"Slow down, Becks. He didn't say. It's probably the assistant to the assistant undersecretary to God-knows-what," Michael said, afraid to get too excited just yet.

"No, I have a feeling on this. Woman's intuition. You're going to be offered the vice presidency. He's facing a tough election and Jensen's a drawback," Rebecca said, her tone indicating that there would be no debate.

"Pretty sure of ourselves, aren't we? Well, if you're right, and that's a pretty big if, do you think I should take it?" he asked. "Being a heartbeat away will mean no more private life. If I don't correctly spell all of my vegetables, I'll be crucified. Are you ready for that?" he asked.

"Michael, of course you should take it. You could really make an impact. And God, I have to catch by breath just to say this, but you could very well be president someday. Do you realize that, Michael? Yes, I think you should accept. And I'll be there right by your side."

"What if he really does offer me some low-level position?" Michael asked.

"Then I'll leave you and run away with Craig Jensen," she deadpanned, breaking out into waves of laughter. "Michael Madigan, I love you."

☧　☧　☧

Krupp arrived in Baghdad and was scheduled to meet with the Iraqi leader in about an hour. He had met him once before, just prior to the allied bombing the previous January. Frederick had met and dealt with him on many occasions but he was not available. So Krupp came alone.

Although over a year had passed since the end of the war, Baghdad was still a war-torn city. Many buildings had been damaged by the bombing and had never been repaired. The facial expressions of the people in the street indicated pain and uncertainty.

Krupp had predicted earlier that the Iraqi leader would be overthrown, after the people realized that it had been his foolishness that had led to such devastation. But incredibly, he appeared secure in his job.

Krupp was escorted to the presidential retreat and was given a short time to clean up before his meeting with the Iraqi leader. Krupp and the other members of the Six had no great love for the Arabs, but they could serve a purpose. Initially, the goal had been to destroy Israel. Now, there was a new objective, to cause the United States and the United Nations to focus their energies on Iraq.

When he was finished cleaning up, he let his hosts know and he was immediately summoned. It was now lunch time and they would share a meal while they talked.

Krupp would speak in English, a language that the president understood. Upon seeing the Iraqi leader, Krupp summoned all of the feigned respect he could muster.

"Hello, your excellency. It is a pleasure to meet you again," he said.

The Iraqi leader merely nodded and gestured to Krupp to be seated. "Are you hungry?" he asked.

"Yes, I am. I would be honored to dine with you," Krupp said, wondering how much of this congeniality he could take without vomiting.

After a silent fifteen minutes while they ate, the dictator indicated that he was finished. Several servants jumped up and cleared away all of the dishes and food.

"What can we do for you?" the Iraqi leader inquired.

Krupp looked around and felt slightly ill at ease, since there were seven or eight subordinates present.

"Your excellency, would it be possible for us to be alone for a few moments?" Krupp asked.

The president moved his head almost imperceptibly and everyone but the interpreter quickly left.

"So, we are alone now. What's on your mind?"

"As you know," Krupp began, "I'm not Israeli. I'm German and my organization supported you during the war last year. Your men fought bravely but it was just a question of overpowering force." He stopped and looked for a reaction but saw none. "We can perhaps make the difference in the future," Krupp said intensely.

"What do you mean?"

"Your nuclear capabilities were dealt a severe setback. We could help you recover," Krupp said. "We can provide to you weapons grade plutonium-239 as well as uranium-235. Many of your calutrons at Tarmia and Al-Sharqat, as well as your calutron component and assembly plants at Al-Dijjla, Al-Dura, Al-Rabesh and Augba-bin-Nafi were destroyed in the war."

Krupp knew that the Iraqi was impressed. "We can help you to rebuild your centrifuge factory at Al-Furat, which, as you know, would allow you to enrich uranium. We can provide to you high-grade metals that could be used to encase bomb devices. We can give you HMX explosives that can compress uranium cores in a fission reaction. And we can provide capacitors that control charges and krytrons, switches that set off implosions," Krupp explained.

The Iraqi leader merely stroked his beard. "And what do you want in return?"

"Your excellency, I don't mean to preempt your leadership," Krupp said, with all of the respect he could muster. "But it's not clear what your intentions are concerning the UN demands and the American threats of force. The American president is in a real quandary and although the war last year made him very popular, the people do not support a return to hostilities. Every step he takes, he is accused of acting for political reasons and he desperately wants to avoid lending that appearance."

"What are you suggesting?"

"My organization has a plan that is some forty years in the making. We would appreciate your assistance and in return, we will help you acquire nuclear weapons," Krupp said. "We hope to be able to carry out our plans in the next three to six months. The American election is coming up and the president is preoccupied. This is what we would like..." he said, pausing for a moment.

"We would ask that you not take any actions that would invite a full-scale response by the U.S. But walk the line, get in their hair and on their nerves, not making clear what it is you want. Defy them, dare them, challenge them but do not go too far. Just keep the U.S. distracted." Krupp was wondering if he had offended the proud Iraqi who might resent being treated as a smoke screen.

"I apologize for asking of you this but please keep in mind the end result," the German emphasized. "If we're able to carry out our objectives, we'll provide to you whatever you want," Krupp said, sitting back and waiting with some trepidation the unpredictable leader's reaction.

"I will give it some thought," he said simply. "I do not like being the mouse but the end result is what counts. I could take some pleasure in playing with Tolbert's mind, seeing him lose his job. Yes, that would be very satisfying," the leader said, smiling. He stood up and put out his hand, which Krupp shook, and said, "How can you be certain we will not use such weapons against your beloved Germany?"

Krupp was not prepared for such a comment, even said while smiling. "Uh, your Excellency, you are above all else, a rational man. There would be no point of such an action. I know you're just joking," he said with a sick feeling.

"You're correct," he said, as he raised his glass, laughing and enjoying the obvious discomfort his comments caused his German guest. Krupp drank and smiled, thinking to himself what pleasure he would derive from slitting the dictator's throat.

✠   ✠   ✠

Michael arrived at the White House right on time, nervous and excited. He still didn't believe that he was going to be offered the vice presidency but just thinking about it was mind-boggling.

Not too very long ago, he was a university professor, one of thousands across the country and just months before that, he was an army colonel, one of hundreds. As his father used to say, "only in America." God, he wished his father were still alive.

Michael waited in a reception area and after a few minutes, was asked by an aide to step into the Oval Office. Andrew Tolbert stood by his desk, smiling, his hand out waiting to shake Michael's.

"Michael, come in. How are you?" Tolbert said, flashing his trademark smile. "Once again, I want to apologize for bothering you and Rebecca. But I needed to talk to you right away."

"No problem, Mr. President," Michael assured him. "It was just an overnight thing anyway. I was planning on working today and so was Rebecca. We just needed a little reprieve. Reporters have been camping out on our doorstep."

"Amazing, isn't it? That's the one thing that I regret about public office," Tolbert said with a touch of sadness. "You sacrifice your privacy. Especially with my job. You know, I haven't driven a car in years or carried a wallet. I can't go to a movie or down to the hardware store. I'm not complaining, mind you. This job also has some pretty good perks. But I have no privacy. I had hemorrhoids last year and it made every paper."

Michael laughed. "Well, being a member of the House isn't quite that bad but I've lost my privacy too. I don't go out of my way to get in the paper, but things just keep happening that land me on the front page. Right now, half the people want to lynch me and the other half want to name their baby after me," he said, smiling.

"Well, I'm too old to have any more little ones, but if I did, I'd probably name him Michael," the president said, laughing. "I can't tell you what a kick I got out of what you did. I have to admit, I hope other House members don't start going on covert missions but, damn it all, I thought it was great. And I wanted to tell you that in person," the president said with enthusiasm.

"Thank you, Sir. I have trouble believing I actually did that mission. But I think a lot of good came of it. We captured the biggest drug lord in the world and sent a message to others to sleep with one eye open because we might get them," Michael responded.

"I don't know why all of those bleeding hearts think that Supreme Court ruling was so awful," Tolbert said. "You break the law, you pay the price.

If you do the crime, you do the time. That's my philosophy. But the world's run by lawyers, you know."

"I have mixed feelings about that ruling," Michael said, "but there are too many attorneys in government."

"Amen. They're always telling you what you can't do. This protocol says you can't do this and that convention says you can't do that. Who needs it?" Tolbert asked in disgust. "You and I are men of action. Sometimes that gets us in trouble but we get things done. Craig Jensen is an attorney, you know. Good legal mind but the man couldn't get anything done if his life depended on it."

Michael perked up at the mention of Jensen. Was there a point to this critique?

"I have a reputation for being blunt and so I'll just say it," Tolbert exclaimed. "Craig Jensen will be resigning and I would like for you to take his place as vice president. I'm facing a tough election and I think that you would be able to contribute to the ticket. What do you say?"

Michael had been prepared for this but still the reality of it stunned him.

"Can I ask you why Jensen is resigning? I've heard reports that you might drop him but why's he quitting?"

"Personal reasons. That's all I'll say. He came to see me yesterday and explained his situation and I agreed that it would be best for him to resign."

Michael wanted the job badly but didn't want to appear too eager. "You know I don't have a whole lot of political experience. There's so much that I don't know. Do you really think that I would help the ticket?"

"Listen, Mike, this government is filled with thousands of people who know things," the president said with contempt. "You wouldn't believe some of the policy geeks we have who can recite from memory thousands of facts and figures about the most obscure things. But the important thing about this job, Mike, is presenting an image. I hate to put it like that, but it's true. My job is to set forth a vision of where I want to take the American people. That's what leadership is."

"Leadership," Tolbert continued. "is what it's all about. There are many things I don't know. That's why I have a staff and a Cabinet and hundreds of policy nerds who tell me the facts. Then I decide and convince the American people that I'm right. I delegate everything except setting out the big picture. I know the ends I want to achieve. My aides help me with the means," the president explained.

Michael was trying to give an impression of being calm. "Do you think the country is ready for a Jewish vice president?" he asked.

"That doesn't mean a damn thing in my book and I don't think it matters to the voters either," Tolbert said candidly. "I don't think being Jewish helped you land that airplane or capture Ramirez. It's a non-issue."

Michael was quiet for a few seconds. "Have you consulted with your staff on this?"

"Of course. And almost everyone concurs. Phil Gordon is a little concerned about your lack of experience but still approves," said the president.

"I see." Michael hesitated as he thought about running for a new office so soon after his election to the House.

"Let me make one thing clear," said Tolbert. "I don't intend to lose. Next January, I'll still be here. But I need a fighter on my team. Will you join me?"

"Yes, I will, Sir," Michael said with a smile.

"Congratulations, Mr. Vice President," said Tolbert, extending his hand. "Welcome to the team."

✠ ✠ ✠

"Sign it, you black bastard," yelled the guard, kicking Matt in the ribs again. Matt's hands were tied and he was doubled over in pain, in a dimly lit room that served as his prison cell.

"I can't even read what it says. It's too dark in here," Matt protested.

"It doesn't matter. If I have to say it one more time, I'll break your neck. Now sign it!" The guard shoved a one-page typewritten letter in front of Matt.

Matt realized that it probably didn't matter after the speech he had made. But it was destroying him to think that there would be thousands who would not understand why he said the things he had. He cursed himself for being so weak. He was doing this for his family. But would they lose all respect for him?

Reluctantly, Matt signed the document. The guard kicked him again and left the cell. Matt passed out from the pain.

He later came to, not aware of how long he had been out, when he heard the door open and the cell was flooded with light. He put his hands over his eyes and slowly sat up.

"Get up, Mr. Connors. We're leaving. Come with me," the guard said. "Now," he added.

Matt struggled to stand up. The guard grew impatient. "Mr. Connors, perhaps you would like a repeat performance of last night to get you in the right frame of mind," said the sadistic guard. "Now move it."

Matt walked out into the corridor, moving as fast as he could. "Where are we going?" he inquired.

"Never mind. Just do as you're told," said the guard. They reached a bathroom and Matt was instructed to take a shower and shave and was given fresh clothes to wear.

"Clean up quickly. I'll be right outside this door. There's no escape from this room and if you don't move fast enough, you will regret it," said the guard in thickly-accented, barely passable English.

Matt stood in the bathroom for several moments before doing anything. The guard was right. There was no way to get out other than the way he came in. And the German thug would be standing there with a gun.

He undressed and stepped into the shower, feeling the warm water pounding his sore back. He had to do something but what? These bastards would lose no sleep over killing his family. He couldn't let that happen. Pam and the kids came first no matter what.

He stepped out of the shower and while still hurting, he felt much better. His head was pounding and his ribs were aching but he was no longer in unbearable pain. His vision remained blurry and he kept shaking his head, as if he could clear it that way.

He noticed an electric razor. He had hoped for a razor blade but his captors weren't foolish enough to supply him with a weapon. He shaved and then dressed in the clothing he had been given. Matt looked in the mirror and hardly recognized his reflection.

His was interrupted by the guard with no name, who resumed his shouting. "Let's go, Mr. Connors. Mr. Klaus wants to see you."

Matt quickly asked, "Do you mean Felix Klaus?"

"Yes."

My God, he thought. The leader of NATO was one of them. Felix Klaus was a Nazi. Numbed, he followed the guard and was joined by two others. He was tied up again and thrown into the back of a truck. This is absolutely unbelievable! Who else was involved in this madness?

Half an hour later, they came to a halt and the back of the truck was opened up. Matt was ordered to get out and he saw that they were parked outside a large two-story house. His hands were still tied and two guns were pointed at him. He walked slowly trying to quickly survey the area for any possible escape. But he saw none.

A servant answered the door and they were escorted into a large study. Moments later, Wilhelm, the leader of NATO, entered.

"Good day, Mr. Connors. I am Felix Klaus. Welcome to my home," said Wilhelm, and extended his hand.

Matt refused to shake it and stood glaring at Klaus.

"Please take a seat," Klaus instructed. He looked at his aides and shook his head. "May we have some privacy?" Immediately the room was cleared.

"Mr. Connors, your little speech has aired in America and has created quite a stir. There have been many reported incidents of racial unrest as your fellow African-Americans, as I think you refer to them nowadays, took your advice to heart. There have been many reports of riots all across America. It is really quite incredible," stated Klaus.

Matt shook his head. "What possible reason could you have to start race riots? You're crazier than I thought," Matt replied with hostility.

"Mr. Connors, I'm afraid that you're unable to see the big picture," Klaus said condescendingly. "These riots will merely serve as a distraction. There are many things going on now that will distract your leaders. Your president is concerned about the election. Iraq is causing trouble and now you have race riots. Your vice president has resigned. We will proceed with our plan very soon and your government will be paralyzed with confusion," Klaus said.

Matt was stunned by the news of Jensen. Was it true? "Why are you telling me this? Now that I know, I suppose that you intend to kill me."

"Mr. Connors, we're not barbarians. If you do what we want, your life will be spared. If not, you and your family will die," Klaus said calmly.

Klaus spoke as if he were discussing the weather. What kind of animal was this?

"So, why was I brought here today?" Matt demanded.

"You signed a letter earlier and we would like you to sign another one. That's all," Wilhelm explained.

"Do you think that I'll keep helping your sick plan forever? You disgust me," Matt said resolutely.

"That's a most unfortunate attitude. Are you willing to let Danielle be raped and tortured and John to be sodomized and beaten? That is what you must consider," Klaus said.

The mention of his children's names sent a shock up his spine and he shook with fear.

"What do you want me to sign? Is it too much to ask if I might be able to read it?"

"Not at all, Mr. Connors. As a matter-of-fact, you're going to write this out in longhand. I will dictate and you will write. Now please go over to my desk and open the top drawer and take out some paper and a pen," Klaus instructed.

Matt walked slowly over to the huge mahogany desk and sat down in the elegant leather chair. He opened the top drawer as he was directed and pulled out a pen and paper.

Wait! He noticed something else in the back of the drawer. It looked like...he couldn't be sure. He pulled off the paper that was obscuring the...gun. My God, it was a pistol! Was this a set up? He looked over at Klaus, who was feeding the fish in his aquarium. Klaus was not in a position to defend himself. And besides, his aides were gone and he was too old himself.

Was Klaus not aware of the gun? That must be it! No purpose could be achieved by leaving a gun intentionally that didn't work, or had no ammunition.

Matt looked around the room and surmised the situation. He knew that he could never get away if he killed Klaus. He would have to use him as a hostage.

He would have to move quickly. He glanced at Klaus, who was still feeding his fish. "Did you find the pen and paper, Mr. Connors?" the elderly German asked.

"Yes, I did. And I also found this," he shouted excitedly, as he pulled out the gun and pointed it at Klaus.

"Are you insane?" Klaus shouted. "Where did you get that? Do you think that you can get away?" He seemed clearly astonished. He must not have known.

"This has to be one of the more stupid things I've ever seen, letting a prisoner get a weapon," Matt said mockingly.

"Mr. Connors, what do you expect to gain? You can't escape," Klaus said, as he pushed a button on the wall.

"We'll see about that. I don't think that your aides will let the leader of NATO be killed. You're my ticket out of here," Matt exclaimed.

"Ah, very clever. But I don't think that it will work," Klaus repeated. Abruptly, the doors swung open and three men brandishing weapons stormed into the room.

Matt quickly put his gun into Klaus' back. "Put your weapons down or Mr. Klaus will die," Matt ordered.

"Do not listen to him," Klaus said.

"Mr. Connors," one of the guards said slowly, "put your weapon down," as he took several steps towards Matt.

"Stop!" he shouted, but they kept coming. Matt pulled the trigger and Felix Klaus collapsed to the floor.

✠   ✠   ✠

Michael went home after his meeting with the president without having called Rebecca. He wanted to tell her in person. He walked in the door of their home and tried his best to stay calm, even though he was bursting at the seams.

"Well?" asked Rebecca, smiling as she saw him walk in. She had been scheduled to work but decided to call in sick.

"Well what?" asked Michael, with a mischievous grin.

"Am I looking at the next vice president?"

"Maybe you are and maybe you're not," Michael teased. "But just in case, I suggest that you use a more deferential tone. You're going to have to learn to be a little more subservient. And you're going to have to master the art of looking at me adoringly while I'm giving a speech," he added.

"You got it, didn't you?" she shouted. "Michael, if you don't tell me right this very second, I'm going to scream."

"You're right, darling. You're looking at the assistant to the assistant undersecretary..." he started, to joke but was interrupted by the phone.

Rebecca playfully began hitting him as he picked up the phone. "Hello," he answered.

"Congressman Madigan, please. This is the White House. President Tolbert would like to speak to him."

"This is Madigan," Michael answered.

"I'll connect you, sir," came the operator's reply.

Michael cupped the phone and whispered to Rebecca, "It's the president." Tolbert came on the line right away. "Hello, Mr. President," Michael said.

"Sorry to bother you again so soon, Michael, but rumors are flying all over the place and I'd like to move on. The election is just over our shoulder and I don't want to waste a single day. I'd like to make the announcement today, at about four o'clock, just in time to get it on the evening news," said the president.

Michael looked at his watch. It was now 2:30 P.M.. He would barely have time to clean up. "That's a little tight, sir. What about 5:00 P.M.?" he asked.

"Five o'clock it is. I'll see you then," Tolbert said, and then added, "bring the whole family. Can you have them all there by five?" the president asked. "Family values, you know."

Michael smiled to himself as he thought about the likely cause of Craig Jensen's resignation.

"Yes, sir, they'll be there."

"O,K., partner. I'm counting on you," said the president.

"I'm confident we'll get the job done. See you at five, sir" Michael added.

Rebecca was able to gather from the conversation that Michael had in fact been offered the job. She grabbed his arm and twisted it sharply.

"Michael Madigan, if you don't tell me right now, I will break your arm. Now, were you offered the job and is there a press conference today?"

Michael feigned a pained look and tried to suppress a laugh. "O.K., I surrender. I agreed to take a job where I do nothing but wait for the old man to die. By the way, do you like to go to funerals?" he asked.

"Oh, Michael," shouted Rebecca, who let go of his arm and hugged him. "I'm so proud of you. I knew that he was going to offer it to you and still it's so unreal. My God, you're the vice president of the United States," she said, hugging him tightly.

It had not really hit him yet. It seemed like a dream. They held each other for several minutes without speaking.

"Our lives are going to change, Becks. Are you ready for it?" Michael asked.

"Yes, I am, Michael," she answered, turning serious. "I know that I've given you some doubt in the past about that but I'm ready for this, darling. I'm so proud of you."

Rebecca yelled for Christina and directed her to make sure the kids were looking their best.

"What about Josh?" Michael asked.

"I'm one step ahead of you, dear," answered Rebecca, who had already dialed him.

"Hello," came Josh's reply.

"Josh, how are you? I've got some big news for you. Are you sitting down?"

Josh had a pretty good idea what the big news was and smiled at Kelly, who was sitting on the couch next to him.

"Yeah, I'm sitting down, Mom. What's up?"

"Your father is about to be named vice president. There's a press conference at five o'clock and I would like for you to be there."

"Well, I don't know, Mom. There's a good basketball game on the tube," he joked. "Of course, I'll be there. Grandpa was right, wasn't he?"

"Yes, he was. I had a feeling that it was going to happen too, but I'm so excited right now, I can hardly stand it," said Rebecca. "Do you want to bring Kelly?"

Josh looked at Kelly and paused. "I don't think so, Mom. She's still at school," he lied.

"Well, O.K. But make sure you're at the White House by five. I'll see you then," she said, hanging up the phone.

Josh smiled at Kelly and they slapped palms. "Success!" he shouted, and kissed her.

Michael tried his best to remain calm but Rebecca was not making it easy.

"My father should be there," she blurted out.

"You know, maybe he shouldn't," Michael cautioned. "Not everyone knows that he's my father-in-law and I'd like to keep it like that. I don't want to convey an image of nepotism or a dynasty or anything like that. I know people will find out but I don't think that today is the best time."

"I guess you're right," she admitted. She glanced at the mirror and proclaimed herself ready.

"I'll see if David and TJ are ready. Christina promised to make sure they were looking their Sunday best." The live-in maid had kept her promise and the kids were both decked out in their finest clothes. They looked so proud of him. He felt an incredible closeness to them.

"TJ, you look stunning," Michael said to his daughter, who was dressing up to go out in public for the first time in quite a long while.

"Thank you, Daddy" she said softly, and then added, "We're very proud of you."

"Are we really going to the White House?" asked David.

"We sure are, champ. And the president's going to name me his 'main man' just like you're my main man."

"All right!" yelled David, smiling from ear to ear.

"Is everyone ready?" Michael glanced out the window and saw a limousine pull up in the driveway. "Let's go," he shouted, as they poured out the door, knowing that their lives would never be the same.

✚	✚	✚

Josh started talking excitedly to Kelly about his father.

"Can you believe it? My father is the vice president of the United States. Is that awesome or what?"

Kelly just smiled as Josh danced around Kelly's cramped apartment in frenzied delight. The phone rang and Kelly answered it.

"Is this Kelly Adkins?"

"Yes, it is. Who is this?"

"This is Columbia General Hospital. Your father has suffered serious injuries and may not survive," said the voice.

Kelly collected herself and asked, "What happened?"

"It's a long story. His neck is broken, among other things. I think you should get here quickly."

Kelly hung up the phone, all color in her face gone. Josh knew something was wrong and grabbed her hand. "My father's dying, Josh. I gotta go see him," she said, and the two quietly left the apartment and drove to the hospital.

After several minutes of silence, Kelly spoke. "I'm sorry that you're going to miss your father's big day."

"So am I. But this is more important. Tomorrow, my father will still be here. Your's might not."

Twenty minutes later, Josh and Kelly arrived at Columbia General and after inquiring at the information desk, found what room Kelly's father was in and headed to the third floor. Slowly they entered room 333 and Kelly saw her father, Michael's old friend, Alan Roberts. They had often been at odds over the years, and Kelly had changed her name from Roberts, but she felt great sorrow at seeing this once-powerful man look so pitiful.

A nurse with large buck teeth was attending to him as they entered. "Are you his daughter?" she asked.

"Yes."

"You can visit for about ten minutes. He's pretty weak."

Kelly nodded and approached the bed and took her father's hand. "Hi, Daddy," she said to the pained man in the body cast.

"Kelly, is that you?" he said weakly.

"Yes, it is. I'm with Josh Madigan," she replied.

Roberts smiled. "How ironic," he whispered.

Kelly didn't understand what he meant. "Daddy, how did this happen to you?"

Roberts was having trouble breathing and he spoke slowly. "There's not enough time to explain it. But there's something that I want you to know," he said.

Kelly leaned over and touched his face. "Go ahead."

"Michael Madigan and I went to West Point together, you know. We were best friends at one time but he ruined my life." Roberts paused for air.

"I swore I'd get him back," he continued. "And I did. I really did," he said with a smile.

Kelly looked at Josh, puzzled. "I don't understand."

He was wheezing heavily now as he became more animated. "Did you ever hear about how his daughter was kidnapped at age three, never to be seen again?"

Kelly responded haltingly. "Yeah. What about it?"

"Well, my dear," Roberts said, "I kidnapped her and her little friend."

"You did what?" Josh said angrily.

"But you don't appreciate the irony," Roberts continued. "You see, what makes this so fitting is that the girl I kidnapped is you. Kelly, your real name is Ellen Madigan, daughter of Michael and Rebecca. I'd like to introduce you to Josh Madigan, your brother," he said, as he slumped back into his bed.

Josh froze in astonishment while Kelly began shrieking hysterically. Roberts smiled. He knew that his time was almost up. He glanced at Kelly as she was mumbling something incoherently, dazed.

"I got him back like I said I would," Roberts said. "I got him." Those were the last words as he collapsed in the bed, his eyes and mouth remaining open. Alan Roberts was dead.

26

att looked at the NATO leader who lay fallen at his feet. He had shot and killed Felix Klaus, one of the Six, and one of the most respected men in the world.

The guards rushed him and threw him to the ground, tieing his hands. One of them checked Klaus' vital signs.

"You'll pay for this, Mr. Connors," said the burliest guard, who picked up Matt's pistol and smashed it into his skull, knocking him unconscious.

On cue, Klaus stood up, quite pleased with his performance. He looked at the guards and asked, "Do you think I was convincing enough? Perhaps I should consider a Hollywood career. What do you think?" he asked jokingly.

"Whatever you say, sir," said one of the guards, rolling his eyes, which brought an immediate laugh to Klaus.

"All right, let's finish the job," Klaus ordered. "Get the film, the letters, and torch the place," he commanded.

The guards gathered up the crumpled deputy national security adviser and carried him to a truck in the garage. They finished loading up everything else and then dragged into the house the dead body of Boris Gunther. The former part-time truck driver would be found charred and ashen. The only way that he could be identified would be by dental records and he now had in his mouth what looked to be the teeth of Felix Klaus. One of the guards dropped the corpse in the middle of the living room and poured gasoline on the body.

Klaus looked at the hapless Gunther and was amazed at the resemblance. He had been dressed in the exact same clothing that Klaus was wearing and his hair had been cut to the same length and style. Klaus slipped his ring off his finger and bent over and put it onto the finger of Boris. He looked at Boris one last time and gave the command.

"Do it," he ordered.

As Klaus and the others quickly exited the room, the burly guard threw a match onto the gas-soaked Boris. A fire erupted and quickly spread, engulfing the room in massive flames. Within minutes, the entire house was on fire, as the NATO leader and his cohorts were driving safely across town. Just as they were leaving, one of the guards had called the fire department and the police. Very soon, the tragic death of the secretary general of NATO would be announced to the world.

✠　　✠　　✠

Michael stood proudly as Andrew Tolbert walked to the podium in the opulent East Room. It seemed like a thousand flashbulbs were clicking simultaneously. Michael looked to Rebecca, who gave him a reassuring glance.

The president began speaking and the room gave way to silence, except for the steady clicking of the cameras.

"Good afternoon. Let me get right to the matter at hand. Craig Jensen, who has served this administration dutifully and with dignity, has resigned the office of the vice president, effective immediately," Tolbert announced to the stunned press corps. "The reason for this sudden departure is personal and family related. I've had great respect for Craig Jensen throughout his tenure and will respect his decision to leave, although with much regret."

He paused briefly before continuing. "This administration has moved quickly to fill the position of vice president. There was only one factor that I used in making my choice. Who would best fill my shoes if something was to happen to me? With that single guideline in mind, I chose a man whom the world has come to know as a man of action and daring, who also possesses a keen intellect and scholarly background," the president explained.

The president signaled for him to come forward and Michael made his way closer to the podium, blinded by flashbulbs. But Tolbert had a few more things to say before turning it over to Michael.

"Let me tell you a few things about my choice before he takes the microphone. He has a beautiful family, who are seated behind us. He was a career army officer, having served in both the Special Forces and Rangers. He served on the National Security Council and earned a Ph.D. in history and for the last couple of years has served in the U.S. Congress. It's with great pleasure that I introduce to you Michael Madigan," Tolbert announced.

Michael looked around the room, which seemed to have a surrealistic look and feel to it. He still couldn't believe this was happening. He knew that he had to display a commanding presence to overcome the feeling that he was an unstable renegade. And he would avoid the arm-waving enthusiasm of Jensen, who four years earlier had flapped his arms and shouted like a game-show host.

"Good afternoon, ladies and gentlemen," Michael began. "I'd like to introduce to you my wonderful family, who have supported me every step of the way and to whom I owe everything."

He turned and gestured to Rebecca and the kids one by one. "First is my beautiful wife of twenty-two years, Rebecca. Next is my daughter, Terri Jean, who has just turned seventeen. And last, but not least, my little champ, David, who's eleven. Our oldest son, Josh, was not able to be here today," he said, trying to hide his disappointment.

"I've accepted the president's offer to serve as his vice president and am very hopeful about the future of this country. It's the strongest, richest and freest nation in history. But we must dedicate ourselves to upholding this standard and improving our country…" Michael continued speaking, as the cameras flashed. He concluded his remarks and was flooded with a barrage of questions.

"Mr. Madigan," began the reporter from the Washington Post, "Can you tell us why Mr. Jensen resigned?"

"Only what the president has relayed to me, that Mr. Jensen has personal reasons."

"Mr. Madigan, you have a reputation as being a loose cannon, a renegade. Do you plan to engage in covert missions as vice president?" asked a GNN reporter.

"I took part in one covert mission because I felt that it was an opportune time and that I was the best man for the job. However, as vice president, such action would be totally inappropriate. But no apologies for this last mission."

"Mr. Madigan, you said that your wife has always supported you but isn't it true, sir, that she left you when you first ran for Congress?" asked an NBC reporter.

Michael glared at the reporter as he answered. "In the future I will not answer such a question. What happens in my marriage is no one else's business. But this one time I will tell you that, yes, we had some problems. I never stopped loving my wife and I believe that she would answer the same way."

"Mr. Madigan," shouted a journalist from the L.A. Times. "Have you talked to Johnny Green lately and do you plan on fighting any gang members as vice president?"

"No!" was Michael's curt reply, as he groaned to himself. Is this what it's going to be like? Isn't anyone going to ask a question that has to do with the issues?

"Mr. Madigan," shouted a CBS reporter. "What do you think of your chances in the upcoming election? Do you think that you'll still be vice president come January?"

Michael smiled and answered, "I wouldn't have taken this job if I thought that it would just be for a few months. President Tolbert has achieved many successes in the last four years and I believe that he deserves another term to fully implement all of the things that have been begun. This administration has a record to be proud of and a strong vision for the future," Michael stated forcefully.

"Yes, I plan to be here in January," Michael added, as Tolbert signaled it was over. The president approached the podium and said, "Thank you." The president, Michael and his family were escorted out of the press room.

Once in the other room, Tolbert said, "Welcome to the big leagues, Mike. You did a good job. Sometimes these reporters are unbelievable, aren't they?" Before Michael could answer, Davis Elliot walked into the room and turned on one of three televisions.

"Mr. President, watch this news report," the national security adviser said.

"We are live in front of the home of the secretary general of NATO, Felix Klaus," said the GNN news reporter to a worldwide audience. "As you can see, it is engulfed in flames. Apparently, Mr. Klaus has been murdered and his killers have set the house ablaze. We've obtained what appears to be a tape of the assassination, incredibly, and it appears that the killer was Matthew Connors, a key adviser to the president. Can we play the tape?" asked reporter Kent Nichols to the anchor, Dorothy Larimer.

Nichols narrated as the grainy film began to roll. "Ladies and gentlemen, we've procured this tape, which shows what happened in the last few minutes of Mr. Klaus' life. Amazing as it sounds, he had video cameras placed in his private study and they were rolling when he was assassinated," explained the reporter.

"As you can see, the tape shows that Mr. Klaus is in his study when three men walk in, including a man that appears to be Matt Connors. Now you can see the other two men leave, Klaus is by the aquarium feeding his fish, and Connors is walking towards a desk."

Tolbert and Elliot looked at the television in amazement. "Why in the world would Matt want to kill someone like Klaus?" asked Elliot.

"Are you sure that's him?" asked the president.

"As sure as I can be given the grainy film. I know his mannerisms and his walk pretty well," answered Elliot.

Nichols continued narrating. "Connors sits down at the desk. Klaus is still feeding the fish. And now Connors pulls out a gun from the desk drawer and points it at Klaus. What appears to be an argument ensues as you can see both men waving their arms. They both appear to be very agitated. Three men with weapons pulled now come into the picture," the reporter continued.

"Now Connors has pulled Klaus close to him and one of the three men is walking towards Connors, apparently pleading with him to put his weapon away. And now you will see his next move," the correspondent said.

The grainy tape showed Matt standing over the collapsing secretary general, who slumped to the floor. The tape came to an abrupt end.

"We've not been able to ascertain what happened next. However, the house was set on fire and a body was found that has been identified as that of Felix Klaus. The face was burned beyond recognition but dental records show it to be the body of the secretary general, Felix Klaus," said the reporter.

"Kent, does anyone have any idea why Mr. Connors would want to kill the head of NATO?" asked the anchor, Dorothy Larimer. "We know that Mr. Connors had abruptly left government service and made an appeal to African-Americans to rise up against the white establishment, but how does killing Klaus connect with that?" she asked.

"Dorothy, we've just received word that a letter was received by the *International Herald Tribune*, an international newspaper here in Europe, purportedly from Matt Connors, saying that he was going to kill Klaus to make a point that America places too much attention on foreign policy and not enough on domestic matters. He states that African-Americans' concerns are secondary to U.S. foreign policy and that he was going to do something to bring attention to that fact," answered reporter Nichols.

"Kent, you said the letter was purportedly written by Connors. What do you mean by that?" asked Larimer.

"Well, Dorothy, the letter was typewritten but signed Matt Connors. Sources tell us that it was indeed his signature but it is currently being analyzed by independent handwriting experts," reported Nichols.

"Thank you, Kent. We'll bring you more as we obtain additional information," Larimer said and signed out.

Andrew Tolbert looked at Michael and Elliot. "My God, what the hell is going on? Michael, you were good friends with Connors, weren't you?" said the president, looking to Michael for an explanation.

Michael was still shaken by what he had seen and replied slowly. "Yes, sir, I was. I considered him my best friend, as a matter-of-fact. He saved my life in Vietnam."

"What's happened to him? I was told by his wife that he signaled a message in code when he gave that speech that he was speaking against his will. But he clearly killed Klaus. Why?" demanded the president.

"I don't know," answered Michael. "The man I know would not be capable of such a thing. The tape seems to speak for itself but I'm sure there must be more to it. My gut tells me it's all part of some crazy plot to get the African-American community riled up and that Matt's an unwitting accomplice."

"Well, it's certainly working," interjected Davis Elliot. "There are angry reports from all over the country about Matt's disappearance. People are getting riled up over this whole situation," said Elliot.

"Do you think this will actually lead to civil disturbances?" asked the president, worried.

"It's hard to say. I don't know how the average black person is going to react to the death of a European leader, but Matt's televised display certainly won't help things, that's for sure," replied Elliot.

The president shook his head. "As if we don't have enough to worry about. Well, Mike, we have our work cut out for us, don't we? Are you up for it?" Before Michael could answer, the president answered his own question.

"I hope you are, or you'll be the answer to the trivia question, 'Who served the shortest term as vice president?'"

Michael replied confidently. "I'm up for it, Mr. President."

"Good. Davis, make sure Mike gets all of the necessary briefings. I'm not going to keep you in the dark like FDR did with Truman. You're going to learn some amazing things, Mike, about the government that even congressmen don't know. I don't plan on kicking the bucket just yet, but if I do, I want you to be ready," Tolbert said with a finality that indicated the meeting was over. Michael and Elliot excused themselves and left the president alone.

Michael realized as he left the room that although he was now "a heartbeat away," there was still an overwhelming gap between his responsibilities and those of the president. Michael had often dreamed of one day becoming president but right now he wasn't so sure he would want the job.

✠   ✠   ✠

General Steigrich was pleased with the development of his army. He had assembled a crack and elite unit, small but highly trained and fanatically patriotic. They were men who believed in Germany, first and foremost.

Klaus had instructed him to proceed along two paths. First, develop a small conventional force and second, stir up anti-foreigner sentiment in the German streets.

It had been decided that Frederick would, after everything was carried out, become the new leader of Germany. He had established headquarters in

Bonn and was coordinating every facet of the Six's plan. He had met on several occasions with the chancellor, key military people, and potential members of a new government. He and his staff were working around the clock on the final details of their plan. He would soon be the most powerful man in the world, the leader of the Fourth Reich.

General Steigrich had been under the impression that Felix Klaus' death was real, so when he received a phone call from Klaus, he was stunned. It took several minutes for Klaus to convince the man that he had not been killed. Klaus then directed Steigrich to meet with Frederick. They were to meet in Bonn and Tommy Schmidt would be joining them.

Steigrich and Tommy arrived at Frederick's palatial estate around 4:00 P.M. as instructed. Frederick himself answered the door.

"Come in, gentlemen. Please make yourselves at home," Frederick said warmly.

"Guten Tag, Herr Roehm," said Tommy. "How are you?"

"I'm just fine, Thomas. Have you heard from your father lately?" asked Frederick.

"He's very excited about how the plan is coming together. It appears that we will soon reach our goals."

"It certainly does," Frederick answered. "Please have a seat," he said, as they walked into an enormous study, complete with multicolored maps of the world plastered all over the wall. "Can I get you anything to drink?"

Steigrich and Tommy both shook their heads.

"Then let's get down to business. General Steigrich, we've not been formally introduced. My name is Alfred Roehm," said Frederick, giving the German general his real name.

"Herr Klaus has told me all about you, sir. I had thought that he had been killed by that American. I was quite distressed and was even more so when I received a phone call from Herr Klaus," explained Steigrich.

Frederick smiled. "Yes, I can see how that might have disturbed you. I apologize for the surprise but it was necessary to keep it quiet. I hope you understand. Despite your obvious talents and loyalties, there are things that we won't be able to reveal. I hope that doesn't bother you."

"Not at all, sir. I'm a soldier. I'm not going to second-guess your decisions. Give me orders and I will see that they are executed," Steigrich said enthusiastically.

"Excellent, General" said Frederick, as he walked over to the bar and poured himself a drink. "I've heard that your army is a formidable fighting force," he added.

"Thank you, sir. It is one of the finest forces in the world, if I may say so," Steigrich replied.

"I'm sure that it is and that it will help us defeat outside enemies. But General, we have many internal enemies. Our country has been invaded by refugees from all over the world. Our strength is being diluted by this constant stream of trash. Africans, Indonesians, Iranians, and the like are preventing us from asserting our true destiny."

"I agree," Steigrich said.

"We've persuaded the chancellor to reduce the flow of parasites into our nation. Once we execute our plan, immigration will be curtailed completely. But there is already an unacceptable number of foreign refugees that have no place here," said Frederick.

Tommy jumped in. "These people are stealing jobs and diluting our race. The number of interracial marriages is sickening. We must stop it now!" he said emphatically, his anger making his metallic voice sound even more alien.

"Exactly," said Frederick. "I want you, Thomas, to cause rioting in the streets, to stir up hatred and intolerance. This will cause many of these dregs to leave. And, we must encourage German nationalism. We're the master race and we must restore that feeling once again in the heart and soul of every German."

"Unfortunately," Frederick continued, "we remain a divided people. But having a common enemy will help. Nothing unites so much as hatred. We must point the blame at the Jews, blacks and Arabs."

Tommy and Steigrich nodded. "One more thing. General, it's impossible for your army, no matter how small, to remain a secret. Therefore, you've been assigned an official task and will report directly to the chancellor."

"To the chancellor?" asked a stunned Steigrich. "Is he involved in this?"

"Of course not. However, Herr Klaus convinced him that there is a vital need for an elite unit to combat riots, terrorism, and the like. That is your official assignment. Thomas will stir up trouble and your unit will 'police' it. If refugees are killed, so be it," he said bluntly.

"Am I to meet with the chancellor?" asked Steigrich.

"Tomorrow afternoon. He's already aware of your unit. But make no mistake, you report to me and Herr Klaus. The chancellor will not be given all of the information and you will cooperate as little as possible, although you will give the impression of total devotion. Is that clear?" he asked.

"Where is Herr Klaus?" asked the German commander.

"Right here," said Klaus, who suddenly entered the room.

"Herr Klaus, you gave me quite a scare," Steigrich blurted out, immediately jumping to his feet.

"As a famous American writer once said, 'the reports of my demise have been greatly exaggerated,'" said Klaus, smiling. "Herr Roehm and I will remain here, making the final coordinations for our plans. We're very pleased with your progress. Soon you will lead all of Germany's forces, and she will be the most powerful country in the world," Klaus said.

These words of praise had the desired effect on Steigrich, who seemed ready to march through hell.

"Gentlemen, I pledge my total commitment to Germany. Long may she reign!" he said emphatically, lifting a glass. They toasted to Germany's rise, confident that the decades-long plan would soon come to fruition.

✠ ✠ ✠

Andrew Tolbert was meeting with his top campaign officials. Only a few months remained and the president was ten points behind in the polls to his opponent, Walt Anderson, the governor of Texas.

"Damn it all," cursed the president. He looked at this chief of staff, "how much money do we have, Phil?"

The normally combative Gordon replied meekly. "Not enough."

Roger Andrews, the boyish-looking campaign chief, responded, "Mr. President, the convention has given us some momentum. We're starting to get some real response now. Labor Day is always when the campaign really begins," Andrews said.

"Well, it's too damn close for me."

"Mr. President, there's a major fund-raiser next week at the Loews L' enfant Plaza. Ernst Turner, the owner, has been a major contributor. It's going to be $10,000 a plate and we expect a thousand people," the campaign chief reported.

"Well, that's more like it," said the president, who finally began to relax a little. "I want Madigan there. People seem to like him."

"He'll be there. Actually, his chief aide when he was in the House was Turner's oldest son," replied Gordon.

"Really. That's interesting," said the president. "Listen, I will not be a one-term president. I'm not going into the history books as a failure. And I will not let this great country of ours be led by that damned liberal. Do you hear me? I will not allow it!" he shouted, the veins in his neck popping out.

✠ ✠ ✠

Michael no longer had to worry about a long drive home after a twelve hour workday. He now lived in the vice president's mansion, a home not quite as palatial as the White House, but a beautiful home nonetheless.

Michael walked into the living quarters and was greatly surprised to see his family dressed up, waving balloons, flags and homemade pennants.

"Surprise, Daddy," yelled out David.

"We love you, Daddy" said Terri quietly.

"Ready to eat?" asked Rebecca. "We're having your favorite dinner," she said, gesturing to the immaculately made-up table that servants had prepared.

"Roast beef?" Michael said, as he sat down and picked up his fork.

"Not so fast," Rebecca said. "Let's say a prayer. We have much to be grateful for," and then led the family in a Jewish prayer.

Michael bowed his head in amazement and repeated the words to the once-familiar prayer that he had not heard in many years. Rebecca had never shown any interest in Judaism and he felt very grateful that she was doing so now.

As she finished, Michael looked at her and took her hand. "That was beautiful and you can't imagine how much it means to me to hear you say it," he said lovingly.

"Michael, I'm a Christian and it's always been a dividing point in our marriage, no matter how much we said it wasn't," she explained. "Now we're back as a family and I want to get rid of all the obstacles that keep us from being closer."

"There's nothing in Judaism that I disagree with." Rebecca continued. "My only problem is what the Jews leave out. I've been taught to believe that Jesus was the son of God. But think about it. Either Jesus was our Savior or he wasn't. Who am I to disregard your beliefs. You're my husband.

Michael listened in amazement.

"I refuse to believe that God will turn his back on either of us," she exclaimed. "My father doesn't know this, but my mother became very serious with a Jewish man and almost married him. Had she married him, she would have converted. Then I would have been raised in the Jewish faith."

Michael listened intently.

"Don't get me wrong. I'm not criticizing Christianity. But I think it's important for our family to be truly united. Michael, I've been thinking about converting to Judaism" she said, taking his hand.

"I don't know what to say," Michael whispered.

"Michael, we've taught our children to love God and to treat people with dignity and respect. We've taught them to make the most of their lives. That's what's important, Michael. Nothing else," she said.

"You're absolutely right, darling. Let's make a toast to the Madigans!" he said, raising his glass.

They all lifted their glasses with enthusiasm.

✠   ✠   ✠

Matt slowly came to consciousness and found himself in a ditch, battered and bloodied. He was somewhere in the middle of a dense forest. It was dark; the sky looked as if it were covered in a shroud of black. He was in great pain and his head was throbbing. He tried to stand up but stumbled. Slowly, his memory came back.

Did he really kill Felix Klaus? If he had, it must be front-page news around the world. This, along with his speeches, would make him an international criminal.

It was too dark to see and so he didn't move. He tried to make himself comfortable, as best he could in the ditch. He decided to wait out the night and then try to make his way to safety. As a fugitive, it would be difficult to get the medical attention that he was sure he needed. Where would he go? He had to call the White House and warn Davis Elliot and the president.

The pain began to numb and he lost consciousness again.

The sun split the darkness as dawn began. An old man was heading out for his daily walk. Actually, he had not walked for some time now, having recently suffered serious injuries that had laid him up for weeks. This was the first time that he had left his house in weeks. He was accompanied by his nurse.

"It's a beautiful day, isn't it?" asked the old man, as they walked along the edge of a running stream.

"It certainly is," came the young nurse's reply.

"You're quite an amazing man. I didn't think that you would ever leave the house. For that matter, I thought that you were dead in the hospital," she said.

"I did all of this just to impress you. If you are, perhaps you will marry me," said the old man, and he laughed.

"I'm impressed but I'm married to my job," she said, laughing, too.

"Of course. I guess that I'm just a foolish old man," he said, pausing. "I've wasted my life. How could you love someone who's thrown away his life?" he said dejectedly.

"Calm down, sir. You mustn't get your blood pressure up again. You've lived a full life and, like everyone, you've made mistakes. Don't let it kill you," said the nurse.

"You're right, of course," he said softly. "I must stay calm. I've had such a chaotic life of hatred and misguided loyalty. I hope it's not too late to live out my remaining days in peace," he said, sighing loudly.

They walked several minutes in silence, taking in the warmth of the new sun and the beauty of the wilderness.

The old man suddenly broke the silence. "What is that? Over there? Do you see?" he said, excitedly.

"Where? I don't see anything!" came the nurse's reply. "Wait. Now I do," she said, and she ran towards the sprawled figure.

The old man followed behind as fast as he could and by the time he arrived, the nurse was checking the man's vital signs.

"Is he alive?" the man asked, gasping from the short run.

"Just barely. He's in shock and has some very serious wounds," she said, as she took her coat off and wrapped it around Matt.

Rita Altheirst looked at the man closely as she wrapped her coat around him to keep him warm. It was Matt Connors, the man she had treated earlier. She had been following the news of the recent days with great interest. She didn't believe that Matt was guilty. She prided herself on her instincts and she had surmised that Matt was a decent person. She couldn't be wrong!

"Herr Weber, it's Matthew Connors, the American government official," shouted Rita.

"My God, it is. We must save him, Rita. He must not die," said the old man, who had been known for over forty years as Charlemagne. Having barely survived his brush with death in Leningrad, he had been snuck back to Germany by some friends to live out his remaining years.

"I've done everything I can. I'm going to get help. You stay here and keep him warm. I'll be back as soon as I can," she said.

"Mr. Connors is wanted by every law enforcement unit in the world. You must get someone who will use great discretion. That is very important, Rita. I must talk to him and I can't do that if he's in jail," Charlemagne said.

"Don't worry," she said. "I know just the doctor. I'll be back soon. Keep him warm," she directed, as she took off sprinting through the woods.

Charlemagne held Matt's hand and prayed that he would not die. He had realized the hypocrisy of the Six and their mission and was sorry that he had devoted his life to it. His close call with death and what happened to his sons had changed him. He no longer desired for Germany to conquer the world. There had been too much damage caused by Germany already. He couldn't be responsible for another world war, this time with nuclear weapons. But most of all, he had renounced his former life on behalf of Gunther and Konrad, whose lives had been taken because of him. Hopefully, he could atone for their deaths.

Rita returned in forty-five minutes with two young men who carried a stretcher to where Matt lay unconscious, going deeper into a coma. They had driven a car to about 100 feet away and walked the last bit to where the old German sat, with his eyes closed and his hand locked with Matt's.

"Sir, we're back," Rita said, waking Charlemagne out of his daydream.

His body quivered at Rita's touch and he snapped out of his brief lapse. "That was quick. I kept him warm as you said, Rita," he said proudly.

"Very good. This is Fritz. He's a friend of mine and an excellent doctor. This is his friend Heinrich," Rita said, as the two young men gently gathered up Matt's crumpled body. They carried the stretcher slowly through the woods and loaded him into the back of Fritz's van.

Rita helped the former Nazi up and told Fritz to go ahead. "We'll catch up to you later. Please save him, he must not die!" she shouted.

"We'll do everything we can," Heinrich said, as he drove away, with Fritz in the back trying to save Matt's life. Fritz heard Rita's exhortation play over and over in his mind. "He must not die!" He would do everything he could to save this man's life.

27

ichael had been on the job one week and except for the one night with his family, he had been on the campaign trail. Rebecca would join him on future trips, but she was currently trying to get them settled into their new lives. Although she had quit her job, she had still been busy. She was beginning to realize that she would see him very little until after the election. Rebecca was looking forward to seeing him this evening, as he was returning for the fund-raiser at Ernst Turner's hotel.

Michael had been giving four to five speeches a day for almost a week now and was relieved to be returning to Washington. Traveling through three and four states a day was exhausting and occasionally he would forget what city he was in. But even though it was tiring, he loved the excitement and its accompanied adrenalin rush.

Michael stopped by his office briefly before heading home and decided to call Alex.

With his appointment to vice president, Michael's gang of students had become unemployed overnight. He felt badly for his former staff. They had been so much a part of his life. They had helped him into his congressional seat. But he knew that the vice president needed a more experienced staff, no matter how bright or how dedicated his students were. He had promised them that he would use his influence to get them new jobs. But he still felt bad.

Hoping that Alex would be staying with his father, Michael dialed the L' enfant Plaza. After going through several people, Alex came on the line.

"Good afternoon, Colonel," Alex said warmly.

"How's it going, Alex?" Michael asked. "I was hoping I'd find you here. I guess you're involved in the shindig tonight. How's everyone doing?"

"I think that I'm going to take some time off and go surfing. Darrell's back at UCLA and Judy's in L.A. too. She's still recovering. I'll eventually go back to school. I'm gonna work towards my PhD, Dr. Turner, how's that sound?"

"Great way to get girls," Michael teased. "But seriously, Alex, I could get you on my staff once I'm elected for this next term."

"No offense, Colonel, but I'm not an Andrew Tolbert fan. I don't trust him. Now if something was to happen to him..."

Michael laughed. "Slow down there, boy. I'm just the new kid in town. Hmm, President Madigan. Has a ring to it, doesn't it?" he said jokingly.

"Yes, sir, it sure does," Alex added enthusiastically.

"Hey, I think we're getting ahead of ourselves here. But you never know. I have to be prepared to assume the presidency. He paused. "Look," he said, "call me anytime. Let me give you my direct number." After repeating the number, he asked, "Have you heard from Judy? How's she doing?"

"I talked to her a couple of weeks ago. She seems much better. She's a tough kid," Alex replied, and then added, "Judy's got one of those new video phones. If you could get access to one, maybe you could give her a call. She could read your lips that way, and I think it would really cheer her up."

"I'll do that, Alex, I'm not sure why but I have felt a real close bond with her. I can't explain it."

"Well, anyway, I'll see you tonight, sir."

"Right. I'll see you tonight," Michael said, and he hung up the phone. He felt his eyes moistening at the thought of Judy. He hadn't known her for that long but they had become very close. He vowed to himself that he would stay in touch with her.

After taking care of some business, Michael rushed home to Rebecca, who greeted him warmly with a kiss. "God, I missed you," she said, throwing herself into his arms. They realized David was standing there, looking disgusted.

"Do you guys have to do that in front of me?" he asked. "You're too old for that stuff."

"Too old? Who you calling old, young man," Michael said laughing. Then he flung himself at David and wrestled him to the ground, displaying the good-natured roughhousing they had done when Josh was just a kid.

As he and David rolled on the floor, Michael shouted, "Do you give up? Give up?" All the commotion brought TJ running into the room, followed by Josh. TJ jumped onto the two bodies rolling across the floor and Michael said, "O.K., O.K., I surrender. I give up." TJ and David exchanged high-fives and got off of Michael, who was feigning to be in great pain.

"We could have used you guys in Kuwait last year," he joked.

"We've got a lot to do," said Rebecca, breaking up the fun. "TJ and David, I need your help. Come with me. And you two," she said, pointing to Josh and Michael, "need to get ready, too."

"The boss has spoken, Josh. Let's get going," Michael said, and he threw a salute at Rebecca as she was walking out of the room. "Yes, ma'am. We'll hop right to it."

Josh was still reeling from the news Alan Roberts had given on his deathbed. He hadn't told anyone yet, because he found it too unbelievable that Kelly could be his kidnapped sister, Ellen. He had decided to wait until after the election to speak to his father about it. But now something else had come to light and this couldn't wait.

Rebecca left the room, and Josh spoke to his father. "I'm not sure how to say this, Dad. I've just discovered something and don't know what to make of it."

"What is it?" Michael asked, worried by Josh's tone.

"Follow me, Dad" Josh said mysteriously.

"Where?" asked Michael.

"To my room," Josh said whispering. "Now be quiet for a minute," Josh scolded. He reached under his bed and pulled out some photographs.

"What are those?" Michael asked, his curiosity thoroughly aroused.

"Dad, I have to warn you. This is going to be the shock of your life. I found these in one of Mom's boxes while we were unpacking. I didn't mean to snoop but I just happened to come across them. Here," Josh said, and handed his father the photographs.

Michael looked at them and began to feel sick. His hands began sweating and his knees started to shake. He instantly developed a headache as he closely examined the photographs.

"Oh God, no" he sobbed, collapsing onto Josh's bed. "This can't be. This is a lie. It can't be!" he cried.

"Dad, I'm sorry. I didn't know what to do or who to tell. At first I thought that maybe it was just some trick photography, like that photo of Oswald holding the gun that killed Kennedy," Josh said.

Michael suddenly perked up. "That must be it," he said, and bolted upright. "That's the only explanation."

"But then I found this diary, Dad" Josh said, showing a handwritten journal to his father. "It's Mom's handwriting. Read this page."

Michael felt as if he were frozen. It took every bit of strength to take the journal and begin reading:

> *Talked to Alan Roberts today...How could Michael have betrayed him? I don't think I can stand being back with Michael. Typical disgusting Jewish brownnose...He makes me sick. Alan proposed joining the KKK. I think I'll do it.*

Michael felt paralyzed. These hate-filled words were definitely her writing. He looked at the photographs again.

There was a picture of Rebecca and Alan Roberts, dressed in full Ku Klux Klan regalia. They were smiling. The second photo showed Rebecca in a Ku Klux Klan outfit, holding a sign that read: *Death to Jews and Niggers.* He was numb. The next photo was of Rebecca behind a giant poster of Adolf Hitler, holding a gun and a whip. Michael stood up and then fainted.

Josh quickly gathered up all the photos and the journal and hid them in his room. He then rushed into Rebecca's room. She was putting on her makeup.

"Mom, Mom, come quick. Dad just fainted," Josh yelled frantically.

"Oh, my God!" she screamed, and ran to Josh's room.

"Michael, darling, are you all right?" Rebecca cried. She threw herself to the floor and picked up his head and cradled it in her arms. He began to gain consciousness.

Still very groggy, his eyes began to focus and he saw his wife's face smiling reassuringly. "It's O.K., darling. Everything's O.K." she said softly.

He instantly shot up and pulled himself out of her grasp, stunning Rebecca by his violent reaction.

Michael brushed himself off. "I'm fine. I'm, uh, just fine. A little tired, that's all," he said, looking at her as if she were a monster.

"Well, you don't look fine. I think we better call a doctor and you should stay home tonight," she said.

"I'm going to that fund-raiser and you can't stop me!" he said, almost shouting.

Rebecca was stunned at his tone. "I'm not trying to stop you, dear. I'm just concerned."

"Concerned. Right. I have to get ready," he said, and bolted out of the room. She stood there in shock, not knowing what to think, and asked Josh in disbelief, "What in the world was that?"

Josh shook his head. "Beats me, Mom."

"I'd better call a doctor. Something's not right."

Not sure how to handle the situation Josh said, "Why don't you wait a little, Mom. I'm sure it's just the strain of the campaign. With a good night's sleep, he'll be fine."

"Maybe you're right. But I want both of us to keep our eyes open tonight, just in case," she said.

"No sweat, Mom. I'll watch him closely. Now, relax. Tonight's a big night. You look great, by the way," he said, holding her hand, hiding his uncertainty.

"Thanks, Josh. You're not my little baby anymore. You're really a man now, looking out for your mother. Thank you, Son," she said, and kissed his cheek.

Michael was in the shower, on his knees, as the hot streams of water pounded his body. It couldn't be, he told himself. His wife belonged to the Ku Klux Klan. His mind began swirling and it seemed as if he were dreaming. He shut the water off and collapsed to the floor, where he cried hard until he fell asleep.

After about fifteen minutes of silence, Rebecca became worried. "Michael, are you all right?" she shouted through the door.

The knocking woke him. He would deal with Rebecca later. Tonight he had to make those fat cats cough up big dollars. There was too much at stake. He wasn't sure how, but he would handle it.

"I'm fine," he yelled back. "I'll be out in a minute."

His voice sounded normal, Rebecca noted to herself, and she uttered a sigh of relief. "O.K., sweetheart. Josh and I are ready. We can leave whenever you are ready."

Ten minutes later, the three left together and Michael tried hard to keep a smile on his face. Rebecca tried to make small talk but Michael appeared to be a thousand miles away.

✠   ✠   ✠

As the Madigans arrived at the hotel, Frederick and Wilhelm were making frantic calls around the world. It was all coming together. Finally, after so many years.

"Have you talked to Baghdad? Are they ready?" Wilhelm asked.

"They've been given the order. Iraq is sending troops into Kuwait," Frederick replied.

"We've waited so long," Wilhelm said.

"This night will go down in Germany's history," Frederick agreed.

✠ ✠ ✠

Michael put the diary out of his mind as he entered the ballroom to the applause of over a thousand well-wishers. The steady clapping continued. Michael felt overcome as he absorbed the admiration of the entire room. He and Rebecca took their seats as Andrew and Mary Alice Tolbert acknowledged the enthusiasm of the guests.

Tolbert bent over and whispered into Michael's ear. "This is for you, Mike. I've been to a thousand of these things and have never heard anything like it. They love you, but don't let it get to your head. In a couple of weeks, they'll hate you," the president said with a laugh.

Finally, the room became quiet as Ernst Turner approached the microphone.

"Ladies and gentlemen, may I have your attention? What a welcome, Mr. President," Turner said, looking at the president. "Don't you believe those polls for one minute. The enthusiasm you've seen here tonight can be found all over this country, in every city, in every state. No matter where you go, you'll hear it: Four more years!"

The crowd began repeating the phrase, and stamping their feet, until the room began to shake.

Tolbert had mixed emotions about such a tumultuous welcome. He knew it was really for Michael. He would have to keep a close eye on him. Send him to a funeral now and then, but otherwise, keep him in the background.

After dinner and speeches by Tolbert and Michael, Tolbert became enchanted with the young lady seated to his right. Victoria Tucker was one of Hollywood's newest leading ladies, an overnight success with her first movie just one year before. Two other movies had catapulted her to superstardom. She was only twenty-four years old, with sultry eyes and a smile that could burn a hole through a man's heart.

The president found himself drawn in by her beauty. Suddenly he was brought back to reality when one of his aides whispered there was a crisis. He would have to leave. Fortunately, dinner was over and everyone had begun dancing. He would try to leave the room without attracting too much attention.

Tolbert started talking to Michael in a loud voice and then whispered, "Something's up. I'm going to leave the room slowly and I want you to follow me a few minutes later, careful not to sound any warnings. Your father-in-law is here and the shit's hitting the fan. Find my military aide. He'll tell you where to go," the president said.

He slapped Michael on the back, feigned laughter and slipped off to talk to a couple of party heads from Illinois, a key state in the election.

Michael did as he was instructed and tried to slip out of the room unnoticed. But it seemed as if everyone wanted a piece of him. The president had left about five minutes before but the crowd just wouldn't let him go.

"Good evening, Mr. Vice President," drawled a tall, lanky man who had clearly had too much to drink. "My name is J.P. Herman. I own the biggest cattle ranch in Texas and I just gave a whole shitload of money to your campaign," he said, stumbling over his words.

"J.P., where are your manners?" scolded his blue-haired wife, Doris. "I'm very sorry, Mr. Madigan, for my husband's crudeness. He just means that we're both big supporters of yours," she said, fluttering her eyes and smiling a mouth full of teeth bigger than the Rio Grande.

My God, this woman is flirting with me and she looks like one of J.P.'s cattle, he said to himself.

"Pleased to meet you and I hope that we can count on the support of Texas. It's a very key state to our winning in November. I'll be out there in a couple of weeks and we can talk more. Right now, you'll have to excuse me, J.P. I really must use the men's room." Michael looked at Doris, the fiercest-looking woman he had ever seen, and said as he was leaving the room, "It was a pleasure to meet you, ma'am."

Michael went out into the hallway and realized that two secret service men had followed him. He then saw the military aide who carried the "football," Major Lyle Morgan, standing outside a nondescript room at the end of the hall.

"The president's waiting for you in here," Major Morgan said, as Michael approached the swarm of secret service men.

"Thank you, Major," Michael said, as he walked into the room and found a very somber-looking president talking to the secretary of defense. Michael noticed that the room looked like a library that one might have in one's house, with many rows of books, a large mahogany desk, some expensive art pieces and a grand piano.

"Hello, Michael," his father-in-law greeted him.

"What's up?" asked the vice president.

"Iraq has moved back into Kuwait, with a force larger than last time!" Tolbert shouted, pounding his fist on the table. "We should have crushed the bastard last year. Why didn't I do it?" screamed the enraged president.

"Don't blame yourself, Mr. President," Karl said, trying to calm him. "It seemed the proper thing to do at the time."

"O.K., what are our options, Karl?" asked the president.

"Mr. President, General Lund is on his way and so is Phil Gordon. They both happen to be nearby. I suggest we wait a few minutes for their arrival," answered Karl Schmidt.

"Why don't we go back to the White House?"

"Because, and stop me if you don't agree, I don't think we should let all these people know there's something wrong. If we all stomp off to the White House, it will cause a panic. I think we should discuss the options quickly here and then you and Michael go back in the party while we start the detailed planning. We can have another meeting later tonight at the White House," advised Karl.

"Good thinking," the president concurred. "O.K., while we're waiting, what comes to the top of your head, Karl? You, too, Michael, don't be shy. I know you were involved in your share of crises when you were on the NSC," Tolbert said, having sat down on a garishly-colored sofa.

"Well, I think we have to move quickly," Michael replied. "The other side will accuse us of acting for political gain but..." his voice trailed off, and he slumped to the floor, grabbing his neck and straining to stay conscious.

"What the hell?" shouted the president, horrified as he saw Michael get hit with a small dart that came from the other side of the room. He jumped to his feet and saw a man with a gun, only half-visible, standing in what appeared to be a hole in the ground. "Who the hell..." Tolbert, too, was unable to finish his words as he was hit with a dart in the neck, causing him to pass out.

"Quick!" yelled Karl Schmidt at the attacker, who surfaced out of a trap door in the floor. Another man suddenly appeared and the brawny assailants grabbed the two unconscious leaders. They disappeared into the trap door, which led to a darkened store in a subterranean shopping mall. They made their way through another opening and walked quickly through a tunnel that led underneath the length of the hotel. Just before closing the trap door, one of the attackers took his gun and aimed it at Karl.

"Sorry about this, Herr Schmidt," said the attacker.

"It's the price we have to pay," Karl responded.

The attacker squeezed the trigger and the secretary of defense slumped to the ground, unconscious.

Underneath the hotel, the two men silently moved as quickly as possible through the tunnel that was about five-feet-high. They shuffled about 300 yards and finally came to the end. The first attacker yelled and within seconds, a manhole cover was removed above him by a third man about ten feet above them.

Silently, the three men passed the unconscious leaders up the ladder and to the ground above, in a dark alley a block away from the hotel. The third man was joined by a fourth, the driver of a nondescript Ford Falcon. The trunk of the auto was opened and they tossed in the two bodies. They then got in the car and quietly and slowly proceeded out of town. Almost every cop in town was outside the L' enfant Plaza, providing security for the president and vice president. But not one of them realized that the men they were protecting were no longer there.

About fifteen minutes later, Phil Gordon showed up, cursing because he had to stop on his way to the hotel to fix a flat tire. The secret service men spotted Gordon and ushered him to the back room where the president and vice president were waiting.

"In there, Mr. Gordon," Major Morgan gestured. Gordon didn't respond and barrelled into the room. He found Schmidt unconscious and the only one in the room. Gordon froze with fear for a second and then opened the door screaming. "Where's the president?"

Morgan's eyes grew wide. "He's in there, sir. This is the only way out and we've been here the entire time."

"Jesus Christ!" Gordon was saying over and over. "He's not in there. Neither is Madigan, you goddamned fools. Get a doctor! I think Schmidt might be dead," said Gordon, almost hysterical.

Morgan and the secret service agents rushed into the room and panicked as they realized what had happened. "How did they get out? There's only one door and we were guarding it."

"Well, obviously, there's another way out, you moron!" screamed Gordon. "Who cares how it happened? Have you called the speaker of the house?" Gordon snapped at Morgan.

"Peter Volhard? No. Should I?" asked the puzzled aide.

"Isn't it your job to carry the football for the president?" screamed Gordon.

"Yes, it is," replied Morgan.

"Well, since you morons let the president and vice president be kidnapped right under your noses, than you better get your ass over to the next man in line!" Gordon screamed.

Morgan realized then what Gordon was talking about. After the president and vice president, the speaker of the house was the next in line to assume the presidency.

"I found a trap door," yelled one of the secret service men.

Gordon was shaking violently. He took a deep breath and said as calmly as he could. "I want all of you to quietly come in this room. Now."

Gordon closed the door after they entered. "They must have gone through here," said one of the secret service men to Gordon.

No shit, Gordon thought to himself. "O.K., listen up. I want three of you to follow this tunnel. I'm sure they're long gone but see what you can find. As I've already told Major Morgan, contact Peter Volhard, and get a doctor in here to look at the secretary. Get the chief justice on the phone and advise the assistant secretary of defense. And has anyone seen General Lund? He was supposed to be here."

No one answered. "Now move!" Gordon shouted "and I don't want any of this getting out yet. I'll go back to the party and make excuses for the president and Madigan. And last, I want to talk to the FBI director. Somebody get him on the phone." Everyone started to leave when the chief of staff yelled again.

"Forget the phone calls to the chief justice and FBI director. I'll handle that myself. What's that?" he said, pointing to something on the floor.

"It looks like the VP's wallet," said one of the secret service men.

"Give it here," snapped Gordon. He looked inside it and found the normal array of credit cards, along with twenty-three dollars. Obviously, he had been on the job only a short time. *What does the vice president need with a wallet?* He looked further and found a paper with some numbers written on it, *10-21-46*. Gordon stuffed it in his pocket.

Gordon's heart was beating so hard he thought he was going to have a heart attack. He walked over to the phone, as a doctor entered the room to look at Karl Schmidt. Gordon called his chief assistant, Hershel Clausen.

After four rings, Clausen answered the phone. "Hello."

"Hershel, the balloon's gone up. The president and vice president have been kidnapped," Gordon said.

This immediately woke the sound-asleep aide. "What? How? When?"

"I don't have time. I want an emergency session of the NSC at the White House in one hour. And don't tell anyone the reason. To top it off, Karl Schmidt has been injured, and that Iraqi lunatic is moving his troops. Jesus Christ!"

"Calm down, boss. I'll meet you at the White House in one hour. I'll tell everyone to be as inconspicuous as possible," responded Clausen coolly.

"Hershel, make sure Volhard's there, too," added Gordon.

"Understood, Chief. Volhard's a good man. He could do the job."

"Maybe. If the world's still here tomorrow," Gordon said, and slammed the phone down.

Before Gordon could leave to make apologies to the guests for the absent leaders, Karl became conscious.

"Is he O.K., doc?" Gordon asked.

"He's fine. He was shot with a tranquilizer dart. See?" he said, holding the dart in his hands. "He'll be groggy for a while but he'll be O.K.," said the doctor.

"Stay with him. I'll gather up the two wives. Could you make sure he gets to the White House?" Gordon asked. "Is he O.K. for a meeting? It's very important."

"Yeah, the tranquilizer will wear completely off in about twenty minutes. He'll have a headache but that's about it. I'll make sure he gets to the White House," said the doctor.

Gordon rushed toward the ballroom, trying his best to remain calm. The second he walked in, some redneck started shaking his hand, talking about the very generous donation he had made. Gordon felt like strangling the large-eared son of a bitch, but politely said, "I'm sure the president will be very grateful, sir. Can you give me a call tomorrow?" He then walked briskly away.

"Be glad to, Phil," he shouted at the chief of staff, and then turned to a buddy. "It's not what you say, it's the way you say it," he explained to a nod of approval.

Gordon sauntered up to Mary Alice Tolbert, who was talking to an NFL quarterback.

"Excuse me, Mrs. Tolbert, may I talk to you for a moment?" he asked, trying not to sound desperate.

"Of course, Phil," she said. Turning to the quarterback, she excused herself, as he kissed her hand. The fifty-year-old First Lady found herself blushing at the young man's charm.

She knew something was wrong. Her husband had been gone too long. "What's wrong, Phil?"

"I don't even know how to tell you. Your husband and Madigan..." he began to stammer.

"Spit it out," said the often acid-tongued First Lady.

"They've been kidnapped. Schmidt was attacked but he's O.K. now. We're having an emergency session of the NSC in one hour," said Gordon bluntly.

The First Lady's reaction was stunned silence. "Listen, Mary Alice," Gordon continued, "I don't know what's happened but it's critical we not cause a panic. Now please get Mrs. Madigan, and tell all of these dancing fools that your husband took sick. Then, you and Mrs. Madigan need to leave here quietly and quickly. Do you hear me?" he asked, as his fingers grabbed her arm tightly.

She nodded. "Good. Now if you want to be at the NSC meeting, you're welcome. But not Madigan, O.K. Your job will be to keep her calm and get her to bed without a nervous breakdown. Tell her that her father's fine but that she can't speak to him tonight. He's too busy. Now put on your best smile and do as I've told you," Gordon ordered.

Mary Alice Tolbert did just as she was instructed. She gathered up Rebecca and after the two had said a few polite good-byes, they exited the room, Mary Alice first, followed by Rebecca a few minutes later. Two secret servicemen accompanied them out to the limousine and they sped out of the hotel parking-lot towards the White House.

"What's going on?" Rebecca demanded. "Where's Michael?"

Mary Alice took a deep breath and tried to remain calm. "Rebecca, they've been kidnapped."

Rebecca didn't understand. The president can't be kidnapped. "Do you mean...?" she asked, afraid to finish the question.

"Yes, I don't know how or by whom but..." Mary Alice Tolbert began calmly. But she couldn't keep it in any longer and started shrieking. Rebecca was stunned at the incredible display of hysteria on the part of the First Lady. She knew that she would have to keep her wits and sat in silence the rest of the trip, patting the almost-deranged First Lady on the back.

The limousine pulled into the White House and a doctor was called to attend to Mrs. Tolbert. Rebecca headed straight for the Situation Room. The large room was barricaded by secret service men.

"I'm sorry, ma'am. You can't go in, orders of Mr. Gordon," came the automatic response.

"Is my father in there? Karl Schmidt?" she demanded.

"Yes, ma'am."

"You tell him that I want to speak to him. Right now. Do you understand me?" she yelled.

One of the guards nodded and another went into the room. Twenty seconds later, Karl Schmidt came out.

"Daddy, what's going on? What happened to Michael and the president?" Rebecca screamed.

"Calm down, Becky," said the secretary of defense. "Come over here," he said, as they walked into the corner of the large foyer. "We were in one of the rooms at the hotel talking, and all of a sudden, this man pops out and shoots all three of us with some kind of tranquilizer dart. I woke up about thirty minutes later. There's a damn tunnel under the hotel and apparently, someone dragged Michael and the president through it. It empties out about 300 yards away into an alley. While practically every cop in town was watching the hotel, these sons of bitches got away. I still can't believe it," he said, lying.

"My God, Daddy. I didn't know you were attacked. Are you all right?" she asked.

"I've got one hell of a headache but I'm fine. I just feel so stupid," he said, continuing the charade.

"Daddy, I don't care what you or Phil Gordon say, I'm coming to this meeting. And if you try to stop me, I will yell at the top of my lungs until you let me in. Do we understand each other?" asked his very determined daughter who stood with her hands on her hips and arms crossed.

He realized there was nothing he could do other than to have her dragged away by the secret service.

"O.K., sweetheart. But please stay quiet. We have a major crisis on our hands, the likes of which this country has never seen. I'll only say this once: the safety and security of this nation will come first. We don't have time to deal with a hysterical wife. If you start with some emotional outburst, I'll have you hauled away. Do I make myself clear?"

"Yes, Daddy," Rebecca said, through clinched teeth.

"All right, now follow me," he said, and walked into the Situation Room, where the highest members of the U.S. government were collectively panicking.

"What is she doing here?" snapped a very peeved Phil Gordon. "Get her out!"

"I said she could stay as long as she stays quiet," said Karl Schmidt with an aura of authority that caught Gordon by surprise.

The meeting was about to get underway. It was 11:55 P.M. Finally, the last person that Gordon had roused out of bed arrived. Randall Koehler, the Chief

Justice of the United States Supreme Court, walked in, surprised to have been included, since he was not a member of the National Security Council.

Gordon brought the meeting to order. "Let me have your attention. We have a crisis upon us that may be unparalleled in U.S. history. I'll be conducting this meeting, but Speaker Volhard will be acting as the interim president and all decisions will be his..." Gordon paused for a moment.

Secretary of State Watkins jumped to his feet. "Where's the president? And Madigan?" he shouted.

"If you would let me finish, I'll tell you all that I know," Gordon shouted at the high-strung Watkins. "President Tolbert and Vice President Madigan were at the L' enfant Plaza tonight, where a large fund-raiser was being conducted. The Pentagon received information on a crisis in the Persian Gulf and Karl Schmidt came to the hotel to brief the president. The three of them began conducting a meeting in one of the rooms at the hotel. The secret service checked out the room and posted a shitload of guards outside of the only entrance. I arrived approximately fifteen minutes after the meeting started, I've been told, and I walked in to find Tolbert and Madigan gone and Secretary Schmidt unconscious."

"My God," said General Lund, chairman of the Joint Chiefs of Staff. "Do you mean they were kidnapped? How did they get out, if there was only one entrance?" he demanded.

All eyes turned to Karl Schmidt, as Gordon gestured to him. "Why don't you fill us in, Mr. Secretary of Defense?"

Karl stood up and walked to the center of the room. "I was made aware of the Iraq crisis and happened to be going by the hotel. So I stopped to brief the president."

"What crisis?" asked Arnold Logan, undersecretary of state.

"Iraq is invading Kuwait again," he said.

"Do you mean to tell me that right now there might be a war going on?" asked the secretary of the treasury, Douglas Wesson.

"I never thought that I would say this, but we've got bigger problems," said Karl.

"I have to agree," said the assistant secretary of defense, Barry Fletcher. "If the U.S. is threatened, we might have a real constitutional problem on our hands."

"What do you mean?" asked Phil Gordon.

"Well, you started off by saying that the speaker has inherited the powers of the presidency. I'm not so sure that's right," he said, stopping to wipe off his glasses.

"Continue," said Gordon.

"Well, the Constitution provides that upon the death or incapacity of the president and vice president, the speaker of the house takes over. First of all, we don't know if the president's dead. He might be missing but I'm not sure that the full power of the executive branch transfers to the speaker. Then there's another problem. And damned if I know the answer to this," he said, pausing again.

"Well, spit it out, man!" barked Karl.

"Article One of the Constitution says the president must be born in America. No offense, Mr. Speaker, but you were born in Germany if I'm not mistaken. I'm not so sure you can assume the presidency," said Fletcher, who had been a constitutional law professor for many years.

"Good Lord," said Gordon, stunned. "I asked the chief justice here tonight for this very reason but I didn't even think of that. Who's next in the line of succession?"

Fletcher was prepared for this and said, "It's the president pro tempore of the Senate, Marcel LeClair. And even though he's been in the U.S. for fifty years, he was born in France."

"Do we have any Americans in this government, for God's sake?" asked Gordon frantically.

"I resent that," said Peter Volhard. "I'm as American as anyone in this room," he adamantly countered.

"No offense, Mr. Speaker. I'm sorry. Who's next in line?" asked Gordon.

"Well, it then goes through the Cabinet, in order of the creation of the department. The State Department was the first one established. So the next man is Chris Watkins," answered Fletcher.

Everyone in the room turned to look at Watkins, whose face was ashen.

Gordon looked to Randall Koehler. "Help us out here, Mr. Chief Justice. Assuming the president and vice president are not dead, what happens? And what about the two men who were not born in the U.S.?"

All eyes were on the chief justice. "There's no absolute answer to your inquiries. Nothing like this has ever happened and the Constitution doesn't gives us a clear answer, I'm afraid. It's clearly an interpretation problem that the whole Court would have to rule on," said the soft-spoken jurist.

"Mr. Chief Justice, we need an answer. Whoever kidnapped these men could very well be launching missiles at us right now. Somebody has to have the authority to respond accordingly. We can't spend all night debating. We need to know, right now, who has the authority to act as the president of the United States," demanded Gordon.

"Well," the frail septuagenarian began, "there are three possibilities. First, assuming the president is still alive, the power might stay within the Executive Branch. That is, with the chief of staff."

Gordon began feeling uncomfortable.

Koehler continued. "The second option would be as Mr. Gordon said initially. That is, with the speaker of the house. And the third option is, taking into account the U.S.-born requirement, Secretary Watkins," said the old man, clearly nervous.

"Mr. Chief Justice, please. Tell us right now so that we can continue this very important meeting. The full Court can give us a formal ruling later," Gordon pressured him.

"I'd say that the intent of the Framers was that the full powers of the presidency would pass on down the line of succession and that the native-born requirement would not apply in situations of such gravity as we are faced with. Surely the Framers would not mean to paralyze the government as its leaders bickered over where they were born. I'd say that the full powers of the presidency must pass to the Speaker," he answered.

"O.K., I'm satisfied with that. Chris, how about you?" Gordon asked the secretary of state.

"I'm satisfied," he said with a sigh or relief, having absolutely no desire to assume the presidency.

"O.K., Mr. Speaker, I'm not sure how to do this formally but I guess that makes you the acting president," Gordon said. "Just to make sure there's no confusion, I want you to roust all of your colleagues out of bed, and tell them to get their honorable butts down to the Supreme Court. Can you do that, sir?" he asked.

"I'm sorry, Mr. Gordon, but the court is in recess. If I'm not mistaken, I'm the only one in Washington at the present time," Koehler informed him.

"That's just great. The country might be under attack and our judges are lying on a beach somewhere," Gordon said, throwing up his hands. "I don't care what you have to do, Mr. Chief Justice, get them back here now!"

"I'll do what I can," Koehler said, and excused himself.

Rebecca couldn't contain herself any longer, and began asking questions.

"Listen, everyone, I know you have some very important decisions but Mrs. Tolbert and I have the right to know about our husbands. Phil, is there anything that you were able to find out?" she asked.

"Let me pick up where I left off," Karl said. "The three of us were talking when I noticed the president was hit with a dart to his neck. Michael and I turned and I saw a man with a gun standing in what appeared to be a hole in the floor. We later found out that it was a trap door. Both of us started to shout, but within a fraction of a second, I was hit. I woke up some time later to find a doctor standing over me. That's all I know," Schmidt recounted convincingly.

Gordon continued the story. "We found this trap door and a tunnel underneath the hotel emptying out into an alley. We sent some men down there but there was no trace of them. The kidnappers are professionals. The only thing we found was Madigan's wallet." Gordon turned and directed his next question to Mrs. Madigan. "I found a scrap of paper in your husband's wallet with numbers—maybe a combination. Does your husband have a safe?"

"Yes, but he rarely uses it. I think there's a gun in there that belonged to his father and our wills and that's about it," Rebecca said, shrugging her shoulders.

"If you don't mind, I'd like the FBI to check it out," said Gordon. He then turned towards the director, Byron Harrison. "Byron, can your boys check it out?"

"Sure thing, Phil," he said.

Rebecca continued asking questions. "Isn't a trap door and a tunnel a little incredible? Ernst Turner must have been in on it. Has anyone checked on him?"

Harrison answered her inquiry. "That was one of the first things we checked. He's nowhere to be found. He was at the fund-raiser but left early, complaining of illness. We went to his house and interrogated his wife, but we don't know where he is. We've also been looking for his son, but he seems to have disappeared as well. Finding them is one of our top priorities," he explained.

Gordon interjected. "If Turner was in on some scheme to kidnap them, then we have a real problem."

"What do you mean?" asked Rebecca.

"The Iraqi situation was the only reason they met in the room. That situation wasn't manufactured. If it hadn't happened, I can't imagine those three men going off into a room by themselves—"

Gordon was interrupted. "Which means," Harrison, FBI Director, continued, "that if Turner was involved in a scheme to kidnap the president, then he was involved in the Iraqi invasion."

"It means no such thing," spouted Davis Elliot, the national security adviser. "That's preposterous!"

"Is it?" asked Harrison. "Let's say Turner had a plan to kidnap the president and it required him to go into a room with a trap door. How in the world could he expect it to work? Did he just hope that some international crisis would occur so that the top two men in the government would scurry off alone to this room with the trap door? No, he knew that some emergency situation was going to occur."

"He's right," added the secretary of state. "Which means that whoever kidnapped the president has the influence and power to move nations. Good Lord!"

"Think about some of the most recent events that we've witnessed," said Davis Elliot. "Like Matt Connors for instance. Rebecca, I believe that you can attest to this. He was one of the most outstanding men I've ever known. And yet he makes an outrageous, racist speech and then murders a diplomat. It's impossible for me to accept. He was forced or framed, to do, or appear to do, those things. But why? I've asked myself that a thousand times during the last few days," Elliot said, standing up and walking across the room.

"Gentlemen, I'm not a rash man, as you know. I don't jump to conclusions but I think that tonight's events and the Matt Connors' incident is connected," said Elliot to the astonished group.

"Davis, what possible connection is there with all of this? These events are as different as night and day," said Karl Schmidt, acting shocked.

"I don't know, Karl. But Matt told me that he was on to something real big. Maybe I'm wrong, but if I'm right, we have a real problem. If there's some group moving nations to war and inciting racist propaganda, then we're in grave danger," Elliot said, shaking his head.

"Davis, I think that we're getting a little out in left field," said Chris Watkins. "I don't see any connection and if there was one, for what purpose? Even if there's some radical group out there, how could they possibly affect a superpower like the U.S." He shook his head in bewilderment. "It's too bizarre. Let's get on with the problem at hand," the secretary of state argued.

Peter Volhard had been quiet throughout the meeting, a fact which everyone noticed. He cleared his throat and finally spoke, causing the roar of heated debate to fall to silence.

"Gentlemen, this is not something I've sought, but now the safety and security of this nation falls to me. So be it," he said convincingly. "We're facing a crisis of unparalleled magnitude. I don't believe that these events are random. I concur with Mr. Elliot, there's some connection. The implications of this are almost unimaginable. We must plan on the basis of worst-case scenario. If an organization exists that is capable of kidnapping the U.S. president, assassinating the NATO chief and causing wars to break out—then, our nation's security is in danger."

"Gather all information possible about the kidnappings during the next forty-eight hours. But do not make this public. Nothing discussed here tonight is to be shared with anyone. I'll work out of my office on the Hill but will stay in constant contact with Phil. Byron, I want continuous updates on what you find," Volhard ordered, looking directly at the FBI man.

"I want another meeting, excluding Mrs. Madigan, tomorrow. Secretary Schmidt, General Lund, I want a full military briefing on the Iraqi situation. And, one more thing..." He paused and looked at every face in the room. "If we don't locate the president by Monday morning, I'll address the nation and declare martial law."

The atmosphere of the room was heavy as Volhard directed several orders to his military aides.

"Karl, I want you and General Lund to brief me tomorrow on the logistics of declaring martial law." He turned to Phil Gordon and said, "Phil,

I want the White House legal counsel to advise me tomorrow morning on the legal aspects."

"Gentlemen," Volhard said gravely, "we can't afford taking half-measures. We have to assume the worst and err on the side of caution. If some future historian wants to say I was a lunatic, fine. But right now, we don't know who our enemy is. There will be absolute panic when the public finds out. Which reminds me of something else."

"Doug, once the public finds out, there will be a real panic," Volhard said to Douglas Wesson, the secretary of the treasury. "I want the banks closed for a couple of days. We have a national security threat that could also precipitate a financial disaster. I don't want the Stock Exchange to open Monday if the president's not found."

"O.K., gentlemen. Grab some coffee, or something to eat and get to your offices," Volhard instructed. "Make sure you have cots so that you can take short naps. I want the president found and the people who did this behind bars. Now let's get to it!" He stood up quickly and there was silence as he left the room.

After Volhard left, the room erupted into heated debate. Rebecca felt faint and bolted for the door. She was followed by her father into the hallway.

"Becky, come here," Karl said. "You've got to believe that he's O.K. He's survived some pretty tough times, you know. Try to get some rest, sweetheart," he said gently, as he kissed her forehead.

"Thanks, Daddy," she whispered, and headed home.

As Rebecca arrived home, she found two FBI men waiting. "Good evening, ma'am. Director Harrison asked us to look in your husband's safe."

"Oh, yeah, the safe," she said absentmindedly. "Come on in." She walked to the bedroom where the safe was kept.

"Here it is," she said.

The FBI man turned the numbers, causing the lock to spring open. Inside, there was a large brown envelope. The agent opened it and found dozens of papers held together by a rubber band. He and his partner began shuffling through the papers, while Rebecca sat on the edge of the sofa.

"My God!" whispered an agent. The other man let out a low whistle.

"What is it?" Rebecca asked.

"Ma'am, we need to take these papers to Mr. Harrison immediately. They appear to be very important."

"What are they? I thought only our wills and some stock certificates were in there," she said.

"There are a few other things I believe Director Harrison would be interested in," explained the agent.

"Whatever," Rebecca said with a sigh. "I'm too tired to argue. I just want to sleep..." she said, as she collapsed on the sofa and fell asleep within seconds. One of the agents took her shoes off and covered her with a blanket as they left for FBI headquarters.

Byron Harrison was seated at his massive walnut desk when the two agents arrived. The door was open.

"Come in, boys. What did you find?" asked Harrison.

"It's a mindblower, boss. Check these out," said agent Velky eagerly.

Harrison leafed through the neatly-arranged papers one by one in disbelief. They indicated that the kidnapping was a scheme planned by Michael so that he could assume the presidency. He grabbed the phone and called Phil Gordon.

Gordon was pacing his office, having already drunk six cups of coffee when the phone rang. He answered it himself.

"Phil, Byron Harrison here. Listen, my men found some extraordinary papers. It's mind-boggling," he stammered.

"Well, what is it, man?" asked Gordon impatiently.

"We shouldn't talk about it over the phone. I'll come right over," Harrison advised.

"I'll be here, Byron."

A few minutes later, Harrison arrived and found a very nervous Phil Gordon chain-smoking cigarettes.

"Those things will kill you, Phil," said Harrison.

"Yeah, I know. What do you have?"

"You're not going to believe it. Let's go through these one by one," said Harrison. "First, this document depicts the room at the hotel, showing the trap door and tunnel. Here's a paper called *Outline of Events*. Look at this, Phil. *Iraq invades*. Next, *Emergency situation in hotel room, no aides*. This is the kicker, Phil. *Next day, MM escapes, becomes hero and president*.

Gordon stared straight ahead and for one of the few times in his life, was totally speechless.

"There's more," Harrison continued. "Here's some documents called: *Road to VP. Bribe Ramirez, fake his capture. Hire Johnny Green, actor, to portray gang member. Frame Jensen with sexy bombshell*. My God, Phil, this was all done by Madigan so that he could become president!" said the FBI director in disbelief.

"It can't be. You mean that this was all some elaborate scheme to...." Gordon couldn't finish his sentence.

"How about Iraq? Did Madigan persuade them to engage in war? And then, as president, cut a deal? It's insanity, Byron," Gordon shrieked and paced feverishly around the room.

"That's what it looks like. I believe we'll soon get a call from Michael Madigan, telling us and the world how he fought off twelve bad guys and barely escaped, to become a national hero and president of the U.S. Put that in your pipe and smoke it," said Harrison, shaking his head.

Gordon sat in stony silence for about two minutes before speaking. "Byron, get the attorney general in here. This is just too much. I..." he started to mumble incoherently.

"Relax, Phil. I'll get the A.G. Do you want to tell Volhard?" asked Harrison.

"Let's wait and see if we hear from Madigan," cautioned Gordon. "I'm not sure why but I don't totally trust Volhard."

28

ichael awoke to find himself in a ditch alongside a barren stretch of road, every bone in his body aching. Where was he? How did he get here? He tried to remember.

Slowly, he sat himself up and managed to look at his watch from the light that was just now becoming visible in the predawn. It was 5:15 A.M. He stood up and tried to walk, noticing that his coat was tattered and his knees and elbows were raw.

Now he remembered. He had been thrown from the car. Or did he jump? He wasn't sure. Wait a second, he had been in the trunk. How did he get out? He cursed.

He started walking alongside the road, trying to recall the events from the previous night. He remembered being summoned by the president to a private room in the hotel. They were talking about Iraq and...then what? He didn't know what happened next. The next thing he knew he was in the trunk of a car, lying on top of another body. Was it the president's?

Had he and President Tolbert been kidnapped? He staggered along the highway.

After twenty minutes of stumbling, Michael heard the sounds of a car coming. He waved his arms madly to flag it down. A pickup truck pulled over.

"Good Lord, man. You look awful," said the driver of the truck, who was accompanied by a boy of about eight. Michael saw fishing poles and realized they were most likely headed for the lake that had now become visible.

"You look like you could use some help, buddy," said the fisherman. "Name's Don Lentine and this is my son, Brandon. Let me give you a hand," said the driver, as he stepped out of the truck. Putting his arm around Michael, he helped him into the truck. The light of the new day hit Michael's face and Lentine's mouth dropped as he realized who it was.

"Good God Almighty. Are you Michael Madigan?" asked the stunned fisherman.

"Yes. I was apparently kidnapped and somehow managed to escape. Will you get me to a phone?" Michael said.

"Brandon, this here's the vice president of the United States. We've got to help him, Son," said the awestruck father.

The Lentines helped Michael into the cab of the truck and raced down the highway.

"Where are we? How far from the White House?" he asked.

"You're in Virginia, sir. We're about thirty-five miles from Pennsylvania Avenue," said the older Lentine.

"Is there a telephone anywhere nearby?" Michael asked.

"There's a service station about two miles from here. We'll be there in a flash," he said driving faster. "If you don't mind my asking, what happened?"

"I'm not really sure. I was at this fund-raiser and got called into a private room by the president and the secretary of defense. Some emergency situation," Michael explained. "And then the next thing I realize, I'm in the trunk of a car. I don't know what happened. I just woke up about fifteen minutes ago in a ditch along the road," Michael said, grimacing as his body was jolted by a bump in the road.

"Sorry. We're just about there. Should I call a doctor?" Don inquired.

"No, thanks. I hate to interrupt your fishing, but could I impose upon you for a ride to the city?"

"No problem. The fish will still be there this afternoon," said Lentine. "Here we are," he said pulling into the gas station parking lot. Michael painfully began to exit the truck.

"Brandon, get out of the truck, Son, and let's give the vice president a hand." The father and son helped Michael to the phone. He reached for his wallet but quickly realized that it wasn't there. Not surprising since he had fallen out of a moving car.

He dialed the operator. "I'd like to make a collect call to the White House. Put me through to Phil Gordon. This is Michael Madigan."

The operator thought it was a gag but did as he requested. The White House operator accepted the charges and put the call through to Gordon.

Before picking up the phone, the chief of staff buzzed his secretary. "Get Byron Harrison on the line right away."

"Gordon here. Mr. Vice President, is that you?"

"Yeah, it's me, Phil. Don't ask me what happened because I'm not sure," said Michael.

"Are you with the president?" asked Gordon.

This confirmed Michael's fear. "No. I assume that means he's been kidnapped," Michael said, feeling his stomach churn.

"Well, weren't both of you? For God's sake, don't you even know?" snapped the chief of staff.

"Listen, Phil, all I remember is talking with the president and Karl Schmidt last night and then ending up in a car trunk. Then about twenty minutes ago I woke up in a ditch. I just got picked up by some guy and his son on their way fishing. They've offered to give me a ride. I don't know anything about the president. We were moving and I was laying on top of someone but I couldn't see a damn thing. It could have been the president but I don't really know," said Michael, knowing how ridiculous this must sound.

Very good, Madigan, Gordon said to himself. Just as Harrison predicted, Michael had a tale of terror that would captivate the public and put him in the White House.

"I can have someone pick you up. Where exactly are you?" asked Gordon.

"Phil, I can be there faster if I just ride with these people. I'll be there in half an hour. I don't want to wait for someone to get me," Michael insisted.

"All right," Gordon agreed. "Let the fisherman bring you in but come right to my office. Nowhere else. There are some important decisions that you have to make. You're the acting president now," he lied.

"Understood. I'll see you in a few minutes," Michael said, and hung up the phone. He started to call Rebecca but then remembered the photos and the journal Josh had shown him.

He began to head back to the truck, when he did an about-face to make one more call. He decided to call the vice president's chief of staff.

"Meyers here. Mr. Vice President, is that you?" asked Michael's top aide.

"Yeah, Ed, it's me. I just woke up in a ditch in Virginia and I have no idea where Andrew Tolbert is. I just talked to Phil Gordon and I'm on my way to the White House. I'm still trying to figure out what happened exactly, and I wondered if you could help," said Michael.

There was a long silence before Meyers spoke. He had known Michael for years. They had worked together at the Pentagon.

"Ed, are you there?" Michael queried.

"Yeah, I'm here. Listen, Mike, we've known each other for a long time," he began.

"Sure. I think about twelve or thirteen years."

"And you're Nathan's godfather."

Michael wondered why Ed would be talking about that at a time like this. Ed and his wife had named Michael and Rebecca to be the guardians of their two children, if anything happened to them.

"You wouldn't betray that trust, would you?" pleaded Meyers.

"Ed, what the hell are you talking about? Of course not! Is something wrong?" Michael asked, puzzled.

Meyers said a quick prayer. "Michael, I hope that I don't regret telling you this," he began, and then hesitated for several moments.

"There were all sorts of top-level meetings last night," Meyers finally said. "Byron Harrison interrogated me last night for about an hour."

"Well with what's happened, I can understand that."

"Michael, this had to do with a scrap of paper found in your wallet."

"I did lose my wallet but what scrap of paper?" he asked.

"The combination to your home safe," Meyers explained.

"There's nothing in that safe except for a couple of legal documents and an old gun my father gave me," Michael replied. "And I've *never* written down the combination. It's easy to remember because it's Rebecca's birthday. 10/21/46."

Meyers tried to detect any quiver or note of deception but Michael seemed sincere. He would gamble.

"Mike, they found documents showing a meticulously-planned plot to kidnap the president. There was a diagram of the room you were in, a picture of the tunnel, and all sorts of details. Also, other documents showed a long range plan to get the V.P. job, including capturing Ramirez for the publicity. Lastly, there were photographs of Jensen and a young blond in the sack that you supposedly used to blackmail him with," explained Meyers nervously.

Michael became sick to his stomach and the pain in his head was now almost unbearable.

"What are you saying, Ed? Do they think I staged the kidnapping so that I could become president?"

"That's what they think, Michael. The papers also say that the day after the kidnapping you'd return after a daring escape," Meyers said, lowering his voice.

"My God, I don't even want the job!" Michael shouted. "What will happen if I come in? Will I be arrested?" he asked in disbelief.

"That's the general idea. Everyone thinks you're the villain, Mike."

"Listen to me, Ed. I swear on my children that I had no involvement in this insanity. I have no idea how those papers got into my safe. For God's sake, if I really had such documents locked up, would I be stupid enough to carry around the combination?" he yelled, and then realized that Don Lentine and his son were watching closely.

"Michael, I've known you too long and I refuse to accept the reports of what happened. Same thing with Matt Connors, I'll go to my grave believing that he didn't kill that NATO man," said Meyers.

Matt. He had completely forgotten. It was just like the thing with Matt. There had to be a connection. He fought the fog that enveloped his mind but he was in terrible pain and in shock over what was happening.

"Mike, we need to think this out," said Meyers.

"I'll call you at exactly six o'clock tonight at this number. Be there to answer the phone, understand?" ordered Michael.

"Got it. Have you talked to Rebecca yet?"

"No, Ed, I haven't. I think she set me up. I can't call her."

"What are you talking about?" Meyers demanded.

"Last night Josh showed me photographs of Rebecca in a KKK outfit carrying a sign saying: *Death to Jews*. And I found a journal that she was keeping describing her feelings, her true feelings. And this thing with the safe, she must have planted those documents," Michael continued. "Who else could have? My God, Ed..." he let the phone fall and stood staring.

"Michael, Michael. Hello? Are you there? Hello?" Meyers screamed but Michael was gone.

Don Lentine hung up the phone and helped Michael into his truck. Michael had fainted, and Don sped toward home.

"Daddy, are we going to the hospital?" Brandon asked. "Isn't it the other direction?"

"We're not going to the hospital. We're going home."

"But, Daddy, he might die," argued the boy.

"Your mom's a nurse. She'll take care of him. Now don't argue with me. I know what I'm doing," said Lentine with determination.

The pickup truck arrived at the Lentine home in less than fifteen minutes and father and son carried Michael into the house.

"Good heavens!" Shirley Lentine shouted, turning off her computer as her husband and son laid Michael on the couch. "What's wrong with that man?" she said.

"I don't know, and it ain't just any man. That's the vice president of the United States," said Lentine.

"Donald, do you really expect me to believe that?" she demanded.

"Look for yourself. That man on our sofa is Michael Madigan," he said.

She took a closer look. "Oh, My God, it is him. We'd better call a doctor right away. And then the White House, I suppose."

"We ain't calling anybody. You're a nurse, you'll attend to him!" he insisted.

"You can't be serious, Don. Obviously, he's been kidnapped and he may be dying. We have to do something," she said, reaching for the phone.

"Put down the phone and I'll tell you why we ain't calling no one," he said, grabbing her arm.

Grimacing in pain, she sat down in shock.

"Shirley, I'm very sorry. I hope I didn't hurt you," said Don. "But we just overheard a very scary conversation."

"What did you hear, Daddy?" Brandon asked.

Don hesitated. He wasn't sure if he wanted Brandon to know all of this. What the hell, he thought. He already knows almost everything anyway.

"Well, I heard him call the White House. He asked the operator to connect him with Phil Gordon," said Don.

"Who's Phil Gordon?" asked Shirley. "Isn't he Tolbert's chief of something?"

"Yes, he's the White House chief of staff."

"Anyway, it seems that both he and President Tolbert were kidnapped last night, except he managed to escape."

"Almighty Father in Heaven," said Shirley, as she crossed herself.

"Then he calls this other number and talks to some guy named Ed. Ed tells him that they suspect him of concocting this whole kidnapping, staging an escape, so that he could become the president," said Lentine.

"I don't believe it," said Shirley.

"Apparently, this Ed guy didn't either. But he told Madigan that if he returns to the White House, he'll be arrested."

"My God, Donald. What in the world are we going to do with him?"

"I don't know. Maybe he's being framed and maybe he's a madman. That's why we ain't calling no one unless we have to. You're a nurse. Look at his wounds and see if he's hurt bad. If he is, we'll call Dr. Lamont. If he's not, we'll tie him up and ask him a few questions," said Don, as he went to the garage for some rope.

Shirley attended to Michael and determined that his injuries weren't life threatening. Don took the rope and tied up Michael, picked up the phone and called the sheriff's office.

"Let me speak to Sheriff Auerbach," he asked the receptionist.

"Auerbach here," said the sheriff in a gruff voice.

"Sam, Don Lentine here. Listen, can you come over here?"

"Don, I'm mighty busy here. What do you need?"

"I can't talk about it over the phone. You're gonna have to trust me. It's something mighty important," Don explained.

"All right, Don. But I can't be there in less than forty-five minutes."

"Sam, you ain't listening, I said it's important! Get your butt over here right now!"

"O.K., Don. I'll be right over. I'll bring Billy with me," said Sam Auerbach.

"Come alone, Sam. Just you and your gun. Do you understand?" Don asked.

"Sure, Don. I'll be right there," said the Sheriff, who immediately sped off to the Lentine house.

The Lentines looked at each other, not believing that they had the vice president of the United States tied up in their living room. Shirley broke the silence. "I wonder if we should call his poor wife. She must be going crazy."

"No, absolutely not. That's another thing I overheard that I forgot about. He thinks his wife framed him and that she's a part of some conspiracy."

"Now, that is truly ridiculous. I've met the woman before. I'm telling you, I know human nature. I know people. And I'm telling you that she couldn't have done it," said Shirley Lentine with no trace of doubt.

"How do you know her?" asked her surprised husband.

"I went to high school with Pam Johnson, who happens to be a close friend of Rebecca Madigan," Shirley explained.

"Who's Pam Johnson?" asked Don.

"Well, that was her maiden name before she married Matt Connors. Her name's Pam Connors now," Shirley explained.

"That's right. I read that the Connors and Madigans are good friends. You know Pam Connors?" he asked.

"I've told you that a hundred times," said an exasperated Shirley. "I swear, Don, you don't listen to a word I say. I wonder how the poor woman's doing anyway with her husband flipping his lid, and everything."

Don thought this over before replying. "Maybe he didn't flip his lid. Maybe he was framed just like Madigan here was framed," Don speculated.

"I suppose it's possible," she responded.

"Listen, Shirley, this might be a long shot, but I want you to call Pam Connors," Don said.

"It's been many years since I even spoke to her. I'm sure that she doesn't even remember me," Shirley protested.

"Maybe she will and maybe she won't. But I want you to get her over here on the double. Tell her anything you want. Tell her it's about her husband. That should do it," Don said, frantically trying to think of his next step.

"Here's her telephone number," Shirley said, pulling out an old telephone address book. "I wonder if she'll even remember me," she added, picking up the phone and dialing.

After two rings, there was an answer. "Pam Connors please."

"This is she," came the response.

Shirley felt flush with anxiety. "You probably don't remember me but this is Shirley Ritter, from Wilson High."

"Shirley, of course I remember you. How could I ever forget someone getting so drunk at our high school graduation that she walked naked through a crowded party?" Pam said good-naturedly.

Shirley winced. She hadn't thought of that unpleasant memory in years and had never told Don. "How are you, Pam?"

"I guess I'm holding up. I don't know if you heard, but my husband was kidnapped and now he's being accused of all kinds of horrible things," Pam said emotionally.

"What? I heard that he just, well, lost it. Sorry, but that's what everyone's saying," Shirley said apologetically.

"No, Shirl, he was kidnapped. I have proof. For God's sake, my son and I were also kidnapped and they let us speak to Matt. He was investigating some drug lords and they grabbed him." She started crying, and said, almost hysterically, "I don't know if I'll ever see him again, Shirl. What am I gonna do?"

Shirley hated herself for what she was about to say, but Don gave her an ice-cold stare.

"Pam, I, uh, might have some information about Matt."

"What are you talking about?"

Shirley closed her eyes and took a deep breath. "I can't tell you over the phone. You're going to have to come to my house," she said, waiting for a violent reaction.

She wasn't disappointed. "Damn it, Shirley, you tell me what you know this very second or I'll...I'll, oh, Christ, I don't know what I'll do." She started to cry again. "Please," she begged.

Shirley felt empathetic to her friend's pain. "Pam, I don't mean to play games with you. Please just come over and I'll tell you everything I know," she said with a determined tone of voice.

"O.K., tell me where you live and I'll be right over," Pam said, with resignation in her voice.

Shirley gave her the address and directions. "I'll see you in a little bit, Pam," she said, but the only response she received was the click of the phone.

"She's going to hate me. Maybe we should talk to Pam first before we get the sheriff involved," Shirley said.

Don thought about it for a second. "You're right, Shirl. But he's already on his way. What can I say?" he asked, already panicking.

"Isn't his birthday soon? I tell you what you're going to do, Don. You're going to wish him a happy birthday and give him your new fishing pole as a present."

"You can't be serious. I never even got a chance to use it!" he started to protest but didn't get to finish because of the knocking on the door. It was Sam Auerbach.

"Give him the fishing pole, Don, and then get him out of here," Shirley said firmly.

Don opened the door and ushered the Sheriff to the garage. "What's so all-fire important?" demanded Auerbach.

"I hope that what you were doing wasn't an emergency," Don started to say, rather defensively. "But I just wanted to tell you in person how much Shirley and I appreciate all that you and Betty have done for us. Here's a little present," Don said, handing him the fishing pole.

The Sheriff rarely shared his emotions but he couldn't resist breaking into a grin. "Shucks, Don, you shouldn't have done that. Thanks very much!"

As Don was showing him some of the pole's unusual features, Pam Connors pulled up. He had to get rid of the sheriff quickly.

Sam had seen Shirley open the door and let Pam in. "Who's that woman, Don?"

"She's an old friend of Shirley's. Listen, Sam, I need to get in the house and you better get back to your job. I apologize for lying to you but I just wanted to give it to you in person," Don said, wincing at his lie and the loss of his new pole.

Sam shook his hand and got into his squad car and drove away. As soon as he hit the pavement, Don sprinted back into the house. He ran into the living room and heard a very angry Pam Connors screaming.

"Damn it, Shirley. I don't talk to you for years and then you tell me some crazy story about my husband and haul me out to this hick place!" she screamed.

Don tried to rescue Shirley from this barrage. "Mrs. Connors, I'm Don, Shirley's husband. Please don't be angry with Shirley. I'm the one who wanted you to come out here."

Pam wasn't satisfied. "Do you have any information about my husband or not?"

"To be honest, Mrs. Connors, I'm not sure, but if you'll follow me, we'll see," Don said, as he walked into the back room containing the unconscious and tied-up vice president.

Pam followed him suspiciously, feeling a shiver of panic go up her back when she saw a man tied-up in the room. Several seconds later she screamed.

"Are you people out of your minds? Oh, Michael, what have they done to you," she said softly. Turning towards the Lentines, she said defiantly, "You people will spend the rest of your lives in prison."

"No, we won't, Mrs. Connors," Don said firmly. "This is going to sound like the craziest thing you ever heard but I swear it's the truth. I got up this morning to go fishing and now I'm caught up in some bizarre conspiracy involving the president. And to top it off, I don't even have a fishing pole no more," he added.

"I'll listen," Pam said calmly, as she sat down.

"Thank you, ma'am. I'm not some big-time conspirator. I'm a simple man, a carpenter. Mrs. Connors, believe me when I tell you that I'm not smart enough to kidnap the vice president of the United States," Don started to explain.

Don told her the whole story just as he knew it. "Now you may be wondering why we got you involved with this."

Pam was shaking with fear. "That's right, I am."

"Well, it's just a gut feeling and I don't rightly know how to really explain it but I'll try my best," Don said, and he got up and started pacing the room.

"You see, I talked to Mr. Madigan this morning. When I found him, he was hurt bad. He wasn't faking it. But even so, he was polite and kind," Don explained.

He continued. "I'm as sure as I can be that Mr. Madigan couldn't have done the things they're saying he did."

Pam was puzzled. "I know him very well and I agree with you. He couldn't have kidnapped the president. It's impossible. But how do I fit in?"

"I remember seeing you on television being interviewed about your husband. And then that Davis Elliot fellow said the same thing, that Matt couldn't have done the things it looked like he had done. And it seemed like too much of a coincidence to me," he said with a shrug of his shoulders.

"I apologize, Mrs. Connors, for hauling you out here," Don continued. "But I had this notion that there's some connection with Mr. Madigan and your husband. I know you and his wife are good friends and I thought that just maybe if the two of you was to talk, well, I don't rightly know. I'm sorry, ma'am," he apologized.

Pam understood now and felt hope for the first time in many days. "Maybe you're right, Mr. Lentine. My God, maybe you are," she said, smiling.

"Why don't we just wait until Mr. Madigan wakes up and talk to him?" Don suggested.

"Can't we untie him?" Pam inquired.

"Mrs. Connors, if he did kidnap Mr. Tolbert, he wouldn't think twice about killing me and my family. I'd never forgive myself if my wife and child were harmed. I'll untie him if I'm convinced of his innocence," Mr. Lentine explained.

"Fair enough," Pam said, as they started into the other room. Just then, Michael began to stir.

"He's coming to," whispered Shirley.

"I got ears, you know," said Don.

They stood in a semicircle around the bed as Michael opened his eyes. He was still groggy and thought that he was dreaming.

"Michael, how are you, dear? This is Pam Connors. Can you see me?"

Michael tried to focus, shook his head, and then spoke slowly and clearly. "Of course, I see you, Pam. You're standing a foot in front of me. Why am I tied up?"

Pam almost laughed but managed to suppress it. "Michael, please believe me when I tell you that I'm here to help you. These people here are the Lentines. Mr. Lentine found you laying in a ditch this morning alongside the highway. Do you know how you got there?"

Michael struggled to sit up and finally managed to sit upright, still tied. "Pam, if I answer your questions, will you untie me?" he asked.

"I'm so sorry, Michael. I'll explain it all to you and yes, I will untie you. But please answer the questions first," she pleaded.

Michael wasn't sure what to make of this but it was no worse than everything else.

"Sure, Pam, I'll answer your questions. After all, I'm probably not really sitting here tied up with you and Ma and Pa Kettle and Opie Taylor. I'm sure this is all a dream. And probably everything I tell you is just a dream, too, because nothing real could ever be so bizarre."

"Let's see," he struggled to remember. "Last night my oldest son tells me my wife is a closet Ku Klux Klanner who hates Jews. And blacks too, by the way. I don't believe him, of course, so he shows me photographs of Rebecca standing in front of a burning cross."

He paused for a moment, fighting to remember. "Then this movie starlet is flirting with me when the president whispers in my ear that there's some crisis. We go into this room down the hall and are joined by the secretary of defense who tells us that Iraq is on the move. And then the next thing I know, I'm in a car trunk, where I can't even see the hand in front of my face, and I'm lying on top of a body. Whose body, I don't know. Andrew Tolbert, maybe."

He paused again and shifted his weight. "Next thing I know, I wake up in a ditch, bloodied and bruised and not sure how I got there. This man gives me a ride and I call the White House to speak with Gordon. He tells me to get there fast because I'm now the acting president and there's big trouble."

Michael rubbed his head and continued. "I don't know what to make of all of this and so I call Ed Meyers, my chief of staff, who tells me that a bunch of documents were found in my safe implicating me to some bizarre plot to have myself declared president, and that as soon as I show up they'll arrest me. And now I'm talking to you with ropes cutting off my blood supply. But I guess it doesn't really matter. This is all just a dream." With that, he laid back down and closed his eyes.

Don and Shirley looked at each other and then at Pam. "O.K., Mr. Madigan, we believe you. I'll untie you," Don said, and with a quick snap of a knife cut the ropes in two.

With a large sigh of relief, he whispered, "Thank you." Michael sat back upright and then stood up. He moved about quickly, trying to get the blood flowing again.

"Pam, it just dawned on me. What in the world are you doing here?" Michael asked.

With a laugh, she said, "It was Mr. Lentine's idea. I thought it was crazy at first but it makes a lot of sense. You see..." she didn't finish. The phone interrupted her.

"That may be for me," Pam said. "I hope you don't mind, but I set up my call-forward here, just in case Matt called," she explained.

Shirley answered the phone. "It's for you, Pam," she said, handing the receiver to Pam.

Don't get your hopes up, she told herself, as she had every time the phone had rung for the past week. "Hello."

"Baby, is that you? It's me, sweetheart. I'm still alive," said the voice, but Pam didn't hear all of it because she was crying so hard.

"Oh, Matt. I thought I'd never hear your voice again," she cried. "Are you all right? Where are you?"

"It's the longest, craziest story that you've ever heard. I wouldn't blame you if you didn't believe me. But I didn't kill that Klaus guy. And you know they forced me to give that speech. I was left for dead in the German woods and some people found me and nursed me back to health. They tell me I've been asleep for over two days. But I made it, babe. I beat them," he said proudly.

"Well, as wild as that story sounds, it's nothing compared to what's happening over here," Pam said, and then told Matt the whole story about Michael.

After hearing the incredible tale, Matt responded excitedly. "Well, that carpenter friend of yours is very perceptive. You bet your ass there's a connection between me and the things with Michael. It's the Germans, babe. The Fourth Reich," he said, talking a mile a minute.

"I don't know what you're talking about. Why don't you speak with Michael," Pam said, handing him the phone.

"Matt, I'm not sure what's going on but we have to move fast," Michael said. "We're both fugitives and the president's been kidnapped."

"I think I'm a step ahead of you, Cube. I know who the one-armed-man is and I know what his plan is. We've got to get together, Mike. Right away. But not in Washington. Don't talk to anyone, Michael, because you don't know who you can trust," Matt said. "Where can we go that's quiet and within a couple of hundred miles of D.C.?" he asked.

Michael thought for a second. "I got it. My mother just bought a spread in Connecticut. I just talked to her last week. It's perfect," he said.

"Don't you think that they're going to be looking for you to go to a relative's house?" Matt warned.

"That's what makes this so great. She's been living in the Washington area for years and out of the blue, just last week, she moves. I'm the only one who knows. She hasn't even sold her other house," Michael explained.

"O.K., you convinced me," Matt said. "We're on the next flight to the U.S. We'll come into Kennedy and drive. Uh, why don't we meet in twenty-four hours at your mother's?"

"You're on. What do you mean, 'We'?" Michael asked.

"I've got a new friend," Matt answered.

"If you want to be mysterious, that's all right. Let me give you some directions," Michael said, and then did so.

"Here's Pam again. See you soon," Michael said, and gave the phone back to Pam.

Shirley turned to Michael. "Can I get you anything, sir?" she asked deferentially.

"I'm pretty hungry, now that you mention it, Mrs. Lentine," Michael said.

"Please call me Shirley," she answered, smiling.

"Only if you call me Michael," he said, and noticed that she appeared a little uneasy at this suggestion. "Shirley, this isn't a normal situation and your husband saved my life. So, it's O.K. What do you say?"

"All right, Michael," she said gamely.

"Mr. Lentine, uh, Don, under the circumstances, would you mind if Pam and I stay here tonight? We'll leave at dawn and drive to my mother's house. Would that be O.K.?" he asked.

"We'd be honored if you stayed in our house," Don said.

"Brandon, go make up the guest room. Mr. Madigan and Mrs. Connors are staying the night," he yelled out to his son, who ran frantically upstairs.

Michael ate ravenously. "Shirley, that was one of the finest meals I've ever had. Thank you very much."

Shirley beamed. "You're certainly welcome, Michael. Would you like to call your mother?"

"Well, I don't have the number but maybe I can get it from information," he said.

"You can use the phone in the bedroom for privacy," Shirley said, showing him where it was.

He called the operator and within seconds had Julia's number. He dialed impatiently.

"Hello," came the frail but familiar voice.

"Hi, Mom, it's Michael. How are you?"

"Michael, is that you, dear? How are you?"

"I'm fine, Mom. The last twenty-four hours have been a little crazy but I'm making it, I guess."

"Michael, no matter how many times I talk to you, I can't tell you how proud I am of you. Imagine, my little boy who used to stick peas up his nose is vice president of the United States."

"Come on, Mom. Listen, the reason I'm calling is that I want to come visit."

"You want to come visit? Of course. You're welcome anytime. Rebecca and the kids, too?" she asked.

"No, just me this time," he said.

"I'll fix up the spare room and I'll fix your favorite dinner. Roast beef and mashed potatoes, O.K.?" she said.

"Sounds great. I'll be there early afternoon tomorrow," Michael told her.

"Are you coming in some military helicopter or like a regular person?" she asked, making him laugh.

"Like a regular person, Mom. I'm going to drive up myself," he added.

"I can't wait to see you, dear. Make sure you stay warm on your drive up here," Mrs. Madigan said.

Michael laughed gently to himself as he realized that a person never stops being a parent. He was the vice president of the United States and his mother was reminding him to stay warm.

"I'll bring a sweater, Mom. I love you and I'll see you tomorrow afternoon."

⚔ ⚔ ⚔

Tommy Schmidt had decided to concentrate in what was formerly Eastern Germany to carry out the plan for racial violence. Eastern Germany was still having difficulty making the transition to democracy. In particular, they seemed to resent the endless stream of foreign refugees claiming political asylum. In Tommy's mind, they were parasites to be eliminated. He would sleep much better if, by some miracle, they all died a horrible death.

Over the previous three weeks he had organized several rallies that would occur simultaneously in various cities. He had assembled hundreds of young and angry right-wing extremists, including skinheads and neo-Nazis, but also many who considered themselves part of mainstream society. Even the middle class had tired of all the refugees.

There would be four places where his troops would make their presence known. They would attack the human flotsam at the so-called refugee centers. First, in Eisenhuettenstadt in East Germany; second, in Luebben, about seventy-five miles southeast of Berlin; third, in Biesenthal, outside the eastern part of the capital; and fourth, in the western city of Leverkusen, where ethnic Germans from the former Soviet Union were housed.

Tommy led a pre-attack meeting of the leaders of the four "battalions" at midnight, hours before the dawn attack time.

Three members of each team gathered to hear Tommy speak. The dozen young men that had gathered were all in their twenties and seemed to wear the same uniform. All had shaved heads and wore black boots with metal-reinforced toes, tight jeans and bomber jackets.

"Guten Abend, mein Freunden," Tommy greeted the others. "We're about to do battle tonight and make no mistake about it. We are in a war. Our nation consists of the finest stock, the most noble of all races and yet we find ourselves diluted and polluted and convoluted by this human trash. No more. It must end," he said emphatically, his metallic voice echoing eerily in the sprawling warehouse that served as their headquarters.

"Just this year over a quarter million of these so-called refugees have poured across the border from God knows where, to steal our jobs, take our women, and dirty our cities," Tommy said contemptuously. "We'll drive them back and make others who consider coming to Germany realize that they're not welcome."

"Especially here in Eastern Germany, with rising unemployment and a severe housing shortage, these people are not wanted," Tommy continued with his harangue. "We have enough problems with the difficulties of reunification. We don't need more obstacles."

"Take heart, my friends, from what happened in Rostock," Tommy declared, referring to the recent riots there. "Two hundred worm-infested Rumanian gypsies had been camping all summer outside one of these refugee processing centers in a residential neighborhood. Good, decent German people complained repeatedly, but to no avail, about the unsanitary conditions and crime. Finally, they could take no more."

"Germans, like you and I, laid siege to the Gypsy camps and forced the authorities to relocate these slugs," Tommy exclaimed loudly. "The amazing thing about this incident, my comrades, is that thousands of everyday people supported the violence. Housewives, factory workers, butchers and bankers. All of society stood up and cheered. Why? Because they've had enough!" The young men watching, nodded their heads in approval.

"Let me assure you that internationally, Germany will see some major changes in the months to come," Tommy pledged. "But we first must cleanse Germany from within. We must expunge these parasites, purge these unwanted boils. Only then can Germany return to its proper place."

"So, gather your soldiers and strike aggressively and violently. Use everything at your disposal, to include arson and explosives. We want to drive these people back to where they came and we want to make the nightly news. Deutschland, über alles!" he said to unanimous cheers.

29

In the Maryland suburbs, the cars drove up one by one. All surviving members of the Six had responded to Rommel's directive that they all be present.

No assistants would be present, no team members, just the principals themselves, although Rommel, as acting president, couldn't get away. He would conduct the meeting by telephone over a secure line. The others had not been together in the same room in some time and were all feeling exhilaration as they were coming closer to the fruition of their dream.

Rommel brought the meeting to order. "Good evening, gentlemen. Our plan is now much closer to full execution. Our goals will soon be realized. The planned kidnapping of Andrew Tolbert and Michael Madigan went even more smoothly than we had hoped. I'm now the acting president of the United States," he said, beaming with pride.

"Hear, hear," his comrades cheered.

"Bismarck, I'm told that you were worthy of an Oscar in the kidnapping. How did you like taking a dart to the neck?" asked Krupp, laughing aloud.

"I was rather impressive, I must say. However, that dart caused one hell of a headache," he said to laughter.

"Speaking of acting, Wilhelm deserves kudos as well for his tragic 'death.'"

Wilhelm, aka Felix Klaus, stood to acknowledge the cheers of his comrades.

Rommel, aka Volhard, chastised everyone. "Friends, we are not there yet. We must not lose sight of our goals. I almost didn't become acting president because of a legal technicality."

"What was that?" asked Frederick.

"The Constitution says that the president must be native-born. The presidency almost went to the annoyingly irritating Christian Watkins, secretary of state. You should have been there," he explained, "all eyes turned to the frail and decrepit Chief Justice. As the sweat poured down his temple and his whole body trembled, he meekly ruled that the presidency was mine. This close call must serve as an example to not become overconfident," Rommel said over the telephone line.

"I would like to report that in Germany, all is moving quickly," Frederick said. "Wilhelm and I are rapidly forming the basis of what will be a new government. General Steigrich is making great progress in forming an army. As we speak, Thomas Schmidt is leading an all-front attack on the refugee problem. Many of these foreigners will be driven out and we've prevailed upon the chancellor to restrict immigration for the time being," reported the future chancellor to the group.

"Also, I'm leading the charge on Europeanization," Frederick continued. "While it's just a ruse that we're seeking a united Europe, it will help us seize a dominant economical position. The deutsche mark is becoming stronger and the dollar is plummeting with each passing day," he explained. "Bismarck, how is your team progressing with its mission of acquiring nuclear missiles?"

"I have wonderful news. My subordinates inform me they've obtained several warheads, both strategic and tactical," reported the secretary of defense.

"Excellent," praised Wilhelm.

"It was not as difficult as you would think," continued Bismarck. "The former USSR is becoming capitalistic, are they not? They were bribed and bought. Several weapons were acquired from a disgruntled army colonel who grew disgusted with the post-coup military. And some from a former top scientist who suddenly couldn't find work and was unable to feed his children," he added, feigning sadness.

"And, lastly, we acquired others from an American admiral whose wife is dying. He gave us weapons that had been earmarked for destruction, ones without arming mechanisms. These weapons can be armed in a few minutes. The process is so easy a child could do it."

Rommel continued. "Let's go over the final plan in the United States. Michael Madigan was allowed to escape and he was supposed to return home as a conquering hero only to discover that he was the main suspect in Tolbert's abduction. Apparently he became aware of this and didn't come in. Fortunately, he's been sighted and will be brought in tomorrow. I will address the nation on Monday, inform them of Mr. Madigan's seditious activities, and declare martial law. Further, I'll deploy approximately one-half of the U.S. Armed Forces to the Persian Gulf to deal with the imaginary war."

"Herr Rommel, why don't we just kill Tolbert and Madigan?" asked Krupp.

"No, no, we've discussed that many times before," Rommel said, becoming a bit impatient. "America is too desensitized. Their attention span is like that of a child. The shock from the death of the president would be over in a week and then it would be back to business as usual. Keeping Madigan alive to try him for his crime will take many weeks and the so-called 'news' media will eat it up. The election will be thrown out of whack, the people will be distracted by the war, there are racial disturbances in every major city, and nobody knows who I am. Lastly, Madigan will be seen as an opportunistic Jew who tried to kill a popular president. With the country in chaos, we'll take maximum advantage of the situation."

"When will we take the final steps?" asked Krupp.

"Soon," answered Bismarck. "First, amidst the chaos that Rommel has described, we'll use our chemical weapons to poison the water supply of London and Paris. We'll mobilize U.S. nuclear forces and I will go to the NORAD facility and insure that it's unable to defend America from nuclear attack. Frederick will take over as the new leader of Germany in a bloodless coup, which will be child's play once the chancellor realizes that the U.S. president is one of us and has nuclear weapons aimed at Germany. And finally..."

"And finally," Rommel interjected, "I will address the American people from an underground facility known as Mount Weather. They will get an ultimatum: capitulate or face destruction. Bismarck and I control the nuclear arsenal whose weapons can be launched by pressing a series of buttons in a prearranged sequence. Nothing can stop them after that," Rommel said.

"The beauty of the plan is that while the world will discover that Bismarck and I are impostors, Frederick will be viewed as legitimate," explained the acting U.S. president. "There will be no connection. The U.S. will be in chaos for decades, the USSR is in shambles already and Germany will rise to the top. Britain and France will be dealing with major health crises because of the poisoned water. They won't know who caused it and will allow us to come to their rescue," Volhard said, almost giddy with excitement. "The deutsche mark will become the dominant currency."

"Germany will fill the vacuum and our strength will be welcomed," he added. "Once our place is solidified, we can decide whether to engage in all-out war. We may not have to. We may inherit the role of the most powerful nation on earth through peaceful means and be revered throughout the world."

"Gentlemen, Herr Rommel is correct. We cannot fail." Bismarck continued where Rommel had left off. "Please stand and raise your glasses. To Germany!" Bismarck toasted.

"To Germany!" came the chorus of voices.

"One last thing, Gentlemen," said Bismarck. "While his foolishness almost destroyed us, he was my friend and was one of us, do not forget, for over forty-five years. He labored as did we all. I would like to say a special prayer for Charlemagne. May God bless his soul."

"Amen," came the weak refrain to Schmidt's request. They, too, had loved him, but they could not forget his foolishness and what it had almost cost them.

Krupp was not so forgiving and thought to himself, may you rot in hell for all eternity, Charlemagne, for that is what you deserve.

✠　　✠　　✠

Michael and Pam thanked the Lentines as they loaded up Pam's car at 4:30 A.M. Shirley had woken up at 4:00 A.M. to fix breakfast and had spent the previous afternoon shopping for a wig for Michael. He was now blond and wore a mustache. He looked in the mirror, with Shirley helping him, and thought that he looked quite distinguished and somewhat younger. He dressed in wool flannels that Don provided.

"You look like a lumberjack, Michael," Pam teased.

"I hear women go for that Jeremiah Johnson look. What do you think?" he asked, unable to keep a straight face.

Michael shook hands with Don one last time.

"Don, I owe you everything. If I can figure a way out of this mess, we'll have you and Shirley over for dinner. Thank you and God bless you," he said, and drove off into the Virginia darkness headed for Connecticut.

✠　　✠　　✠

Meanwhile, Matt and his new German friend landed at Kennedy Airport. Matt was also an international fugitive and unfortunately, did not have as many disguises available to him as did Michael. A black man cannot wear a blond wig. But he had lost twenty-five pounds, had grown a full beard and had added some makeup to lighten his skin color. And he topped off his disguise by wearing thick glasses, which rendered him almost blind.

They cleared customs routinely as Matt used a fake passport that his colleague had acquired for him. His new name was James Jackson. They rented a car and headed for Bridgeport.

✠   ✠   ✠

Michael and Pam arrived at his mother's house around one o'clock in the afternoon. Michael found his sweet, white-haired mother sitting on a porch swing drinking a glass of lemonade.

"Look at that, Pam," he said, as they pulled up in front of the house, pointing to his mother. "Doesn't that look like a Norman Rockwell painting?" he said with a laugh.

He brought the car to a halt and hopped out and ran to give his mother a hug.

"Oh, Mom. I'm so glad to see a friendly face. You wouldn't believe what's happened!" he said, as he squeezed her tight.

"I'm glad to see you as always, Son. How do you like my place?"

"It's beautiful, Mom. Let me introduce you to a good friend of mine. This is Pam Connors, Matt Connors' wife. You remember Matt, don't you? Saved my life in Vietnam?" Michael asked.

"Of course, the one who killed Klaus," she said rather undiplomatically, embarrassing both he and Pam.

"Mom, please. We believe that Matt wasn't really involved in that," Michael said.

"Of course," she said, rather unconvincingly. Then catching herself, she said, "Oh, forgive a foolish old woman. I'm dreadfully sorry, Mrs. Connors."

Pam shook her head gently and said, "No problem, Mrs. Madigan."

"Would the two of you like to clean up, Michael?" asked Mrs. Madigan. "There are two spare bedrooms and two extra bathrooms upstairs," she added.

Pam responded quickly to this offer. "I desperately need to clean up," she said.

As Pam climbed the stairs, Michael asked, "Mom, why did you get such a big place? Why do you need so much room?"

"I don't know. I just got tired of feeling so cramped in that darn match box we had. I just woke up one day and decided I wanted to move," she said. A knock at the door startled Michael.

"Would you get that, dear?" Julia asked.

Something seemed wrong. He moved slowly as his mind couldn't seem to make his feet move. With great effort of will, he opened the door.

Within seconds, he was wrestled to the ground and two pistols were pointed into his temple. One of the three men that burst into the house spoke. "Mr. Madigan, we're with the FBI. You're under arrest for kidnapping the president of the United States, with conspiracy to kidnap. You have the right to remain silent. You have the right to an attorney…" The agent went on with the standard Miranda warning but Michael didn't hear it.

He looked at his mother in shock and disbelief. "Mother, how could you?"

She said nothing and stared right through him, displaying no emotion as the agents hauled him away.

Pam heard the noise and the yelling and glanced downstairs to see the guns pointed at Michael's head. How did they know? No one had seen them come into town, no one had followed them, she was sure.

It was Mrs. Madigan! Pam was in danger and didn't have time to think it through. She had only a few seconds.

Pam ran to the window of the guest bedroom and quickly climbed out onto the ledge. She estimated that it was ten feet to the ground and jumped, doing a somersault as she landed. She ran through the backyard, threw herself over a fence and took one last look at the front of the house, where Michael was being shoved into a government car. She ran into a dense section of woods, cut across a small stream, and came out of the trees on another street parallel to Mrs. Madigan's house.

She wondered how it would look for a black woman to be running madly through a mostly-white neighborhood and decided to walk slowly. If the FBI went the same way that she and Michael had come, they would not go down this street. She would walk calmly to the bus station she could see ahead and get on the first bus out of town. The street she was walking on ran along the woods, and if she were spotted she could disappear into the trees within seconds.

Suddenly, a familiar voice rang out and doubled Pam's heart beat. She instinctively started running, much like she had in college at Oklahoma State.

"Pam!" came the desperate voice again and this time she slowed down. She turned around and looked. It was Matt!

She sprinted toward him, running faster than in her track days. Matt hopped out of the car and sprinted towards his wife. They embraced so tightly that Matt was afraid he would squeeze the life out of her, and as he kissed her lips and caressed her back he felt elated.

"Matt, we're in danger. Let's get out of here!" she warned and hopped into the car, slinking to the floor.

"What are you talking about? I'm supposed to meet Michael at his mother's house," Matt protested.

"Change of plans. Let's get the hell out of this place!" she shouted. Matt did what she said, not knowing why but realizing that something was seriously wrong.

Julia Madigan poured herself a glass of brandy and sat down in her favorite easy chair and started to cry. A man entered the room and put his hand on her shoulder.

"Don't cry, Julia, please don't cry. It was necessary," he said. "It will all work out, you'll see."

Michael was still in a trance as the agents took his fingerprints after they arrived at FBI headquarters. This was all a dream. It couldn't really be happening.

"You want to call anyone, Mr. Madigan?" asked an indifferent-looking agent.

"What?" he responded, still dazed.

"I asked if you wanted to call someone. You have the right to a phone call, you know," repeated the agent.

"Yeah, I do." He struggled, trying to focus. He couldn't call Rebecca. He needed an attorney. He hated the sharks but he desperately needed one now.

The officer walked him to the phone and undid the handcuffs. "Don't try anything funny. Remember, there's a gun right here," he said, patting the bulge in his jacket.

Right. He was going to try to storm out of FBI Headquarters. "Don't worry. I'm not going anywhere," Michael replied.

He dialed the numbers. "Hello," said the soft, female voice.

"May I speak to Sterling Shannon, please?" asked Michael.

"He's in the shower. I'm his wife. Can I help you?"

"Linda, this is Michael Madigan."

"Michael, how are you, darling? Oh, sorry. I guess I shouldn't be so informal anymore. How are you, Mr. Vice President?" she asked.

"Not too good right now. I'm in trouble and need to talk to Sterling right away," he said forcefully.

"Let me go get him," she said, and walked away from the phone. Michael could hear the TV in the background and started to tap his foot, a nervous habit he had never been able to break. Finally, Sterling came on the line.

"What's up, Michael? Linda says you're in trouble. What kind of trouble can a vice president get into?" he joked.

"Quite a bit, believe me. I've been arrested for conspiracy and kidnapping the president," he said bluntly.

"Is this some kind of gag, Mike?" said Sterling.

"This isn't a joke, Sterling. I've been booked and am exercising my constitutional right to a phone call."

"What are you talking about? I haven't heard anything about the president being kidnapped," snapped the lawyer.

"Well, he's been gone since Friday night. I don't know anything more except that I'm scared and need you to come down here immediately," Michael whispered.

"I'll be right there, Michael. Don't worry. I'll be there in a few minutes," Shannon said, and hung up the phone.

Michael looked at the agent, John O'Leary. He signaled that he was through and then followed O'Leary. Moments later he found himself in a cramped cell. The prison guard was a black man named Gus Washington.

"Don't expect any special treatment, Mr. Madigan," said the tall, thin guard with a gray beard. "'Cause you won't get any. But because of who you are, we're going to keep you isolated. You call a lawyer?" Washington asked.

Michael nodded and sat down on the edge of the bed.

"I'll let you know when he's here," said the guard.

Michael lay down and stared at the ceiling, which seemed to be slowly going around in circles. Within seconds, he was asleep. Washington came back, waking him.

"Hey, Madigan, your mouthpiece is here," the guard yelled. "Come with me," he said and led Michael down the hallway. They approached the area where the inmates met with their guests, where they would sit at a table, separated by a piece of bulletproof glass.

Michael sat down and glanced at Sterling Shannon through the glass.

"I don't know what to say," Shannon started, awkwardly. "You don't have to tell me but is there any truth to the charges?" he asked.

Michael shot him a look of disgust and said sharply, "Hell, no! It's absolute nonsense! It's a frame-up. Tolbert and I were both kidnapped. I apparently escaped or was let go and they supposedly found papers in my house that implicate me to some conspiracy to assume the presidency."

Sterling was flabbergasted and had no idea how this case would be handled. Questions raced through his mind but he knew one thing. This case would put him in the history books. A trial charging the sitting vice president with kidnapping the president! It was mind-boggling!

Shannon's mind went back to the powers of the office. Michael was still the vice president. He had not been convicted of anything. If Tolbert was unable to discharge his office, then the powers of the presidency would fall upon Michael, who had only been accused of a crime. He would first have to be impeached.

"Michael, this is incredible. I believe that you're the acting president. You've got to be impeached first."

"It's only been done to one president, and I'm not aware of any vice president ever being impeached."

"Nixon?" Michael asked.

"No, he resigned beforehand, remember?" answered Shannon. "It was Andrew Johnson, back in 1868. The House of Representatives drew up the Articles of Impeachment charging him with abusing the office of the presidency. There was a trial in the House and it was presided over by the chief justice."

"Would the impeachment of a vice president be conducted the same way?" Michael asked.

"That's what's so incredible about this, Michael. I would argue that you're not the vice president. You're the acting president so long as the man who was elected, Andrew Tolbert, is unable to carry out his duties. God, Michael, my head hurts just thinking about it. This is virgin territory, legally speaking," Shannon said, standing up and holding his temples.

After Shannon calmed down, he said, "If you're in this jail cell, then somebody must be exercising the powers of the presidency. It must be Volhard!"

"Michael, the fate of the entire country is at stake. If you're innocent, then some nation or organization is behind all this. We can't wait months for a trial. There must be an immediate impeachment in the Congress," Shannon blurted out. "I'll be back later. I've got a lot of work to do," he said as he stood up and hurried toward the door.

Michael remained in his seat, still in a daze, uncertain of the future. He slowly stood up and headed back to his cell.

"There is one other thing, Mike," said Shannon as he rushed back, just as Michael was leaving the room.

"What's that?" Michael asked.

"We can debate the Constitution forever, but the plain fact is that you're in jail right now," Shannon said.

"No wonder you attorneys make so much money. You're so astute," said Michael sarcastically. He looked around at his surroundings and said, "By George, I think you're right. I am in jail!" he added.

"Sorry, Michael, the first thing that has to be done is to get you out of here," said the lawyer.

"And how do we do that?" he inquired.

"We have to find a magistrate to agree to let you out on bail. The way I see it, you would be able to exercise the powers of the presidency even though charged with a crime but you'd have to be physically able to carry out the job. If you're in jail, you can't do the job and it would go to Volhard. Or maybe Chris Watkins. But we have to get you out of this place first," said Shannon.

Michael thought about the lawyer's last statement. "Watkins? Why him?"

"Because the Constitution requires that a president be native-born. Both Volhard and the next in line after him, Marcel LeClair, were born in Europe. The next American after that is the secretary of state," explained the attorney.

"Oh, My God. I never thought of that. Watkins as president?" he said in astonishment, taking a deep breath and then passing it off with a wave of his hand. "Impossible! Listen, go back to that part about bail. Will I be able to get out of this rat hole?" he asked.

"There's no precedent. But I believe that the normal procedures should apply, and that the regular requirements for release on bond should be followed."

"What are those?" Michael asked.

"Mainly, whether you pose a danger to the public based on this charge and your past history and whether you're a flight risk."

"That's it? No problem, Sterling," Michael quickly responded. "I have an exemplary record of service to my country, no criminal record, and I am, for God's sake, the vice president of the United States. As far as a flight risk, I have my family here and my whole life, for that matter. I'm not a wealthy man. I need the money I earn as vice president to support myself and my family. I can't take off for some desert island and live out my life there. And I can't go anywhere in the U.S. because I'm known throughout the country. The way I see it, if those are the only two obstacles, we've got it made," said Michael.

"Would you be willing to surrender your passport?" Sterling asked. "I think that would help convince the magistrate. As you said, I don't think that you could go anywhere in the U.S. and if you give up your passport, that takes care of overseas," he added.

Michael shook his head. "You know, this whole thing just doesn't make any sense. If I really had done all this to assume the presidency and achieve my place in the history books, I'm not going to run away to Tahiti or something. And if I'm innocent, I'm definitely not going to disappear. Sterling, you've got to convince the magistrate to let me out of here," Michael pleaded.

"I'll give it my best, Michael. I don't want to raise your hopes, but I think we have a good shot," said Shannon.

"When can you do it, Sterling? We've got to move quickly."

"Well, it's early on a Sunday. We're going to have to wait until tomorrow. Hopefully, I can get you out first thing in the morning. So hang in there tonight, buddy," Sterling said, trying to reassure him. Then he added, "Have you talked to Rebecca yet?"

Michael didn't answer at first and finally said, "No, Sterling, I haven't. I don't want to go into it now but I can't talk to her."

Sterling looked at him closely and said, "Michael, you could use her help right now."

Michael looked at the floor while responding.

"I sure could use the help of the person I married. But not the person that I'm currently married to," he said, despondently.

Sterling didn't understand but didn't press it.

"You know best, Mike. Listen, I've got a lot of work to do. Hang in there!"

30

"The people must know. Now is the time. I'll address the nation tonight," Volhard said to Phil Gordon. Speech writers were already working on the speech and had been instructed to have a draft ready by 5:00 P.M. Volhard had directed his aides to arrange for the networks to cover a major presidential address at 9:00 P.M. EST.

It was now five minutes after five. Volhard was getting impatient. He stood up and started pacing and finally yelled for his secretary.

"Get Gordon on the line. I want that draft!" he shouted at Arlene Stewart, his secretary of many years.

"Yes, sir, I'll get him right away," answered his dutiful assistant. Within twenty seconds, Volhard was screaming at Gordon. Before he could finish, an aide brought in the draft speech.

"Never mind. It just arrived," said Volhard.

"Mr. Speaker, have you heard about Madigan?" asked Gordon.

Volhard had not actually heard anything but he had been wondering and waiting. "No, what about him?" he asked.

"Well, he's back, so to speak. He claims he escaped but the FBI found a ton of evidence indicating that he planned this whole kidnapping, including his own escape, so that he could return to Washington as a hero and assume the presidency," said the chief of staff.

"Oh, My God," said Volhard, trying to act shocked. "Where is he?" he asked.

"In the tank. He's been arrested for kidnapping and conspiracy. They are interrogating him now." responded Gordon.

"Good Lord! How does this affect my speech?" Volhard shouted.

"Well, I still believe that you're the acting president. I don't think he'll be released and if he's in jail, then he can't carry out the duties of the presidency," explained the chief of staff.

"I want the attorney general himself to argue against him being released," Volhard ordered. "Madigan can't be trusted with the presidency."

"I'll make sure the A.G. is prepared," replied Gordon.

"Good. Now come over to my office and help me prepare for this speech," Volhard said.

Despite the best efforts of the FBI to keep the matter quiet, the arrest of Michael had spread like wildfire. The press was flooding the White House with questions about Michael's arrest.

"God damn reporters," yelled Gordon, to no one in particular. "They're everywhere." He turned to Volhard. "Listen, Mr. Speaker. You're going to have to go on now. It's only 7:00 P.M. here and I know you wanted to wait until the west coast was in prime time but you've got to do it now."

"Have you got the networks set up? Can we do it at seven thirty?" asked Volhard.

"I think so. It was a bitch to get them to give us the air time without telling them exactly what for. They think Tolbert is going on."

"Speaking of which, I want to talk to the other guy before I go on. Get me Governor Walt on the phone, would you? And then I want to talk to the majority and minority leaders of the House and Senate. We only have a short time."

As he went over his speech, he was buzzed at his desk that Anderson was on the line. Volhard picked it up.

"Governor, this is Peter Volhard. How are you?"

"Uh, hello, Mr. Speaker. I was told that the president wanted to talk to me," answered the presidential candidate.

"Well, that's why I'm calling you. I believe that you have the right to know before the rest of the country finds out in a few minutes that we're facing a grave crisis that is perhaps unparalleled in U.S. history," replied Volhard.

"With all due respect, what the hell are you talking about? Where is Andrew Tolbert?" demanded the governor.

"The president and vice president were both kidnapped late Friday night and I took over as acting president."

"What?" the governor screamed. "They were kidnapped? How the hell can the president and vice president be kidnapped?"

"I don't have time right now to fill you in with all the details. Let me just say it was a professional job. And if you think what I've told you so far is hard to believe, hold onto your seat for this."

Anderson was silent.

"It seems Madigan planned the whole kidnapping," Volhard explained. "The FBI found maps, diagrams, and outlines of the plan. It called for him to escape and return a big hero and assume the presidency for a grateful nation. That's exactly what happened. He returned last night, saying that he had 'escaped' but what he didn't plan on was being arrested and charged with kidnapping and conspiracy. He's currently in the slammer and I'm still the acting president. I plan to address the nation in fifteen minutes about this emergency," the acting president advised.

Anderson's head was spinning. It was unbelievable. Madigan had planned all of this? How would this affect the election, which was only weeks away? If Tolbert were still missing and Madigan in jail, would Volhard automatically be the president, or would he become a new candidate? For Christ's sake, he and Volhard were in the same party. Had all of his work the past two years been for naught? he asked himself, getting a sick feeling in his stomach.

He struggled to think. "Nothing like this has ever happened before but Madigan may be released on bail and then he would be the acting president. He just has to get a magistrate to accept a bond and he's out," speculated Anderson.

"Not going to happen, Governor," said Volhard confidently. "He poses a threat to the safety of the entire country if the charges are true," he said.

"That may be but the bond hearing won't address the merits of the case as to guilt or innocence. The only issue is whether he's a threat to the public or a flight risk," said the governor, a former criminal defense lawyer.

"We're going to focus on his being a threat to the public safety and I'm going to have the attorney general himself argue the bail," replied Volhard. "I just thought that I'd make a courtesy call and let you know what's going on. I really must go now, Governor. Take care," Volhard said, as Anderson muttered something that was undecipherable.

Volhard placed four calls to the leaders of Russia, China, England and France and two quick calls to the Senate majority leader and to the House minority leader. He then had makeup applied so that he would not appear haggard like Nixon in the 1960 presidential debates, and reviewed his speech one last time. Finally, it was time, as he gazed into the camera under the bright, hot lights.

"Good evening, my fellow Americans. I am Peter Volhard, the Speaker of the House of Representatives and tonight I am addressing you from the White House due to an emergency situation that may be without comparison in U.S. history," Volhard began earnestly.

"Late Friday night, at approximately ten thirty in the evening, President Tolbert and Vice President Madigan were kidnapped from the L' enfant Plaza Hotel where they were attending a fund-raiser. An emergency situation involving Iraq had been brought to their attention and a quick meeting was held in a conference room in the hotel between the president, the vice president and the secretary of defense. About ten secret service agents surrounded the only door to the room but a kidnapper came into the room through a trap door that connected to a tunnel."

He continued, trying his best to speak slowly and appear presidential.

"At least one kidnapper, and perhaps more, made his way into the room and tranquilizer darts were shot at the president, Mr. Madigan and the secretary of defense. The president and vice president were apparently dragged away through the tunnel and the secretary was rendered unconscious for approximately twenty minutes, until White House Chief of Staff Phil Gordon arrived."

He proceeded, gaining more confidence with each word.

"It was initially suspected but quickly ruled out that Secretary Schmidt had manufactured a false emergency to get the two men into this room. But in fact, there was a very serious crisis overseas. Iraq has deployed its army and has once again invaded Kuwait. As acting president, I have ordered the secretary of defense and the chairman of the joint chiefs of staff to take the appropriate military measures. Units are being deployed to the Persian Gulf," the acting president declared.

"The unprecedented kidnapping of the president is further compounded and rendered even more bizarre by information that has been obtained by the FBI. This evidence clearly implicates vice president Madigan in the kidnapping," Volhard said.

"Documents, photographs and a typewritten outline of the plan were found in Mr. Madigan's living quarters. The scenario described in the documents indicated that Mr. Madigan would somehow escape from his captors, return to Washington battered and bruised, and claim the powers of the presidency. Amazingly, that is exactly what happened," Volhard exclaimed.

"Michael Madigan has been arrested and charged with kidnapping the president and conspiracy to kidnap. He is currently in custody. With the president and vice president unable to carry out their duties, I have assumed the full powers of the presidency," he said firmly.

"As you know, Article One of the Constitution requires that the president be born in the United States. I was born in Germany, but I have been a U.S.

citizen for many years. At an emergency National Security Council meeting early Saturday morning, the Chief Justice of the Supreme Court ruled that I was the acting president," he said somberly.

"Shortly, the full Supreme Court will rule whether I can act as the president even though I was born in Germany. If not, the next person in line after the Speaker of the House is the president pro tem of the Senate, Marcel LeClair, who is also foreign-born. The next person in the line of succession is the secretary of state, Christian Watkins."

"Meanwhile, because we are in an unprecedented crisis," he continued, "I must take the steps necessary for the good of the country. If this entire sequence of events is the result of a plot of one insanely ambitious man, then that will be easily resolved. On the other hand, if this is the work of some broader conspiracy, the United States is in grave danger, until we can identify who is behind it."

"Accordingly, as acting president, I am declaring that martial law be put into effect immediately. This may prove to be unnecessary, but we must assume the worst. It would be reckless on my part to not take the strongest measures possible. Assuming I am confirmed as acting president by the full Supreme Court, I will immediately name a vice president in accordance with the 25th Amendment.

"The United States will take the strongest measures necessary against any hostilities that may be initiated, and I will not hesitate to use the full powers of this office to prevent any harm to this great nation. We must come together, rich and poor, young and old, Republican and Democrat," Volhard insisted. "Together we can survive this crisis. We shall rely not on individual men and women but on the rule of law and, in particular, the Constitution to guide us. God bless you and good night," Volhard said, looking straight at the cameras.

Volhard suddenly found himself alone in the Oval Office as Gordon and his other aides left one by one. He had finally come close to achieving his goal. This was really beyond the most active imaginations of any of the Six. Surely it was Germany's fate to rule the world, and soon.

✠   ✠   ✠

Michael couldn't sleep. He paced almost all night in his cramped cell. Finally, he succumbed to fatigue until he was awakened at 6:30 A.M. by the guard who ordered him to get up and come to breakfast.

After returning from breakfast, he was told that his attorney had arrived. He was led to the visitor's room and sat down at the table to talk to Sterling again.

"How you doing, Mike?" asked Shannon.

"I didn't sleep much but I'll survive, I guess. You ready for today? Are you going to get me out of this place, Sterling?" Michael asked.

"I'm going to try my best. Do you have any rich relatives or any Swiss bank accounts?" asked Sterling.

"What do you mean?" asked Michael. "I don't think so."

"Well, if the magistrate agrees to any bail at all, it might very well be an astronomical amount. If you want to get out, you'd have to post it," replied his lawyer.

"Let me think. I don't have anything and unfortunately, I'm not aware of any rich relatives," Michael responded.

"What about your mom? Didn't she get a hefty life insurance payoff when your father died?" asked Shannon.

Michael stared at his feet for several seconds without answering.

"Sterling, my mother was the one who turned me in," he said, almost in a whisper.

"You must be mistaken," replied Shannon in disbelief. "I've never met her but I've heard that she's a great lady and that you and she were very close," offered Sterling.

"Well, I always thought so but I'm telling you, Sterling, she called the FBI. The fact that she knew that I was wanted tells you something because it wasn't public knowledge yet," he answered.

Shannon shook his head in wonder. "Mike, you've sure been dealt some lousy cards. It's about time that your luck improved. Let's go see the magistrate," Shannon said, trying to sound more upbeat.

"Do you know who it is?" asked the vice president.

"Hector Rodriguez, a law-and-order type with a reputation for following the rules to a T," answered Sterling.

"Is that good or bad?" Michael wondered.

"I'm not sure. If he plays by the book, he should be able to ascertain that you're not a public threat nor a flight risk, particularly if you sacrifice your passport," mused Shannon. "On the other hand, he could be persuaded that the incredible magnitude of the charges, which if true, would potentially make you a tremendous risk to every man, woman and child in the whole country." He paused, then added, "Are you ready to go?"

"As ready as I've ever been. Let's do it," said Michael. Led by a prison guard, he marched off to the U.S. District Court.

Heavily guarded, Michael and Shannon entered the courthouse through a rarely-used back door. The U.S. Attorney's office was the only party, other than the defendant, Michael, who was aware of the hearing.

Escorted into the courtroom, Michael was surprised to see Leonard Silva, the attorney general who took over the position after the assassination of Anthony Peterson. He whispered to Sterling, "Is Silva going to argue the case?"

"I don't think so. I believe that the U.S. Attorney will make the main argument and the A.G. might be allowed to supplement," speculated Shannon. "I'm sure that this is the first time in history a sitting U.S. attorney general has argued at a bail hearing," he added.

The magistrate entered the courtroom and everyone became silent. Rodriguez was a tall, thin man, with dark black hair. The reading glasses that he wore gave him a professorial air. The bailiff came to attention and spoke loudly.

"All rise and face the flag. This court is now in session. The Honorable Hector Rodriguez presiding."

The magistrate spoke firmly into the microphone. He was determined to prevent this from becoming a circus. So far, the press was unaware but he feared there would be a crash through the doors, finding the participants face-to-face with an army of journalists.

"Appearances, gentlemen, please," stated the magistrate.

"Good morning, your Honor. James Salley from the U.S. attorney's office for the prosecution."

"Good morning, your Honor. Leonard Silva, United States attorney general, appearing specially on behalf of the United States."

"Good morning, your Honor. Sterling Shannon appearing on behalf of the defendant, Michael Madigan, vice president of the United States, who is present in court."

"Good morning, gentlemen," answered the magistrate. "I don't suppose that I have to tell you the significance of today's hearing. I'll fully admit that I'm not aware of another case even remotely resembling this one coming before this court. No doubt, one of you will be very displeased with my ruling. But it's my decision and despite the extraordinary circumstances, I have to let the law and my judgment guide me," he said, stopping to take a drink of water.

"I cannot take into consideration the monumental political aspects of this case and the potential international ramifications. I must treat this like a regular kidnapping, no more and no less. This is a bail hearing. I will ask you to refrain from getting into the merits of your respective cases. I want to hear argument concerning the issue of bail. And nothing else," admonished the magistrate.

Good start, thought Shannon to himself. Keep it up.

"Mr. Salley. Please proceed," the magistrate ordered.

"Thank you, your Honor," responded Salley, who aggressively launched into his argument. "Your Honor, what we have here is an unprecedented situation, perhaps in all of recorded history, or at least American history. Notwithstanding your admonishings, I would offer that the political aspects of this case must be addressed."

Continuing, he said, "The evidence that we have shows clearly that Vice President Madigan planned and executed this plan to kidnap the president and assume the office himself. What we don't know at this time is whether this is the work of a single man or part of a greater conspiracy. Whatever the answer is, it would be ludicrous and potentially dangerous to return this man to the position of the acting president," he said passionately.

"Other than the charges here, do you have any indication of past crimes or violent tendencies on the part of the defendant?" asked Rodriguez.

Salley hesitated since he knew that the answer to that was no. Silva, the attorney general, spoke.

"Your Honor, I would like to respond to your last question. Until now, Mr. Madigan has lived what seems to have been an exemplary life. I am sure that his attorney will tell you of his war service, his family, and so on. However, it appears that everything he's done for years has been calculated to achieve, by any means, the office of the presidency. Our request for no bond is not based on his past but rather the future threat. The entire nation and even the whole world may be in grave danger with Mr. Madigan at the helm. I therefore request on behalf of the administration and the people of the United States that he remain in custody and that no bail be set," Silva concluded and then sat down.

"Your Honor," Shannon addressed the court, "we cannot concern ourselves with crazy hypotheses and speculation. Under the Constitution of the United States that Mr. Silva swore to uphold and protect, Mr. Madigan is entitled to due process of law. My esteemed opponents are asking you to ignore the law and imagine certain incredible scenarios," he said, pausing.

"With all due respect this is a bail hearing to determine if the accused is a threat to society or a flight risk. I strongly assert that the answer to both questions is a resounding No. Mr. Silva made short shrift of Mr. Madigan's past and I would like to have the court hear the full story," Shannon expounded.

"He is a West Point graduate and the son of a former U.S. ambassador," the defense attorney began. "He spent twenty years in the army, rising to the rank of colonel, and served with distinction in Vietnam, winning the Purple Heart, the Legion of Merit, and he survived twenty-seven months as a POW under horrific conditions. During his tenure in the service, he served on the National Security Council, as military aide to the national security adviser."

"Further, he has been married for twenty-two years and has three children. He's a loving father and husband and could never leave his family, especially since his daughter requires constant medical supervision," Shannon continued.

"As this court is fully aware, Mr. Madigan is the sitting vice president of the United States, a job he has only had for a very short time. He had no control over Craig Jensen's resignation, and Andrew Tolbert selected him, out of hundreds of potential candidates. Also, a background check was run by the FBI. Your Honor, the man is clean as a whistle and there's absolutely no proof that he poses a threat to society," Sterling said emphatically.

"Secondly, with respect to his being a flight risk, he will voluntarily surrender his passport to the State Department. As far as fleeing to other parts of the U.S., where can he go?" asked Michael's lawyer. "As a result of his position and the incidents he has been involved in, not to mention the press that will flow from this, he is recognized by almost every citizen in America. Where can he go? The answer is nowhere."

"Your Honor, I have been advised that certain members of the House of Representatives are already drafting Articles of Impeachment for Vice President Madigan," Shannon explained. "After that, if he's not been exonerated, a criminal trial will proceed. The system will work as it is supposed to. He, and the United States, will have their day in court. Today, there is but one issue. But before you render your decision, your Honor, I would like to address a concern that's been raised that Vice President Madigan poses a threat to the country. It was recognized many years ago that an irrational president could plunge the world into nuclear holocaust. As a result, certain safeguards were adopted precluding a president from acting unilaterally in engaging a nuclear war."

Shannon continued. "No one man can launch a nuclear missile. It takes a coordinated effort between the president and the secretary of defense. As far as a non-nuclear war, the president is restrained by the War Powers Act. Which brings me to my last point," the attorney passionately stated.

"We are currently involved in a possible war situation with Iraq. It is imperative that there be clear presidential authority. Mr. Volhard is not the unequivocal next-in-line. There exists some doubt under the Constitution because of his heritage and it will require a full hearing of the U.S. Supreme Court, which is currently in recess. Your Honor, I implore you to release Mr. Madigan on a reasonable bail, as he poses no threat to the public safety and is not a flight risk. Thank you," Shannon said respectfully and sat down.

Rodriguez looked at Salley and asked, "Anything further from the United States?"

"No, your Honor, other than to reiterate our request that Mr. Madigan remain in custody and not be released on bail," said the U.S. attorney.

"Mr. Attorney General? Anything further?"

"Not at this time, Your Honor, other than we strongly and urgently ask of you that bail not be granted because of the severe magnitude of the allegations and the potential threat to the national security of the entire United States. Thank you," added Silva.

Rodriguez took a deep breath and looked directly at Michael. "Mr. Madigan has lived an exemplary life, has raised a fine family and has served his country with great distinction." He wiped his glasses and glared at Salley and Silva. "I cannot bear the responsibilities you have attempted to place on my shoulders. I'm a criminal judge and there have been allegations of a crime. It's not my position to save the world."

Rodriguez took a deep breath. "It is my opinion that Mr. Madigan does not pose a threat to the public safety, and it is my judgment that he is not a risk to flee from this jurisdiction. Mr. Shannon, will you see to it that Mr. Madigan turns in his passport?" asked the magistrate.

"Yes, your Honor."

"Very well. Bail shall be set at $500,000. Good day, Gentlemen," Rodriguez said, as he started to rise, but then stopped and looked at Michael. "Mr. Madigan?" he asked.

"Yes, your Honor," Michael responded.

"I hope you realize that you will be watched very closely," the judge said unnecessarily.

"I am fully aware of that, your Honor."

The magistrate nodded his head, adjusted his glasses, and left the courtroom.

Salley turned to Michael and Sterling. "Your victory will be a short one. We will not roll over, rest assured. You'll be impeached and convicted before you know what hit you," he said menacingly.

"We'll see, won't we?" Michael said bitterly as he turned to walk out of the courtroom. Once in the hallway, he turned to his attorney and vigorously shook his hand.

"Great job, Sterling," Michael said. "I was sweating it there for a while. You'll have to explain a few things to a legal ignoramus like me. I know that I don't have to come up with the full half-mil but just how much do I have to cough up?" Michael asked.

"We get a bond at ten percent, or $50,000. Can you scrounge that up?" Sterling asked.

"I don't have money like that laying around but I suppose we could borrow it," Michael said.

"Well, if you can't get all of it right away, I'll lend it to you, Mike," Sterling offered.

"You don't have to do that. You've done enough."

"It's not altruism," the attorney responded bluntly. "You're going to put me in the history books."

"I would pay you back right away," Michael promised.

"Don't worry about it," said Sterling. "From the publicity that I get off of this case, I'll get it back a hundredfold."

"You mentioned that several House members had drafted Articles of Impeachment. Is that true?" asked Michael.

"It's just hearsay but supposedly the Judiciary Committee is already working on it," replied the attorney. "Michael, I don't think that I can really explain just how difficult this will be. Not just for you but for the whole country. Watergate was grammar-school hijinks compared to this," Sterling added, shaking his head.

"Sterling, for whatever it's worth, I'm innocent," Michael said adamantly. "I don't know how that stuff got into my safe. I can only suspect that it was Rebecca. She probably set me up," Michael lamented.

"Michael, I don't know her that well but I would bet my last dying breath that she's not involved," Sterling guessed. "I just can't believe that she's capable. I've seen you together and how much you love each other. That's something that can't be manufactured, not even in Hollywood. The people who set you up are probably the same sleaze that are framing her."

"You might be right," Michael said. "But if she were being framed, that would mean Josh was involved. That's even worse."

"I don't think we can be sure who it is that we're facing," Shannon said. "Let's get you out of here. We'll figure out everything else as we go along."

Michael asked, "if an impeachment trial begins, and I'm out on bail on a felony charge, do you really think that I'll have the powers of the presidency? And will the public, Congress and foreign leaders pay any attention to me?"

"That's what we're going to find out, Michael. Nothing like this has ever happened. One way or the other, you're going into the history books," Sterling repeated as the two men became lost in their thoughts.

☩   ☩   ☩

Volhard pounded his desk in anger at hearing the news of Michael's release from jail. "This wasn't supposed to happen. He was supposed to stay in prison!" he screamed.

Karl Schmidt shrugged his shoulders. They had clearly been taken by surprise.

"But our plan is not over, by any means," added Michael's father-in-law. "An impeachment trial will begin soon. Troops are being moved overseas and the president is missing with an election coming up, not to mention the threat of race riots. Rest assured, the whole country will be paralyzed with confusion. Things are moving quite well in Germany, also."

Volhard nodded and looked at the papers on his desk. "I just received these. They are articles of impeachment that have been drafted for my review," he said.

"I'm not a lawyer but isn't that a little premature?" asked Karl. "Doesn't some damn subcommittee have to meet first?" the secretary of defense asked.

"You're right. That's why I emphasized that these are just draft articles," answered the Speaker. "The House Judiciary Committee will hold hearings to debate whether there's enough evidence to impeach him. It shouldn't take very long to recommend impeachment to the full House."

"When will these hearings take place?"

"Because of the extraordinary situation, they'll commence tomorrow," replied Volhard.

"Will they have all of the evidence?" Karl asked.

"Yes, my friend, they'll have all of the necessary evidence. Don't you worry," Volhard said, smiling and patting him on the back. "Mr. Madigan will not have his job very long."

"I suppose that he'll feel required to address the public," Volhard speculated.

Karl quickly responded. "If he does, it will confuse everyone and work in our favor."

"You're right, as usual. Nobody will know who is the president," Volhard said laughing.

✠　✠　✠

The onslaught of the reporters was unparalleled. Michael groaned as he realized that it would be like this for quite some time. He headed right for the White House and assembled the president's key aides, including Phil Gordon.

He looked at their faces and realized he had a difficult job ahead of him.

"Some of you are not very happy with my being here and all of you look confused. I understand that if I'm guilty of the things they've charged me with, it will all come out soon enough. But if I'm innocent," he said with emphasis, "we've got some real problems." He walked across the room and all eyes followed him.

"You've got to know one thing," Michael said. "I did not kidnap the president. Whether I'm innocent or guilty, however, I'm the acting president and this country is in serious danger. I need a loyal and dedicated staff. There can be no dissension, no doubt. All those who cannot support me one hundred percent, I would like your immediate resignations."

No one moved for what seemed like several minutes. Michael froze as Phil Gordon stood up and spoke.

"Sorry, Mr. Vice President, but I wouldn't be able to support you. I resign," he said and walked out of the room, four mid-level staffers behind him.

Michael surveyed the room for any other defectors.

"Anyone else? Speak now or forever hold your peace." No one moved. He turned to the vice president's chief of staff, Ed Meyer.

"O.K., Ed, you're the new chief. We've got a lot of work to do. I need to address the nation and I need a speech drafted. Secondly, I want a meeting of the NSC set up this afternoon to address the Iraqi situation. Third, I want to prepare for the coming impeachment hearings. I want Sterling Shannon to be my chief counsel. Any questions?" Michael asked.

One of the White House attorneys, who appeared to be irritated by the news of Shannon coming on board, stood up.

"We just received some subpoenas from the District Court directing you to turn over all documents concerning everything you've done since you've been vice president and while in Congress," said the lawyer.

"Can they do that?" asked Michael.

"They sure as hell can," came the immediate response. "Whether you have to comply is another question. The source of the subpoena was the special prosecutor who was just appointed by the attorney general. There's some question as to whether or not the case is justiciable," the lawyer said.

"In English, please?" Michael asked.

"O.K." replied the attorney. "Since the special prosecutor is a member of the Executive branch, what exists is a dispute between a superior and a subordinate member of the same branch of government. This may not be subject to judicial review," said the aide.

Michael was both irritated and intrigued. "What's your name?"

"Peter Delvecchio," answered the young lawyer.

"O.K., Peter. Will that argument fly?" asked Michael.

"Probably not," came the reply. "Nixon tried it during Watergate and the Supreme Court shot him down. There's another argument that you could try," Delvecchio suggested.

"Such as?" asked Michael.

"Everyone's favorite, executive privilege."

Michael slammed his fist onto his desk. "I'm not going to pull a bunch of legal maneuvers. I have nothing to hide. Give them whatever they ask for. I'm clean," he said pointedly. "O.K., folks, we've got a lot of work to do. Let's get to it," Michael directed.

He looked at Ed Meyers and said, "I don't want to look like I'm trying to take over this job so I'm going to work out of my office, not the Oval Office. I'll continue to use my staff but will utilize the talent that already exists. You'll be in charge over here and I want to meet with you several times each day," Michael directed.

"That's fine, sir. But there are a couple of things you should know, sir," said the new chief of staff.

"Such as?" asked Michael.

"You need to be briefed about the 'football' and the codes so that you can respond to a nuclear attack," explained the crew-cutted Meyers. "I know you've got a million things on your mind but as acting president, nothing is more important than the security of this nation. If this thing really is some big conspiracy, then there's a very real possibility that someone is planning an attack."

Michael all of a sudden felt a very large weight on his shoulders. He was responsible for the safety of an entire country. He was also, for the time being, and maybe a very dangerous period, the preeminent leader of the entire world, since the collapse of the USSR.

Michael nodded. "You're absolutely right, Ed. Set up the briefings. Do whatever it takes. I'll set aside a couple of hours today for that. There really is a chance of someone attacking, isn't there?"

"Yes, there is, as long as you're not the one who planned all this," said Meyers with a wink.

This statement disturbed Michael. "Ed, I know you're joking. I know that you believe me. But I suspect there are many who have doubts. And I don't blame them. If other members of the government aren't sure, if the American public has doubts, how am I going to govern?" he said, staring at the wall.

"You've got to make people believe you. Tonight's speech is not just the most important speech you've ever given, it may be the most important in U.S. history. Because you're right. If the people have doubts, than we'll have chaos. I don't mean to put pressure on you," Meyers exclaimed, "but a collapse of the national psyche could be worse than missiles."

Meyers walked across the room. "There's a lot of confusion all across the country. You've got to stop it," he said emphatically.

Michael tapped his fingers. "O.K., O.K. Uh, give me some time to think. Set up the briefings and get the other things going. Give me about half an hour to prepare my remarks," Michael said. Then he added, "I hope I'm strong enough."

"I think you are," the new chief of staff said, adding, "I hope you are." He then left Michael with his thoughts.

Michael walked over to the window and gazed outside at the magnificence of the city. Washington had been laid out so masterfully, he had thought many times. So geometric, so mathematical. His thoughts were interrupted when his secretary walked in.

"I'm sorry, sir, but there's a man on the phone who has been calling all afternoon and he says that he must speak to you. We've not bothered you until now but we decided he seems to have something important to say," explained the nervous secretary, fearing that she had bothered Michael with some trivial matter.

"Well, Margaret, who is it?" asked Michael warmly, trying to ease her anxiety.

"He says that his name is Billy Shears."

"I'll take it," Michael said simply. It was Matt. Billy Shears was a character created by the Beatles on their Sgt. Pepper album. Michael smiled at the mention of the pseudonym. He waited until she left the room.

"Hello," Michael said into the receiver.

"Listen, we can't talk long. Who knows who's listening?" cautioned Matt Connors.

"Where are you?" asked Michael.

"I can't say," said Matt. "We've got to talk but I don't know how we're going to arrange it. You won't be able to take a crap—much less sneak out to meet with a lowlife like me—without the whole press knowing. But we've got to talk."

"Green, what the hell's going on?"

"We can't do it over the phone. Meet me tomorrow night at Brian McMullen's house at about nine o'clock," said Matt.

"Why?" asked Michael.

"As you probably know, he's the chairman of the Judiciary Committee, which is beginning hearings tomorrow to see if there's enough evidence to impeach you," replied Matt.

"I don't think that it would be real appropriate for me to go over to his house," he added.

"Ordinarily, no, it wouldn't. In fact, it would be very inappropriate. But this isn't your ordinary situation, Cube. Tomorrow night. Be there," Matt said and abruptly hung up the phone.

Now he was even more confused. Matt had implied that there was something drastically wrong but wouldn't say what. He didn't like mysteries. His stomach was in knots and his head was pounding. He felt overwhelmed and didn't know who he could trust. Michael stared out the window again and said a prayer to himself.

Ed Meyers returned and the briefings were commenced. Michael was stunned at some of the things that the U.S. government did and was capable of doing. He knew that there would be specific things that would just blow him away and he found out that he had been absolutely right. He kept shaking his head and wondered if he would ever have the peaceful life that he and Rebecca had longed for. For that matter, he wondered if he still had a marriage.

After the briefings were over, he thought about something that Ed had said. He said that they had an isolated view of what was going on, that they were insulated. He was right. What did the average person think about this situation? He couldn't talk to his family and it wasn't appropriate to go on a campaign-style trip. But he had to get an outsider's view. And he needed to hear a friendly voice. He thought of Judy Solomon, whom he had not talked with since she had returned to Los Angeles. He would give her a ring.

The White House had just installed a video telephone and he had heard that Judy had the same thing. Since she would be able to see him, she could read his lips. He had Margaret contact Ed, who immediately showed him where the video phone was.

It looked like a standard phone but had a flip-up video screen. "Without going into all the details, how does this work?" Michael asked Ed.

"Well, they've had these for a while but finally have come up with one that allows full-motion color videos to be transmitted. In a nutshell, there's a coding device that divides the screen into blocks and analyzes each block about ten times per second. The video portion of the signal is compressed and that data is transformed into an audio signal that can be sent over a phone line. At the other end, the coding device decompresses the signal, sort of like adding water back to orange juice. Simple," he explained.

"Simple. Right. Well, let's give it a shot," Michael said, and dialed the number. Seconds later, Judy answered and he beamed when he saw her image.

"Judy, how are you? It's great to see you. Is this thing cool or what?"

"Hello, Colonel," she said smiling. "I'm doing just fine. Darrell is here, too." Darrell appeared on the screen.

"Hi, sir. I bet you have a lot on your mind," Darrell said. "I'm surprised that you found the time to call."

"The whole world is topsy-turvy and I just had to hear a friendly voice," he said. "How's your recovery, Judy?"

"It's coming along pretty well. I'm doing a lot of physical therapy and there's still a lot of discomfort."

This saddened Michael and he again felt the great bond with this young lady. "I also wanted to get a different perspective on these crazy things that have been happening. What's the word on the street, on the campus?"

"You're certainly the hot topic, Colonel," Judy responded. "It's hard to pin down because opinions are so varied. Some people think you're a criminal, others an innocent dupe and some don't know what to think," she said bluntly.

"Colonel, a group has been formed on campus to support you and it's growing larger each day," Darrell added. "By the way, Judy's got some big news. Tell him," he said as his image on Michael's screen disappeared.

"I got a letter today from the person who pushed me off the balcony," Judy said excitedly.

"Seriously? Who was it? What did it say?"

"I figured out that it was a woman and she said that despite the fact that she hates me and had intended for me to die, there was something that she had to talk to me about. She begged me not to call the police until I heard her out and that if I wanted to turn her in at that point, then she would cooperate," Judy explained.

"That's incredible," Michael remarked. "Where are you going to meet her? And are you going to call the police?"

"I'm going to meet her at the downtown public library at noon and I'm not going to call the cops. Darrell will be close behind. I'm scared but very curious."

Michael sighed loudly. "I don't quite know what to make of that. Be careful, Judy. Listen, I have to go. I just wanted to tell you that I think of you a lot. God bless you and keep in touch."

"I will. Good luck. We're behind you all the way," Judy said with a smile as the video image faded.

31

ebecca was practically incoherent. She had herself driven over to Pam Connors', who was also on edge but the picture of calm next to her longtime friend.

"Pam, I don't know what to do," cried Rebecca. "He won't return my calls. I went to visit him in prison and was told that he didn't want to see me. And I tried to see him today at the White House and was told that he was too busy. I haven't talked to him since before the kidnapping. I'm now the First Lady and my husband won't talk to me."

"Rebecca, Michael's been accused of kidnapping the president and Matt's supposedly stirring up racial wars and killing foreign leaders. This can't be!" Pam shouted, and started shaking Rebecca. "Listen to me. This is impossible. I know Michael and he's not capable of these things. You know Matt. He couldn't do what he's been charged with. There's something going on. I don't know what it is but, Becky, it's big and it won't let go. Matt knows, I think. We've just got to have faith. Our husbands are good men," she said, practically pleading.

"I know, Pam, I know. I don't believe for a second that he planned Tolbert's kidnapping, but why won't he talk to me? I'm a nervous wreck wondering why won't he acknowledge me. Why?"

"I think that somebody wants you to think that. Somebody wants him to think that you've turned on him."

Rebecca hadn't thought of this. "That must be it. This is all an illusion that somebody is masterminding. They're trying to frame Matt for a murder, Michael for a kidnapping and me, for what?" she asked in exasperation.

"I don't know but I think that it has something to do with Germany," Pam replied.

"Germany? What does this have to do with Germany?"

"I'm not sure but Matt referred to the Fourth Reich."

"The Fourth Reich?" she said desperately. "My God, that's what my brother Tommy said!"

"What did he say exactly?" Mrs. Connors asked.

Rebecca strained to remember. "He said, God, what did he say? I remember being so startled that it caught me totally unawares. Let's see." She rubbed her forehead and closed her eyes. "He was explaining to me why he had always been so angry at the world. He said it was because of Dad favoring me and Steven as a kid, because of the war and because of the stress of trying to lead the Fourth Reich. I asked him what he meant and he just blew it off."

Pam walked around the room and said nothing for a few minutes. Finally, she began, "Rebecca, I don't want to jump to any conclusions, O.K.? I'm just talking out loud, you understand?"

"Go ahead," Rebecca urged.

"It's crazy and will probably upset you," Pam said.

"I can't get any more upset than I am right now, Pam."

"No, I don't suppose you could," Pam said with a sigh.

"We know Matt and Michael didn't do the things they've been charged with. But it certainly looks that way. Which means that somebody has gone way out of their way to mastermind some giant conspiracy. We think it has to do with Germans. The next person in line after Michael for the presidency is German. The secretary of defense is German, and he took the job after his predecessor had a freak accident," Pam said, looking to see what reaction Rebecca would have to this statement. Seeing none, she continued. "And apparently the guy who led that coup in Russia is German," Pam said.

Rebecca shot up. "Pam, I'll get to this crazy thing about my father in a second. But you're saying that Russian guy is German?" Rebecca asked in disbelief.

"Well, maybe he is. All I know is that there was an article in the paper yesterday about some little old lady in Bremen, Germany, who's ninety-one years old. She claims Nikolai Ligachev is her son, that he was born in Germany and fought in the war against Russia," she explained.

"You're kidding! Did he respond to it?" Rebecca asked.

"No, he didn't. He's dead and there was a press release saying that she's senile," Pam replied.

"O.K., now let's step back for a moment. Are you implying that my father is involved in some crazy, uh, I don't even know what to call it. What are you saying?"

"I'm not saying it's true. I'm just tossing out ideas," Pam said defensively, realizing that she had struck a chord. "It's just that something's wrong here. Your father got Tolbert and Michael into that room with the trap door. And Volhard lobbied very hard for your father to get his present job. His predecessor dies a violent death and Michael gets set up with things in his own house. Who else would have such access?" Pam continued, seeing the look of horror on Rebecca's face.

"Listen, I'm not saying it's true. But I was kidnapped by people with German accents. Matt went to Germany and supposedly ends up killing a German official. What sense does that make? If he really was a black militant who was turning against the white establishment, why would he go to Europe and kill a foreigner? And if that Russian coup guy really was a German, what the hell does that mean?" Pam said with exasperation.

"You tell me. You're the one with the crazy ideas," Rebecca said.

"Becky, all I'm saying is that something bizarre is going on and I don't know what it is. But all the signs seem to point to Germany. Maybe I'm totally off base and maybe your father bleeds red, white and blue. I hope I'm wrong. But we have to check it out."

"O.K., I'll buy that, I suppose. I can't accept some crazy notion that my father and some other Germans are conspiring to, do what? Take over the world? Christ. It hurts my head just to think of such nonsense," Rebecca said.

"It's just a theory. Where did your mom and dad meet?"

"Oh, let's see. I think they met in Chicago," Rebecca answered, straining to remember. "The south side of Chicago, by Lake Michigan. She was a college student and they met at the University of Chicago. She told me many times that she was attracted to him from the very first second they met. She helped him learn English."

"I can't quite put my finger on it, Becky. I know that you think this is some harebrained theory but on the one in a million chance that I'm right..."

"If you're right, which I'm sure you're not," said Rebecca, "I suppose that we're all in trouble."

"Listen, why don't you spend the night here? Michael's speech will be starting pretty soon. Why don't we watch it and then talk?" Pam offered.

A short time later, Pam turned on the TV. All the networks were about to carry Michael's first speech to the nation. Rebecca felt tremendous pride and overwhelming fear.

Pam and Rebecca listened intently as Michael began to give his speech. "He looks very presidential, don't you think?" asked Pam.

"Sh," admonished the quasi-First Lady.

"Good evening, ladies and gentlemen. We have had thrust upon us a situation that is without precedent in American history. I want to try tonight to curb some of your doubts and ask you to join with me in battling a foe more dangerous than any we have ever had for the simple reason that we do not know who it is."

"As most of you know," he continued, "President Tolbert named me his vice president not too very long ago. On Friday evening, the president and I were both kidnapped. I managed to escape but I never did see any of the kidnappers nor do I know where we were taken. Under the Constitution, the vice president assumes the powers of the presidency if the president is incapacitated," Michael explained.

"We are facing tremendous danger. As I'm sure you are all aware, I've been charged with kidnapping the president. I spent last night in jail but was released this morning on bond. There are many who doubt whether I can serve as president."

"The House of Representatives is about to initiate impeachment proceedings tomorrow. I may be facing a criminal trial. There are many who say that because of all of this I should step down for the good of the country. They say that it will be impossible for me to lead the nation, to conduct effectively the business of governing. I understand those who advocate that position," Michael conceded.

"However, I will not quit. I never sought this job but I now have inherited it. I will not let the American people down. I'm here tonight to tell you that the charges with which I have been accused are absurd and ridiculous. To kidnap a president is inconceivable and would take months of planning. I just became the vice president, and was one of many candidates, a couple of weeks ago. Even if I were so inclined, I could not have planned and carried out this incredible sequence of events."

"Nonetheless, I understand how it looks and I will therefore cooperate with any investigations against me. I have nothing to hide and I welcome the intense scrutiny that will come to bear in the coming days."

"In the meantime, however, I will carry out my responsibilities as the acting president."

"Our legal system has for over two centuries been based upon the premise that a man is innocent until proven guilty. I can guarantee you that those who do not trust me will watch me like a hawk. If I am the mad person some claim, I will never get away with it."

"On the other hand, if I'm innocent and this is merely a frame-up, then it's absolutely critical that this nation have clear presidential leadership," he said emphatically. "I've committed this government, along with state and local governments around the country and with nations all over the world, to use every resource available to find Andrew Tolbert. He is the man that you elected and he is the one who should be in this chair."

"For the time being, I will do everything possible to preserve and protect the Constitution and the United States. Thank you and God bless."

Michael's image slowly faded away and was replaced by a network anchor, who began the process of instant analysis.

"That was very good, don't you think?" asked Pam.

"Yes, it was," said Rebecca. "But I still don't know what to think. Try to put yourself in the shoes of the average person. What's he suppose to think? Last night, Peter Volhard comes on and says that he's in charge. And tonight, Michael says he is and that his major goal is to stay out of jail. What's anybody to think?" Rebecca asked desperately.

"I can't answer that, Becky. All that I can say is that you need to get a good night's sleep and attack it head-on tomorrow. Also, maybe you should say a few extra prayers tonight. That couldn't hurt," Pam suggested.

"No, I don't suppose that it would. God's going to have his hands full the next few days. I'll bet a lot of folks are praying tonight," Rebecca mused as Pam showed her to the guest room. Rebecca undressed and got in bed and lay awake for over an hour. Finally, she got up and walked downstairs in the dark, her heart pounding, her hands quivering. She felt totally out of control and headed for the kitchen.

Like a woman possessed, she grabbed the half-gallon carton of chocolate ice cream out of the freezer and stood by the kitchen window looking into the darkness. She tried to stop herself but couldn't as she feverishly ate one spoonful of ice cream after another. Her bulimic past had returned to haunt her.

After eating the entire half-gallon, she felt dizzy, and staggered about the darkened house. What had she done? The feelings of helplessness that had plagued her years ago were back. She began crying as she stumbled across the living room. Finally, she made it to the bathroom and flicked the light switch on. She stared guiltily at herself in the mirror.

She lifted the lid of the toilet up and forced herself to vomit. She shook violently as she threw up. When she finished, she sat on the toilet, her long hair gnarled and sweaty, her face flush.

✠   ✠   ✠

Brian McMullen hadn't gotten any sleep the previous night and it showed. It was now 7:15 A.M. and he was drinking what seemed to be his fiftieth cup of coffee. As the head of the House Judiciary committee, it was his job, and the committee's, to decide if enough evidence existed to conduct a full-scale impeachment trial. He had been a supporter and admirer of Michael's and initially was reluctant to lead this investigation. But his examination of all of the evidence had left him stunned.

It appeared that there was no doubt of Michael's guilt. But yet this very fact disturbed him. How could there be so much evidence? And how could it have been accumulated so quickly?

This affair was much juicier than Watergate. With the advent of GNN and global TV, the whole world would be watching. He would have to be very careful not to let himself or the other members of the committee pander to the camera or use this proceeding as a means of achieving national prominence. This was an unparalleled crisis and they must be objective. Of course, the limelight couldn't hurt, he admitted to himself.

No, the limelight wouldn't hurt. This could possibly set him up to be the next speaker of the house. Of course, it depended on how he handled it. If he botched the job, it could also cause the voters to throw him out.

He didn't plan to call Michael as a witness. They already had enough witnesses. If Michael were guilty, McMullen wondered how he could have been so stupid to leave such a mountain of incriminating evidence.

In a blur of activity, McMullen made the final preparations for the commencement of the proceedings. It would be nationally televised, of course, and he realized that he would soon be a household name. A gifted lawyer, he had graduated from Stanford Law School eighteen years before and had finished the last part of the Bar exam on the same day that Nixon resigned in 1974. He had watched the Watergate proceedings in amazement, along with much of the rest of the country. Watergate, he thought, had proved that the system worked. No man was above the law.

It was now 8:55 A.M. and he left his office in the Rayburn building for the Capitol. The structures were connected by underground tunnels and he climbed into one of the subway cars. There were four 18-passenger electric cars that ran on two tracks. At twenty miles per hour, the trip from the Rayburn building was a mere minute or so. He got out of the car alone and headed for his date with history. Seconds later, McMullen entered the room where the drama would unfold and found a phalanx of reporters. He took his place at the head table, surrounded by more than a dozen of his colleagues. He whispered to a couple of the members and then turned to address the audience and the nation.

"Good morning, ladies and gentlemen. For the record, this committee's responsibility is to determine whether there exists enough evidence to impeach vice president and acting president Michael Madigan. This is not a criminal proceeding nor is it the impeachment trial itself. This is merely an inquiry designed to assist the full House in deciding whether to exercise its constitutional powers to impeach Mr. Madigan," he declared.

He turned his head in both directions to see that everyone was ready to proceed. "This committee is now in session. The first witness, please."

From the back of the room came a tall, lanky man in his mid-thirties, an FBI agent named Jack Schoen. He took his seat at the witness stand looking somewhat nervous. He was not quite sure what to make of testifying before a national audience and his anxiety showed.

McMullen started the questioning, but first administered an oath. "Sir, would you raise your right hand, please? Do you swear to tell the truth, the whole truth and nothing but the truth?" he asked.

"I do," came the witness' reply.

"Please state your name and occupation."

"Jack, uh, that is, John Schoen. I work as an agent for the Federal Bureau of Investigation," he answered.

"How long have you been with the FBI?" McMullen asked.

"Thirteen years."

"Agent Schoen, were you involved in the investigation and arrest of Vice President Madigan regarding the kidnapping of the president?" he asked.

"Yes, sir, I most certainly was."

"Please tell this committee what you discovered."

"Certainly. Late Friday night, I was dispatched to the L' enfant Plaza Hotel. The word was that the president and the vice president had been kidnapped. I arrived at the hotel around midnight and quickly entered the room where the two men had been," answered Schoen.

"What did you find there?" asked McMullen.

"Chaos, sir. There's no other way to describe it. There were about ten secret service men mulling around in absolute shock. They looked as if they had just seen a ghost. I mean, I don't blame them. It was their job to protect the president and he was gone," Schoen explained.

"Who else was present in the room?"

"Mr. Gordon and Secretary Schmidt," he replied.

"You're referring to Phil Gordon, the white house chief of staff and Secretary of Defense Karl Schmidt?" McMullen inquired.

"Yes, sir. Secretary Schmidt was lying on the ground unconscious and Mr. Gordon was, well, yelling and screaming a lot. He was really upset."

"You then discovered the tunnel?" asked the chairman.

"Well, it was clear as day for anyone to see. A couple of secret service men had already gone down into it and followed it to where it ended," answered Schoen.

"Where did it go?"

"I didn't crawl down there myself but I've heard that it went about three hundred yards under the hotel and emptied out into an alley," he explained.

"Did you find anything in the room?" McMullen inquired.

"Yes, sir, I found a wallet that belonged to the vice president," the agent answered.

"Did you find anything in the wallet?" asked McMullen.

"Just a little cash, a few credit cards and driver's license. You know, things like that. And I also found a small piece of paper with some numbers on it," Schoen told the committee.

"Did those numbers mean anything to you?"

"Not at first but then I thought that it looked like a combination to a safe. It was three two-digit numbers."

"What did you do next?" the chairman asked.

"Well, I did the routine things, dust for prints and so on. I also found Mrs. Madigan and asked her if her husband had a safe at home," he said.

"What was her response?"

"She said that he did but that he didn't really keep anything important in it, just some old papers and a small handgun that wasn't loaded," Schoen said.

"Did you go to the vice president's mansion that night?" McMullen asked.

"I sure did. It was about 2:00 A.M. and Mrs. Madigan was still up. I was with my partner, Miles O'Brien. Mrs. Madigan was real cooperative although you could tell that she was real upset. I'm pretty sure that she had been crying. Her eyes were all red and puffy. But she was real calm when we were there," he answered.

"What happened then?"

"I showed Mrs. Madigan the scrap of paper that we had found and asked her if that was her husband's handwriting. She said she wasn't sure. Then she showed us where the safe was. It was in the vice president's study, under the desk. It was a small one, not built into the wall or anything like that. I tried the numbers on the paper and it opened right up," Schoen replied.

"What did you find inside?" asked McMullen.

"I found several maps, diagrams and a three-page typewritten document. And also the gun Mrs. Madigan mentioned, although it was fully loaded," he answered.

"What did the papers you found depict?"

"Well, the first one was a diagram of the hotel and it showed the room where the president, Mr. Madigan and Mr. Schmidt went into," the FBI agent replied. "And it showed the tunnel. Another page showed where a car would be parked in the alley next to where the tunnel ended. And the typewritten documents appeared to be a planned sequence of events for the kidnapping of the president. It said that the vice president would escape from the kidnappers and return to assume the presidency," he answered, as a wave of astonishment enveloped the room.

A couple of other members of the committee asked the FBI agent a few follow-up questions and about 10:30 A.M., the committee finished its questioning and thanked Mr. Schoen for his testimony and excused him.

"Will the next witness come forward?" McMullen stated.

Karl Schmidt walked from the back of the room and seated himself at the witness table.

"Please state your name and occupation."

"Karl Schmidt. I'm the current secretary of defense."

"Mr. Schmidt, direct your attention to Friday night. Where were you that evening?" asked the chairman.

"I was at the theater with my wife, Katarina."

"How did you end up at the hotel that night?"

"We left the theater about half-past ten in the evening and headed home. On our way, I received a call on the car phone from the under secretary of defense, Jarrett Holmes. He was at the Pentagon and he informed me that Iraq was moving its troops. He gave me a quick synopsis of everything he knew about the invasion," explained Schmidt.

"What did you do?"

"We were at that time just a block or two away from the L'enfant and I knew the president was there. I decided to stop and advise him of what was happening. I sent my aide, who told Michael, uh, that is , Mr. Madigan, that I needed to speak to him. I was in a rest room when Michael came in and I told him briefly what was going on," explained Karl.

"What did he say?"

"He said that there was a room down the hall where we could all meet. He said that he was familiar with the layout of the hotel since the father of one of his former aides owned the hotel. They had had a function there once before," Schmidt replied.

"What was your response to this?" asked McMullen.

"It sounded reasonable to me. We needed a quiet place where we could talk for a few minutes. Michael showed me where the room was and he and I went into it. He then directed one of the secret service agents to quietly get the president. We didn't want panic or speculation about what was going on. I just wanted a few minutes with him and then he could make a decision as to whether to return to the White House or not," Karl stated.

"So what happened next?"

"President Tolbert entered the room with two secret service men and asked me what was going on."

"Your response?" asked McMullen.

"First, the vice president asked the secret service agents to leave. He told the president that they were quite safe and the door was the only entrance to the room, which could be guarded from outside in the hall," Karl answered.

"Is that what happened?" the Chairman asked.

"Yes, it is. The two agents left and it was just the three of us. I gave a down-and-dirty summary of the situation with Iraq to the president and he started asking a few questions," he explained.

"Where were you in relation to what would soon be discovered as the tunnel?"

"At first, we were facing towards where the tunnel would be found. Then, the vice president stood up and walked across the room, acting very animated and asking questions about the situation. We turned our heads to follow him and I started to respond to his questions," Karl said.

"What happened next?"

"I remember thinking how impressed I was with Michael's demeanor. Here we were with a real crisis and he was calm and very assertive. More so than the president, actually. I remember thinking how proud I was. Remember, I've known him since he was in college and he's a member of my family. I've always loved him like a son."

"So you're facing towards Mr. Madigan, responding to his questions. Then what happened?" McMullen inquired.

"It happened so fast it's hard to explain. I was talking to the president when all of a sudden he slumped over. He seemed to have been hit with something in the neck. I turned around and saw a man standing with a gun pointed at me. I started to shout but the next thing I knew I was on the floor looking up at Phil Gordon. That's all I can tell you."

"You said this assailant fired at the president first and then at you. Did he fire at Mr. Madigan?" McMullen asked.

"I don't know if he did or not. All I know is that he fired at the president first and then me. It was a tranquilizer dart and I later found out that I was unconscious for about twenty minutes," Karl responded.

A few members of the committee were curious about the timing of the events and asked questions accordingly.

Congressman Gordon Schaffer from New Mexico leaned forward towards his microphone.

"Mr. Secretary, I'm very curious about how you just happened to be in the neighborhood when all of this transpired," sneered the balding, suspicious representative.

"Congressman, I'm not sure that I like your implication. If you're trying to suggest that I planned all of this, that's absolute nonsense. I was at the theater all night. That can be verified. The theater is very near the hotel and an enemy nation that we engaged in war with just last year had commenced an invasion. Now if you think that I somehow started the invasion as an excuse to kidnap the president, you vastly overestimate my power. I find your suggestion very offensive," Karl said, raising his voice.

"Please, sir, I meant no offense. It's just that a plan like this must have been days or even weeks in the making. Had you not come by at that time with news of a crisis, how would the president and vice president have ended up in that room without their aides?" asked Schaffer.

"I can appreciate the question, congressman, but I haven't a clue. All I can tell you is that there existed what I felt was a crisis of international magnitude that needed the president's immediate attention. I can't speculate about what might have been, or the kidnapper's plan. You'll have to ask someone else for that," Schmidt said with a display of irritation.

A few other members asked follow-up questions but it was decided that he didn't know much else about what had happened. After less than an hour, he was excused.

"Next witness, please," directed McMullen.

All heads turned as Nate Wallace approached the witness chair and took his seat.

"Please state your name and occupation."

"My name is Nate Wallace and I'm an agent for the Drug Enforcement Administration."

"Thank you, Mr. Wallace. You were involved in the covert mission to South America that resulted in the capture of Jorge Ramirez, is that right?" asked McMullen.

"That's correct, Congressman," Wallace replied.

"How did that mission come to unfold?"

"Well, Mr. Madigan and I have been friends for twenty years. We served in Vietnam together. I hadn't talked to him in a few years but I of course heard about his election to Congress. I was real proud of him," Wallace stated.

"Please go on," McMullen requested.

"Well, I had been meaning to get in touch with him, but one day he calls me. We exchanged a few pleasantries, you know, how's the wife and kids, stuff like that. Then he starts asking me about Ramirez and if we at the DEA had any information about him or his whereabouts. I told him that I had just received some intelligence about his location and what he was up to," answered Nate.

"What was his response?"

"He asked me if I was aware of that Supreme Court case that allows U.S. authorities to go into foreign countries to snatch criminals and bring them back to stand trial in the U.S. I told him sure, I was familiar with it, and that there was a plan in the works to go after Ramirez," Wallace said.

"Proceed," said McMullen.

"Well, I wondered why he was asking all of these questions. He said that he was still in agony over what had happened to his daughter, Terri Jean, who almost died from a drug overdose. He wanted to go after Ramirez, who, for some reason, Michael held responsible. I said we all did but that it would take some time. He said that he wanted to participate in a such mission and that he wanted it to take place as soon as possible," explained Wallace.

"What was your response?" inquired McMullen.

"I was stunned. I reminded him that he was a member of the House of Representatives and that if the mission failed or if it became exposed, it could cost him his career and embarrass the U.S. government," the DEA man answered.

"And what was his response?"

"He said that he was the best there was at this kind of thing and that it wouldn't fail," Nate explained. "Remember, he was in the Special Forces and he really was one of the very best at this type of mission. He had been in 100 similar situations, many with me, and he was awesome. And secondly, he said that if the mission was exposed, it wouldn't hurt his career. He said that it would actually help because he would be seen as a man of action. He said in particular that the president would be impressed. And he then said how President Tolbert couldn't stand Craig Jensen and would love to get rid of him. I didn't understand what he was talking about. We met a couple of times to talk about the mission and then we actually went ahead and did it. You know what happened."

"What is the current status of Jorge Ramirez?"

"He was in a maximum security cell at the United States penitentiary in Marion, Illinois, but last week he escaped. We have no idea where he presently is," Wallace said, faking disgust.

"How do you explain that?" asked the New Mexico congressman.

"I can't. All I know is that he had a lot of help. That facility he was in is practically impregnable. In fact, this was the first escape from there ever," added Wallace. "Marion is the only level-six super-maximum security facility in the federal system. The inmates are isolated twenty-two hours a day. The place is surrounded with thirteen rolls of razor-sharp barbwire. It's impossible to escape from without inside help," he said, shaking his head.

"Have you arrived at any conclusions from everything that's happened?" asked McMullen.

"Yes, I have," answered Wallace. "I believe that Michael Madigan arranged the whole thing in advance with Ramirez and promised to help spring him from prison to gain publicity that would help him get the job he currently holds," Wallace stated matter-of-factly to the hushed crowd.

A few more questions ensued and Wallace was excused.

The next witness was an unshaven man wearing wrinkled khaki pants and a blue corduroy shirt.

"Please state your name and occupation," asked McMullen.

"My name is Mark Metcalf and I'm a photographer," he replied.

"Do you know Michael Madigan?" asked the Chairman.

"Yes, I do."

"This committee is interested in any information that might shed some light on Mr. Madigan's present situation and the kidnapping of the president," McMullen said impatiently. "Do you have any information in that regard?"

"I don't know anything about the kidnapping or President Tolbert. But I can tell you about how he became the vice president," he said with a wry smile.

McMullen didn't like this man and stared at him coldly.

"I would suspect that Mr. Madigan became vice president after the president offered him the job. Do you have information to the contrary?" he asked with a sneer.

"You're right, of course, but you must remember that President Tolbert already had a vice president. Craig Jensen. If you recall, he unexpectedly resigned."

McMullen looked up and down the committee table at each of the members before proceeding.

"Mr. Jensen cited, I believe, personal reasons. Do you have anything to add to that?"

"Oh, yes, indeed, I do," responded Metcalf with a grin. "He didn't want to resign, you see. He was forced to. He was blackmailed." Metcalf looked around the room and felt an incredible sense of power as every eye in the room was focused on him.

McMullen asked softly, "What do you mean, he was blackmailed? And keep in mind, that this committee is only interested if it has some connection with Mr. Madigan."

"Certainly, Congressman. Mr. Jensen was caught in bed with a woman not his wife and the whole sordid affair was captured on videotape. When presented with the evidence, he agreed to step down," the cameraman explained.

The roar from the gallery and the press was almost deafening. "How do you know this?" inquired the chairman.

"Because, Congressman, I videotaped the whole thing and it was all planned by Michael Madigan," he said to the shocked panel. "He paid a young girl to seduce Mr. Jensen and for me to film it. I needed the money.

I didn't ask any questions about anything. I just did it and realized later that his objective was crystal clear. He wanted Jensen's job."

"Sir," McMullen started, "how can this committee be sure of what you're saying?"

"Because I have proof," he said. He pulled a brown envelope out. "I have the photographs here if any of you would care to take a look." He knew that the committee members were dying to look at the photos but that their every move was being scrutinized by millions on national TV. Each of them shifted uncomfortably in their seats.

McMullen struggled to remain dignified.

"We will perhaps look at them later if there is any doubt as to your veracity. Can you tell this committee who this woman is?"

"Yeah, I suppose. Young blond bombshell named Kelly Atkins. I didn't know this at the time but apparently her father was a white supremacist. Got killed recently."

Several more inquiries were made and finally they concluded their questioning of Metcalf and he was excused. McMullen looked at his watch and grabbed his gavel.

"Ladies and gentlemen, this committee will now break for lunch. It is one o'clock. We will reconvene at two thirty."

McMullen and his colleagues realized that they were moving quickly towards a historic decision. He asked them to remain a few minutes before going their separate ways.

"It's becoming clear to me that we don't have much choice," the Illinois congressman began. "The evidence is overwhelming. We were planning on several witnesses who would testify as to Mr. Madigan's character and past service. But I wonder if that's necessary. We're not here to quarrel with his accomplishments, for they're many. Our only job is to determine if there's enough evidence to try him for impeachment. I think there is. There's one more witness that I would like to hear. I propose we listen to him and then make our decision," the chairman suggested.

Bernard Kendrick, a committee member from Michigan, stepped forward. "I agree with Brian. I thought that these hearings would take at least a few days but I don't see any reason to drag this out. Let's listen to the next witness and if he can corroborate some of these statements that we've heard, then I propose that we draft Articles and recommend a trial. There's too much at stake. We must move quickly."

All heads nodded. Each exchanged knowing glances with the others and slowly walked out of the room. They had mixed emotions about these proceedings, knowing that the exposure would help their careers but that such a trial would almost certainly hurt the country.

Michael watched the hearings from his office and was stunned at the complexity of the frame-up. Nate, his friend of twenty years, was in on this? It couldn't be! And Kelly was nothing but a whore. He felt true hatred towards her but also great sadness because he knew that Joshua had been deeply in love with her.

But he was most distressed that they had been lovers. It didn't really matter, he supposed, because Rebecca was probably out of his life. And it paled in comparison to the things he had been accused of doing. Yet it filled him with a burning rage. He closed his eyes and told himself that it was all an elaborate lie and that the truth would come out eventually. But he had slept with Kelly and nothing would ever change that. God, please forgive me, he prayed.

The committee members slowly took their places and when the last of them were seated, McMullen again called the proceedings to order.

"Good afternoon, ladies and gentlemen. We will now continue with these hearings."

"Will the next witness come forward?"

A short man with close-cropped hair approached the witness table and took his seat.

"Please state your name and occupation," said McMullen.

"Vincent Donnelly. I'm an agent for the Federal Bureau of Investigation," came the man's reply.

"Agent Donnelly," said McMullen "did you to enter the vice president's quarters during your investigation?"

"Yes, sir. After Agent Schoen discovered the safe, my partner, Sara Cooper, and I were dispatched to the vice president's mansion to investigate further," he explained.

"What did you find?" asked McMullen.

"We found an electronic bug that had been placed beneath the bedroom bureau. It was the size of a lump of sugar and was a frequency-modulated transmitter, the kind that consumes about three milliwatts of power and transmits a signal power of one milliwatt to a remote location where conversations can be recorded on magnetic tape," said Donnelly. "And we also found some tapes."

This revelation resulted in gasps from the audience and a couple of committee members became pale.

Congressman Wayne Burroughs from Maine bolted upright in his chair. "Was this a government authorized wiretap?"

"Not to my knowledge, Congressman. It wasn't one of ours and we have no idea who placed it."

Congressman Gerald Cook from Louisiana leaned towards his microphone.

"Mr. Chairman, this isn't a criminal proceeding and we need not adhere to the strict rules of evidence. And there's no accused here that must be afforded the protection of the Constitution. But I have some serious problems if this committee is considering listening to some God-knows-what tape," argued the former defense attorney.

Burroughs responded to his colleague's concern.

"As you said, this is not a criminal proceeding but merely an inquiry. It's our job to view and listen to all of the evidence to determine whether there exists enough to conduct a trial. This wiretap may not be admissible in a formal trial but I want to hear it," said the congressman.

McMullen interrupted. "It's the decision of this committee to listen to all possible evidence, including any wiretaps." Directing his attention back to the agent, he said, "Agent Donnelly, have you listened to the tapes?"

"Yes, sir, I have," was his brief reply.

"If the wiretaps revealed something outside the scope of these proceedings, we're not interested. This committee has no desire, for example, to consider any sexual liaisons or anything of that sort. Now, please tell us if they produced any information that would shed light on our investigation," directed the committee chairman.

"Certainly, Congressman," replied the agent. "One tape reveals a telephone call from Mr. Madigan to vice president Jensen. Mr. Madigan's voice has been analyzed by our best experts and it's their opinion that it's his voice."

The FBI agent had brought a tape recorder and started to play the machine. "One thing, Mr. Chairman. This first tape has a gap. I can't explain it. Whether you can read anything into that, I don't know," he said with a shrug.

"Very well. Proceed," said McMullen.

Donnelly started the machine and fast-forwarded it. "The beginning is just routine conversation between Mr. and Mrs. Madigan. Let me get to the part with Mr. Jensen," he added. "Keep in mind that the bug wasn't actually on the phone and therefore it didn't record the person on the other end. This tape only has Mr. Madigan's voice on it."

After several seconds, he stopped the machine. "Here it is," he said, and pressed the play button.

"Mr. Vice President, we've never met, but I'm Michael Madigan, a new congressman from California."

"Listen, there isn't time to talk about that now. I'm calling about something that is of the utmost importance, unparalleled in American history. You must believe me."

"Of course not. O.K., I'll try to calm down. Listen, what I'm about to tell you is almost incomprehensible but you must believe me. I swear I'm telling you the truth."

"This is where the gap is. It lasts for about a minute," Donnelly said as the tape ran silently. "O.K., this is where it picks up."

"Andrew Tolbert must be killed immediately. Do you hear me? He must be assassinated for the good of the country and the vice president must quickly take over. There is no other solution. That man in the Oval Office, whoever he is, must die, or this country will never survive. Do you understand what I'm saying?"

"If you're not going to do anything, then I'll kill him myself. For the good of the people of the United States, I will kill that impostor in the White House."

Donnelly stopped the tape recorder. "The rest is just more routine conversation. That's the only part we thought was relevant,"

McMullen and the rest of the committee sat in stunned silence. The words on the tape were mind-boggling. Finally, McMullen spoke.

"I propose that we adjourn for today and get Craig Jensen to corroborate this." He picked up a gavel and banged it on the table. "We stand adjourned."

The press corps bolted out of the hearing room in a mad, chaotic sprint. McMullen watched them with contempt but admitted to himself that this could be the biggest news story in American history. Never had he thought that he would be involved in such a bizarre proceeding. If all of this were really true....

McMullen shuffled along in a zombie-like trance and suddenly didn't feel like talking to the press. He had never wanted to exploit the situation for his own political gain but had decided earlier that he might as well use it to his advantage.

But now he couldn't bear to face the microphones, the cameras and the inane questions from the army of reporters. He whispered to Congressman Cook, the vice-chair, and asked him if he would talk to the press.

"Sure, Brian. You don't look so good. Are you O.K.?"

"I don't know, Jerry. I feel like I just went fifteen rounds with a heavyweight champ. I need some peace and quiet and I just can't face those jackals in the press. I'd appreciate it if you'd cover for me," McMullen said.

"You got it. I'll take care of everything. You get some rest. I'll see about contacting Jensen. I had heard he was on vacation on some island in the South Pacific but I'm not sure. See you tomorrow," said Cook, slapping his colleague on the back. This was one assignment that he would gladly handle. He could use a little publicity. With an extra bounce in his step, he strode towards the press to communicate with the masses, as he watched McMullen slide out a back entrance.

ichael sat staring in front of the television in his office. Next to him was Ed Meyers, his new chief of staff. He wanted to believe Michael but it was becoming more and more difficult.

Finally, Michael snapped out of his reverie and responded to Meyers' awkward silence.

"Ed, I wouldn't blame you if you didn't believe me. But I've never in my life spoken to Craig Jensen and especially not about some ridiculous crap like we just heard," he said, his voice cracking.

"Sir, I want to believe you. But that sure sounded like your voice, you have to admit," replied Meyers.

"It certainly did," Michael said, standing up and walking across the room. "That was my voice and yet I never really said those things."

"That would seem to be a contradiction, wouldn't it?"

"No, I think I know what happened," Michael started to explain. "For the last couple of years, I've had these bizarre dreams about Nazi Germany. It's been the weirdest thing. I always meant to go to a doctor but never did."

Meyers looked confused. "What's the connection?"

"I've been told by Rebecca that during these dreams, I often speak out loud, sometimes hysterically and sometimes calmly. That was a recording of a dream of mine. All we have to do is get a hold of Jensen. He'll say it never took place because it never really did," Michael said, smiling for the first time all day.

"But what you said on the tape had nothing to do with Nazi Germany. It was just a threat to kill Andrew Tolbert," stated the puzzled chief of staff.

Michael rubbed his temples. "No, no. There was more to it. Remember the gap? Someone erased part of it. Oh, I'm trying to remember," he said, desperation in his voice.

"That's right," Meyers shouted excitedly. "The gap. Can you remember the rest of the dream?"

Michael paced the room furiously. "It's starting to come back to me. I've had so many bizarre dreams," he said as he rubbed his forehead. "I remember now. I got a call from the President and he summoned me to the White House. I went there and the place was empty. I walked right in and headed towards the Oval Office. I remember just as I was about to walk in, I heard some voices coming out of the President's office. They were all in German and I remember being very surprised so I stood behind the door and listened for a few minutes," he said excitedly, pausing for a moment.

"What happened next?" asked Meyers.

"Let's see. O.K., I took a quick glance into the office and saw Tolbert, Phil Gordon and Chris Watkins. And they were all speaking fluent German. Oh, God, I remember now," Michael said excitedly.

"Go on," Meyers said.

"Tolbert was sitting at his desk when he reaches up with his hand to his face and pulls off a mask. You know, the kind they used to wear on *Mission Impossible*. And he pulls off this mask and it was..."

"Who was it?" demanded Meyers.

"It was Adolf Hitler. I remember running like mad out of the White House, praying that no one would see me. I ran out onto the street and dashed into the nearest phone booth. And I called Craig Jensen. I remember it all. He said that I was crazy. And I said that the President was really Hitler and that he must be stopped. That he must be killed." Michael stopped for a moment. "That part about Hitler was erased. They just kept in the part where I said the President must be killed," he blurted out.

"It did say that the man in the Oval Office, whoever he is, must die," Meyers said, quoting the tape. "I remember that because it didn't make sense. And there was another part where you said that you would kill that impostor in the White House. Impostor! I didn't understand that, either. But now it makes sense. Will Rebecca confirm these dreams?"

Michael suddenly became dejected. "Who knows? For all I know, she's a Nazi. Or someone's trying to make her look like a Nazi. I don't know what to think."

"Is there anyone else who knows about these dreams?"

Michael shook his head. "No, it's not something I was real proud of. I always thought that dreams like this were a sign of mental weakness or some such nonsense. I never told anyone else," he said. Suddenly, he jumped to his feet.

"There is someone else. Damn it, it was that little tramp Kelly," he screamed. "It was all part of a plan from the start. I always thought that she and Josh made a weird couple. She was using him to get to me all along."

"What are you talking about?"

"Ed, when Rebecca and I were divorcing, I took David to Israel. That's when the plane was hijacked. Well, when I came back, I called Josh to come get me and his girlfriend Kelly answered. The Kelly that the photographer was talking about. She said he wasn't home and she ended up meeting me at the airport. I was dead tired and fell asleep in the car. She dropped David off at Rebecca's and drove me home. She said she had left something in the house. You see, Josh and I were living together then," Michael explained.

"Well, she came in and it was about 2:00 A.M., I think," he continued. "I had just been through the ordeal of my life and was exhausted. Just as I'm about to collapse into bed, this young vixen takes all of her clothes off and starts saying some very suggestive things. As tired as I was, Ed, I couldn't resist. I thought my marriage was over," Michael said, trying to justify his actions.

"Hey, you don't have to explain to me. I don't think that I'd be able to resist either," the aide replied.

"Anyway, the next morning, I wake up and see her laying next to me. I panicked. Can you imagine being caught by your son in bed with his girlfriend?" Michael asked.

"So, I try to rush her out of the house before Josh returns and she tells me that I was talking in my sleep. Something about the Nazis. So I told her that I had been having those dreams for sometime. God, how could I have been so stupid?" Michael said, pounding the table.

"When was the first time you met this young lady?"

"Let's see. Uh, I guess it was the time Josh took me skydiving. Of course," he said, balling his hand into a fist and punching the air. "That was the day my parachutes failed. Do you know the odds of having both your main and reserve fail? I knew that it was deliberate sabotage but I couldn't figure out who could have done such a thing or why. Now I know," Michael said in a near whisper.

Meyers stared at Michael for several seconds and looked closely into his eyes. Like Michael, Meyers was a religious man. Meyers believed that he was being told the truth.

"For whatever it's worth, I believe you," the aide said.

"Thanks, Ed. That means a lot. But they're almost certain to recommend impeachment. And I'll have no power. Congress will ignore me, and foreign leaders will want no part of dealing with a possible madman," Michael said sadly. "I know that this is all some elaborate setup, some sinister plot. But I have no idea who's behind it or for what purpose. I don't know if I have the strength to get me through this," Michael lamented.

"Yes, you do, sir, if for no other reason than your faith in God. This nation is in grave danger and needs your strength. I know you can do it," the chief of staff said, patting Michael on the back.

"Thanks for the pep talk, Ed," Michael said, feeling a rise in his confidence. "I'm the acting President. I guess I better start doing the job."

✠   ✠   ✠

Brian McMullen sat in his study staring at the brightly colored fish in his aquarium. He was sipping from a wine glass, his fourth or fifth, he wasn't sure which. He normally didn't drink and usually didn't shout at his wife. But he was not himself this evening. The day's proceedings had drained him mentally, emotionally and physically. So he sat in silence, staring at the fish and drowning himself in alcohol.

McMullen's silence was interrupted by a knock at the door. He looked at the clock on the mantle. It was a few minutes past eight. No reporter would have the nerve to knock on his door. Or could they? He would give them a tongue-lashing like no one had ever heard before. No damn reporter would dare interrupt him at home again.

The congressman walked slowly to the front door and was surprised that he twice stumbled and almost fell. He had not drank to excess in many years and had not realized the alcohol's numbing effect until he tried to stand up. There was no doubt about it, he realized. He was flat drunk.

Tomorrow he would be the dignified statesman but this evening he would allow himself a temporary reprieve from the world's insanity.

McMullen opened the door and at first didn't recognize the caller. "Are you a reporter?" he shrieked. "If you are, get the hell off my porch and leave me alone."

Matt Connors had not been sure what kind of response he would receive from the congressman, but he had never expected to be greeted like this.

Matt cleared his throat. "Excuse me, Congressman. I'm not a reporter. I'm Matt Connors, from the NSC," he said, and then braced himself for the reaction.

McMullen struggled to focus at the fugitive standing in front of him. "Connors?" McMullen shouted, and immediately tried to close the door.

Matt stuck his foot in before the door slammed and pushed his way into the house. "Listen to me, Congressman. I have some very important things to tell you. If you don't believe me, then you can call the police and I'll go quietly. But you must listen to me. Please," he pleaded.

McMullen's wife Marie ran into the room, having heard the disturbance. She recognized Matt and let out a stifled scream. "What do you want? Don't hurt us, please."

Matt shook his head. "I'm not going to hurt you, ma'am. I have to talk to your husband. It's extremely urgent. I swear to you that I'm not guilty of the things they think I am. I told your husband that if after listening to me, he doesn't believe me, then he can call the FBI and I'll go quietly. But please hear me out," Matt begged.

Marie looked at her husband. "What do you think, Brian?" she asked.

"What the hell?" said the drunken congressman. "Let's go into the study."

The three of them walked into the massive room and Matt nervously sat down and started to explain.

"I know that I have a credibility problem. But what I'm about to tell you is the absolute truth," Matt began.

"Before you start," McMullen said, "Why of all the people in the government did you pick me to tell your tale to?"

"Because part of it has to do with Michael Madigan. He's innocent and so am I. We've both been framed as part of a very complex plot designed for Germany to take over the world," Matt said, determined not to sound like a lunatic.

McMullen raised his eyebrow and shook his head. "What in the hell are you talking about? You're the one who killed that German. How do you expect anyone to believe you after you've caused the worst race rioting in this country's history?" snapped the intoxicated and angry congressman.

Matt took a deep breath. "I feel very badly about the riots that have taken place. It's something that disturbs me greatly. But I was forced to say those things. They were going to kill my family. And as much as I love my country, my family comes first. I knew that speech would cause trouble but I couldn't risk losing my wife and kids," Matt pleaded.

Marie suddenly lost the fear she had and extended warmth towards Matt. "Mr. Connors, it's O.K. Please continue."

"Thank you. I'm sorry," Matt continued, "I didn't kill that German leader. He's still alive. It was set up to look like I killed him but I'm telling you the man is not dead."

"What are you saying?" asked McMullen. "The whole world saw you pull the trigger. And they did an autopsy on the body, for God's sake," he added impatiently.

"I swear to you, Congressman. It was all an act. The body that was found was someone else's. Same basic size and shape. If you recall, the body was burned beyond recognition," Matt explained.

"Who do you think you're fooling, Connors?" McMullen responded. "They matched the body through dental records. There's no doubt that was Klaus."

"That may have been Klaus' teeth but it wasn't his body," Matt declared.

"That's impossible," shouted McMullen angrily.

"I'm telling the truth, Matt said.

McMullen remained skeptical. "O.K., let's say that this ridiculous thing is true. How does Germany plan to take over the world?" he asked, somewhat sarcastically.

"After the war, six young German officers pledged themselves to Germany's return to triumph," Matt began the incredible tale which even he had trouble fathoming. "They knew it would take several decades, at least, and were prepared to wait. Two stayed in Germany and the others went to other countries. They've each risen to the highest levels of government and industry in their respective countries. They call themselves the Six, and one is thought by the others to be dead. But he's very much alive and is willing to testify," Matt exclaimed.

"About what?" asked the still cynical McMullen.

"Among other things, that two of the top people in the American government are these former Nazis," Matt replied.

McMullen raised an eyebrow almost imperceptibly. "Who are they?" he asked.

"Peter Volhard and Karl Schmidt, I think."

"You think? What the hell does that mean? Are they Nazis or not?" shrieked the very perturbed congressman.

"I don't mean to be coy but my German friend has been somewhat mysterious about revealing names. All indications seem to point to them, though," Matt answered.

"All indications, huh? You want to accuse two of the most respected members of the U.S. government of being Nazis. Is that what you're saying? You, someone who's started race riots across the country and is an accused murderer. That will work just great," he stated.

"I don't expect you to believe me. But everything that I say will be backed up and then elaborated upon by my new friend. Remember, he's one of the Six," Matt responded.

"Oh, how could I forget?" McMullen declared. "One of the Six? Or should I say the Five, since one of them is presumably out of the picture. So, five German senior citizens are going to take over the world. I hate it when that happens."

Matt knew he wasn't making any inroads with the crusty and drunken congressman.

"This is all that I'm asking. I want to testify, to be followed by my German friend. You can believe us or not but please just give us the chance to testify," Matt pleaded.

"What's the German's name?" McMullen asked.

"His real name is Wolfgang Weber but he's been known for years as Nikolai Ligachev," Matt explained.

"Ligachev? The Russian who led that botched coup? Are you serious? Who the hell's going to believe him?"

Matt knew that it all sounded ridiculous. "Congressman, you've just got to believe me. Please."

"If I do let you testify, I can't let you go," McMullen said, getting to the bottom line. "You're wanted for murder. You'll be taken into custody," he warned.

"I have no problem with that because I'm not guilty. And that will soon be found out," Matt said.

McMullen paused for several seconds and appeared uncertain. Matt noticed the hesitation of the congressman.

"Trust me, you can't lose. I'll either be vindicated or arrested."

McMullen's head was hurting.

"I'll probably get strung up for this but you can testify and so can your Weber or whatever the hell his name is," the congressman said impatiently. "You better not make a fool out of me."

"Don't worry about that," Matt said excitedly. "You probably should have the FBI keep an eye on Volhard and Schmidt because the second they find out that their colleague is ratting on them, they'll disappear."

"Don't tell me how to do my job," replied the drunken congressman, almost falling down.

Marie touched Matt's shoulder and showed him towards the door. As they got out of earshot of her husband, she whispered to Matt.

"For whatever it's worth, Mr. Connors, I believe you," said the silver-haired Marie McMullen. "It's almost inconceivable what you've said about Peter Volhard, though. We've known him and his wife for many, many years and he's always seemed the most perfect gentlemen. But you say this new friend of yours can prove it?"

"I believe so," Matt said, looking at his watch. "Well, I've taken up enough of your time. I'd better be going. Have a pleasant evening, Mrs. McMullen," he added.

"You, too, Mr. Connors. May God be with you," she said as he walked down the steps to his rented car.

Yes, he thought to himself, may God be with me. I could use the extra help, he thought to himself.

Matt had gotten himself and Ligachev a room at a YMCA in a small town in Maryland. He was very tempted to go home but couldn't take the chance. It would just be for one night, the fugitive realized, and tomorrow night, he would either be in a prison cell or would be a national hero. He would have to convince the committee and the American public that he was telling the truth.

He was a bit angry that Michael had not attended the meeting as he had promised. Maybe it had been asking too much. Perhaps it was impossible for him to break away. He didn't dare call him. He'd just wait it out. Tomorrow would be a watershed in American history, he was sure.

Matt returned to his small room about ten o'clock and opened the door quietly, taking care not to awaken his sleeping friend. He undressed and turned out the light and stared out the window for a few minutes, staring up at the stars in the sky. Having gone most of his life without praying, he decided to give it a shot. He surprised himself by getting on his knees and talking to his creator.

"I haven't been the most devoted, or the most worthy person, Lord," he whispered gently. "But I now realize that you do exist. And so, please help me tomorrow because I'm not strong enough," he prayed and then quietly fell asleep.

✠   ✠   ✠

Even though the hour was late, McMullen's staff was busy finishing the final version of the Articles of Impeachment. Gerald Cook, an attorney, had been asked by McMullen to head this particular assignment. Cook had been a freshman legislator during Watergate and he recalled the intense excitement that had hung over the city, despite the fact that the government was being torn apart. And although certain individuals crashed in humiliation, the government itself was raised higher, a victor over those who would dare not follow the law.

"Smitty, take a look at this and tell me what you think," Cook said to his chief aide, Marv Smith, handing him the latest draft. Smith was a tall Georgian with a slow drawl.

"O.K., Mr. boss man, let's see what we have," he said slowly, smiling as he spoke. He realized that the report of the committee was very short and that they had not deliberated all that long. In contrast, he recalled that the Watergate committee had held six days of hearings and had issued a 528-page report. But Watergate was a different animal, with hundreds of offshoots and dozens of players. In this case, one man, it seemed, had acted almost alone.

The Articles read as follows:

The Committee on the Judiciary, to whom was referred the consideration of recommendations concerning the exercise of the constitutional power to impeach Michael Madigan, acting President of the United States, having considered the same, recommends that the House exercise its constitutional power to impeach Michael Madigan, and that articles of impeachment be exhibited to the Senate.

RESOLUTION

Impeaching Michael Madigan, acting President of the United States, of high crimes and misdemeanors, Resolved, That Michael Madigan is impeached for high crimes and misdemeanors and that the following articles of impeachment be exhibited to the Senate....

Smith noted that there was one article for general abuse of presidential powers and one for obstruction of justice. He paused for a second, realizing the impact these pages would have on history and then continued reading.

Article I. In his conduct as vice president of the United States, in violation of his oath to faithfully execute the office and to the best of his ability, preserve, protect and defend the Constitution of the United States, and in violation of his Constitutional duty to take care that the laws be faithfully executed, has prevented and obstructed and impeded the administration of justice, in that:

Smith quickly glanced over the three pages summarizing the alleged kidnapping of Andrew Tolbert and the supposed conspiracy. He was intimately familiar with the facts and yet he broke out in a cold sweat as he reflected upon the accusations. The second article for general abuse of powers was even more blunt in its accusations of serious crimes supposedly committed by Madigan.

Smith looked at his boss. "I guess that will do it, Congressman. It seems a bit weird to call a kidnapping a general abuse of power but I guess it's no worse than calling the MX missile the Peacekeeper or the contras 'freedom fighters,' " he said with a laconic smile.

"Yeah, well, you know how us lawyers are. It's our job to make simple things complicated," Cook said with a laugh.

Smith let out a yawn and tried to stifle it. "On that note, Congressman, I think that I'll hit the road. Morning will be here sooner than you think. Who will be the lead prosecutor for the House?" Smith asked.

Cook responded somewhat dejectedly, and Smith realized that his boss had wanted the job.

"This is the year of the woman, you know," Cook said. "What's her name from Michigan? You know, the former U.S. Attorney?" he asked.

"Gretchen Powers?" asked Smith.

"Yeah, she's the one," said Cook bitterly.

"I've heard a lot of good things about her and she's a pretty darn good lawyer. It's too bad that you didn't get the call but she'll do a great job," he predicted.

"Yeah, I guess," said Cook. "Now go on home and get some rest. Tomorrow's a big day," added the congressman.

✠   ✠   ✠

Matt had been exhausted and slept soundly for almost nine hours. He awoke about 7:00 A.M., stretched his long body and tried to clear the cobwebs in his brain. He quickly panicked when he didn't see Ligachev.

He bolted out of bed and threw on a pair of pants. Oh God, where is he? What if he had had second thoughts about testifying? Nobody would believe Matt's testimony without the German providing backup.

Matt ran out of the room, struggling to button his shirt. His shoes weren't tied and the top button on his pants remained undone. He had to find Ligachev.

Approximately three blocks away from the YMCA, Ligachev walked peacefully through a beautifully-kept city park.

Today would be a day like no other in his life. He had spent forty-five years working towards a singular goal in a manner that had bordered on obsession. The Six had been a family to him and today he would betray them.

Whether it was revenge for the attempted murder or sorrow for his sons or the failure of the coup, he had undergone a complete change of mind. Violence and war were not the ways to change the world. And although he never thought that he would say this, Germans were no better than anyone else.

Suddenly, he was too old to fight anymore and too weak to pretend that Germans were superior. His former colleagues had to be stopped.

He felt something in his back. His heart began pounding and his vision became blurred. His legs collapsed and he hit the ground with a resounding thud, gasping for breath. He clutched his chest and tried in vain to undo his belt. He knew instinctively what was happening and looked up in a clouded daze and saw what appeared to be a tall man with a gun.

"Good morning, Herr Charlemagne," said Gerrhard Meyer, as he pointed a gun at Ligachev's face.

"What do you want?" the trembling man cried out.

"Do not be so distressed. I am here to give you some good news," Meyer said menacingly, but with a smile.

"What good news?"

"Your son Konrad is still alive."

"Konrad? He's alive? Do not lie to me about such a thing. I would rather you kill me," Ligachev gasped.

"I'm not lying," Meyer said innocently. "But..."

"But what?"

"But if you were to do or say anything to hurt us, he would not be alive much longer."

"How do I know you are telling me the truth?"

"Here's Konrad holding yesterday's newspaper. You can see the date," Meyer said, handing him a photograph.

"My son, he's still alive," the old German said, crying.

"Do you want him to stay that way?"

"Please," Ligachev pleaded. "Let me see my son."

Meyer looked with pity at the old man. He had admired him for many years and was unable to carry out what he had been assigned to do.

Meyer grabbed the former Nazi by the shirt, yanked him upright and stuck the gun against his temple. "Listen to me very closely. I was sent to kill you. But I don't want to, although I will if I must. Assure me that you will not speak of the Six and I will spare your life and you will see your son," he promised. "But if you do not convince me, this will be your last minute on earth," he added, pressing the cold steel of the pistol against his cheek.

"I swear, I will not breathe a word," he said. "Let me see Konrad and I'll say nothing," he begged.

"I'll be watching you, old man. Don't be a hero or both you and Konrad will die. Do you understand me?" Meyer warned.

Ligachev tried to respond but was unable to do so. He grabbed his chest again and struggled to reply but everything became black and he lost consciousness.

Within minutes, a crowd had gathered and an ambulance raced towards the scene, as Meyer calmly walked away. Paramedics arrived shortly and began administering CPR to the ailing man, who was placed into the ambulance, which then sped away towards the nearest hospital.

Matt ran as fast as he could up and down the streets for over ten minutes. He suddenly put his hands on his knees and bent over in near exhaustion. He was out of shape, and a man with only one real leg could run only so fast.

As he fought to regain his breath, he told himself that Ligachev would be back in time. The old man wouldn't let him down. He just couldn't. Matt suddenly pictured himself being dissected by aggressive House lawyers and laughed at by millions of people. It looked like he was right all along. There really is no God.

Matt's heart was racing wildly, his mind much faster. "Calm down, Connors," he said out loud.

Ligachev had made it clear that he wanted to testify and stop his former colleagues before World War III started. He wanted to avenge his sons' deaths. Perhaps he was now returning to the hotel room after a brisk morning walk. He raced back to the YMCA, hoping that the German had returned.

It was now 8:15 A.M., as Matt sat on his bed in the small, cramped room. He would have to leave within the next few minutes. If Ligachev didn't show up, should he testify? Matt looked outside a couple of last times for the former Soviet leader before getting into his rental car and heading for Capitol Hill. Brian McMullen had given him a pass for House staffers to insure that he would be able to get in. The beard that he had grown, he hoped, would allow him to slip in unnoticed.

$\mathfrak{I}$n the giant planning room of the Six's German-based headquarters, Wilhelm and Frederick were finishing up last minute plans with General Steigrich and Tommy Schmidt.

It was 2:55 P.M. and they had gathered to discuss the final parts of their mission, and to watch, via GNN, the impeachment hearings of Michael Madigan.

"Today, I'm certain," said Wilhelm, "that Madigan will be formally impeached and a trial will commence immediately. He'll be removed from office and for a short period Rommel will be the acting president. Then we'll carry out our plans," he said with relish.

Steigrich was eager to commence the fight. "Just tell me when and my troops will be ready. They're not many but are certainly the best soldiers in the world. They're tough, well trained and highly motivated. They're prepared to die for Germany," he said excitedly.

Frederick tried not to become too excited. He looked at Tommy, who seemed withdrawn. He walked over to where Tommy was sitting and placed a hand on his shoulder.

"Thomas, you're uncharacteristically quiet. We're so close to realizing our dreams. While Wilhelm and I will initially rule the new Germany, we're old men whose days are numbered. We'll look to the future, to you and others like you. And yet you seem unsure, hesitant. Speak what's on your mind."

"I'm just tired," the younger Schmidt explained. "We've struggled for so long. I haven't fought as many years as you but still I've devoted half of my life to the cause. I'm proud to play a role in Germany's return to power," Tommy said, trying to display enthusiasm.

Wilhelm interjected. "Quiet, everyone. Let's take our seats. It's truly amazing that the whole world can watch such events, is it not?" he said with a smile. "Let's watch Thomas' brother-in-law twist in the wind as his own government prepares to hang him," Wilhelm whispered, taking his seat to watch the drama unfold.

✠   ✠   ✠

McMullen brought his gavel to a crash three times on the committee table. "This Committee does not wish to make a hurried recommendation without contemplation and debate. The ramifications to the United States and to the world are too great but we have come to a decision. However, before we render it, in the interests of justice, the committee will call one additional witness," explained McMullen.

McMullen paused and looked around the room. He saw someone staring at the ground that looked like Matt but he couldn't be sure. If it wasn't him, it would just be too bad. His whole story was probably a farce anyway. If Matt didn't appear, it would save him the embarrassment.

McMullen's voice rang loudly through the hearing room. "Will the next witness come forward, please?"

The other committee members were under the belief that there would be no more witnesses and were caught off guard by this action by the chairman. Burroughs tried to catch McMullen's eye but to no avail. Burroughs looked at Cook and shrugged his shoulders.

Matt slowly approached the witness table. Matt took his seat. Cook sat next to McMullen and whispered to him.

"Brian, who the hell is this?" he said.

McMullen spoke loudly into his microphone as the whole room listened in silence. "Please state your name and occupation," he directed the witness.

"Matthew Connors, deputy national security adviser."

A wave of astonishment reverberated throughout the hearing room. Burroughs shot to his feet.

"Mr. Chairman, I strongly protest allowing this man to address this committee. He's wanted for murder and has incited race riots throughout the country. This is a travesty!" screamed Burroughs. "I would direct the sergeant at arms to place this man under arrest immediately," he shouted, banging his fist on the table.

McMullen restored order.

"Mr. Connors will be turned over to the authorities. We're all aware of the crimes he has been accused of. But he'll testify first. Is that clear?" McMullen firmly said.

"Mr. Connors, do you have any personal knowledge about the charges that have been made against Mr. Madigan?"

"Yes, Mr. Chairman, I certainly do," Matt said. "Vice President Madigan is innocent. He's been framed just as I've been set up. Michael Madigan didn't kidnap Andrew Tolbert and I didn't kill Felix Klaus. Mr. Klaus is still alive today," Matt testified firmly.

A buzz of disapproval rang throughout the room. Congressman Burroughs again shouted out, ignoring the protocol of obtaining permission from the Chair.

"How do you expect this committee to believe anything that you say, Mr. Connors? You encouraged riots and you want us to listen to you?" shouted the angry congressman.

"I did give that speech," Matt admitted. "But I was being tortured and my wife and son had been kidnapped as well. I painfully regret the speech but my family's lives were at stake," said the defiant Connors.

McMullen tried to get back on track. He didn't want this to be a trial of Connors. That would come later.

"Mr. Connors, please tell this committee how it is that you believe Vice President Madigan was framed."

Matt sighed before responding, looking nervously around the room for Ligachev. He was afraid that no one would believe him without corroborating testimony from one of the Six. But he could not turn back now. He decided to tell what he knew.

"Vice President Madigan was framed by a group of former German SS soldiers whose goal is to conquer the world."

"Would you please elaborate?" asked McMullen.

"After World War II, a group of young SS officers met together and swore to dedicate their lives to returning Germany to power. They realized that Germany had been soundly defeated and so they split up and headed off in different directions, including two to the United States, but with the same goal," Matt said.

"How did they expect to carry out this plan?" asked a skeptical McMullen.

"At first, there was no specific plan except for each of them to reach high-levels of government and business, to ascend to positions of power and authority in each of four countries. No specific plans were made until the last few years when several of them reached the highest posts within their respective governments," Matt said emphatically.

Congressman Cook interjected. "Could you tell us, sir, who the American Germans are, if that's the best way to phrase it?" he said with some sarcasm.

Matt had been dreading this question because while he knew the answer, he didn't have any details. Once he responded with the names, he knew that a huge furor would result and that he would be crucified if he was unable to answer the follow-up questions. He looked around one last time for the elderly German before responding.

"The Germans that came to America are Peter Volhard and Karl Schmidt," Matt said softly.

A loud roar reverberated through the room and the committee members looked at each other in astonishment.

Burroughs jumped to his feet. "Mr. Connors, I certainly hope that you can substantiate these very serious charges."

"I can," he said, trying his best to appear confident. "I have befriended one of the original members of the group and he has stated his willingness to testify and to do everything in his power to stop his colleagues. His two sons were killed by his comrades when they discovered the true nature of the group and were not willing to go along. This, combined with serious health problems, has made him change his mind. He has told me that he no longer wishes to be a part of a group that will cause a third world war," Matt said.

"This is complete hearsay," shouted attorney Cook. "Where is this mysterious German?"

Matt fidgeted in his seat. "He was supposed to be here this morning. I anticipate his arrival any moment," he said with feigned confidence.

"What is his name?" inquired McMullen.

"His real name is Wolfgang Weber although he changed his name when he went to the Soviet Union, where he became a general. He has gone by the name of Nikolai Ligachev for the last forty-odd years," Matt said cautiously.

"Ligachev," shouted Burroughs, his face red. "Do you mean to tell us that your corroborating witness is that lunatic who led that fiasco in Russia? For God's sake!"

"Congressman, it was all part of their plan to acquire power in several different countries. Unfortunately for them, the coup in Russia failed," Matt said, struggling to sound confident.

"I see," responded McMullen. "Why don't you tell us a little more about the Americans involved in this group and how they relate to Vice President Madigan?" he asked.

"Peter Volhard's code name is Rommel and Schmidt's is Bismarck. You see, they all have code names." He continued, "They both came to the United States, shortly after the war. I've been told that their real names are something different, that they assumed new identities upon arriving here and totally immersed themselves in their American lives. Because of their Nazi beliefs, they, of course, do not approve of Jews and blacks and have been very involved in the Ku Klux Klan and a group called the Knights of the White Camelia," Matt boldly stated.

"The Knights of the White Camelia?" asked a bewildered McMullen. "What exactly is that?" he asked angrily.

"It originally was a group formed shortly after the Civil War dedicated to stopping former slaves from assuming full rights as American citizens. It was eclipsed in influence by the Ku Klux Klan and for the most part became a mere footnote in American history. But they were intrigued by the group's history and have attempted to apply its purpose to their objectives of making Germany a racially pure nation, superior to all others," Matt replied.

"Do you mean to tell us," shouted Congressman Cook," that the man who may very well be the acting president, as a result of these proceedings, Speaker Volhard, is actually a Nazi who has been a closet member of the KKK and God knows what else?" yelled the incredulous congressman.

"Yes," said Matt confidently.

McMullen shook his head in disbelief. "Mr. Connors, I'm having a very difficult time believing any of this. I've known Peter Volhard personally for twenty-five years and have always found him to be an outstanding American, dedicated to public service," answered the congressman.

"Please tell us how this alleged conspiracy to conquer the world is to occur and specifically, how Vice President Madigan is involved," he instructed.

Matt was sweating heavily now. Nobody was believing a word he was saying. But he had no choice other than to press on with charges he could not substantiate.

"As I said, there was no specific plan at first other than to assume positions of power, which all members of the group did. One of them was head of Black Operations of the International Commerce Bank until it was shut down. His code name is Krupp and he is the group's expert in guerilla warfare and terrorism. I've already mentioned Volhard and Schmidt. Felix Klaus is another member, as well as the man who is scheduled to be here today, Mr. Ligachev," explained Matt.

"By my count, that's five, Mr. Connors," said McMullen. "Who is the other one?"

Matt was sinking. "I don't know, Congressman. I do know that the original plan was to foment hostilities between the Soviet Union and the United States and possibly even cause a war. Additionally, the plan called for causing distractions in the two countries by advocating violence and inciting riots between the various races and ethnic groups. When I was forced to give that speech, I didn't really understand what they were trying to do," Matt exclaimed. "But the whole plan is to conquer by division. Every day we hear about new countries being formed and the coming year will bring more. Germany is the only country that is consolidating, growing stronger," Matt replied forcefully.

McMullen was becoming more and more agitated, as were his fellow committee members, who could not believe what they were hearing.

"I will ask you again, Mr. Connors, what this has to do with Mr. Madigan?" he demanded.

"Well, after the collapse of the Soviet Union and the apparent death of Mr. Ligachev, the plan's emphasis was shifted to America," Matt spoke gamely. "At first, because of his Jewish heritage, Mr. Schmidt despised Michael Madigan and did not approve of his marriage to his daughter. When he was first elected to congress, certain efforts were made to dispose of him. In a skydiving incident, his parachute was sabotaged. Before that, his father was killed," Matt explained.

"So, his own father-in-law was trying to kill him?" asked a doubting Burroughs.

"That's correct. It wasn't until the hijacking incident, when Mr. Madigan achieved hero status among the American public did they decide to use him to their advantage," Matt replied.

"What do you mean?" asked McMullen.

"I mean that once they saw how popular he had become and since Craig Jensen was viewed as a great disappointment, the goal then became to get Michael the vice presidency," Matt responded.

"Why specifically the vice presidency?" inquired McMullen, suddenly more interested.

"They knew that the presidency wasn't possible. What they wanted was access to the president. Simultaneously, they pursued for Mr. Schmidt the secretary of defense position. His predecessor, General Swanson, was deliberately murdered. His car was sabotaged. Peter Volhard then lobbied the president very hard to name Mr. Schmidt as the successor," Matt answered.

Again, a roar spread across the room. It was now lunchtime but no one was about to call a break. McMullen continued the questioning.

"Why the secretary of defense?" he asked.

"Well, first of all, since he had no political experience, it was the only position that, as a weapons manufacturer and businessman, he had any background justifying a cabinet position. The secretary of defense is also a participant, along with the president, in the launching of nuclear weapons. There is a complicated series of codes that must be inputted to launch a strike," Matt explained. "It was thought that by having Michael as the VP, a situation could be arranged where a kidnapping would be possible. And that's exactly what happened," he added.

"Why not just kill the president and the vice president then?" asked McMullen. "And what about Madigan's escape?"

"Remember, what they wanted most were distractions," Matt said, gaining momentum. "They felt that if they let Madigan escape and make it look like he had planned it all, the country would be so confused that it would make their job easier. Now was the perfect time to execute their mission because of the election, which serves as another distraction. The Iraqi invasion was influenced by this group also. Again, the goal was to disrupt, as was the goal of the race riots," Matt explained, as he gained more and more confidence.

"But we've seen a considerable amount of evidence seemingly implicating Mr. Madigan," protested Burroughs. "How do you explain that?" he asked.

"A dual objective came about. They wanted to expedite Madigan's political career and at the same time, frame him at some point in the future," Matt proclaimed. "For example, the mission to Peru was all set up by the group. Ramirez was paid handsomely to participate in exchange for being sprung later, which is exactly what happened. This mission helped Madigan be offered his current position by the president, and at the same time this very matter is being used against him to destroy him."

"How about the girl who supposedly seduced Jensen at Madigan's request, and also, what about the tape with his saying that the president should be killed?" asked McMullen.

"That girl is a member of the group. You see, besides the six main members, there are dozens of other younger participants. All of the original six are about seventy years old and do not have much more time. So they've recruited young people to help carry out their mission. She is a German American with a neo-Nazi past," Matt explained. "She first became friendly with Madigan's son and then, seduced Craig Jensen. Madigan had nothing to do with it."

McMullen seemed at a loss for words. Never in his wildest imagination did he anticipate the bizarre and incredible testimony that he and millions around the world were hearing. Had he known that Matt was going to testify in this fashion, he would have conducted the questioning in secret, not on national television. If what was being said was even close to being the truth...

McMullen whispered into the ear of his two colleagues on either side of him. He then picked his gavel up and slammed it hard on the table.

"This committee will recess until two o'clock."

This whole thing was out of control, McMullen thought to himself. As Matt stood up from the witness table, he was approached by two FBI agents, who quickly advised him of his rights, and handcuffed him.

McMullen saw their confusion. "Bring him in the back room. I think we need to question Mr. Connors a little bit more," said the chairman forcefully, although he really didn't have a clue as to what to do next.

The committee members adjourned to the back room and huddled around the handcuffed Connors.

"I don't know what to think, to tell you the truth, Mr. Connors. I tend to think that you have been feeding us 100 percent bullshit. But," McMullen said, "if you are telling the truth, we have a serious problem."

"Dennis, please get Mr. Volhard on the phone. Secretary Schmidt, too. ASAP," he ordered his chief assistant, Dennis Haley.

"Right away," was the immediate reply.

McMullen shook his head. "Why didn't one of you guys stop me? Jesus Christ, if what he's saying is true, this country is probably in a panic right now. If he's making this all up, we all look like horses' asses. I'm sure that people are asking right now, who the hell is running this country?" McMullen said to no one in particular.

"If distraction was what they wanted, that's exactly what they got," McMullen continued. "This country doesn't know whether it's coming or going. The acting president is being impeached, but is also being exonerated by someone who is wanted for murder who blames everything on the next guy in line, a closet Nazi who wants to conquer the world. And the one person who can supposedly confirm all of this can't be found," he said in exasperation. "I've got one hell of a headache."

"Brian, you're not the only one who has known Peter Volhard for a long time," interjected Cook. "My wife and I have been close friends for over twenty years. I refuse to believe this nonsense. This is coming from someone who we all saw kill a foreign leader and someone who admits to having incited race riots. He gives us some ridiculous story about Knights of the White, what was it, Camelia? And dreams about Nazis and a bunch of senior citizen former SS guys who are going to take over the world," he said, with clear contempt. "Unless this alleged German steps forward, I say we throw Mr. Connors' ass in jail and do what we intended to do today—recommend that Mr. Madigan be impeached," he added.

The other committee members felt the same as Cook, except for one. The only black on the committee, Ronald Johnson from New York, spoke up in defense of Matt.

"I have to admit that for the most part what Mr. Connors has been telling us seems to be some deranged fantasy," said Johnson, a former district attorney. "Now, I don't want to make this a case of race, siding with him because he's black. But I'm telling you that I know this man and I can't believe he's lying," he said passionately.

Johnson stood up and walked around the room, excitedly waving his hands.

"I refuse to believe that he was acting all of these years. Or that he would throw away his lifelong philosophy that knowledge and hard work were the keys to success. No matter how it looks, I feel that this man is incapable of acting in a manner that would jeopardize the hard-fought accomplishments of tens of thousands of blacks," he said emphatically.

Matt smiled at Johnson. "Thanks, Ron," he said.

Johnson continued. "I don't know anything about these alleged Nazis or about Michael Madigan. I want you to know that my professional opinion as a government representative is that this is all a little too bizarre for me. But as a black man, I feel that it's impossible for Mr. Connors to act so destructively towards blacks. If he's discredited, it will set the black movement back years," he said, pounding his fist on the table.

"I don't know about that," McMullen answered. "But it's all just too mind-boggling," he added.

Burroughs spoke up. "We don't know what the truth is. But we have to err on the side of caution. Mr. Connors is wanted for serious charges that have been brought against him and must be taken into custody. On the other hand, if he's speaking the truth, then this country is in severe danger. Volhard and Schmidt have to respond immediately," he said.

Haley ran back into the room and headed towards a television that was on a shelf.

"Volhard is giving a press conference right now about Connors' charges," he said as he turned on the television.

All of the committee members and Matt watched intently as the image cleared and they saw Volhard beginning the press conference with a statement.

"Ladies and gentlemen, I would like to address the ridiculous comments of Mr. Connors this morning," Volhard started. "Never in my life have I heard such nonsense. The only thing that he said that has a grain of truth to it is that Mr. Schmidt and I were originally born in Germany. And that's it."

He quickly answered a couple of questions and looked irritated when asked if he ever served in the SS. He shook his head in disgust.

"You can look it up. Neither Peter Volhard nor Karl Schmidt ever served in the SS. Actually, neither of us ever served in the army for that matter. To say that we are former Nazis bent on takeover of the world is absolutely preposterous and slanderous. All I can say is that you have to consider the source. This is a man wanted for murder. I find it abhorrent that he was allowed to testify in the first place!"

"What about the claim that there's a man who will testify substantiating everything Mr. Connors said?" asked a reporter with one of the networks.

"Where is he? No such person will appear because no such person exists," replied Volhard.

McMullen and Burroughs looked at each other puzzled. Maybe it had been a mistake to let Connors testify, especially without the mysterious German to verify his testimony. "Hey, Brian, don't worry. What did you expect Volhard to do? Verify it himself? I think that Connors is telling the truth," said the congressman.

"So do I," McMullen concurred. "But we need more than a gut feeling, more than intuition. We need hard evidence or that damn German that he keeps referring to," he said.

"So now what?" asked Cook.

McMullen shrugged his shoulders and spoke with some reservation. "There's nothing else we can do. We need to let the FBI do their thing and check out these wild accusations of Connors. But in the meantime, we have to do our job. I can't see any way around it. We have to recommend impeachment," he said with resignation.

"I agree," said Burroughs. "Reluctantly, but I agree. Maybe there's something to these charges of Connors. Who knows? But our job seems quite clear. Impeachment. There's no other choice."

McMullen looked at Matt, who was sitting on the other side of the room, in handcuffs. He had seen Pam in the gallery and having once had much respect for the deputy national security adviser, he decided on extending one last courtesy.

"Mr. Connors, listen up," McMullen started. "I want to believe you, I really do. And I'm sure that the FBI will look into your accusations in their normal exhaustive manner. But we have a job to do here, and without substantiation from your German friend there's really not much choice. We're going to reconvene in a little bit and will advise the House to impeach Mr. Madigan. Also, you'll be turned over to the proper authorities," explained McMullen. "You may speak to your wife before you go."

Matt smiled a sad smile. "Thanks, Congressman. I appreciate you letting me testify and saying that you don't think I'm crazy. I swear to you that what I've said is the truth," Matt said, as he walked slowly out of the room with two armed escorts.

One of the FBI agents sought out Pam and brought her to a room where they were allowed to talk. Not alone, however, and the presence of the guards made both very nervous.

"I love you, babe," said Matt in a near whisper.

"Me, too, darling. I can't stand to see what they're doing to you. You're trying to save this country and they treat you like some kind of lunatic," Pam replied, trying desperately to hold back the tears.

"Listen, Matt, I've been talking a lot to Rebecca. I don't know if you know, but Michael won't talk to her. And she doesn't know why. But we think that the Germans are behind it," said Pam in a low voice. "Her brother Tommy told her recently something about the Fourth Reich, just like you mentioned. It really spooked her. She thinks that he has something to do with it and since it looks like Michael won't talk to her and it looks like you're going..." She couldn't finish the sentence, and started crying.

"It looks like I'm going to jail," Matt said. "Listen, it's not exactly what I want to do but it won't destroy me. I know in my heart that I'm not guilty. What about Germany?" Matt asked.

Pam tried to put on a brave front. "Rebecca and I plan on going to Germany. I don't know if we can stop them, but we can try."

"You two can do anything once you put your minds together. I'll support whatever you do. All that I ask is that you be careful, babe. I might be in here for a while and someone has to take care of the kids. They need their mamma, you know," he said.

"They need their daddy, too," Pam responded. She saw the FBI agents signal that it was time. "I love you, Matt. With all of my heart," she said, brushing back the tears.

"I love you, too, babe. May God bless and keep you," Matt said.

The agents escorted Matt out of the room and left the building to formally book him. He stared out of the window of the car as it sped away, wondering if it was too late.

✠   ✠   ✠

Pam raced off to the vice presidential mansion and found Rebecca packing. She was shown to Rebecca's bedroom and the two old friends hugged each other.

"I'm in," said Pam. "This is probably something I'll really regret later but count me in."

Rebecca smiled. "Thanks, Pam. Just knowing that you'll be with me makes me a whole lot braver. Maybe we'll be wasting our time. But I've got to try. I'm just spinning my wheels here. Michael won't talk to me and Matt's in custody. And my brother who I've hardly seen for twenty years tells me that he's tired of being a part of the Fourth Reich. I don't know what to think or who to believe but I've got to try. Thanks for supporting me," she said.

"I know you've only been the vice president's wife for a short time but even so, won't it be impossible for you to get away?" Pam asked.

"That's why we're going to leave late at night, Pamela. Why don't you go home and meet me here at ten thirty tonight. O.K?" said Rebecca, giving Pam a hug.

"O.K., Becky, I'll be here. I'm sure I'll need some serious psychoanalysis when I return but I'll be here," said Pam.

Upon returning, Pam laughed out loud when she saw Rebecca. She was wearing a wig and some very loose-fitting clothes, concealing her figure. Rebecca spoke in a rather defensive manner.

"Come on, now. We can't let anyone know who we are. I had to go to considerable lengths to persuade my normal compliment of bodyguards to take us to the airport tonight. I told them that we were going to meet someone and that I had to go there. They don't know I'm going anywhere."

"Oh, God, do you mean we have to lose the secret service?" she asked in horror. "I knew that I was going to regret this," she answered, shaking her head. "I don't want to be a party pooper, but even if you manage to lose those boys, they're just going to have some fellows meet you when you get off in Germany. You won't be able to get rid of them that easy, you know," Pam said.

"There's a flight to Boston that we're going to get on. Then, we'll fly to Atlanta and then to Germany. We'll lose them, I guarantee it," said Rebecca confidently.

"Good God, Becky, I think that you've watched too many movies."

"Maybe. Let's go. We have to travel real light. I'm not going to carry anything except my purse. I want you to carry a small bag, with only a few basics for both of us. We can buy some more stuff over there if we need to," Rebecca announced. "O.K., it's time to go," she said, looking at her watch. It was 11:00 P.M.

Pam had tried very hard to not watch the news but she had to at least once before taking off on this crazy trip. "I've just got to see a couple minutes of the news. Can we watch just a little bit?" she said, practically begging.

"O.K.," replied Rebecca, curious herself. She turned on the TV and they both sat down as the announcer led off the newscast with Matt's testimony and the Judiciary Committee's recommendations.

"Good evening, ladies and gentlemen. This is Channel 8 Eyewitness News. Samantha Reilly reporting. Tonight's lead story concerns the dramatic but unbelievable testimony of former deputy National Security Council adviser Matthew Connors. Let's go live to Capitol Hill for an on-the-scene report by correspondent Neil Hutton. Neil?"

"Thank you, Samantha," said the reporter broadcasting just outside from where the testimony took place earlier in the day. "Just a few hours ago, this nation heard some of the most incredible testimony that has ever been uttered in the annals of American history. Former top official Connors, having somehow eluded capture, shocked the viewing public with tales of Nazi conspiracies and world conquest. His accusations named, among others, Speaker of the House Peter Volhard and Defense Secretary Karl Schmidt as two of the men responsible for what Connors claims is part of a forty-five year plan to restore Germany as leader of the world," said Hutton.

"Is there any evidence that Mr. Connors is suffering from any delusional thinking or anything else that would tend to support his latest actions?" asked the anchorwoman.

Pam was infuriated. "They've already made up their minds, damn it, and they think that he's crazy. That's enough. Let's go, Rebecca," Pam said.

Rebecca stood glaring at the TV for a couple of minutes more, knowing that they would soon get to her husband.

"The Judiciary Committee has recommended that a full impeachment trial be initiated. Because of the urgency and the extreme circumstances in this particular situation, the trial will start tomorrow. The House of Representatives will act as the prosecutor and will be led by Gretchen Powers from Michigan, a former U.S. attorney of many years. Mr. Madigan will be represented by Sterling Shannon, a senior partner in a large D.C. firm. The Senate will act as the jury and the trial will be presided over by Chief Justice Koehler," explained Samantha Reilly.

"Tomorrow's hearings and those that follow will be without precedent as a desperate and puzzled nation looks for some answers," said Reilly. Rebecca punched the remote and watched the picture disappear.

"Are you ready?" asked Rebecca.

"As ready as I can be under the circumstances," said an ambivalent Pam. She gamely tried to look enthusiastic. "Let's go."

Rebecca told Pam to meet her at the airport, deciding their plan would work better if they didn't arrive together. Pam purchased a ticket for Boston and got on the flight. Rebecca pretended to be looking for someone arriving and she was followed by two secret service men. At the last possible second, she sprinted onto the plane that was just preparing to taxi onto the runway, heading for Boston. The secret service men were stunned at this act and for a couple of seconds didn't know what to do. They had never had one of the people they were guarding try to lose them before.

Pam and Rebecca found each other towards the back of the half-empty flight and they then took turns going into the ladies' room. Being about the same size, they switched their clothing and Rebecca donned her blonde wig. She put on a pair of sunglasses and affixed some makeup to her face. She now didn't look anything like she had just minutes before.

The two women exited the plane in Boston, and Rebecca saw a couple of men who had the obvious look of secret service all over them. Shaking inside, she kept walking and let out a huge sigh of relief when they didn't try to stop her. They then got onto a flight that left a few minutes later for Atlanta and having gone undetected once more, they then embarked for a flight to Germany. They had been flying for a couple of hours but only now that they were on their way to Germany, did they relax and let down their guard.

"Whew! We made it," she said with exhilaration.

"Becky, now that we've done all that, I guess the question that pops into my mind is why? You're the First Lady, sort of. You can go where you tell them that you want to go," Pam said, trying to make sense of it all.

"Sure, I could. But that's not the point. Being the First Lady, especially under these circumstances, means that you can't do anything without making the headlines or the six o'clock news. Particularly after Matt testified that it's Germany that's behind it all. It couldn't be known that I headed off to Germany. We'd be escorted by half the German police and three quarters of the European press corps," Rebecca explained.

"I guess you're right," Pam replied. "This is probably a question that I should have asked before, but just where are we going? Are we looking for the 'Hall of Former Nazis Bent on World Domination,' or what?" she asked sarcastically.

Rebecca laughed. "We're going to find my brother, silly," she answered.

"Well, if I'm not mistaken, you don't know his address, do you?" she asked.

"No, I don't," Rebecca responded.

"I knew I should have stayed home."

"Pamela, give me some credit. We're going to visit my godfather, Alfred Roehm. He's been a friend of Daddy's for years and years and I'm sure that if we find him, we'll find Tommy right behind," Rebecca said.

"You know, of course," Pam said, "that if I'm correct about this German conspiracy, then that would probably mean that your godfather is in on it. Right?"

"That's probably true," Rebecca replied. "And if they find out our true reason for being here, they'll probably kill us."

34

r. Duc Le arrived at Columbia General hospital early that morning. He had had little sleep having stayed up much of the night listening to GNN. He had been a political science student in college and had received a prestigious White House Fellowship seven years before. He had worked with the National Security Council and had met Matt. He had greatly respected both Matt and Michael and was astounded that they were being charged with such crimes.

He had listened to Matt's testimony over and over and was thinking of it as he began to make his morning rounds. There was something gnawing at him, something that stuck in his gut. God, what was it?

He entered a room and looked at the sleeping elderly man. The man was Wolfgang Weber, but as he carried no identification, no one was aware of this. He looked at his chart and saw that it had been a routine night. The elderly man should be waking soon. He stared at him for many minutes and suddenly was struck with a wild hunch. Could it be?

Dr. Le grabbed his hand and was somewhat stunned when his eyes popped wide open. He played a hunch and spoke. "Guten Morgen, Herr General."

"Guten Morgen," came the immediate reply. Dr. Le froze.

"Sir, I'm your doctor, Duc Le. How do you feel?" he managed to say, his heart beating rapidly.

"I feel fine. I really do," he said, pausing. "Why did you speak to me in German just now and call me general?"

"It was just a crazy hunch, sir," Dr. Le replied. "Listen, yesterday Matt Connors testified on Capitol Hill about some crazy things concerning a conspiracy of former Nazis to take over the world. He said there was one man who had belonged to this group but who was going to testify against it," he said, shaking. Trying to keep his courage up, he asked, "Are you that man?"

Weber hesitated before responding. "Yes, it was me. I was supposed to testify. I went for an early morning walk as has been my habit for many years and I was accosted by a member of the group. He put a gun to my head and told me that I would be killed if I testified. And also..."

"And what?"

"Well," said the elderly man, "I had thought earlier that my sons had been killed but apparently one of them is still alive. I was told that I could see him if I remained silent but that we would both be killed if I spoke up. The next thing I knew, I was here. Did you watch the hearings?" he asked.

"I watched the late night news. Mr. Connors was pretty much made to look like a fool and they're starting with the impeachment trial of Mr. Madigan this morning," explained the young doctor.

"Oh, God," he said. "He was telling the truth, you know."

"If he was telling the truth, then you must do something," said the doctor.

"I can't," he stammered.

"Sir, if all of this is true, millions could die, including your son. You must tell what you know."

"Doctor, you're absolutely right. I can't allow the deaths of innocent people to be on my conscience. You must help me to go to Capitol Hill. I must be allowed to speak," he pleaded.

"I'll make the arrangements to get you over there," Dr. Le said excitedly as he quickly exited the room.

Ligachev tried to sit upright and felt a sense of peace of mind. They must be stopped. He would have to speak. It was the right thing.

A man dressed in a doctor's smock walked in and looked at the patient, who was attempting to get out of bed.

"Mr. Weber, what you need is bed rest," said Gerrhard Meyer, as he pulled out a gun, silencer already attached. "You were told that you would be watched. I gave you a chance and yet you still wish to act foolishly. Auf Wiedersehen,

Herr Charlemagne," he said, as he pumped three rounds into the former Nazi's chest. The elderly German slumped to the ground and died instantly.

Meyer walked calmly out the door into the hallway. As he got onto the elevator, an excited Dr. Duc Le got off and headed toward Weber's room.

✠ ✠ ✠

Pam and Rebecca landed in Bonn and quickly hailed a taxi towards Alfred Roehm's, aka Frederick's, residence. Rebecca had been rehearsing over and over what she was going to say if she actually found Tommy.

Rebecca paid the driver and asked him to wait and to be ready for a quick exit. The driver was very reluctant as he realized whose house he was sitting outside of, but the very generous amount of deutsche marks placed into his hand by Rebecca changed his mind.

Pam and Rebecca got out of the taxi and walked quietly towards the desolate-looking mansion. With a nod of Rebecca's head, the two women scaled the fence and moved in stealth-like silence towards the house. The lights were on in a large room on the bottom floor. They made those lights their destination as they crept closer.

After Rebecca pressed her face to the window she saw Tommy, Alfred and another man whom she didn't recognize. They were engaging in a heated exchange in German. She peered at the TV and almost cried out when she saw Michael's image on the screen. They were watching the impeachment trial that had begun. It made sense now.

Rebecca gestured for Pam to come closer. Suddenly, both women heard a clicking noise and they found themselves with the barrel of a gun pressed hard against their temples. They were told in guttural German that if they screamed out, they would be killed immediately.

Pam didn't understand German but she managed to catch the drift of the warning. Their new captor switched to perfect English as he said, "Please follow me ladies," in an almost pleasant tone.

Seconds later, the gunman and the two American women entered the large study where the others were. Tommy saw his sister and uncharacteristically looked worried.

"Rebecca, what are you doing for God's sake?"

Frederick recognized Rebecca and addressed her.

"My dear Rebecca, this is quite a surprise. It's always a pleasure to see my god-daughter. But I must wonder what has caused her to sneak around my yard like a common criminal," he said, the tone in his voice turning menacing.

Wilhelm had never met Rebecca but he recognized her as well as Pam. "Well, this is quite an honor. The illustrious Mrs. Connors has honored us as well. What can we do for you ladies?" he said sarcastically.

Rebecca replied, struggling to maintain her composure. "I would like to talk to my brother. That's all. I thought that perhaps you would know where I could find him, Alfred. I didn't really expect him to be here," she said truthfully.

"And what do you wish to talk to him about?" Wilhelm said. Before she was able to respond, Frederick shouted out at the television. The afternoon session was just about to begin in the impeachment trial of Michael Madigan. Karl Schmidt had been on the stand all morning as prosecutor Gretchen Powers questioned him for two and a half hours as he repeated in greater detail what he testified to during the initial hearings. The afternoon would see his cross-examination by Michael's attorney, Sterling Shannon.

The GNN reporter summarized the morning's events. "Good afternoon, ladies and gentlemen. This is Bradley Lynch reporting live from the Capitol. Before the afternoon session begins, let's recap the historic first morning of this incredible impeachment trial of acting President Michael Madigan. With the entire Senate acting as the jury, and the chief justice of the Supreme Court as the judge, the House prosecutor began the government's case with an impassioned and stirring opening statement. This was followed by an equally emotional opening statement from Mr. Madigan's attorney, after which the first witness was called. Secretary of Defense Karl Schmidt responded confidently to the prosecutor's questions."

"Excuse me, Bradley," said Dorothy Larimer, interrupting him, "but has there been explanation as to what happened just before the lunch break?"

"No, there hasn't been, Dorothy," Lynch responded. "For those who are just joining us, right around noon, an aide whispered into the secretary's ear and Mr. Schmidt then asked if it would be all right to recess at that point. Ms. Powers indicated that she was through with her questioning anyway and Mr. Shannon acquiesced. Mr. Schmidt was seen leaving the Capitol in a great hurry, refusing to answer questions. That's all we know, Dorothy," stated the reporter. "The chief justice and prosecutor have just taken their places and it looks like we are about to begin."

Chief Justice Koehler asked, "Are we ready to proceed?" When both sides acknowledged that they were, he said, "Mr. Shannon, I believe you wish to cross-examine the first witness?"

"Yes, your honor, I do," said the defense attorney. His client, the acting president of the United States, was not present but was watching intently from the White House.

"Would the witness please retake the witness stand?" asked the chief justice, and Karl Schmidt did just that. He looked much more nervous than he did during the morning session. "I would remind you, sir, that you are still under oath," the chief justice said to the witness, who nodded.

Sterling Shannon approached the witness and began his questioning. "Sir, is Karl Schmidt your real name?"

"No, it is not. My real name is Hans Mannheim."

Shannon was shocked at the answer and hesitated for a second.

In Bonn, Germany, several viewers were even more stunned. "What is he doing?" said an incredulous Frederick.

Shannon recovered and proceeded. "How is it, sir, that you have repeatedly said that you are Karl Schmidt?"

"I've never said any such thing," said the witness.

"Excuse me, sir, but I was at the Senate confirmation hearings before you were named the secretary of defense. You said that your name was Karl Schmidt."

"I am not the secretary of defense," replied the witness.

The judge and jury looked on in hushed silence and momentarily, Shannon was uncertain.

"Well, sir, let me direct your attention to your testimony of just a few hours ago. You said..."

"That wasn't me."

Wilhelm was screaming incoherently at the image on TV. "What in God's name is he doing?"

Chief Justice Koehler looked down at the witness, visibly angry. "Sir, you are very close to being held in contempt of this court. I would suggest that you..."

"I'm sorry, sir, I mean no disrespect. I can explain everything. Every word that Mr. Connors spoke yesterday is true and there is much more of which he's not aware. I know because I was the leader of this group of Six that Mr. Connors referred to. I was the one known as Bismarck and am the one who originally had the idea of bringing Germany back to her place as leader of the world. I came to America to put our plan into place in 1946, but something happened to me and I've not been a part of this group in over forty-five years. Again, I am not the secretary of defense. I'm his brother, Hans. And his real name is Otto Mannheim."

A collective gasp echoed through the room. The chief justice wasn't sure how to proceed.

Frederick shrieked loudly and Rebecca thought he was going to have a heart attack. He began cursing in German. "Traitor! The back-stabbing traitor. He has signed our death warrants," shouted an almost delirious Frederick.

Wilhelm tried to remain calm, although he too was totally caught off guard. "Otto, I don't understand. You mean that all these years it has been Otto we have followed? Then where has Hans been all of this time?" he said dazedly.

"We've come too far to be defeated." He rushed to the phone and quickly dialed.

"General Steigrich," Wilhelm barked into the receiver. "This is Felix Klaus. An extreme emergency has taken place. We must resort to backup plans, plans that we have never discussed with you. I don't have time to explain it to you but you must do exactly as I say," he commanded.

"Yes, sir. Give me the order and I will carry it out."

Rebecca stared at her brother in disbelief. "Tommy, is this true? Is daddy..." she muttered, unable to finish.

As Wilhelm prepared to give the order, Frederick instructed Tommy to tie the women up. Tape was placed over their mouths so that they could not yell out.

"General Steigrich. Listen to me carefully. Everything that we've planned for so many years is at risk. We must resort to drastic action. A nuclear ICBM will be launched towards America immediately. The missile is aimed at Washington. Prepare the missile, and on my order it is to be launched towards the designated target. Do you understand me?" asked Wilhelm.

The normally imperturbable general was suddenly panic-stricken. "Herr Klaus, I was not aware of any nuclear attack scenario..."

"Wait for my command," Wilhelm said forcefully.

Pam and Rebecca were shoved to the floor. They listened as orders were given by Frederick. Nuclear war?

Wilhelm quickly dialed another number and within seconds had Volhard on the line.

"What the hell is going on? Is that Hans or Otto? Can you believe the son of a bitch? He is destroying our whole mission," screamed Wilhelm. "You must get out of there immediately. I've already instructed General Steigrich to prepare missiles for launching towards the U.S. I want you to do the same."

"You idiot," shouted back Volhard. "Apparently, you've been asleep. It was determined that Madigan was the acting president, remember? I cannot order a nuclear strike. But that is not Bismarck on your TV screen. He and I were just informed a short time ago that the man he killed when he first came to the U.S. has been identified, and that this death has been linked to him through some new technology involving DNA. Bismarck and I will be heading for Mount Weather within minutes. We'll resort to other means. We still have the chemical weapons."

"Do not launch yet. I will contact you within one hour. Rommel out," ordered Volhard.

Wilhelm cut back to the anxious Steigrich. "Belay that order but be prepared to launch within one hour. Gather all troops and report to the bunkers."

"Yes, sir," came Steigrich's reply.

Frederick was pacing furiously, cursing at the image on the television. This Hans, or whoever he was, was providing more and more detail about the Six and their mission. He was beside himself and looked at the two Americen woman with consuming rage.

"Thomas!" he called out at Tommy.

"Yes, sir," responded Rebecca's brother.

"Please dispose of this Jew-lover and her black friend. Now. They know too much. Here is a gun. Get it over with quickly. We have much to discuss," Frederick said, as he handed a pistol to Tommy.

They both glared at Tommy who showed no emotion. "Yes, sir," he said coolly.

Tommy walked over to the two women and then glanced back at Frederick and Wilhelm who were giving orders over the telephone. On the back wall of the study, a giant map of the world appeared. Germany and the United States were highlighted with many bright lights. Tommy realized that World War III was about to begin.

He stood over the two women and cocked the weapon. Pam passed out and Rebecca began silently reciting the Lord's Prayer to herself without taking her eyes off of Tommy.

Tommy abruptly turned around and aimed the gun at Frederick. He squeezed the trigger and a bullet caught the German leader squarely in the head, splashing blood all over the wall. Tommy calmly pulled the trigger again, and a bullet punctured Wilhelm's chest. He collapsed onto the floor and was dead within seconds.

Tommy stood still for a few seconds and dropped the gun to the floor. He ran his fingers through his hair and closed his eyes. Until just a few seconds before his fateful decision to pull the trigger, no such thing had been planned. It was totally spontaneous. He had his doubts lately, yes, and he had even voiced them to Rebecca, but he was to be one of the new leaders of Germany in a short time. He had been part of this plan for over twenty years. His heart was pounding and his hands were sweating.

He looked at his sister and walked over and pulled the tape off of her mouth. He untied her and helped her to her feet.

Tommy suddenly did something he had never done before. He hugged his sister and patted her gently.

"It's O.K., Becky. Everything's going to be all right," he said.

Rebecca couldn't stop shaking. Finally, she mustered the strength to speak. "Was that Daddy on the TV screen?"

Tommy nodded. "Yes and no. That was your father but not mine," he said sadly and she didn't understand.

"Tommy, what kind of monsters are they? How could you have been one of them? You're not even German, for God's sake!"

"It's hard to explain. I know that Vietnam messed me up a lot and then I got involved with this dude that Michael used to know named Alan Roberts. He convinced me that the cause of the world's problems could all be traced to Jews and blacks. Then Steven and I found out accidentally about Dad and his friends. We got sucked up in the excitement of it and I gave up my entire life to work towards the goals of the Six. But in the end, I couldn't do it, Becky. I couldn't kill you, even though you're only my cousin and not my sister. And I couldn't allow a nuclear war," he said.

Rebecca looked at him, momentarily paralyzed with ambivalence.

"You're my cousin? I don't understand."

"You see, Karl Schmidt is my father, but he's your uncle," Tommy explained. "Your father is that man on TV now, whose real name is Hans Mannheim. He was the original leader of this group and was supposed to come to America and assume the identity of an American. That is, he was supposed to kill someone and take over that person's life. But he couldn't bring himself to do it and decided to forsake the group. But his brother came to the U.S. and killed a young man named Karl Schmidt and framed his brother for the murder. Your father was convicted of the killing and has spent forty-something years in jail. My father passed himself off to the others as Hans. None of them knew about Otto," he said, his voice trailing off.

Rebecca couldn't believe what she was hearing. "What about mother?"

"Katarina is your aunt. I don't know what happened to your real mother. Her name was Elena," Tommy replied.

Tommy continued. "I'm a traitor to the cause," he said sadly. "I feel so empty."

"Tommy, whatever you've done is in the past. You've realized that and have taken steps to remedy it," Rebecca said, trying to reassure his recent change of heart.

"No, no, there can be no excuse for what I've done and there can be no justification for my life," he said, and he suddenly pulled the gun from his jacket, put it in his mouth and squeezed the trigger.

Rebecca screamed as blood splattered onto her.

✠   ✠   ✠

At the White House, Michael watched the television.

"Mr. Chief Justice, I insist that this man be arrested for impersonating a Cabinet officer," shouted Gretchen Powers.

"He did no such thing. He never said that he was Karl Schmidt. To the contrary, he denied it right away," yelled an equally excited Sterling Shannon.

"At the very least, this witness has not been sworn and has not been called as my witness. Therefore, Mr. Shannon has no right to cross-examine him," argued the prosecutor.

"You're right, Ms. Powers," replied the chief justice, who then turned towards the witness. "Sir, would you raise your right hand, please? Do you swear to tell the truth, the whole truth and nothing but the truth, so help you God?"

"I do, your honor," he replied.

"Please state your name for the record."

"My name is Hans Mannheim."

"Your honor, I will raise my objection once again. Mr. Shannon has no right to cross-examine this witness at this time," said the congresswoman heatedly.

"Under the circumstances, this witness must be examined. I will question him myself," said the chief justice stoically.

"I object," asserted the prosecutor.

"Objection noted but overruled," the Chief Justice replied. Turning to the witness, he began his questioning.

✠   ✠   ✠

Michael's secretary interrupted his thoughts. "Mr. Vice President, it's Matt Connors for you."

Michael grabbed the phone. "Matt, is that you? I thought you were in jail." he said excitedly.

"Michael, I don't have much time," Matt said nervously. "The shit is hitting the fan. I'm gonna play a hunch. I think that Volhard and your father-in-law, or whoever he is are going to bug out of town ASAP. I think that I know where they're going. If I'm right, the place can be sealed and no one can get in. There's no time to waste. You need to get over there now. If I'm right and you don't stop them immediately, it may be too late," he said, out of breath.

"Matt, what are you talking about? The only place that I know of that's sealed is NORAD. Are you talking about NORAD?" he shouted.

"I gotta go, Mike. I guess that it shouldn't surprise me that you weren't briefed. Ask Ed Meyers about Mount Weather. Grab him and General Lund, and the three of you get your asses over there now!"

"Whoa. Just a second, Matt. I'm the acting president and can't go playing Rambo," Michael protested.

"You don't understand, Michael. There's no time to argue. Mount Weather can be sealed and is practically indestructible. If Volhard and Schmidt seal the mountain, they won't be able to be stopped," he shouted.

"Stopped from what?" asked an agitated Michael.

"They still have access to chemical weapons and there are still some guys running around in Germany with nukes. They very well might launch them towards the U.S. There's some of the best communications gear in the world there. You can address the entire nation. Michael, it's virtually a city. It has a dozen buildings with just communications equipment. It has an on-site sewage-treatment plant and underground ponds. It's the world's greatest bunker," Matt continued.

"Where is it?" asked Michael.

"It's in a mountain ridge between Loudoun and Clarke counties, and it's on a twisting stretch of County Route 601, past Heart Trouble Lane. Get over there with Meyers and Lund by helicopter. Michael, there's not much time," Matt said.

"What if you're wrong?" Michael said.

"If I'm wrong, then you'll only waste a short bit of time. But if I'm right and they seal it up, it will be too late. Behind it is a solid-steel door that is five feet thick, ten feet high and nearly twenty feet across," Matt exclaimed. "The door rests on wheels and can be closed electronically. Now don't worry about losing contact with the White House. There's a direct link with the White House Situation room," he added.

Matt paused, gasping for breath. "Ideally, you'd get the whole Cabinet and all your top aides over there. But there's not enough time. Now, Michael, please. Just do it."

Michael buzzed his chief of staff, who entered the Oval Office within seconds. "What's up boss?" he asked.

"Get General Lund on the line. Tell him to meet you and me at Mount Weather ASAP," ordered Michael.

"Mount Weather? For what?" asked the stunned aide. "I didn't even know that you were aware of it," he said.

"Well, I am and I want to get out there immediately."

"Do you want the rest of the NSC and Cabinet notified?"

"There's not enough time. I want a helicopter leaving the White House lawn in five minutes. Now move," ordered the acting president. Meyers jumped, and within a couple of minutes they were whisked away to the secret mountain facility.

Michael told him how Matt suggested going to Mount Weather immediately, that Volhard and Schmidt would most likely be going there.

The helicopter finally landed on a small helipad, and Michael saw dozens of microwave antennas protruding skyward. They exited the aircraft and Michael shouted to Meyers. "Where's the entrance?"

"Over there," the chief of staff pointed.

Michael began running when he saw another helicopter prepare to land. It must be Lund. Meyers shouted, desperately trying to be heard over the deafening roar of the rotary blades. "Are we going to wait for Lund?"

"No time," Michael said, and continued running towards the front entrance.

There were guards running frantically about in near complete chaos. One man came to a complete stop when he saw Michael. "Mr. Madigan? Is that you, sir?" screamed the man, who Michael surmised was a scientist.

"Yes, it is. I have reason to believe that Peter Volhard and Karl Schmidt are taking over this facility. They are enemies and are extremely dangerous," Michael said.

"Well, I don't know what to think anymore. Mr. Schmidt himself just gave the order to seal the mountain. That's why everyone is running like mad. We've only got a few minutes. Follow me. And hurry," the man said.

Michael and Meyers followed this heavyset man and suddenly were in sight of the front entrance. Horns were blaring and they saw the huge door closing. They only had a few seconds. They might barely make it. General Lund wouldn't stand a chance.

The overweight scientist-looking man was gasping for breath. They were only about fifteen feet away as the monstrous steel door was seconds away from sealing. Michael and Meyers sprinted inside and just as the door was sealing, the fat man with no name dove inside, making it with only inches to spare.

Inside, there was a maze of activity but no one stopped to notice the acting president. Michael wanted to get out of sight immediately.

He gestured to Meyers to a room behind some huge mainframe computers. They ran silently to one of the doors and stepped inside, where the overweight man was still gasping. It was pitch black and Michael began looking frantically for a light switch.

Michael shouted out to their new comrade. "Hey you, I don't know what your name is but where are we? Do these rooms have lights?" he said, and then they were suddenly enveloped in light as Meyers struck a light switch with his hand. They were in what appeared to be a television studio.

The overweight man was still bent over, gasping for air. He tried to speak but was having trouble.

"My name is Edgar Barton. We're in a room that was designed to address the nation in case the Emergency Broadcast System had been knocked out by a nuclear strike," he explained. "I'm a communications expert and it's my job to maintain the equipment, the stuff that you're looking at right now."

"The obvious question is what the heck are you doing here sneaking around?" Barton said.

"These are unusual circumstances Barton. We don't have much time. You mentioned that Mr. Schmidt was here. Where exactly is he?"

"On the other side of the pond," Barton said, referring to a huge man made reservoir 200 feet across. "There are a bunch of offices over there, including one for the president," explained the man.

Meyers knew as much about Mount Weather as almost anyone in the government. He had served in the CIA for many years and had been involved in the war-game scenarios. But even with his vast knowledge of it, there was still much that he didn't know. "Could this place really withstand a nuclear strike?" he asked of Barton.

"I've never been through a nuclear strike but that's what they tell me. The roof areas of the tunnels and rooms have been reinforced with 21,000 iron bolts sunk eight to ten inches into the rock," Barton replied.

"What's the pond for?" Michael asked.

"There are a few of those. One's for drinking water and the others are used to cool the air pumped through the mainframe computers to keep them from overheating."

"We have a lot of work to do and not much time, Edgar," Michael said. "Mr. Schmidt and Mr. Volhard must be stopped. Are there any weapons in this facility?"

"Weapons? You mean, like guns? Let's see. There's an armory that has rifles but I don't really know what's in there, and I don't even know who has the keys," said Edgar.

"How does the air circulate in here?" Michael asked.

"An air shaft was dug from the main tunnel to the top of the mountain and pumps and fans were installed for air circulation," the bureaucrat explained.

"That's what I thought," responded Michael. "Are there any chemicals here anywhere? Could we smoke them out by placing some chemical solution into the air shaft?"

"That's an interesting idea but I don't know where we'd get any chemicals. It was never imagined that this place would fall into enemy hands," Barton answered.

Meyers, who had been leaning against the door, suddenly jumped up. "Sh! There's someone coming."

"Quick. In here," said Barton, motioning them into a closet. Just as the three men closed the closet door, into the room walked Rommel, Bismarck and Krupp.

"Thanks to your brother we are fugitives. The U.S. mission has failed," Rommel said solemnly.

"I will not walk away from a lifetime's endeavor. We've come too close. We still have the chemical weapons and we still have Andrew Tolbert," he said.

Michael was shocked to hear that the president was here.

Bismarck continued his harangue. "Mr. Speaker, you'll inform the nation that the government will capitulate or the chemical weapons will be released and Mr. Tolbert will be killed. Also, you'll inform them that unless they turn power over to Frederick and Wilhelm, certain cities and military installations will be obliterated with tactical nuclear weapons," he spat out.

The men cowering in the closet couldn't believe it.

Volhard activated an intercom and called to a subordinate. "This is Volhard. Bring Mr. Tolbert in here."

There was silence for about two minutes. Then, the door opened and two men escorted a tied and emaciated Tolbert. "Good evening, Mr. President," Schmidt said.

Tolbert responded with a tired, wan voice. "You won't get away with it," he warned.

"Maybe. Maybe not," said Schmidt philosophically. "But this nation will never get over witnessing their president being killed on live TV. And Germany will be ours."

"You're all insane," growled Andrew Tolbert.

"That may be but we're the ones calling the shots, unfortunately. Now sit down and shut up," Krupp shouted pushing the president to the floor.

Volhard began setting up the network that had been designed for a president to address a nuclear-war-threatened nation.

"Where's Barton?" he cried out.

Michael held his breath but was blinded by the light that suddenly flooded the small closet. All that he could see was a gun pointed at his head by the overweight Barton.

"It seems you can't trust anyone, can you, Mr. Madigan?" said Barton, smiling sinisterly. "Now get going," he ordered, and the three men marched into the studio.

"Here I am, Mr. Volhard. And look what I have for you," Barton said, pointing to Michael as if he were a trophy.

"Well, who do we have here?" asked Krupp, who began laughing. "Hello, Michael. How are you?"

Michael looked at Schmidt, who he had, for the last twenty-two years, referred to as his father-in-law. Then he glanced at Krupp and nearly passed out.

"Ariel," he muttered.

"Yes, my nephew. Don't look so shocked. I'm not your real uncle," Krupp explained. "You see, Ariel Madigan was killed in 1946. By me, I must admit. We looked very much alike and I assumed his identity. The only living relative was Benjamin. But he and I had grown apart, should I say. I wrote him a rather vicious letter and he never made an attempt to communicate again. A pity," Krupp said, smiling a wicked smile.

"What is so ironic," Krupp continued, "is that Ben had become obsessed with finding a certain Nazi prison guard and Ariel said to forget about it. Were you aware of this?"

Michael was a whirl of emotion. "I know he dedicated his life to find the guard who killed his parents. A butcher named Herman Kepler," Michael spat out.

Krupp managed an almost imperceptible laugh. "Even you will have to appreciate the irony, Michael. My name is Herman Kepler and I knew your grandparents well, until their untimely demise, that is," Krupp said laughing.

Michael was consumed by anger. The man who killed his grandparents and whom his father had searched for all of these years had been posing as his uncle.

"That's enough of a trip down memory lane," shouted Rommel. "We have a job to do. Barton, tie Madigan up and put him next to Tolbert. Then get the TV hooked up."

Barton pointed his gun at Michael and Meyers and pushed them to their knees. Suddenly, they all became aware of three men standing over by the pond. Each wore a different uniform. It slowly became apparent that the men were standing not just near the pond, but were actually on the water.

The three men began moving closer, walking on the water. As they got closer, their identities became known, almost causing everyone—the three Germans in particular—to gasp in disbelief.

The first man wore the uniform of a World War II Nazi field marshal. He was lean and his hair was slightly gray. He had dark, menacing eyes and tight, pressed lips. His red epaulets contrasted against the gray uniform, the black Iron Cross hanging from his neck. He was the "Desert Fox," the man who beat Montgomery at Tobruk. Erwin Rommel stood before them.

"My God," whispered a stunned Karl Schmidt. "It's Rommel."

The man next to the Nazi general was massive with thick, bushy eyebrows and a full mustache and sideburns. He was bald, and wore his uniform—with its double row of buttons and thick round collar—with pride and dignity. He stood with his chest out at attention.

"It's Bismarck," Peter Volhard said with awe in his voice. Otto von Bismarck, the Iron Chancellor of Prussia, stared intently at the twentieth century onlookers.

The third man was of average size and wore not a military uniform but another type, unique in its style and distinct in many ways. He was dark, with large hands. He was the man whose family had armed the Germans for over five centuries—Alfred Krupp, the weapons manufacturer that had supplied the Second and Third Reich.

"I cannot believe it," said Volhard softly. The three Germans stood frozen in disbelief, unable to move or to think of their next move. They were face to face with their heroes. But it couldn't be since all three men were dead.

Suddenly, a loud hissing noise was heard.

"What's that sound?" asked Krupp.

Everyone looked around and saw a gaseous substance pouring out of the vents. Krupp instantly knew what it was and ran for the steel door, which was now locked.

Michael realized that gas was pouring into the room and they all began gasping, as the gas chafed their lungs and mouths. Oddly, he distinctly heard music, a light and merry tune that he had heard before.

Everyone was on their knees now, choking and coughing, except for the three men on the pond, who remained motionless. Then the door opened and was quickly shut. Michael saw someone dressed in a chemical suit come toward him. The man untied him and handed him three gas masks. Michael donned his mask, untied the president and Meyers and gave them masks. Meyers took the other mask gratefully. The three German men and Barton writhed on the floor, begging for their lives.

From above, Michael heard a voice coming from the loudspeaker. It was a familiar voice.

"Good afternoon, gentlemen. Herr Rommel, Herr Bismarck and most of all, Herr Krupp. It's a pity to see such powerful men in such an undignified manner. Certainly, your heroes who stand before you must be laughing at your weakness. But I do not understand. Are you not members of the master race? Don't tell me that hydrogen cyanide affects you the same way as it did the Jews at Auschwitz? There must be some mistake," said the voice with hatred and contempt.

Michael said, "Dad, is that you?"

"Yes, Michael,"

"Dad, don't do this. Please," Michael begged but received no response. Michael looked at the figure in the chemical suit but also received no response.

After about a minute of silence, the door opened and Benjamin Madigan walked in, wearing a full protective suit. He walked directly to Krupp, whose eyes were burning as he begged for air.

Ben took off his mask and Michael felt a shiver go up his spine. His father was alive! Ben spoke to Krupp. "You are Herman Kepler? You killed my parents and my brother?" he said, as he began to cough. Quickly, he put his mask back on.

Kepler was convulsing as the gas was about to end his life. They would all be dead within minutes.

"Yes, I'm Kepler. Don't kill me," the Nazi choked.

Michael watched aghast. He walked over to his father and took off his mask. "Dad, please don't do it. Don't give in to the hatred. Please stop it," he begged, and began choking. He quickly put his mask back on.

Ben gestured to the other person in the protective suit, who quickly left the room and the door wide open, causing the gas to dissipate. Seconds later, it stopped completely.

Once the gas cleared, everyone took off their masks. Michael sighed in relief as he saw that the three former Nazis were still alive. He looked towards the pond and the images of the three figures from German history slowly faded and seconds later, they were gone.

Michael let out a sharp gasp as the identity of the other person in the protective suit became apparent. The man in the suit wasn't a man at all, it was Elizabeth.

"Dad, Elizabeth, I don't understand," Michael said, as he rushed towards them and hugged them both.

"Come here, Michael. I'm sorry for the past couple of years but it was necessary," explained Ben. "I found out about these monsters and went underground. I had to fake my death and still couldn't have pulled it off without the help of one of the best CIA agents ever," he said.

"Who's that?" Michael asked.

"Elizabeth, of course."

"Liz? CIA? You're kidding," Michael said in disbelief.

"Come on, big brother," said the agent, also known as Sgt. Pepper. "Didn't you ever wonder why I never finished that novel?"

Michael stood with mouth agape. "I guess that I just figured you weren't very good," he said, causing all three Madigans to roar with laughter.

The president walked over to them, and said, "would someone mind filling me in?"

Barton and the three former Nazis were starting to recover. Michael began to tell Meyers to take care of them but Elizabeth had it well in hand. With a pistol in one hand and rope in the other, she expertly had them tied up within a few minutes. Michael still couldn't believe it.

"What about the figures we just saw?" Michael asked. "They sure looked real."

"Nothing like a few holograms to stop a few reincarnation believing Nazis cold in their tracks," Ben explained. "My good friend Pam Connors assisted us."

"Incredible," Michael replied.

Tolbert shook his arms and legs, attempting to get his blood flowing again, after having been tied up for weeks. He then picked up a telephone that he knew was connected right to the White House, but handed it to Michael. "You do the talking. I'm a little tired," he said as he sat down.

Seconds later, Michael heard a familiar voice. "White House, Connors here."

"Matt?" Michael asked. "I thought you were in jail."

"Well, after your real father-in-law's testimony, they let me go. This place is going nuts, Mike."

"Matt, we're coming home. It's over."

35

ichael couldn't believe what had just happened. But now the insanity was over. And best of all, his father was still alive.

In between the hugging and backslapping, Michael made arrangements to have a helicopter take them back to Washington. Several armed soldiers handcuffed Volhard, Karl and the man Michael had thought was his uncle Ariel, as well as Edgar Barton. Michael kept staring at his father and Elizabeth.

Finally, they boarded the marine chopper and Tolbert directed the pilot to the White House.

Looking at Ben, he turned to Karl to ask the question that was burning in his mind. "I gotta know. Was Rebecca part of the KKK or was she framed?"

Karl hesitated for a moment before answering. "It was a frame-up, Mike. She's pure as the snow. Even though she's not my daughter, I came to love her very much. She didn't turn on you," he said.

"Thank God," Michael said. Turning to his father, he shrugged his shoulders and gestured with his hands, struggling desperately for the right words.

"Dad, I don't even know where to begin," he said in a near whisper. "I was at your funeral. I saw you get shot."

"Pretty convincing, wasn't it?" Ben asked as he smiled broadly. "Michael, I'm sorry about keeping all of you in the dark but it was necessary. I had become aware of this group of Six a few months before, from, of all people, a man in jail. I went to visit him and he told me about their plan. You see, he was their original leader," Ben explained.

"Who was he?"

"Rebecca's real father, Hans. This man that you've thought of as your father-in-law killed a man named Karl Schmidt in 1946 and framed his brother for it. The man you know as Karl is Otto Mannheim. None of the other members of the Six realized that they had been following Otto all these years. They thought it was Hans," Ben explained.

"My head hurts," Michael said, running his hands through his hair. "But I saw them lower you into the ground."

"CIA men can pull off damn near anything," Ben replied proudly. "And I had the help of one of the best agents the agency's ever known. Take a bow, Liz," he said, winking at his petite daughter.

"Liz, I always thought that you were afraid of your shadow. I can't believe it," Michael said in amazement.

"You can't always tell a book by its cover, can you big brother?" she said with a grin.

Michael smiled but then suddenly turned somber. "What about Mom? She turned me in."

"Michael, your mom was acting on my instructions," Ben responded. "It killed both of us but there was no choice. We were getting close to cracking it and they found out where you were. We had to let them take you in. I was in the back when you were taken away that day and I've never seen your mother so despondent, as if someone had stuck a dagger in her heart. But I told her that it had to be that way. I'm sorry. I hope that you can forgive us."

The White House came into sight.

"Mr. President, I'm sorry to have ignored you, sir. Are you all right?"

"Yeah, I'm fine now," President Tolbert said as the chopper landed on the White House lawn.

Barton and the former Nazis were taken into custody, while the others were greeted by staff members who lined the perimeter of the White House and by those who filled every balcony and open window.

Tolbert and Michael, along with Ben, Elizabeth and Ed Meyers, were rushed into the Oval Office, where they were met by Matt and General Lund. Matt rushed towards Michael and the two old friends hugged each other.

"We survived, Mikey boy. They almost got us, but we made it," Matt said joyfully.

"We sure did, buddy," Michael exclaimed.

"Mike, there's someone who wants to see you," Matt said, and walked toward the door to the massive office and opened it. Standing in the hall was Rebecca.

"Rebecca," he whispered, as he rushed toward her. They embraced tightly.

"Becks, I'm so sorry," Michael pleaded. "I thought you turned on me. I should have known that you couldn't. But..." he stuttered, unable to finish the statement.

"I don't blame you, darling," Rebecca cried. "I finally got a look at the pictures and so-called diary that you saw. They seemed so real, especially the handwriting. It must have taken someone weeks to make it appear so authentic," she said.

"Becky, I've been informed that there are a couple of other people who would like to see you," President Tolbert said, as he put down the phone on his desk.

"Who?" Rebecca inquired as the president's secretary showed an elderly couple into the office.

"Mrs. Madigan, as strange as this may sound, I would like to introduce you to your parents, Hans and Elena Mannheim," said the secretary, as Rebecca's mouth dropped.

"Rebecca," started the frail woman, "perhaps you'll never understand but your father was sentenced to life in prison for a crime he didn't commit before you were born. Your uncle Otto threatened to kill me and chased me back to Germany. I was young and scared and spoke no English. Katarina is my sister and she promised me that she would raise you well. She never knew anything about the Nazis," Elena said haltingly.

"I just got out of prison recently after forty-five years," Hans explained. "All that time, I dreamed of this day. I hope it's not too late," Hans pleaded, unsure of his daughter's response.

Rebecca felt a shiver up her spine. "It's not too late, Daddy," she gushed. She threw open her arms and wrapped them around the parents she never knew.

Andrew Tolbert suddenly felt like an intruder in his own office and quietly cleared his throat. "Excuse me, everyone," he began, "but I'm afraid that we have some work to do. The world has been turned topsy-turvy these last few weeks and we better do something about it. Michael, I want..." But before he finished his thought, Mary Alice Tolbert walked in the room and made a dash for him, embracing him tightly.

General Lund, the ramrod-straight chairman of the joint chiefs of staff, stood silently in the background.

✠　✠　✠

Michael and his family walked hand-in-hand into the National Cathedral, the most impressive building in all of Washington, located on the highest point in the city. Michael marveled at the gothic architecture of the structure known officially as the Cathedral Church of Saint Peter and Saint Paul.

Though actually an Episcopal church, the cathedral had always been a national place of worship, open to all denominations. This night, a Friday, one of its chapels was opened to celebrate a Jewish service.

Michael smiled as he looked around and saw hundreds of familiar faces. Darrell Johnson and Alex Turner were accompanied by Johnny Green, the gang leader from Los Angeles. Andrew and Mary Alice Tolbert were present, as were Matt and Pam Connors, Don and Shirley Lentine, and Brian and Marie McMullen and many others.

The conversation was suddenly silenced by the opening comments of the rabbi. "Good evening my friends," the rabbi began. "Let us be thankful that the madness is finally over. Let us thank God that the world has been spared another holocaust. Let us sing in joyous praise," he bellowed as the cantor led the congregation in song.

Midway into the celebration, the rabbi turned in Michael's direction and spoke to him. "Mr. Vice President, would you please join me?" he asked as Michael approached the podium to thunderous applause.

Michael gazed sheepishly at the congregation and fought to hold back his tears as he glanced at Rebecca, the kids and his parents. His parents were both beaming with pride.

"Ladies and gentlemen, so much has happened that I barely know where to begin," Michael said haltingly. "It might be easy to become bitter and angry at the recent events but we have to move on. Although we cannot allow ourselves to forget, we must forgive," he said eloquently. "We've been manipulated by outside forces, dangled like puppets by unseen hands. People of every ethnic group, of every religion, were incited by invisible agents of evil. We've lashed out at each other, ready to kill, to destroy, to burn. In the process, we've come close to self-destruction. We almost burned our bridges. And *that*, ladies and gentlemen, is something that must never happen."

"If we burn the bridges to our future, to our hopes, to each other, then each and every one of us shall surely die."

After several seconds of silence, Michael continued. "For those of you who know me, I've always been a frustrated musician. If you will bear with me, I would like to sing a song. If my family would join me, and if all of you would turn to the yellow sheet that was passed out, we'll sing a song I wrote for this day of worship."

Slowly, Michael was joined by Rebecca, Joshua, TJ, David, Ben and Julia, Elizabeth and Hans and Elena. They huddled around the microphone as Michael placed a guitar around his neck and began to sing the lyrics that he hoped would serve as a form of national catharsis. Thinking back to the poignant high school play, *Knights of the White Camelia*, he hoped that maybe someday the hatred would stop.

Gazing from my window to the streets below
I feel the fires burning, I see the embers glow
The smoke-filled ruins of my memories and yours
Victims of hatred, casualties of wars
Burning bridges, all of us
Burning bridges into dust
Which blows away with the gust
Leaving no one that we can trust
Blaming others while pointing fingers
Solving nothing while despair still lingers
It was them, the others say
It's all their fault and they must pay
And on the street the corpses lay
Burning bridges makes no sense
Killing ourselves in self-defense
Bloodied bodies along the ridges
Is all we find when we burn our bridges

Just as the last words were being sung, Michael saw two young ladies walk up the aisle. It was Judy Solomon and Kelly Atkins. They walked up the steps to where Michael and the others were and the whole congregation was silenced.

Michael felt as though his feet were frozen as Kelly approached the microphone. She began to speak.

"Good evening everyone. My name is Kelly Atkins. I was a member of the neo-Nazi organization responsible for the recent events. As soon as I finish what I have to say, I will turn myself over to the authorities." She paused for several seconds and looked at Michael briefly.

She then continued. "It had been my desire for Germany to take over the world and I didn't care how many people died. But then something happened," she said softly, almost in a whisper. "The man I thought was my father told me on his deathbed that he wasn't really my father. He told me that he had kidnapped me when I was three years old, along with a neighbor. He told me that he did this to get back at someone. This man's name was Alan Roberts and he told me a few weeks ago that my real parents were Michael and Rebecca Madigan, and that my real name was Ellen."

Michael's jaw dropped and Rebecca let out an audible gasp. Kelly continued. "His last words were, 'I got him back like I said I would.' It shook me to the core but for some reason I couldn't believe it. I spent weeks in the library, researching newspaper articles and hospital records. I found out something yesterday that I would like to say to the Madigan family." She turned and looked at Michael and Rebecca, both of whom were crying, although for different reasons. Michael was unable to speak.

"Mr. Vice President and Mrs. Madigan, I've discovered that contrary to what I was told several weeks ago, I am not your daughter Ellen," Kelly said, pausing briefly. Michael let out a sigh of relief.

"My real name is Amanda and I was Ellen's friend who was kidnapped by Alan Roberts almost twenty years ago. Ellen is here with me and I would like to reunite her with you," Kelly said, and the tears streamed down Michael's face. Rebecca gasped loudly. Kelly gestured towards Judy Solomon. "Mr. and Mrs. Madigan, this is your daughter, Ellen Madigan. She's home."

Ellen's mouth quivered with emotion as she stepped first hesitantly and then confidently toward her parents—her real parents. Tears were moistening her cheeks before she met their warm embrace. TJ, Josh, and David joined the circle. Together they clung, suspended in time, a picture of completion. Amanda, who had been standing awkwardly on the outskirts was included into the group by Ellen, who reached out her arm and gently pulled her toward them. Amanda joined the Madigan family as they held on to one another, as though this moment could reclaim all the lost years between them.

The madness was over and their family complete.

Alfred Krupp

Frederick the Great

Charlamagne

Kaiser Wilhelm II

Otto Von Bismarck

Erwin Rommel